STEPHE⬚⬚⬚⬚⬚⬚⬚⬚⬚⬚⬚⬚⬚⬚⬚⬚⬚ e winner of three World Fantasy Awards, four ⬚⬚⬚⬚⬚⬚ ⬚⬚ers Association Bram Stoker Awards and three International Horror Guild Awards as well as being a twenty-one-times recipient of the British Fantasy Award and a Hugo Award nominee. A former television producer/ director and genre-movie publicist and consultant (the first three *Hellraiser* movies, *Nightbreed*, *Split Second*, etc.) he has written and edited more than 120 books, including *Coraline: A Visual Companion*, *The Essential Monster Movie Guide*, *Horror: 100 Best Books* and *Horror: Another 100 Best Books* (both with Kim Newman), and the *Dark Terrors*, *Dark Voices* and *The Mammoth Book of Best New Horror* series. A Guest of Honour at the 2002 World Fantasy Convention in Minneapolis, Minnesota, and the 2004 World Horror Convention in Phoenix, Arizona, he has been a guest lecturer at UCLA in California and London's Kingston University and St Mary's University College. You can visit his website at www.stephenjoneseditor.com

PSYCHO-MANIA!

Edited by STEPHEN JONES

Introduction by ROBERT BLOCH,
author of *Psycho*

ROBINSON

Constable & Robinson Ltd
55–56 Russell Square
London WC1B 4HP
www.constablerobinson.com

First published in the UK by Robinson,
an imprint of Constable & Robinson, 2013

A copy of the British Library Cataloguing in Publication
Data is available from the British Library

ISBN 978–1–78033–026–6 (paperback)
UK ISBN 978–1–78033–027–3 (ebook)

Printed and bound by
CPI Group (UK) Ltd, Croydon, CR0 4YY

1 3 5 7 9 10 8 6 4 2

CONTENTS

ACKNOWLEDGEMENTS

Special thanks to my editor, Duncan Proudfoot, for not going crazy; and to Dorothy Lumley, Richard Henshaw, Chuck Verrill, Stephen King, PS Publishing, Peter Atkins and all the contributors, especially John Llewellyn Probert, for their help and support.

"The Man Who Photographed Beardsley" copyright © Brian Lumley 1976. Originally published in *Star Book of Horror No.2*. Reprinted by permission of the author.

"Hollywood Hannah" copyright © Lisa Morton 2013.

"I Spy" copyright © Paul McAuley 1999. Originally published in *White of the Moon: New Tales of Madness and Dread*. Reprinted by permission of the author.

"Reflections on the Critical Process" copyright © Mike Carey 2006, 2013. Originally published in different form in *Mike Carey's One-Sided Bargains*.

"The Finger" copyright © David J. Schow 2013.

"Hot Eyes, Cold Eyes" copyright © Lawrence Block 1978. Originally published in *Gallery*, 1978. Reprinted by permission of the author.

"Hush . . . Hush, Sweet Shushie" copyright © Jay Russell 2013.

"Case Conference #2" copyright © John Llewellyn Probert 2013.

"The Gatecrasher" copyright © R. Chetwynd-Hayes 1971. Originally published in *The Unbidden*. Reprinted by permission of the author's Estate.

"That Tiny Flutter of the Heart I Used to Call Love" copyright © Robert Shearman 2013.

"The Tell-Tale Heart" by Edgar Allan Poe. Originally published in *The Pioneer: A Literary and Critical Magazine*, Vol.1, No.1, January 1843.

"Got to Kill Them All" copyright © Dennis Etchison 2001. Originally published in *Cemetery Dance Magazine*, Issue #34, 2001. Reprinted by permission of the author.

"Essence" copyright © Mark Morris 2013.

"The Beach" copyright © Michael Kelly 2013.

"Yours Truly, Jack the Ripper" copyright © Robert Bloch 1943. Originally published in *Weird Tales*, July 1943. Reprinted by permission of the Estate of Robert Bloch.

"Case Conference #3" copyright © John Llewellyn Probert 2013.

"See How They Run" copyright © Ramsey Campbell 1993. Originally published in *Monsters in Our Midst*. Reprinted by permission of the author.

"Manners" copyright © Conrad Williams 2013.

"Bryant & May and the Seven Points" copyright © Christopher Fowler 2013.

In memory of
Robert Bloch
(1917–94),
a kind and gracious man
who always held on to
that heart of a small boy

ROBERT BLOCH

Introduction

IN 1958 I wrote a novel called *Psycho*, wherein my heroine was suddenly and shockingly killed while taking a shower.

So much for cleanliness.

In 1960 Alfred Hitchcock filmed my novel. It follows the plot of the book faithfully, though in a few cases the movie dramatizes or lengthens events I merely report in the novel. One example, of course, is the shower sequence. I startled readers with a shockingly abrupt murder. Hitchcock jolted audiences by prolonging it. Each of us employed the tempo most effective for our medium.

But neither the film nor the novel is a story about a girl being killed while taking a shower. *Psycho* is a story about the killer – a character named Norman Bates.

And Norman Bates *is* a character. To mislead my mystery readers I created him as middle-aged. Hitchcock achieves deception visually by depicting him as a dozen years younger. Again, our intentions were identical, and appropriately executed for the medium in which we worked. But despite the disparity in age, and dialogue changes supplied by the script-writer adapting the book, the basic character of Norman Bates remains unchanged, right down to my last line, and the film's.

Hitchcock's shower sequence is masterful indeed, but in the past thirty-odd years it has been constantly surpassed in gory, graphic detail, which Hitchcock was adroit enough to convey through suggestion.

Some of the more explicitly violent films are admittedly frightening – and/or nauseating and revolting. Many of their on-screen atrocities are perpetrated by serial killers who do away with victims by the most fiendish methods which low-budget or hi-tech can devise. Moreover, many of these choppy-chappies prove to be immortal: after meeting gruesome (and usually, quite noisy) fates, they tend to come back to life at the drop of a sequel.

But despite the miracles of modern make-up and special effects, it's Norman Bates who has apparently emerged as a symbol of the serial killer – not because he's super-ugly or super-natural, but because he's seemingly just your average face in the crowd until an alternate personality takes over. He could be anybody. Or somebody. Somebody you know.

I refer, of course, to the original Norman – not to the retreads offered in subsequent sequels on-screen, or even a prequel in which character becomes self-caricature.

It's the inevitable self-caricature element which makes many of today's "mad slasher" films meaningless. When characters are unbelievable their deeds lack credibility. And the films (or books, for that matter) offer a series of momentary shocks but leave no lasting imprint on our long-term memory. Short jabs for people with short attention-spans.

To be effective in this genre, the writer or director must aim not for the reader's/viewer's eyes, but for their imaginations. And for emotional rather than mere visceral impact, it is important that the story is more than a dramatized body-count. Whatever the medium, its audiences must be led to care about the victims as human beings – and to understand the "psycho" as a human being too.

Which means that the films that endure must offer us something more memorable than a loud soundtrack, zoom-shots, jump-cuts and an endless chain of crudely contrived examples of death-by-special-effects.

Hopefully, with these criteria in mind, it is possible to evaluate the contents of this book. Fiction and films have come a long way from the standard mystery/horror offerings where the most kindly and intelligent cast-member was finally fingered as the culprit and instantly turned into a raving maniac.

Today, even Hannibal Lecter manages to keep a civil tongue in his head. It's just his teeth we have to watch out for.

The same, of course, could be said for Count Dracula, but in the out-and-out supernatural fantasy the monsters generally advertised their identities or concealed them only clumsily. The problem with the real-life psychopath or sociopath, as well as with many outright dangerous sufferers from psychoses, is that they're not always easily recognizable. They can – and all too frequently do – live just down the street, or even next door. Some may knock on your front door or (worst-case scenario) even move in with you.

Correction: that's not the worst-case scenario after all. Because for some there comes a time when they catch their first glimpse of a psycho by looking into a mirror.

And for many of us who don't necessarily catch a full glimpse, there's always the possibility on occasion of seeing a glimmer.

There's still a great deal which society doesn't know about the problems of psychopathology and psychosis. Perhaps books and films may eventually impel us to learn a little more about our psychos. And ourselves.

JOHN LLEWELLYN PROBERT

Prologue: Screams in the Dark

IT WAS AN old building, fashioned from weathered red brick and held together with mortar that was crumbling almost as quickly as the minds of many of those confined within. The corridors echoed with the flickering whispers of a thousand lonely souls, condemned to reside in the ever-lengthening shadows that would one day coalesce and consume the building in a darkness of never-ending despair. The anaemic green paint on the walls had cracked and split as if in empathy with the patients' sanity, the greying plaster beneath saturated with over a century's worth of screams from the lost and the forgotten.

There were over a hundred rooms, not all with padded walls, not all with three sets of locks to keep their residents within and the staff safely without, not all with red discs on their foot-thick steel doors to indicate that on no account were they to be opened without at least three members of staff present.

Not all.

But most.

"This is an asylum for the criminally insane."

Robert Stanhope's eyes widened at these words, spoken by the much older, and far better dressed, man sitting on the other side of the huge, ornate writing desk. It was one thing to have driven here through the pouring rain, the huge rambling complex of Victorian buildings rising from the moors as he approached like some beast in waiting, the bars on the windows and the signs everywhere forbidding those without permission to come any further, but it was another entirely for the institution's director to be quite so blatant about its purpose. Now, having been shown through a maze of corridors, each with a pair of locked doors at either end that had to be negotiated in keeping with the building's security regulations, he was finally here.

He eyed the man sitting opposite. Dr Lionel Parrish's hands were clasped neatly on the cherry-red leather of the desktop, a pale blue silk handkerchief arranged meticulously in the breast-pocket of the jacket of the blue pinstripe suit he was wearing. The man's demeanour radiated authority, and with only a single sentence he managed to make Stanhope feel partly guest but mainly intruder.

The younger man presumed Parrish's ensuing silence meant he was intended to respond.

"Yes," he said, drawing out the word in a way he hoped suggested he was politely disagreeing. After all, it was possible he was being tested. "At least, my understanding is that's what they used to be called. Nowadays there are more reasonable, under-standing, tolerant terms for places like this."

He looked around the vast, dark study, the shelves filled with medical tomes, the filing cabinets beside the door behind him crammed to bursting with case files. "And for the patients they treat," he added with a smile.

Dr Parrish leaned back in his swivel chair. The creak made Stanhope jump. "I have been the director of this institution for a long time," Parrish said eventually, "and I have been a doctor for far longer than that. And one of the many things I have learned during my career is that it doesn't matter how frequently one renames something, the word or phrase one uses will, gradually but inevitably, take on the same stigma with the general public as that which preceded it."

He folded his hands behind his head. The chair creaked even more ominously as he leaned back further, but his gaze never left the young man opposite. "Lunatic. Insane. Psychotic. Disturbed. Challenged. Different. Special. Crazy." He seemed to be enjoying saying each word. "It doesn't matter what you call them so long as you have no misconceptions about what you are actually deal-ing with." The director narrowed his eyes. "The patients in this place are dangerous, Mr Stanhope. Exceedingly dangerous. You may have come here with very high ideals about kindness and understanding, about hope and optimism, but up there . . ." he gestured above him ". . . you will find nothing and no one to respond to those ideals, except to use them against you."

Stanhope's hands twitched. This wasn't how he had anticipated the meeting starting off at all. "I'm aware that these patients can be violent," he said. "After all, they wouldn't be here otherwise."

"Not all of them are violent," said Parrish. "Some of them are dangerous in other ways. A few are exceedingly manipulative, and will have the coldest heart bleeding for them while they gently slit your throat. Others will turn you against yourself without you even realizing it. There are some very, very clever people in here, young man. Engineers who have devoted their lives to devising new kinds of torture devices, teachers who have delighted in driving their own students to suicide. We have one man upstairs who, before he was caught, managed to manufacture an entire orchestra's worth of instruments from the flesh and bones of his many victims."

"Are there any doctors who are patients?" Stanhope could not help but ask.

"That last one *is* a doctor," Parrish replied with a small smile. "We do have one or two others. No psychiatrists, though, which is interesting, don't you think?"

All Stanhope could do was nod. In the silence that followed, he fancied he could hear a very faint wailing coming from somewhere upstairs, before Parrish eventually nodded at the dictating machine Stanhope had placed on his desk.

"Shall we get started on this interview of yours, then?" the director asked.

Stanhope raised his eyebrows. "I was under the impression we had already begun," he said.

Parrish snorted, picked up the little tape player and squinted at the tiny see-through plastic window in its casing. The wheels of the cassette mechanism were indeed going round. "Good grief, no," he said, pushing the stop button and setting the tape to rewind. Stanhope, taken aback by this, reached out for the device, but Parrish held it away from him.

"Before we properly begin, Mr Stanhope, I would like you to answer a question for me," said the director, his manner confrontational now that he had realized the recorder had been switched on without his permission.

Stanhope suppressed a shudder and forced a nod. "Go on," he said.

"At what point in your own medical career did you decide that you couldn't stand the patients any more?"

Stanhope's eyes widened as Parrish continued.

"Did you really think I wouldn't have done some research of my own before agreeing to let you in here? I am well aware that before you decided to pursue a career writing tabloid-friendly articles for, shall we say, the less-discerning members of the general public, you were a member of this profession yourself." He reached into his right-hand desk drawer and produced a collection of clippings of some of Stanhope's more hysterically headlined articles. "I know you call yourself a medical journalist because that sounds slightly more reputable than the type of tabloid degenerate I sometimes get asking me for an interview, but you are a journalist nevertheless. So . . ." He steepled his fingers and pushed himself away from the desk a little. The chair creaked again and Stanhope was no more prepared for it this time than he had been the first. "Tell me."

"I got my medical degree," said Stanhope, coughing to clear the frog that had suddenly taken up residence in his dry throat, "worked in a couple of junior training posts in various specialities, but then I decided that I preferred writing, so that's what I did."

"That's what you did." Parrish repeated the words slowly and deliberately, savouring them with all the liquid menace of someone who knows that they have only been given a tiny fragment of the true story. For now.

Stanhope nodded. "I'd had a few articles published in the *British Medical Journal, Healthcare Matters, International Ageing*—"

"Comics," said Parrish with a dismissive wave of his hand, "and ones that don't pay well either, if at all."

"I know, which is why I realized that if I wanted to make a living at it, I'd need to broaden my horizons."

"That's how you would refer to it, is it?" said Parrish. "Broadening your horizons?"

"It's as good a way as any," said Stanhope, starting to get riled by the man's attitude. Usually it was he who was the one asking the questions, he who was the one probing and investigating, causing his interview subject the maximum of discomfort to elicit the juiciest information. But, he supposed, that was one of the reasons he had accepted the invitation. An interview with the director of Crowsmoor Institution regarding the alleged mistreatment of its inmates would do his career a world of good, and it wouldn't hurt his bank account or his ego, either. But it obviously wasn't going to be easy.

"You may be wondering why I've asked you here," said Parrish abruptly.

It wasn't difficult to guess. Stanhope glanced at the clippings. "I imagine those may have had something to do with it," he replied.

The director nodded and pushed them towards the journalist. Stanhope didn't need to pick them up to see they were the series of articles he had written for a major newspaper on the alleged incompetence of the staff in large mental institutions.

"I only wrote what I was told," he said. "Ex-patients, cleaners, porters. They all had stories to tell."

"Oh, I don't doubt that," said Dr Parrish, leaning forward. "What always worries me in all these articles you've written is the unquestioning belief that what you have been told is true."

"It's unlikely that they all lied independently," replied Stanhope.

"No," said Parrish, "but this was a series of articles published over many months and under such circumstances it's conceivable that some of them may have got wind of just how much your paper was paying for such information, and realized they might be on to something if they could come up with the kind of story you were looking for."

Stanhope crossed his legs, a slight smirk on his face. "And have you invited me here today to prove them all wrong?" he asked.

"As you are well aware, not all these articles were about my institution," said Parrish. "But a couple of them were and, Mr Stanhope, I can tell you now that I and my staff were deeply offended by the claims made within them. Deeply offended. And as for the patients . . ."

"You're not trying to tell me your patients were upset by them?" Stanhope replied, stifling a chuckle.

Dr Parrish narrowed his eyes. "Most of the patients at Crowsmoor are going to be here for a very, very long time, Mr Stanhope. It is therefore not unreasonable for many of them to think of this place not as a prison but as a home." He pointed at the clippings. "It can be most upsetting to see this sort of thing written about the place where you live and about the people who care for you."

"Fine, fine," said Stanhope, once again wondering where this was leading. "So you asked me here for an interview and here I am." He pointed at his Dictaphone. "And there's my machine, all ready and waiting now that you've turned it off. So perhaps we could stop procrastinating and get started? Or are you hoping if you delay things for long enough, spin out how hurt and upset you and all your patients are, that I'll get fed up and leave?"

"Oh, you're not going anywhere," said Parrish with such vehemence that Stanhope turned and looked at the door. "I don't mean that." Now it was Parrish's turn to chuckle. "What I mean is, there is so much for me to tell you that we are both going to be here for quite a while. Would you like some tea?"

Stanhope shook his head.

"Let me assure you, it won't be drugged. You're not going to wake up in some white-walled room with no chance of ever seeing the outside world again. The thought makes you nervous though, doesn't it?"

Stanhope stopped fidgeting in his seat. "All right then," he said defiantly. "I will have a cup of tea. Lots of milk and two sugars."

"I might have guessed," said Parrish, reaching for his intercom and relaying the instructions to his receptionist.

"Well?" said Stanhope, once Parrish had finished.

"Well what?"

Stanhope reached out a hand. "Can I have my dictating machine back?"

Parrish grinned. "Surely the correct usage is '*May* I'?"

Once he showed no intention of relinquishing the device, Stanhope gave in. "Okay, may I have my machine back?"

"Of course!" said Parrish, handing it over. "We wouldn't get very far if you couldn't record what I was going to say, would we?"

"Thank you," said Stanhope, pressing record and giving the machine his details, the date, and an index number for whichever secretary back at his paper would presumably be typing it up. "I'd like to start by asking you your name, and how long you have been the director of Crowsmoor?" he said, pointing the tape recorder at Parrish.

The director sat in silence for a moment before shaking his head.

"What's the matter now?" said Stanhope, pressing the off button.

"That's not the way we're going to do things," said Parrish. "You are going to have to earn the answers to any questions you want to ask me."

"And how am I supposed to do that?" Stanhope was starting to get annoyed now.

"Oh, it should be fairly easy," said Parrish with a trace of amusement. "You see, my concern is that you can't tell truth from fiction, or at least these articles of yours seem to suggest as much. So I have a proposition for you."

Stanhope didn't look taken with the idea. "Go on," he said.

Parrish gestured to the rest of the room. "In this office are all the case records of all the patients who are here now or ever have been here, including those who have been released and those who, sadly, ended their days within these walls."

Stanhope looked around him at the towering bookcases crammed with ring binders and box files, and then at the filing cabinets behind him. "And . . .?" he said.

Parrish got to his feet. "Over the last few months, in fact since I began reading those articles of yours," this time he pronounced the word "articles" with disdain, "I have been adding a few cases of my own. Fictional ones. Ones I have created, made up with the intention of inviting you here to put you to a little test."

"What sort of test?" Stanhope sneered, not at all happy that Parrish had once again taken control of his interview.

"I propose to read some of them to you, and all you have to do is tell me whether or not you think the case I am describing actually happened, or whether it is, in fact, the product of my somewhat overactive imagination."

"You have one then, do you?" said Stanhope. "In my experience most of the doctors I've met don't even read."

"Do you think if they did they would tell you about it?" said Parrish with a raised eyebrow. He crossed to the bookcases on Stanhope's left and rested a hand on a battered lilac-coloured box file. He glanced at his desk, and then at the bay window behind it.

Beyond the glass lay gloomy rain-washed fields, the few bare trees battered and twisted by the constant buffeting winds of this exposed place. "You'd be surprised how much time there is to think up such things in a place like this, Mr Stanhope, and no – you are not allowed to put that in your interview. At least, not yet."

"Go on then," said Stanhope, realizing there was nothing for it but to accede to the man's wishes. He looked at his watch and found himself wishing the tea would hurry up. "Read me a story and I'll tell you what I think." After all, how difficult was it going to be to tell the difference between a proper clinical case history and some nonsense this man had made up in a hurry, to try and prove some sort of ridiculous point?

"Good!" Parrish lingered by the bookcase for a moment as if considering something, and then moved to the filing cabinet nearest the door. He pulled open the top drawer and began to leaf through manila folders, talking all the while. "What shall we begin with? I wonder," he said, giving no sign of whether he was talking to Stanhope or himself. "A wife-beater? A child-strangler?"

Stanhope shrugged. "I don't care, but let me warn you right now – if you start reading me something that's filled with maniacal gibbering laughter, I'll know you're making it up from the start."

Parrish put down the file he was holding and gave Stanhope a severe look. "Let me assure you, Mr Stanhope, that there is not much laughter of any kind in these files. Tears – yes, sadness – of course, and screams . . ." Parrish paused, a faraway look in his eyes for a moment. "Too many screams, Mr Stanhope, all locked away here in the dark." He gave the filing cabinet a pat that was almost affectionate. "All locked away in the dark, all waiting for someone like me to come along and read them to someone like you. Are you ready?"

Stanhope nodded.

Parrish looked through the cabinet drawer once more before taking a battered folder from the very front.

"May as well begin at the beginning," he said with a smile, as he took out two sheets of paper held together with a rusty paper clip in the top right-hand corner. "How does a little whipping sound?"

Stanhope narrowed his eyes. "Not really my sort of thing," he replied. "But somehow it doesn't surprise me that you'd want to start with something like that."

Parrish took the case notes back to his desk, sat behind it, and adjusted his desk lamp so he could better see the hand-written confession that began the document.

"In that case," he said, "let's begin . . ."

JOE R. LANSDALE

I Tell You It's Love

For Lew Shiner

THE BEAUTIFUL WOMAN had no eyes, just sparkles of light where they should have been – or so it seemed in the candlelight. Her lips, so warm and inviting, so wickedly wild and suggestive of strange pleasures, held yet a hint of disaster, as if they might be fat red things skilfully moulded from dried blood.

"Hit me," she said.

That is my earliest memory of her; a doll for my beating, a doll for my love.

I laid it on her with that black silk whip, slapping it across her shoulders and back, listening to the whisper of it as it rode down, delighting in the flat pretty sound of it striking her flesh.

She did not bleed, which was a disappointment. The whip was too soft, too flexible, too difficult to strike hard with.

"Hurt me," she said softly. I went to where she knelt. Her arms were outstretched, crucifixion-style, and bound to the walls on either side with strong silk cord the colour and texture of the whip in my hand.

I slapped her. "Like it?" I asked. She nodded and I slapped her again . . . and again. A one-two rhythm, slow and melodic, time and again.

"Like it?" I repeated, and she moaned, "Yeah, oh, yeah."

Later, after she was untied and had tidied up the blood from her lips and nose, we made brutal love; me with my thumbs bending the flesh of her throat, she with her nails entrenched in my back. She said to me when we were finished, "Let's do someone."

That's how we got started. Thinking back now, once again I say I'm glad for fate; glad for Gloria; glad for the memory of the crying sounds, the dripping blood and the long sharp knives that murmured through flesh like a lover's whisper cutting the dark.

Yeah, I like to think back to when I walked hands in pockets down the dark wharves in search of that special place where there were said to be special women with special pleasures for a special man like me.

I walked on until I met a sailor leaning up against a wall smoking a cigarette, and he says when I ask about the place, "Oh, yeah, I like that sort of pleasure myself. Two blocks down, turn right, there between the warehouses, down the far end. You'll see the light." And he pointed and I walked on, faster.

Finding it, paying for it, meeting Gloria was the goal of my dreams. I was more than a customer to that sassy, dark mama with the sparkler eyes. I was the link to fit her link. We made two strong, solid bonds in a strange cosmic chain. You could feel the energy flowing through us; feel the iron of our wills. Ours was a mating made happily in hell.

So time went by and I hated the days and lived for the nights when I whipped her, slapped her, scratched her, and she did the same to me. Then one night she said, "It's not enough. Just not enough any more. Your blood is sweet and your pain is fine, but I want to see death like you see a movie, taste it like liquorice, smell it like flowers, touch it like cold, hard stone."

I laughed, saying, "I draw the line at dying for you." I took her by the throat, fastened my grip until her breathing was a whistle and her eyes protruded like bloated corpse bellies.

"That's not what I mean," she managed. And then came the statement that brings us back to what started it all: "Let's do someone."

I laughed and let her go.

"You know what I mean?" she said. "You know what I'm saying."

"I know what you said. I know what you mean." I smiled. "I know very well."

"You've done it before, haven't you?"

"Once," I said, "in a shipyard, not that long ago."

"Tell me about it. God, tell me about it."

"It was dark and I had come off a ship after six months out, a long six months with the men, the ship and the sea. So I'm walking down this dark alley, enjoying the night like I do, looking for a place with the dark ways, our kind of ways, baby, and I came upon this old wino lying in a doorway, cuddling a bottle to his face as if it were a lady's loving hand."

"What did you do?"

"I kicked him," I said, and Gloria's smile was a beauty to behold.

"Go on," she said.

"God, how I kicked him. Kicked him in the face until there was no nose, no lips, no eyes. Only red mush dangling from shrapnelled bone; looked like a melon that had been dropped from on high, down into a mass of broken white pottery chips. I touched his face and tasted it with my tongue and my lips."

"Ohh," she sighed, and her eyes half-closed. "Did he scream?"

"Once. Only once. I kicked him too hard, too fast, too soon. I hammered his head with the toes of my shoes, hammered until my cuffs were wet and sticking to my ankles."

"Oh, God," she said, clinging to me, "let's do it, let's do it."

We did. First time was a drizzly night and we caught an old woman out. She was a lot of fun until we got the knives out and then she went quick. There was that crippled kid next, lured him from the theatre downtown, and how we did that was a stroke of genius. You'll find his wheelchair not far from where you found the van and the other stuff.

But no matter. You know what we did, about the kinds of tools we had, about how we hung that crippled kid on that meat hook in my van until the flies clustered around the doors thick as grapes.

And of course there was the little girl. It was a brilliant idea of Gloria's to get the kid's tricycle into the act. The things she did with those spokes. Ah, but that woman was a connoisseur of pain.

There were two others, each quite fine, but not as nice as the last. Then came the night Gloria looked at me and said, "It's not enough. Just won't do."

I smiled. "No way, baby. I still won't die for you."

"No," she gasped, and took my arm. "You miss my drift. It's the pain I need, not just the watching. I can't live through them, can't feel it in me. Don't you see? It would be the ultimate."

I looked at her, wondering did I have it right?

"Do you love me?"

"I do," I said.

"To know that I would spend the last of my life with you, that my last memories would be the pleasure on your face, the feelings of pain, the excitement, the thrill, the terror."

Then I understood, and understood good. Right there in the car I grabbed her, took her by the throat and cracked her head up against the windshield, pressed her back, choked, released, choked, made it linger. By this time I was quite a pro. She coughed, choked, smiled. Her eyes swung from fear to love. God, it was wonderful and beautiful and the finest experience we had ever shared.

When she finally lay still there in the seat, I was trembling, happier than I had ever been. Gloria looked fine, her eyes rolled up, her lips stretched in a rictus smile.

I kept her like that at my place for days, kept her in my bed until the neighbours started to complain about the smell.

I've been talking to this guy and he's got some ideas. Says he thinks I'm one of the future generation, and the fact of that scares him all to hell. A social mutation, he says. Man's primitive nature at the height of the primal scream.

Dog shit, we're all the same, so don't look at me like I'm some kind of freak. What does he do come Monday night? He's watching the football game, or the races or boxing matches, waiting for a car to overturn or for some guy to be carried out of the ring with nothing but mush left for brains. Oh, yeah, he and I are similar, quite alike. You see, it's in us all. A low-pitched melody not often heard, but there just the same. In me it peaks and thuds, like drums and brass and strings. Don't fear it. Let it go. Give it the beat and amplify. I tell you, it's love of the finest kind.

So I've said my piece and I'll just add this: when they fasten my arms and ankles down and tighten the cap, I hope I feel the pain and delight in it before my brain sizzles to bacon, and may I smell the frying of my very own flesh . . .

REGGIE OLIVER

The Green Hour

"NO! I CAN'T. I've had too much already. It's getting late."
"Every hour is a green hour if you want it to be. Drink."
"Oooh! I'm feeling all fuzzy . . . So what do you want with me, as if I didn't know?"

"Have a little more. This way, mademoiselle."

"Where are we going?"

"To the Egyptian Pyramid."

"Won't it be all shut?"

"Not to me."

"It's dark. What's happening?"

"Have another drink, *ma petite chérie*."

"No. I don't really like it. Nasty green stuff. What are you going to do then?"

"Drink. You won't feel the pain so much."

"What pain?"

"Are you a dirty girl?"

"What d'you mean? Of course not! I'm a clean girl, I am."

"No, you're not. I can smell the filth on you."

"Here, what are you doing with that?"

"You dirty girl! I'm going to make you sing . . . That's better. Now I shall sing to you, my little one, while you still have ears to hear."

Paris, June 29th, 1867
It was five o'clock, the absinthe hour, sometimes referred to by Parisians as *l'heure verte*, and Commissioner Viardot had a good idea where to find his old friend Auguste Dupin. He would be seated at his usual pavement table at the Café Momus. Viardot

was not mistaken. As he approached the café from the direction of the Church of Saint-Germain l'Auxerrois he could see a tall elderly man with a full head of white hair, sitting very upright, one hand resting on a silver-topped cane as he watched the passers-by with a curious stillness and intensity.

In front of him on the table was a glass half-full of a pale green fluid that looked like a distillation of young grass in sunlight. There was also a pitcher of water, a small plate of sugar cubes and a silver absinthe spoon. Dupin poured a tiny measure of the water into the glass. The liquid immediately turned an opaque milky colour delicately tinged with green. He then placed a sugar cube on the spoon which he gently dipped into the mixture, releasing the sugar to let it sink into the cloudy bottom of the glass. Finally he brought the glass up to his nose to scent the delicate herb-flavoured brew.

"My dear Viardot, do sit down. You evidently have something on your mind." The Commissioner who had approached Dupin from behind, thinking himself unobserved by the great detective, was disconcerted.

"I doubt, however," continued Dupin, "if I can be of any assistance. You know that I have long since renounced the active business of detection. My life has been one of observation and deduction, now I merely observe. I am like the Persian Poetess who said: 'For fifty years I wrote poems to the moon; now I will simply sit and look at it.' Besides, where are the criminals of yesteryear? The Lacenaires, the Madame Restells, the Abbé Guibourgs and the poisoners of the Grand Siècle? All gone.

"The criminals nowadays, like their crimes, are commonplace. We live in an age of bourgeois banality, my dear Viardot, of Second Empire insipidity, which I prefer to contemplate through a pale green cloud in a glass." He took a beatific sip of the green liquid. "Would you care to join me?"

"My dear Dupin, you know I have strong views about absinthe."

"Commissioner Viardot, you have never had a strong view in your life, only received opinions. That is both your tragedy and the secret of your success. That is why you come to me when you are in difficulties. Unfortunately I am not interested."

"But what if I were to tell you that your beloved absinthe may be at the heart of this mystery? May even be in a sense the guilty party in the most atrocious series of crimes ever to have been committed in this city?"

For the first time Dupin looked Viardot full in the face. The Commissioner was glad to see that those piercing blue eyes had lost none of their sharpness, despite his old friend's deplorable addiction.

"You have my attention, Viardot, but remember, I am very easily bored these days."

"As you may know," said Commissioner Viardot, "I have been granted the dubious honour of being in charge of all security and police matters to do with the Paris Exhibition. My jurisdiction, so to speak, covers an area of over one hundred and fifty acres on the Champ de Mars and Billancourt. We opened in April and though it has been seen to be in all respects a glorious triumph for His Majesty the Emperor and for France, it has not been without its problems.

"My immediate superior who has been on Prince Jérôme's committee from the first is the Marquis de Saint-Loup, a most zealous man, if somewhat erratic. He became very exercised about the great number of prostitutes to be found at the Exposition at all times of the day and night. He gave me the order that such women (and indeed men) were to be cleared from the site. But it is a vast area! And one cannot simply arrest and deport a woman because she looks like a harlot. I have done my best, but the best is not good enough for Saint-Loup and the committee.

"Then one night some two weeks ago the situation took an even graver turn. One of my gendarmes, Ventroux by name, was patrolling the area around the Spanish Pavilion. (As you know, each nation in the Exposition has its own pavilion or area assigned to it in which it may display its goods and advertise its achieve-ments.) It was close on midnight when he heard a cry. Immediately Ventroux went to investigate. Believing that it came from the Pavilion itself, he tried to gain entrance but found it locked. Having forced his way in he was met with a horrific spectacle. A woman of easy virtue who was known in her circle as La Brouette [the wheelbarrow], for reasons that I need not explain to you as a man of the world, was lying dead in front of a fantastic display of artificial Seville oranges made from wax. She had not been undressed, but her skirts were up and she had been mutilated in the genital area with a knife. Moreover her eyes had been extracted, her ears sliced off and her tongue cut out with a similar instrument."

"Was the knife found?"

"No. But a scrupulous examination of the wounds suggested that it was about six inches long, narrow-bladed and excessively sharp. It might have been a chef's knife, or indeed one to be found in any well-appointed kitchen."

"Proceed." Dupin, eyes almost closed, was staring with furious concentration into the cloudy depths of his undrunk absinthe.

"Naturally I immediately reported this frightful incident to my superiors and received strict instructions that news of the murder was to be kept from the public at all costs, and that every effort should be made to apprehend the assassin. But what were we to do? The evidence was so bizarre. The usual motivations for the crime of murder were so lacking. It was clear only that we were looking for a maniac."

"I assume that La Brouette was just the first victim."

"You have guessed it, my dear Auguste, as I suspected you would. The next was found but two days later in the Algerian Souk. Then one in the Scottish Hall. The portico of the Temple of Greek Arts was the next location. Then last night the murderer struck again in the Egyptian Pyramid. All the victims were ladies of the night; all had been similarly mutilated. The deaths, as far as we can ascertain, occurred at about midnight or in the early hours of the morning at roughly two- or three-day intervals."

"Were there any other similarities between these deaths?" asked Dupin, who had been making pencilled notes in a small *carnet*.

"I now come to perhaps the strangest thing of all, and not the least horrible. In their mouths we found one of these."

The Commissioner threw something on to the table. It was a crude little brooch which consisted of a pin attached to a flat brass disc, the size of a large button, coated in enamel. On a white background a bright green figure was seen hovering. She – or possibly he, it was hard to tell which – had on a long floating gown and the attenuated oval-shaped wings of a dragonfly. An attempt at artistry was marred by the coarseness of workmanship and materials.

"I have seen one of these before," said Dupin.

"Of course you have! They are everywhere. It has been impossible even to track down the manufacturer."

"*La Fée Verte* . . . the Green Fairy," murmured Dupin. "It is the popular name for absinthe. Sometimes people, mostly women, wear objects like this to demonstrate their lifelong devotion to the beverage. It is something of a fashion."

"Moreover the smell of absinthe was in the victims' mouths. An autopsy has revealed considerable quantities of it in their stomach and bloodstream. Evidently the killer is some crazed addict of the drug and plied them with it before their deaths," said Viardot.

"Oh, evidently!" said Dupin. "Then why do you need me, my dear Commissioner? You must simply find a homicidal drinker of absinthe and your case is solved."

"You mock me, monsieur. This is far too serious a case for your satire and irony, Dupin. What am I to do? In two days' time, on the first of July, the Emperor Louis-Napoleon officially commemorates the mid-term of the Exhibition. He will attend a great concert in the Grand Pavilion. Maestro Rossini has composed a new Hymn for chorus, soloists and orchestra. The whole occasion may be blighted by these dreadful incidents. Already some of the national representatives are up in arms. They cannot be kept quiet indefinitely. I have been commanded to find the culprit. Unless I do so I am ruined!"

"I apologize, my dear Viardot. You asked for help; *noblesse oblige*, I will assist you. Was anything else noticed by anyone at about the time these incidents occurred? Any suspicious persons? Suspicious activity?"

"Nothing, I regret to say. And my gendarmes have been most diligent in stopping any suspicious-looking person and searching them for knives or other offensive weapons."

"Unfortunately the killer in question is unlikely to have looked suspicious. On the contrary. Is there nothing else? However slight?"

"One thing perhaps – but it is hardly worth mentioning." Viardot glanced at Dupin, who nodded at him vigorously to proceed. "On the night of the first murder, the gendarme Ventroux who was alerted by the cry of the victim also heard something else."

"Yes?"

"Shortly after the cries came from the Spanish Pavilion, Ventroux was sure he heard someone whistling. There was no one else about at the time, so it could have been our killer."

"Could you tell me what was being whistled?"

"A tune of some kind, I believe. I really could not say. I didn't ask."

"Then you should have done, my dear Commissioner! Come! We must ask this Ventroux at once, before his memory of the event becomes totally corrupted."

While they were driving to the exhibition site Viardot asked Dupin what was so important about the whistling.

"It is clear that the killer is leaving clues deliberately, is it not?" said Dupin. "Well, this is another clue. If we can piece it together with the locations of the killings and the other evidence, we will have a picture of our criminal."

"Do you means he wants to be caught?"

"He or *she*, Commissioner. We do not know which yet. Not exactly. The killer is seeking attention: the miserable ego must be fed, and to that end risks will be taken. The killer is already caught in a net of his or her own fantasies and frustrated desires."

As they approached the Champ de Mars, they could see the great city that had sprung up on the old parade ground. It was a fantastic mélange of nations and cultures: spires, tents, pyramids, minarets, palaces and pleasure domes, triumphal arches and temples had been conjured out of wood, canvas, paint and plaster: all pristine, all transient. That was the Paris Exposition, a miracle of artificiality. To Dupin the whole affair had a vulgar fragility that was wholly appropriate to the bogus Emperor, the *Faux-Napoleon* who had decreed it. To Viardot it was a vast and glamorous headache.

When they arrived at the exhibition site they found that Ventroux was just beginning his tour of duty in the north-west sector of the Champ de Mars. After the briefest of introductions Dupin asked him about the whistling.

"Well, monsieur," said Ventroux, meditatively stroking his fine moustache, "it was something like a tune, something like the whistle one makes when calling for a dog or a cat."

"Like a trill of repeated notes, you mean?"

Ventroux nodded.

"Please demonstrate, if you would be so good."

The gendarme obliged. It did indeed sound rather like someone summoning a dog, or the trill of a bird, but not quite.

"Are you sure it wasn't like this?" said Dupin, and he proceeded to whistle an almost similar series of notes, but more rhythmically.

Ventroux was astonished. "That's it, monsieur! That's it exactly."

"Yes, but what *was* that?" asked Viardot.

"You did not recognize it, my friend?" said Dupin with a touch of condescension. "Then you are clearly no devotee of the opera. It was part of the tune of '*Una Voce Poco Fa*', Rosina's cavatina from *The Barber of Seville* by Rossini."

"But what possible—?"

"You *still* do not understand? The Spanish Pavilion? Seville oranges? Then there was the girl found in the Algerian Souk – *The Italian Girl in Algiers*. The Scottish Hall – *La Donna del Lago*, based on Sir Walter Scott's poem. *Le Siège de Corinthe*, under the Greek Temple (Corinthian columns, I believe). The Egyptian Pyramid – *Mosè in Egitto*. All these unfortunate girls were found on sites representing locations used by the composer Gioachino Rossini in his operas. And if I am not mistaken, they are all Rossini operas that have been performed at the Paris Opéra in recent years. You can confirm this for me. Meanwhile I must pay a call."

"On whom?"

"On Maestro Rossini, of course!"

"You do not suspect him, do you?"

"Great heavens, no! He is far too old and infirm. On the contrary, I suspect someone who has a connection with the Maestro and possibly bears a grudge against him."

"But why?"

"Did you not say that in two days' time, on the first of July—?"

"The Emperor attends a public performance of Rossini's new Hymn to inaugurate the Exhibition! You mean someone is trying to prevent this from happening?"

"Oh, it goes deeper than that. Far, far deeper. *À bientôt*, my dear Commissioner!"

Viardot contemplated his old friend Dupin as he hailed a *fiacre*. At least I have done one good thing, he thought, I have extricated him from his alcoholic stupor and given him a new lease of life.

Paris was bathed in warm evening sunshine when the *fiacre* stopped on the edge of the Bois de Boulogne in front of a villa, pleasantly situated in its own grounds. Dupin paid and dismissed the driver, and bounded up the steps to the front door with the agility of a man half his age. He presented his card to the servant who opened the door to him and was asked to wait in the hall.

Presently a tall, imposing woman in her fifties, with suspiciously jet black hair, entered. Though he had not met her before, Dupin identified her at once as Rossini's long-established mistress and guardian, Olympe Pélissier.

"Monsieur Dupin?" she said, glancing at the card. "I am afraid I have not had the pleasure of your acquaintance. I regret to say that Maestro Rossini is not receiving today. He is recovering from a slight chill. Perhaps if you would put your request in writing we will see what we can do."

"Who is that, my dear?" said a voice from one of the rooms leading off the hall. The door opened and through it waddled a very stout old man, wearing a brocade dressing gown over his day clothes and Turkish slippers on his feet. He was adjusting a wig of a rich auburn colour on his gigantic egg-shaped head.

"Why, it is the great detective, is it not? Monsieur Auguste Dupin? Hero of the Rue Morgue! Solver of the mystery of Marie Rogêt! My dear friend, it has been many years, so many years! Far too long. Come in! Come in!"

"Maestro—" began Olympe.

"My dear madame, you need not worry. I feel better already. Come into my salon, my dear Auguste, and we shall have a tisane together."

Once they were both seated on either side of the fireplace in the salon, Dupin explained the situation while Rossini listened intently. Dupin noticed that physically the great composer had deteriorated considerably since they had last met at the Opéra over a decade ago. He had become flabby and corpulent and most of his teeth were gone. The famous wig looked more grotesque than ever on his seventy-five-year-old head, but the shrewd little eyes were still bright.

"Believe me," he said when Dupin had finished, "I do not wish to make light of these horrible events, but if someone is truly trying to prevent a performance of my Hymn I should be in their debt. It is a terrible piece. Truly one of the sins of my old age. I shall not be attending the performance."

"I do not think that, but I believe someone is trying to exploit their acquaintance with you to make a point. Do you know of anyone who bears a fanatical grudge against you, or even a fanatical obsession *for* you?"

"Alas, no! Those days are long past. Success of course breeds enemies, but once one becomes eclipsed, as I have been by the likes of Signor Verdi and Herr Wagner, one's foes lose interest. In the past there were people whom I have had to cross. There have been divas of course! Ah, those delicious sirens! Those fearful harpies! There was that soprano at the Opéra, La Santelli, who lost her upper register almost overnight and became a contralto. She was very indignant about having to play supporting rather than *prima donna* roles as a consequence. But then, she was always insupportable even as a soprano. She had to go.

"Then there are the aspiring composers. Oh, dear! How can one let them down gently? I had one come to me, a gentleman too, the Marquis de Saint-Loup, a friend of our Emperor, I understand. It was three years ago, shortly after the death of my poor dear colleague Meyerbeer, and this Saint-Loup had written a solemn funeral march in his honour. After he had played it through to me on my pianoforte he asked my opinion and I said: 'Well, my dear Marquis, I think on the whole it would have been better had you died and Maestro Meyerbeer had composed the march.'

"Sometimes my wit gets the better of my good nature, I am afraid, but I do not consider those to be grounds for such atrocious homicides. My dear friend, I am afraid I have been of no help to you."

"On the contrary, Maestro, you have given me much food for thought."

"Do not wait another ten years before you visit me again, my friend. I hardly dare admit it to myself, but I am not long for this world. Olympe tries to hide the truth from me, but I know it well enough. The sins of youth have caught up with me."

The sins of youth! *Les péchés de la jeunesse!* The phrase echoed in Dupin's mind. But then, why *now*?

Dupin took a carriage to the Commissioner's office in the Faubourg Saint-Germain as he had promised. When he arrived there the place seemed to be in some confusion. In the Hall Dupin made himself known to the Commissioner's Deputy who was glancing apprehensively up the stairs. The sound of a violent argument could be heard coming from the office on the first floor.

"Commissioner Viardot is up there with the Marquis," said the Deputy Commissioner.

"Saint-Loup?" suggested Dupin.

The Deputy Commissioner nodded.

"I should like to meet the good Marquis," said Dupin and, before the Deputy Commissioner could prevent him, he was bounding up the stairs, two steps at a time. He knocked at the door of Viardot's office and, without waiting for a reply, entered.

Standing either side of a desk was the robust form of Commissioner Viardot and that of a tall, dandified, red-faced man in his late-fifties, with elaborately coiffed ginger mustachios and whiskers. His once-handsome face was now raddled and scarred by drink and debauchery, but his pale blue eyes burned fiercely. He turned on Dupin.

"How dare you enter without permission, monsieur!"

"Is this *your* office, Monsieur le Marquis?" enquired Dupin coolly.

"Is this—! How dare you, monsieur! And who are you, may I ask?"

"This is the Chevalier Dupin, Monsieur le Marquis. The man I told you about. The celebrated private investigator."

The Marquis de Saint-Loup jammed a monocle into his left eye socket and studied Dupin with what he imagined to be a highly satirical expression.

"Ah, yes, indeed! The *soi-disant* hero of the Rue Morgue, eh? And what are your conclusions this time, monsieur detective? Is it to be another homicidal orang-utan?"

"I assure you, Monsieur le Marquis," said Dupin smoothly, "that no one answering to your description is under suspicion at this present moment."

For some ten seconds Saint-Loup was speechless and his face went an even deeper shade of red. Finally he muttered: "If you were not utterly beneath my notice, Dupin, I would demand satisfaction from you."

"If I had not more pressing matters on my mind, Monsieur le Marquis, you would receive it," replied Dupin. A cold silence followed.

"I have told Viardot here," said Saint-Loup eventually, "that I want to see an arrest for these outrages within twenty-four hours. He may make use of your services, for what they are worth, if he so wishes. He may call upon the Devil himself for all I care, but let this matter be cleared up without any further delay. Is that understood? You seem to forget that the honour of France and of the Emperor are at stake. Good night to you!" And with that he swept from the room.

"You should not have provoked him," said Viardot.

"I apologize."

"Sometimes I think he is not quite sane. Especially when he is in liquor. You doubtless noticed—?"

"Yes. I caught a whiff of his breath as he went past. He too is a devotee of the Green Fairy. But there is all the difference in the world, my dear Viardot, between a gourmet and a gourmand. Well, what have you discovered?"

"You were quite right. The Rossini operas that you mention have been performed at the Opéra in recent years, but there were others."

"In heaven's name, which others?"

"I do not remember."

"Then find out! Find out their casts, the circumstances of their production. Anything you can. Don't you see? If this killer strikes again, it will be in the pavilion of a nation where a Rossini opera has been set. There is some method to the killer's madness, but I cannot yet quite see what that method is. Meanwhile, your men must be vigilant both tonight and tomorrow night. I feel sure that the killer will strike again before July the first, the day on which Rossini's Hymn is to be performed. One more thing: did you notice the Marquis's teeth?"

"His teeth? What about them?"

"They are black."

"So they are. What of it?"

"There, I believe, you have the key to the whole mystery. As yet, I can prove nothing, but a little more research may yield results."

"But black teeth—?"

"*Les péchés de la jeunesse*, my dear Viardot. The sins of youth! Till tomorrow. Be vigilant!"

"I don't do anything funny like that. I'm a nice clean girl, I am."

"But I have heard different, mademoiselle."

"Oh, who from? I've got my principles same as everyone else. There are certain things I will not do."

"I pay in gold. Look!"

"Well, I might. But I want to be treated with respect."

"You will receive the respect you deserve, *ma fille*. Have another drink."

"I don't mind if I do."

"That's better. We could have a little singsong afterwards, couldn't we?"

"You're a strange one and no mistake."

"And you're a dirty little girl, aren't you? Dirty down below. Dirty all through. But I'm going to clean you out. Good and proper. With my little—"

"No—!"

Paris, June 30th, 1867

That morning Dupin rose early and went to the Opéra. There he spent time talking to whomever he could find: scene painters, stage hands, musicians, singers, particularly those who had served in that great theatre for a long time. Several times he dispatched messages to Commissioner Viardot's office requesting that he be informed of any developments.

Finally he returned to his apartment in the Rue Saint-Honoré to wait impatiently for Viardot to summon him. He barely touched the exquisite little supper that his manservant Marcel placed before him. The clock in the façade of the nearby church of

Saint-Roch, where in 1763 the Marquis de Sade had been married, chimed eight . . . nine . . . ten . . .

Suddenly there was a knocking at the apartment door. Marcel let in Commissioner Viardot and showed him into the library where Dupin was sitting disconsolately over a fine Armagnac. He looked up eagerly.

"He struck again last night. The same hideous methods," said Viardot.

"Last night! Then in God's name, why have you only just told me?"

"We found the body but an hour ago. Yet it has been there for eighteen hours at least. It had been hidden by a display of regional crafts in the French Pavilion. A member of the public, a lady, discovered it quite by accident."

"Have you detained the lady in question?"

"No."

"Ah! Never mind. In which part of the French Pavilion was the body found? Devoted to which region of France?"

"Does it matter?"

"It could matter very much. It could mean everything."

"The body was found hidden under a display of wines."

"Wines! But from what district?"

"The Loire Valley, I think."

"The Loire! Of course! And close by, models of châteaux—"

"Correct—"

"Amboise, Chinon, Fourmentieres? The district of Touraine."

"Yes, but what—?"

"Of course! *Le Comte Ory!* Then tonight the killer will strike once more, and I know where. Is your carriage waiting down below?"

"It is."

"Then we haven't a moment to lose. We will stop off at your office only to summon as many men as we can."

"But where then?"

"To the Swiss Alpine village in the Exposition, of course! Pray God that we are in time!"

In the carriage, as they hurried once again towards the Exposition in the Champ de Mars, Viardot turned to his friend Dupin.

"I know that you like to keep your reasoning to yourself, but I must beg you to explain why we are hurrying towards the Swiss Alpine village."

"It is very simple. *Le Comte Ory* is set in the district of Touraine in the Loire Valley. It was the last but one opera that Rossini wrote specifically for the Paris Opéra. (I exclude the *pasticcios* of course.) The two previous ones were *Moïse* (a version of *Mosè in Egitto*) and *Le Siège de Corinth*. So the last three victims were killed in the locations of these three operas in sequence. And what is the last opera that Maestro Rossini composed for Paris?"

"Of course! I know that. It was *Guillaume Tell*. And so, the Swiss Alpine village!"

"Precisely. But there is a further question. Why did the killer conceal the last body, a thing that had not been done before? My conjecture is that our criminal reckoned that we would guess where the next assassination would take place. The clues had become too obvious. Therefore the killer needed to delay our arrival at the scene until the dreadful work was done."

"It seems a very risky procedure in any case. There must be something more behind it than that."

"Oh, I agree! Dear God, can't your coachman go any faster?"

At the entrance to the Champ de Mars Dupin and Viardot alighted and were met with about twenty gendarmes. Viardot instructed them to make their way as swiftly and unobtrusively as they could towards the Swiss section.

There were still plenty of revellers about, wandering through the strange, artificially cosmopolitan avenues and piazzas. Few people noticed the purposeful way in which Dupin and Viardot hurried towards the Swiss Alpine village in the far west of the Champ de Mars.

On arrival they found that most of the gendarmes had got there before them.

With brisk efficiency Viardot spread out his forces and the posse embarked on a thorough search of all the dwellings in the Swiss section. It was a kind of street, decked out with all the picturesqueness of an idealized mountain community. Bright flowers (mostly artificial) erupted from window boxes and hanging baskets. At the end of the street was a wooden chalet with a veranda and, set into its steeply pitched roof, a gigantic cuckoo clock.

"Stop!" said Viardot, pointing to the chalet. "Do you hear singing coming from that building?"

It was a faint sound, but eerily clear in the half-darkness. A deranged sound it was, cracking at all the high notes, half-sobbing at times. Its tones were drunken, self-pitying and desolate. All those who heard it shuddered.

Dupin murmured: "If I am not mistaken it is '*Ah, Mathilde, je t'aime et je t'adore*' – Arnold's aria from the first act of *Guillaume Tell*. But execrably sung."

"Dear God! And I know by whom!" said Viardot.

The next moment he was expertly directing his men to surround the chalet while he, a revolver in one hand, a lantern in the other, mounted the steps of the chalet. Dupin followed him, unsheathing as he did so the blade from his silver-topped cane.

The door was ajar and they entered. Viardot's lantern threw fantastic shadows around the dark interior, and up into the imprisoning latticework of its roof beams. Lying on the black, polished wooden floor in front of them lay what looked at first like a confusion of lace petticoats and tawdry finery, dashed and slashed with blood. It was the body of a young woman, almost a girl. The face when at last seen was too horrible to contemplate. The eyes were mere holes of scrambled dark red sinew, the ears had been severed and were lying neatly to one side along with the girl's tongue. Her mouth was filled with bloody froth. Over this was crouched a tall man in dandified clothes, still crooning his wretched approximation of Rossini's aria.

It was the Marquis de Saint-Loup.

He looked up slowly at Viardot and Dupin, blinking a little. He appeared to be in a dream, not fully aware of the situation in which he found himself.

"Ah, good evening, messieurs," he said in a breathy, quavering voice. "I have been expecting you."

By this time the room had become filled with gendarmes, many carrying lanterns, all stunned into silence by the spectacle that confronted them.

"Monsieur le Marquis de Saint-Loup," said Viardot in a sonorous voice, "I arrest you in the name of the law for the brutal murder of this unfortunate woman and for the slaughter of six others."

Saint-Loup was becoming conscious of his position. He began to rouse himself; his eyes flashed with indignation.

"This is an outrage! Ridiculous! How can you think this has anything to do with me?"

"Then how do you come to be here, Monsieur le Marquis?"

"Damnation take it, because you and that fellow Dupin summoned me here!"

"We did nothing of the kind, Saint-Loup, and you know it. Have you any proof that we did?"

"Ten thousand thunders, Viardot, I don't need any proof! I am the Marquis de Saint-Loup and you, monsieur, are an impudent beggar who is about to be relieved of his position."

"I think not, Monsieur le Marquis. Officers, take him away!"

Paris, July 1st, 1867
At ten o'clock that morning Dupin was sitting in Commissioner Viardot's office. Viardot's manner was brisk and complacent, but his friend noticed a residual sense of unease.

"Of course," said Viardot, "it is something of an inconvenience that the culprit is the Marquis de Saint-Loup, a favourite of the Emperor himself and on the steering committee of the Exposition. However, there is no doubt about his guilt. I have had him thoroughly examined by a doctor and it is quite clear that he is clinically insane."

"The consequence of the tertiary stage of syphilis, no doubt."

"That is correct. How did you know?"

"His teeth. I told you they were black: the blackening occurs as a result of ingesting mercury. Mercury is believed to be a cure for the disease, though I have my doubts. You know the old grim jest: one hour in Venus, and the rest of your life in Mercury."

"It explains everything. He was taking collective vengeance on these girls for giving him the disease. That was his motive. His position gave him access to all the national pavilions: his means. The obsession with opera and the works of Rossini gave him his method. Finally, he is discovered almost red-handed as it were. Thanks to you, my dear Dupin, we have an open and shut case from which not even influence in high places can extricate him."

"So it would seem."

"You have your doubts, Dupin?"

"I have no doubt that the Marquis de Saint-Loup is the ultimate cause of these dreadful events, but was he the perpetrator? That is a different matter."

"How so?"

"Consider the murders, Viardot. All planned and executed with meticulous care down to the last detail. Mad but methodical. And then with the last killing he allows himself to be caught on the spot in a state of drunken stupor. It makes no sense. Saint-Loup is a physical and mental wreck, Viardot. He has not and never has had the capacity for these crimes."

"Then how and why was he present at the scene of the crime?"

"It was as he said. He received a message supposedly from us, but in fact from the killer. Being deranged and almost certainly drunk at that time of night, he went there. Of course the killer was taking a risk, but fantastic arrogance is part of the extreme criminal's nature. Besides, the killer undoubtedly knew Saint-Loup and was thereby able to obtain or purloin private access to the requisite pavilions, temples and chalets."

"Then in God's name who is it, Dupin?"

"I believe I know, but we need to flush out our culprit. If this fails then we must be content with our result. There may be no more murders, but I don't think the game is quite over as far as our killer is concerned. I want you to do something for me, Viardot. I want you to make it known that the Marquis has died in custody – perhaps even committed suicide – and that we are fully satisfied that that is the end of the matter."

Viardot gave his consent with a small shrug and Dupin then issued further instructions.

Dupin spent the day making more arrangements. He told his manservant Marcel to visit his mother and stay the night with her at her house. In the evening Dupin dined at Bignon's. There he met the poet Stéphane Mallarmé, who was working on a translation of Poe's "The Raven". Dupin dared to suggest to his literary friend that "*Le Corbeau dit Jamais plus!*" was an accurate but otherwise wholly inadequate rendering of "Quoth the Raven, Nevermore!"

"My dear Stéphane, not even a French raven would ever say '*Jamais plus*'," said Dupin, but his advice fell on deaf ears.

The church of Saint-Roch was chiming the hour of nine when Dupin returned to his apartment on the Rue Saint-Honoré.

As he stepped into his own hallway he paused to scent the air; then, detecting an unfamiliar perfume, he took up the lighted oil lamp that Marcel had left for him on the hall table and entered the library. He was expecting company.

A slight movement of the shadows in the corner of the room convinced him that he was not alone.

"Good evening, madame," said Dupin. "You are here a little earlier than I had anticipated."

"I saw your servant go out. I thought I would take my chance."

Out of the shadows stepped a tall, statuesque woman with a heavy veil over her face. It was, as a result, hard to tell her age, but she must have been somewhere in her fifties. She wore a dress of shimmering silk, dark green like a dragonfly's wing, trimmed with black lace.

"You know who I am then?" she said, her voice trembling a little.

"I believe so. You are Eugénie Santerre, better known to the world as Eugenia Santelli, the opera singer."

"I am, or rather *was,* La Santelli. *Prima Donna Assoluta* of the Paris Opéra."

"Why have you come here?"

"I have come to tell you that you are wrong. You, the great, the one and only, the first of all detectives who penetrated the secret of the Rue Morgue, who unravelled the affair of Marie Rogêt and many others, are utterly mistaken. You are nothing but a doddering old fool. Whatever powers you may once have possessed have been dribbled away in absinthe and idleness.

"In your vanity you imagine you have solved the great mystery of the Paris Exhibition Murders of 1867, but you have not! The Marquis de Saint-Loup who has died in your custody is absolutely innocent, and I can prove it."

"Innocent is hardly a word I would use with reference to the Marquis, madame, but if you mean that he did not perpetrate those murders, I know that and never for a moment imagined that he was guilty of them." Dupin heard Santelli gasp, but she stood her ground. "However, I would be most interested to know how you can prove that he was not the killer."

"Simple! I was with him at the time of the murders."

Dupin laughed. "I see! You were going to go to the jail, tell the authorities that you were with him and have him released. Then he would at last be truly in your power. You may even have fondly imagined that he would marry you as he had promised all those years ago in the days of your glory. But this is foolishness, madame. You were not with the Marquis at the time of the murders."

"How can you possibly know that?"

"Because you committed the murders yourself, madame."

There was a silence in the room. Both Dupin and Santelli remained utterly still. It was as if each were daring the other to make the next move.

"You can prove nothing, Dupin."

"On the contrary, madame! It would be a matter of the utmost simplicity, for example, to establish that it was you who discovered the body in the French Pavilion, thereby alerting the authorities, deliberately too late, to the whereabouts of your final atrocity. Need I go on?

"But there is one thing I have yet to understand, madame. Why did you want to draw *me* into this business? All that mystification with the Green Fairy. That was for my benefit, was it not? Why did you want to humiliate me so much?"

"My brother was Alphonse Santerre. Perhaps you remember him?"

"Ah! The great Banque de Paris swindle. I remember it."

"It was your evidence that convicted him. If you hadn't insisted to the police that the clerks Gatinet and Fauvinard were too lowly and stupid to have devised the whole scheme, and that there must have been a mastermind behind it, he might have escaped justice. I even came to you, to this very apartment here, and begged you on my bended knees not to pursue the case against my brother. Dear God! I even offered myself to you. And I was beautiful then."

"Yes, I recollect now. Vaguely. And did I . . .?"

"No, you did not."

"I am relieved to hear it."

"You're not a man at all, Dupin. You're a machine! A mere calculating, detecting machine. You have no heart!"

"And you, madame, who butchered and mutilated those wretched women in cold blood, to humiliate me and to spite and take possession again of your precious Marquis, you accuse *me* of having no heart?"

"My heart is broken. I have suffered more than any woman deserves to suffer. And it goes on! My brother is out of prison now, but his life has been ruined. He lives with a drab on the Rue de Lappe and cries like a baby if there is no money to buy him the oblivion of drink.

"I went to Saint-Loup to ask if he might do something for Alphonse and he merely laughed in my face. That man for whom I sacrificed so much! He possessed my very soul, but then he threw it away on a whim, and before he left me he did something else to me that I can never forgive."

"As I thought! It was the Marquis de Saint-Loup who made you a contralto."

"My God! You understand everything!"

"It is well known in musical circles, madame, that the venereal infection of syphilis can affect the vocal cords by deepening their register, and this is truer among women than men. Many years ago Maestro Rossini told me of it."

"It is true. I hated being a contralto. When you have been a great soprano, a *Prima Donna Assoluta*, everything else is dust and ashes in the mouth. And it was not only my voice it affected. Look!"

She drew aside her veil. The left side of her face was redder than the other side. Little clutches of broken veins blossomed on her cheeks and forehead, and it looked as if on that side, the features had somehow slipped downwards. The left-hand corners of her mouth and left eye were pulled down, so as to resemble one half of a badly made Mask of Tragedy.

"So you planned to mutilate others as you had been mutilated," said Dupin. The tone of his voice surprised Santelli, even Dupin himself, because it was not angry or indignant, merely sad, meditative and infinitely weary. "But where will it all end, madame?"

"Here!" said La Santelli, and Dupin saw that she had drawn from her *réticule* an elegant pearl-handled pistol of American make. She pointed it at him, but he made no move. At last he too was in her power, she thought, but only for a moment.

She couldn't help noticing that Dupin was not looking directly at her any more but at something behind her right shoulder. A trick of his?

Almost involuntarily she began to turn to see what it was he was looking at and at that moment a voice behind her said: "I'll take that, if you please, madame!", and her pistol arm was seized in a firm grip by Commissioner Viardot.

A gendarme appeared as if from nowhere and put handcuffs on La Santelli, who by now had begun to scream. The screams transformed themselves into hysterical laughter as she was being led away.

Auguste Dupin's library has several entrances, not all of them immediately visible to the naked eye.

Paris, July 2nd, 1867, a little before five
Commissioner Viardot and Dupin were seated at a table in the Café Momus drinking coffee.

"I must congratulate you, my dear Viardot," said Dupin. "I understand you are to receive a commendation from the Emperor himself for your resolution of this case."

"Are you sure that I can say nothing about your part in the affair?"

"I absolutely forbid it. If you do I will be besieged by nuisances requesting my services as a detective. Old ladies will be demanding that I find their pet dogs for them and I shall never know another moment's peace. One of the few blessings of old age is that you cease to crave celebrity."

"Very well, my friend, I shall leave you to your absinthe and your obscurity. But tell me one thing. You seem to have known from the start that the perpetrator was a woman. How was that?"

"It had to be a woman. The crimes were simply too elaborately conceived for a man's mind. Male and female criminalities have different motives. In men it is always the desire for power, for control pure and simple. In women vindictiveness is the ruling motive: getting even. What is that line of Congreve about 'a woman scorned' that the English always misquote?

"In some cases this longing for vengeance becomes a mania, a disease of the psyche, as you might say, especially when it is exacerbated by a disease of the body like syphilis. La Santelli saw an opportunity to wreak vengeance both on me and the good Marquis. She almost succeeded."

"But at what cost!"

"A cost she wanted to pay. All such killers are out to take vengeance on the world, and that means, ultimately, that they must take vengeance chiefly on themselves, for the world has shrunk to the size of their own diseased brain. But the real clue to the sex of the killer, as you yourself intimated at the very beginning, my dear Commissioner, was in the absinthe."

"How so?"

"Each of those wretchéd women had been plied with the Green Fairy before being killed, so that they were rendered weak and could offer up no resistance. That implied a weak assailant. No male killer would ever have done that. It would have offended his vanity to suppose that he could not overpower a woman by sheer strength and without the adventitious aid of a drug. The whole object of the venture would have been defeated; but a woman's motive, even a madwoman's motive, is more subtle and devious. *Ma se mi toccano dov'è il mio debole, Sarò una vipera, sarò.* Cross me in love and I become the deadliest of vipers."

"Dante?"

"No, Rossini. *The Barber of Seville.* I can remember La Santelli as Rosina singing those very words." Dupin looked at his watch. "Ah! Five o'clock. It is time, my dear Viardot, for you to go to receive your commendation from the Emperor. You must hurry. The great and powerful wait for no man because they know their greatness and power is as fleeting as a fairy's flight. I must also hurry, for it is *L'Heure Verte. Garçon!*"

As if by magic the waiter appeared with Dupin's glass of absinthe. It was the Green Hour and Viardot left his friend to perform, priest-like, his ritual with the water, the sugar cubes, the silver spoon, and a glass half-full of a pale green fluid that looked like a distillation of young grass in sunlight.

STEVE RASNIC TEM

The Secret Laws of the Universe

ED THOUGHT THE toaster had a disapproving aspect. "Have you told your wife yet?" It was difficult to tell which part of the toaster the voice was coming from.

Ed sought to avoid eye contact, but had no idea where not to look. "I don't want to worry her."

"Human beings like to be prepared, or at least to have the illusion. It's characteristic of your race."

"They're not my race." When the toaster began to harangue him, demanding some sort of explanation, Ed left the kitchen. He'd been speaking emotionally, not logically of course. Often he didn't feel like part of the human race, and he didn't expect anyone to understand this, but he wasn't about to be embarrassed in his own home by an appliance.

Behind him, he heard his toast pop up with a ding: done. The toaster sighed.

"It'll get cold if you just leave it there." His wife glanced over the paper at him. She had her own breakfast spread out over her end of the dining-room table – ham and scrambled eggs, a carafe of black coffee, bagel and cream cheese, and a bowl of freshly sliced fruit, all the colours artfully arranged.

"I don't like my toast hot. Cool is fine with me."

"Well, nobody likes it cold."

"I said cool, not cold. And with a little bit of strawberry jam on top, it tastes great."

"I'd be happy to fix your toast when I make my own breakfast, however you want it fixed, Ed. I'll even stick your toast in the freezer, if that's what you really want."

"Well, I appreciate that." It was a marriage lie, and marriage lies don't count. "But you have a job to get to. And I have to be able to do a few things for myself."

Jillian gazed at him with her head slightly tilted. "I guess I can't argue with that."

The coffee carafe said, "Tell her you're going to kill her, Ed. You owe her that much, for all she's done for you." Or perhaps it was the chandelier. One of the bulbs blinked and buzzed, sending painful pulses directly into Ed's brain.

They all acted as if he *wanted* to kill her. Clearly no one understood. He went back into the kitchen and retrieved his cooling toast from the top of the toaster. It caught on the edge of the slot until he ordered, "Let go, dammit." He slapped it on a plate.

Back in the dining room he stared at his plate with the burned square of bread. He'd forgotten his table knife.

Was it okay to put the jam from the serving spoon directly on to his toast if he hadn't touched the bread with his lips? He reached over and took the spoon out of the jam, loaded it, and deposited the bright red spread on the edge of his plate, cognizant that Jillian was watching him, waiting for any mistake so that she might instruct him in some fine point of etiquette. He guided his toast across the protruding jam, being careful not to let any of it spill on to the table.

Of course he knew this convoluted methodology couldn't be the way things were normally done, but at least he hadn't contaminated anything or messed up the tablecloth. She couldn't call him on that. Sometimes he had to jump through hoops simply to avoid the tiniest of mistakes. The jam wasn't evenly spread but at least he'd achieved some coverage.

"You're calling your doctor today, right?" She sipped her coffee, gazing at him unblinking.

"That's the plan."

"Those headaches aren't going to go away by themselves."

Ed didn't say anything. His toast was frowning at him. Whether that meant the toast agreed with Jillian and was expressing its disapproval, or the toast wanted Ed to say something back to Jillian, anything that meant he was a man with his own voice, Ed did not know, because unlike the toaster, the chandelier, and the carafe, his toast apparently had no speaking apparatus.

But the displeasure of the toast was palpable, even more so because of its silence. Unable to eat anything so disapproving, Ed picked up his plate and the jar of jam and returned to the kitchen.

"I'm hardly surprised you're not hungry," the toaster said. "Guilt rarely whets the appetite."

In response Ed pushed the unhappy toast into the garbage disposal and turned it on. The toaster cried out in alarm.

Ed stood with hands on either side of the sink and stared out the window. It was a bright morning, the sun lending its glow to flowers and lawn. It was the kind of day he would have loved to just lie down in the grass and take it all in, letting the warmth spread through his limbs and set fire to his blood. That was one of the few perks available to temporary life forms, experiencing that interchange between air and sun and flesh, one's body a soup of cells thriving and cells dying. A toaster could never know this pleasure, or a chandelier, and yet a toaster could be repaired endlessly, if one ignored practical economics, or its bits recycled into some other machine. And that chandelier might hang in the house for the next family, or the one thereafter, long after Ed was gone. Longevity had always been unfairly distributed. Shouldn't his life be worth more than a stone's?

He should have been out there, enjoying his temporary time, but that would have been irresponsible, and impossible to explain to Jillian. "She really has done everything for you," the jar of jam said from the counter. "She's been very patient. Not everyone would put up with your eccentric behaviour."

Ed found a sharp knife and stabbed it down into the sweet strawberry goodness. The jam attempted to expound further, but Ed churned the knife blade, eviscerating the aborted speech. He heard the TV go on in the living room. Jillian enjoyed watching a few minutes of television every morning before going in to the office, usually programmes recorded the day before which she fast-forwarded between the more interesting segments. She liked the shows about "real people" the best, a kind of programming which appeared to have completely taken over the airwaves.

A young woman was talking about becoming a professional singer. She said it was her dream and she refused to have a back-up plan. Ed felt badly for her. Everyone he knew, practically, had been forced to live their back-up plan, and all too often it was not of their own design, but handed to them. "Here," the world said. "Go do this instead."

Someone was trying to talk over the young woman. People could be so rude sometimes, so callous and uncaring. There was even laughter in the background. Then Ed realized it was another soundtrack laid over the first.

"Now would be a good time, Ed," the TV said. "She's watching some of her favourite shows, enjoying herself – what better time for her to die?"

"But she has to get to work," he offered lamely. "She's going to be late."

"Do you really think she wants to be at work? Wouldn't she rather be famous? Wouldn't all your kind much rather be famous?"

"She loves her work. She says it all the time."

"She's learned to make do. If you kill her now, it should make the evening papers. Don't you think she would like that? And if you continue, if *you* become famous, then she will as well. Famous people, they live for ever."

"I don't think she'd rather—"

"You have the knife in your hand already, Ed. Now why don't you use it?"

Ed looked down at the knife clutched in his right hand, strawberry jam melting off the blade and dribbling on to the clean white tile floor. He backed away from the sound of the television, turned and ran to the back door, jerking it open with his left hand, confused about what he should do with the knife.

The man from the dairy was bent over the milk bottles on the back porch, replacing the empties with full ones of an impossibly white colour, the milk so bright in hue it could only be a motion-picture effect. The man straightened up, his white suit so perfect with nary a wrinkle, and when he saw the knife stained with still-dripping strawberry jam he looked as if he would scream, and if he were to scream Jillian would come out there, and she would miss her shows and be late to work, but most of all she would be so terribly disappointed in him, when all she'd ever done was her very best for him.

The milkman looked down and Ed's gaze followed. The knife was embedded slightly above mid-abdomen, at an upward angle.

And all that red couldn't possibly be jam. The dairy man fell back against the railing and toppled to the ground.

Ed waited anxiously as Jillian gathered her purse, keys, briefcase, and a compact, fashionable lunch tote with flower designs which looked a bit like eyes elaborated with fanciful make-up. Several of these eyes now looked up at him in despair. The jangle of her keys said, "Do it, do it when her back is turned!" He had a hammer he'd retrieved from the closet hidden behind his back for that very purpose, but he knew he would not be doing it. Not this time.

"I don't know why these people waste their time on these impossible dreams," she was saying with a kind of aimless annoyance. "Even if they're talented, well, what difference does that make anyway? Most people are unlucky, or they lack the connections. You have to know how to work the system, you know?"

Ed was anxious for her to leave, but the conversation had veered so closely to what he pondered each and every day he couldn't quite let it go. "So how do they learn how to do that? How do they find out?"

"How should I know? Do I look like a success to you? Some doors close, you leave them closed. You can't re-open them." She was obviously furious now, and he didn't know why. She frightened him when she was like this – he couldn't have swung the hammer at her even if it had been the right time. "I'm just a working girl, remember?"

"I'm sorry, I—"

"Just call your doctor, make an appointment, okay? And make a few job contacts today – you can do that for me, can't you?"

"Of course," he said softly, also annoyed now, stepping back so she could leave. He could have swung the hammer as she turned, but he would not kill her in anger. No matter what, it could not happen like that.

As soon as he heard her car pull away from the front of the house he returned to the back yard where he'd stashed the dairy man beneath an old quilt. He went to his knees beside the body and started to cry, but then furiously wiped his tears away and began to roll the quilt up with the body inside. He had a little bit of old twine – he didn't think it would hold – but he wrapped it around the legs and head anyway. Then with considerable strain he began dragging the awkward package toward the garage along the side of the house, the head-end snagging on the edge of bushes and flowerbed fencing, forcing him to stop now and then to wiggle things free. At least the overgrown bushes around the edge of the yard shielded him from the neighbours. Jillian had nagged him for months to trim them back – perhaps he hadn't gotten around to it for a reason? Could this be working the system?

"Where are you going with that?" the house said.

Ed knew it was the house because of the weight the words made in his head, and because something along the lines of the foundation had shifted and shifted back, even though it hadn't been visual exactly, but more like a movement between dimensions, like travelling through time. In any case it frightened him, because of the depth of structural instability it suggested.

"I'll put it into the trunk of my car. Then I plan to drive it somewhere, get rid of it somewhere."

"Good, I wouldn't want it just lying around here. Is that Jillian in there?"

"No. No, it's someone else." Ed was slightly surprised at the house's ignorance of what had recently occurred in its own back yard. Was that what happened when you lived longer? Your perspective changed so much you didn't even notice the daily tragedies?

"I thought the plan was to kill Jillian, and that would open up some doors, some possibilities for you to have a different life?"

"It's not that cut and dried, but yes, obviously if the life you're living goes away there's now room for a different one. You don't even have to think about it – it will just happen."

"And yet you've killed someone else?"

"It was an accident."

"You're avoiding what you know you need to do to get that other life – you don't want to kill her. You'll kill everyone else in the world first to avoid killing her."

"Of course I don't want to kill her. We have some problems, but I've always loved her, still do. But I don't know what else to do. This *can't* be my life."

"The secret laws of the universe are a conundrum. Why do some get what they want and some do not? The laws mean even less to a house. We are simply here, and then one day you people make a decision to tear us down."

"I have no such plans." Ed was thinking he had no more control over such decisions than over anything else in his life.

"You could travel to her place of work and kill her there. It would be most unexpected," the house said.

Rather than answer (Could he? Would he?) Ed replied, "I have no problem with rules *per se* – rules, laws, principles, that's what makes mathematics, chemistry, physics, work, right? And without those things the world would not function."

The house appeared to have fallen back asleep, or into whatever meditative state architecture is prone to. Ed did not want to discuss things further anyway, instead busying himself getting the body into the trunk of his car, and his car out of the garage. The vehicle ran sluggishly. Ed had not driven it in weeks.

Body disposal was actually not a topic Ed had seriously considered before. He certainly wouldn't have tried to dispose of Jillian's body – you don't do that kind of thing to someone you love. Although he hadn't thought it completely through he'd always assumed he'd claim an intruder had killed her, or that she'd fallen down the stairs. Faking grief would have been no problem because his grief would have been completely genuine. In fact he'd always thought that killing her might fall under the general category of natural causes. Anticipated, certainly, but hardly desired.

So he drove around awhile, hoping to see some options. "I thought we were going to your wife's office," the car said. "I thought you were going to kill her there."

"You've got a pretty good radio. It's been a while since I listened to it – let's turn it on. Full volume."

"You're changing the subject."

"There are people at her office. They would see."

"But have you thought about trying to live in that house after having killed her there? That would be stressful, don't you think?" Ed hadn't considered that. "You didn't think about it because you never seriously thought you would go through with it."

Ed leaned forward and switched on the radio.

"You're not going to be able to avoid this," the car said from the radio and from everywhere else. Ed turned the radio off to kill the echo.

He gradually began to realize that he was in an unfamiliar neighbourhood. It was an older suburb with mature trees, the houses built in the late-sixties, maybe early-seventies. Split-levels and tri-levels mostly. Not very expensive – he supposed they'd be called cheap by some, but very well kept. Perhaps too well. When he considered all the painting and countless specific repairs to old wood and siding and plywood, the effort to keep casement windows usable, all the lawns mowed and hedges trimmed and leaves raked, and the incremental landscaping improvements – the borders and gazebos and fountains and walks and statuary – the time spent keeping up these dolls' houses, these pleasant appearances, it boggled the mind. Wasn't there a better way to spend your time than devising temporary façades in order to put the best possible face on your world?

The street was quiet, empty. The kids would be in school, he supposed, the adults off at their jobs. There would be a few retirees, no doubt – this was the kind of neighbourhood some would retire to – the top of the ladder, the end of the chain, the penultimate destination and the final goal. For some, this was what life would amount to.

An older fellow – dressed in a furry rust-coloured sweater and corduroys, a bit warmly for the weather – shuffled down one of the neatly paved and edged driveways toward the street, leaf rake in hand. He didn't look happy or particularly sad, but there was fatigue in the way he began to rake at the few leaves spilling off his lawn into the gutter. He used short, deliberate strokes precisely overlapped so that every bit of lawn was covered, his almost aggressive focus tiring to watch. Once he got all the leaves into the gutter he herded them toward one particular pile along the curb. For what reason Ed could not imagine.

His property seemed to be the most perfect, the most refined of any of those very refined properties on the block. It must have taken him days, a lifetime of days, to obsessively groom his realm, this relatively tiny area of the universe.

"He's got it all sorted," the car said. "At last he thinks he's got it all figured out."

"I understand the impulse," Ed said. "During these spells of unemployment I'd go out and work in the yard. Not just because Jillian nagged me to do it, but because that way I could show all my neighbours I actually had things to do. It was the only time I ever talked to any of them, really. We'd talk about the weather, and what needed to be done, and how good it would all look if we could only get it all done, but we knew we couldn't get it all done because it was so constant. It made me feel like one of them, but it was depressing. I kept asking myself, 'Is this what it's really all about? Is this what a human life amounts to?'"

The car began to roll forward. Ed never could decide if the car did it on its own (surely a car that talks was capable of driving itself), or if he had deliberately put it into gear and stepped on the gas pedal. In fact, he couldn't even remember if he'd pulled over and parked in order to observe the neighbourhood more closely, or if he'd been driving the entire time, but cruising slowly.

As the car came upon him, the elderly man looked over his shoulder in mild surprise. Not fear, really, and not true surprise. It was the kind of surprise you experience at the moment even though this was something you'd really been expecting all along.

The man went down quickly, and the bump the left front tyre made as it rolled over him was much smaller than Ed would have expected.

Ed drove along in silence for a time, out of that neighbourhood and into another, another still. The car appeared to have nothing to say. Then, as Ed searched for the on-ramp, the car spoke up. "See how easy that was? Quick and painless."

"We don't know there wasn't any pain."

"I didn't hear any screaming, did you? You could have done the same thing with Jillian – it could have been finished by now."

"I don't think I could handle it if Jillian looked at me the way that old fellow did. His last sight was of me behind the wheel. I'd hate for the last thing Jillian ever sees is me behind the wheel."

"It's only a moment. A second. She might even think she was hallucinating it."

"That doesn't help any."

"That old man should have been Jillian. Are you going to kill everybody in this city before you get around to killing your wife? I thought you wanted a different life for yourself. I believe you once said *this* just couldn't *be* your life."

"I'm going to her office now. We'll just have to see what happens."

"You have to *choose*, Ed," the car said plaintively. "I know you love her and it's a terrible thing, but you only get *one* life. People get trapped because they settle for feeling *just a little* happy, or being *just a little* successful." The car horn blared suddenly, painfully. "Wake up, Ed!" the car screamed unmercifully. "Wake yourself up!"

If he drove the car head-on into the next tree would he feel any pain, and for how long?

He found the on-ramp to the interstate bypass that led downtown, a narrow single lane hidden behind a row of trees, as if this part of town wanted to pretend it was out in the country. The highway was rather full for a Thursday morning, and he found himself veering close to the other lanes, sometimes crossing lines, as he attempted to get a good look at the other drivers, and assess in some way their purpose, their intentions, or at least their mood. Periodically someone would honk their annoyance, and the car would honk back in kind, on its own and independent of Ed's wishes. It occurred to him that this might be a dangerous strategy, and indeed some vehicles made their own incursions into Ed's lane.

"Look at all these people with nothing to do," the car said.

"Some of them drive for their jobs, and some of them have important errands to run, I'm sure."

"And some are just driving aimlessly around," the car said. "I'm an expert at this, remember? I can tell when a driver has no business being out on the road."

"I don't know that you can say they have no business . . ."

"They can't stand or sit still. They find their own little patch of ground, the area beneath their shadow, an intolerable place to be in. They'd rather do anything than fill their own space. They can't be satisfied anywhere. If they could jump out of their own skin, believe me they would. Travelling around aimlessly in a car is simply a substitute for jumping out of your own skin."

Ed had been paying so much attention to the car's speech he hadn't noticed their relative position in the lane. He looked out the driver's side window and saw the man in the next car, just a few feet separating them, as he mimed a performance of the radio's latest hit single. The man turned his head suddenly, as if now aware of being watched, and stared at Ed with his mouth open.

The side of Ed's car rubbed the other vehicle. "Scrape!" the car said, followed by a high-pitched metallic chuckle. The other car went up on to the concrete divider and flipped over just as Ed passed it. He watched in his rear-view mirror as other cars crashed into the first, spinning it on its rapidly crumpling hood.

His car took the next exit, accelerated down the off-ramp and trundled over two homeless people stationed there with their cardboard signs. One of the wheels caught and spun, damp red debris spraying out from the wheel well. Ed began to scream.

"Calm down! I'm trying to drive here!" the car said.

The car took side streets and alleys, cutting across the occasional parking lot. Bits of metal and other trash dropped off here and there. Finally they pulled behind a building near a service entrance.

"This is Jillian's building. How did you . . ." Ed began.

"You've taken me here before, remember? Now go do what you have to. I, unfortunately, won't fit in the elevator." With that the car sputtered and stalled out.

Ed climbed shakily from the car. Clearly, at least in this small part of the universe, there had been a rule change. He walked around his old automobile, now silent except for the steam escaping from the engine compartment. The paint was scraped off the length of it in several inch-wide, wavy silvery stripes that showed white-hot as they reflected the sun. They might even have been called "cool" under some new system of rules. Blood was spattered here and there with that randomness that never looks entirely random, but more like an artist's interpretation of random.

Clearly he'd have to kill Jillian now. Better to kill her than to have her see what he'd done to the car.

He came into the building through the janitor's entrance, which they never locked. Will the security guy, who'd once been a grocery-store manager until he retired and then gone back to work in security because he couldn't survive on his small savings, dozed soundly at the front desk. There was no one else down in the lobby – most of the companies here conducted their business by phone or over the Internet. Ed reached down and removed

Will's gun from its holster. Will started, opened his eyes and looked at him. "Whoah," he said. "You're – you're Jillian's husband, right?"

"Shoot me," the gun said. Ed was confused. "Shoot me," the gun repeated, then Ed understood.

"You want me to *fire* you, right? Fire you and shoot him," Ed said patiently. Will sat up quickly. "Are you even loaded?"

"I feel loaded," the gun replied, "but I always feel loaded."

"Will, is this gun loaded?"

"Don't . . . don't point that at me!"

Thinking that probably answered his question, Ed now wondered if he could even shoot a gun. He never had before. He looked for the safety – he'd seen pictures. He flipped it off.

The recoil jerked his arm, so he missed where he was aiming. But he was so close, he took off part of Will's head.

He expected a great deal of alarm when he stepped off the elevator into the office where Jillian worked. Surely they'd heard the explosion downstairs? But everyone walked around as if nothing were wrong. Didn't they understand that there was always something wrong? Several people nodded and smiled, no doubt recognizing him from an appearance he'd made at the last company picnic. He'd gotten quite drunk and Jillian hadn't spoken to him for days.

They didn't even notice he had a gun hanging from his hand. Didn't say a word.

"Watch this guy, he's coming too close," the gun said, raising its long neck, staring up with its singular, deep dark eye. The fellow almost stumbled into Ed, and the gun shot itself, or rather fired itself, somewhere into the man, who fell screaming, and the bullet continuing, blasted through the desk of one of the secretaries.

Now everyone noticed, and ran and screamed, and Ed continued down the hall toward Jillian's office, feeling vague and headachy and a little sick to his stomach. "It's not supposed to happen this way," he told the gun. "Now she's going to know everything."

"Secrets are a bad thing," the gun replied. "Better to get everything out in the open and clear the air. Time to empty the gun, Ed."

Ed made a right at the corridor and walked briskly toward the end to where his wife's office was. He held the gun out limply in front of him despite its admonitions to "Get a grip on that handle! Straighten out the barrel! A *child* could knock me out of your hand the way you're holding me!" But he didn't think he could withstand *anyone's* attempts to disarm him, however firmly he held the weapon. He felt as if he could hardly walk as it was.

With a last burst of energy (and bolstered by the gun's cries of "Charge! Charge!") Ed indeed charged the door. Then stopped short of its surface and knocked, none too loudly.

"Come in." Muffled. He knew the tone. Jillian was occupied with some important business or other, unwilling to spare more than a sliver of attention.

He opened the door gently and slipped inside, pulling it shut behind him. The gun banged against the door and he stiffened, but Jillian didn't even look up from her papers. "What was that noise out there, do you know?" She was looking down and busily writing. "Did someone knock over the water cooler again?"

"Jillian." He held the gun out, his finger trembling against the trigger. She looked up.

"Jesus Christ, Ed!" She jumped up and scattered the papers everywhere.

"Sorry, sorry," he said, going to pick the papers up off the floor, the gun dangling loosely from his thumb.

"That's no way to hold a firearm," the gun grumbled.

"Ed!" He looked up – she'd run into a corner. "What are you doing!"

"I love you, Jillian. You know that, don't you?"

"What are you *doing* here?"

"I love you but sometimes two people can't live together even if they do love each other. Sometimes one person can't be who they should be, live the life they might have, as long as they're in that relationship with the other person."

"Ed, are you saying you want a divorce?"

"No, of course not! It's just that sometimes two people are so close, or at least one of them feels so very strongly about the other, that that person can't *be* who they should be if the other person even exists, anywhere on the planet."

"Ed!"

"You're always taking care of me, Jillian. You're always giving me great advice even if that advice isn't always so great for me, personally. So I'm, I'm trying to think that maybe this—" He waved the gun at her. "This whole thing is just another way you can take care of me. I'm sorry, but I think maybe that's just the way the universe works. Not much we can do about it."

"Less talking, more shooting," the gun said.

Ed took aim at the corner where Jillian was standing. He was pretty sure he couldn't hit her from that distance. He was pretty sure he would have to advance on her, get much much closer, before he had any chance at all of hitting her. Which he did not want, to be so close he could see the fear in her eyes.

He glanced at the huge window behind her, and then the other huge window along the adjacent wall. He'd always known Jillian was important to her company – he just hadn't realized she was *this* important.

But beyond the fact that she had such views it was the city itself, seen not quite as he had seen it before, all those windows, and behind those windows a countless number of secret rooms where people lived, breathed, died, as if their lives had been swallowed whole by this immortal creature, an immortal creature, of course, which all these mortal creatures had given up their lives to create, and in thanks it had stared at them all their lives with its universe of eyes, and eaten them, and condemned them to anonymity.

"I would give anything to see you reach your dreams, Ed, whatever they might be, even if they didn't include me. Don't you know that?" Jillian said behind him.

"I know, I know," Ed said, and began firing, thrilled as all that glass began to shatter and fall into the downtown streets. He heard the blare of the car horns, and the screams of the people, and Jillian's own pleas behind him, and it was as if they were all cheering him on, as he threw the gun out of the pane-less window, and he himself moments later tried to follow it into the tumult below.

BASIL COPPER

The Recompensing of Albano Pizar

I

AFTER LEON FREITAS had been dead for several months, a literary agent of notorious dubiety, determined to extract the last ounce of gold from the great author's accumulated dross, tracked down his widow, who was living in seclusion in a small resort in southern Italy. The Palazzo Tortini, though dilapidated and in disrepair, a relic of the great days of the Borgias and the Medicis, was real enough and the rent, modest in terms of today's money, meant little to Mme Freitas who was more than well provided for from her husband's estate.

A well-preserved woman in her late-forties, Mme Freitas still retained traces of great and original beauty; her days were spent not in idle reminiscence or in vain recall of time gone by, as might have befitted a great man's widow, but in the writing of her own memoirs, the annotating of her husband's papers and in the indexing and cross-referencing of his work.

Though she might have employed an army of secretaries for this purpose – thirteen volumes of her husband's still remained to be issued posthumously – she preferred to do this herself and so found her days filled with satisfying literary labour and her nights with agreeable and diversified social life.

Her only close friend in the small community in the resort she had chosen was a Dr Manzanares, who had once been called in to treat her for a minor ailment and had become her most intimate companion. Dr Manzanares, in addition to being an admirer of the work of Leon Freitas, was also a doctor of philosophy and had himself written a number of monographs on obscure philosophers.

The atmosphere of the Palazzo Tortini was agreeably outré to one of his tastes and predilections; the charm of Mme Freitas undeniable; her cuisine excellent; and, above all, the ambience of literary endeavour and past greatness fascinating to a man of his character.

The Palazzo Tortini stood on the banks of a canal, which gave it the atmosphere of Venice; the canal in turn drained into the sea at no great distance. It was thus necessarily tidal and indeed the canal overflowed into the great vaulted cellars of the Palace so that at the height of the two tides, every twenty-four hours, all the gloomy lower portions of the mansion were filled with the melancholy echo of the sea.

Mme Freitas recalled little of Albano Pizar and it was her infallible rule not to see persons on business connected with her late husband's estate; all his literary properties were pledged to the splendid houses in half-a-dozen countries who had published him during his lifetime. And yet there was something about Pizar's cleverly worded prefatory letter that touched a chord of compassion somewhere in her being. As she read on, she remembered something of him, and recollected a pale, almost ethereal-looking young man who had originally been a publisher's reader in Rome.

But he had aspired to greater things and after – no one knew how – purchasing a share in a minor but greatly respected publishing house in Paris, had edited and issued finely illustrated collections of her husband's then little-known short stories. That had been in earlier days, of course, when Pizar had become a prosperous and fairly successful young man and her husband had yet to make his way; ironically, as the name of Freitas had ascended and had eventually become one of the most resplendent in European literature and *belles-lettres* so Pizar's star had gone into eclipse.

The publishing house had failed, he had disappeared into obscurity for a time; but then, as sometimes happens when men of little talent but keen business acumen fall on hard days, this had acted as a spur to his industry and a sharpener of his abilities so that, like a drowning man, he had once again managed to raise himself above the flood.

This time he had started a small literary agency; as is the way with many such businesses where partners come and go and authors, as they become successful, pass on to greater things, his fortunes had fluctuated. From year to year it had not been possible to foresee the swing of the pendulum, he wrote to Mme Freitas; presuming on an old friendship he hoped to visit her at a convenient date when he had a proposition to discuss.

She gathered that, recalling with some emotion the success of the early short stories which had been issued under his imprimatur, Pizar was again hoping for a similar miracle. Among Freitas's old papers he trusted to find some fragments not thought worthwhile by more august houses; these, with some introductory notes and addenda by himself, he would then bring out through a publishing house in which he had some interest and so retrieve his fortunes.

All this, of course, he did not put into his letter, but that was what Mme Freitas read into it. When she had finished she put down the closely written pages with a sigh and clasped her hands together on the red-leather surface of the heavy desk on which she customarily worked. The brilliance of the Italian sun fell through the oriel windows of the big study and sparkled on the gilt bindings of the ancient leather volumes of the classics, which her husband had gathered together during the course of a long literary career.

For more than an hour Mme Freitas hesitated over the contents of this letter; her secretary arrived at the study at the time she usually took notes, waited for a while, and was then dismissed. At last Mme Freitas became aware that her day, which usually ran so smoothly from dawn to its predestined end among the silver, brandy glasses and Sèvres coffee cups of her dining room, was fatally disrupted. She rang for her car and was swiftly driven to the home of Dr Manzanares.

The conversation, after passing lightly over topics which concerned them, at last turned to the literary agent Pizar; the letter was produced and the problem discussed. Normally Mme Freitas would have dictated a gentle letter of refusal but she felt she owed something to the shadowy figure that Pizar had been in those far-off days in Rome and Paris. And he had been instrumental in launching the earlier works of Freitas to the wider world. If he came to the Palazzo there could not be much for him; Freitas's output was bound to certain publishing houses for ever.

But there might be a few crumbs; the question was whether it would be worth his while to come. Mme Freitas did not want to hold out too much hope lest he might be disappointed.

Dr Manzanares was not enthusiastic; his only contact with literary agents had been little short of disastrous. His voice rose and he gesticulated frequently as the conversation went on. His cry of ten per cent began to sound like a knell to Mme Freitas's deafened ears. Eventually she burst out laughing; an outburst in which the learned doctor was at last persuaded to join. She would write then, she decided; she would leave it to Pizar as to whether he came. She would promise nothing; but there might be something. The friends left it at that.

Mme Freitas wrote a short note to the agent and then, in the general press of a busy life, forgot the matter; she had no reply and as week succeeded week Pizar's request faded to the back of her mind. But she had gone through some of her husband's papers; there was little of value that was not already committed. An early poem or two; some youthful letters; two or three essays which had appeared in obscure magazines and had never subsequently been reprinted.

Something might be made of this mélange, but she doubted it. Looking at the racks of bound memoirs, correspondence and confidential documents that flowed across the great room in unbroken ranks of blue, red, green and yellow, each colour denoting a different genre of her husband's life-work, Mme Freitas rather hoped that Pizar would not come. The little that she could spare from this vast oeuvre would seem incomparably mean; then she shrugged her shoulders. Business was business and if Pizar could make a little from the scraps flung him – in any event there was no need for her to feel guilty. And she had not asked him to come.

More than a month had gone by before she got the letter; Pizar had been away from Paris; he understood her position; he would be delighted to make the trip. He suggested a date, said he would telephone when he arrived at the station. One afternoon of torpid heat when the sun shimmered like molten metal in even the darkest recesses of the cool rooms of the Palazzo, Mme Freitas was informed by her secretary that Pizar had telephoned to announce his arrival. She despatched the car to meet him, vaguely uneasy at something which could be only a routine matter. She went upstairs to change her dress; ordered some lemon tea, some minute sandwiches, the kind she liked most of all, and some éclairs, for an hour's time. Then she went to her study and composed herself to wait.

Mme Freitas rose to greet her guest when the woman secretary brought him to her; her first feeling was of ludicrous disappointment, though what she'd expected of the interview it would be hard to say. For Albano Pizar was a pompous man of decidedly vast proportions; the remains of a handsome head rested on massive shoulders, but the rest of him had run to flesh and the elegance of his well-cut grey suit could not conceal the huge pouches of his capacious stomach. The pale, interesting youth he had once been fled before Mme Freitas and in place of this blurred memory was the hard reality of the present: a commonplace fat man with hard blue eyes and a limp black moustache.

But his manners were beautiful and she soon forgot the grossness of his exterior envelope as she rang for the tea and they chatted like old friends; for his own part Pizar was estimating the value of the documents, private papers and other debris of Leon Freitas's long and rich life which had been left behind, much as the receding tide leaves its deposits on the shore, and his shrewd glance was raking across what seemed to be acres of shelving.

In the meantime he munched delicately at the sandwiches, mentally cursing his hostess's sparse appetite – the train journey had been long and slow, as is the Italian custom, and there had been no buffet car – tinkled his silver spoon against the rim of his china cup and listened to Mme Freitas's small-talk with feigned interest. That had always been infallible in his line of business, especially with ladies from whom there was much to be hoped; so Albano Pizar, who had a thousand dreams riding on the wings of this interview, crossed his plump ankles encased in the silver-grey silk socks, nodded wisely from time to time and continued to rake the shelves with his seemingly lethargic gaze; estimating, assessing, scheming, devouring, while all the time he kept up the polished mechanisms of polite conversation expected in the world in which he usually moved.

After the éclairs, which were more to Pizar's taste, the talk passed almost imperceptibly to business, and at length, after more than two hours, to the subject of Pizar's visit. Without raising too many hopes, said Mme Freitas – after all, none should know better than her visitor that the whole of her husband's literary estate was committed to existing publishers – she had been able to scrape together some material; part of it previously unpublished. She did not know whether it might make a small volume, perhaps two, if he cared to take it on; she was sorry, it was all she could offer.

Though seemingly calm, Pizar was inwardly excited and hardly able to contain himself; his hopes had been rising throughout the interview. However, he remained master of his nerves, merely looked at his hostess with narrowed eyes and continued to puff with empty confidence at the cigar he had lit at Mme Freitas's graciously extended permission. He was well aware, he said, of madame's generosity; more than he could say. It would be impossible to know what might be made of the material without careful examination; could he borrow the documents if madame raised no objection?

He had already engaged a room at a nearby hotel and intended to spend that evening in going through the papers to see what sort of book they would make. He would then call on madame the following day, if she were agreeable. He thanked her for her offer of accommodation at the Palazzo but the arrangement he had already made would do nicely; he had already taken up too much of her time. If he could have the material, he would take his leave and return the following afternoon.

Mme Freitas agreed to Pizar's proposals without raising any objection, much to the latter's surprise; she excused herself for a moment and unlocked a drawer of the desk. She took out a red leather folder containing the documents in question; the clasp was locked. She handed the folder to Pizar, together with the key, enjoining him to take great care of the contents. Scarcely able to credit his good fortune Pizar stammered his thanks. Five minutes later, in Mme Freitas's car on his way back to the hotel, he was unlocking the folder with trembling fingers.

II

Punctually at three the following afternoon Pizar was back at the Palazzo Tortini. The interview again took place in the great study where Mme Freitas worked. Pizar had spent long hours the previous evening on the contents of the folder, his heart sinking lower as the night progressed. A cursory examination of the original material had left him with very little hope that his visit had been successful; later and more detailed examination had confirmed it. He had returned to the Palazzo with a desperate plan half-formulated in his mind.

The interview passed much as before, except that on this occasion Mme Freitas offered him stronger refreshment. Ice clinked coolly in the glasses and, as the oddly assorted couple discussed the possibilities for a book, Pizar awaited the opportunity which he knew must come if only he had the patience. So he spun out the conversation as long as he decently could; went into much pretend detail over the projected manuscript; world rights, royalties and so forth; and all the while as Mme Freitas bent over the desk, studying the legal points he had enumerated for her approval, his eyes were searching the crowded shelves.

His chance came much sooner than he had supposed. The secretary appeared at the door of the study to say that Dr Manzanares had called to see madame; she hesitated a moment and then excused herself. To Pizar's delight the secretary followed her, closing the door behind herself. Pizar sat very still, the drumming of his fingers on the surface of the desk the only outward sign of his nervous tension; he opened the red leather folder, left the key ready in the lock. His eyes once again raked the shelves, the red, the green, the blue and the yellow whirling into one blurred effect to his overheated gaze.

He was still sitting at the desk, the folder locked, when Mme Freitas returned ten minutes later. She excused herself, with many apologies; asked if he would stay to tea. Pizar declined with thanks, glancing at his watch; it had been a great pleasure. He had much to do, but he would write. A few minutes later he had left, the leather folder clutched firmly under his arm, while Mme Freitas went back into the drawing room to attend to the needs of her second guest.

Later that night, when Dr Manzanares telephoned the hotel, he was told that Pizar had left on the eight o'clock train. Doubtless he would be in Rome by this time. The doctor smiled grimly to himself. Doubtless. He consulted his watch, rummaged in his timetables. Pizar would have just made the connection for Paris. He drew the telephone towards him and dialled the Palazzo Tortini.

The matter was serious enough; for, two hours after Albano Pizar had departed from the palace so hurriedly, Mme Freitas, returning to her study, had discovered that some of the files had been disarranged. Slowly, but with mounting alarm, she had gone through the documents with her secretary. A number were missing; the loss was not serious so far as their records were concerned. Mme Freitas had copies of everything on file. But most of the missing documents were letters Freitas had once written to a lady with whom he had become rashly involved; they were of a sensational nature and were marked not for publication during the lifetime of Mme Freitas.

The implications were plain; by a lucky coincidence Pizar, the type of man for whom fortune occasionally relents, had lighted on the two files which were immediately saleable for his purposes. Mme Freitas turned white; she was a Sicilian and of proud stock. She had a long memory and a hard, unforgiving nature. She breathed in deeply when she saw the extent of the damage Pizar might be able to inflict, and Dr Manzanares was immediately recalled to the Palazzo. Then followed various phone calls culminating in the information that Pizar was presumably on the Paris express.

Little could be done at that moment but what might be managed through legal and other channels was immediately put in hand; scandal threatened the great author's reputation and Mme Freitas spent lavishly in order to bring Pizar's plans to nothing. But he seemed to have disappeared; no information was forthcoming. There was silence for more than two months and then the explosion occurred.

Despite the risk of libel, the copyright nature of the letters and the embargo on their publication, certain scandalous magazines, notably in London, Paris, and Rome, printed simultaneous articles on Freitas, obviously based on the contents of the letters. So carefully had the matter been dealt with that Mme Freitas's legal advisers were powerless to act. The storm grew and the press were actually besieging the doors of the Palazzo at the height of the publicity.

Mme Freitas, accompanied by Dr Manzanares, fled to a retreat in the Umbrian Hills until the clamour should have died away; in the meantime Pizar was interviewed on the television and radio channels of several European countries, more stories followed, and even learned and respectable journals in more than a dozen countries were running speculative articles on what had become one of the most interesting literary memoirs of the century. To all the publicity Mme Freitas maintained a deaf ear and a stone face. But she passed many hours of quiet reflection; she had been duped and exploited by a man of mean spirit to whom she had intended to do a kindness, and she could not and would not forget.

She and Dr Manzanares, in their endless conferences, estimated that Pizar could not have made less than £25,000 to £30,000 out of the stolen letters and this fact burned with a sort of sullen inflammation in the widow's mind. Pizar's solicitors had eventually replied to her own lawyers and the ineffective exchanges of ponderously worded letters had dragged on over the months without coming to any definite conclusion. In the end Mme Freitas had given instructions that any projected suit should be dropped and the literary furore gradually died down.

But Mme Freitas had not forgotten and she was dumbfounded to receive for her approval, some three months after this, proofs of the book Pizar had originally solicited from her. All during the long months of scandal and notoriety she and Pizar had never exchanged a letter and the receipt of the projected volume assumed an air of complete unreality in her mind. Dr Manzanares's indignation had no end but he was completely stupefied when Mme Freitas merely initialled the proofs and sent them back to Pizar's publishers. Surely Madame did not intend to let this unspeakable rascal exploit her further, he spluttered.

But Mme. Freitas smiled a cold, quiet smile which promised many things and Dr Manzanares was persuaded into silence. The widow thought long on the topic. Like all Sicilians she had infinite patience and she waited with confidence for an opportunity to strike at the man who had done her family name such harm. In the event it was a whole year after the publication of the Pizar-inspired Freitas work before the widow made her move. In the meantime she had received a considerable sum in royalties from Pizar and a personal letter – the first since his flight from her house.

He mentioned nothing but business matters, hoped she was well and rendered a strict account of all sales. He was her devoted servant, etc., etc. Mme Freitas smiled a colder smile than ever.

A month later she replied. Dr Manzanares was never able to discover what she had written in the letter; it must have been couched in such subtle and enticing terms that Pizar could not, as a man of business, afford to ignore it. Even so, he must have sensed a considerable amount of danger in again venturing into the Palazzo Tortini and Dr Manzanares guessed that his deliberations had taken agonizing days and nights before cupidity won out over his natural fears.

Dr Manzanares was astonished to hear from his old friend one sultry afternoon in July that Mme Freitas had received a reply from Pizar; he was on his way, he would be there that afternoon.

Once again Pizar was driven out from the station in Mme Freitas's car; he was sullen and on guard, not unprepared for scenes and arguments. His fleshy face looked more debased with the grosser pleasures of the world than ever. To his surprise Mme Freitas made no reference to the letters. She received him in the study as before and had evidently put herself out to be charming to him. She congratulated him on the success of the Freitas volume and on the perspicacity and understanding with which he had edited and introduced it.

Pizar bowed stiffly; the inside of his collar was wet with cold sweat; he was ill at ease and something told him that the situation was very wrong. They drank tea and ate sandwiches for an hour. Then Mme Freitas kindly thanked him for his visit and dismissed him. Pizar was stunned. He blinked, his eyes turning to her curiously, as though he had heard amiss.

"Pardon, madame," he stammered, rising to his feet. "But I understood from your letter . . . There were to be other documents released . . . it says here . . ."

"I do not care what it says there," said Mme Freitas coldly, her manner completely changed. "I have no more to say to you."

"But madame . . ." Pizar began again. Sweat ran down his forehead into his eyes, momentarily blinding him.

"I have made this long and expensive journey from Paris for a specific purpose. I have hotel and other expenses. I shall have wasted a week . . . I demand recompense for my trouble and monetary outlay."

"Recompense!" exploded Mme Freitas. She looked at Albano Pizar and her eyes roved over him in a cold and knowing manner which sent tremors coursing through his blood.

"You demand recompense, Monsieur Pizar?"

She stood up with a brusque movement that transfixed him where he stood.

"Very well," she said at length. "You shall be recompensed. Come with me. My husband left other bequests, which I think may interest you. Only this time you must pay the full price."

She led the way out of the study and along a corridor hung with tapestries and lit by crystal chandeliers which were now turned over to electric light. Pizar panted alongside, momentarily regretting his outburst.

"Pardon, madame," he said. "If I inadvertently said anything—"

"Enough, Monsieur Pizar," said Madame icily. "You have made your choice. You demanded recompense. And recompense you shall have."

The pair went down an ornate iron staircase; the contrast here to the rest of the Palazzo was marked and severe. Dusty, naked electric bulbs made harsh shadows as they descended and the silhouettes of the great author's widow and the literary agent were grotesque and distended on the discoloured walls. She was silent until they came out on to a stone-flagged corridor at some distance below the house.

"My late husband had a little cabinet here, Monsieur Pizar," she said. "Here he devoted himself to experiments in coarser fields of literature . . ."

She did not enlarge but her meaning was plain. Pizar's eye began to glisten. Pornography? Was it pornography she meant? If so . . . He sucked in his breath and then had to hurry to keep up. It was a curious room, Pizar saw, when she opened the door; evidently part of the great days of the Palazzo Tortini. Chandeliers with huge candles, now thick with dust; sagging bookcases, seemingly held together by the weight of the rotting leather volumes they held; red leather walls. He stared, fascinated. He had never seen anything like this. He bent to the bureau Mme Freitas indicated. The curtains billowed behind him but his greedy eyes had time only to see the spidery handwriting before him. Then the world spun and consciousness faded.

Dr Manzanares stepped out from behind the moth-eaten curtain and looked ruefully at the sprawled form of Pizar on the carpet. He put down the heavy candlestick on the bureau and bent to feel for the literary agent's heartbeat. Reassured, he turned to Mme Freitas. "Recompense!" he growled. "He'll have recompense enough . . ."

"Save your strength, my friend," said Mme Freitas with a cold, tight smile. "We have much to do tonight. The tide will soon be on the turn."

III

Albano Pizar awoke to confused roaring, sickness in his head and the taste of blood in his mouth. Blurred shapes flickered grotesquely in front of his eyes and the soft slurp of water came to his ears. A groaning noise translated itself into pain and the pain apparently proceeded from himself. He attempted to move and was brought up short with a clanking noise. He opened his eyes and was fully awake.

He gazed into the hard eyes of Mme Freitas and Dr Manzanares. He was leaning against a cold rock surface and the air smelled damp and foul. Electric bulbs gleamed high up in glass globes bolted to a dark, Romanesque ceiling. In the distance the sun burned itself out smokily in water; dark water, which swirled among the piles and through iron gratings to lap sullenly on a shelf of stone a dozen yards away from him.

"The tide is turning," said Dr Manzanares with satisfaction. "The flood will soon begin."

"What is the meaning of this?" said Pizar stiffly, some of his old confidence returning. "There are laws in this country against assault."

He fingered his throbbing skull as he spoke and felt his left hand arrested. A stab of surprise shot through him as he saw that there was a manacle locked round his left wrist. He followed the new steel chain down with his eyes. He saw that the linked length, which was about ten feet long, was locked to an ancient ring sunk into the granite wall at his back. It was impossible to escape. He felt little fear as yet, only curiosity. He looked back to Mme Freitas and the doctor.

The latter stood in shadow but the great author's widow seemed to be brooding over him. Pizar stepped forward to the length of his chain. The two merely retreated before him. He had his right hand free but they stood just beyond his reach.

"What is the meaning of this?" he asked again. He began to laugh as though they were having a joke with him. But the words died with a whimper in his throat.

"Let me out of here," he called, his voice echoing unpleasantly under the high vaulting of the roof. The noise seemed to stir something in the shadow. The lapping of the water was louder now and with sick numbness he saw eyes watching him down near the water's edge. He turned back to the two in front of him, their menacing immobility combining to strike into his consciousness.

"What do you intend to do?" he said. Or at least he intended to speak calmly, but his words came out in a withered shriek.

"Nothing," said Dr Manzanares softly. The banal word struck the prisoner with more terror than any violent denunciation could have done.

He cast his eyes round desperately and then saw the meat cleaver. It lay on the cold stone floor in front of him, new, freshly sharpened and deadly. Just within reach of his fingers. He slid his right foot out quietly, slowly, inch by inch; if only he could keep them talking. But his foot tinkled against the cleaver and the heartless couple before him burst out laughing. Pizar was more bewildered than ever when Dr Manzanares kicked the cleaver towards him. He picked it up with his free right hand, the metal wet and chill against his sweating flesh.

"That's right," said Mme Freitas. "Take it. It's intended for you."

"What is this, a game?" demanded Pizar quietly.

"That's right," the doctor agreed. "A game, in which your wits will lead you to a decision and your life is the prize."

Pizar saw that the vault in which he was chained was becoming darker; looking down at the shadowy waters of the canal he became aware that the sun was beginning its swift decline into the sea.

"You are in the vaults beneath the Palazzo, my friend," the doctor went on. "The tide is coming in. But you have a weapon with which to defend yourself."

Pizar still did not comprehend the doctor's words; he looked back towards the iron gratings on the seaward side of the vault, then strained at the chain. It held firm. There were eyes and darting shapes down at the water's edge. Pizar looked more closely and began to feel sick. Rats! There must have been hundreds of them, being driven in by the encroaching tide. Already the trapped man could see that the sullen wash of the water had reached the lowest of the ancient steps.

"You have two excellent choices," went on Dr Manzanares, as though he were giving a lecture on philosophy. "As you will see, the construction of the vaults must drive the rats past your pillar, where they will assuredly attack you at the slightest movement. Remarkably bold, these sewer rats, I'm told. But, as you see, you may defend yourself with the cleaver. We are, it goes without saying, humanists and you have a first-rate chance of surviving an attack."

Pizar did not reply. With a dead heart and trembling limbs he looked along the floor of the vault; it was just as Manzanares had said. It was a sheer six-foot drop to the level on which he was standing; he could see that Mme Freitas and the doctor had descended by a wooden ladder, which they would no doubt pull up after them.

With a white and twitching face, he began, "If I returned the money . . ."

"Too late," said Mme Freitas, with a terrible smile. Pizar retreated to the pillar at his back; the chain rattled as he moved and the red eyes of the rats twinkled in the gloom at the water's edge. He could hear their squeaks and furtive movements, almost smell their carrion stench. They had thick black mud coated on their filthy bodies. He clutched the cleaver to his chest and blinked as the doctor spoke again.

"As I said before, my friend, you have two choices. Oh, we are being generous. You may be eaten by the rats. But we have guarded against that. You have ample defence in your hands."

But here he turned and pointed up the slope behind the pillar to which Pizar was chained.

"Though if you escape the rats, another problem faces you. They go some way farther up the slope, where they congregate to escape the tide. I am afraid you cannot, for your chain is more than twenty feet short of the high water mark. So if you elude the rats you may drown."

A scream as though he were already drowning escaped from Pizar's parched throat.

"I *may* drown?" he shouted. "You know I will drown."

Mme Freitas moved then and looked Pizar quietly in the face.

"There is a third choice, you know," she said with dreadful emphasis. She moved away and climbed up the ladder. As she went Pizar could see she wore thick leather thigh boots, a protection also afforded the doctor.

Manzanares lingered. The sun was almost gone now, only a faint carmine tinting the surface of the water. The waves slapped the edges of the worn steps, leaving an oily scum, and the rats shifted uneasily at the margin, curious and afraid of the human being who barred their path. But Pizar knew, with horrible certainty, that their fear of the water would certainly outweigh their fear of man.

"If we could only come to some arrangement . . ." he began quickly. One look at the doctor's hard eyes counselled him to save his breath.

Dr Manzanares looked him up and down with something like satisfaction.

"I am sure you will think of something," he said.

He moved away to follow Mme Freitas and pulled up the ladder after him.

"I hope you can swim," he called cheerily to the man chained to the pillar.

Pizar heard the distant clang of a closing door and the sound fell on his soul like the long weight of eternity. He moved and the chain clinked; the light on the outer surface of the canal died and it was night. The tide slopped on the foul floor of the vault, damp air blew in and he caught the foetid smell of the rats. They crouched at the water's edge, moving closer now, scuttling with mincing steps as the tide menaced their feet, their red, unwinking eyes watching his face with quiet confidence. He breathed shallowly and sickly, felt he might scream and clutched the cleaver tightly in his right hand.

He braced himself against the pillar, praying that he would not trip on the chain; the tide crept in inexorably; the putrid mass of the rats shifted and changed shape before his dazed eyes. The first wavelet burst foaming on the floor of the cellar and then they were coming at him, squeaking to themselves, their red eyes murderous, their foul, slime-encrusted bodies brushing his as they leaped for his eyes and throat.

Pizar shrieked and screamed as he wielded the blade, the handle slippery with blood, slashing and hacking with the courage of a man in whom all faith is dead, hoping that he would not become entwined in the chain and fall. Froth was on his lips and madness in his heart when he paused in his blind rage; he tested the edge of the cleaver against the links of the chain but it was high-grade steel and only blunted the blade.

He awaited the next onslaught of the rats, balanced on the balls of his feet, caught his breath deeply and began hacking for his life.

IV

There were enquiries, threats, police investigations and intimation of legal proceedings, of course; all the makings of a first-class scandal. But to all accusations Mme Freitas and Dr Manzanares maintained smiling denials. Albano Pizar had never been to the Palazzo Tortini after his visit regarding the book; was his return likely after the scandalous way in which he had treated the dead author's widow?

Certainly, the authorities could visit the vaults of the house. The authorities did visit the vaults – but found nothing suspicious and retired with apologies. The servants were no help; no, they had never seen M. Pizar at the Palazzo; perhaps the authorities were confusing the occasion? The chauffeur could not recall ever having driven him to and from the station, other than in the one instance. The authorities shrugged and retired; after all, there were more important things to investigate. Mme Freitas and Dr Manzanares exchanged secret smiles of satisfaction and referred to the matter no more.

Albano Pizar returned to his office in Paris a year or so later, paler and thinner than before; in fact, very much more like the young man he had been in the distant past. He would never indicate to any of his friends or business associates how he came to lose his left hand, which seemed to have been hacked from the wrist, but everyone noticed how much better he treated his authors thereafter. And women clients he would not handle at all.

DAVID A. SUTTON

Night Soil Man

THE EAST END was gettin' too hot, so I left with just the clothes on me back, me cart and donkey, and walked the slow miles back to the Black Country. Following on, the loathsome thing? I 'ope not. He knows I knows, see.

The night sky was a-glow with the red fires from the furnaces at Russell's gas-tube factory and brown chimbly smoke clotted th' air and choked me throat. But the iron-tastin' smog, foul as it were, meant I 'ad distanced meself from the pea-soup and what it 'id in the night down south. Least I 'oped so. Obscurity was round about guaranteed hereabouts. Factories and iron foundries, mine works, eight pubs on me birth street alone. I dae wanna go there, so I got me a billet as a lodger with the Mole family on Loxdale Street.

At three I'm emptying the privies on the 'olyhead Road and the stink is worse than the stench of them sliced-up women. Me nice noo calico cap got coated in muck when it fell off into one of the pots. Ne'er mind, it'll be plastered in soot soon enough. On'y doin' the job for enough money until the sweeping pays off.

At foive I'm toutin' for business along Bridge Street. The 'ouses are big and so too the chimblys. I'm thin and short, so's I fit up 'em real neat. At half-six I'm in the darkness, scraping away the burned-on, hardened coal cinders. Heave up, and brushing soot now, me cap black, me face black, me shirt and breeches black, coal dust itchin' me balls, the smell of the soot in me conk. From the chimbly top high above an engine hoots and there's a clatterin' of metal wheels on rails as the train on the Great Western line passes nearby the 'ouse.

Then silence agin and I'm thinking, me sensitive emotions harking back to *him*, the beast I left behind. And I start t' get the collywobbles. As if he was still around. Hauntin' me. But he'd never find me, not once I'd come off the turnpike road, the dark towns too many, each of 'em wi' 'undreds of dark alleys and courts, the people crowded in them back-to-backs, a swirlin' mass of 'uman bodies. *He* was out o' luck.

But I'm up the chimbly, black as night with the burned smell and that *other* smell's coming back and I'm seein' 'im . . . Dropping down, sliding wi' his mardy bulgin' eyes and 'is 'ands clenchin' at me, drivin' cinders into me eyes, chokin' hot . . . He'd got up there somehow, *up there* and still follerin'!

I'm down in a sec', coughin' an' heavin', and the missus of the 'ouse is open-mouthed as she sees me standin' and shakin' in a load of soot in the fireplace. A'ter I tendered me apologies, I tidied up and bagged me soot and got paid and pitched the sack on the cart.

The donkey woke up and eyed me. I was lookin' at him funny-like. He knew I was sore terrified. He knew me. And I was shiverin' still.

Mrs Mole was makin' gloves when I opened the duwer to her 'ouse, and she were sittin' by the winder in the kitchen, for the meagre light. On the hob a pot of something cookin'. I'd sold the soot and clinker, supped two pints in The Cross Guns t'steady me nerves, and took a pinch or two of snuff, and given up sweepin' for the day. Mrs Mole eyed me with a peculiar eye and I told her I was feelin' crook. She told me to stick the wood in the 'ole and to tek some tea and that her husband wouldn't be home till ar'ter seven. Why'd she say that? Her eye caught me agin. It was akin t'the donkey's. I'd had to bash 'im a few times since I'd owned 'im and his look was always a-fear. Mrs Mole had the same eye; the same but different. Like it was dread and yearnin' at the same time. Like me donkey.

Mrs Mole's 'usband Thomas had married her just two months past and they'd set up home across the court from her dad. They needed lodger's money to pay the rent as his wages from the iron works wouldn't cover all the outgoings. I'd come along at just the right time. The missus had a bump of a belly too, so there was another mouth to be fed on the way.

Wednesb'ry's a town of minin' and iron works. It's where I come from, original like, where I was born. Me dad was a gun maker – a trade now gone from the town – and he got me an education; should say he had a way to keep me attendin' school, wi' a leather strap. Me cousin Harry was a sweep and I started as a 'prentice to him soon as I could. No middlemen, like what Mrs Mole had to contend with sewing her gloves, not wi' sweepin '. I did me *own* hours and finished early in the day, and I gambled and drunk a fair bit too; fighting me corner sometimes. In any argy-bargy I could tek a few knocks.

Then I upped and went, to mek a new start in the East End, and lodged in Miller's Court. Don't know what made me leave 'ome that spring. Weren't money; 'ad enough o' that, that's for sure – me cousin didn't see all's the cash I took as 'is journeyman! I'd 'ad a dizzy spell or two, maybe that was it. Yes, them wobbly spells; drunked waster, Ma said afore she piped it.

It were dowen in London I was learned in the ways of women. Wasn't never right, they always had the eye on me and they smelled of the privies. I tried, but was no good at it – and them women, they 'ad no patience and no tender feelings. Then *he* came on the scene and the smell got worse. Dunno why. He'd bin in all the papers. Mitre Court, the Whitechapel Road, Hanb'ry Street. I could smell 'im through the soot, I could. No matter how filthy I got with cleanin' the flues, the raw burned smell couldn't 'ide it. I got faint with it and me 'ead went funny-like and though I read it all in the papers, it seemed like I already knew what he was doin' on them secret nights in them shit-wet streets . . . and I 'ad t' get out. Away from the sinfulness. I'm not a church-goin' man, but it were loathsome seein' 'im at work; in me 'ead like.

In the night I woke up to the smell of muck.

I could hear the furnaces goin' on Portway Road, keepin' sleep away, that and the reisty stink. At fower, I was up and tipping privies on to the dung cart with the gang I worked alongside, and we'd soon taken our 'uman waste t' the privy midden. At foive I was happy to be on me own agin and working the chimblys, scourin' cinders and brushing soot. Whistlin' t' meself . . .

. . . And then he was on me agin, in the dark space, me one place that I coulda called me church, me sanctuary. The tight black bricks crushin' me in, holdin' me arms, so's I couldn't fend him off. The soot turnin' t' shit, the riffy smell overpowerin', drippin' down the chimbly. Me breath a-heavin', throat choked, the air full o' it. *His* face black and eyes a-bulgin'. He'd done summat and he wanted t' tell me about it. He was in me 'ead and I knewed what it was, I cud *see what* he'd done.

The old turnpike road out o' Wednesb'ry was rutted with a muddle-up of snow and mud and me donkey was rooted, the cartwheels half-buried. Even as I lashed him, and gi' 'im a thud on his 'ead with me cosh, I knews he was goin' no further. His eye was on me and it was like *hers*. I'd 'ave to leave him rooted, freezin' to his death, servin' hisself right.

I'd got to leave me new 'ome. Now that *he'd* found me agin. *He* didn't want no witnesses, just an accomplice. I could find another town. I'd be a'right, for a while.

I grabbed one of me empty coal sacks from the cart and shook snow off it. Threw the loaf o' bread I'd took from the larder and bottle o' gin in with it, and me tools and the guttin' knife, and slung the sack o'er me shoulder. And set orf, trudgin' through the snow and mud.

Me brain was dull and I 'ad bad thoughts. *Her*. Mrs Mole on her mattress, mixed with the horsehair; like dog mess turning to wool. Hair and purple blood and them *other things*.

The vile thing. He's always follerin'. I shan't never get rid of *'im*.

Gawpin' back along the road I can sees me donkey, kneelin' down in the snow now, shiverin' and brayin', still tethered to the cart, like he's a-prayin'.

Hope he's prayin' for me soul. Hope he's sayin', Jack, God have mercy on yer soul . . .

BRIAN HODGE

Let My Smile Be Your Umbrella

FORGET EVERYTHING YOU think you know about yourself. Forget those twenty or twenty-five years of assumptions. However old you are. Instead, try looking at yourself from someone else's perspective for a change. My perspective. Empty out all those pitiful preconceptions and just look at yourself. Look at the effect you're having on the world.

What do you see then? Do you see what's really there? Can you even be that honest with yourself?

If you could, then I think you would agree that there's not much choice of what to do about it, is there? The end result? You've been claiming all along it's what you want.

What I see, it's not a question of saving, not any more. It's too late for that. Now it's come down to quarantine and eradication.

So it'll be the same with you as it's been with the others:

I'll take more pleasure in killing you than you take in being alive.

Who gave you the right to not be happy, anyway? Where did you get the idea that it was okay to throw all that back in the face of a loving, benevolent universe? It's your birthright, for god's sake. It's inscribed right there in the constitution of this great land of opportunity we live in: *life, liberty, and the pursuit of happiness*. So if you squander your liberty by refusing to pursue anything of positive worth, then really, haven't you forfeited your right to life?

And remember: according to you, that's what you've wanted for a long time.

Well, just wait, because I'm on my way.

I mean, what kind of attention whore are you, that you would do what you did? Starve yourself to death and blog about the experience so the entire world can share in your sickness – who thinks of a thing like that? If you want to be dead, you just do it, you don't throw a party and invite the world to watch.

And not to belabour the obvious, but if you want to be dead, there are a lot faster ways than starving yourself. Starvation takes a long, long time. As I'm sure you realized. As I'm sure you knew damn' well before you ever decided that you'd had your last bite of food and now it was showtime.

Dehydration, now that's a lot quicker. Three or four bad days, then you're done. But obviously that didn't suit your timetable. Obviously you didn't feel inclined to call water and power, and tell them to turn off the taps, nope, won't be needing those any more.

So I don't know whether or not you're genuinely suicidal. For sure, I believe you're miserable. You don't have to convince me on that account. But more than anything, you're an exhibitionist. You want the attention. You wanted to be found out, and then just *found*, period, before it was too late, because you picked the slowest way possible to kill yourself and gave the world plenty of time to catch up to you. Just sitting in your apartment there in Portland not eating, oh, poor me, poor pitiful me, waiting for the cavalry to ride in and save you, take control of the situation and remove your choice in the matter.

Goddamn sociopath.

Photo updates too. That was a nice touch. One a day, so the world could see your ribs and hipbones standing out a little farther each morning. Like anorexia porn. Just so you could convince the pictures-or-it-didn't-happen sceptics who were calling bullshit on your little experiment. Like, okay, maybe I'm suicidal and masochistic, but don't anyone dare call me a liar.

And they found you. Of course. Well played, applause all around. Hiding your online account behind proxy servers during those first three weeks, so they *couldn't* trace your identity . . . until you weren't. Until you mysteriously "forgot". Because all that hard work of not eating made you loopy and forgetful. Maybe it did, maybe it didn't, but you sure sounded plenty cogent in those last few blog posts.

What a difference three weeks makes, huh? You went from complete anonymity to international celebrity in three weeks. Everybody wondering what was going to happen to HungryGirl234. Everybody loves to watch a good train wreck. You turned viral in the worst sense of the word.

I said three weeks? Less time, actually. Your audience was *huge* before the plug got pulled. Or maybe it was the other way around. The plug got jacked back in. No more worries about life support for *you*. The main thing I wondered was how the hoping was split. What percentage of people was hoping that someone would get to you in time, and what percentage wanted you to follow this thing to its logical conclusion.

As to which side I came down on? Do you even have to ask?

Wait, wait, don't tell me – you were one of those girls who spent your high-school years writing poetry so embarrassingly awful that it would shame a soap-opera diva. Yeah, your blog posts had that whiff about them. I bet your favourite colour was black and your favourite mood was mope and your classmates voted you Most Likely to Cut Notches Up and Down Her Arms.

Please don't misunderstand. I'm not saying there's anything wrong with being sensitive. Only when you gouge out your eyes to everything on the plus side of the meter, and dramatize and catastrophize everything on the minus side. You live to suffer, and that's all, don't you? You have no interest in dining from life's rich bounty, the good along with the bad, right? All you want to do is revel in eating the shit. Just look up from your dinner table with your helpless sagging shoulders and a shit-eating sob-smile, like you're asking, "Why does this keep happening to me?", except you're not the tiniest bit aware of the gigantic ladle waving around in your hand.

You know what it is that I really can't stand about people like you? It's that you're toxic and contagious and you don't even care. You're the runny-nosed moron who wanders up and sneezes on the salad bar. You're the addict who shares the dirty needles even though you know what the test results said.

Can your pathetic little pea-sized soul even begin to compre-hend the magnitude of your callous indifference to the effect you're having on the world? It can be hard enough for people to keep their spirits up even when all they have to contend with is the day-to-day mundanity of seeing their dreams end up on the deferred gratification plan. Then they see you, *you*, someone who would seem to have everything to live for, see you squander the most fundamental gifts you've been given and in the process tell them that they might as well not try either. You apparently can't stand the idea of a world going on without you, never even noticing your absence, and now you've made it your mission to drag down as many people to your level as you can.

Misery loves company, and you're living proof. You're a professional sufferer and you hung out your shingle years ago: *Abandon hope all ye who encounter me.*

Converts, that's what you want. You want followers. You want to be Queen of the Suicides, only you'll never quite manage to get around to ending the suffering for yourself, will you? No, for you, it would be enough to hear about other people following your lead, only with more commitment. Every casualty you inspire just reinforces your negative worldview that much more.

What a pity.

What a waste.

What a tragic perversion of priorities.

I'd ask if you have no shame, but I'm afraid you'd only give me a blank stare and ask what the word means.

I wish you could look up, just once, and see the sun the same way I do, and know its light rather than the shadows. I wish you could take in the first blue of the morning sky and see it as the wrapping paper around the gift of another beautiful day.

And now you're at again, aren't you? HungryGirl234 rides again.

But why use that, when I know your name now? Deborah. You probably hate it, though, don't you? Such a wholesome name. Deborah. It's a cheerleader's name.

Not that you've forced the world to put you back on suicide watch. You've chosen to use more subtlety this time. You have to know what resorting to the same old hunger strike routine might get you, now that you're a known head-case. You no longer have the luxury of anonymity, the option of teasing the world along, rationing out only as much information as you want it to have about you. You've lost control of that much.

People know who you are now. They know where to find you if they have to.

So you've taken a more measured approach. Every day, another litany of woes. Every day, another dispatch from a world that to your eyes is as colourless and grey as ashes. Every day, further confirmation that life for you really must be a tale told by an idiot, full of sound and fury, signifying nothing.

You're good at it, I'll give you that. You could do this for a living, if there was actually a paying market for it. You're the Devil's propagandist, and I don't mean to flatter you when I say that you're dangerous. A person hardly has to get past the titles of your posts to fathom all they need to know about your agenda:

10 Reasons I'm A Cosmic Joke and You May Be Too.

Why Leaving Las Vegas *Was Really a Comedy.*

Why This? Why Me? Why Now?

I Still Resent Eating.

You, Me, and Everybody We Know = God's Chew-Toys.

If your descent into nihilistic spectacle had just been that first time, I would've been willing to overlook it as a cry for help, one that finally ensured that you got what you needed, and once you were discharged, your thinking had been corrected to the point where you could see what a nut-job you really were: *Hoo weee, am I ever glad that's over!*

I would've been willing – deliriously happy, actually – to give you the benefit of the doubt that you were at least going to try. I would've been happy to wish you well, and a life of contentment, from the other side of our shared continent, and we'd each go on our way, and you would never even have to know that I exist.

So remember: you've brought this on yourself.

You have *summoned* me.

What you've been doing all along is a kind of prayer. You've been petitioning the universe, and the universe is kind, so you shouldn't be surprised when it responds via the only avenue you've left open for it. Over time, you have given it all the instructions it needs to see your final wish carried out.

Do you see the beauty of this? Are you even capable of appreciating the wonder of the grand design? You lack the courage to act on your professed convictions, so the universe employs another route to see them carried out. Once again, you're

awaiting the arrival of someone who will show up and take control
of the situation, and remove your choice in the matter. Only this
time, you don't realize it.

It isn't all about you, you know. It's bigger than you, and always
has been.

I want to tell you a story, as long as I'm in transit and have nothing better to do than ignore the so-called in-flight entertainment.
It's supposed to be a comedy, but I can't say I find it particularly
amusing. It's kind of mean-spirited.

But there was this boy, you see, in the neighbourhood where I
lived before. He was old enough that he probably should've been
called a man but, for reasons of his own choosing, that label never
seemed to fit. He appeared never to have graduated into manhood,
or even to have considered that he should, so I call him a boy.

You remind me very much of him. He was dismal, just like
you. He was self-absorbed and sour, just like you.

And every time he stepped outside the house, it was like the
day suddenly got cloudy. By his demeanour alone, he could steal
the sun from the sky and the moon from the night. You expected
flowers to wilt in his wake, grass to die under his footsteps. His
projection of negativity was so pronounced it was having an
actual visceral effect on me.

He was contagious. Just like you.

I like to think I choose my neighbours carefully. The people
you surround yourself with are important. I appreciate the kind
of people who look forward to what each day is going to bring. I
esteem the company of people who keep it cheerful and
positive.

But seeing this dismal, sour boy pollute my environment . . .
this disturbed me. It gnawed at me. How could I have been so
wrong? How could I have missed this? How could this *weed* have
sprouted in my garden? And you know that, before long, there's
never just one weed. They spread.

I did try to help, I really did. I asked him why he never smiled.
He had black hair that hung down over one eye, and kept flipping
it out of the way, but it kept falling right back, and might as well
have been stuffed in his mouth for all he managed to
communicate.

I really did try to think of something I could do for him. If he would've just made an effort to stand up straight, it might've made a difference. It might've demonstrated a willingness to try and get better. Posture has an enormous effect on mood. But he seemed perfectly resigned to letting his shoulders hang as steep as a couple of ski slopes. And he completely misunderstood my intentions. There's no point in recounting what he called me.

So it became obvious there wasn't anything left to do but pull this noxious weed.

They say it takes forty-three muscles to frown, and only four to smile.

Anybody with a good knife can carve a smile into someone's face before they lose their nerve.

It takes real dedication to immortalize the frown.

But I think you'll find that keeping myself motivated is nothing I've ever had a problem with. Especially when I deeply believe in the outcome.

Can you feel my eyes on you, now that I'm finally here? They say people can, sometimes. I've heard that army scouts, observers, snipers – the ones whose success and even lives depend on not giving their position and presence away – I've heard they're trained to avoid letting their gaze linger directly on their enemy for very long. To the side is better. Because some people really can feel eyes on them, following them. The hair on the back of their neck prickles up and they just know.

But I don't think you do. You'd have to be a different kind of person. You'd have to be fully alive.

Here in your neighbourhood, there must be a hundred ways to blend in and places to watch you from, and I'd be amazed if you're aware of even a handful of them. It's a busy place, full of life going on all around you, and if you'd just opened up to it and worked to make your disposition a little sunnier and meet the world halfway, we wouldn't have to have this encounter we're about to.

As I watch you, it becomes clear to me that even though I tell myself I'm doing it to learn your habits and timetables, what I'm really doing is giving you one last chance to change my mind. So show me something. Give me a reason not to follow through.

Reveal to me some heretofore unsuspected capacity for joy beyond your masochistic perversion of it.

But you're giving me nothing here. *Nothing.* If anything, you're making this too easy. This shouldn't be such a cut-and-dried decision. I should wrestle with this, for God's sake. I should anguish over it.

Instead, I can't help but think it would be a kindness. When you left to go out for another coffee a few minutes ago, I almost expected you to melt under the onslaught of the rain. I've heard it can be like this in Portland. Which doesn't bother me in the least – I love a good rainy day – but even if it did, I still would refuse to let it. But maybe that's just not you. If weather has an influence on mood, and with some people it definitely does, then it may be that this goes some way toward explaining yours. So why have you never thought to just move away?

Although it can't be like this *all* the time. And you, if you're anything at all, are consistent. So let's just dismiss that right now. HungryGirl234 is not a foul-weather creation.

Really, it's unprecedented how much I'm bending over backward for you here. No one else would be giving you the kind of last-minute leeway that I am. It's not very many people who would break cover into the rain, and hurry along the sidewalk on the opposite side of the street to get ahead of you, to beat you to the coffee shop just in time to open the door for you.

And do you offer me a smile for this kindness? No. But then, neither do you act as if you're somehow owed it. You nod, okay, but it's barely perceptible, and looks to be an effort, almost painful.

In you go, just as I decide this has to be your final test. The very last chance to win your future. With the coffee house not two blocks from where you live, you're obviously a regular here. They would know you here. They have to, all of them. So, one laugh with the *barista* . . . come on, I'm pulling for you. I know you can do it.

Except you don't.

You just stand there encased in your green rain slicker, the hood like a monk's cowl dripping water to the floor, your head down as you count your change, then seem to decide as an aftermath to drop it all in the tip jar. A nice touch, close, but by itself it's not enough to change anything. The condemned and the terminal often give away their worldly goods, although if you don't realize that's what's actually going on here, that's the least of your problems.

And it's a shame, really, that you don't get to notice the look on the *barista*'s face as you turn from the counter. She knows you, knows you better than you think, maybe even knows who you really are, that you're an Internet celebrity of the sickest kind. She knows what matters, and wishes better for you.

You really should've contributed more to her world, you know.

And look at this! You've at least got one surprise tucked away inside. Your stop with your to-go cup at the spice island? All along I've had you figured for the no-frills, black coffee all the way type, but you're a cinnamon girl. Who knew?

And it's an extra large for me, because I've got every reason to think it's going to be a long night ahead for both of us, one that I trust we'll both find purifying.

But then you're not even gone two minutes before everything goes wrong. I'm barely out the door and back on the sidewalk myself, so all I can do is watch. Watch, and can't help but think that I've failed you. If I'd been closer, maybe I could've . . .

It's not even your fault. You've got the walk light at the corner. It's yours. Anyone can see that. Even knowing you as I do, there's nothing in me that believes you have any other idea than that you're going to cross from one side of the street to the other, without incident, the same as the hundred thousand times you've done it before.

The thing is, I know what's going to happen even before it does. Look over and see the car, and the hair on the back of my neck prickles up and I just *know*, know that the car's going too fast, that it can't stop in time, and I'm running along the sidewalk, and if I'd been closer I would've pushed you or pulled you, whatever it took to get you clear. Because this isn't the way it's supposed to be.

You were meant for so much more than *this*.

The driver is aware, at least, for all the good that does, the brake lights smearing red and the car fishtailing on the wet pavement. But you don't know any of this. You never even see it coming, and I wonder if you had, if there was time, even just a moment to react, if looking at the *genuine* prospect of your mortality, would it have made a difference where nothing else has?

Instead, lost inside that hood, you're blindsided. One devastating impact and there you go, tumbling into the air in the rain and the brown fan of coffee. It's not enough that you're hit the once, is it? No, you have to land on the windshield of the car passing by in the opposite lane, and bounce spinning off that one, too.

Even I have to wince, and shut my eyes for a moment.

And does it verify your worst suspicions about the world and everyone in it, that nobody seems to want to touch you now? They'll crowd around, they'll look, but you're used to that. But I'm used to things they're not, so it doesn't bother me, not in the way it bothers them. I don't mind joining you on the pavement. I don't mind touching you. I don't mind holding you. I don't mind the parts of you that leak on to me.

Or are you even aware of anything at all?

I've never seen anybody breathe that way. This can't be good. A sharp little gulp of breath every few seconds, like a fish drowning in the air. The way your eyes are roving around, they're like a baby's, trying to find something to focus on, and it would surprise me if you have much of any idea what's happened. If you don't, that's okay, and I don't want to tell you.

"Stay with us, Deborah."

Right, that's me saying that. And I *think* it's me you're seeing now. At least your eyes don't leave me, but in a way, that's even worse, because I can see the million questions behind them and I don't know how to begin to answer them. Not here, not now, not this.

I can't even begin to answer my own.

This would've happened whether I was here or not.

I haven't changed anything. I haven't *affected* anything. I haven't had the chance to make one single point to you.

So I was brought here to what? To witness? That's it? *That's it?*

Sometimes all you can do is kneel in the rain and ask what it is that the universe is trying to tell you. But me, I'm supposed to be way beyond that by now.

You don't mind that I've let myself into your apartment, do you? It's almost like the keys crawled out of your pocket and into my hand.

I thought I'd be seeing the place under such different circumstances. Thought you'd be seeing it anew for yourself, the way it goes when we're with someone seeing something for the first time, and we imagine what it must look like through their eyes.

That's all gone now. The today that never happened.

I have to admit, never in my wildest imaginings did I expect lemon yellow walls.

Maybe you *were* trying, in your way.

I'm talking to you like you're still alive, but right now, I don't even know. I just don't know. It didn't look good, down on the street. The state you were in, it didn't look like there was much reason to hope. That's funny, coming from me, isn't it? I always find a reason to hope. I'm the quintessential hope-springs-eternal guy. So if you don't mind, I'll keep the dialogue open for now.

Lemon yellow walls. Bugger me sideways. You really had me fooled.

But it's the posters that are the illuminating part.

It takes a while to sink in. At first I wasn't grasping what it is you've really been doing here in the main room, what these posters mean together. I didn't see them as related at first. At the west end of the room, the one of some forest, either early morning or late evening, everything foggy, that one lone figure standing in the middle. And at the east end, the poster looking out on the opening of some enormous cavern, with a tiny boat sailing out into the slanted beams of sunlight coming through. At first glance, who would think these had anything to do with each other?

But it's the one in the middle of the north wall that ties them together, isn't it? That's the link. Except for the crescent moon, it's so dark and indistinct I can't even tell where the person kneeling in the middle is supposed to be. What is that? Is it a prison cell? A dungeon? A storm drain? A log fucking cabin? I'd really like to know.

The title, well, that makes sense. *The Dark Night of the Soul.* If you're going to give the thing a title, that's as good a name as any. And the quote, too, what's that for, just to rub it in? *The mystic heart senses that suffering and sorrow can be the portal to finding the light of what is genuine. Run not from the darkness, for in time it ushers in the light.*

Look. Don't you dare talk to me about the dark night of the soul.

Honestly, this is why I'm here? What kind of joke is this?

From what garbage pit did you dredge these deceptions, anyway? Who told you you had to go through these things? They're just illusions. What garden of lies did you pick from to settle for the notion that pain and sadness are anything other than unnatural states of being that it's our duty to repel? What malfunction sent you on this detour, and convinced you that this shadow path you're on was remotely normal?

Me, I was raised better than that. I was promised better than that. I was *promised*.

That is my birthright. *That* is my due. And I *will* have the happiness I deserve.

But you? No, you fell for the worst sort of propaganda.

And look at you now.

It didn't have to be that way. It's not *supposed* to be that way. Not for you, not for me, not for anybody, and all of you who think you're going to convince me otherwise, you all find out that the light fights back, don't you? The light doesn't want to go out.

It's so clear now. I was giving you credit for being way more dangerous than you really are, when all you are is another empty puppet. You're a casualty of endless failures of imagination, and your own savage torpor. You just couldn't conceive that you live in a world so generous that everything was yours from the beginning and all you had to do was say "yes". You had to make it so much harder than it really is.

If you can't deal with my exceptionalism, fine, but that doesn't mean you get to try to rob me, or drag me down to your level.

You will not rob me.

Not. Not. Not. Not. Do you hear me? *Not.*

You know, I really should leave here, because you've got nothing to teach me and this whole thing's been nothing more than a clerical error, so yes, I should just turn around and leave, but then again, you should take it as a back-handed compliment that it's so hard to turn away.

Because it's not just the posters. No, it's the fine print. My God, what kind of obsessive-compulsive are you? Until this moment I'd been wondering if you'd even seen the comments people left for you during your escapades in starvation, and now it's obvious that you did. And have, every day since.

I'll hand it to you, it's impressive, the patience it must've taken to print out every single hateful thing anyone had to say to you, and tape it to the wall around the forest poster. And then do the same thing with every kind thing someone had to say, and tape those around the cavern picture. Hundreds of them. That's patience.

You know, before, I suspected you hadn't read a word of any of it because I had you pegged for such a narcissist that you wouldn't even bother taking someone else's opinion under advisement.

And I was absolutely right, you *are* a narcissist, just a bigger one than I even dared imagine you could be. Every time your printer spit out some hate mail or a love note, and you tore off a little strip of tape, that's somebody telling you you matter, even the ones who wished you'd just die already, because at least you got a reaction.

Well, you don't. You *don't* matter. Your opinion doesn't matter. Your deluded sense of identity doesn't matter.

Really, I should leave now, but I've just got to read these first, and laugh.

Because I haven't had a laugh this good in a long time. I should be thanking you.

And I really should leave. But I need you to know that no matter what you do, now and for ever, you can't rob me.

And what's the rush, anyway? I can read these and read these, up and down, across, they're all the same, empty empty empty, and it still feels like I just got here.

And I really should leave. But not until I know how you did it, how you got the walls to start changing colour, from lemon yellow to . . . to . . . to whatever the opposite of that is called.

And I really. Should. Leave.

Only your windows are all covered with bars.

And the doors are nowhere to be found any more.

SCOTT EDELMAN

The Trembling Living Wire

I Z SLOWLY TIGHTENED his grip around Mozart's pulsing neck, savouring the last moments of life that remained. He paused, offering to the dog the gift of several final panting breaths. The beagle had earned that. After all, Mozart had been the key to unlocking Juliet's heart.

Yet what difference did one breath more or one breath less really make? Iz thought. All lives, however short their sputter, however long their flame, still seemed ridiculously brief. And except for the lives of a very special few, poignantly pointless as well. Rare those were, extremely rare, but rarer still the ones who could be shepherded to ripeness under his tutelage. One of those was young Juliet, and as soon as he accomplished this final step, all he'd need to do was pluck her.

As the eyes of the dog whom he had trained to trust him widened in response to the narrowing circle of his fingers, Iz became aware of a second, more human, gaze upon him. He dropped his hands from the animal and moved back, suddenly both alert and confused. It had been decades since he had last felt off balance like that – or had it been centuries? – and the unfamiliar emotion prickled.

He had trained himself to leave no witnesses behind to the sort of action that he was about to take, yet . . . how could there even be any? He considered the unfolding of his previous hours, perfect and tantalizing.

The evening's plans had proceeded smoothly. Juliet was now innocently asleep down the hall, slightly drugged, resting that beautiful, budding instrument of hers, and she would not rise until the timing was right, a timing Iz alone would control. Her parents, at the foot of whose bed he had been ready to act, were more deeply drugged, and would be unconscious at least until morning, if not beyond.

If there was any gaze upon him, it should only be that of the pet itself, and nothing more. But as Mozart lay there, one ear twitching eagerly as it anticipated what it mistakenly thought would be a comforting caress, it looked off toward a dark window on the far wall, eyes narrowing as if making a connection with the eyes of another.

Iz stood, and moved carefully, quietly, to the window outside of which something had apparently captured Mozart's attention. With long, delicate fingers, he slowly widened a gap in the curtains by a few inches so he could peer out from the darkness of the room to the darkness of the street. As he searched the night for a hypothetical unknown observer, his heart was the darkest of all.

The streets were empty, as they should have been in the town he had chosen, at least for this decade, to call home. It must have just been nerves, nothing more. Ever since the local paper had sewn together seemingly random incidents over the years into a string and called it a pattern, tensions had emerged in the town. No one had yet deciphered what it all meant (how could they?), but there was just enough unease floating freely there that Iz had begun to have his own fleeting moments of worry.

Perhaps it was now time for him to move on, to choose a new feeding ground, as he had been forced to do countless times before. But those intermittent feelings were quickly suppressed, for who would suspect *him*, kindly Mr I, apparently old, outwardly frail, wanting nothing more each day than to pluck the heart-strings of his students until a bolder note might swell?

He closed the curtains more completely this time, leaving no gap to be used by a potential prowler. As he turned back to the bed, he momentarily considered Juliet's parents. If he could only explain to them what this sacrifice would buy, they would understand, he knew, in their hearts and souls, if not their minds. He was certain of that. But he could never share that piece of information, for his voice was not up to the telling. That task was beyond him. Though vocal gifts were his to be given, they were never his to possess.

And so best be done with it, and done with it quickly. He could already see through the blackness of the deed to Juliet's shining future. The short, sharp sound of a snapped neck would inevitably be followed in the days ahead – as so many other snappings and smotherings and shortenings had been followed – by the most beautiful sounds of all.

But Mozart was no longer atop the folded blanket at the foot of the bed. Which was itself as much an impossibility as any witness, for if the creature had moved, Iz would surely have heard the scratching of its nails on the hardwood flooring. No sounds escaped his ancient ears, which was both his blessing and his curse. He searched the rest of the house for the wandering beagle, but Mozart was nowhere to be found.

It was a puzzling absence, which Iz did not like, but what was more distressing than that oddity was what it meant – he would need to end his mission. He supposed he could suddenly and spontaneously escalate things, shift his attack from animal to man, but it was not yet time for him to move on like that. His life's work must not be rushed. For Juliet's sake, this composition was to be performed *con adagietto*, not *con affrettando*.

Never *con affrettando*.

He took one long, last look at Juliet asleep in her bed, tucked in by his hand. Not that she would remember. If he had calculated the dosage correctly (and he always did), that moment would be gone, now possessed by him alone, though if he had been especially precise she might still dimly remember the dinner which had preceded it. He curled over her, a question mark awaiting its answer. He caressed her throat, and leaned forward even more deeply to listen to the shallow breaths emanating from her lips, out of which such wonders were meant to spring.

That evening's music lesson would have to wait.

But not for long.

As Iz took attendance the next morning at Helen Keller Middle School, the faces which ringed his own filled him with nothing but disappointment. That day, they failed to remind him, as they so often did, of the possibilities held out by the hours ahead. Instead, they only brought him back to the fact that his previous night had not gone as planned.

The classroom left him with no way to avoid that conclusion, for all of the faces which had been there the day before were with him still. Juliet, one foot tucked beneath her while she twirled this way and that in her seat and chatted with her neighbours, should have been missing. She should have been at home stewing in her pain and growing more flavourful for the private concert to come, but instead, there she was, her eyes offering no sign that she remembered his hands on her from the night before. Her presence – poignantly tender, intensely innocent, little knowing of the shadow which had almost passed across her face – distracted him as he tried to remain casual while taking the head count, but none of the students seemed to notice his estranged mood.

Not that they ever noticed much of anything, even on those rare occasions when he managed to prod them into more elevated and focused conditions.

He moved behind his podium and tapped his baton, attempting to rouse them from their electronics-induced fugue states. Their relationship didn't have to be this way, which Iz knew better than anyone living could, because it *hadn't* always been this way. Unlike once upon a time, students and teachers seemed to exist these days in separate worlds, a hard, unyielding membrane keeping them artificially apart, and though the two groups could occasionally peer across at each other, they usually could not touch, and having any sort of impact was nearly impossible.

But luckily, Iz had found a way to continue affecting change. As the text messaging and gum chewing gave way to the first tentative notes, each student seeking to find the proper key, he was grateful for his discovery, that such a way existed. For there were times that the music each produced was so excruciating that he saw not children, but merely many broken instruments in need of his expert repair, and in the absence of such an answer . . . well. Then there would have only been despair.

Iz started off the period with a quick run-through of the number which the chorus was to perform for the parents at the following week's Spring Concert, a song taken from a Broadway musical in which the singers looked forward to those better times which would surely come tomorrow. Considering the limitations of the talent pool before him, and the failure of his most recent mission, Iz felt that his own tomorrows were running out. He did not see how the group could possibly be ready by then.

As he moved his hands through the air, trying to knit the discordant collection of children together into a voice that spoke as one, Iz glanced from one round, open mouth to the next, feeling a bit like a mother bird about to feed its chicks. But at the same time, he acknowledged that he lacked the true rearing instinct, for he did not see the need to save them all. He was always judging, constantly winnowing, looking to separate those with potential from those who could never, even with his tutelage, be more than merely adequate. And no matter how closely he examined his flock, the pick of the litter was always Juliet, poor Juliet, whose sweets and sours flavoured his otherwise dull days.

His heart broke for her as he picked out her tone from the rest, her voice a crystal. However, it was a little bit too clear, not yet purified by the life experiences which seasoned one's soul. She was supposed to have been changed the night before, her spirit transformed by mortal inevitabilities, but instead, here she was, the same as always, good but not yet great, a sterling example of promise unfulfilled.

As Juliet stretched for each note, projecting them one by one to the back of the room with a tone and control with which the average music teacher would have been satisfied, Iz was constantly aware of the potential there, and of how it could be wasted, always cognizant of the gap between what she could yet become on her own, and how far short that destination would fall of what he could make of her. He managed to hold those fates in his head simultaneously, both how much she had achieved on her own and what she might never achieve. Not without his guidance, a guidance which had given so much to so many.

As his fingers continued to dance, leading the choir along, he was able to hear not just the ones who that day performed bodily in front of him, but all the others who had come before, a long, unbroken string of everyone whose instruments he had tuned. In his mind, they were arrayed about him in a holy ring, interspersed with the contemporary chorus.

There was Ruth, whose voice had been merely pleasant, until the time she woke to find her favourite horse gutted beneath her bedroom window, and then it became magnificent. Michael's airiness grated, but after his house mysteriously burned to a husk, taking with it all the child held dear, his nature was properly grounded. Alyx, whose soul had appeared forever stunted, was one of those who required more extreme measures; an offering of her younger brother was required before she could break free of the bounds of the mediocre. And nearby was Rose, with a sweetness that could be treacly, until her father's death endowed her with a maturity well beyond her years, which encouraged her timbre to follow.

He had nudged them all, and countless others like them, to the fullness of their talents, and in his mind's eye they joined the serenade. They did not judge him for what he had done, and he believed that was not just because they did not know that the characters each accredited to chance had instead blossomed because of his more directed intent. Even if they'd known, Iz felt they would have forgiven him. Anything could be forgiven in the service to art, if one loved that art enough. After all, the world had tolerated *castrati* for centuries (no, more than tolerated – embraced) as a necessary sacrifice to music, as a gift offered up to the Lord, and what Iz had done, what Iz still did, was more or less the same, kinder even, as no one was left physically unmanned. Not that there might not yet be someone out there who might someday have to be.

The music, both that in the room and that only in his head, wafted him away to a place more like Heaven, but the slamming of a door clipped his wings and brought him harshly back down to earth. His hands froze, and without his direction the singers came to a ragged stop. He spun from the podium, prepared to snap at the intruder, but then held his tongue. It was Principal Trottle, whose status shielded him from the abusive outburst Iz had been prepared to give. A shadow of a girl stood beside the man, her head down, straight hair obscuring her face, her spirit so withdrawn that it took Iz an extra beat before he registered that she was even there.

"Good morning, class," said Trottle, and then gestured for Iz to approach.

"Excuse me, class," said Iz. He turned his back on his first-period choir and joined the visitors in a corner near the classroom door.

"This is Cecelia," said Trottle. "Cecelia, this is Mr I."

Cecelia did not look toward Iz, but instead studied the rest of the class with an expression that resembled fear bordering on terror. Iz wished the girl would instead look at him directly, so he could gauge her prospects, make his first guess as to whether she would give the choir lift, or only weigh it down, but she would not meet his gaze.

"She's just moved to the area," continued Trottle, "and she'll be attending our school from now on. She's supposed to be quite a singer."

From anyone else, Iz might have accepted that evaluation, but Trottle was a moron, who wouldn't recognize good singing if entertained by the starry choir itself. Iz would have to be the judge. The girl didn't seem like much, and at first glance, didn't appear to have the self-confidence necessary to be a decent singer. Oh, perhaps Iz could whip her into passing shape for the upcoming mandatory performance before the parents, but he doubted that she'd be worth any more of his attention than that. He could likely tweak her to fool an untrained ear – he could do that with anyone – but he probably couldn't make her of interest to the only one who truly mattered.

"Thank you," said Iz. "I'll make sure she feels at home."

Once Principal Trottle was gone, Iz led the girl to the front of the class and placed her to stand with her back to the other students. Maybe the illusion that the two of them were alone together would assuage her fear and lend her an unconstricted voice.

"So the principal tells me you can sing," he said.

"Yes," she whispered, barely projecting far enough that he could make out her answer.

Iz sighed, and rapped his baton sharply.

"Then let's see what you can do."

Before he could steel himself against the stillborn tone he was sure she would utter, with a volume that would barely register and a pitch that would wound his ears, Cecelia tilted her head, the curtain of hair parting but slightly, revealing her mouth, if little else. She threw open that mouth and sent forth a pure and perfect note, and as it washed over him, its beauty was such that he almost sang a perfect note himself, that note which he dreamed about, and which he thought he could never utter, but only struggle to prod into existence in others.

Startled, he dropped his baton and gripped the podium tightly, offering up a prayer of thanks for its support, for without it he might have toppled backward. The silence once her note had been completed was staggering, the void that followed it too blank for him to dare to fill with his own voice. All eyes were on him, waiting for him to speak, but he could not, for language had fled.

He slowly raised one hand, urging the class back to the song which Cecelia's arrival had interrupted. Cecelia did not move from where he had placed her, just stood there, the veil of her hair hiding her face once more. Iz wished that she would join in with the rest – didn't any teenager already know at least part of that song? – but she remained silent as the class continued at the same level of competence at which they had begun.

This time, however, he did not care about the uneven tempo or occasional forgotten word, nor that their tone had become, by sudden contrast, hollow. Iz had grander things in mind.

He had them repeat the tune endlessly until the bell rang to dismiss them. As the other students started to shuffle out of the classroom, returning to their electronic distractions, he asked Cecelia to remain. He needed to provide her with the sheet music and other paperwork she'd need to catch up with the rest of the class, though even if there had been no reason to speak to her privately, he would have manufactured one. But before he could begin speaking to Cecelia, Juliet stepped up beside them.

Juliet. He had to think for a moment before he could remember her name. Cecelia's arrival had caused him to forget that she was even there.

"How did I do today, Mr I?" she asked eagerly. Her words returned to him memories of her rich voice, but suddenly, today, that voice was no longer sufficient to excite him.

"Fine, fine," he said absentmindedly, waving her off.

"But, Mr I, don't you have any more tips for me? Don't I need to—"

"Hurry along, Juliet," Iz snapped, interrupting her. "You mustn't be late for your next class."

Juliet glared at them both before heading out to join the throng in the hallway, not quite sure what had just happened, ignorant of how much happier her life would end up being in the future from the accidental gift of being ignored.

Once Iz was sure that they were alone together, he pulled a chair over to where Cecelia stood, and sat beside her so that their heads would be level. He handed her a quickly assembled packet while attempting to pierce the veil she had created and look into her eyes. But it was useless. She had built a shell around herself, whether intentionally or unconsciously he could not tell, but either way, he could not get inside. He would though. In time, he would.

"Your voice is remarkable," he said. "Let's talk about how you'll best fit in."

"But don't I need to get to my next class, too?" said Cecelia. "I don't want to be late either. Especially not on my first day. I want to make a good first impression."

"You're right," he said, returning to the professional persona which had served him so well for so long. It wouldn't do for his true self to show through yet. Not now, with such a prize at hand. "You run along. We'll talk later. Very nice to meet you, Cecelia."

Iz sat where she left him, quiet, thinking of nothing but her, and a first impression which had almost stripped him down to his soul, until the students for his next period exploded into the room and tried to flush her from his mind.

But they could not.

At day's end, Iz rushed from the school to the employee parking lot in back. He pulled out ahead of the other teachers, who, though equally motivated to put the school behind them, had merely mortal reasons for their desire to escape, and thus did not have quite his speed. Driving slowly to the side of the red-brick building, he parked alongside the string of school buses and watched the children as they boarded for home.

He knew them all, as the district forced each child to take a music class of some kind, even those for whom the experience was obviously pointless. He'd heard them all sing – or at least, attempt to sing – at the beginning of the school year as part of the sorting process to determine whether each would struggle with a tuba or limp along with him, though he rarely noted their names. He tended to remember them only by their flaws. There stumbled the boy whose low notes reminded him of a hyena with something stuck in its throat, here ran a girl who could only hit the proper key after first sampling all the other ones. They were defined by their shortcomings, and once Iz knew those, he was free to forget all else.

Scattered randomly through the sea of mediocrity that pulsed before him were those few who mattered, rare children who had potential. He watched them board, too, such as Sarah, who had surely swallowed bells, Travis, whose voice had just that year begun to change from broken glass to stained glass, surprising them both, and Juliet, poor Juliet, with tones of honey and spice, who until the start of the day he had thought his finest.

He watched them vanish into their buses with no sense of loss, because now he cared only for one remarkable voice, hoped to spot just one special face. It had only taken a single note to tell him that. He had played this waiting game before with others, and now it had become her turn. His anticipation had never been so high, but then, neither had been the reward.

When Iz finally spotted her, Cecelia was walking slowly down the front steps of the school, her eyes on her feet as the other students swirled around her. Instead of boarding one of the buses, she ignored them each in turn, and walked past the line to exit the school grounds and take to the streets.

Iz waited impatiently for her to proceed a few blocks ahead before he pulled out to follow her slowly. Did she understand how lucky she was to carry such a gift, to have been chosen like that to fly so high, to have come so close to touching the sky? He doubted anyone her age could, which was why the gifted always needed him. This one had come the furthest on her own of any he had seen before save one, but that only meant that she also had the furthest still to go.

Cecelia paused every few blocks, as if she had forgotten something, at which point she would then kneel to paw through her knapsack. She apparently would find nothing, or so it seemed to Iz, no matter how often she looked. Each time she stopped, he would tap his brakes as well, trying to blend in among the parked cars of the suburban streets. He knew what he would have looked like to anyone who could have seen and connected the two of them, but no matter. He needed to track that voice back to its source, perhaps to hear the sound of it once again so he could better envision the advance that would surely come after he had exercised his craft.

After one more stop to rummage Cecelia turned suddenly, and started walking back in the direction of the school, which also meant that she was walking toward *him*. He turned the steering wheel, but before he could pull out, make a U-turn and avoid any confrontation, she caught a glimpse of him and began heading his way. He surveyed the street. They were alone. He tried to calm down. Perhaps he could use this accidental encounter to his advantage.

Cecelia came up to his car and tapped on the glass. He lowered the window, and hoped that he was not blushing with love.

"Hello, Mr I," she said, as if she saw nothing extraordinary in finding him there, parked in a car along her path home. She let her book bag drop solidly to the pavement, and grunted.

"Hello, Cecelia," he said. "What a surprise."

Cecelia shrugged, nearly imperceptibly.

"My backpack is heavy, Mr I," she said. "Teachers load you up with so much stuff the first day."

"Then you should probably have taken the bus, Cecelia," he said. "Why didn't you? Isn't that what your parents were expecting?"

"I don't . . . I don't like buses," she said. Even with their faces close together as they were, he could not make out her expression. "Do you think you could drive me home, Mr I? It would just be this once. I'll figure something else out for tomorrow."

"Will your parents mind?" he asked, feigning concern for anyone's desires save his own. And God's.

Cecelia looked down for a moment, which he could barely make out through her curtain of hair.

"There's only my father," Cecelia said, in a whisper that belied the voice he knew was there. "My mother died, Mr I. That's . . . that's why I don't like buses. Besides, why would he mind?"

Iz surveyed the street, and finding them unwatched, decided . . . why not? When God provides you with an opportunity, you should take it. He quickly cleared the passenger seat of the stacks of private records he was never supposed to have removed from school property in the first place, and she climbed in next to him.

"Make sure to fasten your seatbelt, Cecelia," he said, out of sincere concern. If anything were to happen to her . . . it would be like trampling a Stradivarius. "Now, which way do we go?"

Cecelia directed him, and as they zigged and zagged, he tried to fill the small space that enclosed them with small talk, but none of his usual patter seemed to work with this girl. Could it be because whatever had caused the soulfulness of her voice had already lifted her beyond the usual childish concerns? Whatever the reason, their talk as he drove was elevated far beyond his usual chatter.

"So what is it that you don't like about buses, Cecelia?" he asked. Because she was looking out the passenger window, her head tilted away from him, and did not answer at first, he wasn't sure that she had heard him. "Cecelia?"

"My mother," she finally answered. "My mother was killed by a bus. She was crossing the street and didn't see it coming. That's why I don't like buses."

"I'm sorry, Cecelia," he said.

But he was not. He was glad that Fate had pushed Cecelia so far before he'd arrived to intervene. The special qualities in her voice were there for a reason. She only needed one final push, but what should it be? Iz could not take from her her other parent, because if he did, she might then be taken from *him*, sent away to a relative or a foster home, and he'd never get to personally experience the fruits of his labours. But he wasn't worried. Once she led him to her house, he would surely find the special something he was meant to remove from her young life, a taking which she would someday come to realize was really a form of giving.

He could almost hear her future song, and so abandoned his attempts to make conversation, lapsing into silence so that he could attend to that promise as he drove. He didn't stop listening to it until Cecelia's cry of, "Right over there, Mr I!"

The house looked like many another in the neighbourhood. There was nothing remarkable about it, and even from just a glimpse of the outside, he could tell that Cecelia and her father had obviously not been there long enough to individualize it. There were no curtains at the windows, no decorations on the porch. In fact, if Cecelia hadn't led him to it, if he had just passed it in his wanderings, he would have taken it to be abandoned. Iz could visualize its layout easily, for he had surely been in one like it over the years, meeting with unsuspecting parents, bonding with children in preparation for his special sessions. Perhaps he had once even been in this very home, helping develop a unique talent in his unique way.

Before he could unlock his door and walk her to the house – he'd hoped that he'd be able to steal his first peek inside to begin his calculations for the next step – she had already sprung from his car and was up the path, giving him no time to follow. Cecelia turned in the doorway as if only as an afterthought, waved at him, and then slowly shut him out.

No matter. He now knew where she lived. There would be plenty of time to get acquainted later.

Iz called in sick the next day, the first time he could remember doing so, surprising both the school administrator and himself. He had just never found it necessary before. Not that he was actually feeling ill – he didn't know whether that was even possible – but suddenly, he was not content to wait for the workings of his relationship with Cecelia to play themselves out at the usual pace. His need to better understand what was to come, and understand it quickly, had become an urge, and so instead of showing up at work to pretend that he cared any longer about the other students, he instead stole the time to retrace his path of the day before.

He rolled slowly by Cecelia's house, then turned a corner on to a side street and parked as far away as he could while still being able to keep an eye on the front door. He watched intently as Cecelia left, walking in the opposite direction toward the school, keeping to her decision to avoid the bus, followed shortly thereafter by her father, leaving for whatever dead-end job of which he was still capable. Iz could not make out the man's face as he drove off. He knew what the mother's death had done to Cecelia. But what had it made of the husband? The inside of the house would tell him soon enough.

Iz circled the car around to a more remote section of the subdivision, one where it was less likely to be noticed, and walked through a dense stand of woods to approach Cecelia's property from the backyard. The door and windows of the house were locked, but he entered easily anyway, one of the tricks that time had taught him. Once inside, he moved through the home slowly, for after all, he did have all day. As he pored over their possessions, he interpreted the meaning of each object, inventorying her soul, looking for that thing which when subtracted from her would add to her the most. His task that day wasn't as easy as it usually was, however, because the environment into which he stepped had not yet developed a personality. The messy canvas of life was blank. The rooms were mainly filled with moving boxes, the contents accrued by father and child still hidden. Very little had yet been unpacked.

By Cecelia's bedside was a family photograph, seemingly taken not that long ago, for Cecelia was basically unchanged from how Iz had just seen her. Both parents were hugging her, one on either side of the child, three smiling faces. The mother was beautiful, and Iz could see a sadness there, even with the smile, but it was a sadness that would be as nothing compared to that which would eventually visit Cecelia.

But how best to deliver it? He could not kill Cecelia's mother, because the woman was already gone in a bizarre traffic accident. But if Iz studied Cecelia long enough, he knew that he would find something. He always did.

Iz spent the rest of the day peering into boxes, seeking a sign. But he could sense no direction in clumsily made summer-camp ashtrays, posters of movie stars too distant for any affecting tragedy to be possible, and paperback romance novels; or in the cache, found hidden under stained work shirts smelling of tobacco, of the father's pornography. It was a good beginning, but with the heart of the home still hidden by the move, he saw that he wouldn't be successful that day, no matter how much time he had to devote to it. He would have to wait as the house blossomed into a home, as the placement of each object told tales of their significance, to see if any further clues would be delivered.

When he felt he had lingered long enough, he moved the car back to his earlier vantage point and watched as first Cecelia, and then her father, returned home. He sat there until the skies grew dark and the lights inside Cecelia's home spilled over on to the front lawn.

Then he closed his eyes and trembled.

*   *   *

The following week pulsed to a steady rhythm, one to which Iz tried with great difficulty to surrender. It was difficult to remain *adagio* when his heart screamed that all should proceed *allegro*. Too much time had to be spent in pretence, keeping up the outer shell of his life, but he had lived that way for too long to abandon the face the world knew, not even with the stakes so high. So he continued to spend his days attempting to teach the unworthy, while the afternoons which followed were filled with rehearsals with those he had cherry-picked for the Spring Concert performance. Only the evenings were truly his, and he devoted them to studying Cecelia.

He would park in the secluded back street he had found and walk to her house, always approaching the same way, from the woods by its backyard, and never from the street. Once he did what had to be done next, he did not want to have left behind the memory of any chance encounter with a bystander, which might expose his involvement.

He found a stump, well hidden and topped to just the right height, to act as his perch for the evening. He would stare at the well-lit windows that dappled the darkness, glad that the mother was gone, even though that meant he could not take her to give Cecelia the push she needed, because a woman would have put up curtains immediately upon moving in, and he would then have been unable to play voyeur. From this side of the house he could make out the kitchen and the den downstairs, and the two bedrooms upstairs. He watched for hours, rapt by the silent shadow play.

The action would begin on the first level of the house as Cecelia prepared dinner for her father, who sat dumbly in the breakfast nook, head down, while his daughter worked. Because of his angle of observation, Iz could not see just *why* his head was down. Was he lost in a fog of mourning for his wife? Or just reading a newspaper spread out upon the table? Iz hoped it was the former.

After they ate, they would sit together in the den, watching television. He could not make them out at all, just the flickering of the screen. He could not hear the sound of it, nor their conversation, but as he imagined it, there wasn't any; they had been cut off from each other by the great tragedy which had staggered them both.

Occasionally, Cecelia would get up and move to the kitchen, returning with a beer for her father, then once more vanishing from view. After several hours of this, and more than several beers, the downstairs lights would be extinguished, and the two moved upstairs to their separate rooms. The father paced for a few minutes, then quickly became invisible. Iz imagined him falling asleep atop the unseen bed with the lights on, unable to bear the darkness.

Cecelia, however, would sit at the desk Iz had seen there, her face perfectly framed by the window. Alone in her room, with nothing to hide from, she would run her fingers through her hair, pushing it away from her face. She was beautiful, too, like her mother, but unlike her mother, she was one of those girls, would become one of those women, who obviously did not know she was beautiful. Sometimes she looked down, perhaps reading a book, or doing her homework, or even writing in a diary, for that last was what he had learned all young girls did, even though he had not found one yet.

Sometimes she just stared off into the darkness, not knowing that this time, the darkness was staring back. Iz would stay that way, soaking in her unconstructed essence, until her light would go off, and then he'd sneak quietly away, sleeping but little until the cycle resumed again.

Iz took Cecelia aside after class one day and offered to tutor her privately. She would need it, he told her, to catch up with those he had been teaching far longer and to be ready for the concert, even though she was in truth far more advanced than any of the others. But she seemed to accept what he had to say. He could not tell whether she actually agreed with him, or was just too stunned by life to care one way or another any longer about how that life proceeded.

During one of their sessions, while running Cecelia through her scales, scales which Iz had never heard performed so perfectly before, he thought that he could make out the incursion of a certain . . . coarseness. And so he stopped her.

"What is it, Cecelia?" he asked. "You seem distracted."

"It's nothing," she said, from beneath her curtain of hair. Now that he was seeing that face each night, even though it was from a distance, he found that her veil did not disturb him quite as much.

"I don't believe you, Cecelia," he said. "It's something. Something is bothering you. A music teacher can always tell. You should know that. Your music teacher is the only one in the school who can truly see into your soul. No guidance counsellor, no school psychologist, can do that. You can't hide from me, Cecelia. Now, what's wrong?"

"It's my father," she said, so quietly that he would not have been able to hear her had his ears not been so well trained by the ages.

"Yes?" he said.

Her mouth opened, but no sounds came out. Her silence extended for many beats.

"What is it?" he asked.

But she would not reply further, no matter how many times he prodded her.

"Is your father hurting you?" he asked. "Is that what's going on? You can tell me."

Even as he told her that, Iz could see – no, she couldn't tell him. There was just no way. So they sat there in silence until a tear dropped from her chin. He hadn't even been able to tell that she'd been crying.

"Let's just sing, Mr I," she finally said.

"Yes, let's," Iz said. "You don't have to worry any more. I know just what to do."

And he did, realizing suddenly, as they returned to the scales, that the answer to how next to temper Cecelia's talent was now his. He knew the final step. Whatever it would mean for his ability to see Cecelia in the future, the father had to go. Her voice demanded it.

Iz decided that he would take action the night of the Spring Concert, an event which would provide just the distraction he needed.

It had become a Helen Keller Middle School tradition that once any concert was over, the teachers would take the children out to Skiddoo's for ice cream, with a few parents tagging along as chaperones.

Iz knew that Cecelia's father wasn't going to be one of them, but then, based on what Iz had seen, he had never expected him to be. Iz wasn't even sure that the man was going to be able to stir himself to attend the concert itself. He had been lost to a fugue state ever since the death of his wife, and apparently hadn't been really fully present since. Iz had no idea how the man had been able to summon the energy to move his truncated family to a new town. He barely had enough energy to make it to work each day. Iz didn't see that Cecelia's father would be that much worse off after what he had planned for him than he currently was.

Iz was too distracted to be fully present himself for the concert, because as far as he was concerned, the true performance would not be until later that night. If any of the children noticed, they didn't show it, and as for the audience, most of them were too busy tinkering with the controls of their cameras and camcorders to be present themselves. After it was all over, the principal thanked him as usual, hollow compliments indeed. Iz then excused himself from the pack of squealing children, and hurried off to Skiddoo's. He needed to arrive there first, so he could make sure that all was ready for his unseen departure.

Once the children and their chaperones were present, and having been served their rewards for having survived the experience, Iz tapped his spoon to one side of his ice cream sundae and stood.

"I'm proud of you all," he said, surveying the children as he spoke, while struggling against dwelling overlong on Cecelia. "I know that, for many of you, it wasn't easy. But nothing worth doing ever is. Enjoy yourself. You've earned this night."

As the restaurant filled with applause, Iz slipped away to the men's room, sneaking from there through a window he had previously made sure was unlocked. He sped out of the parking lot and rushed to Cecelia's neighbourhood, and then returned to the house via his usual route, picking his way through the underbrush in the darkness. He would be quick about this, and be back with his group before it was time to settle the bill.

As he approached the home, the lone light inside came from the glow of the television. The father was obviously hypnotized by it, as he usually was of an evening. Iz slipped into his gloves, and opened the back door slowly and quietly, not that he'd have been heard over the din from the television even if he'd slammed the door open and rushed in.

He moved silently down the hall, wafted along by his memories of Cecelia's voice earlier that day, pulled forward by the even greater song which would spring from tomorrow's sorrow. Before entering the den where he planned to extinguish the father, Iz pulled a bowling trophy down from a nook where it had been placed during the previous week.

What was to occur had to look like the work of a random intruder. Iz would be there to comfort Cecelia, to show her what solace was to be found in music. He flexed his fingers around the base of the trophy, raised it over his head, and stepped quickly into the den.

Only – Cecelia's father was not there. Just Cecelia herself, seated calmly on the couch, hands folded in her lap.

Then . . . darkness.

When Iz woke, his head aching, the first thing that filled his field of vision was Cecelia's face, fully revealed, her hair swept back and tucked behind her ears. They were no longer in a dark room lit only by a flickering television. He could see that they were now in the basement, where she knelt beside him as he lay on his back.

When he tried to touch the pulsing area behind his right ear, he found that he could not move his hands. Tucking his chin into his chest, he looked down the length of his body to see that he had been bound by piano wire. Iz heard a thud of footsteps behind him, but he could not turn to see the source. Then Cecelia's father shambled into view, a baseball bat in one hand, the bowling trophy which Iz had last been holding in the other.

"What's going on, Cecelia?" said Iz, speaking as steadily as the situation would allow.

Perhaps it would have made more sense to have talked to the adult in the room, but from the leaden look on the man's face, one far more dull than any Iz had yet seen on him, no one was home to hear any appeal.

"You know, you're not the only one who's figured out how to sneak out of a party, Mr I."

"Untie me, Cecelia."

Iz struggled against the wires wrapped tightly around him, but no matter how much strength he put behind his movements, they would not snap. His years spent in exile might have given him the accrued knowledge he needed to plan his tasks, and a certain canniness necessary to carry them out, but he had never been made as a repository for might. He remained as vulnerable as any mortal. As he wriggled against his restraints, he knew that there was only one way out, and that was through Cecelia.

"Let me go," he said to her.

"I don't think so, Mr I," she said. "For once, I think you're exactly where you need to be."

And then she closed her eyes and began singing a song so sad, he wept. Not for himself, even though that should have been the most proximate cause for weeping, with the wire cutting into his wrists and his future uncertain, and with a hulk of a man looking down at him blankly, a bloodied bowling trophy now hanging in his hands. Not for Cecelia either, who had in his presence *become* the song, transformed into a channel for sorrow. But rather for the whole human race, that it could produce such a voice. He cried for its beauty, and for those who would never get to hear its beauty, and for the miracle that he was lucky enough to be there in its presence, however bound.

And as Cecelia held the final note, stretching it out so long that Iz thought it might go on for ever, almost as if it promised that there might be no other moment on the other side of it, he remembered once teaching that same song to another. Another young girl whose raw talents demanded instruction, in another city, at another time.

"You recognize my song," Cecelia said. "I see it in your eyes. That's good. You're starting to remember. But do you remember it all? Do you remember teaching it to my mother?"

He should have known, but he'd been too swept up by the remarkable voice, too distracted, to have picked up on the resemblance between the faces, so similar at similar ages even with her attempts to hide it. He should have known.

"Cecelia, I—"

"Do you remember the other things you did to her? I do. She told me all about them before she left us."

"I'm sorry that she died, Cecelia, but—"

Cecelia suddenly leaned in so close she could have bitten him if she chose. Or kissed him.

"My mother didn't just die, Mr I. She killed herself. She tried, after all of the torment you put her through, to have a normal life. She married. She had *me*. But it was too much for her. You had worn her down. That was no accident that killed her. She left us a note, telling us everything. She stepped in front of that bus willingly. She just couldn't go on."

"But don't you see, Cecelia?" Iz said, tears of joy streaming down his face. "I may not have planned for your mother to have been snuffed out that way, but the grief was all for a greater good. Listen to yourself! If not for me, moulding first her, and then through her you, you wouldn't have been blessed with this magnificent instrument. I was meant to find you someday. This is part of an eternal plan."

"No, Mr I," said Cecelia. "I was the one meant to find *you*. You think our move to this town was a coincidence? You think anything that happened here was accidental? While you were watching us all week, I was watching, too. This all went according to plan. *My* plan."

She stood, and backed away from him until she was at her father's side.

"You're close, Cecelia," he cried out. "So very close. Let me keep teaching you. I promise you, God Himself will weep. I'll give you a voice to silence the stars."

"Oh, there'll be silence, all right," she said.

Cecelia nodded to her father, and as the man approached, lifted the trophy high over his head, and brought it crashing down, Iz himself finally uttered the perfect note which had eluded him for centuries.

JOHN LLEWELLYN PROBERT

Case Conference #1

"WELL, THAT ONE'S probably true," said Stanhope, shifting in his chair to ease some of the pins and needles that had begun to accrue during the telling of the last story.

"You think so?" Parrish uncapped his fountain pen and poised the nib above the document he had been reading from. "Last chance to change your mind," he said.

"The only thing that makes me wonder is: whose case notes are you reading this from?" Stanhope winced as the feeling began to return to his lower limbs. "I mean, it can't be Mr Iz, can it?"

The doctor didn't seem to agree. "And why not?"

"Because he died, didn't he?" Stanhope spluttered. "At the end of the story Cecelia's father bopped him over the head and he—"

"—and he sang," said Parrish, "quite beautifully according to the case notes. Who is to say that after that little episode he didn't end up being transferred here, perhaps as part of a witness protection programme designed to keep him away from the understandable lust for vengeance of a husband and daughter, whose wife and mother he had driven to her death in the name of art?"

Stanhope shrugged. "I suppose that could be what happened," he said. "Anyway, whichever way you cut it, I certainly agree that a story like that could be true. Music has been known to induce insanity, hasn't it?"

"Perhaps, but I don't think we can wholly attribute the poor gentleman's lack of mental stability to music in this case," said Parrish, making a mark on his notes and popping the cap back on his pen. "Rather it was his obsessive love of one certain aspect of it that drove him to do the things he did."

Stanhope's eyes followed the doctor as Parrish returned the case file to a low shelf behind his desk. "But surely you would agree that music can cause insanity under certain conditions?" the journalist insisted. "Or at least particular types of music can? There are always stories of kids going mental at rock concerts. Drugs, heavy metal, you know the sort of thing."

"I'm afraid I don't," said Parrish, taking the opportunity to stretch now that he was on his feet. "And what you have just come out with is, if you will forgive me for saying so, just the kind of hysterical nonsense the newspapers you work for demand, so that their middle-aged readership can feel shocked and horrified at something they pretend not to understand. It's very rare that young people are capable of the kind of atrocities I have documented here. Now if you'll just wait a moment . . ."

The doctor went over to a low cupboard near the door. It had been fashioned from dark wood and was held shut with a small but robust-looking padlock. Parrish opened it with a tiny key he took from his jacket pocket. The hinges made a noise like mice being put through a mangle.

"Hasn't been oiled in a while, I'm afraid," Parrish said as he rummaged about within.

"What's in there then?" Stanhope asked, the furrow in his brow deepening as he saw the object that was lifted out.

Dr Parrish carried the battered, crumbling violin case to the desk with infinite care, and once he had laid it down he opened the rusting catches as gently as possible. The lid didn't so much open as lift off, its hinges brittle and broken by decades of use. Parrish put the crumbling wood safely out of the way before turning his attention to what lay inside.

If anything, the violin that nestled within the folds of rotting green velvet looked even older than the case that protected it, and Parrish unwrapped the instrument with the care one might afford a new-born child. Finally, divested of its protective coverings, the violin was lifted from its resting-place so that Parrish could display it to Stanhope.

"Beautiful, isn't it?" he said.

Stanhope shrugged. "If you want me to be honest," he said, "and I'm sure you do, it looks like something one might find in a downmarket antique shop."

Parrish tutted. "If you did," he said, "that would be a great shame, for this violin has a history so fascinating and yet so terrible that its story will never be written down."

Stanhope looked amused by his words. "Not even in your case files?"

Parrish shook his head. "Not the full story, anyway."

The journalist reached out to touch the violin, but Parrish wouldn't let him.

"Be careful," said the doctor. "We wouldn't want you to be captivated by whatever power it is rumoured to possess, now would we?"

Stanhope's twitching fingers were still poised to make contact with the instrument when Parrish's words made him laugh out loud. "So you think you've got a magic violin there, do you?"

"I don't," said Parrish. "But I have a very strong personality and I'm not easily influenced by such things. Professor Mortenhoe, to whom this particular piece belonged for a short while, and who is now resident upstairs for the rest of his natural life, is a weak man who knew the history of this violin when he purchased it and, I believe, was unduly influenced by what he believed it capable of."

Stanhope chuckled. "Well, this is the most novel method of presenting one of your cases to me yet!" he said. "Go on then, tell me. What exactly did he think it was capable of . . .?"

Parrish held the violin higher and plucked one of the three remaining strings. It produced a note as pure and as perfect as Stanhope had ever heard. But there was something else about the sound as well, something hypnotic, ethereal. Before he could stop himself, Stanhope asked if Parrish wouldn't mind plucking the string again.

"Oh, no." The doctor smiled. "Once is quite enough. I can see that from your eyes. Twice will have you attempting to wrench this instrument from me so you can play it yourself – do you play the violin, by the way?" Stanhope didn't. "In that case it's just as well I haven't let you touch it. Professor Mortenhoe could play . . . when he still had fingers. In fact, he could play very well. Not well enough for concert standard, but enough to hold a teaching position at a well-known university. Of course, as we have just seen, if one is obsessed with music to the extent that it is driving one slowly insane, it is never a good idea to be around those who might be vulnerable to one's . . . little eccentricities."

"Well, that last story you told me proved that," said Stanhope. "Not that it really needed proving. So what did Mortenhoe do?"

"No one knows, exactly," said Parrish. "The professor was discovered in his study, keening over this very instrument. He was totally uncommunicative, and has remained so ever since."

"Why was he so upset?" Stanhope asked, leaning forward to get a better look at the violin. "Was it because he'd broken a string?"

"Partly," said Parrish, "and partly because he had tried to replace it. And failed. His attempts to do so were what led to his being secured here."

Stanhope gazed at the instrument, fascinated by the scratches on the wood. "He killed someone, then?"

Parrish placed the violin back in its case and secured the lid. Stanhope's grunt of dissatisfaction as he did so did not go unnoticed.

"Several people, in fact," the doctor replied. "All girls, all blondes. Mind you, they didn't have the lovely long hair they started out with by the time he had finished with them. One of the rather strange stories that seems to have grown up around this violin is that the beautiful sound it can produce is a result of the strings having been fashioned from the treated hair of virgins. In a fit of rather over-zealous playing, the professor broke one of the strings and presumably tried to replace it in the only way he could think of.

"When his donors proved to be unwilling to have their heads shaved he killed them, and when their hair proved unsatisfactory, presumably because of the . . . unsuitable nature of the girls themselves, he had to find more. He got through five of them before he was stopped." Parrish grinned. "Apparently he kept the bodies locked in the part of the music library devoted to the sixteenth-century stuff because no one ever went in there. Poor old Palestrina, eh? Good thing his ghost didn't haunt the place, or it would probably have been very annoyed by having dead girls dumped next to his manuscripts. Or who knows? Perhaps he would have got a kick out of it."

"You're saying the other strings on the violin are made from human hair?" Stanhope said.

The doctor shook his head. "I am not. I am saying that Professor Mortenhoe believed that to be the case. As far as I am aware the remaining strings have not been tested and, besides, I'm not sure if it would be possible to tell the difference between the ancient keratin that would be the main constituent of years-old human hair, and the catgut that was used to string such instruments in those days."

"Well, if you need my thoughts on that one, I'd say it's probably true," said Stanhope.

"Really?" Parrish was back at the cupboard now, locking away his museum piece. "Just because I showed you a battered old violin and gave you the impression that you might be in danger of coming under its spell? And told you a story without the benefit of any case notes, a story that for all you know I might have been making up off the top of my head?" Parrish tutted as he returned to his desk. "I do hope I'm not beginning to convince you that everything I say is true."

He regarded the reporter's disbelieving stare and broke into laughter.

"My goodness me, it appears I might be!" Parrish clapped his hands. "How delicious! And talking of delicious, my dear fellow, would you care for something to eat?"

Stanhope stared at him open-mouthed. "I beg your pardon?"

The doctor indicated the empty tea tray in the corner. "All you've had since you came here is some tea and biscuits. Would you like me to get you anything else?"

"I'm fine, thank you." Stanhope felt incensed by the joke that Parrish had just played on him. If, of course, it was a joke. The fact that he was still undecided made him even more angry, but he was determined not to show it.

"You're quite sure?"

Stanhope was.

"You should, you know," said Parrish, "you won't want to eat anything after this next story." He was already searching through one of his lower desk drawers. Finally he produced a worn manila folder with a few scraps of paper inside. "It's a short case from more than fifty years ago, but nevertheless one that might put even those with a strong stomach off their food. You're absolutely sure?"

"Get on with it," said Stanhope, crossing his legs.

"Very well, but it's your funeral," said Parrish with a giggle. "Or rather, it isn't, but I'm sure you would have been invited if they had felt it was appropriate . . ."

ROBERT SILVERBERG

The Undertaker's Sideline

T HE FUNERAL SERVICE for the late and sorely lamented
Thomas F. Underhill of the town of Reeseport was drawing
to its close. A hundred citizens of Reeseport were on hand to hear
the final praises of the late Thomas F. Underhill, who had been
taken from this world by a heart attack at the untimely age of
forty-seven. Thomas F. Underhill had been one of the town's
most substantial citizens, in more ways than one. He had left a
good deal of money behind. And he had tipped the scales in the
funeral parlour at a plump, rotund 216 pounds.

A very substantial citizen indeed, thought the solemn person in
black frock coat who stood at the rear of the auditorium. He was
the highly respected J. Michael Tenneshaw, Mortician – the town
undertaker of Reeseport for more than thirty years.

J. Michael Tenneshaw had supervised the burials of most of
Reeseport's substantial citizens since some time in 1925. He had
grown quite wealthy in that time, since his trade was one that
rarely lacked for customers. He stood now surveying his handiwork. The departed lay serenely in his luxurious coffin. J. Michael
Tenneshaw had worked hard over the dead man's face, lightly
covering it with wax to conceal the mottled purple effects of his
fatal heart seizure. It now looked as if Thomas F. Underhill had
died peacefully in his sleep – whereas Underhill had actually gone
to his repose while screaming and clawing at the air.

Tenneshaw was a craftsman at his trade.

The funeral service was ending. They were closing the coffin
lid; weeping relatives, still tense about the not-yet-disclosed terms
of the dead man's will, flung themselves piteously down on the
burnished coffin to sob out a few gasps of mourning.

Then the pallbearers were carrying the coffin through the hall outside, placing it aboard Mr Tenneshaw's gleaming, flower-bedecked hearse. Then came the ride to the cemetery, where the open grave awaited the coffin of Thomas F. Underhill.

The minister said the proper words; the mourners wept appropriately. The newly dug earth was shovelled over the coffin in a few minutes.

Thomas F. Underhill had gone to his eternal rest.

Or so the people of the town of Reeseport were happy to believe. Gradually, the funeral attendees dispersed. Mr J. Michael Tenneshaw returned to his sumptuous mortuary establishment and occupied himself for a while by preparing a bill for funeral services. The bill would be discreetly delivered to the Underhill family in a few days, after the will had been read. They were more likely not to notice the size of the bill once they realized how much money they had come into.

Mr J. Michael Tenneshaw was a wealthy man, of course. But he believed in providing for a secure old age by continuing to amass wealth. This was why he was not content merely to run a funeral parlour. Mr J. Michael Tenneshaw augmented his earnings from the undertaking business by operating a sideline – in another town, of course.

Night descended slowly over the town of Reeseport. Mr Tenneshaw returned to his own large house on the outskirts and occupied himself until dark by reading; he had obtained a rare edition of von Juntz's *Unaussprechlichen Kulten*, in the English translation of 1876. When only the light of the distant stars broke the town's darkness, Mr Tenneshaw divested himself of his starched and impeccable black funeral garb, and donned in its place an odd and contrasting outfit: a white jacket and white trousers, along with a white apron, all somewhat stained with blood.

He descended to his garage, where he ignored his personal car and instead climbed into a medium-sized truck of elderly vintage. Mr Tenneshaw drove out into the night. A dog ran baying at him along the road for a while, but soon was left far behind.

Mr Tenneshaw retraced his path of earlier that day, driving out to the cemetery. Since it was night, the front gate was locked; but

Tenneshaw drove round to the back gate, where the graveyard attendant sat reading in his shack, and honked his horn.

The graveyard attendant was a man named Smathers, short and stocky, seemingly with no neck at all. He had held his job at the graveyard for longer than anyone in the town but Mr Tenneshaw remembered. Mr Tenneshaw had been instrumental in getting Smathers his job, early in the fall of 1928. Smathers had been wanted for a certain crime in Illinois, and for that reason he was eternally indebted to the angular, lean undertaker of Reeseport.

At Mr Tenneshaw's signal, Smathers came stomping out of his shack, swinging his searchlight.

"Oh, it's you, Mr Tenneshaw."

"Of course it's me!" snapped the undertaker testily. "Who else would you expect to find visiting this place at half-past ten in the evening?"

Smathers chuckled. "You're right, Mr Tenneshaw! You're always right."

He unlocked the gate and swung it open, allowing Mr Tenneshaw to drive his truck through and into the cemetery.

"Is it all taken care of?" Mr Tenneshaw asked.

"Hours ago," Smathers said.

As the night watchman at the graveyard, Smathers went on duty at nine. He had thus had only an hour-and-a-half to perform his special duties for Mr Tenneshaw this evening. Mr Tenneshaw smiled. It was good to have a loyal employee like Smathers! he thought.

"Where is it?" Mr Tenneshaw asked.

"Back there in the icebox," said the stocky graveyard attendant. He led the undertaker into the small watchman's shack and through the main room into a back one, which served as a kitchen for the night watchman. There was a very small stove and a very large icebox.

"Open it," Mr Tenneshaw commanded.

"Yes, sir."

Smathers yanked hard on the icebox door-handle. The lid gave. Within, cradled comfortably on the ice, was an object wrapped in burlap and securely tied with thick hemp cloth.

"Let me see the face," Mr Tenneshaw commanded.

"Yes, sir."

Smathers peeled back the upper folds of the burlap. The serene and plump countenance of the late Thomas F. Underhill peered sightlessly forth.

"You're always afraid I may do something wrong, aren't you, sir?" Smathers asked anxiously. "But I always dig up the right one. I'm not as stupid as people think I am! I—"

"Hush," Mr Tenneshaw said coldly. "Did you pack down the soil and leave it as it should be?"

"Of course."

"Very well. Give me a hand with it, now."

"Yes, sir."

In silence the two of them lifted the burlap-clad figure of the late Thomas F. Underhill from the icebox and carried it through the darkness to Mr Tenneshaw's truck. In the back of the truck was a box some six feet long which might have been a coffin. It was partially filled with ice. Gently Mr Tenneshaw and Smathers deposited their burden on the ice, and lowered the lid once again.

It was after eleven o'clock when Mr J. Michael Tenneshaw reached the town of Plattville, eleven miles from the Reeseport graveyard. In Plattville, Mr Tenneshaw operated another business under a slightly different name. He was known here as Mike Tenny. And, while the undertaker of Reeseport was a bleak and somewhat forbidding man, Mike Tenny ran a prosperous butcher shop in Plattville, and was the soul of friendliness.

His butcher shop was not quite in the heart of the small town. That way he avoided the zoning restrictions that made it impossible for anyone to reside in the commercial district of the town. Mike Tenny, when he was in Plattville, lived in a small and simple apartment on the floor above his butcher shop.

At eleven o'clock most of the residents of Plattville were long-since home, and most of them asleep. It was a town not given much to night-life. Mr Tenneshaw parked his truck in front of Mike Tenny's butcher shop, and, after looking carefully in all directions, lowered the panel of the back of the track, lifted the body of Thomas F. Underhill from the ice, and dragged it into his store. Since Mr Underhill in life had weighed 216 pounds, it was no easy matter to do so.

Still, Mr Tenneshaw succeeded. Entering the store, he dragged the body into the back room, closed the door, firmly, and switched on the light. From the street it would seem that no activity was taking place in Mike Tenny's butcher shop.

What followed was difficult and untidy work, but long years of practice had made Mr Tenneshaw's hand skilful. With a deft flip he tossed the heavy corpse up on to the stained and bloody surface of his carving table. Taking a keen blade from a rack on the wall, he slit open Mr Thomas F. Underhill's burlap wrappings and put them to one side, and then carefully undid his funeral vestments and laid them aside.

The late Mr Underhill had been pleasingly plump – and thanks to Mr Tenneshaw's practice of preserving the dead on ice, there had been no deterioration of his body. Mr Tenneshaw carved swiftly and efficiently, prying the tender pale meat away from the body. He hummed a tuneless little jingle as he worked. Tomorrow the citizens of Plattville would once again have Mike Tenny's "special cut of lamb". It was a pale, tender, juicy meat, which tasted best when cooked rare, and the good folk of Plattville had not the faintest idea what they were actually eating. But they swore by their butcher, cheerful Mike Tenny, because his prices were reasonable and his meat was delicious.

Mike Tenny had one odd and inflexible rule: he sold only meat, never bones. At least, not with the "special cuts". If you wanted soup-bones or ribs, you could have them with the beef, but not with the lamb.

There was a good reason for this. When Mr Tenneshaw finished his carving job on the late Thomas F. Underhill, he took good care that the skeleton was left intact. After he had placed the meat carefully in his big freezer vault, he painstakingly dressed the now-denuded skeleton in the funereal vestments once again, wrapped it in burlap, and carried it outside to place in his truck.

At eight the following morning the sign was posted in the front window of Mike Tenny's store:

WE HAVE SPECIAL CUTS OF LAMB TODAY
45 CENTS A POUND

At eight-thirty the first customers arrived. Mr Tenneshaw was behind the counter, clad in his butcher's clothes, and he smiled and bowed and made little quips as he measured out the meat, wrapped it, and rang up the sales.

"Nice to hear you have lamb in stock again, Mr Tenny," the woman told him. "My family loves it so much, you know."

"It isn't easy to obtain. The supply isn't as easily available as I'd like it to be."

"That's too bad. It's *so good* with just a little dash of mint sauce!"

Mr Tenny laughed and packaged the meat. Within less than an hour, his supply of special cuts from the cadaver of Thomas F. Underhill was gone. At ten that morning, Mr Tenny's assistant, a Plattville youth named Leverson, showed up to take over the store. Mr Tenny rarely stayed in Plattville past ten in the morning. Young Leverson handled the sales during the day as well as the purchasing of the more orthodox cuts, and he locked up the store each night at six. He knew nothing of the true nature of Mr Tenny's "special cuts of lamb". He was simply a young butcher's assistant, who was allowed to run the store because the proprietor had business elsewhere every afternoon.

Mr Tenneshaw might have carried his double life on unobserved until, indeed, it was his own turn to become some other mortician's client. But, unfortunately, an inquisitive young man spied on Mr Tenneshaw at work one night, with distressing results.

His name was Ronnie Rudbeck, he was seventeen, he lived in the quiet town of Plattville and he was as curious as a cat. One afternoon some three weeks after the funeral of Thomas F. Underhill, Ronnie Rudbeck spent the better part of an evening visiting the home of a Plattville girl named Maribeth Wheeler, who otherwise does not figure in this narrative.

It was a fine evening, lit by a full moon, and Ronnie Rudbeck was in a cheery mood as he left Maribeth's house at half past eleven. He decided to walk the two miles to his own house, since at this hour the public transportation system in Plattville was highly irregular. His route happened to take him past the street on which was located the butcher shop of Mike Tenny.

As for Mr J. Michael Tenneshaw, this had been a long and busy and fruitful day for him. During the afternoon he had aided to his eternal sleep the mortal remains of yet another Reeseport citizen, one Gilbert Gosseyn by name. The late Mr Gosseyn had been carried off of over-exertion on the golf course at the age of fifty-three.

By the usual procedure Mr Tenneshaw had obtained the cadaver of the late Gilbert Gosseyn, and was in the process of bringing that cadaver into his butcher establishment at the moment Ronnie Rudbeck turned the corner into that street.

Mr Tenneshaw was too preoccupied with his task to notice the boy. Ronnie Rudbeck stopped short. He saw a tall, thin man whom he recognized as the butcher, engaged in the job of juggling a burlap-wrapped object into his store. To the boy's utter amazement, the burlap wrapping parted slightly as a result of Mr Tenneshaw's struggles with the heavy corpse.

A pale arm tumbled from the burlap shroud and dangled inches above the sidewalk.

Ronnie Rudbeck drew back into the shadows and watched in growing alarm as Mr Tenneshaw successfully manoeuvred the burlap-wrapped object into the store and closed the front door.

A body!

Murder!

A current of excitement throbbed in the boy's heart. The butcher had no business dragging corpses about at this time of night. Ronnie grinned to himself. He felt no fear. He would investigate this strange incident. Perhaps, he thought, he might even distinguish himself heroically.

He tiptoed forward.

He nudged the door of the butcher shop. It creaked open. The boy leaped back, but no one came to investigate.

Reassured, the boy edged forward again, into the store. He saw the crack of light coming from beneath the closed door of the inner room. In there, he knew, was a man and a corpse. A murderer? He had to find out.

A full assortment of butcher's tools hung over the counter in the outer room. Ronnie Rudbeck picked up a substantial cleaver. Thus armed, he tiptoed toward the closed door.

He placed one hand on the door.

He pushed.

The door opened.

The boy gasped. A moment later, Mr Tenneshaw looked up and gasped as well.

Ronnie Rudbeck saw a slab-jawed man of about fifty or sixty, dressed in a butcher's outfit, bending over a bloody and dismembered corpse. Gore was spattered everywhere; a great revolting heap of intestines lay coiled like snakes at one side of the carving table. This was more than murder, the boy realized in a flash; it was some kind of ghoulish fiendishness!

As for Mr Tenneshaw, he saw in one mind-shattering glance that his long years of successful toil had ended now in damning exposure! He was caught in the act! A bulky, square-shouldered teenage boy stood in the doorway, armed with a gleaming cleaver.

"You killed him," said the boy accusingly.

"Hardly. He died naturally. Too much golf, I'm afraid. I'm simply preparing him."

"Preparing him for what?"

"For eating," Mr Tenneshaw said.

He eyed the boy casually. But inside Mr Tenneshaw's mind all was in turmoil. He had been discovered at last. All was ended. His dreadful secret was no longer his own. This blundering boy had ruined everything.

There was only one thing to do.

"Put down that cleaver," Mr Tenneshaw said commandingly, "and tell me how much money you'll want to keep quiet about this."

The following morning, the sign was in Mike Tenny's shop window once again:

WE HAVE SPECIAL CUTS OF LAMB TODAY
45 CENTS A POUND

But the first customer that morning was not one of the town's housewives, but a member of the Plattville police, Brewster by name.

"Morning, Mr Tenny!"

"Good morning there, Officer Brewster. What's on your mind today?"

The policeman shrugged. "Making a check-up, I'm afraid."

"Oh?"

"It really isn't worth bothering you about. But orders are orders. Boy named Ronald Rudbeck – you know him?"

Mr Tenneshaw remained calm. "I know the family. He a big kid with dark hair?"

"That's the one."

"He's been here a couple of times, yeah. What about him?"

The policeman frowned. "Disappeared late last night. Last seen leaving the Wheeler house, a few blocks down the way, at half past eleven. He never got home last night. His parents are all het up about it."

Mr Tenneshaw said, "So why come here about it? I haven't seen him."

"Just checking anyone who might have been up late in the neighbourhood. We figure the boy must have run away from home, or something."

"Wouldn't be surprised. These kids today—" Mr Tenneshaw began, leaving the sentence unfinished. "Is that all you wanted to ask me?"

"Just about." The policeman grinned. "Oh, and the missus asked me to have you put aside a couple of pounds of the special lamb for her. She'll be in around nine to pick it up."

Mr Tenneshaw grinned. "Of course. Be glad to put a little away for Mrs Brewster."

Although, he thought, there was a particularly large supply today. Much larger than usual.

"Hope you find the boy," he said, as the policeman sauntered toward the shop door.

"He'll turn up," the policeman said with confidence.

Mr Tenneshaw nodded and went to the cupboard in back to wrap some of the meat for Mrs Brewster. He gave her nice choice cuts.

He smiled to himself.

He thought of the incident of the night before. How eager the boy had been for money; how avidly he had agreed to accept the cash Mr Tenneshaw offered. But Mr Tenneshaw was no fool. He knew that a blackmailer never settled for one payoff.

He remembered how surprised the boy had looked when the mild middle-aged man had lifted the cleaver and brought it whistling through the air toward its mark. Mr Tenneshaw sighed. He was tired. He had been working nearly half the night to carve all the meat from both the bodies.

Of course, it had left him with no time to dispose of the bones in his usual manner. There hadn't been time for a trip back to the graveyard. But Mr Tenneshaw wouldn't have liked the idea of putting Ronnie Rudbeck's bones in the same coffin as Gilbert Gosseyn's in any case.

So he had taken a chance, just this once. And it wasn't such a big chance . . .

The door opened. Mr Tenneshaw – as Mike Tenny – hustled forward, smiling broadly, rubbing his hands together. But instead of another of his favourite customers, there stood in the butcher shop doorway, looking very grim, the same policeman who had left a few moments before.

"Mike Tenny," said Officer Brewster. It was not a greeting, or a question. It sounded more like a judgement, and a verdict.

"Yes . . . yes," Mr Tenneshaw said, looking around in bewilderment, wondering if anything could possibly have gone wrong.

The policeman held something white in his hand. "I just found a dog in your alley," he said. "The mutt was chewing on this. He must have found it in your garbage.

"It's a human bone!"

Mr Tenneshaw tried hard, but he felt his air of injured innocence vanishing rapidly. He had made one careless mistake at last. The undertaker, he realized grimly, had finally come to the end of his sideline.

JOEL LANE

The Long Shift

THERE WAS NEVER enough light. The railway cut through increasingly bare landscapes, bones poking through skin and tearing the white sky like paper, but Jim still felt trapped. The world was an open-plan office. Bilingual signs told him this was another place where he didn't belong. Despite the radiator close to his feet, he was shivering. No room booked. Only one thing gave him a sense of self, and that was carefully hidden between the clothes in his suitcase. He'd used a half-brick to dent and nick the blade so it wouldn't come out clean.

The one thing that had kept him going. That had made him dry out, got him through the puppet-show of rehabilitation, the nights when only vision could keep you alive. Made him come back to the flat and clear out the rubbish, mop the floors, scrub the walls, fight the sense of being poisoned and lost. All the time, one thought: *Baxter. No mourners. A cost-effective funeral.* Let the gulls scream over Tyseley Dump like fading porn stars. Let the rats creep in the shadows. He had a reason to go on.

Cold sunlight gleamed from mountains too sheer or barren for trees to take hold of them. Darkness had pooled in the valleys where the towns were, creeping up through the woods. From time to time he caught a glimpse of the sea, a wrinkled sheet of tinfoil. Even through the sealed train windows, he could hear the gulls. Everything was directing him towards his purpose. Why else had Baxter moved out here? He had no Welsh past or family that Jim knew of. It was a long journey from the Midlands, for anyone who wanted to find him. Shorter by car, no doubt. But on the train, with every stage along the bare coastline of Cardigan Bay taking you closer to the elements, it was a preparation.

Ritual was everything for Baxter. Timesheets, precise routines, meetings for their own sake. If your socks were the wrong shade of grey he'd call you into his office and say he'd had *comments* from your colleagues. Nothing ever came from him: it was always *a little bird* that had told him. Before each meeting, he briefed his sycophants to make whatever points he wanted to get across. Once he'd ghost-written a whole report damning the performance of another department for a junior editor to read out. No matter how late you'd worked the day before, if you were a few seconds late in the morning he wouldn't speak to you – he'd just tap his watch twice, then turn back to his in-tray.

Coming in midweek gave Jim a better chance of finding Baxter at home, and without visitors. It was a pretty safe bet that Baxter lived alone. His failed marriage was many years in the past, and he referred to his ex-wife as *the error*. In his world, all women were *professional victims*. He wasn't keen on men either. He didn't flirt with his staff, let alone chase them. What he liked to do with young employees was impair them: destroy their confidence, their self-respect, their sense of purpose. His weapons of choice were the meeting and the appraisal. That ghost-written report had got Jim's department closed down in a management review of efficiency, but at least he'd never faced a Baxter appraisal. Twelve people had been forced out of the company in nine years by having their efforts trashed in his immaculately typed reports. A few had complained to HR, and HR had advised them to leave Neotechnic.

Night was falling as the train drew into Fishguard. The silhouettes of boats in the harbour were tinged with red. The breeze off the dark water was cold enough to make Jim wish he'd matched his outfit to the bay. Its fresh, salty taste reminded him that he'd eaten nothing since breakfast. He wasn't staying here overnight – that would be too easy to trace – but a quick meal was worth the risk. A few streets away from the station, he found a quiet pub and ordered fish and chips with a glass of Coke. The local beers called to him in melodic accented tones, but he refused to listen. Maybe afterwards, and not here. As he'd expected, the fish was excellent. But maybe his nerves were playing up, because it didn't stay in his system for long. As he sat in a draughty toilet cubicle, pain hollowing his guts, a message stood out from the many inscribed on the back of the door: THERE ISN'T A LORRY DRIVER IN FISHGUARD WITH A DRINK OF FUCK TO SATISFY ME. That cheered him up somewhat.

When he walked back into the twilit bar, the optics added their higher voices to the choir. Jim paused, suitcase in hand, and let his eyes run across the row of pale, tortured faces behind the barman's head. It was time to go.

Baxter lived in an old farmhouse several miles inland of Fishguard. Even if there was a bus, Jim didn't want to be noticed getting off there. His Google map had some worrying blank spots, but the same helpful website had shown him the house and barn by daylight: no barbed wire or high railings, only a battered dry-stone wall between the road and the bare farmyard. Somehow, despite the rural setting, Baxter's home had the look of an office: gravel-covered drive, entry phone, Venetian blinds. The barn, only part of which was visible in the photo, appeared to have been sealed up with metal panels. The Welsh Nationalists would have been pretty angry about an English businessman doing that, once upon a time; but maybe their measured doses of self-rule had made them more passive.

Beyond sight of the town, he could still hear the gulls and the dusty vinyl crackling of the sea. The street-lamps became less frequent and then ceased altogether. Jim had to use his small pocket torch to see where he was going. The distant barking of a dog made him break into a sweat. If anything stopped him now, he wasn't sure he'd ever find the nerve to try this again. The weak beam showed him dreamlike glimpses of wire and stonework around fields of Braille. He kept switching it off for a few seconds to save the batteries. But he could never remember what he'd seen, because the afterimage of the torchlight kept resolving itself into the faces from behind the bar. The jury from his dream.

In the dark he cried out: *It wasn't my fault. Don't blame me.* But there was no response. That was why he'd come here. Despite the risk, he opened the suitcase a second time and felt between the shapeless underclothes for the blade. Its tip cut his finger and he licked the blood, feeling a sense of renewed control in the taste of his own pain. That was how nights like this usually went. But this time the haunting would end. He remembered buying the knife on the way home from work, after reading Baxter's memo. A small kitchen knife with a black wooden handle and a razor-sharp blade. He could see his own eyes reflected in the steel. So far he'd cut nothing with it except himself.

Gary had been the youngest of Baxter's victims. Everyone at Neotechnic had liked Gary. He'd been the most helpful of the IT team, the one who always found the answer but never made you feel small while doing it. A few of the designers had their eye on him, but he was happily engaged. And then Baxter took over the IT team. Within a month a shadow had fallen over Gary. He'd seemed nervous, preoccupied, much less inclined to give people his time. A colleague in his department said Baxter was "cracking the whip" on all of them. And in April, the appraisal season, Gary had been signed off with stress. Jim knew the union was defending him in a tribunal, but the details were confidential. Around that time, Baxter purchased a popular business book called *The Stress Myth* and was keeping it on his desk at all times. Gary lost the tribunal and was dismissed. That kind of thing was happening a lot and the union seemed unable to do much about it.

A few weeks later they'd heard that Gary had been found dead in his flat. Some of his Neotechnic ex-colleagues went to the cremation, though Baxter made a point of insisting that the usual daily targets had to be achieved. Jim hadn't been able to face going. Funerals left him cold, quite literally: he wondered if the departing spirit took some energy from the mourners to help it cross the black river. He experienced grief as an injury rather than an emotion. No doubt that had to do with him being insane. At the funeral, one of the IT team was told that Gary had left a suicide note in which Baxter's treatment of him was mentioned. The next day, Baxter sent out a memo to the entire site, saying: *Neotechnic will not tolerate irresponsible rumours being spread to the detriment of the Company and its values. Anyone spreading such rumours can expect to be dealt with via the Company's disciplinary procedures.*

After that, Jim had dropped out of the union. Just hadn't seen the point of dragging out more inevitable defeats. When his department was shut down, he'd taken the redundancy cheque with a sense of relief. It had got him out of there after nine years. No more of Baxter sitting vigilant at his desk, like the hawk in the

Ted Hughes poem they'd included in an English textbook. No more of his mock-weary presence at the end of the day: *You go home. I'm here for the long shift.* It was only later, when Jim had drunk most of the money, that the anger came back. And by then Baxter had taken early retirement, sold his Warwickshire home and relocated to North Wales. He might have been hard to track down if he hadn't put the name of the place on Facebook. *Falcon Lodge.*

As if that memory had a power of its own, the roadway turned upward. In the starlight, Jim could make out bare trees or telegraph poles on either side of the steep hill, and a dark mass ahead. It felt strange to see the stars clear of light pollution, adding to his sense of this being inevitable. The climb made his legs ache. He wanted to hide in the shrubbery, curl up to sleep like a fox. But he'd promised himself the heat of blood on his hands, in his mouth. *Promises to keep.* At last he reached the wall, and checked with his torch: no wire or broken glass along the top, and a few missing stones that would make it easier to get over. The front gate had a tight grid he couldn't hold on to, but that didn't matter. There was no name above the gate, but he could see Baxter's white Volkswagen behind it. Whatever security system the house had wouldn't save Baxter. Jim wasn't there to rob.

His sweat cooled as he paced around the dark wall, and he began to shiver. At the back of the farmyard, the bare ground was muddy and streaked with grass. The barn was alongside the house, a long featureless block part-cased in dull metal. Further out, trees were clustered on a slope that continued upward – he couldn't see what to. The wall would be climbable if he left his suitcase behind, and there wasn't much he needed from it. There were clothes for him to change into later. Stepping carefully over the rough ground, he took the suitcase into the trees and hid it as best he could. Then he crouched for a while, looking up at the house.

Something was moving through the trees behind him, scratching near the ground. It was probably a squirrel, but Jim hastily unfastened his case and took out the knife. He remembered that terrible morning in his Tyseley flat, a few months into his abortive attempt at going freelance. He'd been working late, drinking later.

It was a wet autumn day; he carried his hangover into the kitchen to feed it some painkillers. When he opened the door his first thought was: *What did I do last night?* A bin-liner full of rubbish had been torn open and its contents scattered over the floor, including scraps of decaying food. As he'd knelt to pick up the dustpan, something had moved in the nest of black plastic. A grey wedge-shaped head that stared at him for a moment before its owner ran past him into the living room. Where had it gone? He never found out. Traps remained unsprung, trays of poison untouched. He'd kept all the doors shut overnight but still dreamed of rats foraging in the dark, fistfuls of clay that crept over his body and then broke into a foul wet mush.

For weeks he'd barely gone out except to buy alcohol or biscuits, done a few hours of work each evening and spent the rest of the time drinking and watching videos. The work had dried up and he'd run out of films. Friends had tried to help, but he'd ignored them. And then the dream had come. The rat dreams were endless and confused, but *the dream* was crystal clear and happened once only. Like a voice from something inside him that wasn't yet dead. It had made him go to his doctor, spend months on antidepressants, spend the last of his redundancy money on a private alcohol rehab programme. Then he'd come home, sorted out the flat, and started planning the death of Baxter.

And now, sitting in the dark among the bare winter trees, he kissed the knife blade and quickly became aroused. Had he needed to want to kill in order to realise it was what he'd always wanted? Whatever, it didn't matter, because what happened to him after killing Baxter didn't matter. He'd stabbed the bastard so many times in his mind, he'd become a serial killer with a single victim.

In the dream, he was falsely convicted of a murder. It had to have been one of two people, and there was no evidence either way, so the court decided on the basis of character witnesses. Those on Jim's side all admitted under questioning that he was a cold bastard who'd let everyone down. He was found guilty and didn't appeal, because the trial had left him feeling his life was worthless. The judge sentenced him to death by lethal injection. The execution took place in a clinic that was part of a railway station, with hundreds of people coming and going. After the injection they set him free, knowing he had less than an hour to live. He wandered around the station and slowly realised the pain, sickness and dizziness were wearing off. The poison had failed. A police officer stopped him, and he told her he wanted to appeal. She said: *It's too late. All you can do is go back to the clinic and let them finish it. The world is a better place without you.* Jim had woken up with the faces of the jury in his mind. They were the twelve people at Neotechnic whom Baxter had forced to leave.

The rustling and scratching in the trees had stopped. Everything was asleep. Jim checked his watch: almost two a.m. No window in the house was lit. He stood up, slipped the knife under his belt and the hammer into his pocket, then wrapped a T-shirt around his left arm and started towards the wall.

There was no sound from within the house, no flicker of light. Jim ran his fingers down the cold glass of a back window. Very carefully, he stretched the T-shirt over the pane and struck it once with the hammer. Fragments of glass stuck to the Venetian blind or trickled on to the carpet. If that had triggered a burglar alarm, the police still wouldn't be here for ten minutes at least. He slashed at the cords of the blind; the plastic slats rattled as they fell. Putting the knife back in his belt, he broke enough glass away to let him climb through. There was no response from inside.

The room held a desk, a computer, a few filing cabinets. Had Baxter turned his home into an office?

After the chill of the open road, the central heating was like a blanket wrapped around him. Jim wanted to lie down and sleep. A clock ticked on the wall somewhere. He stepped through into what appeared to be the living room: the pale torch beam showed him a sofa, a monochrome rug, a bookcase. It didn't seem real, didn't seem lived-in. But he couldn't expect other people to be as untidy as him. To one side, a staircase ran up the wall. It was uncarpeted, but there was no point in creeping. He didn't want to kill a sleeping Baxter anyway.

Painfully aroused, he pushed open the first door on the narrow landing. A web of starlight in frosted glass; a long bath like a sarcophagus. The next room had a wardrobe, a chest of drawers, a single bed by the window. Knife in hand, Jim ran the torch beam up the crumpled duvet to the pillow, which bore the imprint of a head. He cried out with frustration.

Baxter must have got up after hearing the window break. He'd be downstairs, probably armed. So be it. There was no going back. Jim could smell the man's expensive aftershave in the small bedroom. And what the aftershave had hidden: the smell of Baxter. He wasn't aroused any more, just tense with cold rage. This was one meeting where the boss couldn't dictate the outcome.

The trapped voice of the water-pipes moaned as Jim paced through the still house. No sign of him. Was he hiding to wait for the police? Increasingly desperate, the intruder ran back and forth, looking for alcoves and doors. Then he noticed a pile of boxes at the back of the staircase that wasn't flush with the wall. Baxter could have squeezed in there. He played the torch along the floorboards. Nothing. An irregularity in the bare wall made him look again. Just an inch from the floor, a tiny wooden knob.

It was a cupboard, but the back had been hollowed out into a narrow passage. The torchlight was waning. He crawled into the space, which led downward beneath the floor level. If Baxter had come this way, he must have lost some weight. After a few yards the passage began to curve back upwards. He climbed painfully, unable even to kneel, until he reached a sheer brick surface. Was this a trap? Was the tunnel about to fill with rats?

He reached upwards and touched a wooden panel, pressed and felt it give way. Dazed with relief, he stood up and climbed out into what he immediately sensed was another indoor space. He shone the flickering torch around him.

In the middle of the tiny room, a figure sat at a bench. It was a young woman, dressed in faded green overalls, her hair tied back. She was operating some kind of lathe. There were some panels of metal on the bench to the left of the machine, and some thinner strips to the right. The failing torchlight glittered from metal shavings scattered over the room. The figure was quite life-like, except that her eyes were shut. As well, Jim noticed, her left arm was badly twisted and her face had a dull blue tinge. There were smears of dried blood on her frozen hands. Was the model plastic or wax?

He reached up and touched its curved neck. It was flesh, cool but not cold. He put his fingers to the motionless lips and felt a trace of breath.

I'm sorry, he whispered. He should call the police – and he would, once he'd done what he came to do. It was a long shift but soon he'd be clocking off, and what happened to him then wouldn't matter.

He scanned the walls, which were lined with recent brickwork, and saw a narrow doorway behind the lathe. The door was open. He stepped around the bench, feeling scraps of metal crunch under his feet.

The next room was the same size. It held a desk where a teenage boy was frozen in the act of answering the phone. His immaculate business suit contrasted with his torn and clumsily stitched face. The grey plastic receiver was an inch from his swollen mouth. On the desk, a single bloodstained tooth lay on a pile of memos like a minimal paperweight. On the wall was a square clock, its luminous hands giving the time as half past two.

This must be the barn, Jim realized. No wonder it was sealed from the outside. The third room was almost completely filled with a tangle of black wires and pulleys. A giant toothed wheel was outlined against the wall, turning slowly. The whole system was in gradual motion. Two pale youngsters in shapeless protective clothing were almost buried within the machinery, their limbs contorted and broken. It wasn't clear whether they were driving the machinery or it was driving them.

How many more rooms could there be? Jim bit his lip as he stepped through the doorway, afraid he would scream and alert the museum's curator. But the next room was empty. Through the doorway on the far side, a faint light was gleaming. He paused, allowing himself one more moment of ritual, raised the knife and brushed his lips against its twisted blade. The torch battery was nearly dead: he pressed hard on the switch with his left thumb, trying to hold on to his vision.

This was the only room with plastered walls. There was even a curtain where there could not be any window. On a black leather sofa with red cushions, Baxter was lying asleep. He was dressed but looked almost child-like, at peace with the world. He had indeed lost some weight. Trying not to breathe, Jim stepped forward. He pressed the point of the knife into the soft hollow of Baxter's throat, then tapped on the sleeper's arm to wake him up.

Baxter's eyes opened and he looked up at Jim, then past him, as the intruder felt hands grip his arms from behind and twist hard. A boot came down inside his calf – a *dead leg*, they'd called it in his schooldays – and he fell to his knees, shuddering with pain. Baxter looked down at him and tapped his watch twice, then turned away as the beating started.

BRIAN LUMLEY

The Man Who Photographed Beardsley

GENTLEMEN, MY VERY own darling boys in blue. If, as you seem so determined to avow, there has been about my work an element of the grotesque and macabre ("criminal" I simply *refuse* to admit), and if, in order to achieve the perfection of ultimate realism, I have indeed allowed myself to become a "fanatic" and my art an "obsession" . . . Why! Is it any wonder? I find in these things, in your assertions, nothing to excite any amazement or stupefaction. Nothing, that is, other than the natural astonishment and fascination of my subject matter.

And yet, in his own day, Beardsley's work excited just such – yes, horror! "His own day!" An inadequate cliché, that. For of course he had no "day"; his work is as fresh and inspiring now – and possibly more so, as witness the constant contemporary cannibalization of his style and plagiarism of his techniques – as when first he put ink to paper. His art exists in a time-defying limbo of virtuosity which will parallel, I am sure, the very deathlessness of Tutankhamun as glimpsed in the gold of his funerary mask.

Times change, my dears! Does Aubrey Vincent Beardsley's art excite any such powerfully outraged emotions now? Except in the most naïve circles, it does not! Admiration, yes – delight and fascination, of course – but disgust, revulsion . . . horror? No. Nor, I put it to you, will my art fifty years hence. No, certainly not in the finished, perfect article; neither in that nor in the contemplation of its controversial construction. I would think it likely that there will be controversy; but in the end, though my name be vilified initially, I will be exonerated *through my art itself*! Yes, in the end my art must win.

I digress? My words are irrelevant? My apologies, my dears, it is the genius in me. Genius, like truth, will out.

I started, in what now seems a mundane manner, void of any airy aspiration or ambition other than that of exercising my art to the best of my ability, by selling pornographic photographs to the men's magazines. Now I say "pornographic", and yet even the most permissive of my pictures – so erotic as to shock even, well, Beardsley himself – were executed with a finesse such as to abnegate any prohibitive reactions from my publishers, and they were undeniably the delight of my public.

Came the time when I could afford to be more choosy in my work, when I commanded the attention of all the first-line publishers in the field, and then I would accept only the choicest contracts. Eventually I was sufficiently established to quit working to order completely, and then I was able to give more time and energy to my own projects. To my delight my new photographic experiments went down well, better in fact than even the best of my previous works. Pornography became a thing of the past as I grew ever more fascinated with the exotic, the weird, the *outré*.

Following the Beardsley Project I had plans for Hieronymus Bosch, but—

Pardon? I must try not to wander? The Beardsley Project . . .? Once more I apologize. Well, gentlemen, it came about like this: I had long been disillusioned with colour. Colours annoyed me. Without motion they somehow looked untrue, and they certainly did nothing to enhance the sombre quality of my more sepulchral pieces. Oh, the greens and purples were all right, when I could get just the right lighting effects – Rhine Castles and Infernal Caverns and so on – but as for the rest of the spectrum, I couldn't give a damn! And yet Beardsley had ignored colour without sacrificing an iota of feeling, in perfect perspective, with the result that his black-and-whites are the wonders of intricate design that they are. But if I was to take a lead from Beardsley in tone, why not in texture? Why not in my actual material?

It was then that I began to photograph Beardsley.

At first there was no pattern in my mind, no plot as to the development of my theme; I simply photographed him the way I found him. My "Venus between Terminal Gods" became an instant success, as was "The Billet-Doux"; indeed in the latter picture I actually beat A.V. at his own game! The absolute intricacy of my work was a wonder to behold. The delicate frills and ribbons of her négligée, the Art Nouveau of the headboard, the perfect youthful beauty of the girl herself . . .

Ah, but "The Barge" was my *pièce de résistance*. Oh, I was already well on the road towards that type of success I craved, but "The Barge" made me. It took me six days to set the thing up, to get the studio balcony absolutely *right*, to have the costumes perfected and find the perfectly skeletal gent (profile) to match the young woman (the girl from "The Billet-Doux") with the great fan. And the wigs, my dears, you'd never believe the trouble I—

But there . . . I mustn't go on, must I?

That was when Nigel Naith of *Fancy* asked me for a series. A complete series, pre-paid and entirely in my own time, and I literally had *carte blanche*. The one stipulation Nigel did make – and it made me really *furious* – was that there should be colour. *Well . . .*!

I determined to do the entire series on Beardsley the Weird, commencing with "Alberich"! The trouble I had finding just the right shape of ugly, shrunken dwarf! I went on to "Don Juan, Sganarelle and the Beggar" – and it must be immediately apparent that my difficulty in obtaining a decent beggar was enormous. In the end, to obtain a skull of such loathly proportions and contours, I turned to a local mental institution with the tale that I was preparing a photographic documentary of the unfortunate inmates of such refuges.

Fortunately the custodians of the place did not know my work; eventually I was allowed to borrow one Stanley, who was allegedly quite servile, for my purpose. And he was absolutely ideal – except that he didn't like having to dress in rags. I had to beat him, and it was necessary to dub the two normal models in for they simply refused to pose with him; and moreover he *bit* me, but in the end I had my picture.

Pardon? Well, I *know* I'm taking my time, sweetheart, but it's my story, isn't it?

Yes . . . Well, the first real difficulty came when I was working on the last picture of the set. Yes, *that* picture. "The Dancer's Reward". Now the costumery and props were fairly easy – even that wafer-thin, paint-palette table-top, with its single supporting hairy leg – but I knew that the central piece, the head, was going to give me problems. Ah, that head!

And so I looked around for a model. He or she – I'm not fussy, my darlings – would have to have long black hair, that much was obvious. And I would like, too, someone of a naturally pale complexion . . . Naturally.

Eventually I found him, a young drop-out from up north; long black hair, pale complexion, rather gaunt; he was the one, yes. And he was short of money, which of course was important. I managed to get hold of him on his first day in town, before he made any friends, which was also important. That first night he stayed at my place, but it worked out he wasn't my type, which was just as well in the circumstances. I mean, well, I couldn't afford to get emotional about him, now could I?

The next morning, bright and early, we were up and about; I took him straight downstairs to the studio, unlocked the door and let him in. Then I lit the joss sticks, sat him down in a studio chair and went out to get the morning milk from the doorstep. That was so I could make us both a cup of coffee right there in the studio. Coffee steadies my nerves, you know . . .?

When I got back in he was complaining about the smell. Well, of course, that put me on my guard. I told him I liked the studio to smell sweet, you know, and pointed out all the air fresheners I had about the place and the sprays I used. And I explained away the joss sticks by telling him that the smell of incense gave the place the right sort of atmosphere. He had me a bit worried, though, when he asked me what I kept in the back room. I mean, I just couldn't *tell* him, now could I?

Anyway, I set up a three-minute timed exposure on my studio camera and then kept one eye on my watch. While I was waiting I took a few dummy shots of the lad against various backdrops: getting him in the mood, you know? Then I had him lean over the work-bench with his arms wide apart, staring straight ahead. He was getting fifteen a shot – he thought – and so he was willing to oblige; you might even say overjoyed. I took a few more dummy shots from the front, then moved round to the side.

So there we were: me clicking away with my little camera, and no film in it and all, and him all stretched out over the work-bench staring ahead.

"That's it!" I kept saying, and "Just look in front there", and "Money for old rope!" Stuff like that. And click, click, click with the empty camera. And I moved behind him and got the cleaver from behind the curtains, and his eyes had just started to swivel round when—

I got him first time, and clean as a whistle, which was just as well for I didn't want to mess the neck up. Believe me, it was quick. You've seen the groove in the bench? And still a full minute to go.

On with my wig, with all its tight little ringlets; and the costume, all pinned up just so. Then over to the table with its hairy leg and ornate band. The blood slopping; the head tilted back just so; my left hand held thus and my right holding his forelock; the slippers in exactly the right position. And, my dears, his mouth fell open of its own accord!

Beautiful . . .!

And that was when I realized that in my excitement I had made a dreadful mistake. Such a silly little thing really: when I brought the milk in I forgot to lock the outside door. The studio door, too, for I'd been distracted by the lad's complaints about the smell. And that, of course, was all it took to undo me.

It was the new postman: a nosy-parker, just like the old one. In through the studio door he came, waving a pink envelope that could only contain a letter from Nigel Naith; and when he *saw* what lay across the work-bench! *And* what I had in my hand—

I couldn't let him get away, now could I, my dears? No, of course not.

But he did get away – he did! Oh, I managed to grab the cleaver all right, before he'd even moved. I mean he was still standing there all gasping and white, you know? But damn me if that costume of mine didn't let me down! Halfway across the room I tripped on the thing and went over like a felled oak; at which the postman seemed to come to life again, let out one *terrific* scream and ran for it.

And so there was nothing left for me to do but read Nigel's letter while I waited for you dears to come. Poor Nigel: when was I going to send him the goodies? He wanted to know! Ah, but there'll be no more of my work in *Fancy*, I fear.

What's that, my love? The back room? Yes, yes, of course you're right. The joss sticks? Yes, of *course*, my dear. And the

– thing – on the bed? Ah, but now, I really must protest. That was a *model* of mine! "Thing", indeed!

Yes, yes, a model, something else I was working on. The theme? Why, "Edgar Allan Poe's Illustrators", my darling. Harry Clarke was the artist, and—

You do? Why, you clever boy! Yes, of course it was "Valdemar", and—

Who was he? Why, the old postman, who else! The first one, yes. Of course he still had another week or so to go to reach a proper state of—

You've got all you wanted? Well, anything to help the law, I always say. But isn't it a shame about Nigel – I mean about him paying me in advance and all?

Tell me: is the *Police Gazette* a glossy?

LISA MORTON

Hollywood Hannah

"YOU'LL BE LUCKY to survive this movie," the producer told me two weeks before the end of shooting.

She feigned a joking tone, but I wasn't laughing. Even then, I knew Hannah Ward might literally be the death of me.

Two months ago (God, was it really only two months ago?) I was a recent film-school grad about to take a job as a waitress when a friend told me about an internship program with Hannah Ward – or "Hollywood Hannah", as the industry trades liked to call her. She was the most famous female producer in Hollywood, and at fifty-something she hadn't lost any of her fire. After growing up in a rich Hollywood home (her father had also been a producer), she'd produced her first film at twenty-three – my age, in other words.

"She's supposed to be a bitch on wheels," my friend Allison had told me, "but you'd learn a lot from her."

I applied for the internship, expecting nothing ... but I managed to score an interview. I showed up at her West LA production company offices on a Tuesday morning and was taken into a small nondescript boardroom, where I expected to meet with an assistant or secretary.

I was nervous; at heart, I was still a girl from a Midwestern small town who loved movies, and this was my first real job interview (even though the internship was unpaid). I plucked at my skirt and scanned my (bleak) résumé again, then jumped when the door opened – and I nearly choked when I realized the person entering the room and taking a chair across from me was Hannah Ward herself.

She was still close to beautiful (she'd started as an actress, but had given it up early), with thick strawberry-blonde hair and ice-blue eyes that had frozen stronger men and women than me, but I did my best to smile and look perky as she stared me down. After a few seconds, she asked me, "So, Jennifer – why do you want this job?"

I had prepared an answer for this, but it wilted under that crystalline scrutiny, and I blurted out, "School taught me how the business is supposed to work, but now I need to learn how it *really* works. And I want to learn from the best."

I saw a glimmer of amusement at the corners of her mouth (still unlined, and I thought it was natural, not the work of an expensive surgeon), and she leaned forward then, taking on a posture that was strangely masculine – elbows on knees and fingers curled into fists. "Why am I the best?"

I'd done my homework before the meeting, and now was my chance to show off. "In 1996, you won a fight with the studio head over control of *Meeting Mike*, and you were right, because the movie went on to gross $240 million domestically and $350 world-wide. In 2003, you turned down a chance to run Twentieth Century Fox and opened your own production company, and you were right again, because your first film under your own banner, *The Truth of It All*, won the Academy Award for Best Picture. Your first foray into television, the HBO series *Dreamers*, won the Emmy for Best Dramatic Mini-series. And you once punched out a junior development executive at Fox."

She nodded, then leaned back, never taking her eyes off me. "Do you know what one of my secrets to success is? I always work straight from the gut. And my gut is telling me to forget the other thirty-seven applicants I've already interviewed for this program and go with you."

Hannah Ward stood up, smiled, and stuck her hand out. "Welcome to my team."

"Stunned" would have been an understatement. I'm sure I gaped for a moment, then leaped to my feet and gave her my hand.

She crushed it. I don't mean that in the friendly bear-hug kind of way, or that she gave it an intense but fleeting squeeze. No – she had large, powerful hands, and she wrapped her fingers around mine and applied such pressure that I thought bones were about to snap. I struggled to keep smiling, to not wince or yank my hand back . . . or gasp in relief when she finally let go.

"This is going to be very good for you, I think," she said, before turning and leaving the room.

When the door closed behind her, I waggled my fingers to make sure they weren't broken. I could already see that working for Hannah Ward was going to keep me on my toes . . .

. . . provided she didn't smash them into pulp first.

She had just started pre-production on a new small-budget movie called *The Lowdown*; it was a crime thriller, written and directed by a young Englishman named Ned Tierney who'd won the Audience Award (Dramatic) at Sundance last year. He was an intense fellow who was plainly somewhat intimidated by Hollywood Hannah, but I thought perhaps that would bode well for me as her intern.

The picture's biggest star was Aaron Jakes: he'd made a splash on the last season of some cable drama called *One for the Money*, and he was (of course) very good-looking, and (of course again) somewhat arrogant and not at all intimidated by Hannah or anyone else. The movie's budget was $20 million; a tenth of that was going right into Aaron's pocket.

At first, Hannah was generous in granting me access to everything; as long as I kept her supplied with grande lattes and charged smartphones, I got to sit in on phone calls, production meetings, and even the first read-through of the script. There were at least forty people present for that – the entire cast, the director and producer, the heads of every department, and me – and it went well until we reached page sixty-eight, when Aaron questioned his character's motivation. Ned tried to explain it to him, but Aaron had obviously already decided he didn't like the scene, and he refused to read any further until it was removed.

Even though it was only ten past eleven in the morning, Hannah called a lunch break and dismissed everyone except Aaron. I admit that I was more interested in seeing the outcome of this than eating, so I didn't file off to the food tent with everyone else, but hung around just outside the door of the stage where we were holding the read-through. There was no sound of shouting or arguing from within, but after a few moments the door burst open, and Aaron Jakes – six-foot-tall, chiselled-features, built-like-a-brick-shithouse Aaron Jakes – came out *crying*. He didn't see me, but turned and headed for his car.

After a few seconds, Hannah came out. "Everything okay?" I asked.

Her smile reminded me of the time my dad had taken me fishing and I'd caught a barracuda, and had dreamed for nights of its vicious teeth. "Fine. Where'd he go?"

I nodded after Aaron. "His car, I think. Is he . . .?"

"It's fine. He'll be back by the time lunch is over."

"How . . .?" I started to ask, but Hannah was already thrusting her empty coffee Thermos at me. "Refill that, will you? Oh, and then get yourself some lunch."

She was right, of course – Aaron returned after lunch, the rest of the read-through proceeded without incident, and the scene stayed.

Hannah Ward was always right.

Hannah started asking for my opinion.

The first time was during a meeting with the costume designer; when they'd reached an impasse over different designs for a dress the female lead had to wear in one scene, Hannah asked me to decide. A few days later, she brought Ned into her office, told him I would be reading the latest draft of the script, and that he was to take my notes seriously.

"Why on earth should I? She's nothing but a bloody kid," he said, as if I wasn't even in the room.

"That's exactly why – because she's the perfect demographic for this film. And I respect her opinion."

Ned shrugged and left the office. When he was gone, Hannah offered me the closest thing I'd ever seen to a genuinely warm smile from her. "You remind me a lot of myself when I was your age," she said.

Some part of me sensed the manipulation behind those words, but the biggest part wanted to believe them. I wanted to believe that I was Hannah Ward's spiritual heir – that I would study at the feet of Hollywood Hannah and take over when she retired. I felt bonded to her, and would have done almost anything for her at that point. I was Hollywood Hannah's bitch, very happily so.

Which was proven a week later, when she asked for help with a suitcase.

"Can you stay late tonight and help me with something?"

It was a Friday afternoon, and shooting was ready to begin on Monday. We were in Hannah's meticulously neat office; I'd just finished making notes of a few gifts she wanted to buy for the cast members to celebrate the start of shooting.

"Sure. Whatever you need."

I said that confidently, but when I looked up, my gut clenched – because for a split second, before she caught herself, Hannah Ward looked anxious, and I'd never seen Hannah Ward look anxious about anything.

She took me out to dinner at a favourite small Hollywood eatery where everyone knew who she was and catered to her every whim, and then she asked me to drive her to an airfield in the Valley. The destination was strange enough, but the fact that she asked me to drive was the strangest thing – she *never* asked anyone to drive her. It was a matter of great pride to Hannah Ward that she never used a chauffeur or driver, but always drove herself. I knew better than to ask her why, though, and so we travelled in silence to the Van Nuys Airport.

When we arrived, she directed me to drive right on to an area of the tarmac where a private jet waited, the passenger stairs already in place and the hatch open. "Wait here," she said as she climbed from her Hummer. She stepped out, then turned back and looked at me. "No matter what happens, don't get out of the car. Even if someone tells you to – *don't*."

"Okay, Hannah," I said, trying not to sound as scared as I felt.

I watched, then, as she walked the short distance to the stairs, climbed up, and met a man at the top. He handed her a large suitcase, glanced once at the car (and me), then nodded to Hannah and went back into the plane. She lugged the suitcase down the steps and back to the car, tossing it into the rear before climbing up the passenger side. "Now, get us the fuck out of here before he changes his mind," she said.

I didn't waste any time. Once we were safely away from the airfield and on the 405 freeway, she exhaled and laughed. I glanced at her curiously.

"Know what's in the suitcase?" she asked.

"Not a clue."

She laughed again, a loud, triumphant bark, then said, "Most of the movie's budget."

I'd heard rumours for years that some of Hannah Ward's movie money came from organized crime, but I hadn't really believed them . . . or at least, I certainly would never have pictured anything as low-rent as a midnight suitcase exchange. And I'd been the getaway driver.

I was getting an education, all right.

The first crew member disappeared a week into shooting.

He was the bottom-ranking grip, and staggered in late one morning as drunk as the proverbial skunk. The key grip tried to cover for him, until the idiot knocked over a heavy light stand during shooting, destroying an otherwise-good take and narrowly missing one of the actors.

Hannah walked the key grip off the stage, but she wasn't very happy when she returned a few minutes later.

"Can I get you something?" I asked, both curious and hoping to mollify a brewing tempest.

"A way out of the union contract I signed, maybe." And I'm not exaggerating when I say she *snarled* that.

It turned out the drunk was the key grip's brother-in-law. The key grip wasn't going to fire him, and suggested that the IATSE union would crawl straight up Hannah's ass if she tried. Even Hannah didn't want to mess with the unions.

Besides, she had something better in mind.

The brother-in-law didn't turn up for work the next morning. That afternoon, a security guard doing a routine patrol found him dead in an empty sound stage. It looked like he'd climbed up into the catwalks for some reason, and then fallen to his death.

I accompanied Hannah to the empty stage when the police arrived. The first thing I noticed was the dead man – he looked like he was asleep, except that his legs twisted the wrong way and his eyes were open and milky. A tiny trickle of blood had leaked from the corner of his mouth and crusted over. I couldn't understand why there wasn't more. He didn't look as realistic as the corpses in most horror movies.

But more interesting to watch was my boss and the cops – they greeted her with smiles and called her "Hannah", and she grinned right back at them. She palled around with them like she was just one of the boys, making jokes about other producers, LA's mayor, and the dead man. They told her they thought he'd been dead about sixteen hours, which would put the time of death last night at about nine p.m.

"Oh," Hannah said, turning those Arctic Sea eyes on me, "we were next door watching dailies until ten last night, weren't we?"

We weren't. She knew and I knew that we'd knocked off by eight. But for some reason I smiled and nodded. I even improvised, "Yes, they were great last night."

Hannah gave me a warning look, which I knew meant "don't overdo it", then returned to her police friends. "Well," said the sergeant, "I'm sure toxicology will find this guy's bloodstream reading more like 'Mary' than 'Bloody'."

And that was it. We said our goodbyes, returned to our stage, and got back to work. Hannah even gave the key grip the afternoon off, so he could "cope with this terrible tragedy".

The next day, she presented me with the latest state-of-the-art tablet computer and a year's worth of prepaid 4G access. She said it was so I could do an even better job of helping her work.

I knew what it was really for, of course.

I'd spent the night without sleep, running over the possibilities in my head. Maybe she really hadn't killed him; maybe he'd crawled up on to that catwalk, looking for a quiet place to drink, and had fallen. But I could imagine it all: her telling him something important had been left up there and he had to get it; following him up, and he was drunk and never even saw her, or felt those big hands on his back until it was too late . . .

But there was no proof. She was too smart for that. I knew the tired crew had been heading home after wrapping out the day, that no one had noticed her or the grip, that there were no clues except what they'd find in his toxicology report.

So I rationalized staying quiet. And tried not to hate myself.

It wasn't long after that when Hannah Ward said to me, at the end of a particularly long and difficult day of shooting, "You'll be lucky to survive this movie."

She patted my shoulder, and I asked, "Are they all this bad?"

"Oh, most of them are much worse," she said, winking at me before she walked away.

I was looking forward to the end of shooting on *The Lowdown*, because I figured it meant my internship would be over; but as we neared that fateful day, Hannah asked me if I'd like to stay on to see some of the post-production, and she even offered me a small salary. I seriously needed money – my credit card was close to its limit and for some reason my landlord still wanted rent every month – so I said yes.

Hannah's next film was already set: it was called *Yank!*, and was a rather (*ahem*) liberal re-telling of Twain's *A Connecticut Yankee in King Arthur's Court*. The script was in its eighth draft (with its fifth new writer), and Hannah had just starting talking to directors and stars. She said Will Ferrell and Seth Rogen were both interested.

I was in her office early one morning, taking notes (on my new tablet computer, of course) from her about the *Yank!* script when she glanced down at an entertainment news blog and froze. I saw her eyes scan the screen for a few seconds, then she blurted out, "That fucking bastard!"

I waited; I'd never seen her this furious before. Her face darkened, her eyes narrowed. She suddenly spun her laptop around for me to see the screen. "Look at this!"

The blog claimed that Jeff Minsky over at Dragonstar Pictures was developing an updated version of *A Connecticut Yankee in King Arthur's Court* called *Art and the Yank*.

Hannah had plenty of history with Jeff Minsky – he'd been the development executive she'd once punched.

"He doesn't really want to make this movie," she said, peering at the screen again, "he's just doing this to piss me off."

"What a dick," I muttered, although I was really thinking, *Is this whole movie business run on idiotic pettiness?*

Hannah held a finger up at me. "Stay right there – I want you to hear this."

"Okay."

She pulled out her cell phone, thumbed through her address book for a few seconds, then punched a number and raised the phone to her ear. She looked at me with gleeful anticipation when she said into the phone, "Jeff, it's Hannah."

I only heard her side of the conversation, but she made it pretty clear that he was denying that his project had been influenced by hers in any way, and that he had no intention of giving up *Art and the Yank* . . . and Hannah made it equally clear that she didn't believe a word he said.

When she ended the call she went blank for a few seconds, and somehow that frightened me more than the way blood had suffused her face earlier.

"So he won't give it up, huh?"

She grinned then and said, "Doesn't matter. It's time to do something about Jeff Minsky."

A week later, Hannah called me on a Sunday night and asked if I could meet her at her place in twenty minutes. I was relaxing in sweats, but of course I said I could.

I was five minutes late getting to her Brentwood estate, and was surprised to find her waiting for me in the driveway. "Hope you didn't have anything planned for tonight – I'm afraid it's going to go late."

"Sure," I said, and then hopped into her Hummer.

She drove us down the 405 to the 10 freeway headed east. It was already late – after ten p.m. – on Sunday night, and was one of the few times traffic in LA was sparse. We drove in silence for twenty minutes, then Hannah put on music – she liked classic jazz, which I didn't know at all. It was something with a fast, frantic saxophone, and it didn't do much to help me relax.

We kept going east, past downtown LA and through the towns of the San Gabriel Valley – Monterey Park, Rosemead, West Covina, Pomona. There were fewer cars on the road with each passing town, and Hannah picked up speed – soon we were doing 90 m.p.h., headed for . . . where? If we kept going, we'd soon reach nothing but desert and Palm Springs. I tried to remember if she was working with a writer out here, or searching for a location . . . but at eleven p.m. on a Sunday night?

We kept going. We passed Palm Springs, Indio . . . and then left the 10 freeway and headed south, towards the Salton Sea. I'd never been out here before, and I mainly knew of the area only because of how the noxious, stagnant pond that passed for a "sea" was occasionally stirred up by storms that sent its rotten-egg stench 150 miles west to blanket LA. I guess it had once been planned as a major resort, but from what I could see as we sped through the desert night, it was little more than a collection of abandoned shacks and miles of wind-blown emptiness.

Hannah finally slowed down and turned off the main road. We bounced along a rutted dirt track for another mile or so, until she finally spotted an ancient rusted sign with a lot number painted on it. She parked there and killed the engine.

"We made good time getting out here – we're early."

I couldn't hold my silence any longer. "Early for what, exactly?"

She didn't look at me as she spoke, just stared straight off into the night. There were no lights visible around us – no one lived out here, and I could see why – but in the distance I caught the faint glimmer of starlight on water: the Salton Sea.

"You know, I started as an actress. I was pretty then – a pretty piece of meat. I got tired of it quickly. One day a studio head – doesn't matter which one – called me into his office and told me he'd give me a leading role if I gave him a blow job. Instead I grabbed his crotch, squeezed, and told him I'd keep squeezing unless he let me produce the film instead of starring in it. He agreed, and I was done with acting for ever . . . but there were still plenty of men who thought I was a pretty piece of meat and who needed their balls squeezed regularly, and it hasn't changed much since."

She turned and looked at me then, her eyes glinting from the soft lights of the dashboard . . . but from what she carried inside her, too. "So how's *your* grip?" she asked me.

Why were we here, in the desert by an abandoned sea, at one in the morning? So she could ask me this? No, she could've done it in LA.

"Why did you pick me, Hannah?" I'd finally voiced the question that had circled around my thoughts like a carrion bird ever since I'd interviewed for the internship. What had she seen in me? Was it something I didn't see in myself? Something I didn't want to see?

Before she could answer, something distracted her, something she was looking at beyond me. "Ahh, good – our company has arrived."

I spun in my seat and saw headlights approaching. The new arrival thumped to a halt next to us, and a man got out. He was big, tattooed, short dark hair, a leather jacket. He nodded to Hannah as she walked up to him.

"You got him?" she asked.

The thug – because he fit that description perfectly – smirked, then went around to the back of his car, fingering the release for the trunk. I hadn't left the sanctuary of the Hummer yet, so I couldn't see what Hannah was laughing at as she looked down.

"Jennifer, come here," she called out, waving me over.

I wanted to vomit. Run. Refuse. Instead, of course, I got out and walked up to join them.

There was a man in the trunk, bound and gagged, looking the worse for wear after being in the trunk for three hours, but still alive, squirming. Something about him looked familiar . . .

"Jennifer, meet Jeff Minsky. Nice of him to agree to this meeting, isn't it?" She motioned to the thug. "Haul him out of there."

The kidnapper lifted Minsky out easily, but Minsky couldn't stand – he fell to the sand, then managed to push himself up to his knees, making frantic noises behind his gag.

Hannah gazed down at him impassively, eyeing him as if he were some ugly but amusing little dog. "You know, Jeff," she said after a few seconds, "the people who've already invested in *Yank!* didn't find your little stunt very amusing."

He shook his head back and forth so violently that he almost fell over again, catching himself at the last second.

But he froze and went quiet when the thug handed Hannah a gun.

She eyed it critically, hefted it, pretended to aim along the barrel, made a motion with her thumb that I figured was probably flicking off the safety. "You've been a thorn in my side for too long."

Jeff started to cry behind the gag; his sobs came out as stifled grunts.

Hannah considered the gun for another moment . . . then held it out to me.

I stared from the gun to her and back to the gun, in utter disbelief. She was surely joking, not serious, not—

"Take it," she said.

I did.

It was heavier than it looked, and I nearly dropped it.

"Use both hands," Hannah said. She was clearly experienced in these things.

I wrapped both hands around the grip. I was shaking, but even I couldn't miss at this range.

"Now shoot him."

"I don't know how to use it."

"Just point it and pull the trigger. It's got a hell of a recoil, so be prepared for that."

I wondered how many times she'd done this, maybe even in this same place, with this same enforcer for the investors' money. How many had she killed herself? How many people knew? If I refused, would I be the next victim?

I thought the answer to that was obvious.

So I tried to lift the gun, to point it at the man on the ground below me, a man who'd tried to compete with Hannah Ward and who found himself sobbing on the desert floor as a result. My fingers felt too weak to tear a piece of paper, let alone pull the trigger that would end a man's life (and save mine).

I had to try something else. I flipped the gun around and tried to smile as I returned it to Hannah. "I think this should really be your moment, Hannah. I'm afraid you'll regret it if I do it."

But she didn't take the gun. Instead, she gently pushed the barrel back until it was pointed at Minsky again, and said, "Pull the trigger and you'll be producing *Yank!*"

"But you . . ."

"I'll stay on as Executive Producer, but it'll be your baby."

There it was: everything she knew I wanted. I'd be making movies fresh out of college. The American Dream, the Hollywood dream, my dream. If I just pulled the trigger.

"Jennifer," she said, as I struggled with the gun, "this is how the industry – hell, the whole world – works."

I was surprised at how sad she sounded just then, as if she still had a speck of conscience, as if some tiny part of her was still capable of guilt and regret and sanity.

But I knew that wasn't the case. It was another movie lie.

I braced myself and pulled the trigger.

PAUL McAULEY

I Spy

I SPY FOR a living. That's why I know what you are. That's why I know what you do. That's why I humbly lay this confession at your feet.

Childhood is supposed to be the happiest time of your life, and once they have put it behind them, for most people it is. They remember the good times. They remember Christmas and birthdays. They remember sunny days and freedom and laughter. But my childhood was a hell with no redemption. I grew up resenting the way my schoolmates were cosseted and aimed towards adulthood by caring parents. I had to find my own path. It was no easy one.

My father was a Polish ex-airman. He had fled the Nazis when the tanks rolled over the border in September 1939. He was not a coward. He wanted to get out so he could have his revenge on those who had destroyed his country.

He joined the RAF and flew more than fifty sorties against the Luftwaffe at the height of the Battle of Britain. After the war he settled down and became an accountant. He was well respected in the little Gloucestershire town where we lived. He was a prosperous small businessman. He was a war hero. But he was also a violent bully. He missed the certainties of war and hated the contingencies and random mess of civilian life. He became a martinet who exerted fanatical and rigid control over his family.

Everything in our little bungalow had its place and everything had to be kept spotlessly clean. Meals had to be provided punctually. His clothes had to be ironed and starched in a certain way and had to be laid out for him each morning in the correct manner. He spent most of his evenings at the British Legion club. He drank heavily and came home and beat his wife after he failed to fuck her. He stood in the doorway of the bedroom of his only son and cursed him and listed perceived transgressions and the punishments he would deliver. In this he was as methodical as in everything else. He devised a tariff of discipline which he carried out to the letter.

I hated my mother more than my father because she never complained or stood up to him. She explained away the bruises as falls. Our neighbours accepted this because she was so prone to narcolepsy and epileptic fits she was not allowed a driving licence.

She was a mouse of a woman. Someone who should have protected me and could not even protect herself. She had no friends in the town. She was an only child and her mother was widowed. My father forbade her to have any contact with her meagre family. She was allowed out only to shop. My father would ring from the office at odd times to interrogate her.

I grew up fearful and quiet. I had been taught to speak only when spoken to. Any hint that I might be lying brought swift and terrible punishment. My father once broke a broom handle on my head because he thought I had stolen a £10 note. He later found it on the bureau and beat my mother for misplacing it. The world was constantly thwarting him.

I had concussion for three days. I did not mind. The world was pleasantly out of focus. Everything seemed an inch from my grasp. For the first time in my life my sleep was deep and dreamless.

My father was a burly man. Drink coarsened his face and added a swag to his belly but he remained hale and hearty until he died. He had excelled in all sports as a young man. Although he could easily have afforded a car he walked everywhere. He walked at the same fast pace whether it was raining or gloriously sunny.

I took after my mother. I was slightly built and short. My eyesight was poor. My father forced me to do Canadian Air Force Exercises each morning. He made me use Indian clubs to build up my muscles. They had little effect. He could circle my upper arms with his fingers. Once I tried to defend my mother because he was still beating her after she had been knocked unconscious.

Blood was coming out of her ears. He threw me the length of the living room with a flick of his arm.

I learned how to evade the worst of my father's anger. I found many places to hide. Sometimes I spent the night away from home. The beatings I received upon my return were fearsome but they were a small price to pay for a respite from my father's drunken rages and the aching quiet of my mother's fear. I found that if I pretended not to care about the beatings my father would lose interest. In truth he was getting old. He had married late. He had been fifty when I was born. There had been another child ten years before that. My brother had died when only two months old. He had been my father's true heir. My father blamed my mother and often told me that I was a mistake. It was the only one of his cruelties that I believed long after his death.

I did not seek out friends. I was mostly left alone at school. I was too weird for the bullies to bother with and too scary for the other misfits. A few of the teachers recognized my intelligence and tried to draw me out but I refused to respond.

I turned in essays and other work on time but otherwise I drifted through school. There was nothing to hold my interest. I spent most of my time daydreaming. I drew elaborate patterns inside the covers of my exercise books. Classes dragged slowly towards release at four-fifteen each afternoon. The school was a grammar school with public-school pretensions. It displayed silver trophies in a glass cabinet next to the door to the headmaster's study. The names of the dead of two world wars were engraved on walnut shields hung in the assembly hall. The names of those who had gone on to university were painted on varnished pine boards that lined the main corridor. In its traditions and discipline I saw only a weak reflection of my father's regime. I despised it.

I spent most of my free time as a teenager reading science fiction and Marvel comic books. I read Alfred Bester's *Tiger! Tiger!* and Theodore Sturgeon's *More Than Human*. I read Robert Heinlein's *Stranger in a Strange Land* and John Wyndham's *The Midwich Cuckoos*. I loved Roger Zelazny's *Amber* series of novels. They were about an ordinary man who discovered that he was a powerful prince of a hidden realm realer than our own world.

I used this raw material to construct my own fantasies. I was an orphan of star sailors who had abandoned or lost me for complex reasons. I was an experimental subject unknowingly adopted by my parents. Although I was outwardly an ordinary boy I would slowly realize my powers. I would be able to read minds or move objects by mental power. I would be able to see into the future and amass a vast fortune. I would be able to hypnotize girls and do whatever I wanted with them (the phrase *he bent her to his will* woke a particular thrill for me). I would found a new religion and be surrounded by loyal friends and beautiful compliant women. I would allow my mother and father to be employed in some lowly and humiliating position.

I read James Tiptree Jr's story "Beam Us Home". My father did not own a television and I knew nothing about *Star Trek* but the story rang true at a deep level. For many weeks I dreamed that a great golden ship would one day sweep down out of the sky and hover over my town. Everyone would be tested and everyone but me would fail. I would rise in a beam of light to the wonder of all.

And then there were the comics. Their dramas were centred on weaklings or cripples who were imbued with secret identities and superpowers. Spider-Man – his alter ego a misunderstood teenage loner like me. Iron Man – a millionaire afflicted with a near-fatal heart ailment. Thor – otherwise a cripple. The X-Men – mutant teenagers who hated the difference their superpowers bestowed upon them.

Unlike the X-Men I wanted to be different. I knew that I was better than those around me. I was better than the ordinary teenagers who had loving homes and went on dates and were good at sport. I could not believe that my suffering and my father's punishments were for nothing.

Were you already living in the town? Did you select me? Were you moulding me through those fantasies? Were you beginning to turn me into your disciple?

I will prove myself worthy of you. I will show you that I am capable of deeds of true and absolute justice. I will show you how I triumphed over my father.

I practised telepathy. I tried to control the flight of birds by willpower. I shuffled packs of cards and tried to guess their order. I collected coincidences and wondered if the whole world was a conspiracy. I imagined that it was peopled by actors in a drama centred on me.

I was sixteen. I cut an eccentric figure around town. I craved attention but was too introverted to seek it out. I thought that people would recognize and love my uniqueness. In this respect I was not unlike other teenagers.

In summer I wore an orange jacket and green trousers. In winter I topped this off with a quilted navy blue anorak. Like everyone in the seventies I wore my hair long. I did not often wash it. It was greasy and spangled with dandruff. I had thick-lensed National Health spectacles with thin blue metal rims. I cultivated a wealth of acne by long sessions of pinching and prodding before the bathroom mirror.

I was given no pocket money except for a few odd coins my mother managed to hoard from her meagre housekeeping. I spent her gleanings on second-hand Panther and Pan paperbacks at jumble sales. It left a little over for the bag of chips I shared with the pigeons in the park by the church. After I had used up the public library I needed to steal to get my fix of pulp thrills. I stole Marvel comic books from the revolving wire rack in the newsagent's. I stole Four Square and Star paperbacks from Woolworths' bargain bins. I wrapped my books and comics in plastic bags and hid them in various places in the bungalow's unkempt garden.

I did not know that comics and science fiction were popular culture. I knew nothing about popular culture. We did not own a television. My father kept the radiogram permanently tuned to Radio 4 and listened only to the evening news. I believed that the books and comics were schemes for an ideal world which would one day rise through the quotidian. I believed that they contained secret messages that only the Illuminati could understand.

I began to patrol the town at night soon after I took up shoplifting. I was looking for secrets. I did my homework early and went out after my father left for the British Legion club. Sometimes I followed him. He revealed nothing. It was not until later that I discovered his secret.

But there were plenty of places of interest. I planned my excursions like military operations. I haunted the common. I made furtive raids on the perimeter of the American airbase. I walked the corridors of the hospital. I wandered about the yards of the factories that backed on to the railway line.

I picked up a pair of binoculars in one of the jumble sales. The magnification ratio was feeble and both lenses were badly scratched. It did not matter. I watched ordinary domestic routines through lighted windows. I knew where all my classmates lived and where their girlfriends lived. I watched them in bus shelters or chip shops or in the patch of waste ground where they drank Blackthorn cider and VP sherry. I knew where the older teenagers went in the woods above the town. I knew that the dairy regularly tipped unsold milk back into its tanks. I knew that stolen goods were distributed in the yard of the Prince of Wales pub by the bus station after hours. I knew where dope was sold and I knew who bought it.

I made notes on different coloured paper. I made elaborately coded dossiers. I believed that they held the key to all of the town's secrets. All I had to do was scry the patterns.

There were other rewards. Sometimes I glimpsed through half-drawn curtains a girl or a woman taking off her clothes. I saw Janice Turner take off everything but her bra, and then she turned and with one hand reached behind her long white back and began to unfasten the strap and with the other switched out the light. She was one of the girls at the High School who were rumoured to "do it". She became the subject of my humid private fantasies for weeks afterwards.

Spying did not satisfy my need to know things. The sixth form had its own house in one corner of the school grounds. It was easy to bunk off school between lessons without being missed. I knew the routines of the householders and always carefully checked that they were out by telephoning them before going into action.

It was surprisingly easy to break into houses in those days. Very few people had burglar alarms or security locks. I avoided houses with dogs. People hid spare keys under flowerpots or doormats. They hung them on strings inside letterboxes. In summer they left windows open.

I took nothing. I wanted only to be in the spaces inhabited by ordinary lives. It was like being on stage in an empty theatre. I read letters and bills. I found diaries. I learned all their dirty little secrets. I printed my authority on the commonplace domestic interiors through minor transgressions. I lay in the fragrant beds of teenage girls and masturbated with their underwear around my penis. I pissed in baths but washed it away afterwards. I walked naked around other people's houses.

Although I took nothing from the houses I broke into, I sometimes found rabbits and other small pets in sheds or out-houses. Once I found half-a-dozen new-born kittens blindly moving over each other in a cardboard box lined with newspaper. I killed these helpless creatures in various slow and interesting ways using the dissection kit I had been issued with for biology classes. I smeared their blood on my face. Sometimes I drank a little of it. The thick salty taste made me ill. I was not yet worthy. I left the remains of these small sacrifices in various places at the edge of town. I impaled them on bamboo canes or on branches of certain trees. I was marking the place as my own.

I returned to the sacrifices again and again. Sometimes I discovered that the corpses had been further mutilated. At the time I thought that foxes or crows had found them. Now I know that you were leaving signs of your presence.

Are you lost or did you come here deliberately? Are you experimenting with the town? Or did you come here because of me? Did I draw you here? Perhaps we are the first of a new kind of being.

You have much to learn about me. You should know that after dark the town is mine. I see everything.

I was too unworthy to recognize any messages you left me then. I had not yet ascended to a higher level. I will tell you how I began that long climb. I will tell you how I killed a man.

I was still obsessed with Janice Turner. I broke into her house several times and found her diary. I learned the names of the men she was having sex with. One was an American sergeant from the airbase. She met him every Sunday evening. Her parents believed that she was practising the clarinet at a friend's house or that she had gone to the cinema. In fact she was fucking her boyfriend.

He was a burly man with a thick moustache and a severe crew cut. He drove a red Mustang. It had left-hand drive. The American Air Force allowed their men to ship their cars over. His name was Kowalski.

He had a flat in a big house at the edge of town. The relatives of the old woman who died in it had sold its large garden to developers. Unfinished yellow-brick houses stood where the orchard and lawns had once been. These houses overlooked Kowalski's flat and it was easy to keep watch from the outside.

One day I decided to break in.

All that week I had practised being invisible. It was a matter of sidling along and not meeting other people's eyes. It was a matter of concentration. I was sure that I could do it long enough to see what Janice Turner and her boyfriend were doing. I wanted to see Janice having sex. I wanted to see him fucking her.

I dressed in black. I rubbed coal dust on my face. The lock on the front door was a cheap imitation of a Yale. I knew how to open it using a slip of plastic. My heart was beating fast as I eased inside. My chest felt very full. I was taking many small breaths.

It was very hot inside. It stank of cheap perfume and booze. I could hear a TV roaring at full volume. There was a kitchen to the right. The cooker was black with grease. The sink was full of pots and pans and dirty plates soaking in grey water. The main room was to the left. In a later era estate agents would call it a studio flat but it was really a glorified bed-sit.

Candles burned everywhere. They were stuck to flat surfaces with their own melted wax. A gun lay in front of a half circle of red candles on a side table. I picked it up. It was very heavy. Its cross-hatched metal grip was oily and cold. It was real. TV light flickered over the pull-down sofa where Janice Turner lay.

She was naked. Her white skin shone with sweat. Her thighs were slick. Her big sloppy breasts rolled on her ribcage as she looked up at me. Her eyes were glassy and black. She looked at me and my heart beat even faster. Then I knew that she was looking *past* me. She was looking at the half-open bathroom door.

Kowalski was in the bathroom. He was naked too. His back was to me. Black hair swirled over it. He bent over the bath. One end of a taut strip of cloth was in his mouth and the other wrapped around his arm. He had a glass hypodermic and was searching for a vein. There was old blood spray on the white tiles.

I must have made a noise because he turned. I stepped backwards. Despite the noise of the TV I heard the hypodermic clatter in the bath. He said something and reached for me and the top of the bathroom doorframe exploded in dust and splinters. The gun had gone off. I had not heard it but I felt the shock of it in the muscles of my arm. Kowalski was screaming. His hands were over his face. Blood squirted between his fingers. I shot him twice and he went down.

Janice Turner giggled. I dropped the gun and ran.

I know now that you recognize me. I know that you have read this poor confession.

I first saw you running from one side of the high street to the other. You had taken on the appearance of a naked man. You vaulted a parked car and disappeared down the side of the library. You moved so quickly that by the time I zoomed in you were gone.

I saw you again four weeks later. This time I remembered to use the video. But when I played it back it showed only the street and its pools and light and shadow. You did not register. You have the true power of invisibility.

But I saw you.

I remember your face. It flashed ghostly white as you passed beneath a streetlight. I saw the round dark moon pools of your eyes. I saw the slather dripping from your pointed teeth.

You came again last night. I found your sacrifice. I hid it for you. It took all night but it is done. No one will find it.

You know me now.

You know what I am.

I wait for you to come to me. The others are like sheep. They are blind to our true nature. I am the only free man here. I am too tired and too excited to write more. Be patient. Tomorrow I will write about how I broke free from my father.

There was a huge scandal after Kowalski's death. It was revealed that he had been supplying heroin to many of the personnel of the American Air Force base. He had injected heroin into Janice Turner's arm that night. She was convicted of manslaughter but the sentence was suspended.

At first I was scared and then I was elated. I fed on my fear and turned it to strength. After three days I knew that Janice Turner had not really seen me. I had been the invisible man. I had rescued her from Kowalski. I had delivered justice. I lost myself in fantasies in which Janice remembered what I had done and came to me in gratitude.

I grew bolder. I sneaked out of the bungalow at night and roamed the town. I broke into houses and stood by the beds of sleeping people. Sometimes they woke and stared at me in sleepy confusion but they always went back to sleep. Sometimes I masturbated over them. I violated their dreams.

I was twice stopped by the police. I told them that I had been seeing my girlfriend. They drove me home in their patrol car and watched as I went in through the front door. I stole from the piles of change that people left on bedside tables and chests of drawers. I had stolen money in my pockets when the police stopped me. I bought a knife from the Army surplus store in Bristol. Its blade was as wide as my hand. One edge was serrated and one edge was razor sharp. There was a notch for cutting twine. I found a medical supplies shop. I bought straight scalpel blades and heavy curved scalpel blades. I bought a surgical saw and heavy forceps. I said that I was a medical student. The shop assistant did not question me.

I left many sacrifices in the woods where now surveyor's tapes stretch between iron poles, and yellow crosses of spray paint mark the trunks of trees which will be cut down to make room for new houses.

I finished school that summer. I scraped passes in three A-levels without much effort. It did not matter. I did not want to go to university. In any case my father would not pay for it. He found me a job in the paper mill where he audited the accounts. I worked as a labourer on shifts. I volunteered for the night shift. I came home at dawn and slept for a few hours and then roamed about town. I read the novels of Philip K. Dick. I read Frank Herbert's *Dune* series. I came to believe that most people were zombies or androids. They were no more than machines. Only those who could pass specific tests were human. I had a sudden insight that felt so right everything in my life locked around it. I was the only real person in town because I had passed just such a test. I had murdered a man for true and absolute justice. I began to look for other tests.

I did not know about you then.

I did not know that you were my secret sharer.

I took to following my father. I found out his secret.

It was very simple and very banal. He was fucking his secretary in the lunch hour.

She was a spinster. She was only a few years younger than he was. She was heavily built and had a large mole by the side of her nose.

I watched them several times. They did it on the desk. They pulled down the blinds but in their haste they often left them askew. My father's offices were on the first floor over a butcher's shop. I watched from the flat asphalt roof over the refrigerated store in the rear extension. I was Spider-Man. I tingled with a premonition of absolute justice.

I knew I had to expose this crime. I made several sacrifices in preparation. My father brought in a pest-control firm. He thought there were rats in the building and that some had died under the floorboards. I sanctified the space and made it my own and then I confronted him.

He always locked the office door at lunchtime. One Saturday I stole his key and had a spare made. When I came into his office two days later he tried to rear up from under the weight of his secretary. Then she saw me and screamed and fell to the floor. Her nylon petticoat was bunched up around her flabby white thighs. Her grey hair hung around her face. My father's face was white and red. His penis deflated in little throbbing jerks. I stared at him and went out.

My father said nothing that night. He did not need to. We both knew I had taken away his source of power. He no longer went to the British Legion club. He drank at home. He drank a bottle of Teacher's whisky every night. He raged at my mother but no longer hit her. They were sleeping in different rooms. I realized that my father was an old man.

I came and went as I pleased. I left dead animals on the desk in my father's office. I dissected them to the bones and spread them on his blotter.

I saw my father's defeat as vindication of my power. I knew that I could use my power to do good. I would become an avenger.

Stolen goods were dealt openly in the Prince of Wales pub. I kept watch and learned that one of the local police detectives was involved. He turned a blind eye and was rewarded with cash.

Sometimes he brought in radio cassettes taken from crashed vehicles or jewellery taken from burglarized houses. He brought pornography confiscated from the sex shop in Gloucester.

I determined to expose him. It was my undoing. I overestimated my powers.

I broke into the shed at the back of the pub. Stolen goods were stored amongst crates of empty bottles and carbon dioxide cylinders. I taped pornographic pictures to the windows of the detective's car. I left a stack of VCRs on the step of his house.

Superheroes left villains tied up for the police to deal with. I thought that justice would flow naturally after the crime was exposed.

The police came for me.

I was framed. Stolen goods were planted in my locker at the paper mill. All the recent local burglaries were pinned on me. There was a false confession. The fact that I had been stopped twice in suspicious circumstances added weight to the charges. My father cooperated. I believe that he used his business connections to get rid of me.

I was over eighteen and considered an adult. I was given a five-year prison sentence. Crimes against property were taken very seriously in the county. I was taken to Birmingham prison. My parents did not visit me.

Prison terrified me. Prison gave me discipline. Prison taught me that justice is arbitrary and administered by fallible men.

I had to watch myself every minute of every hour. I had to watch what went on around me. It was lucky that I already knew how to become invisible.

Most of the men inside were recidivists who wanted to do their time quietly. I learned to keep away from the few blowhards and troublemakers. The others left me alone. I was not worth bothering with.

I cultivated my isolation. I knew that I was a political prisoner amongst criminals. I read my way through the library. I listened to men talk. I learned how to hot-wire cars. I learned which alarms could be deactivated. I learned how to pick locks.

I still had a misplaced sense of justice. I learned that one man controlled the flow of drugs through the jail. I snitched him to the warders. Two days later I was ambushed in the showers by two men and severely beaten. In a last flash of lucidity I recognized my assailants and then they were both wearing my father's face. I screamed and writhed under his blows.

The men who beat me were warders. No doubt they were the men who brought the drugs into the prison. This time I kept quiet. My nose and jaw and cheekbones were broken. I almost lost the sight of one eye. I had to have surgery to reconstruct my face. I recovered in hospital and was transferred to Wormwood Scrubs.

I did the rest of my time quietly. I was promoted to the kitchens and ate as much prison food as possible. It was much better than my mother's cooking. I exercised. My frame filled out.

I served three years of my sentence. I was taken into the chaplain's office a few weeks before I was released. He told me that my father was dead. He asked if I wanted to apply for compassionate leave to attend the funeral. I shook my head. I looked down at the institutional carpet to hide my dry eyes.

I had learned of several security firms which employed ex-cons. I got a job with one of them. It was run by a retired police inspector. The word was that he had retired because he had been caught taking bribes from sex shops in Soho. The pay was low. You had to buy your own uniform.

I loved it.

I was rotated through several low-grade assignments. I stood night watch in an empty office block. I patrolled the grounds of a hospital. I patrolled an engineering factory. I took pornography from the workmen's lockers and burned it.

I got a job in another security firm. I was working under a false name. The firm prospered. It won a contract to staff one of the new privatized prisons. I guarded prisoners between prison and court.

Five years passed and then I saw the advertisement which brought me home to you.

I knew at once it was mine. I applied. My references were good but I knew that they were irrelevant. My old sense of certainty surged back. I knew I was one of the masters of the world.

And so I returned home. I returned to you.

*   *   *

The town has changed. There is a housing estate where beech woods once stood. There is a triple set of mini-roundabouts on the site of the old brewery. A bypass skirts to the west. Warehouses and supermarkets are strung along it. It could be anywhere. There is much unemployment and crime is high. The police do not dare patrol parts of the council estate at night.

There was a small riot in the town centre. Youths refused to move on after the pubs had closed. They sat around the market cross. They were drinking and shouting and playing ghetto blasters. The police were outnumbered. Someone threw a petrol bomb. A police car was overturned and set alight.

The council responded by putting in a system of closed-circuit television cameras. I am one of four security officers who keep permanent watch on the bank of TV screens in the little office in the council building.

I spy for a living. No one knows who I am. My face has been changed by the beating and by time. I keep my hair in a Number Two crop. I wear contact lenses. I am no longer skinny. I have followed my mother down the street several times. She did not recognize me. I keep watch on her.

I have visited my father's grave. He can no longer harm me. He is in my power now.

I keep watch on those of my former schoolmates who have not left town. The police detective still works here. I watch him. I watch everyone.

I spend my nights watching TV screens that glow with intensified black-and-white images of the streets of the town centre. I can pan and zoom on anything. A video recorder makes a time-stamped recording of any behaviour I feel is criminal or suspicious. I have an open line to the police station.

That's how I saw you. That's why I know what you are. That's why I know what you can do.

I last saw you four weeks ago. I was just coming on shift. I always arrive a few minutes early. Roland Miller was on duty. He is a scruffy and overweight young man. He had the radio tuned to a pop music station and was flicking through a tabloid newspaper.

I saw you on Camera Sixteen. I saw you run from out of the scruffy bushes that line the patch of ground by the war memorial.

You ran very fast and by the time I had slapped Roland's hand from the joystick and taken command you were already off-screen. I switched through Cameras Fifteen and Twelve and saw you again. Roland was complaining loudly. I shut him out. I saw you run beneath the halo of a streetlight and the camera over-loaded. I backed the sensitivity down but you were gone.

Roland did not see you. I ran back the videotape but there was nothing there.

Roland laughed at me but I knew then that I was the chosen one. Because I had practised invisibility, I alone had the power to see you.

For the first time I deserted my post and went to see your handiwork. The pitiless white moon shone down on her. I marked myself with her blood and went back to work. I watched a police patrol car pass by without knowing she lay a few feet from the road.

I returned at the end of my shift. I took your sacrifice to the churchyard and buried it in my father's grave. No one will find it. My mother never visits the grave and it is in an overgrown corner of the churchyard.

I know that I have found someone worthy of my worship.

The woods are almost gone but I have left sacrifices in a belt of scruffy sycamores beside the ring road. I broke into my mother's bungalow and took back what was mine. I dug up the caches of my precious comics and books. They were swollen by water and mould but burned easily once they had been soaked with petrol.

I have sacrificed my childhood to you.

Now it is full moon again. I have left signs. Only you will know their import.

My mother's head lies at the site of your sacrifice. In the last moment of her life she knew who I was. I have had revenge for her failure to protect me from my father.

I buried her body with your sacrifice.

My father's decomposed body lies amongst the faded poppy wreaths on the steps of the war memorial. He is dressed in my security officer's uniform. I dug him up a few days after I took up my post here and I kept him in my flat. Now I know that every-thing was meant to be.

I have been purified.

I have cast off my past.

I wait for you. I switch from camera to camera. Moonlight gleams on the windows of the shops along the high street. The supermarket at the edge of town burns with a fever light. The trees in front of the churchyard are restless. A group of teenagers are drinking by the side of the town hall. I should report them to the police. Instead I think that they will be the first sacrifice we make together.

I know that I am worthy. I know that you will come to me. I know that we will achieve a glorious synthesis.

Together we will change the world.

MIKE CAREY

Reflections on the Critical Process

MANDELSON AND ME arguing across a table.
I tell him he has to up his game, and he shoots me.

I wake up in hospital, groggy but healing. It's three days later: three days since I last sat down and wrote. Over the whining protests of the doctor, who belongs to a type I despise, I sign the releases and discharge myself on my own recognizance.

Outside, on the street, I flag down a taxi. It swerves in my direction, but doesn't slow. As I bounce off the front bumper, I catch a glimpse of Mandelson at the wheel, grinning like a maniac.

This time it's only two days before I wake up, and it's a nicer ward with a south-facing window. But Mandelson has sent me flowers, which bring me out in a hideous allergic rash when I touch them. I go into anaphylactic shock, and it's another week before I surface.

Is the man disturbed? I wonder. This seems a disproportionate response to a negative review. But as my bloated, blood-swollen face deflates towards its normal proportions, some of my natural indignation drains away too. This is surely nothing that can't be settled over a hearty meal and a selection of fine wines.

I walk home – it seems safer than hailing a cab. When I get there, I find that the door of my apartment has been booby-trapped: I can quite clearly see the scrape marks in the wood of the jamb where Mandelson – for I assume it is he – has been meddling with the hinges. Were I to insert my key in the lock, it seems probable that some very unfortunate consequences would result. Explosives? Poison gas? Discretion, plainly, is the better part of valour.

The elevator doesn't come when I call it, so I take the stairs. The loose board has been more expertly camouflaged than the tampering with my door, so I come down the last three flights arse-over-tip, with gathering momentum. That turns out to be a blessing in disguise, because I sail right over the bamboo stakes and am only brought to a (somewhat painful) halt by the street door.

Limping down the steps into the street, I narrowly escape being run over for a second time. This time Mandelson is driving a truck, and things seem set to go very badly for me, but with great presence of mind I dive behind a potted palm. Mandelson is a keen gardener and fervent conservationist, who favours the re-wilding of urban habitats: he swerves to miss me.

What can I do? My revolver (which I purchased a long while ago, and have never used) is up in my apartment, and therefore inaccessible. In any event, I don't believe I ever acquired any ammunition for it.

I retire to a coffee bar further down the block to consider my options, and while I'm brooding over a lemon tea, the phone behind the counter rings. The waiter who picks up shouts my name, but as I stand to take the call there is a screech of brakes from outside. I have time to drop to the floor before the street window shatters and – to the accompaniment of a sound like a typewriter shod in pig-iron – a hail of machine-gun bullets chews up the counter, the waiter and the people and fittings at the front three tables.

Surely, now, we are beyond the limits of normal hurt feelings.

I lie low for a week, in a repulsive rented room in a dockside hovel, tended to by an obese Armenian woman whose three words of English are "pay", "eat" and "cockroach".

Then, when I judge that the time is right, I begin to stalk my prey.

I buy a Minim .14 hand pistol – small, and probably inaccurate over long distances, but still serviceable at close quarters.

I visit a theatrical costumier's, where a bowler hat, blond wig and Fu Manchu moustache render me entirely unrecognizable.

I go to Mandelson's apartment on 28th Street, and gain entrance by telling the concierge that I am Mandelson's homo-sexual lover. He is out, and so I steal his mail from the pigeonhole in the building's lobby. There is a fat wodge of letters, which I take out into the street and then stop to examine at a bus stop a few blocks down.

The bulk of Mandelson's mail consists of bills, which I am about to discard until I see that one of them, from a disreputable shipping and forwarding agency, is for two female Bengal tigers. These beasts have cost Mandelson $15,000 and some odd change, inclusive of a $22 handling charge. A sizeable sum for a man whose last three novels have struggled to make the bottom of the moderate sellers list. Does that sound harsh? I say what must be said.

I look at the remaining bills a little more closely. I see that Mandelson has rented the Andreas Capellano sports centre on 12th Street for a month, which adds another ten thousand bucka-roos to his burgeoning expenses. He has also cornered the market in stainless-steel razor blades. This intrigues me, for Mandelson has a beard as dense as a hawthorn thicket.

There is also a letter which is not a bill. It is a request from an engineering firm for further specifications. I am not surprised that further specifications are required: what Mandelson has apparently asked for is a layout of interlocking iron plates making up into a rectangle 75 by 150 feet, with an insulated semi-circular area of radius five feet on one of the shorter sides.

I resolve not to go within a dozen blocks of the Andreas Capellano sports centre until Mandelson's lease expires.

My stalking has come to a dead halt, more or less. I visit Mandelson's apartment again later in the day, find nothing more. The next day I call for a third time, with the same result. I ques-tion the concierge. She is abusive. She hasn't seen Mandelson for almost a week: moreover, people keep coming around and demanding money for things she's never seen and knows nothing about. What sort of things? I ask. Things like five thousand gross of stainless-steel razor blades. Things like steel plates, and breed-ing pairs of king cobras. I sympathize. She tells me that she doesn't need my damn' sympathy, and that I'm a sodomite son-of-a-whore who (on that sweet day when God reigns on Earth) will surely be stricken with leprosy and hysterical blindness. I leave with my dignity intact.

I am by nature phlegmatic and slow to wrath, but by this time I am experiencing something akin to perturbation. My choice is this: I can either go to Andreas Capellano and confront my tormentor, or I can roam the city, exiled from my own apartment and from the life I knew, until he picks me off with a combine harvester, a garbage wagon or a snow plough.

Over a cup of coffee in a less than salubrious diner near my less than salubrious dockside rooms, I brood over this conundrum for a long time without bringing it to a solution. But then, as luck would have it, the decision is taken out of my hands. As I stand up to leave, something hard and cold and rounded in cross-section – an aluminium baseball bat, perhaps, although I'm far from being an expert in such things – hits me on the back of the skull and sends me into sudden and complete oblivion.

Mandelson has anticipated me again, the frothing lunatic. How do you even argue with someone like that?

It is dark when I wake up. It remains dark even when I remember to open my eyes. My head is hurting, but when I sit up and probe it anxiously with trembling fingertips I discover that it has been bandaged. As I squint into the darkness, the lights come on. Raw: far too bright. Arc-lighting, as though for a stage.

What I see is this: a long room, the floor of varnished wood and marked out with white lines. The markings are consistent with a five-a-side football court, and I am sitting on the centre line. Around me, the walls are draped in black, except at the far end of the room where there are two doors. There are many things about this set-up that I do not like.

Mandelson says hello over a crackly PA system. I ignore him. I know that he cannot resist the urge to explain the situation, and that he will do it badly, heavy on the bombast. I probably already know more than he intends to tell me, so I can afford to let my attention wander, as you do on a plane when the stewardess delivers the safety demonstration.

"Are you comfortable, Peasey?" he crackles.

"I survive, Mandelson," I reply coolly. I throw my coolness in his teeth. Let him chew on it and take what nourishment he can.

"How did you describe my novel again?"

Two doors. That's interesting. And the drapes draw attention to them by concealing everything else.

"I believe I said that it was a Gothic cock-up, Mandelson."

"'A prime Gothic cock-up; a puerile resurrection of a literary form that should have been allowed to die with Lewis and Shelley.'"

"I never write middle-of-the-road reviews, Mandelson. You know that."

"And yet you may still get to be roadkill."

Bwa ha ha! No, he doesn't go quite that far, but a bwa ha ha is strongly implied. Sitting there on the basketball court, I think of those who have suffered in the name of art. Many of them I tortured myself, for that is a reviewer's task in life.

"Well, if you disliked *House of Blood*, Peasey, you're going to hate the sequel. I call it *Sports Centre of No Return.*"

"I should work on the title, Mandelson. It sounds a little . . . dare I say it . . . jejune."

"At the end of the chamber," he snarls, "there are two doors. Do you see them?"

"I see the doors, Mandelson."

"They mean life or death to you, according to how you choose. Behind one is the back staircase leading out of this place. Behind the other is a Bengal tiger, starved and savage. Decide quickly which door you will open. In a minute's time, if you haven't made a choice, the floor will open beneath your feet and pitch you into oblivion!"

I consider. First of all, he is lying about the doors. Possibly he is also lying about the floor, and the time limit. I glance down and inspect the perfectly polished wood, find a thin line running up the centre of the room which has been recently cut and sanded and indifferently varnished. No, he isn't bluffing. The floor will open. There will be some sort of gesture towards oblivion.

Back at Mandelson's apartment, I assume, the bills must be piling up and up and up.

Fifteen seconds have now gone, and I have no intention of choosing a door because I believe, doubter and cynic though I am, that you don't buy two Bengal tigers if you're only planning to use one.

I straighten up – slowly, because my headache persists – and walk across to one side of the court. I take a fold of the black drapes in my hand and pull them aside. Behind them there are nets, and behind the nets, climbing bars: Andreas Capellano doubles up, as most sports centres do, and the main arena is furnished for pretty much every sport there is.

It's possible to put my feet on the climbing bars, even through the nets. It's possible to take my full weight off the floor and wait there, like a monkey in the rigging, for further developments to eventuate.

The floor pivots on its unseen hinges, breaks open at the centre and falls away into black nothingness below me. I allow myself to feel a little smug: the clean logic of the enlightenment has cut through Mandelson's welter of Gothic excesses.

I swarm along the nets, surprising myself with my skill. Crab-scuttling from one set of bars to the next, I arrive at length at the nearer of the two doors. Once there, I lean out over the black gulf, turn the handle, and pull the door open.

There is another darkness beyond: a narrower space, which stinks of musk and urine. Something stirs in the gloom, gathers itself, and whips past me almost before I'm aware of it. A flash of light on sleekly muscled flesh, sheathed in dark fur, is the limit of what I perceive. It drops out of sight, beyond line or plummet, sending up from the depths below a tinny whisper and a sudden roar of rage or pain.

The next bit is complicated. Since the door opened outwards, I am forced to climb around it before I can actually gain entrance to the room it leads to. This takes me some minutes, and Mandelson makes another "Hello, campers" broadcast over the PA system before I'm done.

"You didn't play by the rules, Peasey."

"Didn't I, Mandelson? That must be because the rules are asinine and arbitrary. But in any case, I did choose a door."

"You can't escape me. Every square inch of this building is a trap, and there's no escape."

"Every square inch? That would be one hundred and forty-four traps per square foot, Mandelson. Surely you exaggerate."

Scrambling in through the doorway, I enter the musky dark-ness. Within it there are faint glimmers of light, which take the form of lines drawn on the air. Straw rustles under my feet: my outstretched arm touches a metal bar, traces it up and down. The vertical glimmers resolve themselves into further bars, extending before me on both sides. I am in a cage: semi-circular recesses at the corners tell me that it is on wheels. A sort of animal transporter.

At its further end there is a door which is bolted, but since the cage was only ever intended to contain animals the bolt is easily reachable from the inside, through the bars. I slide the bolt, push the door wide and step down into – what? A wide, empty space. A floor of ceramic tiles, visible in the light from a skylight over my head, and a white-painted pillar very close to me on which there is a sign I can't read.

Again, I wait for my eyes to adjust. I find that the sign bears no words, only a stick figure walking down some stairs, and an arrow pointing off to my left. I follow the arrow and, yes, there are the stairs. They only lead down, so that is where I go, skirting the sprung bear traps with which the landing is littered. Every square inch! There are only a couple of dozen bear traps at most, and one has already been sprung by a luckless janitor. He has passed out from the pain, so I skirt around him and continue.

The stairwell is much darker than the room above. I grip the banister rail very firmly as I descend now into near-unrelieved blackness, losing the faint glow from the skylight after the first turn. There is a light switch, but even in the dark I can see the supernumerary wires trailing away from it, up and to the left. Mandelson has rigged an axe to swing down when the switch is pressed, positioning it so that it will embed itself in the skull of anyone standing on that particular step. I could pull the wires loose, but that might trigger a further unwanted sequence of events. I choose instead to go on in the dark.

Two floors down and I can go no further. There are no more stairs. I hope that I've reached ground level: it's always possible, of course, that this is a basement, in which case I'll have to memorize the position of the stairs and retrace my steps.

I am walking along a corridor now. There are more tiles under my feet, and – I ascertain – on the walls. The corridor slopes down a little, and there is a faint smell of chlorine from up ahead of me. Abruptly I step into a narrow well in the floor and find that it's filled with water to a depth of four or five inches. This is a footbath, and therefore I'm about to enter the pool area.

The larger darkness ahead of me talks to itself in metallic whispers; in hollow scratches and clicks like the claws of tin crabs on the bed of a dry ocean. Turning a corner, I find the light: it's fierce, but it's high overhead and angled so that very little of it reaches me down here in these nether regions. I am once again in a very wide, very high-ceilinged space. The massive trapdoors from the basketball court two storeys above hang down to either side of me, and something in front of me smells of straw and musk and bodily fluids.

As I shuffle out into the light, I see the rim of the pool as a black slash directly ahead of me. Beyond it, prismatic splinters of yellow and blue slice the air into ionic froth. The swimming pool is filled with razor blades, and the tiger is dying a few feet from the nearest edge: almost close enough to touch, but much, much too far to swim.

I sit by the side of the pool for a while, thinking. It seems that Mandelson has laid no further snares in this particular room, so I am undisturbed except by the tiger's death throes. Taking stock of my situation, I realize for the first time that I am still dressed in the clothes that I was wearing before I was brought here. Is the Minim hand pistol still in my jacket pocket? No, it is not. Nothing else is either: cell phone, wallet, keys, all gone. Nothing to work with except what is here already. I need a base of operations, and for that I need a detailed plan of the building; for which, I imagine, I need the entrance hall.

I do not find the entrance hall. Apart from the brilliant spotlights above the pool, the building remains in darkness, and an understandable caution prevents me from turning on the lights. What I do find is tiger spoor: I tread in it. I infer that the second tiger has been released from its cage, which lends a certain urgency to these proceedings.

I come to another sign, read it with my fingers. It indicates the location of the fire exit, but the corridor towards which it points is hissing ominously. I have no wish to encounter a breeding pair of king cobras: some things ought to be private.

I am feeling a strong sense of trepidation and paranoia now, but I try to keep it from spiralling into panic: I cannot afford to panic. I feel that the second tiger is stalking me through the dark, and that my every step may bring me face-to-face with it. It would be easy, therefore, to stop moving and go to ground. Easy, but fatal, I tell myself, and I keep moving.

When, finally, I reach a door at the head of a long flight of stairs, I am beginning to feel the strain of all these melodramatic and over-coloured events. The sign on the door is shallowly embossed on shiny, varnished wood, so once again I can run my hand over it and read it by touch. This is the supervisor's office. It will do as my base of operations. I open the door and enter.

It is Mandelson's base of operations. He is sitting at a bank of CCTV monitors, but now he swivels his chair and we stare at one another, mildly embarrassed, like women who have come to a party in the same dress. Then he scrambles for his pistol and shoots at me again, splintering the door-post.

I turn tail and run back the way I've come, along nighted avenues, across great rooms that could be anything, could house anything. When I pause I hear running footsteps from somewhere that could be very close by or very far away: the darkness conceals and confuses. When I run I hear nothing but the beating of my own heart.

At last, I see a light up ahead of me, growing stronger as I approach. Turning a last corner, I am face-to-face with it. An open door. I step through and find myself in the building's chapel – an odd thing to find in a sports centre, but I speak as a confirmed atheist. Others, clearly, treasure the sense of oneness with God that comes after an intense and sweaty workout.

I walk between rows of removable seating, noting the prayer books on shelves behind each one. The floor rings like a steel drum beneath my feet, and this is unsurprising because it is burnished metal. The points where the individual metal plates abut on to each other are clearly visible, though an attempt has been made to disguise them with some sort of resin.

Ahead of me is the altar, and behind it the handsomely carved mahogany cross in its recess. The recess, I see now, is semi-circular. The room is approximately twice as long as it is wide: I would not be at all surprised to learn that its exact dimensions are 75 by 150 feet.

I vault over the altar rather than walking around it. I step into the recess, ducking my head because its ceiling is low. There is no metal here: or rather, the metal is covered with a layer of springy, foam-rubber-like insulation. To one side of the recess there is a foot pedal at the end of a coiled length of electric flex. Aha.

I turn as Mandelson enters the room. He raises the gun. I say, "Goodbye, Mandelson," and press my foot down on the pedal.

He fries. The smell is of burned bacon on a griddle. Gothic excess.

After he is thoroughly, unfragrantly dead I take my foot off the pedal, return to the supervisor's office and lock myself in. I switch all the lights on and wait until I feel calm and composed, which takes a little more than five minutes. Then I call the police and wait a little longer.

By this time, the tips of my fingers are starting to prickle. The supervisor's computer is already booted up, and though it's mainly set up to monitor the feeds from the many CCTV cameras dotted around the building, it also has a version of Microsoft Word with which I am conversant.

I open a document, type in header and footer information and set line-spacing to double.

I begin to write, critiquing in reasoned and pithy prose everything that has happened to me since I first took Mandelson's bullet. My usual word count is 4,000 and I bring the piece in at 3,889, not counting the title.

I despise the vernacular. It is the progenitor of sloppy thought and flabby argument.

But I own Mandelson. I fucking *own* him.

DAVID J. SCHOW

The Finger

IDIDN'T KNOW it at the time, but my personal monster had flown all the way to Minnesota to murder a woman I had never met, didn't even know. Dead, just because she had phoned me to harass me on behalf of a bank, in dutiful pursuit of one of many outstanding loans. Her job had been working one of those soulless telephonic rat-runs as the voice of authority who "only wants to help you", which is enough to cheese off any normal human.

How I came to have a personal monster is preamble.

In Los Angeles, very few people are pedestrians by choice. But when you walk the avenues and side streets as traffic whizzes past, you notice things on the ground the speed demons will never see, and thus never even consider. Like found objects, for example.

I have a collection.

Stray, random items out in the wilds of the world have always fascinated me. Discards, junk, oddments, lost possessions. A deadbolt, all by itself with no door. A wristwatch with no band, which has ceased to function, cast away not into a bin, but stranded in the world, on the street. Mostly small things – not trash-heaped computer monitors or old furniture, but discoveries you can hold in your hand. A broken porcelain satyr missing a leg. Half a string of fake, formerly flashy costume jewels. Pirate booty at ground level.

Once this object had been new. It rolled off an assembly line or craftsman's table and was packaged to sparkle and attract the consumer eye. *Yeah, I need one of those.* Someone desired it. It appealed to a purpose. It got unwrapped and used. Then it failed, or was replaced by something better, or became lost by accident to end its days in the wilderness, the realm outside of the comfort of a speeding automobile. Forsaken, forgotten by all except those who had learned to watch the ground with a treasure-hunter's eye.

You could make up stories about found objects. Like the enigmatic single shoe, perched on the traffic island, or swept to the kerb, or just sitting there on the sidewalk begging the question, *What happened to the other shoe?* Everybody has seen that single shoe at one time or another in their life. There are more shoes on Earth than people, right? Even the least imaginative of us concoct, in passing, a narrative for that single shoe, because it just seems so odd.

The weirdest part is that when you inevitably see two abandoned shoes together, it seems even stranger.

More often than not, the attraction was a cheat – a shard of cigarette foil crumpled just so as to suggest a more interesting shape, or a broken bottleneck catching the light. Then, next to the useless junk, you'd find a key. Where was the lock? The key had a purpose and was ready to perform its function, but the lock was gone or irrelevant. What if the key had been lost inadvertently? Then it would still unlock something. What did it no longer protect?

A spent brass shell casing, headstamped *Federal .38 Special.* A story there, for sure.

I got the Valley Village house when Samantha left me. She took the more expensive place way out in Agoura, halfway to Santa Barbara. She took the more expensive car. Hers was the bigger bank account, so she saw this as equitable. Her deadbeat children were still living with her, as far as I knew, way out in that suburban purgatory. I like being close enough to the city to feel its rhythms and pulse. Samantha hated the traffic. I would walk a mile for groceries and she detested having to drive a block and a half just for extra milk. The lesson seemed to be not to get involved with a partner who has a previous life, but how often is that going to come your way? Friends and lovers all arrive with baggage and damage, and the challenge of human relationships is the quest to find a cooperative compromise whereby their "ins" fit your "outs".

For example, the offspring from her previous marriage did not seem like a deal-breaker at the time. They bailed early. Minors when we married, they were now adults by definition (if not in practice), supposed grown-ups who only manifested around birthdays, holidays, or any other period that provided a good excuse to ask for more money. When Samantha and I split, they had simply moved back in with her. Not my headache, not any more.

I had the cheaper car, the back-up house, and an aborted career as a software developer and website designer, which is the twenty-first-century nomenclature for "unemployed", the way Hollywood screenwriters who are "between projects" are accepted as jobless. They make up their stories, and I make up mine, and neither of us, it seems, is getting paid for anything these days.

The housing crash flipped the mortgage on my modest home, but banks could not foreclose the entire country all at once, even if they preferred the neatness of such a coup. It seemed unfair that the nation could raise its debt ceiling but I couldn't. The government wasn't paying its bills, so why should I? The tension had stretched out to three years and counting, and while know-nothings nattered about things "getting better", I saw no physical evidence of such an optimistic rally.

Walking allowed mindspace, a vent, a chance to air out my head.

I found the finger right at the corner of Ventura and Whitsett, a stone's throw from the LA River, poking up from a clump of stubborn weed. The lot had been cleared by the demolition of yet another brick-and-mortar bookstore, and was engirded by the usual sagging chain-link fence and plywood construction signs heralding the imminent arrival of something better than a book-store. The dirt had remained unturned long enough for tendrils of green kyllinga to take hold and break surface, and the finger had been lifted from horizontal by the growth until it was nearly upright, as though it was giving *me* the finger, personally, because no one else would ever notice it.

Hey. Fuck you!

It was white and desiccated. Middle finger, definitely. Both knuckles intact. Nicotine-coloured nail, chipped. Humanoid if not human. Sawn off right at the base of the metacarpal bone. Shreds of decomposed flesh, there, but long deprived of moisture. It presented no biological threat; it was dead and dry, almost mummified. Deactivated. I wrapped it up in a shred of newspaper – another common trash item we would soon forget altogether.

Twenty or thirty possible stories there, no doubt. Maybe I could frame it in a light-box for display. People might ask what the story was and would believe anything I'd care to invent.

Except as soon as I got it home, the damned thing started growing.

The morning ritual went something like this: put on sweats. Acquire coffee. Activate monitors. Delete spam, skip blather. Note how few, if any, messages relate to fresh work, then click directly to the latest news of my own imminent job doom. Reconsider smoking. Troll uselessly around the Internet for a stray hour or so in an attempt to feel better about the fact that I was becoming obsolete *while I watched*, within my own lifetime.

Dither over the spec projects for another hour. Check snail mail.

Go for a walk.

In the time it took to accomplish this well-meaning yet empty industry, the severed finger I had found the day before had changed. Before, it resembled a sad little cartoon penis. Now it had a thumb-like extension of jaundice-coloured flesh and looked more akin to a crab claw.

It had also gained a smell – not unpleasant, but the arid, spicy aroma of something alive.

I put it in the refrigerator, inside the hinged transparent hatch for the butter, since I didn't have any butter.

By the following morning – and I'll admit I checked it about a thousand times – the mesh of flesh between the finger and "thumb" had marshalled itself to present the stub of an index finger. A digit, I should say, since it in no way resembled an ordinary human hand. This was more like the talon from a marble statue, bloodless and alabaster, still with that yellow tinge.

Lucerno phoned, leaving a message about some bread-and-butter work helping several digitally challenged clients zip up fresh formats for their antiquated blogs. Lucerno, who works for some big company I can never remember the name of, had always been kind that way, while my wealthier and more accomplished friends forgot about my existence (or utility) until they needed me to do something for them, like right *now*.

The finger – the thing – had mustered into an entire hand by Thursday. I took pictures of its progress until one morning it vanished from the fridge.

I found it in the living room, soaking up sunlight like a cat near the sliding glass door to the back yard. It now had a palm, a wrist and part of a forearm. Either I had completely lost my marbles and put it there, or it had shoved its way out of the refrigerator and spider-walked to the nearest heat source. I picked it up and the new fingers, now three plus the thumb, closed gently on my own thumb with no force or threat. It was not a horror-movie moment. It was just . . . odd.

Odd enough that I stuck it into the freezer, in the garage. It did not try to escape, and nestled contentedly among a few frozen steaks and bags of microwave mung. The freezer was large but not huge – you could not have stashed a corpse in there – left to me because it wasn't modern enough for Samantha to claim dibs on it.

I could enumerate all the ways I tried to distract myself, but let's face it: the hand kept regenerating, even while frosted with ice crystals. It grew a shoulder. I installed a padlock on the freezer.

This was news. I had to keep taking pictures.

From the new shoulder, a wing began to bud.

A new sense of urgency filled my day-to-day life. It had become a project with up-to-the-minute developments that needed to be monitored – a reason, in fact, to get out of bed in the face of a new day that could only offer renewed disappointment on the job front as the calendar eroded in fast-forward and the bills continued to pile up. It worked just fine for me.

Until the morning when I checked the freezer and found the lock hasp broken, and the occupant gone.

I had spent my entire life avoiding this kind of pain. The stress of having your child kidnapped, or seeing your yard suddenly vacant of your favourite pet. You know the million questions already, the ones you use to torture or blame yourself; the journalist's credo. How? Why? When?

I searched the house. Scoured the yard. Crawled under the pilings with a flashlight. Disturbed junk that had a year of dust layered atop it.

The hasp had not merely broken. It had been sundered in two with enough force to dent the freezer lid. The padlock lay twisted, on the floor, useless now except as someone else's found object. In another life I would find such a thing and wonder what its story had been.

The crank-style garage window was broken, its metal interstices bent outward.

My internal commotion ate the day, and when the day was over sleep was an impossibility. There was no authority to whistle up, nobody in a uniform that could be called. This was all mine.

In any house, you grow attuned to the ambient noise. How traffic outside sounds on the inside. How heat or cold makes beams and joists sound off. Which sounds belong, and which don't. So at two a.m., I knew instantly that something was going on in the garage. *Clunk, thud.*

I bolted up, flashlight at hand, a gun unboxed from my closet at the ready. It was a little eight-round .380 Bersa Thunder, one of the few legacies from my late dad. It looked like a purse gun, a toy gun, but at least it was a firearm. It was totally illegal and I had last fired it on a range over a decade ago, back when Samantha and I were still together and both of us were wondering when the social contract of marriage would reveal unto us its secret plan to make us whole.

That was when Samantha realized she had gotten married not for herself, but for her mother, for appearances, because "that's what people did". She had duly reproduced with someone unworthy, and without a mate of current record she had nothing to look forward to except eventual grandparenthood and death. Or pooching out one last foetus, to reset the whole game. We discussed it; vetoed it. Her career had enabled us to have two homes and sufficient timespace for me to rally my own work ethic. She had risen to head of publicity for a movie studio; more than once I had declined her offer of a subsistence job in the same ratbox, because you just don't want to be around even the most loved and trusted person you know 24/7. She understood that I did not want to be her employee or subordinate. Nevertheless, entropy and stasis worked their sorcery and here we were, living in two separate houses. Our split was too reasonable, almost drained of emotion, because we both knew we were already finished.

I had the .380 because I have never understood how people believed they could defend their home turf from one or more intruders by swinging a baseball bat around in the dark. In their underwear. Cite me a single time this technique has succeeded . . . or kept the home invader from shooting off Batman's dick with a Glock. Then let's crucify the imbeciles who keep using this cliché in movies and television.

Yeah, I was all about the truth.

Truth was, Samantha was an emotional parasite. She fastened, fed, battened, and traded up. I was the suitable man-thing to do her donkey-work and heavy lifting until deposed by a *more* suitable man-thing. I occupied the "husband slot". Her idiot fifteen-year-old son Ricky once stole my car and tried to hock it. Her seventeen-year-old daughter Shannon once offered me a blow-job to keep quiet about her indiscretions. They were a nest of vipers who would eventually be forced to eat each other, and I needed to escape their toxic family values.

Gun-first, I stealthed into the garage.

Opened the freezer.

There inside, curled up like a slumbering infant, was the finger-critter. It was nearly three feet tall. It had both arms, a torso, wings, legs and a tiny fist-like head. Its rude slash of a mouth was slathered in dry blood. Tissue gobs were clotted into the ebony nails on the claws and feet. And it held a hank of curly, coppery hair in one hand.

Samantha had curly, coppery hair.

I was so shocked by this that I missed the offering that had been left for me on the workbench, also in a pool of blood. It could have been a stray knob of meat from the freezer, but as I lifted it in my hands I knew that at last, finally, I had won my ex-wife's heart.

I couldn't concentrate on anything that resembled work.

The creature emerged at dusk. I heard the kitchen door to the garage open and close. Nails scratching on the floor.

Shyly, it peeked around the corner until it saw me sitting at the desk. Then in a rush and a flurry of wingbeats, it was right next to me, tilting its head in curiosity just like a cocker spaniel.

Its flesh was nearly translucent now. Fine blue veins. Its eyes were pupil-less black orbs. I wanted to blast off from my chair to clutch the ceiling like a cartoon cat. It sniffed me, hesitantly. Then it yawned, stretching, its wings unfurling and shuddering slightly at the apex of extension. It worried its claws together in a peculiar watchmaker's gesture, rocking from foot to foot.

"Hi there," I said. My body wanted to die.

But it perked up at the sound of my voice, stopped rocking, and commenced an even odder up-and-down motion. I've seen lizards do it.

It *smiled*. Its mouth was full of needled teeth and it still had dry blood on its chin.

Okay, what was the procedure, here?

"So what do I call you?" I said. "What *are* you?"

It seemed to enjoy the sound of my voice.

I almost asked if it was hungry. Bad idea.

"What do you need? Do you need to go out?"

It shook its head *no*. The move was so simple, so human, that it stopped me cold. Stupid question. If it wanted out, it would go out.

It kept looking around my body to see the computer screens. I clicked to change the image and captured his complete attention.

I decided to name him Bob.

When the police showed up to inform me of the murder of my ex-wife, I thanked the dark lords that they had not come bearing a search warrant, since her fresh DNA was spread all over my garage, and they might have confabulated a few idle questions about the little gargoyle sleeping in my freezer, too.

I cleaned Bob up and pitched all the incriminating evidence into the Hollywood reservoir. Bob just brought it back the next day.

Then he brought me parts of Shannon and Ricky.

He also developed a preference for long-form, multi-arc television dramas – the modern soap opera dolled up with feature-film production values and presented to a non-discerning viewership as something exciting and new. It kept him happily occupied when he wasn't napping in the freezer or off on one of his midnight sorties. Religion, as Marx said, is the opiate of the masses, and nostalgia is the soma of the vanquished, but television remains an ideal babysitter, even for your own little monster.

Regretfully, I was already thinking about how to kill Bob. He could not be restrained or deactivated. He seemed to slaughter according to his own interior hourglass. No matter how I disposed of his little keepsakes, he brought them back because they were, well, for me. So I had to destroy them instead, chopping up one and flushing it down the toilet, and shoving another into the maw of the garbage disposal, which clogged and began to back up the kitchen sink. I'd never be able to scotch all the invisible evidence even a lazy forensics team might find. In due course, representatives of law enforcement returned to convey the sad news about Shannon and Ricky, and this time I was scheduled for an interview and asked not to leave town.

As I returned from my interrogation some dipshit in a long-cab Ram 3500 with "truck balls" dangling from the trailer hitch almost T-boned me coming off the 101 as he tried to change lanes and text at the same time. Bob brought back a heart . . . and the fake balls. He snuggled up to them while sleeping in the freezer as though they were his own personal hacky-sack.

Bob slept in the freezer because I had put him there. The cold did not bother him. He never seemed to eat while I was watching. When the faceless female voice called to pester me about my payment plans, Bob decamped for nearly a day and a half. In my own (intact) heart I knew he had flown all the way to Minnesota to disembowel some anonymous drone whose crap job was to hector me. And while this seemed horrific, I could not deny the notion felt really good. Bob was vitally in tune with my feelings. Bob wanted to eliminate anyone and everyone who made me feel bad about myself. He never asked for anything, not that he could speak. He fed, if he ate at all, out of my sight – probably while eviscerating whomever had pissed me off that day. When he wasn't sleeping he watched TV and hung out, always vaguely interested in whatever I was doing. His presence in the house was utterly non-threatening. In a darker humour, I wished for a burglar to chance along ... not that I had anything worth stealing.

And really, how many people annoy you? Do you ever run out of candidates?

The loudmouth ahead of you in line at the supermarket. The street loon who wants change, smokes and a chance to tell you his whole tragedy. The bartender who blows you off or the potential lover who adjudges you as not young, rich, or attractive enough. Jehovah's Witnesses.

Killing Bob had something to do, I was sure, with cutting off his long white fingers. Bob did not like scissors, clippers, or anything that resembled them. I'd had to calm him down once when I was power-shredding another dunning letter from a credit-card company.

I could not sneak up on him and hope to mutilate him. He had never done anything bad to me.

Define love, now. What are its covenants? Strip away the fantasies, lies and bullshit, and tell me what love really is; how it is expressed. Love is acceptance, tolerance, compromise, coordination, and the warmth generated by the subtle dovetailing of those qualities. A comfort zone; a safe house against the brutal world at large. Love requires patience and maintenance.

Which is why I am writing this down on non-edged paper with a soft pencil, behind the locked door of a maximum-security cell. One too many visits from the police is all it takes to get you where I am now. And I wait, because you have to be willing to wait for the best things that ever happen to you. I am waiting for the soft sound of friendly claws, scratching at the window beyond the bars.

Bob will come.

He loves me.

LAWRENCE BLOCK

Hot Eyes, Cold Eyes

SOME DAYS WERE easy. She would go to work and return home without once feeling the invasion of men's eyes. She might take her lunch and eat it in the park. She might stop on the way home at the library for a book, at the deli for a barbecued chicken, at the cleaner's, at the drugstore. On those days she could move coolly and crisply through space and time, untouched by the stares of men.

Doubtless they looked at her on those days, as on the more difficult days. She was the sort men looked at, and she had learned that early on – when her legs first began to lengthen and take shape, when her breasts began to bud. Later, as the legs grew longer and the breasts fuller, and as her face lost its youthful plumpness and was sculpted by time into beauty, the stares increased. She was attractive, she was beautiful, she was – curious phrase – easy on the eye. So men looked at her, and on the easy days she didn't seem to notice, didn't let their rude stares penetrate the invisible shield that guarded her.

But this was not one of those days.

It started in the morning. She was waiting for the bus when she first felt the heat of a man's eyes upon her. At first she willed herself to ignore the feeling, wished the bus would come and whisk her away from it, but the bus did not come and she could not ignore what she felt and, inevitably, she turned from the street to look at the source of the feeling.

There was a man leaning against a red-brick building not twenty yards from her. He was perhaps thirty-five, unshaven, and his clothes looked as though he'd slept in them. When she turned to glance at him his lips curled slightly, and his eyes, red-rimmed and glassy, moved first to her face, then drifted insolently the length of her body. She could feel their heat; it leaped from her eyes to her breasts and loins like an electric charge bridging a gap.

He placed his hand deliberately upon his crotch and rubbed himself. His smile widened.

She turned from him, drew a breath, let it out, wished the bus would come. Even now, with her back to him, she could feel the embrace of his eyes. They were like hot hands upon her buttocks and the backs of her thighs.

The bus came, neither early nor late, and she mounted the steps and dropped her fare in the box. The usual driver, a middle-aged fatherly type, gave her his usual smile and wished her the usual good morning. His eyes were an innocent watery blue behind thick-lensed spectacles.

Was it only her imagination that his eyes swept her body all the while? But she could feel them on her breasts, could feel too her own nipples hardening in response to their palpable touch.

She walked the length of the aisle to the first available seat. Male eyes tracked her every step of the way.

The day went on like that. This did not surprise her, although she had hoped it would be otherwise, had prayed during the bus ride that eyes would cease to bother her when she left the bus. She had learned, though, that once a day began in this fashion its pattern was set, unchangeable.

Was it something she did? Did she invite their hungry stares? She certainly didn't do anything with the intention of provoking male lust. Her dress was conservative enough, her make-up subtle and unremarkable. Did she swing her hips when she walked? Did she wet her lips and pout like a sullen sexpot? She was positive she did nothing of the sort, and it often seemed to her that she could cloak herself in a nun's habit and the results would be the same. Men's eyes would lift the black skirts and strip away the veil.

At the office building where she worked, the elevator starter glanced at her legs, then favoured her with a knowing, wet-lipped smile. One of the office boys, a rabbity youth with unfortunate skin, stared at her breasts, then flushed scarlet when she caught him at it. Two older men gazed at her from the water cooler. One leaned over to murmur something to the other. They both chuckled and went on looking at her.

She went to her desk and tried to concentrate on her work. It was difficult, because intermittently she felt eyes brushing her body, moving across her like searchlight beams scanning the yard in a prison movie. There were moments when she wanted to scream, moments when she wanted to spin around in her chair and hurl something. But she remained in control of herself and did none of these things. She had survived days of this sort often enough in the past. She would survive this one as well.

The weather was good, but today she spent her lunch hour at her desk rather than risk the park. Several times during the afternoon the sensation of being watched was unbearable and she retreated to the ladies' room. She endured the final hours a minute at a time, and finally it was five o'clock and she straightened her desk and left.

The descent in the elevator was unbearable. She bore it. The bus ride home, the walk from the bus stop to her apartment building, were unendurable. She endured them.

In her apartment, with the door locked and bolted, she stripped off her clothes and hurled them into a corner of the room as if they were unclean, as if the day had irrevocably soiled them. She stayed a long while under the shower, washed her hair, blow-dried it, then returned to her bedroom and stood nude before the full-length mirror on the closet door. She studied herself at length, and intermittently her hands would move to cup a breast or trace the swell of a thigh, not to arouse but to assess, to chart the dimensions of her physical self.

And now? A meal alone? A few hours with a book? A lazy night in front of the television set?

She closed her eyes, and at once she felt other eyes upon her, felt them as she had been feeling them all day. She knew that she was alone, that now no one was watching her, but this knowledge did nothing to dispel the feeling.

She sighed.

She would not, could not, stay home tonight.

When she left the building, stepping out into the cool of dusk, her appearance was very different. Her tawny hair, which she'd worn pinned up earlier, hung free. Her make-up was overdone, with an excess of mascara and a deep blush of rouge in the hollows of her cheeks. During the day she'd worn no scent beyond a touch of Jean Naté applied after her morning shower; now she'd dashed on an abundance of the perfume she wore only on nights like this one, a strident scent redolent of musk. Her dress was close-fitting and revealing, the skirt slit Oriental-fashion high on one thigh, the neckline low to display her décolletage. She strode purposefully on her high-heeled shoes, her buttocks swaying as she walked.

She looked sluttish and she knew it, and gloried in the knowledge. She'd checked the mirror carefully before leaving the apartment and had liked what she saw. Now, walking down the street with her handbag bouncing against her swinging hip, she could feel the heat building up within her flesh. She could also feel the eyes of the men she passed, men who sat on stoops or loitered in doorways, men walking with purpose who stopped for a glance in her direction. But there was a difference. Now she relished those glances. She fed on the heat in those eyes, and the fire within herself burned hotter in response.

A car slowed. The driver leaned across the seat, called to her. She missed the words but felt the touch of his eyes. A pulse throbbed insistently throughout her entire body now. She was frightened – of her own feelings, of the real dangers she faced – but at the same time she was alive, gloriously alive, as she had not been in far too long. Before she had walked through the day. Now the blood was singing in her veins.

She passed several bars before finding the cocktail lounge she wanted. The interior was dimly lit, the floor soft with carpeting. An overactive air conditioner had lowered the temperature to an almost uncomfortable level. She walked bravely into the room. There were several empty tables along the wall but she passed them by, walking her swivel-hipped walk to the bar and taking a stool at the far end.

The cold air was stimulating against her warm skin. The bartender gave her a minute, then ambled over and leaned against the bar in front of her. He looked at once knowing and disinterested, his heavy lids shading his dark brown eyes and giving them a sleepy look.

"Stinger," she said.

While he was mixing the drink she drew her handbag into her lap and groped within it for her billfold. She found a ten and set it on top of the bar, then fumbled reflexively within her bag for another moment, checking its contents. The bartender placed the drink on the bar in front of her, took her money, returned with her change. She looked at her drink, then at her reflection in the back bar mirror.

Men were watching her.

She could tell, she could always tell. Their gazes fell on her and warmed the skin where they touched her. Odd, she thought, how the same sensation that had been so disturbing and unpleasant all day long was so desirable and exciting now.

She raised her glass, sipped her drink. The combined flavour of cognac and crème de menthe was at once warm and cold upon her lips and tongue. She swallowed, sipped again.

"That a stinger?"

He was at her elbow and she flicked her eyes in his direction while continuing to face forward. A small man, stockily built, balding, tanned, with a dusting of freckles across his high forehead. He wore a navy blue Quiana shirt open at the throat, and his dark chest hair was beginning to go grey.

"Drink up," he suggested. "Let me buy you another."

She turned now, looked levelly at him. He had small eyes. Their whites showed a tracery of blue veins at their outer corners. The irises were a very dark brown, an unreadable colour, and the black pupils, hugely dilated in the bar's dim interior, covered most of the irises.

"I haven't seen you here," he said, hoisting himself on to the seat beside her. "I usually drop in around this time, have a couple, see my friends. Not new in the neighbourhood, are you?"

Calculating eyes, she thought. Curiously passionless eyes, for all their cool intensity. Worst of all, they were small eyes, almost beady eyes.

"I don't want company," she said.

"Hey, how do you know you don't like me if you don't give me a chance?" He was grinning, but there was no humour in it. "You don't even know my name, lady. How can you despise a total stranger?"

"Please leave me alone."

"What are you, Greta Garbo?" He got up from his stool, took a half step away from her, gave her a glare and a curled lip. "You want to drink alone," he said, "why don't you just buy a bottle and take it home with you? You can take it to bed and suck on it, honey."

He had ruined the bar for her. She scooped up her change, left her drink unfinished. Two blocks down and one block over she found a second cocktail lounge virtually indistinguishable from the first one. Perhaps the lighting was a little softer, the background music the slightest bit lower in pitch. Again she passed up the row of tables and seated herself at the bar. Again she ordered a stinger and let it rest on the bar top for a moment before taking the first exquisite sip.

Again she felt male eyes upon her, and again they gave her the same hot-cold sensation as the combination of brandy and crème de menthe.

This time when a man approached her she sensed his presence for a long moment before he spoke. She studied him out of the corner of her eye. He was tall and lean, she noted, and there was a self-contained air about him, a sense of considerable self-assurance. She wanted to turn, to look directly into his eyes, but instead she raised her glass to her lips and waited for him to make a move.

"You're a few minutes late," he said.

She turned, looked at him. There was a weathered, raw-boned look to him that matched the western-style clothes he wore – the faded chambray shirt, the skintight denim jeans. Without glancing down she knew he'd be wearing boots and they would be good ones.

"I'm late?"

He nodded. "I've been waiting for you for close to an hour. Of course it wasn't until you walked in that I knew it was you I was waiting for, but one look was all it took. My name's Harley."

She made up a name. He seemed satisfied with it, using it when he asked her if he could buy her a drink.

"I'm not done with this one yet," she said.

"Then why don't you just finish it and come for a walk in the moonlight?"

"Where would we walk?"

"My apartment's a block and a half from here."

"You don't waste time."

"I told you, I waited close to an hour for you. I figure the rest of the evening's too precious to waste."

She had been unwilling to look directly into his eyes but she did so now and she was not disappointed. His eyes were large and well-spaced, blue in colour, a light blue of a shade that often struck her as cold and forbidding. But his eyes were anything but cold. On the contrary, they burned with passionate intensity.

She knew, looking into them, that he was a dangerous man. He was strong, he was direct, and he was dangerous. She could tell all this in a few seconds, merely by meeting his relentless gaze.

Well, that was fine. Danger, after all, was an inextricable part of it.

She pushed her glass aside, scooped up her change. "I don't really want the rest of this," she said.

"I didn't think you did. I think I know what you really want."

"I think you probably do."

He took her arm, tucked it under his own. They left the lounge, and on the way out she could feel other eyes on her, envious eyes. She drew closer to him and swung her hips so that her buttocks bumped into his lean flank. Her purse slapped against her other hip. Then they were out the door and heading down the street.

She felt excitement mixed with fear, an emotional combination not unlike her stinger. The fear, like the danger, was part of it.

His apartment was two sparsely furnished rooms three flights up from street level. They walked wordlessly into the bedroom and undressed. She laid her clothes across a wooden chair, set her handbag on the floor at the side of the platform bed. She got on to the bed and he joined her and they embraced. He smelled faintly of leather and tobacco and male perspiration, and even with her eyes shut she could see his blue eyes burning in the darkness.

She wasn't surprised when his hands gripped her shoulders and eased her downward on the bed. She had been expecting this and welcomed it. She swung her head, letting her long hair brush across his flat abdomen, and then she moved to accept him. He tangled his fingers in her hair, hurting her in a not unpleasant way. She inhaled his musk as her mouth embraced him, and in her own fashion she matched his strength with strength of her own, teasing, taunting, heightening his passion and then cooling it down just short of culmination. His breathing grew ragged, and muscles worked in his legs and abdomen.

At length he let go of her hair. She moved upward on the bed to join him and he rolled her over on to her back and covered her, his mouth seeking hers, his flesh burying itself in her flesh. She locked her thighs around his hips. He pounded at her loins, hammering her, hurting her with the brute force of his masculinity.

How strong he was, and how insistent. Once again she thought what a dangerous man he was, and what a dangerous game she was playing. The thought served only to spur her own passion on, to build her fire higher and hotter.

She felt her body preparing itself for orgasm, felt the urge growing to abandon herself, to lose control utterly. But a portion of herself remained remote, aloof, and she let her arm hang over the side of the bed and reached for her purse, groped within it.

And found the knife.

Now she could relax, now she could give up, now she could surrender to what she felt. She opened her eyes, stared upward. His own eyes were closed as he thrust furiously at her. Open your eyes, she urged him silently. Open them, open them and look at me—

And it seemed that his eyes did open to meet hers, even as they climaxed together, even as she centred the knife over his back and plunged it unerringly into his heart.

Afterward, in her own apartment, she put his eyes in the box with the others.

JAY RUSSELL

Hush . . . Hush, Sweet Shushie

TIME IS LIKE a river, some unemployed philosopher mused. It has something to do with not being able to step in the same bit of it twice. I was never big on philosophy, lacking one of my own. I did once go on a silent, meditative retreat at Leonard Cohen's Zen hangout in the Hills, but all I came up with was: "Make it stop!" I kept yelling it until they booted my bored ass right off Tofu Mountain.

On the other hand, I have stepped in the LA River – several times, mind – though famously, of course, it doesn't have any water in it. That seems to me to raise a whole bunch of other deep questions: all that one-hand-clapping, tree-falling-in-forest, who-(who)-who-wrote-the-book-of-love razzamatazz. I don't know, maybe that's the way philosophy is supposed to work.

Or maybe I'm just the wrong person to ask.

If you do ask me – and remember right up front that no one's putting a gun to your head – time is mostly like a big heap of doggie-do: step in it once and no matter how hard you try, you can never scrape all the shit off your shoes.

"Shushie!"

"Hello, Martin."

You could have knocked me over with a steamroller.

"I didn't think you'd recognize me."

"I don't know if I do," I said, frozen in my front doorway.

But that wasn't true. If Shushie was a grain of sand, I'd be able to pick her out of Malibu Beach.

"You look . . . wowie-kazowie."

"Always the sweet-talker. You look good, too, Martin."

"You still lie like a pro, Shush. I'm fatter in the middle, thinner on the top, and all the gunk they've sucked out of Roseanne over the years has somehow ended up in my ass."

Shushie leaned forward, twisted those filthy, fat lips of hers into the smile I've also never forgotten, and warm breath tickling my hairy ear, whispered, "But I bet you've still got the prettiest, sweetest-tasting cock in Hollywood."

I let her in, of course.

Shoshona Elaine Horowitz is what it said on our marriage licence.

Shushie is what I always called her.

We were married for two months three lifetimes ago. We were kids at the time: I wasn't much past twenty and Shushie was three years older than me. I suppose she still is. Maybe you couldn't rightly call us "kids" at those ages, but we sure as hell acted like kids, laughed like them (screwed like them). And getting married six days after meeting wasn't the most grown-up thing to do. Though it sure felt like it back then.

And if God could make a whole universe in six days, it had seemed more than enough time to know we'd be Together 4Ever.

Goddamn God.

Shushie had been a wild child. Me, too. I was on my first bounce-back into The Business after bottoming out following a savage Hollywood adolescence. My child acting heydays had already faded into booze-fed, stardust – ha! Poprock – memories, but I'd miraculously sobered up enough to snag a couple of decent TV parts. I made William Conrad beg for mercy in a killer episode of *Cannon* (he really was a corpulent sonofabitch – Jesus, could he eat!), and all but induced a stroke in Buddy Ebsen in a senses-shattering *Barnaby Jones*. It'd helped me re-establish a bona fide or two. Enough to get me cast in a John Huston pic on location in Mexico. We were shooting around Cuernavaca. Actually, I was mostly chugging Cuervo and Tecates and spending every penny I had on an all-you-can-eat buffet of drugs and Mexican whores (did I mention it was a John Huston film?). There were a lot of pennies, a lot of blow, a lot of whores.

And Shushie.

*　　*　　*

"You live alone."

"Is it that obvious?" I said.

"Mmm," Shushie mmmed.

She strolled around the living room, touching objects randomly along the way: a glass fruit bowl with some over-ripe plums; a framed photograph of me with Héctor Elizondo and Joe Santos; a broken Golden Globe award; an empty package of Goldenberg's Peanut Chews. She wiped her fingertips on a grimy antimacassar and sat herself down on the sofa. She picked up a cushion, sniffed it – I suddenly remembered that Shushie was always sniffing stuff – then tossed it on to the chair opposite.

"Mmm," she repeated. She looked me square in the eyes and smiled.

"You've had your teeth done," I said.

"*Ages* ago. Cost a bundle. Braces are no fun as a grown-up."

"What is?"

She snorted.

"They look good. The teeth. You look good. I repeat that. I might even say it again at some point soon."

Her smile widened. So did mine. Then I let it droop.

"What in the name of the Dark Lord Beelzebub and all his unholy works and practices are you doing here, Shushie?"

She laughed.

I didn't.

The doggie-do was already hardening on my Skechers.

The thing about Shushie – and her name alone should have been the tip off – is that she was nuts. Really nuts.

It was a big part of her charm, at first. But there's a line between zany, Teri Garr eccentricity and menacing, Ray Liotta psychosis. You'd think it would be a thick old, double-yellow line, but it's worryingly thin and fades in bright sun. I see it more clearly now that I'm old and ever so wise (there's a reason why I live alone and it's not just on account of the smell of my cushions), but back then, under the glamours of youth, I didn't recognize it.

I confused self-destruction with free-spiritedness, and mistook vitriol for passion. I got lots of other stuff wrong, too. I thought Shushie was wild and provocative and uninhibited, and all those idiotic characteristics that the immature imagine to be better and more important than an elasticated waist.

We grow too soon old and too late smart, as my mom used to say.

Shushie landed in Cuernavaca on her father's stolen Amex card. She did it all the time, I soon learned. Why her dad – a La Jolla cosmetic dentist – didn't simply pay with cash I never could figure out. But Shushie was his only child and she could do no wrong in his eyes.

Of course, he never saw her giving a blumpkin to a fat First AD, tight ass-naked in an open-air Mexican latrine.

"Who's next?" she'd challenged, raising her head. Her mouth – it needed wiping – was twisted into that fat little smile.

I thought it was the coolest thing I'd ever seen and I was in love. My hand shot up like an eager schoolboy in history class.

I was a festering idiot.

Many would say I still am.

"He's been gone four days," Shushie told me.

She sat on my sofa, sipping green tea out of a mug with my face on it. I chose it deliberately to gauge her reaction. I don't often use mugs adorned with my picture, though as it happens I have a whole case of them left over from my days starring on *Burning Bright*. And I might not seem like a green tea kind of guy, but I've taken to drinking the stuff. It's supposed to be good for you and it doesn't taste as bad as most of what's supposed to be good for you. It also stops me from drinking quite so much beer.

Shushie had accepted the mug with her sweet little smile and offered a delighted "oooh" when she tasted the tea. She seemed so sensible, so grown-up.

Don't forget that thing about me being an idiot.

"Four days isn't long to be out of touch," I said. "How old is he again?"

"He's twenty-two, Martin. I just told you."

"You did. But he's not a kid then, is he? I mean, a twenty-two year old not calling his mom for a few days isn't exactly amber alert time. Maybe he went to Vegas or Ensenada or wherever the hell young people go these days to drink and party."

"*Young* people?"

"Kids. Young adults. *Twilight* readers. Whatever. People whose idea of a good time consists of more than sitting on the sofa watching HBO with an iPad on their lap."

"Do *you* do that, Martin?"

"I don't care to say."

She shook her head a little and smiled briefly. Then she got serious again.

"He's very immature, Martin. And he's been in trouble before."

"You mentioned that."

"The police are not going to be interested, given his ... indiscretions."

"That's a generous euphemism for felony assault. Where the hell do you even get a *jai alai* basket? How do you beat someone with it?"

"It's called a *xistera*, actually. And the damage was done with the *pelota* not the basket."

I shook my head.

"The *pelota* is the ball. It's very hard."

"Great to know. If I'm ever a contestant on *Jeopardy* I'll be sure to take Bizarre Basque Assault Items for two thousand."

"He wasn't convicted."

"You said that, too. 'A technicality. He got lucky,' were your exact words."

"He's a good boy."

"You don't think Mama Manson feels that way about her little Chuck?"

"That's cruel, Martin. He's just mixed up with some bad people, some wrong doings. He's young and he's stupid. Don't you remember how that was?"

I exhaled loudly and shook my head. Shushie was pouting. She had always been a damned fine pouter.

"Someone has to help him find a way back. Someone he can ... *might* trust."

"What is it that you think I can do, Shush? Why in the world are you here? I haven't seen you for ... I can't even count how many years. I'm not a detective any more, you must know that. And I was crap at it back in the day. I don't even play one on TV now. All's I've got are my residuals. And the mugs."

She put the tea down and stood up. She walked around the cluttered coffee table and knelt in front of me. I had a sudden, terrible (wonderful?) flash on the blumpkin that brought us together. She picked up my hand and held it between hers.

"I told ElronD something important just before he disappeared."

Oh, did I not mention the poor kid's name was ElronD? Yeah, with the big "D" at the end. It says most of what anyone needs to know about her, though you'd think someone who'd been saddled with *Shoshona* might have been more clued-in with her own choice of baby name.

"Oh?" I said. I tried to withdraw my hand, but in addition to the sniffing thing, Shushie had always been freakishly strong. I once liked that.

"I told him something about his dad. Something I never told him before."

I shrugged at her as best I could while caught in her vice-like grip.

"I told him it was you," she said.

"Piss. Fuck. Shit," was my restrained reply.

I shook my head at my own stupidity. I shook it quite a lot. But then I am very, very stupid.

The traffic on Jefferson was appalling. Still, why should the traffic differ from anything else in the neighbourhood? I parked outside the address Shushie gave me: a squat, concrete office block just up from the USC campus. Close enough, in fact, that a few white faces even dotted the sidewalks.

I shook my head some more. What the hell was I doing? And what was Shushie doing to me?

John Huston actually married us. I bet there are not many people who can say that (other than his five actual wives, of course). He claimed to have been ordained years before by a pal of Sydney Greenstreet – hell, that was good enough for me – and conducted the nuptials right there in a church on set. It probably wasn't legal – it was only the façade of a church, natch – but Huston did a bang-up job on the ceremony, so yay, Sydney! We went and ruined things by registering it for real back in LA. Kind of a waste since it took longer to annul than the whole marriage lasted.

The point being, as I had felt obliged to mention to Shushie, that while for those few glorious weeks – well, half of them at least

– we had the kind of rampant, almost non-stop sex you can only have when you're of a certain age, that age was some several years prior to ElronD's birth. Game, set and match to Detective Burns, thank you very much.

"And Twentynine Palms?" Shushie said. She fluttered her eyelashes and flashed that little smile again.

"What about it?"

"You've forgotten that weekend, I suppose. There *was* a lot of booze."

I scowled. "What week . . .?"

A primordial memory crawled up out of the ever-flowing river of time and bit me in the ass.

"Piss. Fuck. Shit," I said again.

"You do remember. Sweet."

It was just possible. Not very likely, but just possible. Shushie had appeared at my door then, too, looking for money. I didn't have any, but I had a lot of bourbon. I always had a lot of bourbon in those days, which is why I remember so few of them. I was only ever able to guess what happened from the hotel credit-card bill.

I still couldn't really believe it.

But she showed me his picture. I stared at it for a very long time. There was something . . . I didn't know.

I worried it might be true.

Which explained why I was sitting outside the entrance to the offices of Ludgate Productions in a very shitty part of LA.

Just in case.

The door was opened by a curiously orange woman with a beehive do out of *Hairspray*. She looked as if she'd been embalmed with nicotine and spoke with a trace of the imported.

"Heya?"

"Yeah, hi. I'd like to speak with . . ." I glanced at the piece of paper again, still unsure ". . . O'Leo Resin?"

"Leo's out back. They're still shooting. Something I can do with you?"

I glanced around. The untidy office space was open-plan with piles of DVD cases littering the desks, and cardboard boxes stacked floor to ceiling. There was a funny smell about the place. I thought it was the John Waters lady at first, but it was sickly sweet yet chemically. A scent to mask a worse smell, and omni-present. She must have seen my nose wrinkle.

"Bug spray," she said. "The place reeks of it. They get out, they're everywhere."

I nodded as if that made perfect sense to me.

"I'm actually . . . "

Just then a little wiry-haired guy with a walking stick came in followed by a very tall brunette wearing killer black stilettos, a blood-red fascinator that looked like it had blown off an organ-grinder's monkey, and absolutely nothing else. The shoes were badly stained. She eyed me top to bottom and frowned, then turned back to the little guy.

"I told you I don't like them," she said.

"And I give a tinker's cock because?"

"Because they still ask for me, don't they, Leo? And maybe I've had it with bugs. They bite!"

"They're cheap, all right, bitch? Don't that mean more money in your hole? And don't think you're so special. You're just another gash in high heels. If I say it's day of the locust, you stomp, baby. Don't get precious on me 'cause Talia Shire you ain't."

He looked up at me, turned to the big-haired lady. "Who's this?"

"Marty Burns!" Stiletto Girl suddenly shouted. "I knew you were somebody."

"I was," I sighed.

"You work with this bitch?" O'Leo asked me. "You must be a cunt, too."

"Oh, my," I said. The girl grinned at me, then arched her back. "No, I've never had the pleasure."

He snorted. "You're the only one, then."

"Hey!" she shouted. Before she could get another word in, O'Leo pointed at the door. She began to protest, then thought better of it. She grabbed a long coat off a rack, threw it over her shoulders and drifted out.

"What do you want?" he said. "Who are you?"

"I am Marty Burns and I'm looking for someone."

"God help you if you're looking here."

I nodded. "His name is Ron."

Shushie had informed me that her boy didn't care for ElronD any more – imagine! – and used the simpler variant.

"Horsedick Ron? Cow Tongue Ron? Ron the Ferret? Lot of Rons here. You know, Cow Tongue Ron's actually got a bigger dick than Horsedick Ron? Ain't that just the way?"

The woman laughed.

"I didn't know," I said. "And I have no idea how big my Ron's . . . listen. He's a kid and his name is ElronD but he goes by Ron. Just Ron. I don't think he . . . performs."

The smile fell off O'Leo's face. "No, he don't. You're a pal of his?"

"Not exactly," I said. "I'm just trying to find him. For his mom, believe it or not. A . . . friend gave me this address as a place to start looking."

"A friend, huh? His mom, huh? I see," he said, nodding very sagely. "Lainie sent you here."

"No, it was Shu—" I caught myself. I'm the only one who ever called her Shushie. She used to insist on Shoshona to everyone else, but if ElronD was Ron, it figured that Shush must have a *nom de porn*, too. Because that had to be what she was hooked up with here. "Yeah, Lainie sent me."

"Looking for little Ron. Uh-huh, uh-huh. Well, he sure as fuck ain't here. I'd like to see him, though. Say, if you find him, would you maybe give him something from me?"

"What's that?" I asked.

"Just this."

And smooth as silk on oil, he whipped his walking stick around and smashed it across the side of my head. The kicking started before I'd even crumbled to the floor. I felt – and heard – something crack, then an electric explosion between my legs.

The rest was as lost as a weekend in Twentynine Palms.

"Shushie," I said.

"How are you feeling, Martin?"

"I'm home."

"No place like it. Your ruby slippers are under the bed."

I was lying in my room. My ex-wife sat next to me on the edge of the bed, idly stroking my hair. It kind of hurt.

"How'd I get here?"

"I found you."

"Was I lost?"

"Aren't you always?"

My nose throbbed. I touched it with a fingertip and it ached, but didn't slide across my face. That seemed like a good thing. I tried to sit up and felt pain shoot through my chest and balls. Sitting up, I decided, was *so* last year that I wouldn't do it. Uh-uh, not me. Lying down is definitely the new black in my fashion regimen.

"How did you find me?"

"I didn't, truth be told. Leilani did. She called me and I picked you up."

"Picked me up?"

"Literally. From off the ground."

Just then the bedroom door opened and a familiar brunette head poked in.

"I thought I heard talking. Hey."

It was Stiletto Girl. She'd lost the fascinator and the shoes, but gained my running shorts – don't worry, I've never actually jogged in them – and *Burning Bright* T-shirt (it came with the mugs). The shirt is kind of a collector's item, but it seemed churlish to mention it. And she filled it out pretty good.

"Leilani?" I presumed.

She flashed a nice smile. "How you doing, big guy?

At five-nine with the aid of a Procrustean bed, "big guy" isn't often thrown my way. Especially by six-foot brunettes wearing much-too-small-for-them running shorts.

"I'm good, thanks," I said. "I'm . . . I'm . . . what the hell's going on, Shushie? What are you doing to me?"

Shushie raised her chin at Leilani – she didn't look Hawaiian, by the way – who nodded and withdrew. But not before throwing me a wink.

"I like her," I said.

"She's a brick."

"She called you."

"Yeah. O'Leo dumped you on the kerb after he beat on you. Fortunately, Leilani was still outside. Did you find out anything about ElronD?"

"I'm fine, Shush. Thanks for asking."

"I don't think anything's broken, Marty. I had a feel."

"And how the hell would you know?"

"I did some nursing classes a while back. Almost a year. At Pomona State."

"Really?"

"I flunked out. I screwed too many doctors. I tried a lot of stuff."

"Comforting, then. Your diagnosis."

She leaned in closer. "I had a feel all over, if you know what I mean."

"If you think I am even remotely stimulated by that, you're even crazier than I remember. Not to mention O'Leo kicked me pretty righteously in the goolies."

She stiffened up and looked huffy. "That's not nice," she said.

"No, it doesn't feel nice at all."

"I mean the crazy talk. That's not a nice way to speak about a person, Martin."

"Offence definitely intended, Shush."

She actually looked hurt. Then she saw it wasn't working. She changed her look all over again.

"ElronD called me," she said.

"Hey, hey! Case closed," I said. "Chalk another one up for the boy. My bill shall be forthcoming."

"He's still in trouble, Martin."

"Yeah, well, I'm not so terrific myself," I said. I did manage to raise myself to a sitting position. A wave of nausea later, I could even throw my legs over the side of the bed. Christ, my balls hurt!

"They're threatening to kill him," she said. She put her hand on my thigh, rested her head against my shoulder. I could see dark roots coming through her blonde hair. It smelled nice, though. It always had. "And it's my fault."

"Oh, Christ. What have you done, Shushie? What are you two into?"

She raised her head off my shoulder, squeezed my thigh – a little too hard – and stood up to pace.

"The recession has been difficult for me, Martin," she began. "I took some money that wasn't mine. ElronD . . . helped."

"Christ on a crutch," I muttered. It didn't deflect her.

"ElronD's a good boy but he's had his troubles. Lawyers are expensive. Things get tough. A girl does what she has to do."

"This, too, may strike you as ungallant, but you're not a girl any more, Shush."

Silence.

"Okay, I'll bite: what did you do?"

"I was taking some Zumba classes in Echo Park . . ."

"You couldn't cut back on those?" I offered.

"That's where I met Leilani."

"Ha! And I figured her strictly for Bootie-Bikini."

"This is serious, Martin. We got friendly. Very friendly, if you know what I mean."

She peered up at me.

"Uh-huh," I said. "So what, you're a switch-hitter these days?"

"Always was, Martin. You weren't around long enough to know."

"Oh, do go on, Shush."

"I told her about my money troubles – ElronD's . . . difficulties. She told me she had a great gig, if I wasn't squeamish."

"Someone says that to you – in LA, for God's sake – and you don't run as fast as you can some other way?"

"She said she knew a guy who makes videos. Not porn, though."

It wasn't hard to interpret my look.

"Not *real* porn. You know there's no money in that these days. It's all free on the net. YouPorn?"

"I'm passing familiar with it. So this guy . . . it's O'Leo, right? What is he doing?"

Shushie hesitated. She tried to be cute and bit her thumb.

"Shush," I said.

"Mmm?"

"Do you remember who showed you *The Big Sleep* for the first time?"

She took her thumb out of her mouth.

"What's O'Leo's scam?"

Silence.

"Shushie . . ."

"Crush videos," she rasped. She looked away from me, lower lip aquiver.

I nodded. I reached out and gently touched her forearm.

"I don't have the slightest idea what you're talking about."

"Oh, Martin, you're still such a square. Crush videos, you know. Naked girls, high-heeled shoes. Little things. Crush!"

"I'm sorry, I am very square. I like vanilla ice cream, sometimes with sprinkles if I'm feeling crazy. I eat pizza – thin-crust – with mushrooms and pepperoni; no broccoli, no clams, no dragon fruit or whatever other stupid toppings they try to ruin it with. I watch *The Tonight Show*, though admittedly I don't laugh. And I actually enjoy the missionary position when I can find someone to convert. So what is it exactly that you do, Shushie?"

"*Crush*. I take my clothes off. I put on sexy shoes with big sharp heels. Then I stomp bugs to death while O'Leo films it."

"You are shitting me?"

"Not everyone wants vanilla ice cream, Martin. I seem to recall you used to eat . . . more exotic things."

"And there's money in this? That's what you stole?"

Shushie nodded. "O'Leo does . . . other stuff, too. But I only do Crush. And soft Crush only, no hard. I swear."

"Oh, Jesus, I'm going to regret this. Soft? Hard?"

"Soft Crush is, you know, bugs and stuff. Worms sometimes. I don't think they're actually bugs, officially. But soft things only. Hard is . . . not so nice."

"Not so *nice*."

"Little animals. Mice, gerbils, parakeets, sometimes rabbits. I think even small dogs and cats."

"Jesus, Shushie!"

"I know. I've never done hard, I told you! I mean bugs are just bugs, right? *You* kill ants and flies, don't you? Mosquitoes? Wasps? They're not, like, furry or anything. Not pets and shit."

"Oh, Jesus."

"Please stop saying that, Martin."

"What are you, bi *and* religious now?"

"I have my faith."

"Which obviously does not preclude you flashing your hoo-hah and stomping things to death on camera."

"I'm not proud of it, Martin. But a girl has to live."

"You're not a girl," I said again.

We sat in silence for a while. I even forgot my aches and pains while I thought about what she'd told me. I remembered the stains on Leilani's shoes, and shuddered. I wondered who the

Sam Hill would want to watch such stuff? Then again, people claim to like Ryan Seacrest. An odd thought suddenly swam into my head.

"Fish?" I asked.

Shushie just stared at her painted toes. I wondered if the polish met the demands of some specific bug fetishist. Red for fire ants? She didn't respond.

"Shushie. Did you ever crush a fish? They're soft. Mostly, I think. Other than, like, lobsters."

She burst into tears.

"I have," she shrieked. She was blubbering away. A few seconds later Leilani burst through the door. She looked at me, then at Shushie, then back at me.

"I *have* crushed fish," Shushie wailed.

"We've all done it, darling," the tall girl said, bending down to comfort her. She glared reproachfully at me as she gently rubbed Shushie's back and stroked her head. "We *all* have to crush something. One way or another."

See? Everybody has a fucking philosophy.

"I don't like your car," Leilani said two days later as we drove north on the 405. She fired up a cigarette.

"Aren't you going to ask if I mind?" I said, rolling down the Prius's passenger window four inches.

"No."

"Fair enough."

I exited on to Ventura, heading west. There's that famous line from Sartre about Hell being other people. Clearly he never visited Sherman Oaks or he'd have fixed it in the rewrite.

"Why don't you like my car?" I asked.

She blew smoke out the window, which I thought was at least decent.

"It's . . ." She paused to take another deep drag off her Dunhill; this time she blew the smoke straight up. "I bet your insurance is cheap."

"Cheapish," I admitted. "And that's a bad thing?"

Leilani shrugged. She had on a chartreuse sundress with spaghetti straps. One of them slipped off her ivory shoulder. The way it dangled over the top of her freckled arm was weirdly sexy.

As was the rest of her. Even knowing about the bugs.

"Safe. Predictable," she said. Another long drag. "Boring."

"Boring isn't your style, is it? Is that why you tied up with Shushie?"

Another shrug. "You live once, you're dead a long time."

"I think I read that on a T-shirt in Glendale."

She tossed the rest of the cigarette out the window. I've never understood how smokers feel comfortable doing that. But then smoking is about the only vice I never managed to pick up.

"Don't take it so personal, Marty. Your car isn't your cock, you know?"

"I know – the car seats six. It's also not my ass, so don't blow smoke up it."

She laughed. Her other strap slipped and she adjusted them both.

I did kind of like her.

"Listen," I said.

"I need the money, pure and simple," Leilani said. Before I could jump in, she added: "Please don't: you're not the first to start a sentence at me in that tone. I make no apologies. Ever."

"Really? Never? I apologize all the time. It's a lot easier than people make it out to be. Sometimes I even mean it."

That at least earned a smile.

"Or maybe I just have a lot more to be sorry for," I muttered.

The address was off Topanga Canyon Boulevard in Woodland Hills. I parked up the road a little and we studied the house for a few minutes. There was barely any activity on the street.

"You know Shushie pretty well?" I asked.

"Sure, we're tight. *Lainie* and me."

"And ElronD?"

"He's a good kid."

"Kid. You can't be that much older than he is."

"That's sweet, but I'm strictly MILF material these days."

I didn't like to think what that made me.

"Don't worry about it, you'll like him when you meet him," she said. "I'm sure of it."

"I hope so. It's a little hard to get used to the idea of him, though."

"I bet. But he means everything to Lainie."

"Does he really?"

"Of course. They do so much together. That's how he got into this mess. They look after each other – almost like a married couple, I swear. I even met them together."

"Really."

"Mmm. At an after-hours club off Sunset. I thought it was sweet that mommy and son partied together."

"Real sweet," I said, thinking.

"You're not going all Prius on me again."

"No, no. This is not really a Prius moment."

"Good. Should we go in then?"

"Yeah, let's do it," I said, and I patted her muscular thigh.

She smiled at me and started to open her door. I squeezed her leg admiringly and said: "Wow, that bug-crushing sure keeps you in good shape. Or is it the Zumba?"

"I don't do Zumba," she said, frowning. She got out. "Zumba's for suckers."

Indeed.

On our fourth day of wedded life – my shooting schedule exhausted – I borrowed a production car and Shushie and I sped down the highway to Acapulco, equipped with a case of tequila, a baggy-ful of peyote and songs of love in our hearts. The crew had done a generous whip-round just before we left, and Huston himself – in full Mariachi regalia – stuffed a fistful of Mexican notes down what little there was of Shushie's dress. (He also French kissed the bride.)

We checked into the swankiest beachfront hotel that would take us – we'd broken open both the case and the baggy on the drive – and staked out a Honeymoon Suite. We proceeded to do the stuff that honeymooners do – and I don't mean pal around with Art Carney – aided and abetted by twenty-four-hour room service and our quickly dwindling stash of abusable substances. At some point Shushie produced a marital aid of a type unencountered by me before or since and which I still do not entirely grasp. It sure grasped me, though.

We came up for air about four in the morning on the second day. I had a vague sense that we'd exhausted the money – and a certainty about exhausting my vas deferens – but I'd never felt as thrilled or alive. For the first time since falling from the heights of child stardom, I espied a path I imagined might take me back to a happy life. Maybe even without the peyote.

Shushie led us up to the roof of the hotel – naked as a pair of newlyweds – to see in the fresh day. Someone had conveniently left an inflatable pool float up there and Shushie demanded that we christen it as a rooftop bed. Just before it – and I – punctured, Shushie spotted a large shipping container at the rooftop edge. In a haze, she wandered over.

The crate was filled with large, mirrored disco balls. What the hell they were doing there – or why even an Acapulco hotel would need a whole shipping crate of them – I never did know. Maybe the Bee Gees and Donna Summer were coming for summer vacation. Whatever, Shushie was entranced. She pulled one out and, with a cackle, flung it at me. I somehow caught it and we started tossing it back and forth like a beachball, laughing madly as the quicksilver facets caught the first, fresh beams of morning sun.

It was a Mexican mescaline idyll.

Then I missed an errant throw and the ball bounced off the concrete edge of the roof and exploded into bits before tumbling twelve floors to the earth below. It was sheer magic for a moment as that myriad of glinty glass created a rainbow mosaic of light. The sound was pure music.

The crash from the ground was more sobering.

We both dashed to the edge to peer over. Bits of glass littered the path in front of the hotel. No one, incredibly, had noticed. It was just dawn.

I expelled a deep breath and turned to offer Sushie a look of relief.

She was back at the crate fishing out another ball. Before I could call her name, she'd run back to the edge and heaved it over. I remember still the look of exultation, of crazed delight, on her face. We followed the trajectory of the swirling globe all the way down to the explosion at ground zero.

Shushie cheered as it shattered. I felt something cold at the base of my spine.

She got another. Then another. She laughed like a maniac with every potentially fatal lob.

"Shushie, stop," I told her, reaching for her arm.

She wheeled out of my grasp, screeching like a mad thing. A mad naked thing: some chaos-driven sylph on an unholy spree.

I could hear voices coming from below now and cautiously glanced over the edge. Even as I did so, another silver ball hurtled over my head and another crazed laugh issued from my betrothed.

I ran over and physically tackled her. She tore at my face with her nails and screeched at me until I could think of nothing else to do but slap her.

The shock of it broke the spell.

"They're coming, Shush. We've got to split."

She half-nodded at me and we got up. Blood trickling down my face, I reached out to take her elbow, but she pulled away from me.

"Don't stop me, Martin. Don't ever try to stop me."

We made for the stairwell, but she whirled around again and dug a finger into my chest.

"If you can't keep up, you get left behind."

Five weeks of wedded bliss later that's exactly what happened.

"Should I take the bag?" Leilani asked.

"No offence, but I think I'll hold on to it."

"Cool," she said.

The Dodgers tote bag held $25,000 in cash.

That's how much Shushie said she needed to get ElronD out of trouble. O'Leo and his pals, whom Shushie and Son had grifted, agreed to drop the matter – and ElronD – for a price. Shushie had been a bit vague about the nature of the swindle she'd tried to pull, but swore that they'd "only" stolen $15,000. The extra ten was interest required to buy ElronD out of the mess and avoid other, more physical penalties. The house in Woodland Hills was the drop. We were to leave the money in a storage bin in the backyard. O'Leo had specified that Shushie was not to come along, and that ElronD would be freed once the money was safely in his hands.

"I don't like the smell of that," I'd said. "Why doesn't he want you there?"

"He said he'd beat me with a chainsaw if he ever saw my . . . face again," Shushie told me.

"You don't usually beat people with chainsaws," I noted.

"You don't know O'Leo."

I considered the whupping he gave me with his walking stick. I knew him well enough.

"Twenty-five grand isn't a lot of money," I said.

"Maybe not to you," Shushie said, sharply.

"No, not to anyone in this kind of trade. It's not killing money."

"I told you: you don't know O'Leo. He's crazy."

"Takes one to know one. But this deal still doesn't sit right. And if he really is that crazy, there's no telling what he'll do. What if . . .?"

"I'll go with you," Leilani said.

"What? Why?"

"O'Leo likes me. I'm money in the bank to him."

"If I remember correctly, he referred to you as cunt, gash and bitch. All in one sentence I think."

"See?" she said. "He's clever."

Who could argue with logic like that?

Which is what led us to the front gate of the neat little bungalow on the quiet street in the Valley. We walked on through and, as per Shushie's instructions, saw a neatly tended cobbled path leading around to the back of the house. Leilani started to follow it, but I held her back with a touch on the arm.

"Leilani," I said.

"What?"

"Your name."

"Yeah, it is."

"It's been driving me crazy. Forgive me for judging a book by its cover – I know that *really* doesn't work in the age of Kindles – but you don't look remotely Hawaiian."

"I'm not."

"*Leilani?*" I said again.

"It means 'heavenly lei'," she said. And smiled.

"Right," I said. "Of course."

We followed the Yellow Brick Road.

"There it is," Leilani said, with the kind of wonderment I imagine Columbus's navigator employed yelling "New World, ho!"

She pointed at a grey plastic, all-weather storage box sitting in the middle of the back patio. The patio led on to a set of French doors, but the curtains were tightly drawn and I couldn't see inside. A second, proper door, further along the path, led into a kitchen. I could see in that window, but there was nothing to note other than some dull Kenmore appliances and an open pack of Chips Ahoy on the counter.

"Anything?" Leilani asked.

"They can't be too dangerous," I said. "They like chocolate chip cookies."

"I once dated a guy who beat me with leather dildos. He ate Fig Newtons."

"Fig Newtons are pervy," I said.

"There's a note," she observed.

I strolled over. Sure enough, someone had scrawled the words PLACE MONEY HERE on a sheet of Justin Bieber notepaper and taped it to the top of the box. They'd drawn a little arrow below the words pointing down at the latch. I felt sure if any of those words had contained an "i" it would have been dotted with a little heart.

"Jesus wept," I muttered.

I lifted the lid. Nothing inside but mould, a crushed cigarette pack and a few dead spiders. I closed it again.

"Aren't you going to leave the bag?" Leilani said. She looked worried.

"I don't think so."

"What? Why not? What about ElronD!"

"I got this on Tote Bag Night," I said, patting the rucksack. "The Dodgers one-hit the Giants that game and I ate three – count 'em – three Dodger Dogs. It means a very lot to me."

"What? What are you doing, Marty?"

I glanced around the yard and saw just what I needed: a folded patio umbrella stuck in a weighted stand. I slung the tote bag over my shoulder and yanked the umbrella out. I grabbed the stand by the pole and hefted it – it was pretty heavy so I rolled it over to the French doors.

I knocked on the glass, then called out: "I'm going to count to three, like they do in the pictures. Then I'm going to smash the glass.

"Or you can just open the door," I added.

"Marty . . ."

"One," I yelled.

"O'Leo . . ." Leilani started to say.

"Two."

Leilani held her hands out in front of her like she was directing traffic. Her gaze shifted back and forth between me and the door as if following some madcap ping-pong match.

"Three," I said, and sighed.

Nothing.

I turned to Leilani. "You really should Zumba," I said.

"What?"

"Shit, this is goddamn' heavy," I muttered. But I picked up the stand, took two steps back and started swinging it around as if I was launching a hammer.

I took three good turns and just as I let the stand fly, I saw the curtains flutter and the door slide open.

Too late.

The base of the stand caught O'Leo square in the chest and sent him sprawling backwards into the house, arms flailing. He issued a pained "Oooomph" and I heard a loud crack as his skull connected with a heavy pine dining table. It looked like IKEA. But then they all do.

"Oh my god," Leilani said, walking in behind me.

Blood was colouring his wiry hair. There wasn't too much, though he was clearly down for the count.

"Fuck him," I said. I glanced over my shoulder at Leilani. "Who else is here?"

"What? I don't . . . what do you mean?"

"Is Shush here? She must be. She wouldn't trust anyone else with money. What about ElronD?"

"Marty, what . . . what are you talking about?"

She'd recovered a bit. A bit.

"You'll need bigger stomping boots than those for the likes of me," I said.

Leilani looked at her feet, then up at me. She shook her head some more.

"*My* shoes are big, Martin."

I turned back around. Shoshona Elaine stood there with a gun in her hand and that twisty little smile on her kisser.

It made me very sad.

"I really hoped I was wrong," I said.

"You're smarter than you used to be, Martin," Shushie said.

"I'd pretty well have to be. You're twice as crazy, though."

She laughed. "Crazy is as crazy does," she said and waggled the gun at me.

"Thank you, Shushie Gump."

"Grab the bag, Lani," Shushie ordered.

"Lainie and Lani?" I asked. "You preparing a Don Ho tribute act?"

Shushie shrugged. "We are a pair."

A bit sheepishly, Leilani slipped the Dodgers bag off my shoulder and brought it over to Shushie. Shush gestured at it and the tall girl put it down on a coffee table – also IKEA – and unzipped it.

"What the fuck?" she said.

She pulled out a *San Pedro Beach Bums* beach towel that was folded around an object. She unfurled it on the table.

Shushie started to laugh.

"That's pretty good, Martin. No, that's very good."

"I don't get it," Leilani said. She picked up the *Burning Bright* mug with my face on it and held it up in the air.

"Just how stupid do you think I am?" I said. I pointed at the mug. "Though that really is collectable. The towel, too. Maybe not twenty-five large, but have a look on eBay."

"You bastard," Leilani spat.

"Enough," I said.

"You think?" Shushie said. "I've still got the gun, you know."

"Shush. I've been in The Business since I'm six years old. I've done like thirty cop shows over the years. Not to mention I was fourth lead in *The 'Nam*, thank you very much. You think I don't know a prop gun when I see one? Now let me ask you the only thing I want to know: is there even really an ElronD?"

"There most definitely is, Martin. Oh, yes."

"And is he, is he . . .?" I couldn't bring myself to say the words. What does that say about me?

"Is he, is he . . ." Shushie teased.

I looked at her imploringly.

Shushie twisted her lips in that familiar way. I flashed back to long ago Mexico and felt sick and sad and old.

She laughed very loudly. Then all trace of levity fell off her face.

"I withdraw my earlier statement, Martin," she said. "You're not even one little bit smarter."

That's when she shot me.

Kendall Arlo is the best agent in Hollywood. Not the most famous or successful or rich, but definitely the best.

She's *my* agent – who else would be at my hospital bedside?

Gotta love this town.

"Hey, big guy," she said.

"Do not, under any circumstances, ever call me that again," I said, bringing the world back into focus. "Cedars?"

"They took you to Kaiser, but I had you transferred here once things seemed okay."

"You're a gem, Kendall. I take it that means that I *am* okay?"

"She shot you in the calf."

I peered under the cover at my bandaged leg.

"Holy cow! What a shit shot." I remembered Shushie pointing the gun square at my chest. Then it occurred to me. "So how come I'm so groggy? Why does my head hurt?"

"You fell and smacked your skull on an IKEA bookcase. But the bullet wound was clean. Through and through."

"Still watching those old *ER* box sets, eh, Kendall?"

She smiled. "You're okay, Marty. Lucky, but okay. Yet again."

I slowly sat up, decided that Dr Agent's diagnosis seemed on-the-mark.

"What happened to Shush?"

"Who?"

"Shushie . . . Shoshana. My ex. The lady with the bad aim."

"In the wind. She ran right after she shot you. The police will find her. They got the other girl. Quintangelo."

"So that's her real name," I mused.

"Leilani Quintangelo," Kendall said, nodding.

I shot her a look.

"What?" she asked. "She's an actress. You can IMDb her."

"Maybe later." I leaned back against the pillow. "What happened to O'Leo?"

"Who?"

"The little guy who I laid out on the floor."

"They didn't find anyone else there, Marty. Quintangelo turned herself in. The police will need a statement if you're up to it. There's a lieutenant waiting in the cafeteria. I just schmoozed him over lunch. I paid, of course."

"You're one of a kind, Kendall."

"Yes. I am. Is there anything I need to know before you talk to the detective? Any . . . spillage?"

"Nothing that needs special mopping, I don't think. Though I don't like the thought of Shushie still out on the loose."

"Were you really married to her?"

"I was very young."

"Not me," Kendall said. "Never."

That made me feel so much better.

"She has quite a history," Kendall said.

"Tell me about it."

"No, I don't think you realize. She's been in and out of institutions for the better part of a decade."

"What? Prison?"

"Psychiatric."

"Shit," I shat.

"She had some kind of major breakdown about ten years ago. I couldn't get her records, of course – well, I can, but it will be really expensive – but she's definitely got more than just issues. The police are pretty familiar with her, too."

"How do you know all this?"

"I have my minions. You ever know me to go into a meeting unprepared?" Kendall said.

I smiled, but I wasn't feeling light-hearted. "I spent a few days with her and didn't have a clue. I mean, Shush has always been crazy, but this is . . . something else."

I lay back and stared at the ceiling for a while.

"Marty? Should I get the doctor?"

"No, I'm okay. Just pondering. You'd think after all my years in the business – in LA – my psycho-meter would be more finely tuned. Kendall, how do you tell the genuine crazies apart from . . .?"

"The rest of your ex-wives?" she suggested.

"For a start."

"I better let them know you're up, Marty. You're sure there's nothing else you need to get straight about before you tell your tale?"

"No, I should be safe with the truth this time. They probably won't believe me anyway."

Kendall nodded and made for the door.

"Hey, Kendall?"

She stopped.

"Can you use your ... *minions*, whatever they cost, to look into something for me?"

"Sounds important," she said.

"I don't know ..." I had to confess.

ElronD – the capital "D" at the end is right there on the California birth certificate – Leonard Horowitz was born thirty-seven weeks after my lost weekend in Twentynine Palms with Shushie. He weighed seven pounds, two ounces, and entered the stage at eight minutes past eleven in the morning. He was delivered by a Dr Karen Kendel-Smith, who has a stereotypically terrible signature. The document was in one of three envelopes sitting atop my dining-room table. (I bought it second-hand, from an independent furniture shop in Mar Vista.)

A normal, full-term pregnancy is forty weeks, of course. Had ElronD simply come early? No way to know. Yet.

The second envelope in the package that Kendall had hand-delivered to me contained a couple of dozen photos. They were of ElronD, all taken very recently. Except for one: an archive photo from the *Times*. Kendall's minion had tracked it down, along with everything else. It was of a six-year-old ElronD at Universal Studios. Apparently there'd been a malfunction and ElronD had been hurt on the *Back to the Future* ride. The photo showed a smiling little boy being given a signed Hoverboard by Michael J. Fox and a free lifetime pass to the park in compensation.

I thought I recognized something familiar in the little boy's eyes, his smile.

The third envelope was the only one of the three that was sealed.

"How did you do it, Kendall?" I asked.

She shook her head. "Only for you, Marty. I wouldn't for anyone else."

Just a plain white envelope. Nothing written on front or back.

"Are you sure you want it?" she'd asked before she left.

"No," I said. "Not sure at all."

I balanced it on my palm. The paternity report inside must have been thin: it felt like there was only a single sheet of paper. Was that meaningful?

Kendall's minion had somehow extracted a DNA sample from ElronD.

I started to open the envelope.

I put it back down.

I paced for a while, then picked up and put down the envelope several more times.

After a while, I took all the material Kendall gave me – including the still-sealed envelope – and stuck it in a box of papers I've been meaning to deal with for years at the back of my bedroom closet.

My philosophy? Ignorance may or may not be bliss, but it'll do.

JOHN LLEWELLYN PROBERT

Case Conference #2

"DO YOU HAVE many female patients upstairs?"

Dr Parrish gave a flicker of a smile at Stanhope's words. "What an interesting question," he said. "I must say I have noticed how you become more attentive when the story I'm telling happens to be about a mentally unstable woman instead of a man. Could it be that I've uncovered some hitherto unrealized predilection of yours?"

Stanhope immediately became defensive. "It's not that," he replied. "It's just that ... well ..." He was obviously finding it difficult to find the right words. Parrish allowed the struggle to continue, relishing the journalist's discomfort in the process. Eventually, he decided to put the man out of his misery.

"You've never really understood women anyway, is that it?" he said with a knowing smile. "They've always been a bit of a mystery to you? A bit illogical? Ruled by their emotions – that sort of thing?"

"Yes – that sort of thing." Stanhope seemed reluctant to be drawn further on the subject, but Parrish was having none of that.

"Tell me, Mr Stanhope, are you married?"

Stanhope shook his head.

"Girlfriend?"

"No."

"Boyfriend?"

"Most certainly not."

"But that worries you, does it – that last question? I can see from the way you physically recoiled when I asked it."

Stanhope responded by leaning forward and fixing the psychiatrist with a stare. "I'm not so much worried as irritated, Dr

Parrish. After all, I am meant to be interviewing you, and so far you've been the one asking all the questions."

Behind his desk, Lionel Parrish beamed and held out his hands, palms upward. "I am simply saying what comes into my head," he said. "But if it makes you feel any better, please don't worry. You will find out all you wish to know in good time. Meanwhile, would you care to venture a guess regarding the veracity of that last case report?"

The fountain pen was poised again, ready to make a mark on the piece of paper where Parrish was keeping a record of Stanhope's successes and failures, his right or wrong answers.

"Oh, it has to be true," Stanhope said without hesitating. "The kinds of things that go on in the showbusiness community, that story doesn't surprise me at all."

"I see," said the doctor, making a mark on the paper and putting his pen back into his pocket. "Now let's get back to what we were talking about."

"And what exactly was that?" Stanhope asked.

"Why, you and the opposite sex, of course," Parrish replied with a raised eyebrow. "Or rather, your fascination with female mental disease. It does fascinate you, doesn't it? Don't try to deny it – I am a doctor, you know. I can tell these things. I wouldn't be at all surprised if you've been out with a few ladies you've found difficult to control."

Stanhope smirked at that. "Haven't we all?"

Parrish's expression became grave. "No, Mr Stanhope, we haven't. Did you ever try and control any of those women?"

"What exactly do you mean by that?"

"Did you berate them? Shout at them?" Parrish paused, letting his words sink in, delighting in the way he appeared to be deflating the already cowed-looking reporter. "Did you ever hit them?"

"No," was the reply. "I've always been against physical violence of any kind."

"Just psychological brutality, then?"

"No."

"We have quite a lot of victims of that upstairs, you know."

"That's not what I meant."

"Well, if it wasn't, then why did you imply that it was?"

"I didn't!" Stanhope was shouting now. "I didn't! It was you! You've just made out that that was what I meant. I've hardly said anything and you've manipulated my words to make me look like a wife-beater!"

"Whereas you, of course, have never manipulated anybody's words in your life, have you, Mr Reporter?"

Those last words weren't exactly a snarl, but they were delivered with sufficient vehemence that Stanhope would probably have pushed himself through the back of the chair had it not been of such stout construction.

"My goodness me, I do believe I've touched a nerve!" Parrish held out a hand. "My dear chap, I'm terribly sorry if I've upset you, I can assure you that wasn't my intention at all."

Whether or not Parrish was telling the truth, all Stanhope could find to mumble in reply was, "That's okay. I think it's probably just a bit of everything getting to me."

Parrish's brow creased. "Everything?"

"The stories, you," Stanhope looked around him, "this place."

"Very interesting." Parrish turned to the window behind him. "Would you mind coming here for a moment? I'd like to show you something."

Stanhope got to his feet, circumvented the desk, and joined the doctor to stare through the mullioned panes. He checked his watch. Despite the fact that it was early-afternoon, it already seemed to be getting dark outside. The dim greyness of the day only made the bleak, windswept landscape seem all the more forbidding.

In the distance, close to the trunk of an ancient and stunted oak, a number of crows seemed to be engaged in a macabre dance beneath the tree's naked, twisted branches. And what was that thing they seemed to be congregating around, the one that resembled a pile of wet sandbags? Had that hunched, tattered shape perhaps been chased across the field, made it as far as the safety of the oak, and then met an even worse fate from what lived inside it?

Stanhope eyed the gaping dark hole in the tree's trunk. Had some hideous, spider-like thing emerged, bitten into its unsuspecting victim, and then scuttled back into the warrens beneath the field?

"I think these stories really are starting to get to me," he said, trying to stop his voice from shaking.

Parrish laid a hand on his shoulder. "Good," he said. "I'd be very disappointed if they weren't by now." He pointed to where Stanhope was already looking. "Do you see those birds, there?" Stanhope nodded, trying not to shudder. "Do you see what they're doing?"

"To be honest, I thought they were dancing," Stanhope replied with a nervous laugh.

"I suppose in a way they are. It's a bleak and thankless life for such creatures in this weather. Food is scarce, and the worms stay hidden deep in the earth, where it's warmer. The only way those crows can survive is to encourage their prey to come to the surface. So they pretend to be the rain, the rain that would drown the worms if they stayed where they were. The poor things rush to the surface to avoid a watery death and are instead gobbled up by the hungry monsters waiting above." Parrish smiled. "It's rather a good example of something using fear to get what it wants."

Stanhope looked at the older man, incensed. "And is that what you're doing with me?" he said.

"Perhaps, just ever so slightly," said Parrish with a twinkle in his eyes. "But I rather expected you to be a good sport about it instead of turning into a shivering mass of jelly. Now stop wondering if that's a corpse out there by the tree and sit back down."

It was with a sense of relief that Stanhope resumed his seat.

"Feeling better now?" Parrish asked.

"I am, as a matter of fact," said Stanhope. "Perhaps you actually are a good psychiatrist after all."

"I like to think I know my way around the human mind," the doctor replied, looking away for a moment, the hint of a smile on his face as if he were sharing a private joke with someone. "Anyway, back to business. You were exhibiting an interest in our female patients?"

Stanhope shook his head and chuckled. "I am no more interested in crazy ladies than crazy men," he said. "I just wanted to know if there might be any psychiatric conditions women suffer from that men don't."

Parrish shook his head. "Post-natal depression aside, there's not really much of a difference. Of course there are far more cases of anorexia and bulimia nervosa in women, but neither of those conditions is exclusive to the female of the species."

"What about the other way around?"

"You mean psychiatric conditions exclusive to men?" Parrish rubbed his chin. "Interestingly enough, no, which has made for some rather unusual cases in itself. Even a condition as rare as Ripper Psychosis, which was thought for many years to be suffered only by men, has now had a few female cases documented world-wide."

Stanhope eyed the tape recorder on the desk. The one that was meant to be recording his interview with Parrish; the one that still hadn't been switched on yet, because Parrish wouldn't let him. "Ripper Psychosis?" he heard himself ask.

Parrish nodded. "Do you know what a delusion is?" he asked.

Stanhope shook his head. "Not an exact definition, no."

Parrish pointed at a heavy red volume on a high shelf. "Well, to be precise, a delusion is defined as a fixed, false belief out of context with the social and cultural background of the patient. In Ripper Psychosis, this fixed false belief is that the patient—"

"—believes that they are Jack the Ripper?" Stanhope interjected with a sardonic smirk.

Dr Parrish did not look pleased at the interruption. "In some cases, yes," he said. "Such as the one earlier about the young chimney sweep, and another we will get to later. But not all. Some merely believe that their actions are being motivated or controlled by the spirit of Jack the Ripper, that the terrible things they feel they are being made to do are beyond their control."

"Despite the fact no one still really knows who he was?"

"That's hardly important, is it?" Parrish raised an eyebrow. "No one can conclusively prove the existence of God, Mr Stanhope, and yet there are plenty of people who feel as if their actions are influenced by Him. The 'God Told Me To' psychosis is far commoner than you might think. We have quite a few of those upstairs, actually."

"And quite a few Ripper Psychosis cases as well, I presume?"

Parrish shook his head. "Not that many, no. As I said, it's actually a very rare condition, which in turn makes it all the more fascinating and worthy of study than the more common or garden delusional problems we see a lot of in here."

He bent over, picked up a bulging file from the bottom shelf of the closest bookcase, and laid the crammed and battered box on his desk. "Very fascinating indeed," he said.

"Is that just one case?" Stanhope asked.

"It is." Parrish had the box open now, and was searching through for the case summary. "But very much worthy of all this study. You see, I had never come across a case quite like his before. Outwardly entirely normal. He could hold down a job, he lived in a nice flat, he even had normal relationships with other human beings. And yet for some reason, something triggered inside him and suddenly he was off on a killing spree to rival the famous Victorian serial killer."

Stanhope could not help but look interested. "Do they have any idea what started it?" he asked.

"He's been examined by specialist after specialist. Poked, prodded, tested and re-tested." Parrish picked up a document whose yellowing typed pages were held together by a rusty paper-clip in its top left-hand corner. He handed it to Stanhope.

"Personally," Parrish said as the other man began to read, "I think it all began with the séance . . ."

R. CHETWYND-HAYES

The Gatecrasher

S OMEONE SAID, "LET's hold a séance," and someone else
  said, "Let's," and five minutes later they were all seated round
a table. There was a lot of giggling, and any amount of playing
footsie under the table, and it is possible that the entire idea might
have collapsed if it had not been for Edward Charlton.

He was a tall, thin youth, with a hungry intense expression that
is often peculiar to young men who embrace some burning cause.
He had long-fingered hands that were never still, and his ears,
which were rather large, stuck out like miniature wings.

"I say." No one paid much attention, so he raised his voice, "I
say, let's treat the matter seriously."

This had not been the original intention, and everyone looked
at him with astonishment.

"I mean to say," he cleared his throat, "if one is going to do this
kind of thing, one should do it properly."

Normally he would have been laughed down, but they were in
his flat, and good manners, or what passed for good manners in
that company, demanded the host be given some freedom in his
choice of entertainment.

"What do we do?" asked a blonde girl.

"We all hold hands." He waited for the ribald comments to die
down, then went on. "So as to form an unbroken circle. Yes, and
I'll turn all the lights out except the table lamp."

They sat in the semi-gloom holding hands, and the occasional
giggle was more an expression of uneasiness than one of merri-
ment. Edward felt more confident now the lighting had been
subdued, and his voice was stronger.

"You must empty your minds," he instructed.

"That won't be difficult for some of us," a voice remarked.

"Then," Edward went on, "we must concentrate all our powers on the spirit world."

The young man cursed when a feeble wit asked: "Whisky or gin?", but nobody bothered to laugh.

"Now concentrate," Edward ordered.

They all obeyed him in their different ways, but an undisciplined mind is like a wild stallion when subjected to restraint. Under Edward's continual bombardment of whispered "Concentrate"s, several minds tried to chain thought, but mental pictures manifested in the void, and the senses would not be muted. Hand could feel hand, ears heard the sound of breathing; eyes saw the shaded table lamp; smell sipped at a whiff of perfume, and imagination was never idle.

"Is there anyone here?" asked Edward in a stage whisper.

"Only us chickens," the humorous one could not help himself, and now several voices ordered him to belt up.

"If anyone is there, come in," Edward invited, "don't be afraid – come in."

There was an ungrateful silence; the blonde girl shivered and tightened her grip on her neighbour's hand. Presently the shiver ran round the entire circle, passed from hand to hand, up arms, down legs, leaving behind a paralysing coldness. Consciousness fled, and was replaced by dreams.

Edward walked in the footsteps of a tall man; a great towering figure dressed in a black coat and matching broad-brimmed hat. The man stopped, then turned, and Edward looked upon the lean dark face, the deep sunken eyes, the jutting beak of a nose; the coat fell open revealing a row of knives stuck in a black belt. He heard the distant sound of carriage wheels, and tasted the bitter fog.

The room was like an ice chamber; the table lamp dimmed down to an orange glimmer, and the air was full of fog. All around him he could hear the moans of his companions. Slowly the fog lifted, rose to the ceiling and gradually dispersed, and the coldness went as the lamp grew brighter. Edward looked at the faces of his companions with astonishment that gradually merged into horror. It was as though they had all gone to sleep with their eyes open. The blonde girl had fallen back in her chair and was moaning as though in great pain; one young man had his face twisted up into a snarling grimace, another was opening and closing his hands while staring with unseeing eyes at the overmantel mirror. Edward whispered, "Stop messing about," but without much conviction; then he rose, went over to the wall switch and flooded the room with light. They all returned to the land of the living shortly afterwards.

The mass exodus began some five minutes later; no one said much, but eyes accused Edward of some unspeakable crime; a violation, an act of indecency, an unpardonable breach of human behaviour.

The last man to go out of the front door looked back at Edward with scornful, but at the same time, fearful eyes.

"I wouldn't be you, brother," he said, "not for all the tea in China."

He slammed the door, and Edward was left alone.

His bed stood on a dais situated in the centre of the far wall of his sitting room; during the day it was surrounded by a curtain, but at night he drew this back and by raising his head could see the entire room. As he lay on the bed and put out his hand to turn off the bedside lamp, the fear came to him, and he wondered, in that revealing moment, why it had not come before.

The fear was at first without form. It was just black, unreasoning terror, and he shrank back against his pillow and tried to see beyond the circle of light cast by his lamp. Then he knew. He was afraid of the dark. He lay awake all that night with the light on.

The next day was spent in anticipation of the night which must follow, and when he finally put his key into the lock and opened his front door there was a sense of fearful expectancy. But his flat was empty, was almost irritatingly normal, and he experienced a strange feeling of disappointment. As he ate a solitary meal before the artificial electric log fire, and later tried to read a book, his mind circled the canker of fear, like a bird flying round a snake. He toyed with the idea of going out; perhaps staying the night at a hotel. But this fear took him to the borderline of insanity. If he were to leave the flat, he would be haunted by the knowledge it was empty; his imagination would picture what was moving among his furniture; if his body slept, then surely his soul would return here and bring back some macabre memory to the waking brain.

He did not intend to fall asleep, but he had been awake the entire previous night, and unconsciousness smothered him unawares so he did not hear the book fall from his lax fingers. The icy cold woke him. The limb-freezing, hair-raising chill, and the wild thumping of his heart. He choked, cleared the bitter bile from his throat, gripped the arms of his chair, cried out like a frightened child as his sitting-room door opened, then closed with a resounding slam. The overhead electric lamp trembled slightly, then began to swing to and fro, making a pattern of light circles dance a mad reel across the room. He looked up at the swaying lamp, and as though it had been caught out in some childish prank it suddenly became still; his gaze moved across the ceiling and travelled down to the overmantel mirror, then stopped. A man's face was staring at him out of the glass.

A face that was long, lean, and dark. The sunken, eyes, glittering pools of darkness, stared down at the shrinking figure and betrayed no emotion. Indeed, the entire face was a blank mask; the eyes moved, studied the room with the same unreasoning stare, then looked down again. The thin lips parted, and Edward read the soundless word.

"Come."

Like a sleepwalker, he rose and walked to the mirror.

Greek Street mumbled in the half-sleep that falls upon Soho in the small hours. The after-theatre crowds had long since finished their late dinner and gone home; now only the night-club revellers, or more likely seekers of esoteric entertainment, still moved like maundering snails along the pavement, glancing hopefully into darkened doorways, or looking upwards at lighted windows.

The girl came upon Edward suddenly. She materialized out of a shop doorway and gripped his arm, while gazing up at him with the air of one who has just stumbled upon an old and extremely dear friend.

"Hullo, darling, how nice to see you again."

One blue-painted lid closed in an expressive wink and that part of Edward's brain that still worked took in the words, the expression, and the wink, then came to a decision.

"Let's start walking, darling." The full red lips scarcely parted, and the blue eyes were never still. "You never know when a bloody copper is going poke his nose round the corner."

"Let's walk," said Edward in a flat voice.

She took his arm, and together they walked along the pavement. The girl gave Edward a calculating sideways glance. "Like to come to my place, darling? Five quid and no hurry."

"I would like you to come to my place," said Edward.

"How far?" Now there was a hint of suspicion in her voice.

"Off the Edgware Road."

"Rather a long way. Have to make it worth my while."

"Shall we say thirty pounds?" Edward suggested.

Next time the girl spoke her voice sounded like a cash register.

"You a pussy, dear?"

"A pussy?"

"Yes, pussy – cat – do you go in for the rough stuff? If you do, count me out. I've got me other clients to think about. In any case, I'd want more than thirty pounds."

Edward chuckled and the girl frowned. "Nothing like that. Just your company."

She relaxed. "All right then. Ten pounds down in the taxi, and the rest when we say goodbye. Okay?"

"Okay," said Edward.

He opened his front door and, after turning on the hall light, stood aside for her to enter. Despite the carefully applied make-up, tell-tale lines marred her face and the muscles under her chin sagged slightly; the brash metallic blonde hair was brittle, while her calves were plump and streaked with extended veins. He helped her take off the light blue coat, noting with cold detachment the short, sleeveless, and very low-cut black dress. He then guided her through the sitting-room door and she gasped with pretend, or perhaps genuine, delight at the cosy surroundings.

"You are nice and comfy." She wriggled her bottom and the action made her suddenly grotesque, and a mirthless grin parted his lips. "Do you think I could have a little drinkie?"

"Of course." He walked over to the sideboard. "Whisky all right?"

"Lovely." She rubbed her well-corseted stomach. "Nothing like a drop of the hard stuff to turn me on."

He poured generous splashes of whisky into two glasses, then carried them over to the sofa where she sprawled, displaying a large amount of not particularly appetizing leg. She gulped down the neat spirit with experienced ease, then glanced suggestively over one shoulder.

"I see you've got everything handy. Curtains and all. This is quite a treat after my place ... you know how to treat a girl. I always like dealing with gentlemen. At one time I had an extensive refined clientele, if you follow me. No riff-raff. But times are hard now, what with the Squeeze, and the Wolfenden Report, and all. Thank you, darling, perhaps I will have another. Tell me, have you anything special in mind?"

Edward's eyes were cold, devoid of expression.

"Yes," he said, "something very special."

"Well," she shrugged, "with one or two of those inside me, perhaps I won't mind. But I'll have to put my fee up." She suddenly shivered. "Strike a light, it's bloody cold in here."

He backed slowly to the window bay, an alcove lined with dark red curtains and so masked with shadow. The outward edge of a small mahogany table could only just be seen. With his eyes still fixed upon her face, Edward walked slowly backwards until he was stopped by the table; he reached with his right hand and took something from it. Slowly he brought it out and the overhead lamp reflected its light on the steel blade. The woman, her wits dulled with whisky, giggled softly.

"Oh, no, dear, not knives. I mean, there's a limit ..."

Edward came out from the window bay, the knife clasped firmly in his right hand, and behind him strode a second figure. A tall, dark man, with a bitter lean face, his eyes masked by the shadow of his broad-brimmed hat; together they crept forward, the tall man's hands resting on Edward's shoulders. Their legs worked in unison. Breast to back, thighs to buttocks, legs to legs; the tall man's chin rested on Edward's head, and while his face was white, devoid of emotion, the stranger's lips were parted in a joyous, anticipatory smile, his eyes gleamed with unholy joy, and his hands pressed down on his partner's shoulders, steering him ...

"Gawd," the woman was sober now, and half-rose from the sofa, "not two of you . . .?"

The tall man's eyes willed her to silence, forced her back on to the sofa, where she lay like a plump broken doll with a wide-open mouth and glazed eyes. The four-legged, two-headed monster now stood over her; the two pairs of eyes, one cold, blue, dead fish, the other, black, glittering, stared down. Then the tall man raised his hand, and Edward raised his knife. The stranger's thin lips moved, and from between the tightly clenched teeth came one hissing word.

"Now."

Edward's hand flashed down – then up, then down, then up, then down – until the gleaming knife blade was an unbroken streak of red-blotched silver light.

There was blood everywhere, but no body.

Once the curtains had been pulled back and the early-morning light flooded the room, his eyes refused to be deceived. There was a dark ominous stain covering the sofa and most of the surrounding carpet. In some places the stains were lighter in colour as though they had been scrubbed in a futile effort to remove them. His suit hung in front of the electric fire, shrunken and creased; it was still damp, and although it had clearly been washed, ugly stains darkened the jacket front and trousers. His grey waistcoat was like a screwed-up flannel, and his shirt was missing. He went up close to the overmantel mirror until his reflection filled it.

"Why?"

There was blood in his hair. His face and body had been washed, but the subconscious, or whatever had controlled his body during the dark hours, had not considered shampoo.

"How?"

That one was easy. In the bathroom he found a clean carving knife with a blood-stained towel next to it; the subconscious had not bothered to empty the bath either. The water was pink, red-rimmed and foul; his missing shirt floated on the surface like the upturned belly of a dead fish.

"Where?"

That was indeed the master question. Where was the body that had given forth such a profusion of blood? He stumbled from room to room, searched the six-by-eight kitchen, even looked under the bed, opened cupboards; it took him a full five minutes to summon courage to open the blanket chest, but he did not find a body. His terror became flecked with anger, and he glared at the mirror.

"Where?" He hissed the word. "Where did you hide it?" And instantly there came to him a thought. Maybe the victim had not died, but had managed to escape. If so, why had not the police paid him a visit long since? He went out on to the landing, examined the banisters, stair carpet, even the hall door. There was no sign of blood.

He was about to open the front door when he realized he was still dressed in pyjamas, and the sound of the postman mounting the steps made him scurry back to his top-floor flat. He dressed quickly, then like an unhappy ghost went out to haunt the city.

He walked all day. The sunlight burned up the hours like a fire devouring the last frail barricade, and night was sending forth its first dark spears when sheer weariness forced him to come to rest, and enter a workmen's café. The table at which he sat was situated by a mirror; a long, oblong frame with its surface misty with steam, flyblown, and in some places the quicksilver had become blurred but still cast a reflection.

His coffee had grown cold, and the food on his plate congealed when that familiar face looked at him out of the mirror. He tried not to look into the eyes; made one futile effort to rise from his chair, then the great coldness froze him, and slowly his head came up, and then round.

The thin lips moved, and Edward did not have to read the word.

She was young this time, and walked with pathetic bravado along the pavement, swinging her cheap green handbag with childlike abandon, and recklessly eyeing the men who passed.

The tall young man with a white drawn face stepped out of the shadows, and the girl slowed her pace and looked back over one shoulder.

"You a nosy?"

Her voice had a North-country accent, and her grey eyes, in that pitifully young, grossly over-made-up face, were hard. Like chips of grey flint.

"If you mean, am I a policeman, the answer is no."

"Oh, la-di-da." She relaxed and moved towards him, her hips swinging in what she considered to be a seductive walk. "Are you lonely, then? Looking for a friend, then?"

"I could be."

"You look as if you need one."

She eyed him up and down with some distaste. "You're not down on yer luck, are you? I mean, you've got some of the ready? I mean, I don't do it for peanuts."

The young man smiled and took out his pocket book. The girl's eyes widened when she saw the thick wad of bank notes, and her smile flashed on like a neon sign.

"Oh, well," she patted her Elizabeth Taylor hairdo, "looks as if this is my lucky night."

The young man nodded gravely. "It is indeed."

For the first time the girl betrayed signs of embarrassment.

"Look, have you got a car? Or maybe a place nearby? You see, I haven't been in Fogsville long, and me landlady ain't a regular, if you get my meaning. She won't stand for anything."

"I was going to suggest you came back to my place. It's not very far."

She took his arm and he looked down at her bright red fingernails; the hand was small, plump, and not over-clean; her false eyelashes were long, and stuck out like black spikes.

"We'll get a taxi," he said.

The flat looked like a well-furnished slaughter-house. There was blood everywhere; the bedclothes were sopping wet, again there had been a futile effort at washing; the old stains on the carpet were overlaid with fresh ones; blurred red fingerprints stood out on the pale blue-emulsioned wall; there were even red spots on the ceiling. Another ruined suit hung before the electric fire.

Edward stood against the door and surveyed the macabre scene with curious detachment. He was shocked to find his feeling of terrified disgust was less strong than yesterday. It was as though his senses were numb; his brain seemed to have absorbed its full capacity for horror, and now was willing to view the outrageous rationally. Terror, black dread, still smarting under the first healing skin, but it was just bearable. Tomorrow – next time – the pain would be less, and one day, perhaps when the room was a red cavern and he paced a squelching carpet, there would be the strange sense of peace that comes with normality.

For the second time – was it only the second time? – there was no body. At least almost no body. In the bathroom he caught a glimpse of his white, unshaven face; three long scratches curved down over one cheek. Three red lines that scarcely broke the skin, save in one place, just a little to the left of his mouth. A small fragment was embedded in the flesh. He pulled it out and stared down at that sliver of fingernail; it still retained traces of bright red lacquer, and the horror flared up, burned away the healed scab, and gave him a brief moment of sanity.

"I must confess!" He shouted the words, ran into his tiny hall and screamed his defiance. "I'll give myself up. I'll make them lock me away."

The tall figure came out of the kitchen and moved towards him. The deep sunken eyes glared their awful anger from under the broad-brimmed hat, and the lips were stretched back in a mirthless grin.

"Never again," Edward was whispering now, a harsh madman's whisper, "I'll bring the police up here. I'll let them see it all . . ."

He stopped short as the gaunt head slowly moved from side to side. The voice spoke and his ears heard the word it uttered.

"Mine."

"I'm not yours. Not – not – not . . ."

The words came slowly, with great effort.

"Life – I – now – walk – in – daylight."

The teeth parted and he saw the black nothingness beyond. Then the laughter came, hollow, punctuated by silent pauses, like a faulty radio.

"Ha – ha – ha . . ."

He covered his ears with shaking hands, but the laughter echoed round the limitless caverns of his skull; then the figure was gone, and the laughter was his. Hollow, madman's laughter, that the walls absorbed, the very air contained, and whose vibrations still throbbed long after he had sunk to the floor in merciful oblivion.

The days passed and became weeks. In the world outside questions were being asked, but without great concern, for no mutilated bodies had been found and there were many reasons why a prostitute might find it good policy to disappear.

One person was perturbed, but for a different reason. Mr Hulbert Jeffries stood on the landing outside Edward's flat and gently pressed the bell-push. He waited for a few moments, then pressed again. He heard a door open, then footsteps; a slow hesitant tread. A voice, muffled by the closed door, came to him; a tired, frightened voice.

"Who is it?"

"The chap from downstairs." Hulbert was irritated by all this security. In his world a fellow never spoke from behind a closed door; in fact, if he had any sense he would never lock his door in the first place. There was no telling who you might lock out. "Can I have a word with you?"

For a while it seemed as if his request was going to be ignored, then the door reluctantly opened, and Hulbert gasped when he saw the skeleton face, the sunken eyes that flickered with a baleful light, and almost abandoned his self-imposed mission. Then he remembered what had prompted that mission, and hardened his heart.

"Sorry to bother you, 'specially if you're feeling under the weather, but I had to speak with you."

He paused, waiting for encouragement, but those awful eyes just stared at him, so he swallowed hastily and continued.

"I hope you'll take this in the right spirit, but I wondered if you would quieten things down a bit? I mean, when you entertain your lady friends. I know a certain amount of noise is unavoidable, but there is a limit . . ."

Again he waited for some response; an excuse, even possibly an explanation, however feeble. But the bloodless lips only moved and muttered something that sounded like "sorry", and the door began slowly to close.

"Here, wait a minute!" Hulbert's normally placid disposition became ruffled. "That's not the only thing. There's all that hammering, and if you must throw things, and spill stuff over the floor, for Pete's sake mop up the mess. I've got bloody great patches all over my ceiling."

The door jerked back, and a bony-fingered hand shot out and gripped Hulbert's shirt front; a hollow voice croaked:

"What patches?"

"Watch it, matey." Hulbert gripped the slender wrist and wrenched his shirt free. "You're asking for a punch-up. The patches on my ceiling. It's beginning to look like the map of the world before we lost the empire. You must have knocked a couple of barrels of port over to make a mess like that." He sniffed suddenly. "What the hell is that bloody stink?"

The door was slammed in his face, and he was left pounding out his rage upon its unresponsive panels. After a while he went back to his own apartment, muttering angrily to himself.

He looked up at his disfigured ceiling. The dark red stains were deeper towards the centre; even as he watched, one swelled into a scarlet globule, it elongated, its tip became detached, then fell to a table-top with a minute splash. Another red, glistening driblet yo-yoed down as Hulbert reached for the telephone.

Edward was ripping up his fitted carpet, an easy task for most of the tacks had already been removed, and those that remained slid out of their holes at the first pressure. He rolled back the carpet, tore at the underfelt, and stared at the bare boards. They bore many scrapes, made by a hammer wielded by an inexperienced hand; they were also blood-stained, and in some places not quite flat, like the lid of a suitcase that has been forced down on a too-full interior. Edward stood up as the tall man entered the room.

"Is this the end?"

"I fear so." The tall man bowed his head gravely. "And it is to be regretted that our fruitful association has to terminate. But," he smiled, or rather bared his teeth, "the vessel is, in more respects than one, full, and indeed overflowing."

Fear had long since died, now only curiosity remained; an unsated lust for forbidden knowledge.

"What now?"

The once-lean cheeks were tinted with colour, the lips full and red, the eyes bright with fully charged life.

"Now I am replete, and the wheel has turned full circle – almost. You alone can seal the circle, give me the power to walk abroad. Eighty years ago I suspected the truth, now I know. I too called forth a shade from the dark lands, and I gave him the seven sacrifices that are necessary, plus the ultimate."

"Your master," Edward asked, "he still walks the Earth?"

The eyes sparkled, and the deep voice took on a joyous tone.

"He walks, they all walk, for we are legion. We sit in high places and fan discord until the guns begin to boom, and the bayonets flash. Your lovely wars are a feast, a banquet that charges us for twenty or thirty years. Once past the first barrier there is no reason why any of us should starve."

"What is the ultimate?" Edward knew the answer but he wanted the tall man to tell him. The strong, deep voice went on.

"It is important that the seven initial sacrifices be dispatched in a special way. You were an apt pupil, although at first your tiresome conscience wanted to cover up. That futile scrubbing and washing. But," he glanced round at the blood-spotted, in some places blood-coated, room, "you grew out of that in time."

He pulled his greatcoat open and lovingly selected a long-bladed knife; when he looked up his smile was gentle, his voice soft, comforting.

"How said Brutus on the Plains of Philippi?"

Edward looked into those shining eyes and knew he must follow the path of knowledge to the end – and beyond.

"'Hold then my sword, and turn away thy face, while I do run upon it.'"

"That," whispered the tall man, "is the ultimate."

Edward moved forward and the knife came up; the blade quivered, then was still. The lean face turned and looked back over one shoulder.

"Grip my shoulders and thrust forward. You helped me to come here, it is only right that I should assist you to go there."

Edward gripped the powerful shoulders, then pulled with all his strength. The pain was cold fire that paralysed his body; he sank to the floor and watched his life-blood pouring out over the bare floorboards.

"Have patience," the tall man whispered, then threw wide his arms in a triumphant gesture. "Have patience; you have all eternity."

They tore up the floorboards and took away the bits and pieces. The room was stripped; the bed went to the flames, the furniture was dispersed, the wallpaper removed, but they left the overmantel mirror.

Time had no meaning, and perhaps a year passed before a
new tenant took up residence in the flat; perhaps two, even five.
But one evening that which had been Edward Charlton looked
out of the mirror and saw that a new bed stood on the dais, a fresh
carpet covered the floor, and unfamiliar furniture cluttered the
room.

Night darkened the window, then the sun painted a golden bar
across the carpet, and existence became a panorama of light and
darkness; lamps that went on, then off, the murmur of far-off
voices; the void waiting to be filled.

Tenants came, then departed, fashions changed, furniture
became bizarre, strange contraptions entered the flat, but the
overmantel, now a priceless antique, remained.

Young people dressed in outlandish clothes gathered before
whatever had replaced Edward's electric fire; they danced, made
love, ate, drank, and finally became bored. Suddenly the words
rang out, a clarion call that brought Edward floating to the mirror;
he gazed out at the crowded room.

A young man with pink hair and a spotty face asked: "What
did you say?"

A girl's voice, young, fresh, impatient, repeated the long-
awaited call.

"Let's hold a séance."

ROBERT SHEARMAN

That Tiny Flutter of the Heart I Used to Call Love

KAREN THOUGHT OF them as her daughters, and tried to love them with all her heart. Because, really, wasn't that the point? They came to her, all frilly dresses, and fine hair, and plastic limbs, and eyes so large and blue and innocent. And she would name them, and tell them she was their mother now; she took them to her bed, and would give them tea parties, and spank them when they were naughty; she promised she would never leave them, or, at least, not until the end.

Her father would bring them home. Her father travelled a lot, and she never knew where he'd been; if she asked he'd just laugh and tap his nose and say it was all hush-hush – but she could sometimes guess from how exotic the daughters were. Sometimes the faces were strange and foreign, one or two were nearly mulatto. Karen didn't care, she loved them all anyway, although she wouldn't let the mulatto ones have quite the same nursery privileges. "Here you are, my sweetheart, my angel cake, my baby doll –" and from somewhere within Father's great jacket he'd produce a box, and it was usually gift-wrapped, and it usually had a ribbon on it " – this is all for you, my baby doll." She liked him calling her that, although she suspected she was too old for it now she was very nearly eight years old.

She knew what the daughters were. They were tributes. That was what Nicholas called them. They were tributes paid to her, to make up for the fact that Father was so often away, just like in the very olden days when the Greek heroes would pay tributes to their gods with sacrifices. Nicholas was very keen on Greek heroes, and would tell his sister stories of great battles and wooden horses and fatal heels. She didn't need tributes from Father; she would much rather he didn't have to leave home in the first place. Nicholas would tell her of the tributes Father had once paid Mother – he'd bring her jewellery, and fur coats, and tickets to the opera. Karen couldn't remember Mother very well, but there was that large portrait of her over the staircase. In a way Karen saw Mother more often than she did Father. Mother was wearing a black ball gown, and such a lot of jewels, and there was a small studied smile on her face. Sometimes when Father paid tribute to Karen, she would try and give that same studied smile, but she wasn't sure she'd ever got it right.

Father didn't call Nicholas "angel cake" or "baby doll", he called him "Nicholas", and Nicholas called him "sir". And Father didn't bring Nicholas tributes. Karen felt vaguely guilty about that – that she'd be showered with gifts and her brother would get nothing. Nicholas told her not to be so silly. He wasn't a little girl, he was a man. He was ten years older than Karen, and lean, and strong, and he was attempting to grow a moustache; the hair was a bit too fine for it to be seen in bright light, but it would darken as he got older. Karen knew her brother was a man, and that he wouldn't want toys. But she'd give him a hug sometimes, almost impulsively, when Father came home and seemed to ignore him – and Nicholas never objected when she did.

Eventually Nicholas would say to Karen, "It's time," and she knew what that meant. And she'd feel so sad, but again, wasn't that the point? She'd go and give her daughter a special tea party then, and she'd play with her all day; she'd brush her daughter's hair, and let her see the big wide world from out of the top window; she wouldn't get cross even if her daughter got naughty. And she wouldn't try to explain. That would all come after. Karen would go to bed at the usual time, Nanny never suspected a thing. But once Nanny had left the room and turned out the light, Karen would get up and put on her clothes again, nice thick woollen ones – sometimes it was cold out there in the dark. And she'd bundle her daughter up warm as well. And once the house was properly still she'd hear a tap at the door, and there Nicholas would be, looking stern and serious and just a little bit excited. She'd follow him down the stairs and out of the house, they'd usually leave by the tradesmen's entrance, the door was quieter.

They wouldn't talk until they were far away, and very nearly into the woods themselves.

He'd always give Karen a few days to get to know her daughters before he came for them. He wanted her to love them as hard as she could. He always seemed to know when it was the right time. With one doll, her very favourite, he had given her only until the weekend – it had been love at first sight, the eyelashes were real hair, and she'd blink when picked up, and if she were cuddled tight she'd say "Mama". Sometimes Nicholas gave them as long as a couple of months; some of the dolls were a fright, and cold to the touch, and it took Karen a while to find any affection for them at all. But Karen was a girl with a big heart. She could love anything, given time and patience. Nicholas must have been carefully watching his sister, just to see when her heart reached its fullest – and she never saw him do it; he usually seemed to ignore her altogether, as if she were still too young and too silly to be worth his attention. But then, "It's time," he would say, and sometimes it wasn't until that very moment that Karen would realize she'd fallen in love at all, and of course he was right, he was always right.

Karen liked playing in the woods by day. By night they seemed strange and unrecognizable; the branches jutted out at peculiar angles as if trying to bar her entrance. But Nicholas wasn't afraid, and he always knew his way. She kept close to him for fear he would rush on ahead and she would be lost. And she knew somehow that if she got lost, she'd be lost for ever – and it may turn daylight eventually, but that wouldn't matter, she'd have been trapped by the woods of the night, and the woods of the night would get to keep her.

And at length they came to the clearing. Karen always supposed that the clearing was at the very heart of the woods, she didn't know why. The tight press of trees suddenly lifted, and here there was space – no flowers, nothing, some grass, but even that was brown, as if the sunlight couldn't reach it here. And it was as if everything had been cut away to make a perfect circle that was neat and tidy and so empty, and it was as if it had been done especially for them. Karen could never find the clearing in the daytime. But then, she had never tried very hard.

Nicholas would take her daughter, and set her down upon that browning grass. He would ask Karen for her name, and Karen would tell him. Then Nicholas would tell Karen to explain to the daughter what was going to happen here. "Betsy, you have been sentenced to death." And Nicholas would ask Karen upon what charge. "Because I love you too much, and I love my brother more." And Nicholas would ask if the daughter had any final words to offer before sentence was carried out; they never had.

He would salute the condemned then, nice and honourably. And Karen would by now be nearly in tears; she would pull herself together. "You mustn't cry," said Nicholas, "you can't cry, if you cry the death won't be a clean one." She would salute her daughter too.

What happened next would always be different.

When he'd been younger Nicholas had merely hanged them. He'd put rope around their little necks and take them to the closest tree and let them drop down from the branches, and there they'd swing for a while, their faces still frozen with trusting smiles. As he'd become a man he'd found more inventive ways to despatch them. He'd twist off their arms, he'd drown them in buckets of water he'd already prepared, he'd stab them with a fork. He'd say to Karen, "And how much do you love this one?" And if Karen told him she loved her very much, so much the worse for her daughter – he'd torture her a little first, blinding her, cutting off her skin, ripping off her clothes and then toasting with matches the naked stuff beneath. It was always harder to watch these executions because Karen really *had* loved them, and it was agony to see them suffer so. But she couldn't lie to her brother. He would have seen through her like glass.

That last time had been the most savage, though Karen hadn't known it would be the last time, of course – but Nicholas, Nicholas might have had an inkling.

When they'd reached the clearing he had tied Mary-Lou to the tree with string. Tightly, but not *too* tight – Karen had said she hadn't loved Mary-Lou especially, and Nicholas didn't want to be cruel. He had even wrapped his own handkerchief around her eyes as a blindfold.

Then he'd produced from his knapsack Father's gun.

"You can't use that!" Karen said. "Father will find out! Father will be angry!"

"Phooey to that," said Nicholas. "I'll be going to war soon, and I'll have a gun all of my own. Had you heard that, Carrie? That I'm going to war?" She hadn't heard. Nanny had kept it from her, and Nicholas had wanted it to be a surprise. He looked at the gun. "It's a Webley Mark IV service revolver," he said. "Crude and old-fashioned, just like Father. What I'll be getting will be much better."

He narrowed his eyes, and aimed the gun, fired. There was an explosion, louder than Karen could ever have dreamed – and she thought Nicholas was shocked too, not only by the noise, but by the recoil. Birds scattered. Nicholas laughed. The bullet had gone wild. "That was just a warm up," he said.

It was on his fourth try that he hit Mary-Lou. Her leg was blown off.

"Do you want a go?"

"No," said Karen.

"It's just like at a fairground," he said. "Come on."

She took the gun from him, and it burned in her hand, it smelled like burning. He showed her how to hold it, and she liked the way his hand locked around hers as he corrected her aim. "It's all right," he said to his little sister gently, "we'll do it together. There's nothing to be scared of." And really he was the one who pulled the trigger, but she'd been holding on too, so she was a *bit* responsible, and Nicholas gave a whoop of delight and Karen had never heard him so happy before, she wasn't sure she'd *ever* heard him happy. And when they looked back at the tree Mary-Lou had disappeared.

"I'm going across the seas," he said. "I'm going to fight. And every man I kill, listen, I'm killing him for you. Do you understand me? I'll kill them all because of you."

He kissed her then on the lips. It felt warm and wet and the moustache tickled, and it was hard too, as if he were trying to leave an imprint there, as if when he pulled away he wanted to leave a part of him behind.

"I love you," he said.

"I love you too."

"Don't forget me," he said. Which seemed such an odd thing to say – how was she going to forget her own brother?

They'd normally bury the tribute then, but they couldn't find any trace of Mary-Lou's body. Nicholas put the gun back in the knapsack, he offered Karen his hand. She took it. They went home.

They had never found Nicholas's body either; at the funeral his coffin was empty, and Father told Karen it didn't matter, that good form was the thing. Nicholas had been killed in the Dardanelles, and Karen looked for it upon the map, and it seemed such a long way to go to die. There were lots of funerals in the town that season, and Father made sure that Nicholas's was the most lavish, no expense was spared.

The family was so small now, and they watched together as the coffin was lowered into the grave. Father looking proud, not sad. And Karen refusing to cry – "Don't cry," she said to the daughter she'd brought with her, "you mustn't cry, or it won't be clean." And yet she dug her fingernails deep into her daughter's body to try to force some tears from her.

Julian hadn't gone to war. He'd been born just too late. And of course he said he was disappointed, felt cheated even, he loved his country and whatever his country might stand for, and he had wanted to demonstrate that love in the very noblest of ways. He said it with proper earnestness, and some days he almost meant it. His two elder brothers had gone to fight, and both had returned home, and the younger had brought back some sort of medal with him. The brothers had changed. They had less time for Julian, and Julian felt that was no bad thing. He was no longer worth the effort of bullying. One day he'd asked his eldest brother what it had been like out there on the Front. And the brother turned to him in surprise, and Julian was surprised too – what had he been thinking of? – and he braced himself for the pinch or Chinese burn that was sure to follow. But instead the brother had just turned away; he'd sucked his cigarette down to the very stub, and sighed, and said it was just as well Julian hadn't been called up, the trenches were a place for real men. The whole war really wouldn't have been Julian's bag at all.

When Julian Morris first met Karen Davison, neither of them was much impressed. Certainly, Julian was well used to girls finding him unimpressive: he was short, his face was too round and homely, his thighs quickly thinned into legs that looked too spindly to support him. There was an effeminacy about his features that his father had thought might have been cured by a spell fighting the Germans, but Julian didn't know whether it would have helped; he tried to take after his brothers, tried to lower his voice and speak more gruffly, he drank beer, he took up smoking. But even there he'd got it all wrong somehow. The voice, however gruff, always rose in inflection no matter how much he tried to stop it. He sipped at his beer. He held his cigarette too languidly, apparently, and when he puffed out smoke it was always from the side of his mouth and never with a good bold manly blast.

But for Julian to be unimpressed by a girl was a new sensation for him. Girls flummoxed Julian. With their lips and their breasts and their flowing contours. With their bright colours, all that perfume. Even now, if some aged friend of his mother's spoke to him, he'd be reduced to a stammering mess. But Karen Davison did something else to Julian entirely. He looked at her across the ballroom and realized that he rather despised her. It wasn't that she was unattractive, at first glance her figure was pretty enough. But she was so much older than the other girls, in three years of attending dances no man had yet snatched her up – and there was already something middle-aged about that face, something jaded. She looked bored. That was it, she looked bored. And didn't care to hide it.

Once in a while a man would approach her, take pity on her, ask her to dance. She would reject him, and off the suitor would scarper, with barely disguised relief.

Julian had promised his parents that he would at least invite one girl on to the dance floor. It would hardly be his fault if that one girl he chose said no. He could return home, he'd be asked how he had got on, and if he were clever he might even be able to phrase a reply that concealed the fact he'd been rejected. Julian was no good at lying outright, his voice would squeak and he would turn bright red. But not telling the truth? He'd had to find a way of mastering it.

He approached the old maid. Now that she was close he felt the usual panic rise within him, and he fought it down – look at her, he told himself, look at how *hard* she looks, like stone; she should be *grateful* you ask her to dance. He'd reached her. He opened his mouth to speak, realized his first word would be a stutter, put the word aside, found some new word to replace it, cleared his throat. Only then did the girl bother to look up at him. There was nothing welcoming in that expression, but nothing challenging either – she looked at him with utter indifference.

"A dance?" he said. "Like? Would you?"

And, stupidly, opened out his arms, as if to remind her what a dance was, as if without her he'd simply manage on his own in dumb show.

She looked him up and down. Judging him, blatantly judging him. Not a smile upon her face. He waited for the refusal.

"Very well," she said then, though without any enthusiasm.

He offered her his hand, and she took it by the fingertips, and rose to her feet. She was an inch or two taller than he was. He smelled her perfume, and didn't like it.

He put one hand on her waist, the other was left gently brushing against her glove. They danced. She stared at his face, still quite incuriously, but it was enough to make him blush.

"You dance well," she said.

"Thank you."

"I don't enjoy dancing."

"Then let us, by all means, stop."

He led her back to her chair. He nodded at her stiffly, and prepared to leave. But she gestured towards the chair beside her, and he found himself bending down to sit in it.

"Are you enjoying the ball?" he asked her.

"I don't enjoy talking either."

"I see." And they sat in silence for a few minutes. At one point he felt he should get up and walk away, and he shuffled in his chair to do so – and at that she turned to look at him, and managed a smile, and for that alone he decided to stay a little while longer.

"Can I at least get you a drink?"

She agreed. So he went to fetch her a glass of fizz. Across the room he watched as another man approached and asked her to dance, and he suddenly felt a stab of jealousy that astonished him. She waved the man away, in irritation, and Julian pretended it was for his sake.

He brought her back the fizz.

"There you are," he said.

She sipped at it. He sipped at his the same way.

"If you don't like dancing," he said to her, "and you don't like talking, why do you come?" He already knew the answer, of course, it was the same reason he came, and she didn't bother dignifying the question with a reply. He laughed, and hated how girlish it sounded.

At length she said, "Thank you for coming," as if this were *her* ball, as if he were *her* guest, and he realized he was being dismissed. He got to his feet.

"Do you have a card?" she asked.

Julian did. She took it, put it away without reading it. And Julian waited beside her for any further farewell, and when nothing came, he nodded at her once more, and left her.

The very next day Julian received a telephone call from a Mr Davison, who invited him to have dinner with his daughter at their house that evening. Julian accepted. And because the girl had never bothered to give him her name, it took him a fair while to work out who this Davison fellow might be.

Julian wondered whether the evening would be formal, and so he overdressed, just for safety's sake. He took some flowers. He rang the bell, and some hatchet-faced old woman opened the front door. She showed him in. She told him that Mr Davison had been called away on business, and would be unable to dine with him that evening. Mistress Karen would receive him in the drawing room. She disappeared with his flowers, and Julian never saw them again, and had no evidence indeed that Mistress Karen would ever see them either.

At the top of the staircase Julian saw there were two portraits. One was of a giantess, a bejewelled matriarch sneering down at him, and Julian could recognize in her features the girl he had danced with the night before, and he was terrified of her, and he fervently hoped that Karen would never grow up to be like her mother. The other portrait, much smaller, was of a boy in army uniform.

Karen was waiting for him. She was wearing the same dress she had worn the previous night. "I'm so glad you could come," she intoned.

"I'm glad you invited me."

"Let us eat."

So they went into the dining room, and sat either end of a long table. Hatchet-face served them soup. "Thank you, Nanny," Karen said. Julian tasted the soup. The soup was good.

"It's a very grand house," said Julian.

"Please, there's no need to make conversation."

"All right."

The soup bowls were cleared away. Chicken was served. And, after that, a trifle.

"I like trifle," said Karen, and Julian didn't know whether he was supposed to respond to that, and so he smiled at her, and she smiled back, and that all seemed to work well enough.

Afterwards Julian asked whether he could smoke. Karen said he might. He offered Karen a cigarette, and she hesitated, and then said she would like that. So Julian got up, and went around the table, and lit one for her. Julian tried very hard to smoke in the correct way, but it still kept coming out girlishly. But Karen didn't seem to mind; indeed, she positively imitated him, she puffed smoke from the corner of her mouth and made it all look very pretty.

And even now they didn't talk, and Julian realized he didn't mind. There was no awkwardness to it. It was companionable. It was a shared understanding.

Julian was invited to three more dinners. After the fourth, Mr Davison called Mr Morris, and told him that a proposal of marriage from Julian to his daughter would not be unacceptable. Mr Morris was very pleased, and Mrs Morris took Julian to her bedroom and had him go through her jewellery box to pick out a ring he could give his fiancée, and Julian marvelled, he had never seen such beautiful things.

Julian didn't meet Mr Davison until the wedding day, whereupon the man clapped him on the back as if they were old friends, and told him he was proud to call him his son. Mr Morris clapped Julian on the back too; even Julian's brothers were at it. And Julian marvelled at how he had been transformed into a man by dint of a simple service and a signed certificate. Neither of his brothers had married yet, he had beaten them to the punch, and was there jealousy in that back clapping? They called Julian a lucky dog, said that his bride was quite the catch. And so, Julian felt, she was; on her day of glory Karen did nothing but beam with smiles, and there was no trace of her customary truculence. She was charming, even witty, and Julian wondered why she had chosen to hide these qualities from him – had she recognized that they would have made him scared of her? Had she been shy and hard just to win his heart? Julian thought this might be so, and in that belief discovered that he did love her, he loved her after all – and maybe, in spite of everything, the marriage might just work out.

For a wedding present the families had bought them a house in Chelsea. It was small, but perfectly situated, and they could always upgrade when they had children. As an extra present, Mr Davison had bought his daughter a doll – a bit of a monstrosity, really, about the size of a fat infant, with blonde curly hair and thick red lips, and wearing its own imitation wedding dress. Karen seemed pleased with it. Julian thought little about it at the time.

They honeymooned in Venice for two weeks, in a comfortable hotel near the Rialto.

Karen didn't show much interest in Venice. No, that wasn't true; she said she was fascinated by Venice. But she preferred to read about it in her guidebook. Outside there was noise, and people, and stink; she could better experience the city indoors. Julian offered to stay with her, but she told him he was free to do as he liked. So in the daytime he'd leave her, and he'd go and visit St Mark's Square, climb the basilica, take a gondola ride. In the evening he'd return, and over dinner he'd try to tell her all about it. She'd frown, and say there was no need to explain, she'd already read it all in her Baedeker. Then they would eat in silence.

On the first night he'd been tired from travel. On the second, from sightseeing. On the third night Karen told her husband that there were certain manly duties he was expected to perform. Her father was wanting a grandson; for her part, she wanted lots of daughters. Julian said he would do his very best, and drank half a bottle of claret to give him courage. She stripped off, and he found her body interesting, and even attractive, but not in the least arousing. He stripped off too.

"Oh!" she said. "But you have hardly any hair! I've got more hair than you!" And it was true, there was a faint buzz of fur over her skin, and over his next to nothing – just the odd clump where Nature had started work, rethought the matter, given up. Karen laughed, but it was not unkind. She ran her fingers over his body. "It's so *smooth*, how did you get it so smooth?

"Wait a moment," she then said, and hurried to the bathroom. She was excited. Julian had never seen his wife excited. She returned with a razor. "Let's make you perfect," she said.

She soaped him down, and shaved his body bald. She only cut him twice, and that wasn't her fault, that was because he'd moved. She left him only the hairs on his head. And even there, she plucked the eyebrows, and trimmed his fine wavy hair into a neat bob.

"There," she said, and looked over her handiwork proudly, and ran her hands all over him, and this time there was nothing that got in their way.

And at that he tried to kiss her, and she laughed again, and pushed him away.

"No, no," she said. "Your duties can wait until we're in England. We're on holiday."

So he started going out at night as well, with her blessing. He saw how romantic Venice could be by moonlight. He didn't know Italian well, and so could barely understand what the *ragazzi* said to him, but it didn't matter, they were very accommodating. And by the time he returned to his wife's side she was always asleep.

The house in Chelsea had been done up for them, ready for their return. He asked her whether she'd like him to carry her over the threshold. She looked surprised at that, and said he could try. She lay back in his arms, and he was expecting her to be quite heavy, but it went all right really, and he got her through the doorway without doing anything to disgrace himself.

As far as he'd been aware, Karen had never been to the house before. But she knew exactly where to go, walking straight to the study, and to the wooden desk inside, and to the third drawer down. "I have a present for you," she said, and from the drawer she took a gun.

"It was my brother's," she said.

"Oh. Really?"

"It may not have been his. But it's what they gave us anyway."

She handed it to Julian. He weighed it in his hands. Like his wife, it was lighter than he'd expected.

"You're the man of the house now," Karen said.

There was no Nanny to fetch them dinner. Julian said he didn't mind cooking. He made them some eggs. He liked eggs.

After they'd eaten, and Julian had rinsed the plates and left them to dry, Karen said that they should inspect the bedroom. And Julian agreed. They'd inspected the rest of the house; that room, quite deliberately, both had left as yet unexplored.

The first impression that Julian got as he pushed open the door was pink, that everything was pink; the bedroom was unapologetically feminine. That blazed out from the soft pink carpet and the wallpaper of pink roses on a pink background. And there was a perfume to it too, the perfume of Karen herself, and he still didn't much care for it.

That was before he saw the bed.

He was startled, and gasped, and then laughed at himself for gasping. The bed was covered with dolls. There were at least a dozen of them, all pale plastic skin and curls and lips that were ruby red, and some were wearing pretty little hats, and some carrying pretty little nosegays, all of them in pretty dresses. In the centre of them, in pride of place, was the doll Karen's father had given her as a wedding present – resplendent in her wedding dress, still fat, her facial features smoothed away beneath that fat, sitting amongst the others like a queen. And all of them were smiling. And all of them were looking at him, expectantly, as if they'd been waiting to see who it was they'd heard climb the stairs, as if they'd been waiting for him all this time.

Julian said, "Well! Well. Well, we won't be able to get much sleep with that lot crowding about us!" He chuckled. "I mean, I won't know which is which! Which one is just a doll, and which one my pretty wife!" He chuckled. "Well."

Karen said, "Gifts from my father. I've had some since I was a little girl. Some of them have been hanging about for years."

Julian nodded.

Karen said, "But I'm yours now."

Julian nodded again. He wondered whether he should put his arms around her. He didn't quite like to, not with all the dolls staring.

"I love you," said Karen. "Or rather, I'm trying. I need you to know, I'm trying very hard." And for a moment Julian thought she was going to cry, but then he saw her blink back the tears, her face was hard again. "But I can't love you fully, not whilst I'm loving them. You have to get rid of them for me."

"Well, yes," said Julian. "I mean, if you're sure that's what you want?"

Karen nodded grimly. "It's time. And long overdue."

She put on her woollen coat then, she said it would be cold out there in the dark. And she bundled up the dolls too, each and every one of them, and began putting them into Julian's arms. "There are too many," he said, "I'll drop them." But Karen didn't stop, and soon there were arms and legs poking into his chest, he felt the hair of his wife's daughters scratching under his chin. Karen carried just one doll herself, her new doll. She also carried the gun.

It had been a warm summer's evening, not yet quite dark. When they stepped outside it was like pitch, only the moonlight providing some small relief, and that grudging. The wind bit. And Chelsea, the city bustle, the pavements, the pedestrians, the traffic – Chelsea had gone, and all that was left was the house. Just the house, and the woods ahead of them.

Julian wanted to run then, but there was nowhere to run to. He tried to drop the dolls. But the dolls refused to let go, they clung on to him, he could feel their little plastic fingers tightening around his coat, his shirt buttons, his skin, his own skin.

"Follow me," said Karen.

The branches stuck out at weird angles, impossible angles, Julian couldn't see any way to climb through them. But Karen knew where to tread and where to duck, and she didn't hesitate, she moved at speed – and Julian followed her every step. He struggled to catch up, he lost sight of her once or twice and thought he was lost for good, but the dolls, the dolls showed him the way.

The clearing was a perfect circle, and the moon shone down upon it like a spotlight on a stage.

"Put them down," said Karen.

He did so.

She arranged the dolls on the browning grass, set them in one long neat line. Julian tried to help, he put the new doll in her wedding dress beside them, but Karen rescued her. "It's not her time yet," she said. "But she needs to see what will one day happen to her."

"And what is going to happen?"

Her reply came as if the daughters themselves had asked. Her voice rang loud, with a confidence Julian had never heard from her before. "Chloe. Barbara. Mary-Sue. Mary-Jo. Suki. Delilah. Wendy. Prue. Annabelle. Mary-Ann. Natasha. Jill. You have been sentenced to death."

"But why?" said Julian. He wanted to grab her, shake her by the shoulders. He wanted to. She was his wife, that's what he was supposed to do. He couldn't even touch her. He couldn't even go near. "Why? What have they done?"

"Love," said Karen. She turned to him. "Oh, yes, *they* know what they've done."

She saluted them. "And you," she said to Julian, "you must salute them too. No. Not like that. That's not a salute. Hand steady. Like me. Yes. Yes."

She gave him the gun. The dolls all had their backs to him, at least he didn't have to see their faces.

He thought of his father. He thought of his brothers. Then, he didn't think of anything.

He fired into the crowd. He'd never fired a gun before, but it was easy, there was nothing to it. He ran out of bullets, so Karen reloaded the gun. He fired into the crowd again. He thought there might be screams. There were no screams. He thought there might be blood . . . and the brown of the grass seemed fresher and wetter and to pool out lazily towards him.

And Karen reloaded the gun. And he fired into the crowd, just once more, please, God, just one last time. Let them be still. Let them stop twitching. The twitching stopped.

"It's over," said Karen.

"Yes," he said. He tried to hand her back the gun, but she wouldn't take it – it's yours now, you're the man of the house. "Yes," he said again.

He began to cry. He didn't make a sound.

"Don't," said Karen. "If you cry, the deaths won't be clean."

And he tried to stop, but now the tears found a voice, he bawled like a little girl.

She said, "I will not have you dishonour them."

She left him then. She picked up her one surviving doll, and went, and left him all alone in the woods. He didn't try to follow her. He stared at the bodies in the clearing, wondered if he should clear them up, make things tidier. He didn't. He clutched the gun, waited for it to cool, and eventually it did. And when he thought to turn about he didn't know where to go, he didn't know if he'd be able to find his way back. But the branches parted for him easily, as if ushering him fast on his way, as if they didn't want him either.

"I'm sorry," he said.

He hadn't taken a key. He'd had to ring his own doorbell. When his wife answered, he felt an absurd urge to explain who he was. He'd stopped crying, but his face was still red and puffy. He held out his gun to her, and she hesitated, then at last took it from him.

"Sorry," he said again.

"You did your best," she said. "I'm sorry too. But next time it'll be different."

"Yes," he said. "Next time."

"Won't you come in?" she said politely, and he thanked her, and did.

She took him upstairs. The doll was sitting on the bed, watching. She moved it to the dressing table. She stripped her husband. She ran her fingers over his soft smooth body; she'd kept it neat and shaved.

"I'm sorry," he said one more time; and then, as if it were the same thing, "I love you."

And she said nothing to that, but smiled kindly. And she took him then, and before he knew what he was about he was inside her, and he knew he ought to feel something, and he knew he ought to be doing something to help. He tried to gyrate a little. "No, no," she said, "I'll do it," and so he let her be. He let her do all the work, and he looked up at her face and searched for any sign of passion there, or tenderness, but it was so *hard* – and he turned to the side, and there was the fat doll, and it was smiling, and its eyes were twinkling, and there, there, on that greasy plastic face, there was all the tenderness he could ask for.

Eventually she rolled off. He thought he should hug her. He put his arms around her, felt how strong she was. He felt like crying again. He supposed that would be a bad idea.

"I love you," she said. "I am very patient. I have learned to love you."

She fetched a hairbrush. She played at his hair. "My sweetheart," she said, "my angel cake." She turned him over, spanked his bottom hard with the brush until the cheeks were red as rouge. "My big baby doll."

And this time he *did* cry, it was as if she'd given him permission. And it felt so good.

He looked across at the doll, still smiling at him, and he hated her, and he wanted to hurt her, he wanted to take his gun and shove the barrel right inside her mouth and blast a hole through the back of her head. He wanted to take his gun and bludgeon her with it, blow after blow, and he knew how good that would feel, the skull smashing, the wetness. And this time he wouldn't cry. He would be a real man.

"I love you," she said again. "With all my heart."

She pulled back from him, and looked him in the face, sizing him up, as she had that first time they'd met. She gave him a salute.

He giggled at that, he tried to raise his own arm to salute back, but it wouldn't do it, he was so very silly.

There was a blur of something brown at the foot of the bed; something just out of the corner of his eye, and the blur seemed to still, and the brown looked like a jacket maybe, trousers, a uniform. He tried to cry out – in fear, or at least in surprise – but there was no air left in him. There was the smell of mud, so much mud. Who'd known mud could smell? And a voice to the blur, a voice in spite of all. "Is it time?"

He didn't see his wife's reaction, nor hear her reply. His head jerked, and he was looking at the doll again, and she was the queen doll, the best doll, so pretty in her wedding dress. She was his queen. And he thought she was smiling even wider, and that she was pleased he was offering her such sweet tribute.

EDGAR ALLAN POE

The Tell-Tale Heart

TRUE! – NERVOUS – VERY, very dreadfully nervous I had been and am; but why *will* you say that I am mad? The disease had sharpened my senses – not destroyed – not dulled them. Above all was the sense of hearing acute. I heard all things in the Heaven and in the Earth. I heard many things in Hell. How, then, am I mad? Hearken! And observe how healthily – how calmly I can tell you the whole story.

It is impossible to say how first the idea entered my brain; but once conceived, it haunted me day and night. Object there was none. Passion there was none. I loved the old man. He had never wronged me. He had never given me insult. For his gold I had no desire. I think it was his eye! Yes, it was this! He had the eye of a vulture – a pale blue eye, with a film over it. Whenever it fell upon me, my blood ran cold; and so by degrees – very gradually – I made up my mind to take the life of the old man, and thus rid myself of the eye for ever.

Now this is the point. You fancy me mad. Madmen know nothing. But you should have seen *me*. You should have seen how wisely I proceeded – with what caution – with what foresight – with what dissimulation I went to work! I was never kinder to the old man than during the whole week before I killed him. And every night, about midnight, I turned the latch of his door and opened it – oh so gently! And then, when I had made an opening sufficient for my head, I put in a dark lantern, all closed, closed, that no light shone out, and then I thrust in my head. Oh, you would have laughed to see how cunningly I thrust it in! I moved it slowly – very, very slowly, so that I might not disturb the old man's sleep. It took me an hour to place my whole head within the opening so far that I could see him as he lay upon his bed. Ha! Would a madman have been so wise as this? And then, when my head was well in the room, I undid the lantern cautiously – oh, so cautiously – cautiously (for the hinges creaked) – I undid it just so much that a single thin ray fell upon the vulture eye. And this I did for seven long nights – every night just at midnight – but I found the eye always closed; and so it was impossible to do the work; for it was not the old man who vexed me, but his Evil Eye. And every morning, when the day broke, I went boldly into the chamber, and spoke courageously to him, calling him by name in a hearty tone, and enquiring how he has passed the night. So you see he would have been a very profound old man, indeed, to suspect that every night, just at twelve, I looked in upon him while he slept.

Upon the eighth night I was more than usually cautious in opening the door. A watch's minute hand moves more quickly than did mine. Never before that night had I *felt* the extent of my own powers – of my sagacity. I could scarcely contain my feelings of triumph. To think that there I was, opening the door, little by little, and he not even to dream of my secret deeds or thoughts. I fairly chuckled at the idea; and perhaps he heard me; for he moved on the bed suddenly, as if startled. Now you may think that I drew back – but no. His room was as black as pitch with the thick darkness (for the shutters were close fastened, through fear of robbers), and so I knew that he could not see the opening of the door, and I kept pushing it on steadily, steadily.

I had my head in, and was about to open the lantern, when my thumb slipped upon the tin fastening, and the old man sprang up in bed, crying out – "Who's there?"

I kept quite still and said nothing. For a whole hour I did not move a muscle, and in the meantime I did not hear him lie down. He was still sitting up in the bed listening – just as I have done, night after night, hearkening to the death watches in the wall.

Presently I heard a slight groan, and I knew it was the groan of mortal terror. It was not a groan of pain or of grief – oh, no! – it was the low stifled sound that arises from the bottom of the soul when overcharged with awe. I knew the sound well. Many a night, just at midnight, when all the world slept, it has welled up from my own bosom, deepening, with its dreadful echo, the terrors that distracted me. I say I knew it well. I knew what the old man felt, and pitied him, although I chuckled at heart. I knew that he had been lying awake ever since the first slight noise, when he had turned in the bed. His fears had been ever since growing upon him. He had been trying to fancy them causeless, but could not. He had been saying to himself – "It is nothing but the wind in the chimney – it is only a mouse crossing the floor," or "It is merely a cricket which has made a single chirp." Yes, he had been trying to comfort himself with these suppositions: but he had found all in vain. *All in vain*; because Death, in approaching him, had stalked with his black shadow before him, and enveloped the victim. And it was the mournful influence of the unperceived shadow that caused him to feel – although he neither saw nor heard – to *feel* the presence of my head within the room.

When I had waited a long time, very patiently, without hearing him lie down, I resolved to open a little – a very, very little crevice in the lantern. So I opened it – you cannot imagine how stealthily, stealthily – until, at length a simple dim ray, like the thread of the spider, shot from out the crevice and fell full upon the vulture eye.

It was open – wide, wide open – and I grew furious as I gazed upon it. I saw it with perfect distinctness – all a dull blue, with a hideous veil over it that chilled the very marrow in my bones; but I could see nothing else of the old man's face or person: for I had directed the ray as if by instinct, precisely upon the damned spot.

And have I not told you that what you mistake for madness is but over-acuteness of the sense? Now, I say, there came to my ears a low, dull, quick sound, such as a watch makes when enveloped in cotton. I knew *that* sound well, too. It was the beating of the old man's heart. It increased my fury, as the beating of a drum stimulates the soldier into courage.

But even yet I refrained and kept still. I scarcely breathed. I held the lantern motionless. I tried how steadily I could to maintain the ray upon the eve. Meantime the hellish tattoo of the heart increased. It grew quicker and quicker, and louder and louder every instant. The old man's terror *must* have been extreme! It grew louder, I say, louder every moment! – do you mark me well? I have told you that I am nervous: so I am. And now at the dead hour of the night, amid the dreadful silence of that old house, so strange a noise as this excited me to uncontrollable terror. Yet, for some minutes longer I refrained and stood still. But the beating grew louder, louder! I thought the heart must burst. And now a new anxiety seized me – the sound would be heard by a neighbour! The old man's hour had come! With a loud yell, I threw open the lantern and leaped into the room. He shrieked once – once only. In an instant I dragged him to the floor, and pulled the heavy bed over him. I then smiled gaily, to find the deed so far done. But, for many minutes, the heart beat on with a muffled sound. This, however, did not vex me; it would not be heard through the wall. At length it ceased. The old man was dead. I removed the bed and examined the corpse. Yes, he was stone, stone dead. I placed my hand upon the heart and held it there many minutes. There was no pulsation. He was stone dead. His eye would trouble me no more.

If still you think me mad, you will think so no longer when I describe the wise precautions I took for the concealment of the body. The night waned, and I worked hastily, but in silence. First of all I dismembered the corpse. I cut off the head and the arms and the legs.

I then took up three planks from the flooring of the chamber, and deposited all between the scantlings. I then replaced the boards so cleverly, so cunningly, that no human eye – not even *his* – could have detected anything wrong. There was nothing to wash out – no stain of any kind – no blood-spot whatever. I had been too wary for that. A tub had caught all – ha! ha!

When I had made an end of these labours, it was four o'clock – still dark as midnight. As the bell sounded the hour, there came a knocking at the street door. I went down to open it with a light heart – for what had I *now* to fear? There entered three men, who introduced themselves, with perfect suavity, as officers of the police. A shriek had been heard by a neighbour during the night; suspicion of foul play had been aroused; information had been lodged at the police office, and they (the officers) had been deputed to search the premises.

I smiled – for *what* had I to fear? I bade the gentlemen welcome. The shriek, I said, was my own in a dream. The old man, I mentioned, was absent in the country. I took my visitors all over the house. I bade them search – search *well*. I led them, at length, to *his* chamber. I showed them his treasures, secure, undisturbed. In the enthusiasm of my confidence, I brought chairs into the room, and desired them *here* to rest from their fatigues, while I myself, in the wild audacity of my perfect triumph, placed my own seat upon the very spot beneath which reposed the corpse of the victim.

The officers were satisfied. My *manner* had convinced them. I was singularly at ease. They sat, and while I answered cheerily, they chatted of familiar things. But, ere long, I felt myself getting pale and wished them gone. My head ached, and I fancied a ringing in my ears: but still they sat and still chatted. The ringing became more distinct: it continued and became more distinct: I talked more freely to get rid of the feeling: but it continued and gained definiteness – until, at length, I found that the noise was *not* within my ears.

No doubt I now grew *very* pale; but I talked more fluently, and with a heightened voice. Yet the sound increased – and what could I do? It was *a low, dull, quick sound – much such a sound as a watch makes when enveloped in cotton*. I gasped for breath – and yet the officers heard it not. I talked more quickly – more vehemently; but the noise steadily increased. I arose and argued about trifles, in a high key and with violent gesticulations; but the noise steadily increased. Why *would* they not be gone? I paced the floor to and fro with heavy strides, as if excited to fury by the observations of the men – but the noise steadily increased. Oh God! What *could* I do? I foamed – I raved – I swore! I swung the chair upon which I had been sitting, and grated it upon the boards, but the noise arose over all and continually increased. It grew louder – louder – *louder!* And still the men chatted pleasantly, and smiled. Was it possible they heard not? Almighty God! – no, no! They heard! – they suspected! – they *knew!* – they were making a mockery of my horror! – this I thought, and this I think. But anything was better than this agony! Anything was more tolerable than this derision! I could bear those hypocritical smiles no longer! I felt that I must scream or die! And now – again! – hark! louder! louder! louder! *louder!*

"Villains!" I shrieked, "dissemble no more! I admit the deed! Tear up the planks! – here, here! – it is the beating of his hideous heart!"

DENNIS ETCHISON

Got to Kill Them All

THE SKY WAS getting darker all the time.

I set the red can under the glove box and drove away from the pumps, steering with one hand so I could gulp down some coffee. Then I hit the brakes before I got to the street.

The can worried me.

It was still upright but I heard the gas sloshing. There were a lot of turns between here and the house. What if it tipped over? I'd be sucking fumes before I got home.

I reached into the backseat, grabbed the plastic bag from B&B Hardware and wedged it next to the can. But it wasn't heavy enough. So I had to shut off the engine, climb out and make room in the trunk, between the spare tyre and the suitcase. That way the can wouldn't move around no matter how fast I took the corners. I turned the key again and headed east on Washington, picking up speed, with only one question in my mind:

Which of the following is a Burt Reynolds film? (a) Cannonball Run, (b) Stroker Ace, (c) Smokey and the Bandit, or (d) The Night of the Following Day.

I couldn't remember the winning answer but it didn't matter now. The gas station was history.

The sky was so dark by now that I had a hard time believing it was still early-afternoon. The clock on the dash said the same as my watch, a few minutes past three. Rush hour wouldn't be for a while yet. I changed lanes, weaving in and out, flexing my fingers till the joints popped, the sound like little arcs of electricity below the windshield. I thought I saw a barricade of squad cars at the next corner, coloured lights spinning, but it was only a road crew setting out detour signs. Their red vests glowed in the underpass.

I shook my head to clear it and noticed that the coffee was almost empty.

I worked my way over between the trucks and sport utility vehicles, heading for Venice Boulevard. It would have been a lot easier to take Sepulveda to Lincoln straight out of LAX. I'd be home now. But this way I had everything I needed. I could do the rest in my sleep. As I turned onto Venice another question flashed before me:

In what film does William Shatner appear? (a) The Intruder, (b) The Brothers Karamazov, (c) Big Bad Mama, or (d) Anatomy of a Murder.

That one was easy. It was from Day Two, Show Five, the one we had just wrapped. How many hours ago? I could still see the answer on the card in front of me. I pretended to play the game, jabbing the steering wheel as if it were a buzzer. The horn went off and he glanced up.

The first thing I noticed was that he might have been anyone.

A beach boy, nothing special, the type you see around here all the time. Sun-bleached hair, sweat collecting in his squinty eyes and a walk that said he was not going to slow down for anybody. He stepped into the street and one of us had to stop. I could tell by those eyes it had to be me. He glared back like a hot spot on the glass and didn't move.

Then he did something strange.

He folded his legs and sat down right there in the crosswalk, daring me to hit him. I didn't, of course. The light was red.

I opened the window.

"Hey, you want to move it?"

He shrugged. Not defiantly. He just didn't care.

Cars were stacked up behind me now and they didn't like this game. The light changed. I heard a horn tapping. For God's sake, I thought.

"What's your problem?"

When I leaned out his eyes got big.

"God, you're him!"

I shook my head. "Move your ass."

"Yeah! The guy on *Green!*"

Busted. I didn't even have my make-up on. Did I? No, that was hours ago, in Honolulu. I would have taken it off. I checked the rear-view mirror. My eyes were like two cigarette burns. I had a hard time recognizing myself. The kid's legs unfolded as he got up. But not to move out of the way. He started walking toward me.

He was going to ask for my autograph.

The rest of the drivers leaned on their horns.

I had to make a decision fast so I unlocked the passenger door. I'd drive around the corner and dump him off once we were out of the intersection.

When he got in I took a close look at him. New Nikes, clean T-shirt and jeans, no dirt anywhere that showed. He was not a beach bum and he didn't really have an attitude. He had just plain given up. He probably didn't know he was going to until that moment and then something – the traffic, the sun, all the people on the street who couldn't care less – made him lose it. Now I could see that it wasn't sweat under his eyes. He had been crying.

He closed the door and wiped his face. "Shit, I'm sorry. If I'da known it was you . . ."

"What happened?" I said.

"Oh, nothin'." He tried a laugh to make light of it. "My old lady. We had a, you know, fight. She kicked me out."

"Where?"

"Right here, in the middle of the street. Told me to fucking split. So I did."

"I understand," I said.

"You do?"

"She's a bitch."

"Well . . ."

"Sure, she is. Acts like you're always bothering her. No time to talk. When you call, she's never home."

"How did you know that?"

Which is proof that your wife is cheating? (a) Staying out all night, (b) mysterious stains on her clothing, (c) phone calls from someone who hangs up when you answer, or (d) frequent trips to see her "mother" in the hospital.

"They're all the same," I said. "Think about it."

"Yeah," he said, as if it had never occurred to him, "I guess they are . . ."

Now we were close to Admiralty Way and the grid of side-streets by the marina. It was hard to tell them apart in this light. Got to bear down, I thought.

"Where do you want me to drop you?"

"Wait," he said. "What do I do?"

What should you do once you know she is unfaithful? (a) Make her account for every hour of her day, (b) hire a private detective, (c) hide a Global Positioning Device in her car, or (d) kill her.

"Only one thing *to* do," I told him, "isn't there? How about the corner?"

"It doesn't matter."

"Where's your house?"

"I can't go back there."

"Maybe you should."

"Why?"

"To make it right."

"I don't know how."

"Yes, you do. Think about it."

"Okay. I will."

He squinted at the shadowy rows of condos as we neared the end of the boulevard. We both saw sparks of light like tiny fires starting between the buildings. It could have been the sun on the ocean except that the sky had closed over.

"I have to let you out," I said.

"Huh?"

"I can't take you with me. Not where I'm going."

"That's cool. The market, okay?" There was a Stop 'N Start ahead, at the corner. "I need some stuff."

That was cool with me. I could get a refill on my coffee, as long as it didn't take too long.

I pulled in between a brand-new Land Rover and an exterminator's truck. The mannequin on the roof had a tux and top hat and a big rubber mallet behind his back and he was standing over an innocent-looking mouse. On the way to the glass doors I saw the little rat out of the corner of my eye, twitching his whiskers and scooting away over the hood. Go on, I thought. You can run but you can't hide.

Inside the convenience mart I poured a big 22-ouncer, black. The kid was in the aisle where they keep the dog food and soap and aspirin and Tampax, for when you're running late and she gave you a list and you promised. I popped a lid on the coffee and left a dollar bill on the counter, thinking: *Which method is best for a crime of passion? (a) Gun, (b) rope, (c) knife, or (d) gasoline.*

"Good luck," I said over my shoulder.

The kid had a couple of household items in his hands. He must have wanted to do the pots and pans or something as soon as he got home. So he was going to try and make up after all. He could hardly wait. The poor bastard. I went out while he was paying for his stuff.

The mousemobile was gone. Now a pool-cleaner's truck was parked next to me, the kind I'd seen in the marina, sometimes in front of my own house even though our pool wasn't finished yet. I wondered if it was the same one. If it was, maybe I could do something right here before I drove off and took care of the rest.

Let's see, I thought.

I hadn't figured on this part and didn't have the right tools for the job. It wouldn't take much to give him the message, say a screwdriver stuck in a sidewall or the radiator, like a note on his windshield, only better. He'd know what it was for and look around and I'd be gone. Or I could wait for him to come out and see what his sorry ass looked like. Was he inside? I hadn't noticed. *What should you do to her lover? (a) Make his life a living hell, (b) tie him up and torture him, (c) castrate him, or (d) kill him.* But this was his lucky day. I wasn't sure.

Time to go.

The kid walked around and opened the passenger door like he wanted to get in.

"One question," he said.

"What?" I swallowed hot coffee, put the cap back on and took out my keys.

"Can I get on the show?"

"I don't have anything to do with that," I said, revving up.

"But if you put in a good word . . ."

"I'm out of here," I said. The sky went black like a shadow had passed over the earth. Night was ready to fall. I could feel it in my head. "Close the door."

"Okay," he said and got in.

Now he thought we were friends. He was really innocent. Like the Fool in a deck of cards, too busy smelling the flowers to notice that he's walking off a cliff. I didn't want to tell him the whole truth. He wouldn't be able to handle it.

"I guess you have to be pretty smart, anyway."

"Do you watch the show?"

"Every week!"

"Then you know the rules," I snapped. We were driving again and traffic was heating up. I couldn't waste any more time. "It's not what you know. It's what—"

"You *don't* know!" he finished for me. "That's so cool. All those other shows, you have to get the answer right. But on *Green,* one right answer and you're—"

"History," I said. "Look, I have to be somewhere."

"Sony Studios, Culver City, seven o'clock. Right?"

"Not tonight."

"But this is Friday . . ."

"We tape the shows in advance."

"You do?"

"Five a day. I just flew in from Hawaii. Yesterday San Francisco, Atlanta the day before, New York on Monday. A month in a week."

"Jesus, when do you sleep?"

"It's been a while."

He held out his hand. "Ray Lands, right?"

"Lowndes."

"I thought you were live." He tried to give me some kind of brotherhood handshake but I got out of it.

"I used to be. Now they want it every night. We had to get some shows in the can."

"'Cause it's so popular?"

"Right."

He put his bag of household crap in the backseat, cheered up already, sure everything was going to work out. It didn't take much. Even if she threw him out again he could sleep under a blanket of stars and eat dates off the palm trees while he figured another way to get her back. That would be cool. Somebody needed to burst his bubble but I didn't want to be the one. I had things on my mind.

What is the best way to obtain satisfaction? (a) Catch her in the act and take pictures, (b) expose her betrayal on national television, (c) beat her within an inch of her life, or (d) tie her up and burn the house down.

"All ri-i-ght!" he said.

"What?"

He was still leaning over the seat and now he had his hand on the plastic bag from the hardware store. "You go to B&B, too! Over on Washington, right? They have everything. It's great, huh?"

"Great."

He reached into my bag and took out the long butane lighter. It balanced across his palm like a combat knife. He fingered the switch, ready to test it.

"I like these babies. For when you have to start a barbecue."

"Leave it," I told him.

"Duct tape, nails, rope . . ." He put the bag back down next to his. "Need to fix something?"

"Yeah."

"At your place?"

I stopped the car at the last corner.

"You better get out now."

"Oh, yeah." He took his bag from the backseat, then hesitated. "Need any help?"

"No."

A private security patrol car nosed out of the alley by the gate and sat there idling, the guard watching me behind tinted glass. I hovered for a minute while I downed the rest of the coffee and let it absorb into my bloodstream.

I could see the stars already through my eyelids and then the streaked sky over Waikiki Beach, the way it was outside the window of the hotel room when the storm started moving in, and my hand as I picked up the phone to call her for the hundredth time. I felt the rumbling of the surf. It sounded like a car engine. I opened my eyes and checked the mirror. So far there were no other patrol cars rolling up to block this way, only the one in the alley and while my eyes were closed he had camouflaged the front end so it looked like a trash can in the shadows. I saw waves churning in the marina. The water was blood-red.

"You sure?" the kid said. "I'm good with my hands."

I would have bet that he was. I considered. If she was alone I could handle it and if she was out that would give me time to get set up while I waited for her to come home. But if she was not alone there might be complications.

"Still want to be on the show?" I said.

"Sure. Ten million greenbacks!"

"It's easy. All you have to do is give the wrong answer. Prove that you're an asshole, in other words, like everybody else."

"I know."

"If I gave you something to hold, could you do that, and not ask any questions?"

"Like what?"

"What would you do if you saw a rat?"

"Um, kill it, I guess."

"That's right. You've got to kill them, don't you?"

"Hell, yeah."

"Then come on."

"Where are we going?"

"I want you to meet my wife."

He swung his legs back in and closed the door. "You'll put in the word?"

"Sure."

"When?"

"Next week."

"Cool!"

We drove around to the multi-level ranch houses at the end of Circle Vista.

"Uh, one thing," he said, "just so's you'll know. I'm not into anything weird."

"That's cool," I told him. "Neither am I."

Her lemon-coloured car was in the driveway. I took the hardware store bag from the back and as I climbed out a curtain flapped shut in an upstairs window. The bedroom.

"Wait here," I said.

"You got it."

I started along the flagstone walk to the side of the house. Better check it out, I thought, before you bring the red can from the trunk, just to be sure. Before I got very far the front door squeaked open and I heard a voice.

"Ray . . .?"

I backtracked, holding the bag casually at my side.

"Hi, honey."

I waited for her to ad lib an excuse to keep me outside. Her eyes were puffy, almost swollen shut. She hadn't been getting much sleep, either.

"Ray, I'm so glad you're here!"

"Are you?"

"You don't know . . ."

"What's wrong?"

"It's Mother."

I nodded knowingly. "Your mother? I see. Is she still 'sick'?"

"She's . . . gone."

"Oh, really? Where did she go?"

"She passed away last night. This morning. I tried calling you from Kaiser but you'd already checked out. I don't know what to do. I have to make the arrangements . . ."

I dropped the plastic bag and held her off, feeling her wrists trembling, so thin I could snap them like chicken bones. She came at me again and struggled as I pushed her away. Then her face twisted up and she started sobbing. I grabbed her around the waist and lifted her off her feet, carrying her out of the yard before the neighbours could see our hysterical little scene. The only one who saw was the kid. He watched from the car, taking it in.

"What's wrong with you?" she screamed as the sirens started closing in.

What is a mouse when it screams? I thought. *(a) Still shitting me, (b) scared shitless, (c) full of shit, or (d) shit out of luck . . .*

The next thing I remember is this:

She got her arms around my neck and then I wasn't fighting her anymore. I stood there feeling her lips against my neck and her breath was hot like a child's from the crying and my eyes finally closed all the way. And when they opened again it was like I was waking up.

I smelled her hair and tasted her skin and knew where I was. Everything else had been a dream. The sirens receded and there was only the quiet lapping of blue water behind our house. The weight lifted and the sky opened and there was light again and the pounding in my ears was her heart beating in my chest. Then her legs went out from under her and I had to hold very tightly to keep her feet from dragging as I pulled her inside.

I was sorry the kid had to witness any of this. He would have to walk home from here. I had a vague recollection of the bitter, twisted things I had said to him and felt ashamed. Someday he would understand how burned-out a man can get when he's really exhausted and wired, and how bent out of shape things seem when you're like that, and maybe he'd forget this day. I had been out of my head. It can happen to anybody, I told myself.

Her clothes were so wrinkled she must have slept in them for days on a cold bench somewhere and her hair had come loose and there was no make-up on her pale face. I set her on the couch.

"I'm so sorry," I said, and kissed her forehead.

"I have to call the funeral home . . ."

"Let me."

"And my brother—"

"I'll take care of it. Rest."

"Where are you going?"

"The phone. I'll be right there, in the kitchen. Okay?"

She nodded.

I found her brother's number by the phone. No answer. He was probably on his way. I'd try again in a few minutes if he didn't show up. The next thing would be to call the funeral home. I didn't know which one it was. I started back to the living room and heard her cry out suddenly, louder and more desperate. The sound stopped before I got there.

The kid moved in front of the couch to block my way.

"Everything's cool," he said.

"What is?"

Across the room the front door was still open. There were spatters on his clean white T-shirt. His bag from the convenience mart lay on the carpet with the contents spilling out: a blister pack of cheap steak knives, a roll of twine and a dispenser of wide package-sealing tape. In his hand was a pizza cutter.

She was where I had left her, only now her ankles were bound together with the twine, a piece of the tape covered her mouth and one of her arms dangled to the floor. Blood dripped from the wrist.

"I was gonna save my stuff," the kid said, "for when I get home. But I could tell you needed a hand."

I tried to get past him before the room became any blacker. He stepped aside and grinned.

"You really got it down, man, about the bitches. I guess I always knew. There just isn't no other way . . ."

"*What have you done?*"

"What you said." And he winked at me, his eyes dancing wildly in his skull. "I mean, like, you got to kill them all. Right?"

MARK MORRIS

Essence

A S SOON AS she walks through the door they know that she's the one.

It's like a sixth sense, like they've been genetically augmented to home in on the vulnerable, the uncertain. They play it cool, however, saying nothing, their flat shark's eyes never even meeting in a flicker of mutual recognition. Pa continues to sip his pint of bitter, his solid, weighty body relaxed into a round-shouldered slouch. Beside him, Ma still toys with her rum and Coke, turning the greasy tumbler round and round on the stained wooden table-top. They appear unaware of their surroundings, uninterested in the choppy clamour around them.

But in truth they are focused wholly on the girl, who is still clearly acclimatizing, having stepped from the frosty November night and into the over-warm, sour-smelling fug of The White Hart.

The girl is slight, her complexion too peachy-smooth, her features too delicate, to be from this neighbourhood. The faces that bob and leer around her, gulping at drinks, engaged in braying, aggressive conversation, are coarse, or mottled, or cunning, or sometimes all three. She is like a fallow deer that has inadvertently stumbled into the midst of a wolf pack.

Both Pa and Ma see her eyes widen imperceptibly, her shoulders stiffen with tension, as she looks around, her head making little darting motions, her golden hair shimmering as it flickers and bounces around her face.

Then, as if nervous of making a move which might incite hostility, she tilts her right wrist towards her face and carefully peels back the cuff of her soft grey hoodie. She glances down, then up again. Checking her watch. Then checking to see whether anyone has noticed how expensive it is. In that instant, despite their lack of mutual consultation, both Pa and Ma know her story.

She is new in town, a student maybe, judging by the dinky little backpack she is wearing. A friend has arranged to meet her here, and she is wondering whether she is too early, or too late, for the appointment. Is wondering, in fact, whether she is in the right place.

She probably is. The White Hart is a no-man's-land kind of pub, frequented by locals and occasionally by students, but not particularly cherished by either. Dirty-walled and dirty-windowed, it gives the impression of trying hard *not* to be noticed. Its sign is faded and colourless with age. It perches in a dark, forgotten street of largely shuttered and abandoned businesses, somewhere between the edge of a decaying council estate and a neighbourhood of once-grand houses which have now run to seed, their chilly, high-ceilinged rooms sliced and diced into bedsits for itinerants: students, casual labourers, the dispossessed.

The only reason people come here at all these days is because it is *convenient*. Within walking distance of the main road, and therefore of the bus route into town; grim, but not *too* dangerous; quiet, but not entirely dead. It is a meeting-place, a stopping-off point, a stepping-stone. It serves a similar purpose to a city-centre bus station, and has a corresponding lack of allure.

All of which makes it perfect for the purposes of Pa and Ma. They know they won't be remembered here; they know they can blend in; they know they can move on quickly if things go wrong, to any one of numerous such hunting-grounds dotted throughout the city.

They watch the girl decide whether she's going to stay or not. If she doesn't it's of no importance. They know there will be plenty more opportunities. They know that the city is full of young flesh, impressionable minds. This is a game not of desperation, but of patience, persistence. They are hungry, but they are not reckless. It is better to take small bites, when they can, than to gorge themselves. They know that if they were to feast without compunction, they would risk exposure, and subsequently face a future of nothing but famine.

When the girl eventually takes a deep breath and marches almost defiantly to the bar, they show no response. They watch as she slides her lean frame between bulkier shoulders. As soon as the barman gravitates towards her, Ma finishes what is left in her glass and stands up. Without looking at Pa she walks unhurriedly to the bar, her eyes fixed on her target, her expression blank. She arouses no interest. She is drab, invisible – a plain, dumpy, middle-aged woman in colours that deflect attention. She positions herself directly behind the girl, knowing that she remains unnoticed.

The girl leans forward to take a jingling handful of change from the barman, her tight-fitting jeans stretching over a bottom that is almost breathtaking in its perfection. Ma is close enough to the girl to smell her. She smells of youth and freshness, of spring-time, new growth. Ma breathes it in, relishes it, is aroused by it, even as she feels a giddy, enraged desire to destroy it utterly.

The girl pockets her change, and as she picks up her glass of Coke, Ma steps forward, a practised move, so subtle it is almost balletic in its execution. The girl turns. Instantly surprise and alarm cloud her face as she bumps into Ma, her elbow jolting. Coke splashes out of her glass and down the front of Ma's grey cardigan.

"Oh my God! I'm so sorry. I didn't see you there," the girl says.

She looks distraught, though Ma guesses she is more fearful of the reaction she might provoke than of the fact that she has stained this dull-looking woman's shapeless item of clothing.

"Oh!" Ma says, as though startled by the collision, and drops the purse she is holding. She bends to pick it up, and then staggers slightly. "Oh," she says again, her voice fainter this time.

She feels the girl's hand clutching her arm, hears her anxious voice: "Are you all right?"

What do you care? Ma thinks. *You only ask because you don't want to draw attention to yourself.*

Weakly, raising her head like a tortoise emerging from its shell, Ma says, "Yes, I . . . I'm sure I'll be fine. I just felt a bit dizzy there for a minute."

The girl is biting her lip, an expression of concern on her face. Ma's eyes flicker down to the purse at her feet, and immediately the girl says, "Oh, let me pick that up for you."

"Would you, dear?" Ma says. "That's very kind."

She steps back to allow the girl room to lean forward. Staring down at the girl's blonde head she allows herself a moment of indulgence. She imagines herself naked before the girl, imagines twisting her hands into the girl's shimmering hair and forcing her face into the sour, damp crevice between her meaty, dimpled thighs.

Then the girl rises with the purse and holds it out. Instead of taking it, however, Ma sways slightly. "Oh," she says for the third time. "I think I'd better sit down."

"Here," the girl says, stepping forward quickly. "Let me help you."

She has no hand to spare, though, and Ma sees she is in a quandary. She hesitates a moment, then stuffs Ma's purse into the side pocket of her hoodie. With her left hand now free, she curls it slightly awkwardly under Ma's right arm.

"That's where I'm sitting," Ma says, nodding towards Pa. "That's my husband, Gerald."

Gerald is not Pa's real name, but he'll know that's what she's calling him tonight. They had decided on names earlier, as they always do before a hunt. Tonight he's Gerald and she's Phyllis.

She allows the girl to lead her to the table, knowing that this is the most dangerous time. Knowing that if she and Pa are going to be noticed and remembered, then this is when it will happen. She doesn't think that they *will* be noticed, though. If any of the pub's customers are looking their way right now, their attention will be on the girl. She's the one who catches the eye. She's the beacon whose glare will reduce those she's with to dim silhouettes.

Ma knows that people are spectacularly unobservant. They *think* they remember everything until pressured to recount precise details, whereupon they discover that their recollections are hazy, that the finer points have become smudged and blurred.

Pa is hunched over *The Times*, which he has folded into quarters. He is doing the crossword, holding the newspaper in his left hand, a stub of pencil in his right. Pa has a look of intense concentration on his face, his eyes narrowed behind his spectacles. He doesn't look up as they approach the table. He appears to be lost in thought.

Ma knows that the girl will find the sight of Pa reassuring. The fact that he is engrossed in *The Times* crossword, and that he is wearing spectacles, will give her the impression that he is educated, reliable, unthreatening. The further fact that he appears not to have noticed their approach will cement this impression. The girl will be used to men staring at her, admiring her, assessing her physically. But Pa will seem to be above all that. She will think of him as a fatherly figure, someone to be trusted.

Only when their presence is too close to ignore does he look up. And then he barely glances at the girl before his attention focuses fully on his wife. His face creases in concern and he puts down his newspaper and pencil in one swift motion. Struggling to his feet, and wincing as he does so, he reaches out, as though to catch her should she fall.

"My dear," he says, his voice a gentle rumble, "whatever's the matter? You look terribly pale."

Ma tries to laugh it off, to wave it away, but she knows that the sound she makes is hollow, her movements feeble. "I'm fine," she says. "I just felt a bit dizzy, that's all. It's nothing."

Despite her words, Pa's face looks no less concerned. "Sit down, sit down," he urges, waving towards her chair.

Ma *does* sit down, plumping into the chair a little more weightily than she needs to. Pa's eyes rove anxiously over her face, and only then does he glance at the girl.

As if prompted, she begins to speak, the words spilling out of her. "I'm afraid it's my fault. I accidentally bumped into your wife and spilled my drink on her and made her drop her purse. She reached down to pick it up and went a bit dizzy. I have it here. Her purse I mean . . ."

She snatches it from her pocket, as if afraid that she might otherwise be accused of trying to steal it. She places it on the table, her face flushed.

Pa eyes the purse, and then looks up at the girl again. He takes his time before replying. When he does, his words are accompanied by a warm smile. "Thank you, Miss . . .?"

"Veronica," the girl says. "My friends call me Roni."

"Thank you, Veronica," Pa says. "You've been very kind."

Veronica demurs modestly and haltingly, but Ma cuts across her words with a groan. "I'm terribly sorry, Gerald," she says, "but would you mind getting me a drink? I'm feeling rather faint."

Pa immediately looks away from the girl as if he has entirely forgotten about her. As if all that concerns him now is the welfare of his beloved wife.

"Certainly, my dear," he says. "What would you like?"

"Oh, anything soft," she replies. "It doesn't matter."

"Right you are," he says, and turning awkwardly, he reaches for a walking stick propped against the wall. He hobbles from behind the table, leaning heavily on the stick. Wincing again, he lets out a low but quickly stifled grunt, which gives the impression that he is attempting to cover up the fact that his leg is causing him considerable pain.

Spotting this, the girl puts her glass down on the table and raises her hands, as though to physically impede his progress.

"Please," she says, "let me get you both a drink. It's the least I can do."

Pa smiles and shakes his head. "No, no, my dear, you've done more than enough. You go back to your friends."

The girl pauses. Pa knows he has given her a get-out clause, but he is not concerned; it is all part of the game. Though the pause seems prolonged, it is really no more than a second or two before the girl is shaking her head.

"Honestly," she says, "I'd *like* to buy you both a drink. Besides, my friend's not here yet. I was supposed to meet her ten minutes ago, but she hasn't turned up."

Pa looks at Ma, doubt on his face. Ma sighs, and wearily says, "Don't look at *me*, Gerald. *You* decide. But do it quickly, please. I really do need that drink."

"It's already decided," the girl says firmly. "I'm buying." She swivels to face the bar and throws a question back over her shoulder. "Gerald, what can I get you?"

"Oh . . . er . . . half a pint of bitter, please," he says, grunting as he lowers himself gingerly into his seat. It's a convincing performance, and one he maintains despite the fact that the girl is already marching back towards the bar and doesn't see it.

Ma and Pa sit in silence until the girl returns. They do not look at each other. The game is going well, though their faces betray no trace of triumph. They are both aware that there is a long way to go yet before the girl is theirs. If her friend arrives, which is more likely than not, then the girl will slip from their grasp. But the prospect does not concern them. Many such girls have slipped from their grasp over the years. The majority that do serve only to make the victory of procuring the few that don't all the sweeter.

Indeed, it amuses Ma and Pa to think that there are hundreds of girls alive today who have no idea how thin was the ice upon which they once skated.

No doubt most of those girls don't even remember the nice couple with whom they once had the briefest of encounters. If the friend of this girl, Veronica, appears as arranged, full of apologies for her lateness, Ma and Pa know that they will all too soon be forgotten. It doesn't bother them. It's the way things are. People are inherently selfish, inherently callous. They resent dwelling on the needs and misfortunes of others. Out of sight, out of mind.

The girl returns with the drinks, and after thanking her, Pa casually invites her to join them. The girl glances at the door, as if weighing up her chances of reaching it before they can bring her down (although both Ma and Pa know that she is actually wondering about her friend's whereabouts), and then gratefully accepts their invitation. She clearly feels less vulnerable in their company than she would do if she were waiting alone.

They chat, though because Ma is still feigning recovery, it is Pa and the girl who do most of the talking. Occasionally one or other of them will break off to ask Ma how she is feeling. "A bit better," she replies weakly, or "Not too bad." The girl texts her friend, but after receiving no reply calls her, only to reach a voicemail message. "Where are you?" she asks, her voice thin with frustration and restrained anger. She frowns at the phone as she puts it away. Ma and Pa look sympathetic.

Almost half an hour passes. Eventually Pa lifts his glass, tilts back his head and drains the last of his beer. Placing his glass back on the table with a decisive thump, he gives a gasp of satisfaction.

"That's my lot," he says, and smiles at Ma. "Shall we make tracks, Phyllis?"

Ma nods, then casts an anxious look at the girl. "But what about you, dear? What will you do?"

The girl looks momentarily indecisive, then straightens, shakes back her hair and sighs. "I might as well go too," she says. "It looks as though I've been stood up."

"Oh, dear, I wonder where your friend is," Ma says. "I hope nothing's happened to her."

The girl looks resigned rather than worried. Dismissively she says, "I'm sure she's fine. She's a bit like this, I'm afraid. Unreliable."

"Oh, dear," Ma says again.

The girl smiles, evidently touched by her concern. "It's okay. It's no big deal."

"I hope you haven't far to go?" Pa asks.

"No, not really. Fulwood Park. It's only a bus ride away."

Ma looks almost shyly at Pa. "We could give Veronica a lift, couldn't we, Gerald? We go right through Fulwood Park."

Pa looks a little doubtful. "Well, I *suppose* we could. But she might not want to, Phyllis. I mean, she doesn't really know us from Adam. We could be anyone."

Ma gives a silvery laugh. "Don't be silly, Gerald. You'll accept a lift, won't you, Veronica?"

The girl looks wary. "Well, I don't know . . ."

Frowning at Ma, Pa says, "Of course you don't. Don't pressure the poor girl, Phyllis. You're making her uncomfortable." Turning to the girl with a look of apology, he adds, "Don't feel as though you have to say yes, Veronica. We'd quite understand if you weren't keen. Wouldn't we, Phyllis?"

Ma looks a bit put out, like a child who feels she's been unfairly reprimanded. Glancing at her, the girl says quickly, "Well, obviously I'd love a lift, but only if you're absolutely sure . . ."

Ma beams. "Of *course* we're sure."

Pa looks at the girl and secretly raises his eyebrows in a *what-is-she-like?* gesture, making the girl smile. "That looks as though it's settled then," he says.

They leave with the girl, Pa moving slowly, aided by his walking stick, Ma with her hand resting lightly on his back. They don't look around to see whether anyone notices their departure. They know that even if they *have* been seen, witnesses will remember only false details: Pa's spectacles, his walking stick. Aside from that they'll recall only that Ma and Pa were a normal, middle-aged couple. Plain-looking and drably clothed. Nothing to distinguish them.

The night is cold. Ma thinks of the air like a thin, flexible sheet of ice closing over her face. The white vapour of her breath curls and dissipates, each exhalation a fragment of her life breaking free and instantly, irretrievably lost.

At least, she thinks, the girl's young, sweet breaths, which are currently coiling in the air, are more limited than her own. This pleases Ma. It gives her a sense of longevity, of immortality almost.

"Here we are," Pa says, gesturing down the dark street. He and Ma have parked their car around fifty metres from the pub, deliberately positioning it in the bowl of shadow between one glimmering street light and the next. Cloaked in darkness it is impossible to tell what colour the car is. Like its owners, it is drab and nondescript. Pa takes his key fob from his pocket and presses a button, and the car responds with a brief, complicit flash of its lights.

"You sit in the front, dear," Ma says. "Then you can give Gerald directions."

"Are you sure?" the girl asks.

"Oh, quite sure. Besides, I'll be able to spread out a bit in the back. Put my feet up."

They get into the car, Pa making a big show of easing his stiff leg into the footwell. Finally he's settled, whereupon he hands his walking stick to Ma in the back, pulls his seatbelt across his round stomach and clicks it into place. Beside his bulk the girl, waiting patiently, seems child-like. She has taken off her backpack, which now rests between her feet like a sleeping pet.

"Are we all set?" Pa says, glancing at the girl and then at Ma in the back. They both nod and he starts the engine.

Ma knows the girl will be relaxed, unsuspecting. Like *The Times* crossword, and Pa's spectacles, and his walking stick, she will find the interior of the car reassuring. It is clean and tidy, but not so pristine that it hints at obsession, at a need to control and dominate. There is a National Trust membership sticker in the top corner of the windscreen – symbolic of respectable, middle-class gentility – and a three-quarter-full packet of chewy mints in the shallow well between the seats.

There is nothing visible that is sharp, nothing that can be construed as a weapon. Ma and Pa are very careful about this. They make certain they are never in possession of any of the tools that they use on the girls. Even at home they keep the tools hidden, and restrict their activities to the basement. They pride themselves on their restraint, their attention to detail. It is thanks to their meticulous natures that they have never been caught.

They have been active for almost twenty-two years, and the light of suspicion has never once wavered in their direction. In the eyes of the world they are decent, law-abiding citizens. Good neighbours. Pillars of the community.

They make only one exception to their rule, and although it constitutes a tiny risk it is a necessary one. In a hidden compartment in the lining of her handbag Ma keeps a small hypodermic syringe filled with a strong, swift-acting anaesthetic. As Pa chats to the girl in the front seat, Ma takes the hypodermic from her handbag and removes the plastic cap that protects the needle. Then she leans forward ever so slightly, pushes the needle into the exposed flesh of the girl's neck and depresses the plunger.

So swift and skilled is she at this that the syringe is empty before the girl reacts. By the time she jerks forward in her seat, clapping her hand to her neck as if stung by an insect, Ma has withdrawn the needle and is settling back in her seat. She catches a glimpse of the girl's face as she twists, and relishes the brief expression of shock, accusation, and, yes, terrified realization in the girl's eyes. Then those eyes lose focus and the delicate peach-coloured petals of the eyelids slide closed over them. The girl's head nods forward and she slumps to one side in her seat, limp and compliant, her poise and vitality suddenly gone.

The anaesthetic affects the girls in different ways. The majority merely fall into a deep and abrupt sleep, though some lose muscular control to such an extent that they evacuate bladder and bowels. There was a girl four years ago who had an epileptic seizure, which almost resulted in Pa losing control of the car. And there were two girls who suffered such an adverse reaction to the drug that they died on the journey back to the house – a bitter disappointment for Ma and Pa, as it denied them their pleasure just when it seemed they were home and dry.

Steering the car with one hand, Pa reaches across and pushes the girl's head down so that it is beneath the level of the window. Now anyone who happens to glance casually at them when they drive past will not see an unconscious girl slumped in the front seat.

"I want to take my time with this one," Ma says. "I want to make her suffer."

Pa laughs. "You really hate the pretty ones, don't you?"

"I hate the ones who think they've got it all," Ma retorts. "Who think they're untouchable."

Ma and Pa are both eager to start their night's work, but Pa drives steadily, carefully. It wouldn't do to be pulled over for speeding, or to otherwise draw attention to themselves. In truth they live nowhere near Fulwood Park, and now that the girl is unconscious, Pa takes a right, and then another right, until they are heading in the opposite direction.

They lapse into silence, but are occupied by thoughts of how they will use the girl. Of the implements they will employ to penetrate her. Of how loudly they will make her scream. Of how much they will make her plead.

Their house is neat, modest, unassuming. They live in a quiet neighbourhood, suburban, respectable. The crime rate is low and the local children are generally well behaved. Each house is equipped with a small garden front and back, and its own garage. The streets are sparsely populated at this time of night, and indeed, as they pull into their cul-de-sac, Ma and Pa see only a single figure ahead of them – a man hunched in a bulky overcoat, a dog trotting at his side.

Pa slows the car as they approach the open gate into their own drive and reaches across the girl's body to snap open the glove compartment. He withdraws a slim black device the size of a mobile phone, points it out of the window and presses a button. Almost silently the door of the garage which abuts their house begins to ascend. Pa places the remote control in the well between the front seats and drives smoothly through the gate, up the drive and into the garage.

Even now Ma and Pa do not hurry. Though they are eager, their actions are rehearsed, methodical. Pa gets out of the car and closes the garage door with the remote control, before placing it back in the glove compartment. Ma waits until the door has descended far enough to conceal them from view before clicking on the light. Then, while she unlocks the inner door that leads directly into the kitchen, Pa unclips the girl's seatbelt and lifts her out of her seat. He drapes her over his shoulder in a fireman's lift, her body so limp that she resembles a rag doll. Her golden hair hangs between her dangling arms like a shimmering, silken waterfall.

Ma imagines burning off that hair with a blowtorch, continuing until the girl's scalp is raw and bleeding. She imagines the girl's flesh crisping like roasted pork, hot meat juices running down the girl's face and into her screeching mouth.

She chuckles at the prospect, the sound low and throaty with lust. As Pa carries the girl into the house, Ma snatches up the backpack, locks the car and switches off the garage light. By the time she switches on the kitchen light, Pa is already halfway across the room. He knows the house so well that he has already side-stepped the kitchen table in the dark.

"I'll take her down," he says. "You put the kettle on."

Ma nods. It is part of the ritual. Pa will take the girl to the basement and make her secure, then he will come back upstairs and the two of them will plan their evening's entertainment over a nice cup of tea.

Ma fills the kettle and switches it on. She hums contentedly as she takes two mugs down from the cupboard and drops a tea bag into each. To Pa's mug she adds two spoonfuls of sugar. It is a vice he has been unwilling to relinquish. It is because of him that she still buys biscuits – his favourites are chocolate HobNobs and bourbon creams. She worries about his heart, but at the age of fifty-six he is as strong as an ox. She thinks it is their joint hobby which keeps him young and fit. He does enjoy it so.

The kettle boils and she fills each mug three-quarters full. She pokes at the tea bags with a spoon, stirring them around. Hers she removes first. Pa likes his tea brick-red, just as his own father did, but Ma prefers hers the colour of sun-warmed flesh. She adds milk, then stirs the tea and drops the metal spoon into the sink. Carrying the mugs to the table, she wonders where Pa has got to.

A wriggle of alarm snakes through her. Surely he hasn't started without her? She shakes her head. No, he would never do that, they have always done everything together. Even when Pa is having his way with the girls at the beginning, he knows how much Ma likes to watch. Knows how she likes to savour the terror and revulsion on their faces, to hear them begging him to stop.

Even so, this particular girl is prettier than most, and Pa has his appetites. Perhaps he has been unable to resist a quick dabble with his fingers, or with his tongue. Ma *supposes* that would be understandable, but even so, she feels a little disappointed, a little hurt, at the prospect.

She puts the mugs on the table and turns towards the kitchen door, meaning to go to the top of the basement steps and call down to him. But as she turns she freezes, her heart lurching with shock, her eyes widening with astonishment.

The girl – Veronica – is standing in the kitchen doorway.

She looks neither groggy nor dishevelled nor confused. On the contrary, she appears fresh and alert, her eyes gleaming. There is even a half-smile on her face, as if she enjoys the impact her unexpected appearance has made.

A myriad questions rush instantly through Ma's head. What is the girl doing here? How did she escape? Where is Pa? How has the girl overcome the effects of the anaesthetic so quickly?

Ma wonders whether she should speak to the girl, lie to her, try to bluff it out. But there is something in the girl's expression that tells Ma she knows precisely what has been happening, and why. And so instead of speaking, Ma wheels towards the knife block beside the electric cooker, her hand already reaching for the jutting black handle of the carving knife.

Ma doesn't know how, but suddenly she is lying on the kitchen floor. It happens so abruptly that it is only in retrospect that she recalls being hit by a solid weight that moved so swiftly it might have been a car. Except that that is impossible. So what has happened? Has she been shot? Struck down by a sudden seizure or heart attack? Her ribs and back are hurting, her eyes are unfocused and she cannot move her arms. Then she blinks and sees that the girl is sitting astride her. Peering down at her with eyes that are glittering strangely, the girl's golden hair softly caresses Ma's face.

"You thought you were the hunters," the girl said, "but you're not. *I* am."

There is a blur of movement and suddenly everything goes black.

How long Ma is unconscious for she has no idea. When she comes to she is no longer lying on the kitchen floor. It takes several moments for her vision to focus, and when it does the first thing she sees are stone walls and a stone floor. Her thoughts are so jumbled that she doesn't immediately realize she is in her own basement. It is only when she spots Pa, in the centre of the room, strapped into the iron chair which they call The Throne, that she becomes fully aware of her surroundings.

Pa is slumped forward, groaning slightly, though Ma can see no obvious injuries to his body. There is no blood on his clothes, no bruises on his face. Yet somehow he has been overcome, restrained. How can this be?

It is not until Ma tries to move that the pain kicks in. As if it too has been sleeping, it awakens in her shoulders and back and ribs, threading glassily through her muscles, embedding itself in her bones, her joints. It swiftly rises to such a pitch that she cries out, and instinctively attempts to curl up, to draw her body inwards. But she cannot move. Her arms are locked in an upright position, her immovable feet planted firmly on the ground, a metre or more apart.

As the cramps set in, excruciating enough to reduce her cries to nothing but tortured gasps, she looks down and sees the shackles encircling her ankles. And suddenly she realizes she has been clamped to the wall, just as she in turn has clamped numerous girls to this same wall over the past twenty-two years.

She glances up, and although it is only a small movement it causes such agony to tear through her body that everything whites out for a second.

When her vision clears, seconds or perhaps minutes later, she sees the face of the girl swimming before her. At first she thinks it is an illusion, but then the girl speaks.

"You've been hanging there for a while," the girl says. "I'm sorry it's so uncomfortable. I think the dead weight of your body, pulling downward, has dislocated at least one of your shoulders."

Ma tries to respond, to vent her fury, or perhaps simply to plead for release, but the pain has robbed her of her ability to speak. The girl's face still swims in her vision. Ma sees regret there, compassion. The girl speaks again.

"I expect you're confused. Wondering what's happened. And I *know* you're in pain, for which I truly apologize. I mean, all things being equal, you probably deserve it. But I've never gone in for that eye for an eye Old Testament stuff. Just because *you* like inflicting pain doesn't mean that whoever metes out your punishment should get the same satisfaction from inflicting it on you. It'd be a pretty sick world if we *all* got gratification from the suffering of others, wouldn't it?" The girl smiles, as if she's made a joke. "A *sicker* world, I should say."

Ma watches the girl as she crosses the basement and comes to a halt in front of Pa. The girl peers into Pa's face, as if to check whether he is conscious, and then turns back to Ma.

"I ought to explain who I am," she says. "Or rather *what* I am. Because I can guarantee that you'll never have come across anything like me before. And I don't want you to get the wrong idea. I don't want you to think that I'm doing this because I *like* doing it, or even that I'm some kind of avenging angel, acting on behalf of all the girls you've killed. Although, having said that, I can't deny that there's a certain poetic justice to this situation, or that I don't feel *some* satisfaction in knowing that you'll never torture and kill another innocent girl. But as I say, that's not my main motivation for what I'm about to do. You see, for me, this is all about *survival*."

Ma is not sure whether she's momentarily blacked out, because all at once the girl is standing directly in front of her once more. Earnestly the girl says, "What you have to understand, Phyllis, is that there are two kinds of serial killer in this world. There are those that *choose* to kill, like you and Gerald, and there are those that *have* to. And when I say 'have to', I'm not talking about people who are driven to kill by some form of psychological deviance. No, I'm talking about killing in the same way that you would talk about eating or breathing. I'm talking about killing in the sense that if you didn't kill you would die. And I mean, *literally*, die. Because for some people killing is like oxygen, or food. For some people, there is no way to survive without it."

She pauses, peering into Ma's eyes. "I hope you're getting all this," she says. "I hope you understand what I'm saying. Because you see, Phyllis, *I'm* one of those people. Which doesn't mean that I'm cruel – on the contrary, I'd say I was quite compassionate. It just means . . . well, it's simply the way I am, the way I was born. I'm not a monster. I'm a human being, just like you. But I'm also . . . *different*. A freak of nature, I suppose you'd call me.

"I'm faster and stronger than you could ever be. I live longer – much longer – and I'm pretty much impervious to the illnesses that afflict most human beings, and also to the drugs that you use. I eat and drink only for the pleasure of it, not because I have to. My *real* sustenance, you see, as I've already said, comes from killing – or rather, not from the act of killing itself, but from absorbing the memories and emotions of fellow human beings at the point of death. Absorbing their *essence*."

She shrugs, as if to say: *I know it's crazy, but there you are.* "When I was growing up," she continues, "this was a big problem for me. I didn't *like* killing people, but I had to. For a while I survived on old people, who were nearing the end of their time, or people with terminal illnesses, who just wanted relief from their pain. Then I hit on the idea of feeding off those who feed off others. That way I get not only the memories and emotions of my chosen subjects, but the residual emotions of those on whom they've inflicted pain.

"Because that's the way it works, you see. The more extreme the memories and emotions, the longer they sustain me." She waves a hand between her captives. "I mean, you two will keep me going for simply *ages*. I won't have to kill again for a long time after this. Now, isn't it nice to know that out of all your evil some good will ultimately come? True, it's not much of a consolation to all the girls you've tortured and murdered over the years, but at least there's a *kind* of cosmic balance."

She smiles gently and says, "Right then, who's first? I can't pretend it won't hurt, but at least it'll be quicker than the ordeal you were planning for me." She raises her head and twitches her nose as if sniffing the air. "I'll start with you, Gerald, if I may? I don't wish to be cruel, but your wife is more frightened than you are, and when she sees what's in store for her she'll go out of her mind with terror. And that, frankly, will be all the sweeter for me. Now, are you ready? Brace yourself."

Ma opens her mouth, but she still can't scream, not even when the girl walks up to Pa, places her hands almost tenderly on the sides of his head and pushes her thumbs into his eyes.

Ma can't scream, but Pa certainly can.

Over the next few hours he screams more than enough for the both of them.

MICHAEL KELLY

The Beach

THE LONESOME BEACH. The shrieking gulls. The ceaseless rain.

Elspeth hears the rain, beating against the window in an incessant murmur. Rain is her religion now. Rain and the changing seasons. It's all she has left. It's all she believes in.

All too soon summer is over, she thinks. It's autumn now, the rainy season, and soon it will be winter. The seasons pass quickly. Elspeth sighs. The years pass quickly, too.

She moves to the front window. It's another grey day. For a moment all she can see is herself reflected back at her from the dark pane. She doesn't recognize the face. It's as if someone else, some other Elspeth, is outside on the damp lawn staring in at her impassively, as if there is another her, another world beyond the thin pane. And sometimes, alone in her house, staring out her window, she truly believes there is another world, a thin place of shadows and unreality.

She moves closer to the rain-streaked window, and as she does, one of the Elspeths disappears. Which one is the real me? she thinks.

The cottage is silent except for the rain and the beating of her heart. Outside, she hears a gull cry. She pictures its small red-lidded eyes, its curved yellow beak. Sometimes all she can hear is their shrieking.

There is a pot of stew simmering on the stove, its savoury tang hanging in the air. She's made too much stew – there's only her – but what she doesn't consume in a few days, she'll freeze. She takes her small comforts where she can.

Outside, the rain falls in a steady, soothing rhythm. It puddles on the green lawn, the cracked sidewalk, and bumpy grey road. It runs in the gutters.

On the street, a small child in yellow rain-gear is splashing through a puddle. Elspeth smiles. She can feel her heart beating in time to the rain. Watching the child play, something inside her flares briefly, a sweet pain. She hearkens back to her own childhood, when she still believed. Then she grew up. She wished she'd never grown up.

Elspeth stares out the window, eyes dry and unblinking. She'd imagined a different life, or different lives. She thought she'd marry, have children. Then she thought she'd travel, maybe actually go to China, for her father's sake and for herself. Go to Chile. She'd seen a documentary once about Rapa Nui, Easter Island, thousands of miles off the coast of Chile. Huge carved stone heads covered the island. They were a mystery. Because of their strange proportions and their geometry, everyone assumed they were just heads. But they weren't. They had bodies under the ground. They'd been buried up to their necks. Implacable stone faces peering out to the ocean. It always made her think of her father. She wished she could have gone to Easter Island or China.

The girl, Anna, is walking through puddles, kicking dead leaves, searching for frogs and looking for fat worms. Her mother had told her not to get soaked. "You're too old," she'd warned, "for playing in puddles." Anna hopes she"ll never be too old to play in the rain. Still, she's made sure to put on her mackintosh and galoshes. It wouldn't do to return wet. She would get a smack. Maybe two, to make up for not having a father.

Like Elspeth, the cottage is old and small. It hasn't changed. Even as a child, when the world seemed impossibly big, the cottage appeared small to Elspeth. That was its charm, she supposed. That, and the lonely beach that ran outside the back door. As a child she'd spend her weekends on the warm summer sand with her plastic bucket and shovel, digging, making sandcastles and moats, dreaming of far-off places. Back then, peering out to the far horizon where water met sky, the effect was of a wide, carnivorous smile, a thin wedge of unreality that thrilled and scared her.

The world was vast and cosmic. The cottage was small and insignificant. Still, she thinks, it's big enough for one, for her.

Elspeth watches the child, a girl, she thinks – what boy would wear yellow? – playing in the rain. It's late in the season for children. Most of the families have left. Most everyone has gone. And Elspeth . . . well, Elspeth is used to being alone.

Anna is whistling, poking at a worm with a stick, when the woman appears. The woman has a hood over her head, hiding her face in shadow, but Anna can see that the woman is smiling.

"Shouldn't you be gone?" the woman says, not unfriendly.

Anna straightens, blinks.

"Home, I mean," the woman says. "Away from here. Back to school."

Anna drops the stick, steps closer, squints up at the hooded woman. "We always come late, my mum and I," she says. "It's cheaper."

Elspeth considers, looks up and down the grey, empty street. "You shouldn't be out here," she says.

"I'm allowed," Anna says. "I like the rain. I"m going to be a meteorologist. Or a pilot."

Elspeth barks a laugh. The sound startles her. She can't recall the last time she laughed aloud. Perhaps there is hope for her yet. Perhaps she can reclaim some faith.

The rain is fat and unremitting. It streaks off Elspeth's rain hood and blurs her vision, as if she's crying. Overhead a gull cries, a white speck against the crumpled, dark sky. Elspeth shivers. "Would you like some lunch?" she asks. "Some stew?"

Her father ran away. Years later, her mother died. All she has left is the cottage and her memories.

Elspeth remembers the last weekend she'd spent with her father at the cottage before he left for good. They were on the beach. It was a sunny, cloudless day; blue skies and green water. The cool, salty breeze. The cry of gulls. He'd asked her if she wanted to dig to China. "Let's see if we can dig to the other side of the world," her father said. And they tried.

Her father retrieved a shovel from the bed of his pick-up truck. They took turns digging the hole, laughing in the August sun.

After a time, exhausted but happy, Elspeth stopped. "We'll never make it," she said, feigning disappointment.

Her father smiled, picked her up and placed her in the hole. Elspeth squirmed, kicked her legs, laughed. "We'll bury you," he said. "Just to your neck. Promise." And he began to fill in the hole. Elspeth was in the damp hole, buried to her neck. "Look at you," her father said. "From a distance, you could be a discarded beachball. We best make sure no one tries to kick you." He smiled. "Hmmm, perhaps I'll go in for a bit, leave you to the gulls. 'Bye, El," her father said, turning.

"Dad, no!"

He turned back. "El, I'm joking. You know that." He dug her out of the hole, hugged her tight, kissed her forehead. "I would never leave you."

But he did leave her. A child shouldn't grow up without a father, she thinks. A child should never grow up.

"Is it good?" Elspeth asks the girl.

Anna looks up from the bowl of stew. "Yes. Delicious. My mum doesn't cook. Not like this. Her speciality is grilled cheese. Heck, even I can make grilled cheese. But I like grilled cheese."

"And your father?" Elspeth asks.

Anna blinks, spoons stew into her mouth, swallows. "Don't know," she says. "Mum says he got scared. Took off." She rests the spoon in the bowl. "It's okay. I don't mind. My mum tries."

Elspeth turns to Anna. "Would you like to go to the beach?" Then, "Would you like to go to China?"

"When I'm a pilot," Anna says, "I'm going to travel the world. When I'm grown up."

"I hope you never grow up," Elspeth whispers.

Anna brushes a strand of wet hair away from her eyes, squints at Elspeth, then looks toward the door.

Elspeth stares at the young, skinny thing. "Are you strong, Anna? Can you dig? Will you help me?"

"I have to go now," Anna says.

Once, long ago, when she was a young woman who still had faith in the world, there was a boy, Matthew. She'd met him on holiday, here at the cottage. He was on the beach, alone, tall and tan, blond

and bright-eyed. On the beach, at night, he kissed her. And she
believed in the power of love. Then, like summer itself, it ended.

"It's been fun," Matthew said, smiling, idly kicking the sand,
"but I have to go now."

It was a grey day. The wind howled, and the gulls squawked.
The beach was barren save for the two of them. The sand was a
gritty irritant. It blew in Elspeth's face and brought tears to her
eyes. She blinked, squeezed Matthew's hand. "You'll visit, keep in
touch?" She hated the pleading tone in her voice.

Matthew shrugged his shoulders, released Elspeth's hand. "It
was just a summer fling. Nothing more."

"Please," she said, "don't go."

"You need to grow up, El," he said. "I have to go now."

Then he was gone.

Elspeth stood alone on the dark beach with the wind and the
gulls. Dark clouds filled the sky. Then it rained. Still she stood in
the cold rain, unblinking, unmoving, staring at nothing. Alone.

It's raining, a pounding against the glass like gull wings. Elspeth
moves to the back window. The beach is a thin dark finger of soft
bone. Rain blurs the windowpane, and for a moment all she can
see is herself reflected back to her from the dirty glass. She doesn't
recognize her face. It's as if some other Elspeth is out there on the
dark sand staring in at her.

She moves closer and one of the Elspeths disappears. She
leans against the cool glass, squints.

She sees a pale world like stretched canvas, a thin veil, grey and
unending, no line on the horizon.

She sees the water, dark and rumpled muslin, heaving.

She sees the wet black sand, a dark round shape, and the
shrieking, hungry gulls.

The long, empty beach.

The ceaseless rain.

ROBERT BLOCH

Yours Truly, Jack the Ripper

I

I LOOKED At the stage Englishman. He looked at me.

"Sir Guy Hollis?" I asked.

"Indeed. Have I the pleasure of addressing John Carmody, the psychiatrist?"

I nodded. My eyes swept over the figure of my distinguished visitor. Tall, lean, sandy-haired – with the traditional tufted moustache. And the tweeds. I suspected a monocle concealed in a vest pocket, and wondered if he'd left his umbrella in the outer office.

But more than that, I wondered what the devil had impelled Sir Guy Hollis of the British Embassy to seek out a total stranger here in Chicago.

Sir Guy didn't help matters any as he sat down. He cleared his throat, glanced around nervously, tapped his pipe against the side of the desk. Then he opened his mouth.

"Mr Carmody," he said, "have you ever heard of – Jack the Ripper?"

"The murderer?" I asked.

"Exactly. The greatest monster of them all. Worse than Springheel Jack or Crippen. Jack the Ripper. Red Jack."

"I've heard of him," I said.

"Do you know his history?"

"Listen, Sir Guy," I muttered. "I don't think we'll get any place swapping old wives' tales about famous crimes of history."

Another bull's eye. He took a deep breath.

"This is no old wives' tale. It's a matter of life or death."

He was so wrapped up in his obsession he even talked that way. Well – I was willing to listen. We psychiatrists get paid for listening.

"Go ahead," I told him. "Let's have the story."

Sir Guy lit a cigarette and began to talk.

"London, 1888," he began. "Late-summer and early-autumn. That was the time. Out of nowhere came the shadowy figure of Jack the Ripper – a stalking shadow with a knife, prowling through London's East End. Haunting the squalid dives of Whitechapel, Spitalfields. Where he came from no one knew. But he brought death. Death in a knife.

"Six times that knife descended to slash the throats and bodies of London's women. Drabs and alley sluts. August the seventh was the date of the first butchery. They found her body lying there with thirty-nine stab wounds. A ghastly murder. On August the thirty-first, another victim. The press became interested. The slum inhabitants were more deeply interested still.

"Who was this unknown killer who prowled in their midst and struck at will in the deserted alleyways of night-town? And what was more important – when would he strike again?

"September the eighth was the date. Scotland Yard assigned special detectives. Rumours ran rampant. The atrocious nature of the slayings was the subject of shocked speculation.

"The killer used a knife – expertly. He cut throats and removed – certain portions – of the bodies after death. He chose victims and settings with a fiendish deliberation. No one saw him or heard him. But watchmen making their grey rounds in the dawn would stumble across the hacked and horrid thing that was the Ripper's handiwork.

"Who was he? What was he? A mad surgeon? A butcher? An insane scientist? A pathological degenerate escaped from an asylum? A deranged nobleman? A member of the London police?

"Then the poem appeared in the newspapers. The anonymous poem, designed to put an end to speculation – but which only aroused public interest in a further frenzy. A mocking little stanza:

> *I'm not a butcher, I'm not a Yid*
> *Nor yet a foreign skipper,*
> *But I'm your own true loving friend,*
> *Yours truly – Jack the Ripper.*

"And on September the thirtieth, two more throats were slashed open."

I interrupted Sir Guy for a moment.

"Very interesting," I commented. I'm afraid a faint hint of sarcasm crept into my voice.

He winced, but didn't falter in his narrative.

"There was silence, then, in London for a time. Silence, and a nameless fear. When would Red Jack strike again? They waited through October. Every figment of fog concealed his phantom presence. Concealed it well – for nothing was learned of the Ripper's identity, or his purpose. The drabs of London shivered in the raw wind of early-November. Shivered, and were thankful for the coming of each morning's sun.

"On November the ninth they found her in her room. She lay there very quietly, limbs neatly arranged. And beside her, with equal neatness, were laid her head and heart. The Ripper had outdone himself in execution.

"Then, panic. But needless panic. For though press, police, and populace alike waited in sick dread, Jack the Ripper did not strike again.

"Months passed. A year. The immediate interest died, but not the memory. They said Jack had skipped to America. That he had committed suicide. They said – and they wrote. They've written ever since. Theories, hypotheses, arguments, treatises. But to this day no one knows who Jack the Ripper was. Or why he killed. Or why he stopped killing."

Sir Guy was silent. Obviously he expected some comment from me.

"You tell the story well," I remarked. "Though with a slight emotional bias."

"I've got all the documents," said Sir Guy Hollis. "I've made a collection of existing data and studied it."

I stood up. "Well," I yawned, in mock fatigue, "I've enjoyed your little bedtime story a great deal, Sir Guy. It was kind of you to abandon your duties at the British Embassy to drop in on a poor psychiatrist and regale him with your anecdotes."

Goading him always did the trick.

"I suppose you want to know why I'm interested?" he snapped.

"Yes. That's exactly what I'd like to know. Why are you interested?"

"Because," said Sir Guy Hollis, "I am on the trail of Jack the Ripper now. I think he's here – in Chicago!"

I sat down again. This time I did the blinking act.

"Say that again," I stuttered.

"Jack the Ripper is alive, in Chicago, and I'm out to find him."

"Wait a minute," I said. "Wait – a – minute!"

He wasn't smiling. It wasn't a joke.

"See here," I said. "What was the date of these murders?"

"August to November, 1888."

"1888? But if Jack the Ripper were an able-bodied man in 1888, he'd surely be dead today! Why look, man – if he were merely born in that year, he'd be fifty-seven years old today!"

"Would he?" smiled Sir Guy Hollis. "Or should I say, 'Would she?' Because Jack the Ripper may have been a woman. Or any number of things."

"Sir Guy," I said. "You came to the right person when you looked me up. You definitely need the services of a psychiatrist."

"Perhaps. Tell me, Mr Carmody, do you think I'm crazy?"

I looked at him and shrugged. But I had to give him a truthful answer.

"Frankly – no."

"Then you might listen to the reasons I believe Jack the Ripper is alive today."

"I might."

"I've studied these cases for thirty years. Been over the actual ground. Talked to officials. Talked to friends and acquaintances of the poor drabs who were killed. Visited men and women in the neighbourhood. Collected an entire library of material touching on Jack the Ripper. Studied all the wild theories or crazy notions.

"I learned a little. Not much, but a little. I won't bore you with my conclusions. But there was another branch of enquiry that yielded more fruitful return. I have studied unsolved crimes. Murders.

"I could show you clippings from the papers of half the world's great cities. San Francisco. Shanghai. Calcutta. Omsk. Paris. Berlin. Pretoria. Cairo. Milan. Adelaide.

"The trail is there, the pattern. Unsolved crimes. Slashed throats of women. With the peculiar disfigurations and removals. Yes, I've followed a trail of blood. From New York westward across the continent. Then to the Pacific. From there to Africa. During the World War of 1914–18 it was Europe. After that, South America. And since 1930, the United States again. Eighty-seven such murders – and to the trained criminologist, all bear the signs of the Ripper's handiwork.

"Recently there were the so-called Cleveland torso slayings. Remember? A shocking series. And finally, two recent deaths in Chicago. Within the past six months. One out on South Dearborn. The other somewhere up on Halsted. Same type of crime, same technique. I tell you, there are unmistakable indications in all these affairs – indications of the work of Jack the Ripper!"

I smiled.

"A very tight theory," I said. "I'll not question your evidence at all, or the deductions you draw. You're the criminologist, and I'll take your word for it. Just one thing remains to be explained. A minor point, perhaps, but worth mentioning."

"And what is that?" asked Sir Guy.

"Just how could a man of, let us say, eighty-five years commit these crimes? For if Jack the Ripper was around thirty in 1888 and lived, he'd be eighty-five today."

Sir Guy Hollis was silent. I had him there. But—

"*Suppose he didn't get any older?*" whispered Sir Guy.

"What's that?"

"Suppose Jack the Ripper didn't grow old ? Suppose he is still a young man today?"

"All right," I said. "I'll suppose for a moment. Then I'll stop supposing and call for my nurse to restrain you."

"I'm serious," said Sir Guy.

"They all are," I told him. "That's the pity of it all, isn't it? They know they hear voices and see demons. But we lock them up just the same."

It was cruel, but it got results. He rose and faced me.

"It's a crazy theory, I grant you," he said. "All the theories about the Ripper are crazy. The idea that he was a doctor. Or a maniac. Or a woman. The reasons advanced for such beliefs are flimsy enough. There's nothing to go by. So why should my notion be any worse?"

"Because people grow older," I reasoned with him. "Doctors, maniacs, and women alike."

"What about – *sorcerers?*"

"Sorcerers?"

"Necromancers. Wizards. Practitioners of Black Magic?"

"What's the point?"

"I studied," said Sir Guy. "I studied everything. After a while I began to study the dates of the murders. The pattern those dates formed. The rhythm. The solar, lunar, stellar rhythm. The sidereal aspect. The astrological significance."

He was crazy. But I still listened.

"Suppose Jack the Ripper didn't murder for murder's sake alone? Suppose he wanted to make – a sacrifice?"

"What kind of a sacrifice?"

Sir Guy shrugged. "It is said that if you offer blood to the dark gods they grant boons. Yes, if a blood offering is made at the proper time – when the moon and the stars are right – and with the proper ceremonies – they grant boons. Boons of youth. Eternal youth."

"But that's nonsense!"

"No. That's – Jack the Ripper."

I stood up. "A most interesting theory," I told him. "But Sir Guy – there's one thing I'm interested in. Why do you come here and tell it to me? I'm not an authority on witchcraft. I'm not a police official or criminologist. I'm a practising psychiatrist. What's the connection?"

Sir Guy smiled.

"You are interested, then?"

"Well, yes. There must be some point."

"There is. But I wished to be assured of your interest first. Now I can tell you my plan."

"And just what is that plan?"

Sir Guy gave me a long look. Then he spoke.

"John Carmody," he said, "you and I are going to capture Jack the Ripper."

II

That's the way it happened. I've given the gist of that first interview in all its intricate and somewhat boring detail, because I
think it's important. It helps to throw some light on Sir Guy's
character and attitude. And in view of what happened after that—

But I'm coming to those matters.

Sir Guy's thought was simple. It wasn't even a thought. Just a
hunch.

"You know the people here," he told me. "I've enquired. That's
why I came to you as the ideal man for my purpose. You number
amongst your acquaintances many writers, painters, poets. The
so-called intelligentsia. The Bohemians. The lunatic fringe from
the near north side.

"For certain reasons – never mind what they are – my clues
lead me to infer that Jack the Ripper is a member of that element.
He chooses to pose as an eccentric. I've a feeling that with you to
take me around and introduce me to your set, I might hit upon
the right person."

"It's all right with me," I said. "But just how are you going to
look for him? As you say, he might be anybody, anywhere. And
you have no idea what he looks like. He might be young or old.
Jack the Ripper – a Jack of all trades? Rich man, poor man, beggar
man, thief, doctor, lawyer – how will you know?"

"We shall see." Sir Guy sighed heavily. "But I must find him.
At once."

"Why the hurry?"

Sir Guy sighed again. "Because in two days he will kill again."

"Are you sure?"

"Sure as the stars. I've plotted this chart, you see. All of the
murders correspond to certain astrological rhythm patterns. If, as
I suspect, he makes a blood sacrifice to renew his youth, he must
murder within two days. Notice the pattern of his first crimes in
London. August the seventh. Then August the thirty-first.
September the eighth. September the thirtieth. November the
ninth. Intervals of twenty-four days, nine days, twenty-two days
– he killed two this time – and then forty days. Of course there
were crimes in between. There had to be. But they weren't discovered and pinned on him.

"At any rate, I've worked out a pattern for him, based on all my data. And I say that within the next two days he kills. So I must seek him out, somehow, before then."

"And I'm still asking you what you want me to do?"

"Take me out," said Sir Guy. "Introduce me to your friends. Take me to parties."

"But where do I begin? As far as I know, my artistic friends, despite their eccentricities, are all normal people."

"So is the Ripper. Perfectly normal. Except on certain nights." Again that faraway look in Sir Guy's eyes. "Then he becomes an ageless pathological monster, crouching to kill, on evenings when the stars blaze down in the blazing patterns of death."

"All right," I said. "All right. I'll take you to parties, Sir Guy. I want to go myself, anyway. I need the drinks they'll serve there, after listening to your kind of talk."

We made our plans. And that evening I took him over to Lester Baston's studio.

As we ascended to the penthouse roof in the elevator I took the opportunity to warn Sir Guy.

"Baston's a real screwball," I cautioned him. "So are his guests. Be prepared for anything and everything."

"I am." Sir Guy Hollis was perfectly serious. He put his hand in his trouser pocket and pulled out a gun.

"What the—" I began.

"If I see him I'll be ready," Sir Guy said. He didn't smile, either.

"But you can't go running around at a party with a loaded revolver in your pocket, man!"

"Don't worry, I won't behave foolishly."

I wondered. Sir Guy Hollis was not, to my way of thinking, a normal man.

We stepped out of the elevator, went toward Baston's apartment door.

"By the way," I murmured, "just how do you wish to be introduced? Shall I tell them who you are and what you are looking for?"

"I don't care. Perhaps it would be best to be frank."

"But don't you think that the Ripper – if by some miracle he or she is present – will immediately get the wind up and take cover?"

"I think the shock of the announcement that I am hunting the Ripper would provoke some kind of betraying gesture on his part," said Sir Guy.

"You'd make a pretty good psychiatrist yourself," I conceded. "It's a fine theory. But I warn you, you're going to be in for a lot of ribbing. This is a wild bunch."

Sir Guy smiled.

"I'm ready," he announced. "I have a little plan of my own. Don't be shocked at anything I do," he warned me.

I nodded and knocked on the door.

Baston opened it and poured out into the hall. His eyes were as red as the maraschino cherries in his Manhattan. He teetered back and forth regarding us very gravely. He squinted at my square-cut homburg hat and Sir Guy's moustache.

"Aha," he intoned. "The Walrus and the Carpenter."

I introduced Sir Guy.

"Welcome," said Baston, gesturing us inside with over-elaborate courtesy. He stumbled after us into the garish parlour.

I stared at the crowd that moved restlessly through the fog of cigarette smoke.

It was the shank of the evening for this mob. Every hand held a drink. Every face held a slightly hectic flush. Over in one corner the piano was going full blast, but the imperious strains of the March from *The Love for Three Oranges* couldn't drown out the profanity from the crap-game in the other corner.

Prokofiev had no chance against African polo, and one set of ivories rattled louder than the other.

Sir Guy got a monocle-full right away. He saw LaVerne Gonnister, the poetess, hit Hymie Kralik in the eye. He saw Hymie sit down on the floor and cry until Dick Pool accidentally stepped on his stomach as he walked through to the dining room for a drink.

He heard Nadia Vilinoff the commercial artist tell Johnny Odcutt that she thought his tattooing was in dreadful taste, and he saw Barclay Melton crawl under the dining-room table with Johnny Odcutt's wife.

His zoological observations might have continued indefinitely if Lester Baston hadn't stepped to the centre of the room and called for silence by dropping a vase on the floor.

"We have distinguished visitors in our midst," bawled Lester, waving his empty glass in our direction. "None other than the Walrus and the Carpenter. The Walrus is Sir Guy Hollis, a something-or-other from the British Embassy. The Carpenter, as you all know, is our own John Carmody, the prominent dispenser of libido liniment."

He turned and grabbed Sir Guy by the arm, dragging him to the middle of the carpet. For a moment I thought Hollis might object, but a quick wink reassured me. He was prepared for this.

"It is our custom, Sir Guy," said Baston, loudly, "to subject our new friends to a cross-examination. Just a little formality at these very formal gatherings, you understand. Are you prepared to answer questions?"

Sir Guy nodded and grinned.

"Very well," Baston muttered. "Friends – I give you this bundle from Britain. Your witness."

Then the ribbing started. I meant to listen, but at that moment Lydia Dare saw me and dragged me off into the vestibule for one of those Darling-I-waited-for-your-call-all-day routines.

By the time I got rid of her and went back, the impromptu quiz session was in full swing. From the attitude of the crowd, I gathered that Sir Guy was doing all right for himself.

Then Baston himself interjected a question that upset the apple-cart.

"And what, may I ask, brings you to our midst tonight? What is your mission, O Walrus?"

"I'm looking for Jack the Ripper."

Nobody laughed.

Perhaps it struck them all the way it did me. I glanced at my neighbours and began to *wonder*.

LaVerne Gonnister. Hymie Kralik. Harmless. Dick Pool. Nadia Vilinoff. Johnny Odcutt and his wife. Barclay Melton. Lydia Dare. All harmless.

But that forced smile on Dick Pool's face! And that sly, self-conscious smirk that Barclay Melton wore!

Oh, it was absurd, I grant you. But for the first time I saw these people in a new light. I wondered about their lives – their secret lives beyond the scenes of parties.

How many of them were playing a part, concealing something?

Who here would worship Hecate and grant that horrid goddess the dark boon of blood?

Even Lester Baston might be masquerading.

The mood was upon us all, for a moment. I saw questions flicker in the circle of eyes around the room.

Sir Guy stood there, and I could swear he was fully conscious of the situation he'd created, and enjoyed it.

I wondered idly just what was *really* wrong with him. Why he had this odd fixation concerning Jack the Ripper. Maybe he was hiding secrets, too . . .

Baston, as usual, broke the mood. He burlesqued it.

"The Walrus isn't kidding, friends," he said. He slapped Sir Guy on the back and put his arm around him as he orated. "Our English cousin is really on the trail of the fabulous Jack the Ripper. You all remember Jack the Ripper, I presume? Quite a cut-up in the old days, as I recall. Really had some ripping good times when he went out on a tear.

"The Walrus has some idea that the Ripper is still alive, probably prowling around Chicago with a Boy Scout knife. In fact – " Baston paused impressively and shot it out in a rasping stage-whisper "– in fact, he has reason to believe that Jack the Ripper might even be right here in our midst tonight."

There was the expected reaction of giggles and grins. Baston eyed Lydia Dare reprovingly. "You girls needn't laugh," he smirked. "Jack the Ripper might be a woman, too, you know. Sort of a Jill the Ripper."

"You mean you actually suspect one of us?" shrieked LaVerne Gonnister, simpering up at Sir Guy. "But that Jack the Ripper person disappeared ages ago, didn't he? In 1888?"

"Aha!" interrupted Baston. "How do you know so much about it, young lady? Sounds suspicious! Watch her, Sir Guy – she may not be as young as she appears. These lady poets have dark pasts."

The tension was gone, the mood was shattered, and the whole thing was beginning to degenerate into a trivial party joke. The man who had played the March was eyeing the piano with a Scherzo gleam in his eye that augured ill for Prokofiev. Lydia Dare was glancing at the kitchen, waiting to make a break for another drink.

Then Baston caught it.

"Guess what?" he yelled. "The Walrus has a gun."

His embracing arm had slipped and encountered the hard outline of the gun in Sir Guy's pocket. He snatched it out before Hollis had the opportunity to protest.

I stared hard at Sir Guy, wondering if this thing had carried far enough. But he flicked a wink my way and I remembered he had told me not to be alarmed.

So I waited as Baston broached a drunken inspiration.

"Let's play fair with our friend the Walrus," he cried. "He came all the way from England to our party on this mission. If none of you is willing to confess, I suggest we give him a chance to find out – the hard way."

"What's up?" asked Johnny Odcutt.

"I'll turn out the lights for one minute. Sir Guy can stand here with the gun. If anyone in this room is the Ripper, he can either run for it or take the opportunity to – well, eradicate his pursuer. Fair enough?"

It was even sillier than it sounds, but it caught the popular fancy. Sir Guy's protests went unheard in the ensuing babble. And before I could stride over and put in my two cents' worth, Lester Baston had reached the light switch.

"Don't anybody move," he announced, with fake solemnity. "For one minute we will remain in darkness – perhaps at the mercy of a killer. At the end of that time, I'll turn up the lights again and look for bodies. Choose your partners, ladies and gentlemen."

The lights went out.

Somebody giggled.

I heard footsteps in the darkness. Mutterings.

A hand brushed my face.

The watch on my wrist ticked violently. But even louder, rising above it, I heard another thumping. The beating of my heart.

Absurd. Standing in the dark with a group of tipsy fools. And yet there was real terror lurking here, rustling through the velvet blackness.

Jack the Ripper prowled in darkness like this. And Jack the Ripper had a knife. Jack the Ripper had a madman's brain and a madman's purpose.

But Jack the Ripper was dead, dead and dust these many years – by every human law.

Only there are no human laws when you feel yourself in the darkness, when the darkness hides and protects and the outer mask slips off your face and you feel something welling up within you, a brooding shapeless purpose that is brother to the blackness.

Sir Guy Hollis shrieked.

There was a gristly thud.

Baston had the lights on.

Everybody screamed.

Sir Guy Hollis lay sprawled on the floor in the centre of the room. The gun was still clutched in his hand.

I glanced at the faces, marvelling at the variety of expressions human beings can assume when confronting horror.

All the faces were present in the circle. Nobody had fled. And yet Sir Guy Hollis lay there . . .

LaVerne Gonnister was wailing and hiding her face.

"All right."

Sir Guy rolled over and jumped to his feet. He was smiling.

"Just an experiment, eh? If Jack the Ripper *were* among those present, and thought I had been murdered, he would have betrayed himself in some way when the lights went on and he saw me lying there.

"I am convinced of your individual and collective innocence. Just a gentle spoof, my friends."

Hollis stared at the goggling Baston and the rest of them crowding in behind him.

"Shall we leave, John?" he called to me. "It's getting late, I think."

Turning, he headed for the closet. I followed him. Nobody said a word.

It was a pretty dull party after that.

III

I met Sir Guy the following evening as we agreed, on the corner of 29th and South Halsted.

After what had happened the night before, I was prepared for almost anything. But Sir Guy seemed matter-of-fact enough as he stood huddled against a grimy doorway and waited for me to appear.

"Boo!" I said, jumping out suddenly. He smiled. Only the betraying gesture of his left hand indicated that he'd instinctively reached for his gun when I startled him.

"All ready for our wild goose chase?" I asked.

"Yes." He nodded. "I'm glad that you agreed to meet me without asking questions," he told me. "It shows you trust my judgement." He took my arm and edged me along the street slowly.

"It's foggy tonight, John," said Sir Guy Hollis. "Like London." I nodded.

"Cold, too, for November."

I nodded again and half-shivered my agreement.

"Curious," mused Sir Guy. "London fog and November. The place and the time of the last Ripper murders."

I grinned through darkness. "Let me remind you, Sir Guy, that this isn't London, but Chicago. And it isn't November, 1888. It's over fifty years later."

Sir Guy returned my grin, but without mirth. "I'm not so sure, at that," he murmured. "Look about you. These tangled alleys and twisted streets. They're like the East End. Mitre Square. And surely they are as ancient as fifty years, at least."

"You're in the coloured neighbourhood off South Clark Street," I said, shortly. "And why you dragged me down here, I still don't know."

"It's a hunch," Sir Guy admitted. "Just a hunch on my part, John. I want to wander around down here. There's the same geographical conformation in these streets as in those courts where the Ripper roamed and slew. That's where we'll find him, John. Not in the bright lights of the Bohemian neighbourhood, but down here in the darkness. The darkness, where he waits and crouches."

"Is that why you brought a gun?" I asked. I was unable to keep a trace of sarcastic nervousness from my voice. All of this talk, this incessant obsession with Jack the Ripper, got on my nerves more than I cared to admit.

"We may need a gun," said Sir Guy, gravely. "After all, tonight is the appointed night."

I sighed. We wandered on through the foggy, deserted streets. Here and there a dim light burned above a gin-mill doorway. Otherwise, all was darkness and shadow. Deep, gaping alleyways loomed as we proceeded down a slanting side-street.

We crawled through that fog, alone and silent, like two tiny maggots floundering within a shroud.

When that thought hit me, I winced. The atmosphere was beginning to get *me,* too. If I didn't watch my step I'd go as loony as Sir Guy.

"Can't you see there's not a soul around these streets?" I said, tugging at his coat impatiently.

"He's bound to come," said Sir Guy. "He'll be drawn here. This is what I've been looking for. A *genius loci.* An evil spot that attracts evil. Always, when he slays, it's in the slums.

"You see, that must be one of his weaknesses. He has a fascination with squalor. Besides, the women he needs for sacrifice are more easily found in the dives and stewpots of a great city."

I smiled. "Well, let's go into one of the dives or stewpots," I suggested. "I'm cold. Need a drink. This damned fog gets into your bones. You Britishers can stand it, but I like warmth and dry heat."

We emerged from our side-street and stood upon the threshold of an alley.

Through the white clouds of mist ahead, I discerned a dim blue light, a naked bulb dangling from a beer sign above an alley tavern.

"Let's take a chance," I said. "I'm beginning to shiver."

"Lead the way," said Sir Guy. I led him down the alley passage. We halted before the door of the dive.

"What are you waiting for?" he asked.

"Just looking in," I told him. "This is a tough neighbourhood, Sir Guy. Never know what you're liable to run into. And I'd prefer we didn't get into the wrong company. Some of these Negro places resent white customers."

"Good idea, John."

I finished my inspection through the doorway. "Looks deserted," I murmured. "Let's try it."

We entered a dingy bar. A feeble light flickered above the counter and railing, but failed to penetrate the further gloom of the back booths.

A gigantic Negro lolled across the bar – a black giant with prognathous jaw and ape-like torso. He scarcely stirred as we came in, but his eyes flicked open quite suddenly and I knew he noted our presence and was judging us.

"Evening," I said.

He took his time before replying. Still sizing us up. Then, he grinned.

"Evening, gents. What's your pleasure?"

"Gin," I said. "Two gins. It's a cold night."

"That's right, gents."

He poured, I paid, and took the glasses over to one of the booths. We wasted no time in emptying them. The fiery liquor warmed.

I went over to the bar and got the bottle. Sir Guy and I poured ourselves another drink. The big Negro went back into his doze, with one wary eye half-open against any sudden activity.

The clock over the bar ticked on. The wind was rising outside, tearing the shroud of fog to ragged shreds. Sir Guy and I sat in the warm booth and drank our gin.

He began to talk, and the shadows crept up about us to listen.

He rambled a great deal. He went over everything he'd said in the office when I met him, just as though I hadn't heard it before. The poor devils with obsessions are like that.

I listened very patiently. I poured Sir Guy another drink. And another.

But the liquor only made him more talkative. How he did run on! About ritual killings and prolonging the life unnaturally – the whole fantastic tale came out again. And, of course, he maintained his unyielding conviction that the Ripper was abroad tonight.

I suppose I was guilty of goading him.

"Very well," I said, unable to keep the impatience from my voice. "Let us say that your theory is correct – even though we must overlook every natural law and swallow a lot of superstition to give it any credence.

"But let us say, for the sake of argument, that you are right. Jack the Ripper was a man who discovered how to prolong his own life through making human sacrifices. He did travel around the world as you believe. He is in Chicago now and he is planning to kill. In other words, let us suppose that everything you claim is gospel truth. So what?"

"What do you mean, 'So what'?" said Sir Guy.

"I mean – so what?" I answered. "If all this is true, it still doesn't prove that by your sitting down in a dingy gin-mill on the South Side, Jack the Ripper is going to walk in here and let you kill him, or turn him over to the police. And come to think of it, I don't even know now just what you intend to *do* with him, if you ever did find him."

Sir Guy gulped his gin. "I'd capture the bloody swine," he said. "Capture him and turn him over to the government, together with all the papers and documentary evidence I've collected against him over a period of many years. I've spent a fortune investigating this affair, I tell you, a fortune! His capture will mean the solution of hundreds of unsolved crimes, of that I am convinced.

"I tell you, a mad beast is loose in this world! An ageless, eternal beast, sacrificing to Hecate and the dark gods!"

In vino veritas. Or was all this babbling the result of too much gin? It didn't matter. Sir Guy Hollis had another. I sat there and wondered what to do with him. The man was rapidly working up to a climax of hysterical drunkenness.

"One other point," I said, more for the sake of conversation than in any hopes of obtaining information. "You still don't explain how it is that you hope just to blunder into the Ripper."

"He'll be around," said Sir Guy. "I'm psychic. I know."

Sir Guy wasn't psychic. He was maudlin.

The whole business was beginning to infuriate me. We'd been sitting here an hour, and during all this time I'd been forced to play nursemaid and audience to a babbling idiot. After all, he wasn't a regular patient of mine.

"That's enough," I said, putting out my hand as Sir Guy reached for the half-emptied bottle again. "You've had plenty. Now I've got a suggestion to make. Let's call a cab and get out of here. It's getting late and it doesn't look as though your elusive friend is going to put in an appearance. Tomorrow, if I were you, I'd plan to turn all those papers and documents over to the FBI. If you're so convinced of the truth of your wild theory, they are competent to make a very thorough investigation, and find your man."

"No." Sir Guy was drunkenly obstinate. "No cab."

"But let's get out of here anyway," I said, glancing at my watch. "It's past midnight."

He sighed, shrugged, and rose unsteadily. As he started for the door, he tugged the gun free from his pocket.

"Here, give me that!" I whispered. "You can't walk around the street brandishing that thing."

I took the gun and slipped it inside my coat. Then I got hold of his right arm and steered him out of the door. The Negro didn't look up as we departed.

We stood shivering in the alleyway. The fog had increased. I couldn't see either end of the alley from where we stood. It was cold. Damp. Dark. Fog or no fog, a little wind was whispering secrets to the shadows at our backs.

The fresh air hit Sir Guy just as I expected it would. Fog and gin-fumes don't mingle very well. He lurched as I guided him slowly through the mist.

Sir Guy, despite his incapacity, still stared apprehensively at the alley, as though he expected to see a figure approaching.

Disgust got the better of me.

"Childish foolishness," I snorted. "Jack the Ripper, indeed! I call this carrying a hobby too far."

"Hobby?" He faced me. Through the fog I could see his distorted face. "You call this a hobby?"

"Well, what is it?" I grumbled. "Just why else are you so interested in tracking down this mythical killer?"

My arm held his. But his stare held me.

"In London," he whispered. "In 1888 . . . one of those nameless drabs the Ripper slew . . . was my mother."

"What?"

"Later I was recognized by my father, and legitimized. We swore to devote our lives to finding the Ripper. My father was the first to search. He died in Hollywood in 1926 – on the trail of the Ripper. They said he was stabbed by an unknown assailant in a brawl. But I know who that assailant was.

"So I've taken up his work, do you see, John? I've carried on. And I will carry on until I do find him and kill him with my own hands.

"He took my mother's life and the lives of hundreds more to keep his own hellish being alive. Like a vampire, he battens on blood. Like a ghoul, he is nourished by death. Like a fiend, he stalks the world to kill. He is cunning, devilishly cunning. But I'll never rest until I find him, never!"

I believed him then. He wouldn't give up. He wasn't just a drunken babbler any more. He was as fanatical, as determined, as relentless as the Ripper himself.

Tomorrow he'd be sober. He'd continue the search. Perhaps he'd turn those papers over to the FBI. Sooner or later, with such persistence – and with his motive – he'd be successful. I'd always known he had a motive.

"Let's go," I said, steering him down the alley.

"Wait a minute," said Sir Guy. "Give me back my gun." He lurched a little. "I'd feel better with the gun on me."

He pressed me into the dark shadows of a little recess.

I tried to shrug him off, but he was insistent.

"Let me carry the gun now, John," he mumbled.

"All right," I said.

I reached into my coat, brought my hand out.

"But that's not a gun," he protested. "That's a knife."

"I know."

I bore down on him swiftly.

"John!" he screamed.

"Never mind the 'John'," I whispered, raising the knife. "Just call me . . . Jack."

JOHN LLEWELLYN PROBERT

Case Conference #3

"ANOTHER OF YOUR Ripper Psychosis cases?"
Dr Lionel Parrish smiled but said nothing in reply as the tape recording came to an end. He ejected the cassette and returned it to the box he had taken it from.

"Possibly," he said eventually. "But as I have already explained, the Ripper Psychosis is rare. It's possible that we have three examples of this fascinating condition upstairs, but it is also equally possible that we have only one, or even none at all. Do you think the confession you have just heard is that of a real case?"

Robert Stanhope scratched at his left cheek in thought. "My first impression is that it's nonsense," he said.

"I see," said Parrish. "Your reasoning being?"

"Well, for a start, the events being described took place decades ago," said Stanhope. "If they were true, the voice on that cassette should be that of an old man."

"Not if the patient in question believes himself to be Jack the Ripper," said Parrish. "If he was alive in 1888 and he is alive now, then of course he would have survived all the intervening years and would be bound to have had a few, shall we say, adventures, during that time?"

Stanhope slumped back in the chair, a resigned look on his face. "Well, if you put it like that, I suppose this one could be true as well," he said. "Especially as I also find it hard to believe that you would go to all the trouble of getting someone to make such a recording just for the purposes of deceit."

"Even though your type do that kind of thing all the time?"

Stanhope shook his head. "That's hardly fair, Dr Parrish," he said. "In fact I would go so far as to say that I find that remark quite offensive."

Parrish steepled his fingers. "Oh. Do you?"

That was evidently enough for Stanhope, who got to his feet.

"Yes, I do," he said. "And I'm getting a bit tired of this little game. For all I know, every single case history you've presented me with today is rubbish, a collection of contrivances that you've spent years putting together to relieve the boredom of having to run an isolated godforsaken place like this. Or they might all be true. I have no way of knowing, but I think that's probably all part of your little game as well."

He pointed to the cupboard near the door. "And as if that isn't bad enough, you've also shown me a violin that you claimed might be cursed, but then almost straight afterward suggested that you might have made it all up." His accusatory finger swivelled to the window. "Then you showed me something that might be a dead body in that field out there, and all you did was go on about the bloody birds that were dancing all over it."

He returned his gaze to the doctor, still calmly seated behind his desk. "Well, Dr Parrish, to be honest, I don't care any more. I don't care whether your stories are true – whether upstairs is filled with crazed photographers, or insane film stars, or immortal serial killers, or people who think they're Humpty Dumpty. I have had enough of this, and frankly I have better things to do with my time."

With that Stanhope turned and strode purposefully to the door of Parrish's office.

Which was locked.

"Can you open this door for me, please?"

The doctor shook his head. "I suspected we might get to the point where you found all of this a little too much for comfort," he said. "So a while ago I took the precaution of activating the electronic locking mechanism for that door. It's actually there for my safety, in case the inmates should ever literally try to take over the asylum. To be honest, the chances of that are so infinitesimally small as to be negligible, so I'm pleased I've been able to find another use for it."

Stanhope tugged at the door handle, then turned around and glowered at the doctor. "I suggest you open this door," he said, threateningly. "*Now.*"

Parrish gestured helplessly. "I'm afraid I can't, Mr Stanhope," he said. "Once activated the lock is on a timer. No one can get in or out until the time period entered into the device has elapsed."

"And how long was the time you entered?" Stanhope was clearly seething now, his fists clenched so tight that they were shaking.

Dr Parrish, as relaxed as ever, extended his left wrist and looked lazily at his watch. "Oh, I should say about another two hours," he said.

"That's ridiculous!" Stanhope cried. He turned around and pounded on the heavy oak. "Let me out of this bloody office!"

"Anyone who might hear your cries was instructed to ignore them before you came in here," said Parrish. "As you so rightly intimated earlier, I have spent rather a long time preparing all of this for you. So why don't you be a good boy and come and sit back down? There are quite a few cases I haven't told you about yet."

Whether or not Stanhope was paying any attention it was difficult to say as he continued to pound on the door and demanded to be let out.

"Oh, dear," said the doctor. "It would seem we have a slight case of claustrophobia here." He opened his uppermost right-hand desk-drawer, took out a disposable syringe, and fitted it with a thick white aspiration needle. From the next drawer down he removed a vial of an unmarked solution, punctured its rubber cap with the needle, and proceeded to draw up twenty millilitres of colourless fluid.

"I was hoping I wouldn't have to do this, but I can see I was right to take the precaution of keeping a sedative in here with me," he said, flicking the syringe to remove any air bubbles and changing the needle for a slightly smaller one to perform the injection.

Parrish got to his feet, holding the syringe with the needle pointed towards the ceiling. "I'll ask you once more, Mr Stanhope. Will you sit down and behave yourself?"

Either Stanhope was deliberately ignoring the doctor, or he was lost in the throes of his own mounting panic. Oblivious to Parrish's actions, Stanhope was still hammering on the door as Parrish came up behind him, smartly tapped the external jugular vein on the right of Stanhope's neck twice, and then plunged the needle downwards into the prominent vessel.

With the skill of years of practice, Parrish pulled back on the plunger. A flashback of blood into the syringe confirmed he was in the right place, and he pressed down on the plunger, delivering the sedating medication directly into Stanhope's bloodstream.

Then the doctor stood back, wary that if he had miscalculated the dose the reporter might just fall over, on top of him.

Stanhope staggered a little and took a step back, rubbing at the puncture mark. When his fingers came away red he began to hyperventilate.

"Scared of the sight of our own blood as well, are we?" Parrish tutted. "My, what a bundle of neuroses you're turning out to be, you poor fellow." He helped Stanhope back to his chair, where the journalist sat panting and rubbing at his throat.

"Now give it a minute or so, and you'll be feeling much better," said Parrish, returning to his side of the desk and resuming his seat. He timed sixty seconds on his wristwatch, and then looked up.

"Feeling better now?" he asked.

Stanhope nodded. "I'm sorry," he said, his voice just a little slurred. "I don't know what came over me."

"Oh, just a little claustrophobia, mixed with quite a bit of fear, anxiety and, dare I say it, suspicion," said Parrish. "The human mind is a complex, wonderful and remarkable thing. But tip the balance of the mental processes just slightly in the wrong direction and the results can be, well, disturbing. I hope you have now had the opportunity to see that for yourself."

The doctor reached under his desk and pressed a button. From behind Stanhope there was a hum and a click.

"The door's open now," said Parrish.

Stanhope tried to turn and look, but was a little too dizzy to do so. Instead he looked at Parrish.

"You're a bastard, you know that?" he said.

Parrish grinned. "Perhaps," he said. "But I hope that I have at last convinced you that you shouldn't believe everything you hear, not even from such a figure of authority as my good self."

"Your evil self, you mean," said Stanhope, rubbing his eyes and leaning back in the chair.

"However you prefer to think of me," said Parrish. "But I promise you that what I am about to say is true. If you feel you have had enough and would like to leave, then by all means you may. The sedation I gave you was a very short-acting benzodi-azepine. By the time you make it back to your car it will have worn off."

It was obvious from Stanhope's posture that it was already beginning to. He made to get to his feet, and then shook his head.

"No," he said. "No way."

Parrish gave him an encouraging look. "What do you mean?"

"I've come this far," said Stanhope. "There is no way I am not staying until the end, now. If this is the game you want to play, then I'll play it, but by God I will have my interview by the end of it."

"You shouldn't use double negatives, Mr Stanhope," said the doctor with a smile. "You are a writer, after all."

"A writer who has been assaulted by you, both mentally and physically." Stanhope rubbed his neck again only to find the bleeding had now stopped. "I'll be putting all of this in my story, you know."

"I would be disappointed if you didn't," Parrish replied. "Now, may I take it from what you have just said that you are ready to continue?" Stanhope nodded. "Good. After all that, I think you're probably ready for something really horrible, especially as you've now had first-hand experience of just how suggestible some people can be."

"Forgive me if I don't seem enthused by that," Stanhope replied with a shiver.

"This one's a court case," said Parrish, taking down a set of documents the size of a telephone directory and held together with numerous rubber bands. Some of them were so old they crumbled when the doctor tried to remove them. "It's a most fascinating example of why some people really should stay away from the darker corners that exist in this world."

"Is this one going to be all about the conviction of another serial killer, then?" said Stanhope, eyeing the now-collapsing pile of papers.

"Only partly," said Parrish, leafing through to find the relevant pages. "What was even more interesting was what happened *after* the trial . . ."

RAMSEY CAMPBELL

See How They Run

THROUGH THE READING of the charges Foulsham felt
as if the man in the dock was watching him. December
sunshine like ice transmuted into illumination slanted through
the high windows of the courtroom, spotlighting the murderer.
With his round slightly pouting face and large dark moist eyes
Fishwick resembled a schoolboy caught red-handed, Foulsham
thought, except that surely no schoolboy would have confronted
the prospect of retribution with such a look of imperfectly
concealed amusement mingled with impatience.

The indictment was completed. "How do you plead?"

"Not guilty," Fishwick said in a high clear voice with just a hint
of mischievous emphasis on the first word. Foulsham had the
impression that he was tempted to take a bow, but instead
Fishwick folded his arms and glanced from the prosecuting counsel to the defence, cueing their speeches so deftly that Foulsham
felt his own lips twitch.

". . . a series of atrocities so cold-blooded that the jury may
find it almost impossible to believe that any human being could
be capable of them . . ." ". . . evidence that a brilliant mind was
tragically damaged by a lifetime of abuse . . ." Fishwick met both
submissions with precisely the same attitude, eyebrows slightly
raised, a forefinger drumming on his upper arm as though he
were commenting in code on the proceedings. His look of lofty
patience didn't change as one of the policemen who had arrested
him gave evidence, and Foulsham sensed that Fishwick was eager
to get to the meat of the case. But the judge adjourned the trial for
the day, and Fishwick contented himself with a faint anticipatory
smirk.

The jurors were escorted past the horde of reporters and through the business district to their hotel. Rather to Foulsham's surprise, none of his fellow jurors mentioned Fishwick, neither over dinner nor afterwards, when the jury congregated in the cavernous lounge as if they were reluctant to be alone. Few of the jurors showed much enthusiasm for breakfast, so that Foulsham felt slightly guilty for clearing his plate. He was the last to leave the table and the first to reach the door of the hotel, telling himself that he wanted to be done with the day's ordeal. Even the sight of a newsvendor's placard which proclaimed FISHWICK JURY SEE HORROR PICTURES TODAY failed to deter him.

Several of the jurors emitted sounds of distress as the pictures were passed along the front row. A tobacconist shook his head over them, a gesture which seemed on the point of growing uncontrollable. Some of Foulsham's companions on the back row craned forwards for a preview, but Foulsham restrained himself; they were here to be dispassionate, after all. As the pictures came towards him, their progress marked by growls of outrage and murmurs of dismay, he began to feel unprepared, in danger of performing clumsily in front of the massed audience. When at last the pictures reached him he gazed at them for some time without looking up.

They weren't as bad as he had secretly feared. Indeed, what struck him most was their economy and skill. With just a few strokes of a black felt-tipped pen, and the occasional embellishment of red, Fishwick had captured everything he wanted to convey about his subjects: the grotesqueness which had overtaken their gait as they attempted to escape once he'd severed a muscle; the way the crippled dance of each victim gradually turned into a crawl – into less than that once Fishwick had dealt with both arms. No doubt he'd been as skilful with the blade as he was with the pen. Foulsham was re-examining the pictures when the optician next to him nudged him. "The rest of us have to look too, you know."

Foulsham waited several seconds before looking up. Everyone in the courtroom was watching the optician now – everyone but Fishwick. This time there was no question that the man in the dock was gazing straight at Foulsham, whose face stiffened into a mask he wanted to believe was expressionless. He was struggling to look away when the last juror gave an appalled cry and began to crumple the pictures. The judge hammered an admonition, the usher rushed to reclaim the evidence, and Fishwick stared at Foulsham as if they were sharing a joke. The flurry of activity let Foulsham look away, and he did his best to copy the judge's expression of rebuke tempered with sympathy for the distressed woman.

That night he couldn't get to sleep for hours. Whenever he closed his eyes he saw the sketches Fishwick had made. The trial wouldn't last forever, he reminded himself; soon his life would return to normal. Every so often, as he lay in the dark which smelled of bath soap and disinfectant and carpet shampoo, the taps in the bathroom released a gout of water with a choking sound. Each time that happened, the pictures in his head lurched closer, and he felt as if he was being watched. Would he feel like that over Christmas if, as seemed likely, the trial were to continue into the new year? But it lacked almost a week to Christmas when Fishwick was called to the witness box, and Fishwick chose that moment, much to the discomfiture of his lawyer, to plead guilty after all.

The development brought gasps from the public gallery, an exodus from the press benches, mutters of disbelief and anger from the jury; but Foulsham experienced only relief. When the court rose as though to celebrate the turn of events he thought the case was over until he saw that the judge was withdrawing to speak to the lawyers. "The swine," the tobacconist whispered fiercely, glaring at Fishwick. "He made all those people testify for nothing."

Soon the judge and the lawyers returned. It had apparently been decided that the defence should call several psychiatrists to state their views of Fishwick's mental condition. The first of them had scarcely opened his mouth, however, when Fishwick began to express impatience as severe as Foulsham sensed more than one of the jurors were suffering. The man in the dock protruded his tongue like a caricature of a madman and emitted a creditable imitation of a jolly banjo which all but drowned out the psychiatrist's voice. Eventually the judge had Fishwick removed from the court, though not without a struggle, and the psychiatrists were heard.

Fishwick's mother had died giving birth to him, and his father had never forgiven him. The boy's first schoolteacher had seen the father tearing up pictures Fishwick had painted for him. There was some evidence that the father had been prone to uncontrollable fits of violence against the child, though the boy had always insisted that he had broken his own leg by falling downstairs. All of Fishwick's achievements as a young man seemed to have antagonised the father – his exercising his leg for years until he was able to conceal his limp, his enrolment in an art college, the praise which his teachers heaped on him and which he valued less than a word of encouragement from his father. He'd been in his twenties, and still living with his father, when a gallery had offered to exhibit his work. Nobody knew what his father had said which had caused Fishwick to destroy all his paintings in despair and to overcome his disgust at working in his father's shop in order to learn the art of butchery. Before long he had been able to rent a bed-sitter, and thirteen months after moving into it he'd tracked down one of his former schoolfellows who used to call him "Quasimodo" on account of his limp and his dispirited slouch. Four victims later, Fishwick had made away with his father and the law had caught up with him.

Very little of this had been leaked to the press. Foulsham found himself imagining Fishwick brooding sleeplessly in a cheerless room, his creative nature and his need to prove himself festering within him until he was unable to resist the compulsion to carry out an act which would make him feel meaningful. The other jurors were less impressed. "I might have felt some sympathy for him if he'd gone straight for his father," the hairdresser declared once they were in the jury room.

Fishwick had taken pains to refine his technique first, Foulsham thought, and might have said so if the tobacconist hadn't responded. "I've no sympathy for that cold fish," the man said between puffs at a briar. "You can see he's still enjoying himself. He only pleaded not guilty so that all those people would have to be reminded what they went through."

"We can't be sure of that," Foulsham protested.

"More worried about him than about his victims, are you?" the tobacconist demanded, and the optician intervened. "I know it seems incredible that anyone could enjoy doing what he did," she said to Foulsham, "but that creature's not like us."

Foulsham would have liked to be convinced of that. After all, if Fishwick weren't insane, mustn't that mean anyone was capable of such behaviour? "I think he pleaded guilty when he realised that everyone was going to hear all those things about him he wanted to keep secret," he said. "I think he thought that if he pleaded guilty the psychiatrists wouldn't be called."

The eleven stared at him. "You think too much," the tobacconist said.

The hairdresser broke the awkward silence by clearing her throat. "I never thought I'd say this, but I wish they'd bring back hanging just for him."

"That's the Christmas present he deserves," said the veterinarian who had crumpled the evidence.

The foreman of the jury, a bank manager, proposed that it was time to discuss what they'd learned at the trial. "Personally, I don't mind where they lock him up so long as they throw away the key."

His suggestion didn't satisfy most of the jurors. The prosecuting counsel had questioned the significance of the psychiatric evidence, and the judge had hinted broadly in his summing-up that it was inconclusive. It took all the jurors apart from Foulsham less than half-an-hour to dismiss the notion that Fishwick might have been unable to distinguish right from wrong, and then they gazed expectantly at Foulsham, who had a disconcerting sense that Fishwick was awaiting his decision too. "I don't suppose it matters where they lock him up," he began, and got no further; the rest of the jury responded with cheers and applause, which sounded ironic to him. Five minutes later they'd agreed to recommend a life sentence for each of Fishwick's crimes. "That should keep him out of mischief," the bank manager exulted.

As the jury filed into the courtroom Fishwick leaned forwards to scrutinise their faces. His own was blank. The foreman stood up to announce the verdict, and Foulsham was suddenly grateful to have that done on his behalf. He hoped Fishwick would be put away for good. When the judge confirmed six consecutive life sentences, Foulsham released a breath which he hadn't been aware of holding. Fishwick had shaken his head when asked if he had anything to say before sentence was passed, and his face seemed to lose its definition as he listened to the judge's pronouncement. His gaze trailed across the jury as he was led out of the dock.

Once Foulsham was out of the building, in the crowded streets above which glowing Santas had been strung up, he didn't feel as liberated as he'd hoped. Presumably that would happen when sleep had caught up with him. Just now he was uncomfortably aware of how all the mannequins in the store windows had been twisted into posing. Whenever shoppers turned from gazing into a window he thought they were emerging from the display. As he dodged through the shopping precinct, trying to avoid shoppers rendered angular by packages, families mined with small children, clumps of onlookers surrounding the open suitcases of street traders, he felt as if the maze of bodies were crippling his progress.

Foulsham's had obviously been thriving in his absence. The shop was full of people buying Christmas cards and rolled-up posters and framed prints. "Are you glad it's over?" Annette asked him. "He won't ever be let out, will he?"

"Was he as horrible as the papers made out?" Jackie was eager to know.

"I can't say. I didn't see them," Foulsham admitted, experiencing a surge of panic as Jackie produced a pile of tabloids from under the counter. "I'd rather forget," he said hastily.

"You don't need to read about it, Mr Foulsham, you lived through it," Annette said. "You look as though Christmas can't come too soon for you."

"If I oversleep tomorrow I'll be in on Monday," Foulsham promised, and trudged out of the shop.

All the taxis were taken, and so he had to wait almost half-an-hour for a bus. If he hadn't been so exhausted he might have walked home. As the bus laboured uphill he clung to the dangling strap which was looped around his wrist and stared at a grimacing rubber clown whose limbs were struggling to unbend from the bag into which they'd been forced. Bodies swayed against him like meat in a butcher's lorry, until he was afraid of being trapped out of reach of the doors when the bus came to his stop.

As he climbed his street, where frost glittered as if the tarmac was reflecting the sky, he heard children singing carols in the distance or on television. He let himself into the house on the brow of the hill, and the poodles in the ground-floor flat began to yap as though he was a stranger. They continued barking while he sorted through the mail which had accumulated on the hall table: bills, advertisements, Christmas cards from people he hadn't heard from since last year. "Only me, Mrs Hutton," he called as he heard her and her stick plodding through her rooms towards the clamour. Jingling his keys as further proof of his identity, and feeling unexpectedly like a jailer, he hurried upstairs and unlocked his door.

Landscapes greeted him. Two large framed paintings flanked the window of the main room: a cliff baring strata of ancient stone above a deserted beach, fields spiky with hedgerows and tufted with sheep below a horizon where a spire poked at fat clouds as though to pop them; beyond the window, the glow of street-lamps streamed downhill into a pool of light miles wide from which pairs of headlight beams were flocking. The pleasure and the sense of all-embracing calm which he habitually experienced on coming home seemed to be standing back from him. He dumped his suitcase in the bedroom and hung up his coat, then he took the radio into the kitchen.

He didn't feel like eating much. He finished off a slice of toast laden with baked beans, and wondered whether Fishwick had eaten yet, and what his meal might be. As soon as he'd sluiced plate and fork he made for his armchair with the radio. Before long, however, he'd had enough of the jazz age. Usually the dance music of that era roused his nostalgia for innocence, not least because the music was older than he was, but just now it seemed too good to be true. So did the views on the wall and beyond the window, and the programmes on the television – the redemption of a cartoon Scrooge, commercials chortling "Ho ho ho", an appeal on behalf of people who would be on their own at Christmas, a choir reiterating "Let nothing you display", the syntax of which he couldn't grasp. As his mind fumbled with it, his eyelids drooped. He nodded as though agreeing with himself that he had better switch off the television, and then he was asleep.

Fishwick wakened him. Agony flared through his right leg. As he lurched out of the chair, trying to blink away the blur which coated his eyes, he was afraid the leg would fail him. He collapsed back into the chair, thrusting the leg in front of him, digging his fingers into the calf in an attempt to massage away the cramp. When at last he was able to bend the leg without having to grit his teeth, he set about recalling what had invaded his sleep.

The nine o'clock news had been ending. It must have been a newsreader who had spoken Fishwick's name. Foulsham hadn't been fully awake, after all; no wonder he'd imagined that the voice sounded like the murderer's. Perhaps it had been the hint of amusement which his imagination had seized upon, though would a newsreader have sounded amused? He switched off the television and waited for the news on the local radio station, twinges in his leg ensuring that he stayed awake.

He'd forgotten that there was no ten o'clock news. He attempted to phone the radio station, but five minutes of hanging on brought him only a message like an old record on which the needle had stuck, advising him to try later. By eleven he'd hobbled to bed. The newsreader raced through accounts of violence and drunken driving, then rustled her script. "Some news just in," she said. "Police report that convicted murderer Desmond Fishwick has taken his own life while in custody. Full details in our next bulletin."

That would be at midnight. Foulsham tried to stay awake, not least because he didn't understand how, if the local station had only just received the news, the national network could have broadcast it more than ninety minutes earlier. But when midnight came he was asleep. He wakened in the early hours and heard voices gabbling beside him, insomniacs trying to assert themselves on a phone-in programme before the presenter cut them short. Foulsham switched off the radio and imagined the city riddled with cells in which people lay or paced, listening to the babble of their own caged obsessions. At least one of them – Fishwick – had put himself out of his misery. Foulsham massaged his leg until the ache relented sufficiently to let sleep overtake him.

The morning newscast said that Fishwick had killed himself last night, but little else. The tabloids were less reticent, Foulsham discovered once he'd dressed and hurried to the newsagent's. MANIAC'S BLOODY SUICIDE. SAVAGE KILLER SAVAGES HIMSELF. HE BIT OFF MORE THAN HE

COULD CHEW. Fishwick had gnawed the veins out of his arms and died from loss of blood.

He must have been insane to do that to himself, Foulsham thought, clutching his heavy collar shut against a vicious wind as he limped downhill. While bathing he'd been tempted to take the day off, but now he didn't want to be alone with the images which the news had planted in him. Everyone around him on the bus seemed to be reading one or other of the tabloids which displayed Fishwick's face on the front page like posters for the suicide, and he felt as though all the paper eyes were watching him. Once he was off the bus he stuffed his newspaper into the nearest bin.

Annette and Jackie met him with smiles which looked encouraging yet guarded, and he knew they'd heard about the death. The shop was already full of customers buying last-minute cards and presents for people they'd almost forgotten, and it was late morning before the staff had time for a talk. Foulsham braced himself for the onslaught of questions and comments, only to find that Jackie and Annette were avoiding the subject of Fishwick, waiting for him to raise it so that they would know how he felt, not suspecting that he didn't know himself. He tried to lose himself in the business of the shop, to prove to them that they needn't be so careful of him; he'd never realised how much their teasing and joking meant to him. But they hardly spoke to him until the last customer had departed, and then he sensed that they'd discussed what to say to him. "Don't you let it matter to you, Mr Foulsham. He didn't," Annette said.

"Don't you dare let it spoil your evening," Jackie told him.

She was referring to the staff's annual dinner. While he hadn't quite forgotten about it, he seemed to have gained an impression that it hadn't much to do with him. He locked the shop and headed for home to get changed. After twenty minutes of waiting in a bus queue whose disgruntled mutters felt like flies bumbling mindlessly around him he walked home, the climb aggravating his limp.

He put on his dress shirt and bow tie and slipped his dark suit out of the bag in which it had been hanging since its January visit to the cleaners. As soon as he was dressed he went out again, away from the sounds of Mrs Hutton's three-legged trudge and of the dogs, which hadn't stopped barking since he had entered the house. Nor did he care for the way Mrs Hutton had opened her door and peered at him with a suspiciousness which hadn't entirely vanished when she saw him.

He was at the restaurant half an hour before the rest of the party. He sat at the bar, sipping a scotch and then another, thinking of people who must do so every night in preference to sitting alone at home, though might some of them be trying to avoid doing something worse? He was glad when his party arrived, Annette and her husband, Jackie and her new boyfriend, even though Annette's greeting as he stood up disconcerted him. "Are you all right, Mr Foulsham?" she said, and he felt unpleasantly wary until he realised that she must be referring to his limp.

By the time the turkey arrived at the table the party had opened a third bottle of wine and the conversation had floated loose. "What was he like, Mr Foulsham," Jackie's boyfriend said, "the feller you put away?"

Annette coughed delicately. "Mr Foulsham may not want to talk about it."

"It's all right, Annette. Perhaps I should. He was—" Foulsham said, and trailed off, wishing that he'd taken advantage of the refuge she was offering. "Maybe he was just someone whose mind gave way."

"I hope you've no regrets," Annette's husband said. "You should be proud."

"Of what?"

"Of stopping the killing. He won't kill anyone else."

Foulsham couldn't argue with that, and yet he felt uneasy, especially when Jackie's boyfriend continued to interrogate him. If Fishwick didn't matter, as Annette had insisted when Foulsham was closing the shop, why was everyone so interested in hearing about him? He felt as though they were resurrecting the murderer, in Foulsham's mind if nowhere else. He tried to describe Fishwick, and related as much of his own experience of the trial as he judged they could stomach. All that he left unsaid seemed to gather in his mind, especially the thought of Fishwick extracting the veins from his arms.

Annette and her husband gave him a lift home. He meant to invite them up for coffee and brandy, but the poodles started yapping the moment he climbed out of the car. "Me again, Mrs

Hutton," he slurred as he hauled himself along the banister. He switched on the light in his main room and gazed at the landscapes on the wall, but his mind couldn't grasp them. He brushed his teeth and drank as much water as he could take, then he huddled under the blankets, willing the poodles to shut up.

He didn't sleep for long. He kept wakening with a stale rusty taste in his mouth. He'd drunk too much, that was why he felt so hot and sticky and closed in. When he eased himself out of bed and tiptoed to the bathroom the dogs began to bark. He rinsed out his mouth but was unable to determine if the water which he spat into the sink was discoloured. He crept out of the bathroom with a glass of water in each hand and crawled shivering into bed, trying not to grind his teeth as pictures which he would have given a good deal not to see rushed at him out of the dark.

In the morning he felt as though he hadn't slept at all. He lay in the creeping sunlight, too exhausted either to sleep or to get up, until he heard the year's sole Sunday delivery sprawl on the doormat. He washed and dressed gingerly, cursing the poodles, whose yapping felt like knives emerging from his skull, and stumbled down to the hall.

He lined up the new cards on his mantelpiece, where there was just enough room for them. Last year he'd had to stick cards onto a length of parcel tape and hang them from the cornice. This year cards from businesses outnumbered those from friends, unless tomorrow restored the balance. He was signing cards in response to some of the Sunday delivery when he heard Mrs Hutton and the poodles leave the house.

He limped to the window and looked down on her. The two leashes were bunched in her left hand, her right was clenched on her stick. She was leaning backwards as the dogs ran her downhill, and he had never seen her look so crippled. He turned away, unsure why he found the spectacle disturbing. Perhaps he should catch up on his sleep while the dogs weren't there to trouble it, except that if he slept now he might be guaranteeing himself another restless night. The prospect of being alone in the early hours and unable to sleep made him so nervous that he grabbed the phone before he had thought who he could ask to visit.

Nobody had time for him today. Of the people ranked on the mantelpiece, two weren't at home, two were fluttery with festive preparations, one was about to drive several hundred miles to collect his parents, one was almost incoherent with a hangover. All of them invited Foulsham to visit them over Christmas, most of them sounding sincere, but that wouldn't take care of Sunday. He put on his overcoat and gloves and hurried downhill by a route designed to avoid Mrs Hutton, and bought his Sunday paper on the way to a pub lunch.

The Bloody Mary wasn't quite the remedy he was hoping for. The sight of the liquid discomforted him, and so did the scraping of the ice cubes against his teeth. Nor was he altogether happy with his lunch; the leg of chicken put him in mind of the process of severing it from the body. When he'd eaten as much as he could hold down, he fled.

The papery sky was smudged with darker clouds, images too nearly erased to be distinguishable. Its light seemed to permeate the city, reducing its fabric to little more than cardboard. He felt more present than anything around him, a sensation which he didn't relish. He closed his eyes until he thought of someone to visit, a couple who'd lived in the house next to his and whose Christmas card invited him to drop in whenever he was passing their new address.

A double-decker bus on which he was the only passenger carried him across town and deposited him at the edge of the new suburb. The streets of squat houses which looked squashed by their tall roofs were deserted, presumably cleared by the Christmas television shows he glimpsed through windows, and his isolation made him feel watched. He limped into the suburb, glancing at the street names.

He hadn't realised the suburb was so extensive. At the end of almost an hour of limping and occasionally resting, he still hadn't found the address. The couple weren't on the phone, or he would have tried to contact them. He might have abandoned the quest if he hadn't felt convinced that he was about to come face to face with the name which, he had to admit, had slipped his mind. He hobbled across an intersection and then across its twin, where a glance to the left halted him. Was that the street he was looking for? Certainly the name seemed familiar. He strolled along the pavement, trying to conceal his limp, and stopped outside a house.

Though he recognised the number, it hadn't been on the card. His gaze crawled up the side of the house and came to rest on the window set into the roof. At once he knew that he'd heard the address read aloud in the courtroom. It was where Fishwick had lived.

As Foulsham gazed fascinated at the small high window he imagined Fishwick gloating over the sketches he'd brought home, knowing that the widow from whom he rented the bed-sitter was downstairs and unaware of his secret. He came to himself with a shudder, and stumbled away, almost falling. He was so anxious to put the city between himself and Fishwick's room that he couldn't bear to wait for one of the infrequent Sunday buses. By the time he reached home he was gritting his teeth so as not to scream at the ache in his leg. "Shut up," he snarled at the alarmed poodles, "or I'll—" and stumbled upstairs.

The lamps of the city were springing alight. Usually he enjoyed the spectacle, but now he felt compelled to look for Fishwick's window among the distant roofs. Though he couldn't locate it, he was certain that the windows were mutually visible. How often might Fishwick have gazed across the city towards him? Foulsham searched for tasks to distract himself – cleaned the oven, dusted the furniture and the tops of the picture-frames, polished all his shoes, lined up the tins on the kitchen shelves in alphabetical order. When he could no longer ignore the barking which his every movement provoked, he went downstairs and rapped on Mrs Hutton's door.

She seemed reluctant to face him. Eventually he heard her shooing the poodles into her kitchen before she came to peer out at him. "Been having a good time, have we?" she demanded.

"It's the season," he said without an inkling of why he should need to justify himself. "Am I bothering your pets somehow?"

"Maybe they don't recognise your walk since you did whatever you did to yourself."

"It happened while I was asleep." He'd meant to engage her in conversation so that she would feel bound to invite him in – he was hoping that would give the dogs a chance to grow used to him again – but he couldn't pursue his intentions when she was so openly hostile, apparently because she felt entitled to the only limp in the building. "Happy Christmas to you and yours," he flung at her, and hobbled back to his floor.

He wrote out his Christmas card list in case he had overlooked anyone, only to discover that he couldn't recall some of the names to which he had already addressed cards. When he began doodling, slashing at the page so as to sketch stick-figures whose agonised contortions felt like a revenge he was taking, he turned the sheet over and tried to read a book. The yapping distracted him, as did the sound of Mrs Hutton's limp; he was sure she was exaggerating it to lay claim to the gait or to mock him. He switched on the radio and searched the wavebands, coming to rest at a choir which was wishing the listener a merry Christmas. He turned up the volume to blot out the noise from below, until Mrs Hutton thumped on her ceiling and the yapping of the poodles began to lurch repetitively at him as they leapt, trying to reach the enemy she was identifying with her stick.

Even his bed was no refuge. He felt as though the window on the far side of the city was an eye spying on him out of the dark, reminding him of all that he was trying not to think of before he risked sleep. During the night he found himself surrounded by capering figures which seemed determined to show him how much life was left in them – how vigorously, if unconventionally, they could dance. He managed to struggle awake at last, and lay afraid to move until the rusty taste like a memory of blood had faded from his mouth.

He couldn't go on like this. In the morning he was so tired that he felt as if he was washing someone else's face and hands. He thought he could feel his nerves swarming. He bared his teeth at the yapping of the dogs and tried to recapture a thought he'd glimpsed while lying absolutely still, afraid to move, in the hours before dawn. What had almost occurred to him about Fishwick's death?

The yapping receded as he limped downhill. On the bus a woman eyed him as if she suspected him of feigning the limp in a vain attempt to persuade her to give up her seat. The city streets seemed full of people who were staring at him, though he failed to catch them in the act. When Jackie and Annette converged on the shop as he arrived he prayed they wouldn't mention his limp. They gazed at his face instead, making him feel they were trying to ignore his leg. "We can cope, Mr Foulsham," Annette said, "if you want to start your Christmas early."

"You deserve it," Jackie added.

What were they trying to do to him? They'd reminded him how often he might be on his own during the next few days, a prospect which filled him with dread. How could he ease his mind in the time left to him? "You'll have to put up with another day of me," he told them as he unlocked the door.

Their concern for him made him feel as if his every move was being observed. Even the Christmas Eve crowds failed to occupy his mind, especially once Annette took advantage of a lull in the day's business to approach him. "We thought we'd give you your present now in case you want to change your mind about going home."

"That's thoughtful of you. Thank you both," he said and retreated into the office, wondering if they were doing their best to get rid of him because something about him was playing on their nerves. He used the phone to order them a bouquet each, a present which he gave them every Christmas but which this year he'd almost forgotten, and then he picked at the parcel until he was able to see what it was.

It was a book of detective stories. He couldn't imagine what had led them to conclude that it was an appropriate present, but it did seem to have a message for him. He gazed at the exposed spine and realised what any detective would have established days ago. Hearing Fishwick's name in the night had been the start of his troubles, yet he hadn't ascertained the time of Fishwick's death.

He phoned the radio station and was put through to the newsroom. A reporter gave him all the information which the police had released. Foulsham thanked her dully and called the local newspaper, hoping they might contradict her somehow, but of course they confirmed what she'd told him. Fishwick had died just before 9.30 on the night when his name had wakened Foulsham, and the media hadn't been informed until almost an hour later.

He sat at his bare desk, his cindery eyes glaring at nothing, then he stumbled out of the cell of an office. The sounds and the heat of the shop seemed to rush at him and recede in waves on which the faces of Annette and Jackie and the customers were floating. He felt isolated, singled out – felt as he had throughout the trial.

Yet if he couldn't be certain that he had been singled out then, why should he let himself feel that way now without trying to prove himself wrong? "I think I will go early after all," he told Jackie and Annette.

Some of the shops were already closing. The streets were almost blocked with people who seemed simultaneously distant from him and too close, their insect eyes and neon faces shining. When at last he reached the alley between two office buildings near the courts, he thought he was too late. But though the shop was locked, he was just in time to catch the hairdresser. As she emerged from a back room, adjusting the strap of a shoulder-bag stuffed with presents, he tapped on the glass of the door.

She shook her head and pointed to the sign which hung against the glass. Didn't she recognise him? His reflection seemed clear enough to him, like a photograph of himself holding the sign at his chest, even if the placard looked more real than he did. "Foulsham," he shouted, his voice echoing from the close walls. "I was behind you on the jury. Can I have a word?"

"What about?"

He grimaced and mimed glancing both ways along the alley, and she stepped forward, halting as far from the door as the door was tall. "Well?"

"I don't want to shout."

She hesitated and then came to the door. He felt unexpectedly powerful, the winner of a game they had been playing. "I remember you now," she said as she unbolted the door. "You're the one who claimed to be sharing the thoughts of that monster."

She stepped back as an icy wind cut through the alley, and he felt as though the weather was on his side, almost an extension of himself. "Well, spit it out," she said as he closed the door behind him.

She was ranging about the shop, checking that the electric helmets which made him think of some outdated mental treatment were switched off, opening and closing cabinets in which blades glinted, peering beneath the chairs which put him in mind of a death cell. "Can you remember exactly when you heard what happened?" he said.

She picked up a tuft of bluish hair and dropped it in a pedal bin. "What did?"

"He killed himself."

"Oh, that? I thought you meant something important." The bin snapped shut like a trap. "I heard about it on the news. I really can't say when."

"Heard about it, though, not read it."

"That's what I said. Why should it matter to you?"

He couldn't miss her emphasis on the last word, and he felt that both her contempt and the question had wakened something in him. He'd thought he wanted to reassure himself that he hadn't been alone in sensing Fishwick's death, but suddenly he felt altogether more purposeful. "Because it's part of us," he said.

"It's no part of me, I assure you. And I don't think I was the only member of the jury who thought you were too concerned with that fiend for your own good."

An unfamiliar expression took hold of Foulsham's face. "Who else did?"

"If I were you, Mr Whatever your name is, I'd seek help, and quick. You'll have to excuse me. I'm not about to let that monster spoil my Christmas." She pursed her lips and said "I'm off to meet some normal people."

Either she thought she'd said too much or his expression and his stillness were unnerving her. "Please leave," she said more shrilly. "Leave now or I'll call the police."

She might have been heading for the door so as to open it for him. He only wanted to stay until he'd grasped why he was there. The sight of her striding to the door reminded him that speed was the one advantage she had over him. Pure instinct came to his aid, and all at once he seemed capable of anything. He saw himself opening the nearest cabinet, he felt his finger and thumb slip through the chilly rings of the handles of the scissors, and lunging at her was the completion of these movements. Even then he thought he meant only to drive her away from the door, but he was reckoning without his limp. As he floundered towards her he lost his balance, and the points of the scissors entered her right leg behind the knee.

She gave an outraged scream and tried to hobble to the door, the scissors wagging in the patch of flesh and blood revealed by the growing hole in the leg of her patterned tights. The next moment she let out a wail so despairing that he almost felt sorry for her, and fell to her knees, well out of reach of the door. As she craned her head over her shoulder to see how badly she was injured, her eyes were the eyes of an animal caught in a trap. She extended one shaky hand to pull out the scissors, but he was too quick for her. "Let me," he said, taking hold of her thin wrist.

He thought he was going to withdraw the scissors, but as soon as his finger and thumb were through the rings he experienced an overwhelming surge of power which reminded him of how he'd felt as the verdict of the jury was announced. He leaned on the scissors and exerted all the strength he could, and after a while the blades closed with a sound which, though muffled, seemed intensely satisfying.

Either the shock or her struggles and shrieks appeared to have exhausted her. He had time to lower the blinds over the door and windows and to put on one of the plastic aprons which she and her staff must wear. When she saw him returning with the scissors, however, she tried to fight him off while shoving herself with her uninjured leg towards the door. Since he didn't like her watching him – it was his turn to watch – he stopped her doing so, and screaming. She continued moving for some time after he would have expected her to be incapable of movement, though she obviously didn't realise that she was retreating from the door. By the time she finally subsided he had to admit that the game had grown messy and even a little dull.

He washed his hands until they were clean as a baby's, then he parcelled up the apron and the scissors in the wrapping which had contained his present. He let himself out of the shop and limped towards the bus-stop, the book under one arm, the tools of his secret under the other. It wasn't until passers-by smiled in response to him that he realised what his expression was, though it didn't feel like his own smile, any more than he felt personally involved in the incident at the hairdresser's. Even the memory of all the jurors' names didn't feel like his. At least, he thought, he wouldn't be alone over Christmas, and in future he would try to be less hasty. After all, he and whoever he visited next would have more to discuss.

CONRAD WILLIAMS

Manners

THE RAIN SOUNDS different out here. Deep countryside. Kingfishers and toads. Dad told me I woke up to green so often that my eyes changed colour from brown to reflect it. He shared his love of nature with me, his practical knowledge. He was in the Scouts when he was a boy. I never went; I was far too shy, but I knew the Scout Promise off by heart. It's common sense, really. Thoughtfulness and consideration. *On my honour, I promise that I will do my best . . .*

I could identify all the birds, trees and flowers by the time I was five. I knew my knots and could tie them blindfold. I used to catch small animals – newts and snakes and frogs – and keep them in jars with punctured lids overnight while I studied and sketched them. In the morning I'd let them go. Sometimes we'd take long walks and there'd be something dead in the road. Later, when I went walking on my own and I saw an animal that had collided with a car, I'd place it in a bag (I always took a couple out with me) and take it home to study what it looked like internally.

Mum died when she gave birth to me. Her name was Julia. There's one photograph of her and Dad (Gordon) on their wedding day. She's leaning in to kiss him. She looks mousy. He's a bald eagle. He's holding an umbrella – August wedding; it pissed down – and she's got flowers in her hair. Confetti frozen around them. He always told me I was in that shot too. She was pregnant with me six months when they had the ceremony. I keep it, carefully folded, in my wallet. I don't take it out that often any more. It's been unfolded so often it's beginning to separate along the pleats.

When Dad died he left me the house. I say "house". It's more like a couple of connecting sheds at the edge of a long, thin field that ends at the motorway, which is like a thick, black underscore. Dad lived here rent-free, employed as a handyman by the farmer who owned the land. The farmer died about five years ago when the farm caught fire. There were rumours that it was a botched insurance scam, or that he'd committed suicide. Nobody came to demolish what was left of the building. You can still smell the smoke soaked into the walls of the place. Every so often, especially during nights when the storms come, you can hear bits of it collapsing. The main roof is gone now. Vandals have done for all the windows. Sometimes there is torchlight. Kids mucking about, scaring each other, drinking, taking drugs, having sex. I go in after them in the mornings to see if they left anything valuable behind, wallets, iPhones, but there's never anything worth having.

You'll not see me in town, much. I'm not a people person. I'm a book person. I read a lot, although I never enjoyed my school days and I left as soon as I was able, failing every exam they threw at me, if I was even around to take them. Like Dad, I thought I'd end up labouring around the farm: what's the point of knowing about isosceles triangles when you're knee-deep in pig shit? The farmer was a decent guy to us, even if he did resemble a sad bloodhound, and I was sorry about what happened to him.

I never thought about taking my own life. But I wonder about it. Everybody does, I reckon. People who commit suicide – is it on their minds from an early age, or is it something that creeps up on you? You think about how it might go, how you'd decide to do it, and what would be the least horrible way. Could I take a bottle full of painkillers? Could I jump from a skyscraper? Could I step out in front of a lorry on the motorway? I'd be more scared of getting it wrong than right. And what if I changed my mind?

I spend a lot of time in the woods here. Food is a problem. I don't have any money to buy stuff from the shops, and I'm a good lad. I promised I'd never thieve, so I'm out harvesting whenever I can. Nuts, berries, fruit, mushrooms. I lay traps and catch rabbits. By the pond I can sometimes collect a frog or two. I check the motorway every morning for fresh road-kill and it's here that I find the bulk of my meals. I've bagged magpies, rats, pheasants, squirrels, badgers, foxes, hedgehogs, a swan and, one time, in winter, a deer. I had to borrow a book from the library on how to skin and gut it. I portioned it and kept it in plastic bags outside in the cold, in a tin bath covered with tarp. It kept me going till spring. Sometimes I wish I'd been born in Canada, or Australia. I've never tried crocodile, or bear, or ostrich. Exotica, I think they call it.

I don't eat anything if it looks as though it died from something other than a car's bumper. If it's fresh and not flat, it goes in the pan. The only downside is that you've got to cook it pretty well – no pink meat here – because of the likelihood of trichinosis. Fox is probably my favourite. It's not very fatty, so you need to cook it quick on a barbecue. It's dense meat, but pretty soft, with a salty, kind of earthy taste. Rat is a bit like pork in flavour, but I only tried it once because there's the risk of Weil's disease. Owl's okay, badger's bad and hedgehog's horrid, but you can use their spines as toothpicks. I'll try anything. I had dog once. A Golden Retriever. I think it was an unwanted pet dumped in the country-side that wandered on to the road. I had it in a stew with some beans and potatoes. It tasted like lamb.

I'm not sure how I made the leap to eating what I was study-ing, but it seemed the natural progression. Granted, it sounds a bit grim, but it's the ultimate free-range, organic diet. It won't be pumped full of hormones, or tense and knotty because it's been trapped in a pen. My way, you can taste the surroundings in what's on your plate. You can taste the good soil and the moist fields and the fresh air. You can detect the night on your palate. I'd rather have a toad stir-fry than a chicken injected with steroids to the point of deformity, crushed up against hundreds of others in a shit-spattered battery farm.

When it's dark, because I don't have any electricity, I sit and read by candlelight while a failing wind-up radio plays old American songs from the wartime years; the only station I can find. I like listening to that stuff. I imagine my mother might have enjoyed it as well. She looks like someone who would sway to Johnny Mercer or The Ink Spots or Irving Berlin, her voice fading in and out as she sang a bar or two. "Be Careful, It's My Heart". The news comes on and I fade out. Never anything good. Never something I want to hear.

I continue to draw the animals I've eaten. I'm decent at draw-ing, somehow, despite Dad never having any talent in that area.

Maybe Mum had a knack. Or maybe it skipped a generation. I often think about who my forebears were; I never knew my grandparents, but I know their names were Bert and Olive on my mum's side and Norman and Iris on my dad's side. There are four names you don't hear much nowadays. Everybody dies and sometimes their names die with them. Could Norman ever be a popular name again? Was it ever?

I get down to the road around five in the morning and climb over the fence. I wait on my side of the crash barrier, listening for traffic. There are no motorway lights on this stretch. It's usually quiet for another half-hour bar the odd car, or an HGV. Now's the time to go looking for road-kill; most of the animals I've found are nocturnal and it's usually too early in the day, or too cold, for them to have been worried by rats or birds or for the flies to have filled their moistest parts with eggs.

I find a jay, which is interesting; I've never had one of those before. And a pheasant with just its head crushed. That's promising because sometimes, if they've been run over, you can taste the rubber off the tyres. I put what's edible in a bag. About half-a-mile further south, I see something that gives me pause, something grey near the middle of the road, moving slightly. I hurry along the hard shoulder. Sometimes you can miss out on a decent dinner because the animal is merely stunned. One time, about three years ago, I saw a foal lying still at the side of the road with a broken jaw, its tongue hanging from between its teeth, fat and purple like a partially inflated balloon. When I was about ten feet away, it jerked upright and escaped. It must have starved. Had I been a bit quicker I could have saved it some agony and made my belly a happy place for weeks.

It's a wolf.

I stand over it. This one won't be running away. It's been hit so hard that the flesh has been substantially parted; most of its insides are now outside. I can't quite understand how it can still be moving, but it is, and it is obviously in considerable pain. Its eyes bulge, its jaws stretch in either a scream that is silent or beyond the frequency human ears can detect. I can't pick it up like this. There's nothing to bludgeon it with, so I pull my knife from my back pocket and kneel down alongside. Where the legs meet the body I sever an artery and wait for it to bleed out. It's frustrating; usually I can get a decent *boudin noir* out of an animal, but I don't want to risk distressing it further by carrying it home alive because the suffering can transfer to the meat, making it pale and sweaty. I sling it over my shoulder when the twitching has stopped and trudge back to the shed.

I put the jay and the pheasant in my makeshift pantry for later and get on with the wolf. I strip it and skin it and gut it – well, those that are left – and joint it. I get a big pot on the gas stove and add onions, wild garlic, carrots, rosemary and potatoes. I get the meat in the pot and brown it all over. I pour in plenty of water. My stomach is rumbling. Give it a stir. I wish I had some stock, or a drop of red wine.

I pick up my sketchbook and begin to draw the wolf. I'm wondering about the skin, whether it could be put to good use – Dad always hated waste – and wondering what its name might have been, when there's a knock on the door of the shed. Nobody ever comes down here, not even the farmer when he was alive and it's his gaff, really. A voice, male, deep and purposeful – like Dad's – asking to talk to me. I open the door and there are six or seven policemen standing behind a man in plain clothes. Big eyes. He's an owl. I remember my manners. Dad brought me up to be polite. I invite them in.

The man in plain clothes gestures at the sketchbook. "It's a good likeness," he says. "Just like on the posters."

The pot has started to bubble on the stove and two of the policemen see what's on the chopping board and leave without saying anything, which is simply rude. I start to pick up the clothes from the floor, and I ask if anybody is hungry.

CHRISTOPHER FOWLER

Bryant & May and the Seven Points

"I'VE REACHED THE age," said Arthur Bryant with the weariness of a man who has just realized that his library card's expiry date is later than his own, "when my back has started to go out more often than I do."

"That's because you have no social life," his Antiguan landlady Alma Sorrowbridge pointed out as she passed him a fresh slice of buttered lavender cake sprinkled with hemp seeds. "You spend all your time in that filthy old office of yours. And you do go out. You went to see your old friend Sidney Biddle the other day."

"Alma, I went to his funeral," said Bryant testily. "I don't call that much of a day out. He was as adamantine in death as he was when he was alive."

"I don't know what that word means."

"Unyielding. But the sausage rolls were better than yours. I swiped some from the wake and ran chemical tests on them. Caramelized onions, apparently. You may wish to take note."

"Those who are taken from us don't always leave the earthly realm," said Alma, who had been following a more spiritual line of thought.

"You may be right," Bryant admitted. "I imagine most of them end up working for the post office. Has this cake got nuts in it?"

"Of course not," said Alma. "I know how they get under your dental plate."

Bryant examined his slice with suspicion. "Everything comes with a warning about containing nuts these days. Except the general population. Do you know, there's no common consensus on what constitutes insanity in society?"

"Really," said Alma flatly. Bryant had been poring over a tattered volume entitled *An Analysis of Uncommon Psychoses* all morning. She didn't hold with too much reading.

"Benjamin Franklin said that insanity was doing the same thing over and over again and expecting different results. But psychosis suggests a spectrum of behavioural patterns defined by abnormal thought processes and violations of societal norms, a flagrant disregard for accepted moral codes."

"I'll remember that when I'm doing your ironing. Do you always have to harp on about murderers? You know what I think about all that sort of thing – it's unwholesome." Alma rose and tidied away the tea things. "Why don't you get your mind off all this morbidity? Come to church with me this evening."

"You never give up, do you? I'm not that desperate for something to do," Bryant replied, dusting crumbs from his stained waistcoat. "Besides, I remember what happened the last time I went. The vicar told me off for praying too loudly."

"You made God jump," said Alma. "And your singing nearly deafened us. It would have helped if you'd known the tune. Or the words."

"I couldn't read the hymn-sheet because I'd forgotten my spectacles, so I had to make up the lyrics. I think I did a better job than all that rubbish about winged chariots and spears of fire." Bryant sighed and looked about himself impatiently. "I suppose I could make myself useful, plant the window boxes, scrape the oven out, clear the guttering, put some dubbin on my boots. It's just that I've got no cases on at the moment."

"Then Mr May is probably at a loose end, too. Why don't you give him a call?"

As Alma rose and prepared to wrap herself up against the grim deluges of a blustery February morning, Bryant rang John May.

Don't think too harshly of Mr Bryant; since Christmas, London had been alternately drenched and frozen by squalls heading down from Iceland, until its massed buildings looked like something one would find at the bottom of a stagnant pond. Everyone who ventured out soon became cold, wet and bad-tempered, and Arthur, who took the chill in his aged bones for a sign as ominous as the appearance of Elsinore's ghost, suffered more than most. It is a testimony to John May's persuasive skills that the most senior detective in London's Peculiar Crimes Unit was soon following his partner across the rain-swept upper reaches of Charlton Park, looking for a closed funfair.

"He's been missing for three weeks," said May as they made their way through the wet grass. "Left work at seven p.m. on the last Friday night in January, detoured here for reasons we don't know, and never reached home."

"And it took him all this time to be flagged as missing?" asked Bryant, incredulous. "Slow down a bit. My walking stick's sinking into the mud."

"It's a little more complicated than that. As far as we know, Michael Portheim is a GCHQ officer and mathematician specializing in codes. He was seconded to MI5 from the CIA for reasons no one will tell us, although an inside contact of mine suggested he was involved in certain aspects of counter-terrorism being jointly covered by the two agencies. As soon as he vanished, both sides began investigating."

"How soon after?"

"He was reported missing on Friday night after failing to turn up at a Russian supper club in Mayfair. One of his colleagues made the call that night."

"So it was a business dinner."

"It always is with that mob. Most of them have no friends and very little social life. Confidences aren't encouraged. MI5 sent their bods in to turn over his apartment in Muswell Hill, half expecting to find him zipped into a holdall, but they found nothing disturbed or out of the ordinary. It looks like he never reached home. They traced him here from phone records, CCTV and his travel card. There are no cameras in the park, on the common or in the woods – too many trees – but there's footage of him entering from the street and none of him coming back out the same way."

"So the assumption is that he was killed somewhere inside the park," said Bryant, fighting the ground with his stick.

"It looks that way. A team went over the entire area, but short of turning over every inch of turf with a spade there's no way of knowing what happened. The agencies' internal investigators have no leads to speak of, but the biggest fear is that he was either murdered or kidnapped."

"So what are *we* hoping to achieve in a rainy field in near-zero temperatures?" Bryant demanded to know.

"They've called us in. It's rather clutching at straws, but I went through Portheim's file this morning and found that he came from a military background. He'd been a keen sportsman at college, a free runner, hiker, canoeist, skydiver, good athletic all-rounder. He studied medicine for a while, then joined the army – straight in at officer level – but as part of his training he also learned circus skills. And the only unusual contact anyone has been able to come up with is this."

May pointed ahead through the sleeting gloom at what appeared to be a half-built stage set. As the pair approached, Bryant saw that it was a semi-circle of boarded-up sideshows, the old-fashioned kind consisting of tents fronted by tall painted flats, inset with strings of coloured light bulbs.

"Back when he was learning to tightrope walk and swing from a trapeze, Portheim knew a man called Harry Mills. The chap was his mentor in competitive athletics, taught him a lot about physical prowess and showmanship. There's no evidence to suggest they had any further contact with each other after Portheim was headhunted by the CIA, or when he returned to England. But here's the funny thing. This set-up appeared in the park the week Portheim went missing."

He looked up at a rain-streaked board that read:

HARRY MILLS'S INCREDIBLE ARCADE
OF ABNORMALITIES!

Beneath the red-and-yellow lettering, set in a traditional circus typeface known as "Coffee Tin", were posters painted on to linen and sealed beneath discoloured varnish, vignettes that had probably been produced in the 1930s, when such delights were popular at coastal resorts.

One painting showed a voluptuous young woman riveted into a steel bathing suit, holding a pair of terminals from which jagged streaks of blue lightning arced. Scrolled across the base of the picture was the legend:

YOU'LL BE JOLTED BY ELECTRA
THE 30,000 VOLT GIRL!

Another board showed a painfully thin young man, his ribcage visible under his pale translucent skin like the bars of a xylophone, a dozen lethal-looking steel rods piercing his chest:

NOTHING CAN PREPARE YOU FOR
LUCIO THE HUMAN PIN-CUSHION!

Beside him was an ethereally beautiful depiction of a woman clad in a diaphanous pink silk gown, with large furry wings sprouting from her shoulder-blades. She was balanced on a perch, staring wistfully up at the sky through the bars of her cage. The picture was captioned:

WITNESS THE HEARTBREAKING TRAGEDY OF
MARTITIA THE MOTH WOMAN!

The final vignette showed a green man with an elongated torso and no limbs, green antennae waving from his misshapen, beaked and bug-eyed head. The unfurled lettering beneath him read:

PREPARE TO BE HORRIFIED BY
MARVO THE CATERPILLAR BOY!

"Looks like he was painted by Francis Bacon," Bryant sniffed.

"I suppose it's what people did before television," said May. "Not much different from going to Bedlam to laugh at the insane."

The sideshows themselves were surrounded by a six-foot-high steel-staved fence, which the detectives now circled, searching for an entrance. The rest of the funfair, the waltzers, rifle ranges and coconut shies, stood further back on open ground. Only the Arcade of Abnormalities was sealed.

"I remember these exhibits from when I was a nipper," said Bryant. "I knew they had to be illusions but they always gave me the creeps. Let's see if we can find anyone."

"I guess they closed off this part to stop anyone from sneaking in."

"Or out. Look over there." Bryant pointed with his stick. They glimpsed a malformed figure hopping and running between the sideshows on the far side of the circle, and went after it.

Behind the show-tents, the performers' caravans were arranged like a wagon train. "Hey!" called May. "You there!" But nobody came. Finally he rang his contact and the pair waited for someone to come and open the main gate.

"Sorry about that," said an elderly man with a shock of wild grey hair, unbolting the mesh gate and pulling it aside. He wore leather knee-boots, and the sides of a crimson embroidered gypsy waistcoat struggled to meet over his stomach. "I'm Harry, the owner of this place. Come on in."

He clasped their hands with nervous gratitude and led them to one of the caravans. "We keep the gate locked tight to prevent the dogs from getting out," he explained, ushering them in. "There's been trouble in the past. One of the Alsatians bit a child after being teased."

The trailer's streamlined exterior of blue-and-white steel was misleading; inside it was as cosy and overcrowded as a nineteenth-century Romany caravan, hung about with copper pots, vases, painted jugs and rugs. Mills made thick dark Turkish coffee and served it in tiny steel cups. "There, that'll keep the chill out," he said. "You said you want to know about Michael Portheim?"

"We'll come to that," said Bryant, a luminosity in his eyes suggesting that, as usual, his primary interests lay elsewhere. "Tell me about the sideshows – from the paintings they look like they're originals."

"They are indeed, Mr Bryant," said Mills, settling himself opposite them. A large man with mutton-chop whiskers and a bay-window belly, he seemed ill suited to spending his life in a cluttered interior as snug as an egg. "Most of these illusions date back to the early-1930s. They used to tour the seaside towns: Blackpool in the north, Margate in the south. I've become some-thing of a custodian, and over the years I managed to save a lot of the original props and scripts from bonfires and dustcarts. I try to make sure that each act is performed exactly as it would have been in its heyday."

"Do the illusions still hold up today?"

"You'd be surprised. We can still make the kiddies scream. Once in a while you get a few smart-aleck teenagers in who think they know how it's done, but we have ways of scaring them as well."

"I think I saw the Girl Without a Head in Margate's Dreamland when I was about six," said Bryant. "I have a feeling I wet myself."

"Can we get to the subject of Mr Portheim?" asked May, knowing that his partner would be quite capable of discussing the sideshows for hours if he didn't interrupt. "When did you last speak to him?"

"We've stayed in touch over the years," said Mills. "He said he was having some kind of difficulty in his job. He didn't sound happy. Before he joined the agency he used to tell me everything, but of course that was no longer possible. I spoke to him about a month ago. He wanted to come and see the show."

"And did he?" asked May.

"I believe so, but you'll have to speak to Andrei the Great about it," said Mills. "I was up north, arranging bookings. Andrei the Great is my General Manager; he's in charge of the performances and the staff."

"Could we see him?"

For the first time, Mills looked uncomfortable. "I'm not sure if he's available."

"It's very important," May insisted. "If we can't see him today, we'll have to keep coming back until we do. You understand."

"All right, I'll see what I can work out. It's just that he's very . . . well . . . wait here." Mills lumbered to his feet, narrowly avoiding a collision with a ceiling lamp, and let himself out.

"Curious," said Bryant.

"Why?"

"Something put the wind up him all of a sudden. It's almost as if—"

"Don't prejudge," warned May. "Let's hear them out first."

After a few minutes, Mills reappeared. "Come with me," he said. His earlier cheerful demeanour had vanished. The detectives followed him across the puddled grass, stepping between guy-ropes, and found themselves in one of the sideshow tents. It comprised a series of battered wooden benches placed before a small blood-red stage that was framed in yellow satin curtains.

As Bryant & May seated themselves Mills stepped back into the shadows, as if he had been instructed to make himself scarce. The curtains opened to reveal a pastel-coloured 1960s Lambretta motor scooter with a slender girl seated side-saddle on it. She wore tight three-quarter-length jeans, rope espadrilles and a black halter top that exposed her neck and shoulders, but where her head should have been were half-a-dozen red rubber tubes. These extended up from the stump of her neck to four large glass jars set on the floor, that appeared to contain her blood and organs. As they watched, the girl slowly unfolded her arms and waved to them.

From behind the scooter appeared a squat, broad-chested dwarf with a scarlet goatee and bright red horns. This form of extreme body modification involved the insertion of cones under the skin on his forehead, and gave him the appearance of a miniature devil. His gypsy outfit of clashing indigo and violet silks was strung about with heavy silver chains, and made him appear even more garish and bizarre. Almost every inch of his exposed flesh was covered in piercings and dense black tattoos. He was carrying a black leather whip taller than himself.

But Andrei the Great was not dressed to amuse or entertain. He remained unsmiling and austere throughout the brief interview. "Do you like the lovely Headless Dolores?" he asked in a thick Russian accent. "Her mortification intrigues you? You would not be human if it didn't." He had a surprisingly rich and deep voice for a man of such diminutive stature.

"She does disturb me," Bryant admitted.

"That is the intention. To arouse and upset."

"How is it done?"

"I cannot tell you that." Andrei wagged a fat index finger at them. "We are just poor showmen. All we have in the way of currency is our secrets, and we will never give them up. But I can tell you these displays are a mixture of illusion and physical skill."

"You mean there's something more to them than just a few well-placed mirrors," Bryant said. "Did you show Dolores to Michael Portheim?"

"Yes, indeed," said Andrei unhesitatingly, as if he had been expecting the question. "He was interested in all of the illusions."

"Why did he come here?"

"For old times' sake," said Mills, cutting across Andrei the Great before he had a chance to answer. "To see me, I told you."

"Harry, I will deal with this," said Andrei, his voice soft with menace. "There are always people who want to know secrets."

"Mr Federov, when was Michael Portheim here, exactly?"

"Just over three weeks ago. A Friday night. I'm sure Harry will be able to give you a more accurate date."

"I can check in the diary," said Mills anxiously. "I made the arrangement before I went north."

"So he didn't come to see you," said Bryant. He turned to the dwarf. "If that's the case, you were the last one to see him before he disappeared."

"Then I imagine he'll remember me when you find him," said Andrei smoothly.

"What did he do here?"

"He watched some of the shows and was introduced to the performers. I imagine he left with the last audience at ten. I didn't see him go." Andrei pulled the curtains shut with a flick of his whip, presumably leaving the Headless Lady stranded onstage until they had concluded their business.

"How did Mr Portheim seem to you?"

"Perfectly normal, as much as anyone can be." Andrei's sharp blue eyes slowly closed and he swayed slightly.

"You'd met him before?"

"No, but Harry had told me about him." The dwarf's eyes remained closed. May noticed that he had tattoos of fish on his eyelids.

"If he sought you out, he must have had a reason for wanting to meet you," Bryant persisted. "He didn't just come here to see the show, did he?"

When Andrei snapped back to attention the effect was startling. "He spoke fluent Russian. He wanted to know if I still had connections in the Old Country."

"Why do you think he wanted to know that?"

"I imagine he was looking to sell some secrets," said Andrei with a leering wink. "Isn't that what your British agents always want to do when they start to fail?"

"And did you buy them?"

"I told him what I've already told you. That all information is currency."

"That's not answering my question."

"No," said Andrei, "I did not buy them."

*　　*　　*

"Well, that was creep-inducing," said May as they walked away through the rain across the deserted park. "I'll be happier when we're back under the street lights. There was something very unpleasant about that whole set-up, and particularly that little man."

"Did you notice how scared Harry Mills was around him?" said Bryant. "The poor devil was leaking sweat from every pore. He may be the owner and Andrei his manager, but it's the dwarf who's in charge. Why does Mills need him? You heard him say he's the custodian of the sideshows, the one with the passion. What's the general manager for? We need to do some digging on Andrei the Great. Something tells me he's got a lot to hide."

"I don't know," said May uncertainly. "He certainly seems keen to project a disturbing image of himself. His self-assurance worries me."

"I know what you mean. He's confident enough to admit that he was one of the last people to see Portheim before his disappearance," Bryant replied. "I have a feeling he thinks he's untouchable."

"Don't take it as a challenge, Arthur," May pleaded, "at least until we know more about him. The Russian connection concerns me. What if he arranged for Portheim to defect?"

"He's a circus dwarf," said Bryant, digging out his pipe. "Not very likely, is it?"

Back at the headquarters of the Peculiar Crimes Unit in Caledonian Road, King's Cross, Detective Sergeant Janice Longbright was waiting for them with fresh information. "You were right about Andrei Federov being dangerous," she said, following them along the corridor. "He spent twelve years in a maximum security jail in Irkutsk, Siberia."

"What's on his charge sheet?" asked May, accepting the file as he headed to his office.

"Four murders that anyone could be sure of, possibly many more. The details were contradictory and pretty hard to come by."

"Then what the hell is he doing out of jail?"

"He had his sentence slashed. No reason given." Janice checked her notes. "He was granted compensation by the Russian government."

"They pardoned him?" said Bryant, shocked.

"It seems that way. So he was free to leave his homeland and enter this country. You know how that works, Mr Bryant. If you call someone a thief after they've served their time for theft, it's libel. He served his time and was discharged as being safe."

Bryant was indignant. "Four murders? He didn't exactly serve his time, did he? The compensation means he was either wrongfully accused or he did the government a favour of some kind."

"He managed to escape on three separate occasions. Yet according to his records they still pardoned him."

"Something's not right there. And why on earth would he end up working in a English sideshow?"

"He's a dwarf, for God's sake," said Bryant, poking around for his pipe. "It was that or panto."

"That's not very politically correct of you," said Longbright.

"It's very hard to be PC around dwarves, especially one who's chosen to transform himself into a carnival devil. I understand the term 'midget' is considered offensive because it comes from the word 'midge', but we're talking about someone who runs a sideshow of human oddities, even though they're mostly fake. Is it wrong to say 'headless lady'? I mean, she has no head, what else are you going to say? If a boy has been made up to look like a caterpillar, you'd call him a Caterpillar Boy, wouldn't you?"

Longbright felt as if she had stepped into some kind of Pythonesque conversation to which she could not contribute. "We've just received Federov's medical history," she said instead. "The murders were supposedly committed randomly, without motive."

"Show me." Bryant grabbed at Longbright's paperwork. "Hmm – looks like he exhibits the classic ego-signifiers of a psychopath. I was discussing it with Alma just today."

"Oh, and what did she have to say about that?"

"I don't know, something about ironing. Goodness, whole batteries of tests were conducted by his doctors, and they all said the same thing." He pointed to an immense list of attributes that ran down the page. "Emotionlessness, detached, fearless, dissociated from reality, exhibits a grandiose manner, total lack of anxiety, attitude of entitlement, insatiable sexual appetite, tendency toward sadism. Has no normal responses to punishment, apprehension, stress or disapproval. A risk-taker and an uncontrollable liar."

"You're telling me the last man to see our missing man alive is a clinically certified psychopathic Russian dwarf?" asked May.

"I see what you mean. It might be best not to let the *Daily Mail* get hold of this one."

"We're going back to that sideshow tonight."

"And put them on their guard?" exclaimed Bryant. "What would be the point of that?"

"Why don't I go?" Longbright suggested. These days the Detective Sergeant found herself spending most of her life caged up in the office. "You know I like getting out into the field."

"This will get you out into *a* field."

"I can tell them I'm after a job as an assistant, and while I'm there I'll take a look around."

"All right, but for Heaven's sake, be careful. I don't like the sound of this one," said May, somewhat understating the problem. "You read the doctors' reports. He's duplicitous – an uncontrollable liar."

"I'd be happier if I came along to protect you, Janice," said Bryant, suddenly earnest. The sight of this shrunken, elderly gentleman with an arctic tonsure raised above his wrinkled ears, and wide watery eyes swimming at her through bottle-thick glasses, drew breath into her heart.

"I'll be careful, Mr Bryant, I promise," Longbright told him gently.

The barkers and their charges, the Moth Girl, Marvo the Caterpillar Boy, the Headless Lady, the Mummified Princess, the Human Pin-Cushion, the Girl in the Goldfish Bowl and Electra the 30,000 Volt Girl, were all on their second and third shows of the night. Most of the performances lasted only fifteen minutes, including the barker spiels, and on a good night the artistes would continue until most of the punters had seen most of the sideshows, paying separately for each in turn. But the driving rain had kept the attendance figures down for the fourth night in a row. Harry Mills paced fretfully in his caravan, no mean feat given his bulk and the doll's-house obstacle course of the interior. Finally he could stand it no longer, and stormed outside to find Michelle, the cashier. "We should close it down," he told her.

Michelle ran glittered nails through her frizz of dye-fried hair and puffed out over-rouged cheeks. "It ain't as bad as all that. The rain's easing off. We might get a late turnout."

"I don't care about the bloody attendance figures, we should just end this!" he shouted suddenly, frightening her. But of course, he was in no position to explain his fear. He needed to see Andrei.

He found the Russian dwarf seated at the back of Electra's tent, watching as the bored girl stepped on to her steel plate once more and prepared to produce sparks from unlikely places. A third of the benches were taken with spectators, including some teenaged boys armed with cans of lager.

"Now can I have a brave young man from the audience?" called the barker, a disreputable drunk Cockney who had only joined the Arcade of Abnormalities on this leg of the tour. He worked for booze but, having spent his life in funfairs and circuses, was capable of memorizing his lines perfectly. "You, sir, with the racy haircut, you look like you have an eye for the ladies – would you care to step up here?" The barker pointed so energetically and with such conviction that the boy could not refuse. His friends laughed and pushed him forward. The barker swung him up on the stage to make him look good in front of the crowd; the secret was not to show anyone up, to build expectations but then give them relief after a scare and show the volunteers how brave they'd just been, granting them a round of applause.

The barker produced a shiny metal salver and dropped a set of keys on to it. "These keys," he said, "are the keys to the lovely Miss Electra's hotel room. She's a very lonely lady and likes to have company on these long dark nights."

He handed the salver to Electra, who raised up the tray with a dazzling smile and a flourish for the audience. "Now," the barker instructed, "if you can take these keys from the salver, I think Miss Electra will be prepared to reward your bravery with a night of pleasure."

In the audience, a couple of families with small children looked awkward. The young man grinned out at his mates. To be honest, the arcade's latest Electra had seen better days, but a challenge was a challenge. He blew on his fingers like a safecracker, and prepared to reach out for the keys.

"But first," said the barker, "we must turn on Electra's own safety shield of 30,000 volts, which she needs to protect herself from the attentions of her many admirers." Someone in the audience gave a sarcastic laugh as the switch was thrown. There was a buzz and a crackle, and Electra was illuminated with tall, wavering spikes of blue-white static. The young man suddenly looked a little less confident. His friends egged him on. Stretching out his hand, he went to clasp the keys and received an electric shock. It was only a small one, but the anticipation had paid off and he yelped, jumping away as his mates roared with laughter.

Janice Longbright had seen enough. Some of the illusions were obvious. Electra was standing on a metal plate producing a low level of static discharge, capable of lighting a neon tube when she connected it to the terminal hidden in her palm, enough to scare a punter who had already been unnerved by the spinning dials and jolting needles of the standard Frankenstein-laboratory equipment behind Electra that included a spark regulator and a Wimshurst machine.

While she waited for Andrei Federov to finish overseeing the shows, Longbright wandered across to the other tents. The Half-Bodied Woman and the Moth Girl produced similar effects, one through judicious use of careful lighting and angled mirrors, the other via a rig that disguised her tightly contorted body beneath a framework simulacrum. The princess who turned into a mummy involved two performers with a glass scrim passing between them – although having the mummy break loose at the end was a nice touch. Lucio the Human Pin-Cushion clearly had a skin condition, and she knew that bleeding could be prevented by pinching the epidermis and folding it in such a way that it could be pierced without harm.

The only exhibits that still fooled her were Marvo the Caterpillar Boy, effectively a writhing torso in green shag-haired monster make-up that was either a dressed-up amputee or a disturbing rubber-beaked prosthetic, and the Headless Lady, which she decided most likely involved someone putting their arms through a model of a woman's chest, although she still could not see how the trick really worked.

Longbright went in search of Harry Mills. She found the showman hiding away in his caravan, looking as if the weight of the world was on his broad shoulders. Introducing herself, she gave him her own barker's spiel.

"I was once a magician's assistant in Blackpool," she explained, making sure that Mills got a good look at her infinite legs. "Just during the summer holidays. But I'm very well-rehearsed in the art of prestiges." These were the gestures used by assistants to distract audience members from the magician's activities. The statuesque Longbright had arrived at the Arcade of Abnormalities dressed in a low-cut spangled red leotard she had borrowed from a costume shop in Camden. As much as she disliked using her sex appeal on Mills, she needed to get backstage access in a way that would never be granted to punters. Mills was clearly distracted by her voluptuous figure, but was tense and abrupt.

"If I could just have a meeting with your general manager, I feel sure I'd be able to persuade him to consider me," she persisted.

"I'm afraid that's not possible, love," said Mills. "Andrei is very busy at the moment. Now if you'll excuse me, there's a lot of work to be done before we close up . . ." Rising, he began ushering her from his caravan.

Longbright was a police officer/showgirl who wouldn't take no for an answer. "It's all right," she said cheerfully, "I can see myself out. Perhaps we'll run across each other." Backing to the door, she pushed against the handle and slipped outside before he could stop her.

The audiences had gone home now, and the sideshows were in darkness. Moving between each of the tents in turn, she found that their entrance-flaps were held together with rope and were easily loosened. She checked the stages, but all were emptied and silent. Presumably the "exhibits" had all returned to their caravans. Mingled scents of burned petrol, sawn wood, popcorn, electricity and stale sweat pervaded the canvas rooms, and beneath these lay an animal musk, the tang of something feral and corrupt.

Two fat grey candles still burned behind tin shields in the Caterpillar Boy's tent. Checking inside, she pulled back the yellow satin curtains and found the stage bare. She had just turned to leave when a dark, stunted figure blocked her path at the entrance.

Longbright could see two cones of crimson skin sculpted like horns, broad bow legs set wide apart, a barrel chest topped with an abnormally large head.

"The show has ended. You should not be here." The dwarf remained motionless beneath the flickering lights, watching her. A more bizarre apparition was impossible to imagine, not because Andrei was of diminutive stature but because he had exaggerated his unusual features as much as possible. As he spoke he kept his deep-set eyes fixed tightly on hers. From his right fist he trailed his whip. "I thought you English know that it's rude to stare," he said with soft menace.

"You encourage it," she replied. "The make-up, the piercings, the tattoos, I'd say you set out to deliberately provoke."

"I am not as other people, so I have remade myself in order to increase the difference."

"You mean because you're a dwarf."

"I mean because I am of superior intellect," Andrei replied.

"I was hoping to see you," said Longbright. "I'm trying to get a job."

"You're trying no such thing. You're looking for Michael Portheim."

There was no point in lying, she decided. "What makes you think that?" Longbright assessed the situation, playing for time. Andrei was standing in front of the only exit, and was armed.

"You're a police officer." Andrei sniffed the air. "I can smell them a mile off. I suppose you want to know why he came to see me."

"The information would be helpful, yes."

"Let's just say it concerned the Seven Points."

"The Seven Points? What does that mean?"

"You're the law, you tell me. Portheim works for the secret service. You know most of their agents are psychologically disturbed. Their problems run very deep."

"I guess you'd know about that. I've read your own medical evaluation."

Andrei exhaled wearily, flicking the whip much as a bored tiger would twitch its tail. "Doctors are hardly the best judges of character. Most of them are ill themselves. They lack a sense of vision."

"Is that what Portheim lacked?"

"You know nothing about him other than what your bosses have told you. You've read a screenful of unreliable data posted in a document written by strangers half a world away."

"How do you know that?"

"There is no other access to my medical records from here, only material which the state of my mother country allowed."

"Then tell me what you know about Michael Portheim."

"What do I get in return?"

"We don't make bargains," said Longbright firmly.

"Then you get no information." Andrei smiled tightly.

"We're not supposed to tell you what we think when we're investigating . . . persons of interest," said Longbright carefully. "But these are unusual circumstances, and I'm speaking for myself, not my bosses. I think you killed him."

Andrei's smile broadened, revealing filed teeth. "Now why would I do that?"

"Going from your past record, you don't need a reason. You're mad."

The smile faded. Andrei suddenly raised his arm and cracked the whip in her direction, making her start. "And you are trespassing on private property. Now get out of here before I set the dogs on you. They haven't been fed, and will tear you apart."

"I'll be back with a warrant to take this place down," Longbright warned. "If we find any evidence against you, you won't avoid justice again." She left, knowing that he was watching her every step of the way.

It was nearly ten-thirty p.m. when the detective sergeant found Bryant & May in the Nun & Broken Compass, finishing their pints. "I didn't let him see I was frightened," she said, accepting a frothy pint of Made in Camden Lager from them. "He's certainly arrogant. And there's a stillness about him that's incredibly threatening."

"It still doesn't mean he knows anything about Portheim's disappearance," said May.

"He was taunting me, John. He said Portheim went to see him, not Harry Mills."

"That suggests he was ready to sell secrets. Federov may be a psychopath, but he's well connected."

"He mentioned something called the Seven Points. What does that mean?"

"Well," Bryant began, "the only Seven Points I can think of are the key meditative stages of mind training. It's a system of behavioural modification and self-improvement conducted to awaken the senses, part of Mahayana Buddhism. We know Portheim studied a lot of Eastern belief systems because the contents of his flat list an awful lot of books on the subject, but why would he go to see Federov or Mills about them?"

"Mills may seem a rough-and-ready type, but he has a shared history with Portheim," said May. "They studied together. Maybe they shared other interests."

"So he goes to see Mills about learning meditation and instead Andrei Federov murders him?" scoffed Bryant. "Forgive me, but that doesn't seem very likely. And where's he buried – under the common?"

"Federov is explosively unpredictable – anything could have happened," said Longbright.

"There's something else to take into account," said Bryant. "I dug a little further into his background. Unfortunately most of his files are archived in St Petersburg, and are only made available to authorized visitors who can arrange their appointments in person, but his academic records are online. It seems he was a brilliant student, specializing in code-breaking."

"The same as Portheim," said Longbright.

"I imagine his university achievements singled him out for attention by the Russian Federal Security Service. After he leaves college, there's an eight-year gap in his file. The next time he appears is in court for murder – the case was heard *in camera*."

"So you think he was released with help from his former colleagues?"

"I've no idea," said Bryant. "But you have to admit, it's very suggestive."

"So, what do we do now?"

"Crisps," said Bryant. "Worcester Sauce flavour. Three bags. And a sausage. I'll think more clearly then."

"You won't be able to reason with him," said May nervously, as they pushed open the gate to the park and set off in the direction of the sideshows once more. It was past midnight, and the rain-clouds had parted to reveal a sickly moon.

"Not that you've ever been able to reason. I mean, not properly. You're utterly illogical so maybe the two of you have something in common. And what if you're wrong? What if Michael Portheim left the arcade alive and just – I don't know – fled the country? Or lay down and died somewhere in the woods where no one has found him yet?"

"He didn't leave the park," said Bryant. "The CIA and MI5 couldn't find him."

"And that means we can? Without back-up? I don't understand how."

"The secret-service agencies collate empirical data, but we operate on instinct and emotions," said Bryant. "We can't involve anyone else because we're not even supposed to be involved now. And my ears are tingling, which means I know he's killed again."

"We don't have a warrant yet," May reminded him. "And what do you mean, we're not meant to be involved? Did I miss a meeting?"

"Something like that, yes. I had a bit of an argument with MI5 earlier. But Harry Mills is closing the arcade after tonight," said Bryant. "If he does that, Andrei Federov will disappear and no one will ever know what happened to one of the country's top code-breakers. Slow down a bit, will you? You're very tense tonight."

"Are you surprised?" said May. "Trying to get the goods on a whip-wielding psychopath in the middle of the woods?"

"We're in a London park," said Bryant. "Honestly, I never took you for such a worryguts."

"Do you really think he killed Portheim?"

"If he did, I'd like to know what he did with the body."

"He has an IQ of almost 130, not that I suppose intelligence translates into common sense, but I can't imagine he'd be so stupid as to bury it."

"No," said Bryant, thinking. "The tents are pitched right in the middle of the park, which is bordered on all four sides by main roads, and they're all covered with traffic cameras. I suppose he could have fed Portheim to his dogs, but he's more likely to have hidden him somewhere."

"Why do you say that?"

"Oh, you know," said Bryant, waggling his fingers around his forehead, "twisted mind, likes to play with people."

"I can't get *my* mind around motiveless crimes at all," said May. "There are no reference points to work from."

"Oh, I don't think it was motiveless," said Bryant. "Far from it."

"Can you prove that?"

"I'm going to have a damned good try."

They had reached the arcade entrance. The evening's customers had long been ushered from the area, but the main gate was unlocked. The burning flambeaux that lit the walkways around the edge of the tents were guttering in the rain, throwing odd angles of flamelight across the trodden, sodden grass.

And there he was, waiting for them, as dark and solid and mysterious as an ancient crow-filled oak.

"Mr Bryant, Mr May, thank you for sending me your show-girl. I returned her intact."

"Ah, you met our Miss Longbright," said Bryant cheerfully. "Got a minute? Can we sit down somewhere? My legs are killing me."

"Everything is killing you," replied Andrei. "Your air, your food, your water, but most of all, your beliefs."

"Ah, you're in a philosophical turn of mind tonight, I see." Bryant smiled indulgently as he eased his old bones on to the wooden bench. He was playing for high stakes now, and chose his words carefully. "We find ourselves drawn back here, Mr Federov, because as you admitted yourself, Mr Portheim's story ends here with you."

"That's not quite true. His story goes on."

"We know he didn't leave here. We know you're the last person who saw him alive."

"I'm afraid that's not true either."

"Given your track record, it's not likely that we'll believe you, is it?"

"I don't know. I imagine your belief systems and mine are at variance. On my twelfth birthday I discovered a deep and powerful spirituality within me, and have acted according to its dictates ever since. It was like being touched on the cheek by a butterfly's wing."

"Unfortunately you touched someone on the cheek with something a little sharper than a butterfly's wing. You're a dab hand with a knife by all accounts. Wasn't that why you were expelled from school? And didn't your father kill himself on your twelfth birthday?"

For the first time, Andrei's composure momentarily flickered, like a video transmission briefly losing its signal.

"And this spiritual awakening of yours includes murder," Bryant pressed.

"Not at all. I have never killed anyone." The dwarf's features had recomposed themselves. He was in control once more. "I would not presume to hold the power over life and death. That responsibility is not in the charge of mortals."

"Interesting. Tell me, do you think you are mad?" Bryant favoured surprising his suspects with the kind of blunt questions few officers ever asked.

"Never. I know I'm not."

"How do you know?"

"Because everything I do is for a reason."

"Of course. The Seven Points," said Bryant, realization dawning on him. Jumping to his feet, he made a dash – a slow one, as Mr Bryant is rather old – toward the yellow silk curtain that closed the stage from the public. Andrei spun himself around and raised his whip, cracking it so that the end wrapped itself around Bryant's wrist, but a moment later May was on him. The detectives never carried weapons but, knowing that Andrei was dangerous, May had borrowed Longbright's taser. He cracked it across Andrei's barrel chest, convulsing him.

"A bit more effective than Electra's 30,000-volt static stunt," he said as the dwarf fell to the floor. Bryant flicked back the curtain with his walking stick. There, writhing on the crimson-painted dais in the centre of the stage, was the Caterpillar Boy, a limbless green torso with an absurd rubber beak and bulbous articulated eyes.

Bryant tore at the plastic strips holding the exhibit's mask tightly in place.

Underneath it he found Michael Portheim, his face contorted in agony. His body had been painted green, and his arms and legs had been severed and neatly sutured at their bases. He was held in place on the dais by a single plastic strap.

"Federov was a medical student for two years in St Petersburg," said Bryant, looking for something with which to cut Portheim free. "If that little fellow moves again, stick a few more volts up him."

May looked at the Caterpillar Boy, aghast. "Why would he do such a thing?" he asked.

"Because of the Seven Points. Give me a hand here." Bryant had found his Swiss Army knife, and used the blade to sever the strap. "I knew there had to be a reason why Andrei Federov was released by the Russian Security Service. They wouldn't set a psychopath free and then allow him to leave the country without a purpose. He was dangerous, but he knew exactly what he was doing, and needed cover to operate as an agent.

"Portheim has a head full of counter-terrorist information that Federov needed to unearth and deliver, so he used a technique from the old country to get it. The immobilization of the prisoner by the removal of his limbs. He had to be kept alive until he'd given everything up. He had everything taken away from him except the Seven Points." Bryant indicated his ears, eyes, mouth and nostrils.

"My God, the poor devil," exclaimed May.

"The Seven Points," said Bryant. "I realized that only one of the exhibits was reduced to relying on them. He had to be kept alive until he'd been drained of information. I imagine Mills is the only other person who knows the truth about what's been going on here since the night he arrived.

"I'm willing to bet that Federov perfected his interrogatory technique in Russia. The difference was that there his victims died before anyone could get to them. Technically I suppose you could argue that he didn't kill anyone – his countrymen let them die from their surgery."

"All right, the RFFS want information, but I can't imagine that they'd have asked Federov to put his victim on display in a side-show, for God's sake," said May.

"Well, that was a bit of an own-goal on their behalf, I'm afraid," said Bryant. "They branded him a psychopath when it suited them, but he became one." The last of the plastic strips came away from Portheim's mouth, and he was able to speak.

"He needs water," said May. "He's suffering from dehydration."

Bryant handcuffed the dwarf to a tent-pole with Portheim's strap, and May called for an ambulance.

"They can do miracles with prosthetic limbs these days," said Bryant, not very reassuringly. "Of course, that will deprive the Caterpillar Boy of his career in showbusiness."

"Let's not use the term 'Caterpillar Boy' in Mr Portheim's presence any more, Arthur," May whispered.

"Tricky, isn't it?" mused Bryant. "To define the exact point where sanity ends and madness begins."

"In this job, yes," agreed his partner, feeding the limbless spy water as his partner locked the devil-headed dwarf to a tent-post.

HARLAN ELLISON®

All the Birds Come Home to Roost

HE TURNED ONTO his left side in the bed, trying to avoid the wet spot. He propped his hand against his cheek, smiled grimly, and prepared himself to tell her the truth about why he had been married and divorced three times.

"Three times!" she had said, her eyes widening, that familiar line of perplexity appearing vertically between her brows. "Three times. Christ, in all the time we went together, I never knew that. Three, huh?"

Michael Kirxby tightened the grim smile slightly. "You never asked, so I never mentioned it," he said. "There's a lot of things I never bother to mention: I flunked French in high school and had to work and go to summer school so I could graduate a semester late; I once worked as a short-order cook in a diner in New Jersey near the Turnpike; I've had the clap maybe half-a-dozen times and the crabs twice . . ."

"Ichhh, don't talk about it!" She buried her naked face in the pillow. He reached out and ran his hand up under her thick, chestnut hair, ran it all the way up to the occipital ridge and massaged the cleft. She came up from where she had hidden.

That had been a few moments ago. Now he propped himself on his bent arm and proceeded to tell her the truth about it. He never lied; it simply wasn't worth the trouble. But it *was* a long story, and he'd told it a million times; and even though he had developed a storyteller's facility with the interminable history of it, he had learned to sketch in whole sections with apocryphal sentences, had developed the use of artful time-lapse jumps. Still, it took a good fifteen minutes to do it right, to achieve the proper reaction and, quite frankly, he was bored with the recitation. But there were occasions when it served its purpose, and this was one of them, so he launched into it.

"I got married the first time when I was twenty, twenty-one, something like that. I'm lousy on dates. Anyhow, she was a sick girl, disturbed before I ever met her; family thing, hated her mother, loved her father – he was an ex-Marine, big, good-looking – secretly wanted to ball the old man but never could cop to it. He died of cancer of the brain but before he went, he began acting erratically, treating the mother like shit. Not that the mother didn't deserve it . . . she was a harridan, a real termagant. But it was really outrageous, he wasn't coming home nights, beating up the mother, that sort of thing. So my wife sided with the mother against him. When they found his brain was being eaten up by the tumour, she flipped and went off the deep end. Made my life a furnace! After I divorced her, the mother had her committed. She's been in the asylum over seventeen years now. For me, it was close; too damned close. She very nearly took me with her to the madhouse. I got away just in time. A little longer, I wouldn't be here today."

He watched her face. Martha was listening closely now. Heartmeat information. This was the sort of thing they loved to hear; the fibre material, the formative chunks, something they could sink their neat, small teeth into. He sat up, reached over and clicked on the bed lamp. The light was on his right side as he stared toward the foot of the bed, apparently conjuring up the painful past; the light limned his profile. He had a Dick Tracy chin and deep-set brown eyes. He cut his own hair, did it badly, and it shagged over his ears as though he had just crawled out of bed. Fortunately, it was wavy and he *was* in bed: he knew the light and the profile were good. Particularly for the story.

"I was in crap shape after her. Almost went down the tube. She came within a finger of pulling me onto the shock table with her. She always, *always* had the hoodoo sign on me; I had very little defence against her. Really scares me when I think about it."

The naked Martha looked at him. "Mike . . . what was her name?"

He swallowed hard. Even now, years later, long after it was ended, he found himself unable to cleanse the memories of pain and fear. "Her name was Cindy."

"Well, uh, what did she do that was so awful?"

He thought about it for a second. This was a departure from the routine. He wasn't usually asked for further specifics. And running back through the memories he found most of them had blurred into one indistinguishable throb of misery. There were incidents he remembered, incidents so heavily freighted with anguish that he could feel his gorge becoming buoyant, but they were part of the whole terrible time with Cindy, and trying to pick them out so they would convey, in microcosm, the shrieking hell of their marriage, was like retelling something funny from the day before, to people who had not been there. Not funny. Oh, well, you'd have to be there.

What had she done that was so awful, apart from the constant attempts at suicide, the endless remarks intended to make him feel inadequate, the erratic behaviour, the morning he had returned from ten weeks of basic training a day earlier than expected and found her in bed with some skinny guy from on the block, the times she took off and sold the furniture and cleaned out the savings account? What had she done beyond that? Oh, hell, Martha, nothing much.

He couldn't say that. He had to encapsulate the four years of their marriage. One moment that summed it up.

He said, "I was trying to pass my bar exams. I was really studying hard. It wasn't easy for me the way it was for a lot of people. And she used to mumble."

"She mumbled?"

"Yeah. She'd walk around, making remarks you just *knew* were crummy, but she'd do it under her breath, just at the threshold of audibility. And me trying to concentrate. She knew it made me crazy, but she always did it. So one time . . . I was really behind in the work and trying to catch up . . . and she started that, that . . ." He *remembered*! "That damned *mumbling,* in the living room and the bedroom and the bathroom . . . but she wouldn't come in the kitchen where I was studying. And it went on and on and on . . ."

He was trembling. Jesus, why had she asked for this; it wasn't in the script.

". . . and finally I just stood up and screamed, 'What the hell are you mumbling? What the hell do you want from me? Can't you see I'm busting my ass studying? Can't you for Christ sake leave me alone for just five fucking minutes?'"

With almost phonographic recall he knew he was saying precisely, exactly what he had screamed all those years ago.

"And I ran into the bedroom, and she was in her bathrobe and slippers, and she started in on me, accusing me of this and that and every other damned thing, and I guess I finally went over the edge, and I punched her right in the face. As hard as I could. The way I'd hit some slob in the street. Hard, real hard. And then somehow I had her bedroom slipper in my hand and I was sitting on her chest on the bed, and beating her in the face with that goddamn slipper . . . and . . . and . . . I woke up and *saw me hitting her*, and it was the first time I'd ever hit a woman, and I fell away from her, and I crawled across the floor and I was sitting there like a scared animal, my hands over my eyes . . . crying . . . scared to death . . ."

She stared at him silently. He was shaking terribly.

"Jesus," she said, softly.

And they stayed that way for a while, without speaking. He had answered her question. More than she wanted to know.

The mood was tainted now. He could feel himself split – one part of him here and now with the naked Martha, in this bedroom with the light low – another part he had thought long gone, in that other bedroom, hunkered down against the baseboard, hands over eyes, whimpering like a crippled dog, Cindy sprawled half on the floor, half on the bed, her face puffed and bloodied. He tried desperately to get control of himself.

After some long moments he was able to breathe regularly. She was still staring at him, her eyes wide. He said, almost with reverence, "Thank God for Marcie."

She waited and then said, "Who's Marcie?"

"Who *was* Marcie. Haven't seen her in something like fifteen years."

"Well, who *was* Marcie?"

"She was the one who picked up the pieces and focused my eyes. If it hadn't been for her, I'd have walked around on my knees for another year . . . or two . . . or ten . . ."

"What happened to her?"

"Who knows? You can take it from our recently severed liaison; I seem to have some difficulty hanging on to good women."

"Oh, Mike!"

"Hey, take it easy. You split for good and sound reasons. I think I'm doomed to be a bachelor . . . maybe a *recluse* for the rest of my life. But that's okay. I've tried it three times. I just don't have the facility. I'm good for a woman for short stretches, but over the long haul I think I'm just too high-pressure."

She smiled wanly, trying to ease what she took to be pain. He *wasn't* in pain, but she had never been able to tell the difference with him. Precisely that inability to penetrate his façade had been the seed of their dissolution. "It was okay with us."

"For a while."

"Yeah. For a while." She reached across him to the nightstand and picked up the heavy Orrefors highball glass with the remains of the Mendocino Gray Riesling. "It was so strange running into you at Allison's party. I'd heard you were seeing some model or actress . . . or something."

He shook his head. "Nope. You were my last and greatest love."

She made a wet, bratting sound. "Bullshit."

"Mmm. Yeah, it is a bit, ain't it?"

And they stayed that way, silently, for a while. Once, he touched her naked thigh, feeling the nerve jump under his hand; and once, she reached across to lay her hand on his chest, to feel him breathing. But they didn't make love again. And after a space of time in which they thought they could hear the dust settling in the room, she said, "Well, I've got to get home to feed the cats."

"You want to stay the night?"

She thought about it a moment. "No thanks, Mike. Maybe another night when I come prepared. You know my thing about putting on the same clothes the next day." He knew. And smiled.

She crawled out of bed and began getting dressed. He watched her, ivory-lit by the single bed lamp. It never would have worked. But then, he'd known that almost from the first. It never worked well for an extended period. There was no Holy Grail. Yet the search went on, reflexively. It was like eating potato chips.

She came back to the bed, leaned over and kissed him. It was the merest touch of lips, and meant nothing. "Bye. Call me."

"No doubt about it," he said; but he wouldn't.

Then she left. He sat up in the bed for a while, thinking that it was odd how people couldn't leave it alone. Like a scab, they had to pick at it. He'd dated her rather heavily for a month, and they had broken up for no particular reason save that it was finished. And tonight the party, and he was alone, and she was alone, and they had come together for an anticlimax.

A returning. To a place neither had known very well. A devalued neighbourhood.

He knew he would never see Martha again.

The bubble of sadness bobbed on the surface for a moment, then burst; the sense of loss flavoured the air a moment longer; then he turned off the light, rolled over onto the dried wet spot, and went to sleep.

He was hacking out the progression of interrogatories pursuant to the Blieler brief with one of the other attorneys in the office when his secretary stuck her head into the conference room and said he had a visitor. Rubbing his eyes, he realized they had been at it for three straight hours. He shoved back from the conference table, swept the papers into the folio, and said, "Let's knock off for lunch." The other attorney stretched, and musculature crackled. "Okay. Call it four o'clock. I've got to go over to the 9000 Building to pick up Barbarossi's deposition." He got up and left. Kirxby sighed, simply sitting there, all at once overcome by a nameless malaise. As though something dark and forbidding were slouching towards his personal Bethlehem.

Then he went into his office to meet his visitor.

She turned half-around in the big leather chair and smiled at him. "Jerri!" he said, all surprise and pleasure. His first reaction: surprised pleasure. "My God, it's been . . . how long . . . ?"

The smile lifted at one corner: her bemused smile.

"It's been six months. Seem longer?"

He grinned and shrugged. It had been his choice to break up the affair after two years. For Martha. Who had lasted a month.

"How time flies when you're enjoying yourself," she said. She crossed her legs. A summary judgement on his profligacy.

He walked around and sat down behind the desk. "Come on, Jerri, gimme some slack."

Another returning. First Martha, out of the blue; now Jerri. Emerging from the mauve, perhaps? "What brings you back into my web?" He tried to stare at her levelly, but she was on to that; it made him feel guilty.

"I suppose I could have cobbled up something spectacular along the lines of a multi-million-dollar lawsuit against one of my competitors," she said, "but the truth is just that I felt an urgent need to see you again."

He opened and closed the top drawer of his desk, to buy a few seconds. Then, carefully avoiding her gaze, he said, "What is this, Jerri? Christ, isn't there enough crap in the world without detouring to find a fresh supply?" He said it softly, because he had said I love you to her for two years, excluding the final seven months when he had said fuck off, never realizing they were the same phrase.

But he took her to lunch, and they made it a date for dinner, and he took her back to his apartment and they were two or three drinks too impatient to get to the bed and made it on the living-room carpet still half-clothed. He cherished silence when making love, even when only screwing, and she remembered and didn't make a sound. And it was as good or as bad as it had ever been between them for two years minus the last seven months. And when she awoke hours later, there on the living-room carpet, with her skirt up around her hips, and Michael lying on his side with his head cradled on his arm, still sleeping, she breathed deeply and slitted her eyes and commanded the hangover to permit her the strength to rise; and she rose, and she covered him with a small lap-robe he had pilfered off an American Airlines flight to Boston; and she went away. Neither loving him nor hating him. Having merely satisfied the urgent compulsion in her to return to him once more, to see him once more, to have his body once more. And there was nothing more to it than that.

The next morning he rolled onto his back, lying there on the floor, kept his eyes closed, and knew he would never see her again. And there was no more to it than that.

Two days later he received a phone call from Anita. He had had two dates with Anita, more than two-and-a-half years earlier, during the week before he had met Jerri and had taken up with her. She said she had been thinking about him. She said she had been weeding out old phone numbers in her book and had come across his, and just wanted to call to see how he was. They made a date for that night and had sex and she left quickly. And he knew he would never see her again.

And the next day at lunch at the Oasis he saw Corinne sitting across the room. He had lived with Corinne for a year, just prior to meeting Anita, just prior to meeting Jerri. Corinne came across the room and kissed him on the back of the neck and said, "You've lost weight. You look good enough to eat." And they got together that night, and one thing and another, and he was, and she did, and then he did, and she stayed the night but left after coffee the next morning. And he knew he would never see her again.

But he began to have an unsettling feeling that something strange was happening to him.

Over the next month, in reverse order of having known them, every female with whom he had had a liaison magically reappeared in his life. Before Corinne, he had had a string of one-nighters and casual weekends with Hannah, Nancy, Robin and Cylvia; Elizabeth, Penny, Margie and Herta; Eileen, Gail, Holly and Kathleen. One by one, in unbroken string, they came back to him like waifs returning to the empty kettle for one last spoonful of gruel. Once, and then gone again, forever.

Leaving behind pinpoint lights of isolated memory. Each one of them an incomplete yet somehow total summation of the woman: Hannah and her need for certain words in the bed; the pressure of Nancy's legs over his shoulders; Robin and the wet towels; Cylvia who never came, perhaps could *not* come; Elizabeth so thin that her pelvis left him sore for days; having to send out for ribs for Penny, before and after; a spade-shaped mole on Margie's inner thigh; Herta falling asleep in a second after sex, as if she had been clubbed; the sound of Eileen's laugh, like the wind in Aspen; Gail's revulsion and animosity when he couldn't get an erection and tried to go down on her; Holly's endless retelling of the good times they had known; Kathleen still needing to delude herself that he was seducing her, even after all this time.

One sharp point of memory. One quick flare of light. Then gone forever and there was no more to it than that.

But by the end of that month, the suspicion had grown into a dread certainty; a certainty that led him inexorably to an inevitable end place that was too horrible to consider. Every time he followed the logical progression to its finale, his mind skittered away . . . that whimpering, crippled dog.

His fear grew. Each woman returned built the fear higher. Fear coalesced into terror and he fled the city, hoping by exiling himself to break the links.

But there he sat, by the fireplace at The Round Hearth, in Stowe, Vermont . . . and the next one in line, Sonja, whom he had not seen in years, Sonja came in off the slopes and saw him, and she went a good deal whiter than the wind chill factor outside accounted for.

They spent the night together and she buried her face in the pillow so her sounds would not carry. She lied to her husband about her absence and the next morning, before Kirxby came out of his room, they were gone.

But Sonja *had* come back. And that meant the next one before her had been Gretchen. He waited in fear, but she did not appear in Vermont, and he felt if he stayed there he was a sitting target and he called the office and told them he was going down to the Bahamas for a few days, that his partners should parcel out his caseload among them, for just a few more days, don't ask questions.

And Gretchen was working in a tourist shop specializing in wicker goods, and she looked at him as he came through the door, and she said, "Oh my God, *Michael*! I've had you on my mind almost constantly for the past week. I was going to call you—"

And she gave a small sharp scream as he fainted, collapsing face-forward into a pyramid of woven wicker clothing hampers.

The apartment was dark. He sat there in the silence, and refused to answer the phone. The gourmet delicatessen had been given specific instructions. The delivery boy with the food had to knock in a specific, certain cadence, or the apartment door would not be opened.

Kirxby had locked himself away. The terror was very real now. It was impossible to ignore what was happening to him. All the birds were coming home to roost.

Back across nineteen years, from his twentieth birthday to the present, in reverse order of having known them, every woman he had ever loved or fucked or had an encounter of substance with . . .

was homing in on him. Martha, the latest, from which point the forward momentum of his relationships had been arrested, like a pendulum swung as far as it could go, and back again, back, back, swinging back past Jerri and Anita, back to Corinne and Hannah, back, and Nancy, back, and Robin and all of them, straight back to Gretchen, who was just three women before . . .

He wouldn't think about it.

He *couldn't*. It was too frightening.

The special, specific, certain cadence of a knock on his apartment door. In the darkness he found his way to the door and removed the chain. He opened the door to take the box of groceries, and saw the teenaged Puerto Rican boy sent by the deli. And standing behind him was Kate. She was twelve years older, a lot less the gamin, classy and self-possessed now, but it was Kate nonetheless.

He began to cry.

He slumped against the open door and wept, hiding his face in his hands, partially because he was ashamed, but more because he was frightened.

She gave the boy a tip, took the box, and edged inside the apartment, moving Kirxby with her, gently. She closed the door, turned on a light, and helped him to the sofa.

When she came back from putting away the groceries, she slipped out of her shoes and sat as far away from him as the length of the sofa would permit. The light was behind her and she could see his swollen, terrified face clearly. His eyes were very bright. There was a trapped expression on his face. For a long time she said nothing.

Finally, when his breathing became regular, she said, "Michael, what the hell *is* it? Tell me."

But he could not speak of it. He was too frightened to name it. As long as he kept it to himself, it was just barely possible it was a figment of delusion, a ravening beast of the mind that would vanish as soon as he was able to draw a deep breath. He knew he was lying to himself. It was real. It was happening to him, inexorably.

She kept at him, speaking softly, cajoling him, prising the story from him. And so he told her. Of the reversal of his life. Of the film running backward. Of the river flowing upstream. Carrying him back and back and back into a dark land from which there could never be escape.

"And I ran away. I went to St. Kitts. And I walked into a shop, some dumb shop, just some dumb kind of tourist goods shop . . ."

"And what was her name . . . Greta . . .?"

"Gretchen."

". . . Gretchen. And Gretchen was there."

"Yes."

"Oh my God, Michael. You're making yourself crazy. This is lunatic. You've got to stop it."

"*Stop it!?!* Jesus, I wish I *could* stop it. But I can't. Don't you see, you're *part* of it. It's unstoppable, it's crazy but it's hellish. I haven't slept in days. I'm afraid to go to sleep. God knows what might happen."

"You're building all this in your mind, Michael. It isn't real. Lack of sleep is making you paranoid."

"No . . . no . . . listen . . . here, listen to this . . . I remembered it from years ago . . . I read it . . . I found it when I went looking for it . . ." He lurched off the sofa, found the book on the wet bar and brought it back under the light. It was *The Plague* by Camus, in a Modern Library edition. He thumbed through the book and could not find the place. Then she took it from him and laid it on her palm and it fell open to the page, because he had read and reread the section. She read it aloud, where he had underlined it:

"'Had he been less tired, his senses more alert, that all-pervading odour of death might have made him sentimental. But when a man has had only four hours' sleep, he isn't sentimental. He sees things as they are; that is to say, he sees them in the garish light of justice – hideous, witless justice.'" She closed the book and stared at him. "You really believe this, don't you?"

"Don't I? Of course I do! I'd be what you think I am, crazy . . . *not* to believe it. Kate, listen to me. Look, here you are. It's twelve years. Twelve years and another life. But here you are, back with me again, just in sequence. You were my lover before I met Gretchen. I *knew* it would be you!"

"Michael, don't let this make you stop thinking. There's no way you could have known. Bill and I have been divorced for two years. I just moved back to the city last week. Of *course* I'd look you up. We had a very good thing together. If I hadn't met Bill we might *still* be together."

"Jesus, Kate, you're not *listening* to me. I'm trying to tell you this is some kind of terrible justice. I'm rolling back through time with the women I've known. There's you, and if there's you, then the next one before you was Marcie. And if I go back to her, then that means that after Marcie . . . after Marcie . . . *before* Marcie there was . . ."

He couldn't speak the name.

She said the name. His face went white again. It was the speaking of the unspeakable.

"Oh God, Kate, oh dear God, I'm screwed, I'm screwed . . ."

"Cindy can't get you, Mike. She's still in the Home, isn't she?"

He nodded, unable to answer.

Kate slid across and held him. He was shaking. "It's all right. It's going to be all right."

She tried to rock him, like a child in pain, but his terror was an electric current surging through him. "I'll take care of you," she said. "Till you're better. There won't be any Marcie, and there certainly won't be any Cindy."

"*No!*" he screamed, pulling away from her. "*No!*"

He stumbled toward the door. "I've got to get out of here. They can find me here. I've got to go somewhere out away from here, fast, fast, where they can't find me ever."

He yanked open the door and ran into the hall. The elevator was not there. It was never there when he needed it, needed it badly, needed it desperately.

He ran down the stairs and into the vestibule of the building. The doorman was standing looking out into the street, the glass doors tightly shut against the wind and the cold.

Michael Kirxby ran past him, head down, arms close to his body. He heard the man say something, but it was lost in the rush of wind and chill as he jammed through onto the sidewalk.

Terror enveloped him. He ran toward the corner and turned toward the darkness. If he could just get into the darkness, where he couldn't be found, then he was safe. Perhaps he would be safe.

He rounded the corner. A woman, head down against the wind, bumped into him. They rebounded and in the vague light of the street lamp looked into each other's faces.

"Hello," said Marcie.

RIO YOUERS

Wide-Shining Light

I WOULDN'T HAVE gone to the school reunion but for the fact that Lorna had left me three weeks before, and I felt resentful and disillusioned, and yes . . . in need of company. Perhaps not the best state of mind in which to revisit old acquaintances, but in the raw weeks following a separation – particularly one as volatile as mine and Lorna's – a person will often feel that they are drowning, and at such times will cling to anything.

Thus, I treated myself to some new clothes and a haircut, assumed a brave face, and attended the reunion at the Bellston Mark Hotel (three miles from our old school, but with the distinct advantage of being able to sell alcohol). I had hoped to rekindle a friendship, or, better yet, discover a thread that I might weave into a new beginning. I clung to this possibility as the cold water lapped first around my waist, then around my shoulders, then around my face. It covered my mouth, nose, and eyes, and just when I believed my lungs would burst, a hand reached down and pulled me free.

"Martin? Martin Sallis?"

It had been twenty-five years since I'd heard that voice. I turned, drink in hand, and looked at the man who, as a boy, had been my best friend through primary and secondary school. He'd lost most of his hair and gained a paunch, but his voice – other than it being deeper – was the same. That familiar inflection, and, unmistakably, the interdental lisp, turning the sibilants in my surname into "th" sounds: Thallith. His eyes were the same, as well. Light brown with delicate orange flecks. A person can change stature, hairstyle, even face shape, but their eyes will always remain the same.

I didn't need to look at his nametag. I offered my hand.

"Good to see you, Richard."

We shook emphatically. Red wine spilled over the rim of my glass, on to my hand. The following morning I would find maroon stains on my shirt cuff.

He grinned. "It's been a long time."

"It has."

"You moved to . . .?"

"Thame."

"That's right. I knew it was somewhere in Oxfordshire."

A pause while we looked at each other, smiling. Richard patted the top of his head. "Sunroof," he said, and I told him he looked good for his age, which wasn't entirely true, but he nodded gracefully, enquired into my line of work, and from there we fell into easy conversation, with much laughter, and I felt the years receding like waves having already crashed.

Even then I thought it peculiar how we opened up to one another. The previous twenty-five years had, in effect, rendered us strangers, yet we forsook reticence and shared like . . . well, like old friends. I found it refreshing. Liberating, even. So much of my life with Lorna had been spent behind a wall. One that she had built. Perhaps it was the occasion (or more likely the alcohol), but I relaxed into a space where before there was impediment, and felt that Richard did the same.

Our former classmates danced unabashedly to songs that topped the charts when we were at school, but neither Richard nor I – in keeping with our younger selves – joined them; we had never sought the limelight – were content, both, with our roles of little remark. This reserve was one of many reasons for Lorna's discontent. My "spectacular nothingness", she called it. I preferred Richard's term: under the radar. However viewed, it suited me – suited *us* – and we sat while the music played.

Not that we weren't enjoying ourselves; the discourse flowed as readily as the alcohol, and, in timely fashion, we switched from Zinfandel to Glenfiddich as our conversation turned to matters of the heart.

"How long have you been married?" Richard asked, indicating, with the rounded base of his tumbler, the ring on my finger.

"Seven years," I replied, and sighed. "I should probably take this off, though."

"Oh?"

"We're recently separated," I said. "It's too long a story. One for another occasion, perhaps. Suffice to say our accord has . . . faltered."

Richard's light brown eyes gleamed. "Do you still love her?"

I rattled the ice cubes in my glass, took a sip, and contemplated my wretched heart. If I looked beyond the disillusionment and self-pity, and assessed my marriage for what it was, did love remain? I thought, on my part, it did, but was too drunk and emotional to be certain. I needed time and perspective, both of which Lorna had granted me. She had also granted me torment, of course, and loneliness. Our union had gone from being blessed – witnessed by God, no less – to a tumult of lies and heartaches. I was guilty of spectacular nothingness. Lorna was guilty of abuse, infidelity, and spite.

"She's an unthinkable cunt," I said.

Richard raised an eyebrow. "Perhaps you'll revise that opinion with a sober mind."

I smiled and shrugged, took an ice cube into my mouth and crunched it between my teeth. "And you?" A vague gesture in Richard's direction. "A special someone?"

"Very special," he replied at once, and I watched the emotion touch his face like rain. His gaze faded and skimmed away. "Constance. My wide-shining light. My shelter from the storm."

I swallowed the ice. It leaked into my chest and I imagined it, as bright as dye.

"And you didn't bring her tonight?"

His eyes snapped back to mine. Clear again. "She died eight years ago." He finished his drink with a hiss, showing his teeth.

"I'm so sorry," I offered.

"Not at all." Richard set his tumbler down and ran his finger around the rim until it sang. "I'm a stronger man for having had Constance in my life. And her death was a deeply spiritual moment. Quite beautiful, in fact."

I had no idea how to respond. All I could do was hold his gaze, and even that was challenging.

"Her light saved me," he said.

I nodded; all I could manage.

A rare lull in the conversation, which was lifted when a frightful redhead, her nametag illegible, invited us to dance. We declined, politely of course, and she shuffled away, leaving us to smirk in a juvenile fashion.

Richard tapped the base of his tumbler on the table. "Another drink, friend?"

I replied, "A double, I think."

And so continued our evening, with conversation, always affable, touching upon many topics, and the alcohol flowing with disconcerting ease. The DJ's choice of music ensured the dance floor was always full, and the class of 1987 kept things lively. Beneath whirling lights we saw bravado and coquettishness, ostentation and acquiescence. There was naked skin, stolen kisses, groping, fumbling, embarrassment. Richard and I opined that, of the latter, there would be even more the following morning. We watched it all from our pedestal, wearing smiles some would no doubt consider supercilious, though, again, I prefer Richard's term: detached.

"These people live clockwork lives," he said, flapping a hand at the dance floor. "They do the same thing day in, day out, marking the hours like wooden figurines in a clock."

Needless to say, we exchanged contact information with only each other at the end of the night. The old-fashioned way: with business cards. None of this Facebook nonsense.

"I live in Marlow," Richard said as we walked to the taxi rank. "Not such a drive to Thame. I'd like to see more of you."

"Absolutely," I concurred. "I've had an enjoyable evening. Very much needed." And it *was*. I already felt lighter, somehow, as if a stone, resting against some vital place inside me, had been lifted, or at the very least nudged aside, allowing me access to the man I'd been before Lorna came into my life.

By noon of the next day – before my hangover had even worn off – that stone would fall back into place, and I'd again be secured to the emotional pillory of dissolution. But at that moment, with Richard beside me and my head lightly spinning, I was unbound.

"I can see why we were such good friends at school," Richard said. "We're really quite alike."

"I'll say." I smiled at him.

"The same disposition, politics—"

"Kindred spirits."

"Quite." He laughed, swaying a little, the heels of his expensive shoes clicking off the pavement. His shadow, beneath the street lights, appeared disproportionately longer than mine. "And here we are, into our forties, with women absent from our lives."

"Better to have loved and lost," I offered. "Or so they say."

"So they say."

We arrived at the taxi rank, where our separate cabs were waiting. Mine would take me to a better grade of hotel than the Bellston Mark. Richard's would take him to his home in Marlow, four miles away. I thought, for a moment, that he was going to invite me along, so that we could imbibe into the early hours while Shostakovich blared from Denon speakers.

He didn't though; he held out his hand and I took it, shook firmly. I wasn't to know he had other plans – that Alexandra Locke, his latest victim, lay bound and gagged in his garage, and would be dismembered and disposed of before morning light.

"It's been a pleasure, Richard," I said.

"Absolutely," he agreed, and patted the pocket in which he'd placed my business card. "I'll call."

"Do."

And with that he got into his taxi. I watched as it pulled away, out of sight, wondering if I'd discovered my thread. And I *had* – only it wasn't one I controlled, one I could weave. Rather, it dangled loosely from my state of mind, and Richard had hold of the end.

He pulled. I unravelled.

Is there anything beyond redemption? Without hope or worth? Surely even the cruellest acts have extenuating circumstances, and the cruellest souls a vein of good? This is certainly true of Richard Chalk, my old friend. Yes, I saw his murderous side, but I also saw his kindliness. Small things, like calling his elderly mother to say that he was thinking about her – a thirty-second exchange that doubtless made her day. And much bigger things, like organizing a fun-run to raise money for Huntington's disease.

I wonder, did Richard balance his wickedness because he feared for his mortal soul, or did he genuinely wish to do good? I cannot pretend to understand the mind of a serial killer. Only one thing is for certain: he flashed between light and dark like a coin-flip in the moonlight.

Redemption, perhaps, for the man who murdered eleven women in eight years, but my marriage was beyond salvation. In the weeks following the reunion, I endeavoured to repair what was broken. I first took the old-fashioned approach; I sent Lorna flowers and gifts, and had Steve Wright dedicate "Nights in White Satin" to her on BBC Radio 2.

These things didn't work. If anything, they further soured her opinion of me. So I embraced my spiritual side (something Lorna constantly requested I do) and sought the advice of a medical intuitive. She – her name was Echo – claimed my Prana was agitated and my chakras out of line, and referred me to an energy healer. I went not because I believed it would work, but because I wanted Lorna to see how committed I was to winning her back, and how open to change.

Alas, my efforts were in vain; Lorna had no investment in reconciliation. Our separation had graduated to an irreparable rift – as I was to discover over a "reality-check luncheon" at Gee's in Oxford.

"How do I look?" I asked her, seated, wine in hand. Lorna had ordered tap water – would not allow herself anything as daring as Perrier, and certainly nothing alcoholic, for fear this luncheon be regarded a pleasure. I wanted her to loosen up, of course, enjoy herself, but she sipped water, ate salad, and sat board-stiff throughout.

"The same," she replied. "Gaunt." She had on a flesh-tone lipstick that made her mouth appear a thin, uncompromising line. "Why? Is there a reason you should look different?"

"I've had my chakras aligned," I said.

"Your chakras?"

"I'm energetically balanced." I inhaled vigorously and took another sip of wine. "Feels splendid. Apparently my sacral chakra was in a perilous state."

She sighed and looked away from me, her expression one of disdain. Such an ugly reaction. It twisted her face like a rag. Hard to imagine it the same face that would pulse pleasurably while we made love, and glow afterwards, sometimes for hours.

I wondered if any part of the old Lorna – the one who'd whispered "I do" seven years ago – remained. I reached across the table, perhaps to grasp it, if it were there, but she pulled away, folded her hands, placed them in her lap.

I touched the tablecloth where her hand had been only seconds before. I imagined a cat chasing reflected light.

"This luncheon—" I started.

"Lunch," Lorna interjected. "It's the twenty-first century, Martin. Nobody calls it luncheon any more."

I bit my lip and wished Richard were sitting beside me. We'd have ordered from the luncheon menu with glee. "This lunch," I said. "I'd assumed its purpose was to discuss reconciliation."

She looked at me again and her eyes were chips of granite. "All I wanted was to meet with you. Briefly. Lunch was *your* idea. And no . . . we won't be discussing reconciliation. It's time for a reality-check, Martin."

"You want a divorce?"

"Yes." A quick, unwavering reply.

The waiter came over and Lorna found a smile for him, ordering her sterile salad (she even turned down the vinaigrette) while I – unsmiling – ordered the veal. I could feel my carotid artery thumping as I enquired into the tenderness of the meat. The waiter assured me it was gourmet, and I assured him that nothing less than absolute atrophy of the muscle would suffice.

Lorna raised her eyebrow but said nothing. Her hand – no ring on her finger, I noted – was back on the table. I imagined driving my fork through it.

"Divorce," I said. "What would your mother say?" Lorna's mother was a devout Christian who kept the scriptures closer than her undergarments. No doubt she would decry the putting asunder of that which God joined together. "She'll be beside herself."

"This is not about my mother's contentment, it's about mine." Lorna flicked tawny hair from her brow and sipped her tap water. "Besides, she gave me the number of an excellent solicitor."

"She did?"

A dry smile in reply.

I groaned – more of a growl, actually – and glugged my wine, spilling it down my chin, managing to draw the attention of the

table to our left. I stared at them, eyebrows knitted, chin stained,
until they went back to their meals. Then I reached across the
table and grabbed Lorna's hand before she could pull away.

"Lorna, darling, I—"

"Let *go* of my hand." She kept her voice low, but I could see
the stringy muscle in her forearm tensing as she tried to pull free.

"Let's just—"

"Do you want me to scream?"

I let go and her hand snapped back so forcefully that the table
wobbled and her glass almost toppled over. Again we drew the
attention of other diners. I saw their scowls and heard them
mumble in disapproval. It took a few moments for the general
hum of conversation to resume.

"If you insist on making a scene," Lorna said, rubbing the back
of her hand, "I'll leave."

"You already left," I said.

"Show some dignity, Martin."

"Perhaps if you were to show some compassion . . ."

"Oh, really!" Now it was her turn to scowl. "It was compassion
that brought me here. I could – *should* – have had my solicitor
send you a letter."

I closed my eyes and recalled a breathing exercise my energy
healer – Leaf, his name was Leaf – taught me: four-seven-eight
breath. Slowly inhale through the nose for a four-count. Hold for
seven. Exhale for eight. I repeated until I reached a plain of calm
as broad as a motorway. No, a runway . . . a runway of calm that
I could take off from and soar, jets trembling.

"Your nostrils are flaring, Martin."

Four-seven-eight.

"Martin?"

"I don't want a divorce," I said, and looked at her squarely. "I
believe our marriage is worth rescuing. I can change, Lorna. I
have changed. Let me prove it to you."

I saw something in her eyes. A smoothing of the granite. As
close as she would come to lenity. It made me ache for the woman
who had promised herself to me, and who could make me breathe,
as if for the first time, with a well-chosen word, or the gentlest
touch.

"It's over," she said.

And this ache . . . I buried it, like I would have to bury all hope of reconciliation.

"Over?"

"Yes, Martin."

I'd had more enjoyable luncheons, if truth be told. We sat in near-silence, merely picking at our food (the veal was indeed gourmet, but my appetite, sadly, absent). I looked mostly out the window, but occasionally at Lorna, hoping to see a trace of the woman I had lost. But she was a stone, dull grey and bluntly edged. She avoided eye contact, and the closest she came to conversation was to remark on Alexandra Locke, the Hemel Hempstead woman who'd been missing for four weeks. A chap at a nearby table was reading the *Telegraph*, the pages folded so that her black-and-white image stared woefully at us.

"That poor woman," Lorna said. "I wonder if they'll ever find her."

She excused herself a short time later to use the facilities, and I did something I'm not proud of; I fished her mobile phone from her coat pocket and read several text messages (the phone was password-protected, but you don't share almost one-quarter of your life with someone without learning a little something about them, and I accessed the device on only the third try). I sought evidence of another man, if I'm being honest, reasoning that my solicitor should have all information pertinent to the separation.

I found nothing incriminating, however, only a number of messages to her harridan friends that were unnecessarily spiteful towards me. *He's a pithless cretin and I can't wait to get him out of my life,* one of them read. And another: *I'm doing the right thing, Molly; I couldn't live another second with that pompous arse.* Reading them made me remember the vindictiveness and anger directed at me in the final year of our marriage, how she brimmed with scorn, and pulled away when I tried to get close.

Lorna returned from the ladies' room and grabbed her coat from the back of her chair. The phone was safely back in her pocket by this time, but I still seethed. *Pithless cretin,* I thought. *Pompous arse.* I could barely look at her.

"I should leave," she said.

"Yes," I said. "You should."

Granite eyes and an uncompromising line. "My solicitor will be in touch."

"Don't expect me to make this easy for you." Spoken through clenched teeth, this sounded anything but pithless.

She swept from the restaurant, tawny hair bouncing, and I poured another glass of wine. I considered ordering a Glenfiddich, a double, and then another . . . drinking until the world's hardness was smoothed away, but to do so would be to risk making a scene. So I chose, as ever, spectacular nothingness.

The next few weeks were difficult, a whirlwind of angry phone calls, legal advice, and threats. I sought comfort from my family, who gave as much as they could, but have never really been attuned to matters of the heart.

"An incorrigible woman," my father offered. "If she were a dog, I'd have her put down."

My mother's approach was less cut-throat, but equally unhelpful. "A lot of the time it comes down to a woman's sexual needs," she said. "Perhaps you"ll be happier with someone less . . . particular."

Little surprise, then, that Richard Chalk became my primary source of support, as good a friend – at least to begin with – as one could hope for. I let him into my life and offered my trust. I served it to him, as vulnerable and atrophied, and in as many pieces, as the veal at Gee's. When I needed to spill my soul, he was there, always with the right amount of empathy, and always telling me what I needed to hear.

I invited him into my home.

I showed him photographs of Lorna. So help me God.

"Her eyes," he said. I'm sure there were other comments, but I can only remember those two words: her eyes.

How strange that I should open myself to him so quickly, so readily, given the twenty-five-year gulf in our relationship. A person will experience much in the years between secondary school and middle age, and their character – their state of mind – will adjust, sometimes for the better, sometimes for the worse. Even so, I thought I knew Richard. I thought he was my friend.

"We're really quite alike," he said to me, as he so often would. Perhaps he believed, if he said it enough, he could make it true. I admit, even I started to believe it.

"Quite," I said with a smile.

"What a shame we didn't stay in touch when we finished school," he said. "All those wasted years."

"We can make up for it now," I assured him.

We were sitting outside The Angel in Henley-on-Thames, a beautiful September evening, if a little cool, with the late sun dancing on the river in burned oranges and pinks, and traffic chasing across the stone bridge that arced to our left. I sighed with rare contentment and sipped my ale: Brakspear Oxford Gold, of good body. Richard had ordered the same. And so we sat with our identical drinks, beneath the wing of evening light, cut from the same cloth, you'd think.

"Are you feeling any better?" Richard asked.

"Actually, I am." I looked at him and nodded. "Thank you."

"Good ale," he held up his glass, "and good company. Works every time."

But it was more than that, lovely as these things were. And it was more than the pink light on the river and the somnolent buzz of traffic on the bridge. I felt I'd turned a corner in the last couple of days. Perhaps *many* corners. I was resolute, where before I had been wavering. Strong, where I had been . . . *pithless*. Also, I had grown to loathe Lorna, where once I'd known only love.

We'd had furious exchanges on the telephone, mainly because I'd refused to sign the petition for divorce (some small power, and I revelled in it). Her cruelty shocked me. She insisted, over and over, that she regretted ever having laid eyes on me, and how thankful she was that we'd never had children. She wished a car accident on me. A "crippling" one. And cancer – *cancer!* It was as if she were digging into a depthless sack of curses, and hurling them at me one after the other.

I gauged from this just how deeply she was hurting and how cruel it was not to give her what she sought. Thus, that very afternoon, I acceded – put pen to paper, sealed the petition in one of my personalized toile-lined envelopes, and dropped it in the pillar-box.

Were there tears? Yes . . . many, in fact. But they were not all tears of woe. They fell, and I found strength. They splashed on my shirt, and I found relief. So yes, I wept, and for a long time, but even a cocoon has to crack.

Richard called at precisely the moment I thought some company would be nice. He asked if I wanted to join him for drinks by the river – his judgement, as ever, exact.

The Thames's rippling surface deepened with bronze colour. A boat called *Mystery* sliced through, creating a V-shaped wake that rolled and broke musically against the banks.

"Such fortuity," I said, "meeting you, renewing our friendship at a time I needed it most. This has been arguably the most challenging period of my life, and I'm grateful to have had you beside me."

"Destiny," Richard said, although for a moment I thought, because of his lisp, he'd said, "death to me". He raised his glass and I touched it with mine.

Another boat chopped through, too small to have a name, its engine blatting disagreeably. Both Richard and I cast it reproachful glances.

"And you'll be there for me," he said, once the boat was out of earshot, "when I need you?"

"*Should* you need me," I said. "You're perfectly grounded, Richard. I'm sure there's not a problem you can't handle yourself. But yes . . . I'll be there."

"Thank you." He smiled and sipped his beer.

"That's what friends are for."

"Indeed."

I looked at him carefully, his fist curled around the pint glass, the setting sun casting the same bronze shades into his eyes. The right side of his mouth twitched. His sunken cheeks caught the evening shadows. I saw it then, I think, for the first time. A scarring, but beneath the surface, pulsing lightly against his skin from the inside. The man had issues, and they ran deep. Being his friend, I should have asked about them, but I had too much going on in my own life. I wasn't ready for Richard's problems. Not even close.

And you'll be there for me when I need you?

I turned back to the river. Almost red now. It rippled like a flag and chattered endlessly against the banks, and the traffic on the bridge buzzed and threw javelins of light that were like warnings.

*   *   *

He called at the beginning of October. A stormy, miserable night. I hadn't heard from him in some weeks – he hadn't returned my calls or emails – so hearing his voice came as some surprise. The timbre of that voice was more surprising still. I was so used to a firm, assured tone, which both reflected his character and compensated for his lisp. What I heard that night was altogether different: a trail of meek sound punctuated by sobs and cracked breathing.

"I need you, Martin," he said.

The drive from Thame to Marlow should not take longer than thirty minutes, depending on traffic and your chosen route. I took the M40, and being after nine p.m. – closer to ten – on a Thursday night, the traffic was light. Even so, it took me fifty minutes to reach Richard's house.

The weather was dreadful, with heavy rain lashing my car and ugly gusts blowing me into the next lane. HGVs rumbled by, creating maelstroms that I believed would whip me from the road and carry me away. Dirty water sprayed from beneath their rear tyres, covering my windscreen. I gripped the steering wheel so hard my knuckles throbbed. I wonder now if the elements conspired to keep me away. Given everything that happened that night, I wish they'd succeeded.

Richard's house was small, detached, and surrounded by trees that thrashed in the wind. There was a single-car garage butted on to its east face – an addition, judging by a vague discrepancy in the brickwork. His Volvo was parked in the driveway, but I didn't think this unusual; perhaps the garage was used for storage. I parked on the road and hurried through the rain to his front door.

It took him a while to answer. I thought the doorbell broken, and was about to knock when I saw his image through the frosted glass. The lock rattled and he opened the door, using his weight to keep it from slamming wide in the wind.

"Martin . . ." He appeared, as ever, kempt, dressed in a clean white shirt and corduroys. Following his telephone call, I'd expected to find him in disarray, but the only evidence that something was wrong was his puffy eyes and, as I noted a little later, a single spot of blood on the toe of his left shoe. He stepped back and the door pushed wider. "Do come in."

I was not so together, rattled by the drive, my clothes damp and leaves in my hair. I kicked off my shoes and followed Richard through to the living room, an elegant place, where Beethoven fluttered from stereo speakers and a tot of Glenfiddich had already been poured for me. I sat, and Richard placed a towel over my shoulders as I took several quick and warming sips from the glass.

"Thank you for coming." He sat opposite me on a high-backed Chesterfield, crystal tumbler resting in his palm, his legs crossed. That was when I noticed the drop of blood on his toe.

"Not at all." I looked at him, searching his swollen eyes. "I came as quickly as I could, but the weather—"

"'And I, cut off from the world, remain . . . Alone with the terrible hurricane'."

I frowned, then my eye flicked, again, to that glaring drop of blood.

"William Cullen Bryant." He smiled and sipped his whisky. "'The Hurricane'. It describes aloneness and fear in the face of doom." He followed my gaze, noticed the blood on his shoe, then wet the tip of his thumb and smeared it away. "Doom," he said again.

I finished my whisky, surprised at how quickly it had gone down, and surprised more at seeing my hand tremble as I set the empty glass upon the table. "I'm not familiar with it," I said.

"It's how I feel sometimes . . . isolated, scared, surrounded by darkness." On cue the windows shook, thunder exploding in the wet night. "I just want it to end."

I recalled sitting with Richard outside The Angel, and seeing something beyond his well-dressed, well-spoken exterior, perhaps the hurricane he was referring to. Maybe he had terminal cancer, only months to live, or some deep-rooted psychological concern that could only be suppressed through medication. Again I reflected how little I knew him, yet here I was in his house, in his life. The first threads of anxiety touched me as more thunder cracked outside. I wanted to leave, risk the storm again, but I had promised to help with his problem, just as he had helped with mine.

"I'm here for you, Richard," I said. "Whatever you need."

He took a framed photograph from a side-table close to his chair and handed it to me. "Constance," he said, then grabbed my empty glass and stepped to the drinks cabinet to pour another shot.

"Not for me, Richard," I said. "I have to drive home."

"Nonsense," he said. "You'll wait out the storm."

More anxiety, but I nodded and thanked him, then studied the photograph while the windows trembled and Beethoven's "Symphony No. 5" floated into its fourth movement. She was plain, Constance, to say the least. Not the beauty I'd envisioned, given she'd been described as a wide-shining light. Her marigold hair and clear eyes were offset by a palsied smile and a web of acne scars on her right cheek. Also, her hands were clasped in such a way as to indicate a disconnect in her motor functions.

Richard returned with my drink, which I exchanged for the photograph. I wanted to say something supportive, but all could manage was, "Let's hope there's not a power cut."

"I have candles," Richard said. He sat down, crossed his legs, stroked the photograph. "I never told you how she died."

"No."

He gazed at Constance's imperfect face and sighed, and at once I knew the reason for his call: he was still in mourning. Deeply spiritual though her death may have been, there were times when it consumed him.

"1994 was a terrible year," he said. "The worst of my life, by far, though with a silver lining that blinded me. My sister, to whom I was incredibly close, was killed in a skiing accident. A week later my grief-stricken father threw himself from the top of a multi-storey car park in Wycombe. You can imagine the effect this had on me and my mother. We spiralled into depression, side-by-side, yet so alone. She lost her job. I lost mine. My home, too. One moment everything was intact, and the next it was in pieces. *Everything.* I went from corporate conventions and health spas to psychiatrists and Prozac."

I nodded. Not that I could gauge the level of his despair. All I had lost was a wife who didn't love me, and I felt resentful at the world for that.

Richard snapped his fingers. "That's how quickly the hurricane hits, and your life is flipped upside down."

"Yes." I took a sip of whisky and the thunder boomed again.

"And then I met Constance. The silver lining." His fingers on the photograph, stroking, as if she could feel. "Long story short: things got better. She was the house I lived in. She gave me security, warmth, and comfort. And when the storms came, she gave me shelter. We got married in '96. A fairytale wedding in the Bahamas. Everything was perfect for another year, eighteen months, and then one morning – we were in the conservatory having breakfast – I noticed her hand trembling while she drank her grapefruit juice. Very subtle, but no mistaking it."

He demonstrated, but I knew what a trembling hand looked like; I had two of my own.

"You don't assume . . ." Richard's words faded and he shook his head. A single tear leaked from his eye and he smeared it away with his thumb, reminding me of the blood on his shoe. "You don't assume the worst from something like that. Not immediately. You just get on with your life, and in most cases forget it ever happened.

"But Constance started to exhibit more symptoms, some subtle, others not so. Flashes of irritability and a feverish temper. Distractedness, clumsiness, lots of weeping. I thought it was premature menopause. She told me not to be ridiculous. Anyway, we went to the doctor and ran some tests."

He put the photograph back in its place and drank his whisky. His eyes were distant, still wet. I plucked a leaf from my hair, but didn't quite know what to do with it. I twirled the stem between thumb and forefinger. The leaf flickered, gold and red. I sipped my drink and felt the weight of it – the weight of the night – pull at me from inside.

"Do you know anything about Huntington's disease, Martin?"

"Huntington's . . ." I twirled the leaf. I could see the tiny veins beneath its red skin and thought it looked too healthy a thing to detach and die. "It's like Parkinson's disease, isn't it?"

"There are similarities," Richard said. "Both are neurological maladies. Both are degenerative. Parkinson's affects the central nervous system, while Huntington's – I'm simplifying – deteriorates the areas of the brain responsible for movement, cognition, and personality. It usually begins around middle-age and progresses until there is little or no quality of life."

"How dreadful," I said.

"Indeed." Richard nodded. "Constance was diagnosed in 1998. A tall, strong, intelligent woman – the house I lived in, remember? Hard to believe anything could bring her down. But within five years she was a jerky, slurring shadow of her former self. She fell apart, brick by brick, and once again I felt the storm gathering."

I could hear the trees outside, twisting in the wind. I gathered the towel closer to me. "Miserable." Another sip of whisky. "Miserable way to die."

Richard looked at me. His eyes were clear but they appeared to shake in his skull like the windows in their frames. "Yes, but that's not what killed her." He grinned and I counted his teeth. All six hundred of them. "Not exactly."

"Richard, I . . ." The leaf, still between my fingers, caught my eye, softly glowing. "I'm afraid the Glenfiddich is going straight . . . straight to my head."

"We were living in this house. Not ideal, but it was the home we bought together after we were married, and we loved it. I had the dining room and a portion of the kitchen converted into a bedroom and bathroom so that Constance had no reason to go upstairs. I rarely left her untended, if I could help it. Sometimes I'd nip to the shops or mow the lawn, never longer than half-an-hour, and she was always fine – would sit where you are now and listen to an audiobook, or watch one of her Doris Day musicals.

"But there was one afternoon when I had to go into the attic to replace some damp insulation. It took a little longer than expected – maybe an hour – and when I came down I found her standing at the top of the stairs, not holding on to the banister or wall, just . . . standing there, jerking and swaying, looking down the flight at the hallway below. Maybe she had come up to ask me a question, and forgotten what it was, or maybe she had climbed the stairs to prove she still could. So many maybes, Martin, but what I think – what I truly *feel* – is that she was waiting for me to do exactly what I did."

The room swayed as I waited for him to continue. I thought it peculiar that I should feel squiffy on only a measure and a half of single malt, but put it down to a combination of the alcohol, the harrowing drive, and so many recent stresses. I rolled my hand, gesturing for Richard to continue. The room dipped and the walls seemed too far away.

"She looked at me," he said. "Her face was full of anguish, pain, sadness . . . can you even imagine?"

I could, in fact; I imagined her face like a detached leaf softly glowing, curled at the edges, tiny veins beneath the skin.

"I placed my hand between her shoulder blades." Richard blinked and several tears spilled on to his cheeks. "She nodded, or jerked her head. I'll never know. But I pushed, and down she went. Her head hit the newel post, the bottom wall, and then the floor. I'll never forget the sound – like three gunshots. Then I took a deep breath, walked downstairs, and watched her die."

"Good God, man," I said. Actually, I didn't; I *slurred* it. A crash of thunder echoed my unease. Richard was lowering his mask, showing me the shadowy thing beneath – a thing I had only glimpsed until now. It was all so disturbing.

I tried to stand but my limbs felt loaded with Novocain and I dropped back into my seat with a little gasp.

"Her eyes," he said. "I saw the life leave her body through her eyes, and it was sublime. They shone fiercely for three or four seconds. Exquisite, tiny novas. I almost felt that I could scoop one into each palm and carry them into every dark place. It was awe-inspiring. Invigorating. Then they faded, and I held her hand and stroked her hair. I wept, too." He wiped his eyes and showed me the tears on his fingers, fat as pearls. "Haven't stopped weeping, in fact."

"Please," I said. "I don't want to hear any more."

"It *had* to be done, Martin. You understand that, don't you?"

"No, Richard, I don't."

"Her house was in ruins," he said, a touch impatiently. "It couldn't shelter me any more, so I razed it to the ground. I released her."

Again I tried to stand. Again I slumped, boneless, back into my seat.

"Then I stood alone," he continued. "Yes, I had regular sessions with a psychiatrist. Yes, I was prescribed seemingly countless meds. But they didn't help. When the hurricanes came – as they did, and often – I recalled the light in Constance's eyes. It gave me the strength I needed, and the darkness went away."

His mouth twisted into a strange shape, too wide, too greedy. "At least for a while."

I reached for my whisky and knocked it over, quite deliberately. No more of that.

"What did you give me?" I asked.

"Rohypnol," he said. "Just enough."

"Why did . . .?"

"It will all become clear, Martin."

"Thought you were . . ." I twirled the leaf between thumb and forefinger. Red and gold. Such a pretty leaf. "I thought you were my friend."

Richard smiled and righted the glass. He used three Kleenex to mop up the spilled whisky. "Moonlight Sonata" started to play, a piece I have always loathed, due mainly to it being the one composition that even philistines are familiar with. Now I have cause to loathe it more.

"That light was so alluring, so powerful." Richard disposed of the sodden tissues and strolled over to a handsome mahogany cabinet. From its bottom drawer he took a box, and from the box he took a stack of newspapers. Thunder crashed. The windows trembled. Similarly, I shuddered as Richard stepped towards me and dropped one of the newspapers face-up on the table. It was an edition of the *Bucks Free Press* from November 2005. A young woman's face stared at me from the front page. She had short blonde hair and a smile that could lift your feet from the ground. A memory-feather tickled the back of my mind, but I was too numb to grasp it. The headline – unimaginative but succinct – read: VICKY STILL MISSING.

"Victoria Channing," Richard said, and with her full name the memory clicked into place. She was a local woman who was believed to have been murdered by her boyfriend. He had passionately maintained his innocence, and no charges were brought against him, but Vicky was never found, dead or alive. Now her eyes regarded me brightly and with faint accusation, the way they had for several weeks, until they disappeared from the newspapers altogether.

"From Great Missenden," I said, voicing details as they resurfaced in my mind. "Twenty-three years old. Worked at the Roald Dahl Museum."

"Yes." Richard nodded and grinned and every one of his six hundred teeth glistened. "I stabbed her three times and she died in my arms. I thought the light in her eyes would last for ever."

I jerked in my seat the way I sometimes do on the verge of sleep. That myoclonic spasm. That flash of terror. Only this time the terror was sustained. I looked at Richard with eyes like pools of cracked ice. "No," I slurred, my drumming heart adding syllables to the word. I shook my head and slurred it again: "Nuh-oh-oh-oh."

"I was wrong," Richard continued. "Nothing lasts for ever." He dropped the *Reading Evening Post* on to the table. It landed with a slap. Another young woman stared at me from the front page. "Rosemary Hill. I cut her throat with a Stanley knife in February of 2007. The light in her eyes was brief, but had a russet tinge that warmed me for months afterwards."

"Richard, I—"

Another newspaper. Slap.

"Elaine Emmington. Seventeen years old. My youngest victim. In my defence, she looked so much older."

I screamed. It was more of a warble, really, while "Moonlight Sonata" played and the thunder boomed.

"Her eyes," he said. "Goodness, her *light* . . ."

I wanted to run, of course, but there was no way. My body felt loaded with iron ball bearings, that would slip and roll heavily with even the slightest movement. So I closed my eyes and willed myself to float away . . . out of the seat, through the ceiling, through an upstairs room where Richard may once have made love to the wife he killed, through the roof and into the night. I could be as light as the leaf in my hand, carried for miles, until the storm exhausted itself and I landed in the greenest of meadows.

Richard crippled this fantasy by dropping newspapers on to the table and giving summaries of the women he had killed. His voice was an anchor attached to my delicate stem. I twirled the leaf and concentrated on it, and suddenly I remembered my energy healer – Leaf, his name was Leaf – and the breathing exercise he taught me.

Four-seven-eight. I applied it, but was only midway through my second set when Richard dropped the final newspaper on to the table. "Alexandra Locke," he said, and all the air rushed from my lungs. The fact that she was still in the news, and instantly recognizable, made it all the more real. I looked at her image, my heart thumping against my ribs like a fat fist.

"The police are looking for her," I said ridiculously, as if Richard didn't know this.

"Yes. They'll find her buried in my garden. In fourteen pieces." He paused before clarifying. "Easier to bury if they're . . ." And he made a chopping motion with his hand.

My fear was absolute. I think that if a crocodile had grabbed me in its jaws and death-rolled me to some deep, dark place I would not have been more scared. I made one last attempt to leap out of my seat and actually succeeded, but managed only three or four steps before collapsing. Richard came towards me. He planted one foot on my upper arm and rolled me on to my back.

"Silly," he said.

"Gur," I said. The room swam. Richard stood above me. The light behind gave him a halo. I would have laughed if I hadn't been so drugged.

"Do you know why I called you here tonight?" he asked.

"Going . . . kill me," I blurted.

"Quite the opposite, old boy." Those teeth again. "My house is in ruins and the hurricane is more vicious than ever. I can feel it howling in my head, taking me apart. I can't go on like this." He gestured at the newspapers on the table and then used the same hand to wipe his eyes. "I want you to release me, just like I released Constance."

"Don't . . . understand."

"Suicide is so crass. So classless. And if I could do it, I would have already."

"You want me to *kill* you?"

"Yes."

"What on earth makes you think . . ." my eyelids fluttered; I drooled ". . . could do such a thing?"

Richard smiled. "Because you're not some wooden figurine living a clockwork life."

"Gur."

"You're just like me."

"No!" I growled and shook my head. "I'm *nothing* like you. I could never . . ."

"Kindred spirits, remember?"

"*Never.*"

He crouched beside me and placed his hand on my chest. I wonder what he thought of my heartbeat – a storm unto itself, raging and banging. I faded, gripped his hand, though I didn't want to. The edges of the room closed in until only Richard's face remained, as if seen through a keyhole.

"We'll see," he said. "I think you'll be surprised what a man is capable of."

And with that I drifted away, like the leaf, swirling and gone. Beethoven accompanied me for a while. Beautiful, tormenting notes, but even they faded.

I looked for my green meadow but found only rain, only darkness.

I awoke to find myself in a room I soon recognized as Richard's garage, but there was no workbench, no lawnmower, no tools hanging from nails on the walls. The up and over aluminium door was the only standard garage feature. Polythene sheeting had been tacked to the walls, and the linoleum floor sloped away on both sides to narrow drainage chutes that reminded me of the gutters found on autopsy tables. A bare bulb depended from a length of dusty cord, its glow attracting two moths that repeatedly knocked their plump bodies against the glass.

Lorna sat opposite me, coarse rope binding her wrists and ankles to the chair, a rag pushed into her mouth so tightly she couldn't work her tongue to push it free. There was blood in her hair and smeared across her top lip. I remembered that single spot on Richard's shoe and wanted to scream. Her left eye was a mess of swollen tissue but her right eye was wide and filled with terror. In seven years of marriage – ten of being together – I had never known her to be terrified. It sickened me.

Richard stood behind her, knife in hand, the edge too close to her throat. "You're awake," he said. "Good. Take a moment to compose yourself."

"Richard, what—?"

"Deep breaths help."

"What are you *doing?*"

It was then that I noticed my arrangement: I, too, was bound to a wooden chair, but not completely; my right arm was free. I had a gun in my hand.

"So you don't believe you can take a man's life?" More tears leaked from Richard's eyes. I watched two of them drip into Lorna's hair. "I believe, under certain circumstances, you can."

I shook my head. "Don't do this, Richard." Tears of my own now. Too many of them. "Please."

"What did she call you? A pithless cretin?" Richard used the tip of the blade to flick hair from Lorna's face. "Now's your chance to prove her wrong, and save her life into the bargain."

I looked at the gun, fat and oily and *real*.

"Maybe the love has gone. Or maybe not." He curled his upper lip and shrugged. "One thing is for certain . . . you don't want to see her die like this."

"*Please*."

"I'm going to cut her throat in exactly ten seconds."

"No . . . dear Jesus, *no*."

"Then I'll chop her into easy-to-manage pieces and bury her in the garden."

Lorna screamed through the rag. A raw, muffled sound. Her throat bulged as it filled with air that couldn't escape.

"But you can stop me, Martin."

"Nuh-oh-oh-oh."

"You can save us all."

I whimpered like a scolded dog and considered putting the gun to my own head.

"Ten seconds," Richard said, and pressed the edge of the knife to Lorna's throat. "This is it, old friend. It's time to see how alike we really are."

"Ten."

I wonder, now, if Lorna's uncompromising attitude, not to mention our bitter separation, in some way impacted my hesitance to pull the trigger. It was easy to remember the ember of derision that so often burned inside her – evident in her behaviour at Gee's, when clemency would not have cost anything, and despite my efforts at accord. Nor had I forgotten that she'd

wished a "crippling" car accident on me. Cancer, too. Heat of the
moment, maybe, but still hurtful.

I looked at the gun in my hand as the memory of her cruelties
teetered in my mind. I'm fairly certain that if our marriage was
intact, and blissful, even if Lorna had shown an iota of affection,
that I would have blasted Richard's brains against the polythene
wall. But that wasn't the case; Lorna didn't like me – an understatement; she *hated* me – and I didn't like her much, either.

"Nine."

I could let her die, or kill Richard. Neither choice appealed. It
was like being faced with two doors – one leading to hell and
damnation, the other to insanity and rue. The gun trembled in my
hand, as foreign to me as a Neolithic relic or alien rock. I have no
idea what type it was. Something beastly, with a squat barrel and
a magazine locked into its grip. I didn't know if I had to load a
bullet into the chamber or release the safety catch (if I could find
it). I assumed Richard had made it as simple as possible – just
point and shoot. Not that there was anything simple about that.

"Eight."

After all, what makes someone a killer? What rare ingredient
makes them capable of taking another person's life – of determining who lives or dies? Maybe it's something we all possess, a
chemical or electrical impulse locked deep in the brain, that for
most of us can only be accessed via extreme circumstances . . .
and maybe not even then.

"Seven."

Rain rattled against the garage door. An explosion of thunder
made the roof creak and the bare bulb tremble. Would this storm
never end? I had a feeling that, whichever door I chose, I would
hear it for the rest of my days.

"Six."

Thix. Stupid lisp. Stupid Richard. I looked at him and screamed.
Raw, cascading sound. My throat felt like a rainstick filled with
broken glass.

"Five."

Lorna screamed, too – or tried to, at least. Her throat was dark
with the effort, veins as thick as the ropes that bound her. And how
could her eye – that single, glaring orb – be filled with such terror
and reproach? Yes, *reproach*. For *me*, as if she didn't have more

pressing things on her mind. Her body shook, wrists and ankles pushing against the ropes. She couldn't believe that I hadn't yet pulled the trigger, or that this was even difficult for me. She always said I lacked backbone. *Pithless*, the ever-famous adjective. And here I was proving her right, my spectacular nothingness on display.

"Four."

Yet more thunder boomed outside and I looked at my soon-to-be-ex-wife (maybe sooner than she'd hoped) with broken eyes. I saw things – random details – I'll remember in my nightmares for years to come: the fine hair on her forearms and a loose thread hanging from the hem of her skirt; the scar on her knee she'd got from falling off a see-saw when she was eight years old; the pale band of skin where her wedding ring used to be. There was blood on her blouse. One of the buttons was missing.

It was easy to imagine her getting ready that morning (I knew her routine as well as my own), drying her hair and applying make-up – small things done daily, not knowing that she was doing them, perhaps, for the last time. I saw fresh blood trickling from her swollen left eye, and a damp corner of the rag dangling from her mouth.

"Please, Richard," I gasped. It was a wonder I could speak at all. "Please, I'm *begging* you—"

"Three."

So vivid, her blood, trickling too perfectly, as if it had been painted on. I saw tiny pink sequins embedded in the varnish on her fingernails. Bruises on her legs. A broken shoe strap.

"Two."

I brought the gun to chest level and extended my arm. Tears blurred my vision and I blinked them away, then curled my finger around the trigger. Richard had positioned himself so that his head floated above Lorna like a lunatic bull's eye. I could barely see the curve of his left shoulder, and his right elbow was cocked to the side, but they were such small targets and too close to Lorna. I couldn't risk shooting at one in the hope of disabling, rather than killing, Richard, and couldn't move to a better position because I was tied to the chair. It was a hopeless situation. I closed one eye (possibly the wrong one) and stared down the barrel. The sights trembled somewhere between Richard and Lorna. I tried to steady my hand but couldn't.

It was over. I had failed them both.

"Sorry," I whimpered.

"One."

Everything happened in the next second: Richard's eyes flickered with disappointment and he tightened his grip on the knife's handle. Then darkness – total and sudden – as the storm knocked out the power. Startled, I jerked, pulled the trigger. The gun snapped in my hand like something with teeth. In the muzzle flash I saw Lorna's hair lift at the top (it *bounced,* the way it had when she'd swept out of Gee's) followed by a haze of blood. I sagged. Maybe I screamed. The gunshot rang in my ears and all I could think of were the moths in the darkness, lost, looking for their light.

Including his wife, Richard Chalk murdered eleven women. Alexandra Locke was his final victim. Following my statement, the police found her dismembered corpse buried in Richard's back garden, along with the remains of his other victims (except for his wife, of course, who'd been peacefully laid to rest at a cemetery in Little Marlow). For nearly three weeks Richard's house was in the news, surrounded by police tape and with one of those white tent-things in the back garden. That was how long it took to disinter and correctly match all the body parts.

The press named Richard "The Chiltern Chopper". He's a celebrity now, like Harold Shipman and Fred West.

Me? I'm a mess. A psychological train wreck. Before all of this, I was a successful accountant working from my home in Thame. Recently separated, yes, but with my mind intact. Now I scream myself awake every night. I've lost nearly two stone. My hair is more white than grey. I shake a lot, too, and haven't worked for over a year. The police called my actions heroic, but I don't see a hero when I look in the mirror, and I don't feel like one when I'm fumbling the cap off my Sertraline prescription. My psychiatrist endeavours to dig beneath the anxiety, to whatever supports it – a trestle, perhaps, of weaknesses and woes. Writing this account was his idea. "Explore," he told me. "Uncover." Leaf works to balance my chakras. Sometimes he sweats.

Lorna hates me. Still. The difference now is that she probably has cause to. After all, she would never have been in that predicament if not for me. *I* befriended Richard. *I* showed him her photograph. *I* debated for ten long seconds whether or not to pull the trigger. She wanted to press charges against me, but was told outright that it was a fight she would never win. She went on television, on some gauche talk show, and completely lost the plot. She threw her shoe at an audience member and had to be restrained by a beefy TV bouncer called Tim. Or maybe Jim. Her wig fell off. Everybody saw her scar. Yes, I shot her, but I saved her life, too.

It came down to millimetres, maybe even micrometres. I have a recurring nightmare in which I lower my hand a fraction before pulling the trigger, and in the muzzle flash I see the bullet rip through Lorna's skull. A similar nightmare has me holding the gun a dash higher and watching Richard's face disappear in a cloud of blood and bone. What actually happened was that my hand was at the perfect height, and the gun at the perfect angle, so that when I pulled the trigger I injured both, but killed neither of them.

The shot was analysed by ballistics experts on a BBC *Newsnight* special. According to their calculations, I have a one in two-point-six million chance of doing it again. A ridiculous number, if you ask me. But we'll never know; I'm not doing it again.

The bullet scored the top of Lorna's head. It burned through her hair, separated her scalp, and cut a groove in her skull deep enough to rest a pencil in. She required several surgeries – bone and skin grafts, mainly – and now has a thick scar running down the centre of her head. The bouncy, tawny hair will never grow back there. She buys her wigs from Les Cheveux in Amersham. I've heard they procure their product from human cadavers. I hope that's true.

Richard was not so fortunate. The bullet struck his lower jaw and removed it completely. His tongue, too. Had its trajectory not been altered, albeit subtly, by Lorna's hair and skull, it would have hit him in the throat and killed him instantly. He resides now in one of England's finest high-security hospitals, locked in a tiny room, his hands strapped to the bed-rails so that he cannot disconnect the numerous tubes that keep him alive.

I visited him in the summer. My psychiatrist's idea. "For closure," he said. He wrote to the hospital on my behalf and reluctantly I went along. It was a brief visit. I stood with two of the burliest nurses I have ever seen in a room not unlike Richard's garage: bleak, windowless, a single light in the ceiling glimmering behind mesh. There was a drain in the floor and the walls were coated with something that made cleaning blood and body waste from them easier.

Richard lay in his bed, his eyes (light brown with delicate orange flecks, still the same, even now) fixed upward. Below the nose, his face appeared to have been removed by some kind of human pencil eraser. Smudged away. No teeth. No *mouth.* Just a whorl of scar tissue. A trach tube jutted from a hole in his throat.

I looked at him, this man – "The Chiltern Chopper" – who enjoyed Beethoven and Glenfiddich, and who I once called a friend.

We're nothing alike, I thought. I had intended to say this out loud – for closure, you understand – but couldn't get the words out. I stuttered and covered my mouth.

He didn't look at me. Not once.

"That's what he does all day," one of the nurses said. "Just stares at the ceiling. I've never seen him sleep. He hardly even blinks."

I looked at Richard a moment longer and then turned to the nurses. "That's enough," I said. "I want to leave now."

I drove home with my heart clamouring, beneath a cloudless summer sky, and as I pulled into the driveway of my lonely little house in Thame, it occurred to me that the nurse was wrong.

It wasn't the ceiling Richard was staring at.

It was the light.

NEIL GAIMAN

Feminine Endings

M Y DARLING,
Let us begin this letter, this prelude to an encounter, formally, as a declaration, in the old-fashioned way: I love you. You do not know me (although you have seen me, smiled at me, placed coins in the palm of my hand). I know you (although not so well as I would like. I want to be there when your eyes flutter open in the morning, and you see me, and you smile. Surely this would be paradise enough?). So I do declare myself to you now, with pen set to paper. I declare it again: I love you.

I write this in English, your language, a language I also speak. My English is good. I was some years ago in England and in Scotland. I spent a whole summer standing in Covent Garden, except for the month of Edinburgh Festival, when I am in Edinburgh. People who put money in my box in Edinburgh included Mr Kevin Spacey the actor, and Mr Jerry Springer the American television star who was in Edinburgh for an opera about his life.

I have put off writing this for so long, although I have wanted to, although I have composed it many times in my head. Shall I write about you? About me?

First you.

I love your hair, long and red. The first time I saw you I believed you to be a dancer, and I still believe that you have a dancer's body. The legs, and the posture, head up and back. It was your smile that told me you were a foreigner, before ever I heard you speak. In my country we smile in bursts, like the sun coming out and illuminating the fields and then retreating again behind a cloud too soon. Smiles are valuable here, and rare. But you smiled all the time, as if everything you saw delighted you. You smiled the first time you saw me, even wider than before. You smiled and I was lost, like a small child in a great forest never to find its way home again.

I learned when young that the eyes give too much away. Some in my profession adopt dark spectacles, or even (and these I scorn with bitter laughter as amateurs) masks that cover the whole face. What good is a mask? My solution is that of full-sclera theatrical contact lenses, purchased from an American website for a little under 500 euros, which cover the whole eye. They are dark grey, of course, and look like stone. They have made me more than 500 euros, paid for themselves over and over. You may think, given my profession, that I must be poor, but you would be wrong. Indeed, I fancy that you must be surprised by how much I have collected. My needs have been small and my earnings always very good.

Except when it rains.

Sometimes even when it rains. The others as perhaps you have observed, my love, retreat when it rains, put up the umbrellas, run away. I remain where I am. Always. I simply wait, unmoving. It all adds to the conviction of the performance.

And it is a performance, as much as when I was a theatrical actor, a magician's assistant, even when I myself was a dancer. (That is how I am so familiar with the bodies of dancers.) Always, I was aware of the audience as individuals. I have found this with all actors and all dancers, except the short-sighted ones for whom the audience is a blur. My eyesight is good, even through the contact lenses.

"Did you see the man with the moustache in the third row?" we would say. "He is staring at Minou with lustful glances."

And Minou would reply, "Ah, yes. But the woman on the aisle, who looks like the German Chancellor, she is now fighting to stay awake." If one person falls asleep, you can lose the whole audience, so we would play the rest of the evening to a middle-aged woman who wished only to succumb to drowsiness.

The second time you stood near me you were so close I could smell your shampoo. It smelled like flowers and fruit. I imagine America as being a whole continent full of women who smell of flowers and fruit. You were talking to a young man from the university. You were complaining about the difficulties of our language for an American. "I understand what gives a man or a woman gender," you were saying. "But what makes a chair masculine or a pigeon feminine? Why should a statue have a feminine ending?"

The young man, he laughed and pointed straight at me, then. But truly, if you are walking through the square, you can tell nothing about me. The robes look like old marble, water-stained and time-worn and lichened. The skin could be granite. Until I move I am stone and old bronze, and I do not move if I do not want to. I simply stand.

Some people wait in the square for much too long, even in the rain, to see what I will do. They are uncomfortable not knowing, only happy once they have assured themselves that I am a natural, not an artificial. It is the uncertainty that traps people, like a mouse in a glue-trap.

I am writing about myself perhaps too much. I know that this is a letter of introduction as much as it is a love letter. I should write about you. Your smile. Your eyes so green. (You do not know the true colour of my eyes. I will tell you. They are brown.) You like classical music, but you have also ABBA and Kid Loco on your iPod Nano. You wear no perfume. Your underwear is, for the most part, faded and comfortable, although you have a single set of red-lace brassière and panties which you wear for special occasions.

People watch me in the square, but the eye is only attracted by motion. I have perfected the tiny movement, so tiny that the passerby can scarcely tell if it is something he saw or not. Yes? Too often people will not see what does not move. The eyes see it but do not see it, they discount it. I am human-shaped, but I am not human. So in order to make them see me, to make them look at me, to stop their eyes from sliding off me and paying me no attention, I am forced to make the tiniest motions, to draw their eyes to me. Then, and only then, do they see me. But they do not always know what they have seen.

I think of you as a code to be broken, or as a puzzle to be cracked. Or a jigsaw puzzle, to be put together. I walk through your life, and I stand motionless at the edge of my own. My gestures – statuesque, precise – are too often misinterpreted. I want you. I do not doubt this.

You have a younger sister. She has a MySpace account, and a Facebook account. We talk sometimes on Messenger. All too often people assume that a medieval statue exists only in the fifteenth century. This is not so true: I have a room, I have a laptop. My computer is passworded. I practise safe computing. Your password is your first name. That is not safe. Anyone could read your email, look at your photographs, reconstruct your interests from your web history. Someone who was interested and who cared could spend endless hours building up a complex schematic of your life, matching the people in the photographs to the names in the emails, for example. It would not be hard reconstructing a life from a computer, or from cell-phone messages. It would be like filling a crossword puzzle.

I remember when I actually admitted to myself that you had taken to watching me, and only me, on your way across the square. You paused. You admired me. You saw me move once, for a child, and you told a woman with you, loud enough to be heard, that I might be a real statue. I take it as the highest compliment. I have many different styles of movement, of course – I can move like clockwork, in a set of tiny jerks and stutters, I can move like a robot or an automaton. I can move like a statue coming to life after hundreds of years of being stone.

Within my hearing you have spoken many times of the beauty of this small city. How, for you, to be standing inside the stained-glass confection of the old church was like being imprisoned inside a kaleidoscope of jewels. It was like being in the heart of the sun. Also, you are concerned about your mother's illness.

When you were an undergraduate you worked as a cook, and your fingertips are covered with the scar marks of a thousand tiny knife-cuts.

I love you, and it is my love for you that drives me to know all about you. The more I know, the closer I am to you. You were to come to my country with a young man, but he broke your heart, and still you came here to spite him, and still you smiled. I close my eyes and I can see you smiling. I close my eyes and I see you striding across the town-square in a clatter of pigeons. The women of this country do not stride. They move diffidently, unless they are dancers. And when you sleep your eyelashes flutter. The way your cheek touches the pillow. The way you dream.

I dream of dragons. When I was a small child, at the home, they told me that there was a dragon beneath the old city. I pictured the dragon wreathing like black smoke beneath the buildings, inhabiting the cracks between the cellars, insubstantial and yet always present. That is how I think of the dragon, and how I think of the past, now. A black dragon made of smoke. When I perform I have been eaten by the dragon and have become part of the past. I am, truly, seven hundred years old. Kings come and kings go. Armies arrive and are absorbed or return home again, leaving only damaged buildings, widows and bastard children behind them, but the statues remain, and the dragon of smoke, and the past.

I say this, although the statue that I emulate is not from this town at all. It stands in front of a church in southern Italy, where it is believed either to represent the sister of John the Baptist, or a local lord who endowed the church to celebrate that he had not died of the plague, or the angel of death.

I had imagined you perfectly pure, my love, pure as I am, yet one time I found that the red lace panties were pushed to the bottom of your laundry hamper, and upon close examination I was able to assure myself that you had, unquestionably, been unchaste the previous evening. Only you know who with, for you did not talk of the incident in your letters home, or allude to it in your online journal.

A small girl looked up at me once, and turned to her mother, and said, "Why is she so unhappy?" (I translate into English for you, obviously. The girl was referring to me as a statue and thus she used the feminine ending.)

"Why do you believe her to be unhappy?"

"Why else would people make themselves into statues?"

Her mother smiled. "Perhaps she is unhappy in love," she said.

I was not unhappy in love. I was prepared to wait until everything was right, something very different.

There is time. There is always time. It is the gift I took from being a statue – one of the gifts, I should say.

You have walked past me and looked at me and smiled, and you have walked past me and other times you barely noticed me as anything other than an object. Truly, it is remarkable how little regard you, or any human, give to something that remains completely motionless. You have woken in the night, got up, walked to the little toilet, micturated, walked back to your bed, slept once more, peacefully. You would not notice something perfectly still, would you? Something in the shadows?

If I could, I would have made the paper for this letter for you out of my body. I thought about mixing in with the ink my blood or spittle, but no. There is such a thing as overstatement, yet great loves demand grand gestures, yes? I am unused to grand gestures. I am more practised in the tiny gestures. I made a small boy scream once, simply by smiling at him when he had convinced himself that I was made of marble. It is the smallest of gestures that will never be forgotten.

I love you, I want you, I need you. I am yours just as you are mine. There. I have declared my love for you.

Soon, I hope, you will know this for yourself. And then we will never part. It will be time, in a moment, to turn around, put down the letter. I am with you, even now, in these old apartments with the Iranian carpets on the walls.

You have walked past me too many times.

No more.

I am here with you. I am here now.

When you put down this letter. When you turn and look across this old room, your eyes sweeping it with relief or with joy or even with terror . . .

Then I will move. Move, just a fraction. And, finally, you will see me.

PETER CROWTHER

Eater

"HE'S A *WHAT*?" Doc Bannerman slammed his locker door closed and turned to face Jimmy Mitulak.

"An eater." The word hung in the air with the dying echo of the metal door as though it were a part of the sound. "He eats his victims," Mitulak went on, hanging his black shirt on the back of his door. He shook his head and clunked his teeth together, growling.

Bannerman rolled his eyes in despair. "This fucking city, it gets to me sometimes. Gets so I think maybe I can't take any more of it."

"But still you turn in with each new shift."

"Yeah." He drew the word out lazily. "But maybe one day . . ."

"Yeah, maybe one day you'll win the lottery." Mitulak smiled. "I'll know it before you do, though, 'cos that'll be the day I drive down Sixth and all the lights'll be in my favour." He pulled a crumpled, brown, short-sleeved shirt from his locker and struggled into it. As Mitulak slid his holster over his head, Bannerman saw a cartoon drawing of a bowling ball with a lit fuse coming out of one of the finger-holes and the words BOWL PATROL – and, in smaller letters beneath, MITULAK – emblazoned on the back.

"Nice shirt."

Mitulak turned around and squinted at him. "You serious?"

Bannerman shook his head. "No."

"My sister, Rosie. She designed it."

"I didn't know she was a designer."

Mitulak lifted his jacket off the peg and closed his locker. "She isn't," he said as he slapped Bannerman's back and made a gun sign with his hand. "Keep an eye on him, okay?"

Bannerman nodded. "I'll keep *both* of 'em on him."

"You'd better," Mitulak shouted over his shoulder as he opened the locker-room door. "He 'specially likes eyes."

Bannerman sneered a smile. "Who've I got?"

Mitulak was already halfway out and he didn't stop. His answer floated back through the gap between the door and the jamb, merging with the sound of footsteps already fading down the corridor to the parking lot. "Gershwin and Marty. See ya."

Bannerman changed into his shirt and pants and strapped his holster on to his belt. Then he made a last call into the bathroom and walked out into the corridor, made a right away from the back door and started up the stairs.

The holding cell where they had the beast was on the first floor, tucked against the wall in an open-plan office where the uniforms could write up their collars. Just like in the movies. Above that was a flat roof, looking out on to the oily waters of the Hudson. Below was a walk-through main desk and seven small offices. Below *that* was the locker room and the showers.

The 17th Precinct building was in a derelict area two blocks west of the Port Authority terminal and one block south of the Lincoln Tunnel. It was surrounded by warehouses filled with containers of frozen fish and electrical goods. No people. Particularly at night.

It was three minutes past three a.m. when Denny "Doc" Bannerman signed in at the front desk and walked slowly up the corridor to the rec room.

His nickname came courtesy of a one-year spell doing medicine at NYU Medical Center. It was to there, the eighteen-storey hospital building, that Denny's policeman father had taken a young punk spaced out of his bead on PCP. The punk had laughed and cried, both at the same time, and, in an all-too-brief second when nobody was paying him too much attention, he had pulled a two-handled telescopic wire out of his shoe, wrapped it around Jim Bannerman's neck and, with a swing of his hands, severed the big man's head and sent it scudding across the floor. Then the kid had leaped through a plate-glass window, dropped two floors smashing both legs, three ribs, both collarbones and the hood of a 1963 Studebaker, before trying to scurry away across 20th Street like the stocking-clad torso in Todd Browning's

Freaks. When the delivery van had hit the punk, witnesses said he was still laughing. Denny never went back to the hospital.

Bannerman pushed open the rec-room door and cleared his throat. "Officer Bannerman reporting for duty," he said, clicking his heels to complement the officialese.

"Hey, how you doing, Bannerman?" It made a change from Marty Steinwitz's usual greeting of "What's up, Doc?" which he usually supplemented with a munching chuckle *à la* Bugs Bunny.

"Just fine." Doc lifted the night's call-sheet from the desk. Steinwitz returned his attention to a thick slab of coagulated pizza which he lifted from a *Sbarro* bag perched precariously in front of him on a maze of papers and forms alongside a polystyrene cup of milky coffee, its top edges pinched tight with teeth marks.

"What's the pizza?" Bannerman asked without turning his attention from the papers in his hand.

Steinwitz held up the steaming mess and belched. "Pancreas and large intestine."

Bannerman glanced up and grimaced. "Ho-fucking-ho."

Steinwitz shrugged and continued to eat, getting the mess all over the lower part of his face.

Bannerman read on. Pinned to the back of the call-sheet was the eater's record details. The guy was a bona-fide head-case. No doubt about it. The record itemized the contents of his freezer – various entrails and intestines contained in see-through bags – a wardrobe of custom-made "clothes" and several items of undeniably avant-garde "furniture", which included an occasional lamp fashioned out of a mouldering leg stump, two torsos bound together with garden twine and used, or so it would appear, as a footstool, and three arms, suitably bent at the elbow and attached to the living-room walls in a grim parody of exotic boomerangs or headless geese flying to sunnier climes.

He wanted to feel revulsion but couldn't. That was the worst part of the job right there: the way it shaved off a person's ability to shake his head at the weird and the absurd. Here, nothing was weird any more. Nothing was absurd. Things just *were,* that was all. He settled back into his chair, removed the gun from his holster for comfort and propped his feet on his desk. "There any coffee?" He opened a drawer and dropped the gun inside.

"I was just gonna make a fresh pot."

"Sure could use it."

Steinwitz nodded and bit into his pizza. "Just let me finish up my supper, and I'll get right on to it," he said through a full mouth.

Bannerman returned his attention to the call-sheet as he shook a cigarette out of a crumpled crumple-proof pack. "You seen him yet?"

"The eater?" The word came with a thick half-chewed wedge of what looked like cheese and anchovies that landed with a thud on the open file in front of him on the desk-top.

Bannerman lit the cigarette and threw the burning match into a full ashtray next to his arm. "Yeah." He blew out smoke. "His name's Mellor."

"I know," Steinwitz said as he gathered the expelled food between two fat fingers and slid it into his mouth. Just for a second it looked to Bannerman as though it were alive, like a long, stringy worm, folded in on itself time after time and hanging with thin bubbly veils of cheese, twisting in his grip. "What's he like?"

"What's he *like?* You mean, does he like have horns and a tail or something?"

"No, I mean what's he like? How does he talk? How—"

"Kind of deep." Steinwitz spoke in a throaty baritone, his ample chin resting on his shirt collar. "How the fuck do I know what he talks like? Go talk to him yourself, you're so interested." He lifted the glop to his mouth again and then stopped. "Hey, that's an idea. You like cooking . . . go compare some recipes." He sniggered and pulled off a piece of anchovy that looked like a wriggling worm and slurped it up into his mouth.

The call-sheet said they had found the remains of thirty-two bodies. It had to be some kind of record. The sheet also said that some of the bodies seemed to date back a long ways, but that the condition might have something to do with the lime content of the ground in which they had been buried. Basically, not a lot could either be done or determined until they had the forensic results back. Then they might be able to pin a few names to the remains.

Bannerman shook his head and blew out smoke. "Thirty-two bodies. Jesus Christ."

Steinwitz burped and wiped his mouth on the back of his hand. "*He* almost certainly wasn't one of them."

"*Who* wasn't – oh, right: Jesus Christ. Hey, that's funny, you know that? You ever think of going into vaudeville?"

Steinwitz stopped eating for a second and looked straight at Bannerman. "That's what this is, isn't it?" He waved a greasy hand in a wide arc, taking in the room, the station and maybe even more beyond that. "A routine? A stand-up routine?" He seemed to produce another piece of food from the side of his mouth and started to chew again.

Bannerman shook his head and stared at Steinwitz. "I swear I don't know what's gotten into—"

"And, anyways, there's more than thirty-two."

For a second, it seemed mightily oppressive in the small room. Bannerman watched Steinwitz eat his pizza. It sure had a lot of tomato on there – the stuff was all over Steinwitz's hands.

"How d'you mean, more than thirty-two?"

"*Bodies.* More than thirty-two *bodies.* I mean, what are we talking about here?"

"I know *bodies,* okay? I mean what makes you say there are more than thirty-two?"

"Because—" He paused for maximum effect. "That's the way it is. There are more."

"Says who?"

Steinwitz smiled, his mouth a thick smear of pizza topping, and jabbed a runny finger against his chest. "Me says, that's who."

"And who are you?"

Steinwitz chewed, swallowed and stared. He smiled and said, "What about all the stuff in the freezer? Where'd that come from?"

Bannerman's shoulders relaxed. "Oh," he said, "yeah. Forgot about that."

Steinwitz wiped his mouth on a napkin and waved a finger. "Shouldn't forget about stuff like that," he said. "Gotta think about the promotions. Gotta think like Sherlock Holmes."

Bannerman threw the call-sheet on to the desk. "Yeah, right. Sherlock Steinwitz."

Steinwitz laughed and stood up.

Bannerman laughed along with him, suddenly realizing that it sounded forced, unnatural.

Steinwitz said, "Coffee?"

"Yeah—" Bannerman stood up and followed Steinwitz out of the room, watched him walk to the front desk. "Hey, where's Gershwin?"

Steinwitz reached across for the coffee-pot and switched it on. He shrugged without turning around. "Gershwin? Oh, he went to check on the prisoner."

Bannerman shook his head. "Five'll get you ten he's on the goddamn telephone again. Who's he call at this time of night, anyway?"

"Beats me."

"I'll go and get him down here."

"'kay."

"You got the phones geared to come in down here?"

"The phones are fine."

Bannerman turned and walked along the corridor, away from the front desk. He pushed open the swing doors and started up the stairs. A half a minute later he walked into the squad room and paused, looking around the main office.

The desks were strewn with piles of papers, cardboard cups partly filled with cold coffee, and greaseproof paper packages of unfinished deli feasts. He figured that the *Marie Celeste* had probably looked a lot like this. Round-backed chairs sat at angles to desks, a television set picture glowed in the corner – Lee Marvin smashing a new car into thick concrete pillars, each impact making no sound at all – while a radio across the office advertised second-hand cars at knockdown prices. Bannerman smiled at the timing and looked across at the far wall. At the cage. It was empty.

He stepped into the squad room – suddenly wishing he hadn't removed his gun – and walked slowly between the desks, keeping his eyes wide. Then he saw the figure, lying on the bunk at the back of the cage, wrapped in a thick blanket, his face turned to the wall. He hated the relief he felt. He just hadn't been able to see Mellor because of the surrounding desks. That was all. What the hell was wrong with him?

He turned around to face the office. "Hey, Gershwin?" he shouted. "You on the goddamn' telephone again?"

There was no answer. He turned back. What seemed somehow even worse was the fact that Mellor hadn't moved.

Bannerman turned his full attention to the figure and called again, louder, directing the words over his shoulder. "Gershwin?"

Still nothing.

He walked over to the cage and stared at the prisoner. *Was* he moving? Could he see the faint traces of the man's back rising and falling? Maybe he was in a deep sleep. After all, it must have been one hell of a day for him.

On the radio, a woman with a come-to-bed voice started talking about McCain's pizzas like they were sex aids.

Pizzas. *Sbarro* closed at midnight. And yet the pizza that Marty had been eating had looked hot, or warm at least. Bannerman remembered seeing it steaming. He frowned. The microwave. That was how Marty had done it. The frown disappeared. What was *wrong* with him?

He turned off the radio and the television set and lifted a plastic mug from a nearby desk, rattling it across the bars of the cage, like he had seen Jimmy Cagney do a thousand times. "Hey, Mellor – you want anything?"

"How about a plate of liver 'n' eyeball risotto?" said a voice behind him.

Bannerman spun around to see Marty Steinwitz holding out a steaming mug of coffee.

"I brought it up to you in case you'd gotten involved with the prisoner. Here."

Bannerman took the coffee and nodded thanks. He took a sip. It tasted good and strong, though there was a faint metallic undertaste.

Steinwitz sat down heavily and rested his feet against an open desk-drawer. "That good?" he asked.

"Mm, hits the spot." He smacked his lips a couple times. "Tastes a little metally, though."

"Metally?"

Bannerman shrugged and waved a hand dismissively.

"New blend," Steinwitz said. "Chicory and soya."

"Ah." Bannerman nodded, feeling inexplicably easier.

"You seen Gershwin?"

Bannerman shook his head.

Steinwitz made a clicking noise with his mouth and then thrust a finger between his teeth and his cheek. "Maybe he's out in the storeroom," he said around the finger.

"Yeah." Bannerman took another sip of coffee, swallowed and noticed a piece of grit on his lip. The coffee was more metally than he thought. He picked it off and studied it, then threw it into a nearby basket. "Guy's out like a light," he said, looking across at Mellor. The figure had not moved during their entire conversation, he was sure of it.

"You ever wonder what makes them do it?"

"Kill people?"

Steinwitz nodded and clasped his hands on his stomach. "And eat them. That's the thing. Eating *people*."

Bannerman shrugged. "Maybe he gets a charge out of it."

"A charge?"

"Yeah, you know – a thrill, kind of. Some kind of sexual turn-on." Bannerman drained the coffee and put the mug on the desk. "I can't figure it."

Steinwitz sighed and moved his hands behind his head, cradling it. "You ever wonder what it tasted like? Human meat?"

"Same as any other meat, I guess." Bannerman walked across to the cage and held on to the bars, rattling them, making sure they were securely locked.

"I think it's power."

"Huh?"

"The reason he does it. Maybe it gives him some kind of power, an edge. Maybe—" He stopped talking and turned his head sharply.

Bannerman followed the other man's gaze and looked at the door. "What? What is it?"

Steinwitz sat up on his chair. "Thought I heard something."

"Like what?"

"Dunno. Wait here a minute." Steinwitz stood up and walked across the room. When he reached the door, he opened it slowly and looked out. He turned back, shrugged, and mouthed, "*Wait*." Then he stepped out and closed the door behind him.

Bannerman waited.

Suddenly, the precinct house seemed impossibly big and he inside it impossibly small. Impossibly small and *very* vulnerable. He waited a little longer and then shouted, "Everything okay?" But there was no answer. What had Steinwitz heard? Bannerman wished his partner had at least given him some idea before he had just gone off like that. It wasn't like him. It wasn't like him at all. Damn me for leaving the fucking gun downstairs, he thought.

He strained to listen. He strained so hard he imagined he could hear the clock near the front desk ticking. But that was two sets of doors, a flight of stairs and two corridors away. Maybe it was his watch. Bannerman lifted his arm and looked at the watch-face. It was a little before four a.m. He lifted it all the way to his ear and listened for a gentle ticking. There was no sound.

He turned around to the cage and watched Mellor's body for signs of movement. Had he moved? Had Mellor turned around and watched him while he had been watching the door? He didn't like to think that. He didn't like to think of Mellor quietly turning around, quietly standing up and oh-so-quietly shuffling across the cage towards his back. His unprotected, unsuspecting back. Sure there were bars between the two of them but were bars enough? Maybe the prisoner could have reached through those bars and grabbed him . . . maybe he could have ripped his—

He shook his head and scattered the black thoughts away like crumbs from the table. "Hey, Mellor!" He banged on the bars again. "Hey, Sleeping Beauty . . . rise and shine. Come on!"

The body just lay there, didn't move a muscle.

He was dead. That was it. The guy had up and died on them. Here they were, jumping at the slightest sound, and all because of some guy lying dead in the cage, stiffening up right now, probably. Maybe he should check on him.

Bannerman looked around for the keys and saw them hanging from the hook on the wall beneath a large, hand-drawn sign that said POKEY in big letters. He walked across and lifted the keys, feeling something slide in his stomach as he held their coolness in his hand. He jingled them and watched for some sign from Mellor. Nothing. He walked back to the bars and rattled the keys across them. Nothing.

He shuffled through the keys until he hit on the right one and then inserted it into the lock, turning it slowly.

"Hey, I ain't sure you wanna be doing that, man," said Gershwin from the door. "I ain't sure you wanna be doing that *a-tall.*" He slammed the door behind him and strolled across the squad room. Bannerman watched him, suddenly aware of the dumb look he must have on his face.

"Where you been? Didn't you hear me calling you?"

Gershwin frowned, raised his shoulders and splayed out his hands. "Hey, I'd heard you, man, I'd've answered. What's up?"

Bannerman pulled the key from the lock and checked the cage-door again. Just to be safe. "I'll tell you what's up," he said. "Marty heard something downstairs and—"

"Wasn't anything." .

"Wasn't—"

"I just saw Marty, downstairs. He said to tell you it wasn't anything."

"What was it then? Must've been *some*thing."

Gershwin answered with a shrug. "He didn't say. The wind? Who knows, man? Nothing."

"Where is he now?"

"Downstairs. He's still downstairs."

"What's he doing?"

"He didn't say."

Bannerman rubbed his face with his hands. "God, I don't know . . . this whole thing is spooking me."

Gershwin sat down at the desk that Steinwitz had been sitting at and pulled open the desk-drawer, propped his feet on it. Just like Steinwitz. He clasped his hands behind his head – again, just like Steinwitz – and nodded. "What whole thing is that, man?"

Bannerman watched him for several seconds and then smiled.

"What's funny?"

Bannerman laughed.

Gershwin returned the smile. "What is it, man?"

"It's you . . . you guys." Bannerman shook his head.

Gershwin joined in the nervous laughter, only his contribution didn't seem to sound quite so nervous. "*What?*"

Bannerman felt the smile slip from his face and, as it slipped, he watched the smile on Gershwin's face slip, too. Yeah, *what*? he thought. What the hell was so funny?

"Nothing," he said. "Forget it." He turned to the cage and felt Gershwin's eyes watching him. He rattled the bars, though he knew there would be no response. Then he looked across at the squad-room door.

"You want another coffee?" Gershwin said.

It was like somebody had encased Bannerman's back in ice. He wanted to ask how Gershwin had known he had already had a coffee; he wanted to ask why Gershwin had plopped down into exactly the same chair at exactly the same desk as Steinwitz; how he'd known which drawer to pull out; why he'd propped his feet up in just the same way as Steinwitz; why he'd clasped his hands behind his head, just like Steinwitz again. But then he didn't want to ask those things. There was a large part of his head that said: *No, let's not play their game; let's not show them we're falling for it.* And there was a small part of his head, a tiny, darkened part, where the sun never shone and where things – even the most ridiculous things – were simply accepted ... where questions were never asked. That part said, *Don't let him know you know.*

Know what? said the big, rational part.

Just don't let him know, came the answer.

Bannerman heard Gershwin stand up from his chair. "I said, you want another—"

"No!" Bannerman turned around quickly and, just for a second, the other man seemed to falter. "No," Bannerman said, calmer now. "Thanks."

"Is anything wrong?"

Bannerman winced inwardly at the suspicion in the question. It oozed suspicion. He'd blown it. He glanced back at the door, irrationally considering his chances of making it. Then he looked back and started to laugh. At first, it was forced but then it just seemed to flow naturally. The ease with which it flowed amazed him. Hysteria, he guessed. He laughed so loud and so hard that it hurt. He leaned back against a desk and folded his arms across his stomach. "Is anything *wrong*! Hell, is anything *right's* more the question," he said between laughs that came dangerously close to out-and-out sobs. "We're holed up here," he said, "the three of us, with some whacko who eats people for a hobby – " he pointed to the body in the cage *(Who is it in there?* that dark part of his head wondered) "– and the dude up and dies on us while he's in custody." He took a deep breath. "Now, how's that gonna look in the morning? Huh?"

Gershwin watched him, his head tilted slightly to one side.

"I'll tell you how it's gonna look," Bannerman said, standing up and walking towards the other man, hoping Gershwin wouldn't be able to hear his heart thudding, "it's going to look *bad*." He laid emphasis on the last word like it was cement.

Gershwin continued to stare at him.

Bannerman turned around and started towards the door, mentally counting the steps, mentally humming, mentally praying, mentally waiting.

"Where are you going?"

"To tell Steinwitz we have a problem," he said without stopping. "A fucking big problem." He pulled open the door, holding his neck so tight that the muscles would ache for days. If he was lucky. He walked along the corridor to the stairs, forcing himself not to run, forcing himself not to turn around.

The door clicked shut behind him. There was no other sound. Walking down the stairs, he muttered to himself. He wasn't sure what he was muttering, but he made sure the word "problem" cropped up in it several times, and the phrase "up and died on us", too. He imagined that Gershwin was right behind him, could almost sense his breath on his exposed neck . . . breath from his open mouth . . . his *wide* open mouth.

He walked along the downstairs corridor as loudly as he could. Bannerman, man with a mission, man without fear. Yeah! "Hey, Marty?" he yelled. "Marty, we got a problem. It's a fucking big problem, *mi amigo*." He kept walking. Through the downstairs doors. Towards the main desk. Still walking. "Marty," he yelled again, "you listening to me? You hear we got a problem?"

There was no answer. Of course.

The precinct house doors loomed ahead of him.

He kept on walking.

"Yeah, the problem we got is—" He reached the doors, reached out. "It's big, Marty. It's—" His hand touched the handle, grasped it firmly, and turned.

The doors were locked.

"It's one big fucking problem," he said in a soft voice that somehow seemed very alone.

Bannerman looked down at the lock and saw there were no keys. He hadn't expected any.

He turned around, half-expecting Gershwin to be standing watching him, a knife and fork in his hands, chanting "*Chow time!*" over and over. The place was empty.

He started to walk back the way he had come, mentally cursing the security of the station: barred windows, steel doors . . . you name it. "Hey, Marty? You gone back upstairs?" he shouted. Then, his voice lower, "What the fuck is the lieutenant gonna say when we hand over a dead body, for crissakes?"

Halfway along the corridor he turned into the side office he and Steinwitz – or whoever Steinwitz was *now* – were in earlier. He was still muttering when he picked up the receiver. Still muttering when he jabbed the numbers. But he stopped muttering—

the phones are fine

—when he heard the silence from the earpiece. He had always thought that statements like *the silence was deafening* were ridiculous. But here it was, real, honest-to-God deafening silence. That explained what had been bothering him earlier: no incoming calls. No complaints about domestic fights; no robberies; no shootings or knifings. *Just eatings*, the dark part of his head observed.

He replaced the receiver as gently as he could and leaned on the desk-top with both hands. Then he saw the file on the desk, the file that Marty had been looking at while he ate his pizza. There were stains all over it. He leaned over and read upside down:

HOBBIES – music, golf, and cooking.

That was—

hey, that's an idea. You like cooking – go compare some recipes

—his own file. His own personal file. Steinwitz had been reading his own personal fucking file! Bannerman reached out to pick up the file and throw it across the office but managed to stop himself. Instead, he pulled open the drawer of the desk he was sitting at. His gun wasn't there. He checked to make sure it hadn't slid to the back, but the drawer was completely empty.

He straightened up and considered his position. It didn't take long. Locked doors, barred windows, dead telephones, no gun – all the other firearms were locked up in a metal cabinet that only the lieutenant had a key for.

Steinwitz was walking along the corridor when Bannerman stepped out of the office. "What you—" Steinwitz started in Gershwin's Brooklyn drawl; then he cleared his throat and said, "What're you doing down here?" The replacement nasal tone was Marty Steinwitz's.

"Looking *for you*," Bannerman said, all but placing his left hand on his hip and wiggling his right index finger like a fourth-grade school teacher. He hoped Steinwitz's dialect-slip hadn't been intentional – which would mean Steinwitz wanted him to comment on it – and he hoped that, if it were unintentional, Steinwitz wouldn't think he had noticed it.

"Problem?"

Problem? Bannerman wanted to ask where Steinwitz had been, wanted to rub his nose in it. But—

don't let him know you know

—he didn't dare. He forced himself to walk up to Steinwitz, stand right in front of him, like he was going past, then he stopped. "I was looking for you."

Steinwitz glanced at the office Bannerman had just left and returned his attention to his face. "I was taking a dump."

Bannerman nodded. "Thank you for sharing that with me. Was it a good one?"

Steinwitz pulled a face and rubbed his stomach. "Think I might've eaten something disagreed with me." (Was that the hint of a smile tugging at the edges of his mouth?) "What's up?"

Bannerman slumped back against the wall and thrust his hands – his increasingly sweaty and shaky hands – deep into his trouser pockets. "Oh, nothing much. Nothing except I think maybe we've got a dead prisoner in the cage."

Steinwitz narrowed his eyes and watched him. "Dead?"

He's playing for time, Bannerman thought. He's weighing up what kind of a threat I am to him. He's wondering if he should stop the game right now. Does he know I know the phones are dead? Does he know I've tried the doors? Does he know I've seen that he was reading my personal file? Does he know I've been looking for my gun? He looked deep into Steinwitz's eyes, searching for a sign, a sign that he was wrong, that he was being stupid and everything was a-okay. But though the eyes were Marty's eyes – a conviction that came to him not without an element of surprise; after all, why would he study another man's eyes, even over the many years he had known him? – then again they weren't. They were the right colour, sure, but they were darker and without depth. Fish eyes, lacking in . . . lacking in *soul.* He nodded. *He knows,* said the voice in his head. "Yeah, dead. Why don't you go see?"

Steinwitz watched him, shuffled from one foot to the other.

"Gershwin's up there," Bannerman added.

Steinwitz smiled. "Better take a look then, I guess."

"Why don't you do that?" He stood up from the wall and started back to the main desk.

"You not coming up?"

Bannerman replied without turning around. "Yeah. First I'm gonna brew up some fresh coffee. Looks like it's going to be a quiet night."

"That's the way I like it," Steinwitz said softly behind him.

Bannerman nodded slowly as he walked towards the coffee-maker and, just for a second, he felt like giving up. He felt like turning around and telling Steinwitz, *Okay, you win. But kill me first, okay?* But he didn't think that whatever it was that occupied his friend's body now would observe such a display of generosity. Such *weakness*. He kept walking and felt a wave of relief when he heard the door at the end of the corridor behind him swing closed.

As he reached the desk he turned to look behind him. Steinwitz had gone. He leaned against the counter containing the coffee-maker, coffee and various mugs, and forced himself to think. What now? He looked up at the front doors, checking for signs of a key hanging somewhere next to them. Nothing. He looked across at the barred windows and, though he couldn't see them, thought about all the empty warehouses in the streets beyond. No life anywhere.

He had to get out.

Suddenly, he jolted upright. Downstairs! He could get out from the basement. What had taken him so long? He switched on the hot water and then walked calmly but quickly across to the stairs leading down to the basement. Checking the corridor to the stairs leading up to the squad room, he placed his hand on the basement door, grimacing as he expected it to be locked.

The handle turned.

The door came open.

Another quick check to see that the corridor was clear and he slid inside and started down the stairs.

As he travelled down the air got fresher, cooler. He ran, now, taking steps two and three at a time. When he reached the bottom he stopped and looked back up the staircase, half-expecting Steinwitz or maybe Gershwin – or maybe even a bizarre hybrid of the two of them – to be thundering down the stairs wielding an axe, with Bernard Herrmann's violins screeching in the background. But there was nothing.

He saw the spare key hanging beside the door. Bannerman bit into his bottom lip as he considered running back up the stairs to lock the door. Would he get halfway up and the door suddenly open, though?

Chow time!

He decided against it and turned to the corridor leading past the changing rooms to the back door. Halfway along he stopped and listened for sounds of those *Psycho* footsteps clumping down the stairs. But all was quiet.

He reached the back door, took the handle in his hand, turned the dead-lock and pulled. It opened.

"Where the hell *you* going?" Jimmy Mitulak said.

Bannerman stopped dead and stared.

"What the hell's the *matter* with you?" Mitulak said.

"What are *you* doing here? You should be home."

Mitulak frowned. "I forgot something. What are you, my mother?"

"What did you forget?" Bannerman said backing down the corridor.

"My bowling shoes. We got a match tomorrow . . . actually, today now. Look, what the hell's the matter?"

"You could've picked them up in the morning."

"Doc, what *is* this? I gotta be in Buffalo by— Hey, since when do I gotta tell you everythin—"

Bannerman grabbed hold of Mitulak's jacket and pulled it open. "You still got your gun on."

"Yeah, I still got my gun on. Come on, now, what's—"

"Get inside."

Mitulak stepped warily into the corridor, still frowning.

"Let me see it."

Mitulak frowned some more.

"The gun, let me see your fucking gun."

Mitulak smiled and started to shake his head.

"Jimmy, I'm not playing around here. Let me see the gun."

Mitulak flipped the harness catch and removed the gun, held it out to Bannerman. "Doc, you're making me nervous here. I hope I'm not going to regret this."

Bannerman took it gingerly, checked the cartridge. It was full. He secured the cartridge and handed it back to Mitulak with a visible sigh of relief.

"You wanna tell me what's going on?"

"He's out."

"Who's out?"

"The eater, Mellor. He's loose in the station."

"*What?*"

Bannerman nodded. "But . . . it gets worse."

"How worse?"

"He's disguised."

"How can he be disguised? There's only you and—"

"He's disguised as Marty."

"Marty?"

"And Gershwin."

Mitulak started to laugh. "Hey, I don't know what you're smoking, Doc, but how about passing it around?"

"Listen to me, goddamnit!"

Mitulak's smile faded.

"He's taken their appearance," Bannerman said. He shook his head tiredly. "I know, I know," he added as Mitulak looked at him like he was going mad. "It sounds crazy, but he has."

"How?"

"How the fuck do I know how? Maybe he's a fucking Ymir or a face-hugger . . . maybe he can assume the identity of whoever he eats . . . you know? Like the Indians? They ate the hearts of their enemies because they thought it gave them their enemies' strength. Maybe this guy gets the full thing . . . hair, face, looks . . . everything."

"He's *eaten* Gershwin and Marty?"

Bannerman shrugged. "Maybe. All I know is that they're never together."

"Never together?"

"Never together in the room at the same time. And when Gershwin came into the squad room he sat down in the same chair as Marty . . . propped his feet on the desk just the same way as he had been doing a few minutes earlier. And . . . yeah, and Mellor's dead. In the cell. He doesn't move or speak or anything."

"You just said that Mellor was loose."

"Jesus Christ! He *is* loose. But he's left his body in the cell, curled up so it's facing the wall."

"You sure it's him? In the cell?"

"Sure as I can be without going in there and checking him out."

"You haven't even checked the body?"

"Hey, I've seen *Silence of the Lambs*, okay? I wasn't going to go in there and have him wearing my head like a Hallowe'en mask."

Mitulak thought for a moment. "But, if Mellor's out and about, what's the problem with going in the cell?"

Bannerman was breathing heavily, almost panting.

"Well?"

Bannerman shrugged tensely. "I wasn't sure then. I'm sure now. Okay? I didn't want to go into the cell when I thought that, maybe, Mellor was playing possum. But then all these other things happened—"

"Like Gershwin and Marty sharing a chair?"

"Yes! It sounds crazy . . . I *know* it sounds crazy, okay? But my gun."

"Your gun?"

"It disappeared. And Marty was reading my personal file . . . and the phones are dead . . . and the front doors are locked . . . Look, we have to do something, Jimmy."

Mitulak made noises with his mouth as he considered. Bannerman shook his head and ran both hands through his hair, turning around and walking to and fro in the corridor.

"Okay."

"You believe me?"

"Let's say I believe *you* believe, and leave it at that for now. Maybe it's worth checking it out."

Bannerman suddenly felt as though all of his problems were over. Then, just as he felt like hugging Jimmy Mitulak, he remembered that they still had to confront Steinwitz. Or Gershwin. Could he move both of them at the same time, this eater? He didn't think so. It would be one or the other.

"So what do we do?" said Mitulak, interrupting Bannerman's thoughts.

Bannerman glanced longingly at the back door and then turned to face him. "We go up."

Mitulak nodded. "Right." He slipped off the safety catch on his gun and hefted it slowly in his hand, like he was weighing it. "Right," he said again. "You lead the way."

Bannerman turned around and walked back along the corridor to the stairs.

Taking them slowly, stopping after every couple of risers to listen for any sound of movement, took time. In fact, it took too much time. Halfway up, Bannerman started to wonder what Steinwitz was doing up there. Had Steinwitz discovered that he wasn't there? If so, where did he think he'd gone? Surely by now he would have checked all the possible hiding places – there weren't many, for cris-sakes – and would probably have concluded that he was downstairs. If so, then why hadn't the eater come down after him?

He stopped and listened: all quiet. He pressed on.

Maybe Steinwitz had suddenly remembered the downstairs door, and had gone out from upstairs and snuck around the back of the parking lot to wait for him outside. Shit! Maybe the eater had tried the door and discovered it was open . . . then sneaked in, sneaked along the downstairs corridor, taken a look around the corner of the staircase, real quiet, and seen Mitulak and him creeping up the stairs.

Bannerman stopped again and turned his head slowly. There was only Mitulak behind him. The rest of the staircase was empty. He shook his head and carried on. Two steps further and he was at the top, his hand on the door handle.

"Hey . . ."

Mitulak's sharp whisper almost made Bannerman jump out of his skin. He held on to the handle tightly and hissed, "What?"

"You want maybe I should go first?"

"Why?"

"Because I got a gun. If this guy is round the corner when you open the door – and if he knows you're on to him – he's gonna start shooting as soon as we show ourselves."

It made sense. "That makes sense," Bannerman whispered, and he changed places with Mitulak, staring intently at the door handle while neither of them was holding it.

When they were in place, Mitulak gently turned the handle and pushed. The door eased open silently.

"See anything?" Bannerman whispered.

"Nothing." Mitulak pushed it a little wider and stepped on to the top step, folding his body into the door, his gun flat against the handle.

"Anything now?"

"Just wait, for—" He stopped.

Bannerman drew in his breath. "What? What is it?"

Mitulak jammed his head between the door and the jamb and tried to look up the corridor to the right.

"What is it?" Bannerman asked again.

"It's Marty."

"Jesus Chri—Where? Where is he? Can he see you?"

Mitulak pushed the door wider and looked around it to the left. Then he stepped back and turned to Bannerman.

"Now I believe you."

"Huh?"

"It's Marty. He's dead."

"Dead?"

Mitulak nodded. "Far as I can make out."

"Where is he?"

"Lying on the floor right in front of us."

"Any sign of Gershwin?"

Mitulak shook his head. "God. Marty. Dead." The three words came out slow and punctuated into tiny sentences, each with a poetic, grim resonance.

"What do we do now?"

"We go out – what else *can* we do?"

Bannerman grunted. There was nothing else.

"Ready?" said Mitulak.

"Ready."

"Right!" He pushed open the door and ran, crouched over, to the main desk on the left.

Bannerman stepped up on to the top step and looked around the door-edge. Marty stared at him. He was naked, lying face-down on the floor about fifteen feet from the door, his head tilted to one side like he was watching them. His legs were splayed out behind him, his arms stretched in front of him. One half of his face had gone, exposing teeth and gums and part of his cheek-bone. His left arm ended just above the wrist in a fray of skin and cartilage. There was no blood.

Bannerman closed his eyes and blinked away the tears, then opened them again. The horror was still there. He pushed open the door and stepped out into the corridor without thinking.

"Hey," Mitulak whispered loudly. "What the hell you doing?"

Bannerman didn't answer. He walked across to Marty Steinwitz's body and looked down at it. There was a folded piece of paper lying on his back. He bent down.

"What is it?" Mitulak whispered.

Bannerman read the words on the note, four lines, carefully typed on one of the machines up in the squad room:

> game over
> you have gun now
> now weer even
> lets finnish it

He waved the sheet to Mitulak. "Come read it yourself. He knows you're here."

Mitulak stood up from behind the desk, warily watching for any signs of movement from anywhere. "Huh? How's he know I'm here?"

"He knows I've got a gun." Bannerman shrugged. "How the hell do I know how he knows anything?"

Mitulak reached him and took the note. He read.

Bannerman turned Steinwitz's body over and jumped back. "Jesus H. Christ!"

Mitulak looked up from the note and then down at the body. The whole of Steinwitz's chest had been ripped open, pieces of snapped bone jutting out.

Bannerman said, "He's eaten his heart."

Mitulak said nothing.

"Let's go. He's waiting for us."

Bannerman led the way along the corridor to the doors. They pushed open the doors together and looked up the staircase. Gershwin was hanging from one of the lights. He, too, was naked, his chest similarly destroyed and both legs gone from the knees. As they got closer, they saw that his eyes were missing. A note taped across his stomach read:

getting warmer
the end *is* nere

Neither of them said anything.

At the top of the stairs, his heart pounding fit to burst out of his own chest, Bannerman turned the handle on the door.

"Wait."

Bannerman turned.

"Let me go first. I'll go left, over towards the cage, you go right."

Bannerman nodded.

"Right!" said Mitulak.

Bannerman threw open the door and both men fell into the room, crashing in two directions behind the desks nearest the door. But the hail of bullets Bannerman had expected didn't come.

Bannerman lifted his head above the desk and looked around. He couldn't see anything.

Mitulak did the same.

"Hey . . ." Mitulak said.

"What?"

"I thought you said the guy was dead in the cage."

Shit, Bannerman thought. He knew what was coming next but he had to respond. "He was."

"He ain't now, man," said Mitulak. "Cage is empty."

Bannerman stood up slowly, staring around the squad room. "He's gone back to his own—" He stopped. Over by the far wall, Mellor was sitting against a radiator. He still had the blanket wrapped around him, like an Eskimo or an Indian Chief. Pulled down over his head was a large, brown evidence bag, one side of which was blown apart and stained a red so dark it looked almost black. The wall behind the bag looked like somebody had thrown a pizza at it.

"What is it?" Mitulak asked.

"Just wait where you are," Bannerman said. "And cover me." He moved to the side and walked slowly around the desk. As he moved, more of the body came into view. Mellor was holding a gun in one hand. In the other hand was another note. He looked around at Mitulak. Mitulak frowned and mouthed, *What?*

Bannerman shook his head. *Cover me,* he mouthed back. Mitulak nodded and waved the gun.

Bannerman edged his way along the side wall, keeping Mellor in sight all the way. At last he had reached a point where there were no more desks to provide cover. But he had watched the body very carefully and there was no sign of any movement. Either the guy *was* dead or he could hold his breath a very long time.

He crouched down on to all-fours and crept the final few feet towards the body. When he reached it, he leaned over and took hold of the barrel of the gun and gently pulled.

"You okay?" Mitulak whispered from behind him.

The gun came away, and Mellor's fingers plopped against his stomach.

"Yeah, I'm okay," Bannerman said. He put the gun in his pocket and reached for the note. Behind him, he heard Mitulak moving between the desks.

Bannerman unfolded the note, a roster sheet, and looked at the other side. It was blank.

"You still okay?"

Bannerman nodded, frowning. "He left a note."

"What's it say?"

"It doesn't. It's blank." He turned it over. It was this week's roster. He looked at the grid and the pencilled names in the boxes. One of them was ringed, the one for tomorrow – *today,* now. The box was for ten a.m.; the name in the box was J. MITULAK.

Bannerman frowned and looked at the evidence bag, reached up and lifted it off. The eater had left just enough of Mitulak's face – the *real* Mitulak's face – for Bannerman to recognize who it was, even without the eyes. "Jimmy . . ." he whispered, sadly. Behind him, he heard desks moving as though something large was making its way across the floor.

He saw it all, now, in his mind's eye.

He reached into his pocket and lifted out the gun.

Then he discovered that the cartridge was missing.

"Let's eat," said a voice behind him. It didn't sound like any accent or dialect he had ever heard before.

JOHN LLEWELLYN PROBERT

Case Conference #4

"DEFINITELY SOMETHING TO put you off your food, don't you think?"

Robert Stanhope said nothing as Lionel Parrish closed the bulging document folder. Throughout the telling of the story the journalist had been staring at the floor, his eyes following the complex geometric patterns woven into the rich red fabric of the rug that lay beneath Parrish's desk. He fidgeted with his hands for a moment, then looked the doctor in the eye and said, "False."

Parrish gave him an encouraging look. "The story, you mean?"

Stanhope nodded. "That one's just too extreme, too over the top. It couldn't possibly be the creation of someone whose mental state is so impaired that they have ended up in here."

The doctor held up the folder, failing to notice the scrap of paper that had been stuck to its underside. It fell to the desk, skimmed the red leather, and then slipped to the floor making less sound than a whisper.

"On the contrary," Parrish replied. "Many of the members of our little community are here exactly because their fantasy lives have become rather *too* vivid, because what is going on in their minds has taken over their real lives to the extent that they have caused significant harm to others, as well as sometimes to themselves."

"All right," said Stanhope, happy to play along. "Supposing that story is true? If it is, how do you know that I'm not Mellor? How do you know that I haven't transferred my personality into the body of a journalist so that I can take my revenge on the man who was finally able to keep me locked up?"

Parrish shook his head. "Very, very unlikely, Mr Stanhope. I know all my patients too well, and if Mr Mellor is upstairs I can assure you he is still there. Unless, of course," and at this he gave Stanhope a meaty grin, "*I* actually am Mr Mellor."

Stanhope suddenly felt so uncomfortable that he found himself searching for anything to change the subject. His eyes alighted on the paper lying on the floor.

"You've dropped something," he said.

"Have I?" Parrish was in the process of getting to his feet to replace the folder on the shelf. He bent down, picked up the document, and peered at the heading. "My goodness me," he said. "Thank you for spotting that. It would never have done to have left it lying around."

Stanhope asked what it was, only to be rewarded with a dismissive gesture.

"A little bit more about our Mr Mellor," said Parrish, "but seeing as you are so disturbed by the case, it's probably better we just put it away."

Parrish was about to return it when Stanhope stopped him.

"Read it," he said.

Parrish looked shocked. "My dear chap, are you quite sure?" he said. "You do seem rather upset."

"I want to hear what happened next," said Stanhope. "Please read it."

And so the doctor did.

PETER CROWTHER

Mister Mellor Comes to Wayside

THE FIRST DAY of May had come and the promise of a summer to follow filled the countryside. Mister Mellor had been here for a couple of weeks, during which time he had not been idle. He had discovered a solitary homestead and he had spent time there, talking to the man and the woman and the three children and even the dog. They had been unable to help him. Now they were resting. The police would call it different when they finally found them, but for Mister Mellor, "resting" was a reasonable catch-all.

He drifted into the nearby town – with the rather quaint name of Wayside – with the first hot day, not fully formed and completely undecided of what he wanted to be ... crouched down on all fours and slinking in, feral and deceitful, alongside the wire-mesh fencing by the town dump.

For the past day he had been holed up in the fields and the valley down along the Interstate between Carver and Durphin, playing with shapes and preening himself like a wily old cat just waiting for the right time to come along. That time was now, first day of the month, and he felt energized by his rest, felt frisky and ready for action.

He stopped at the sign and looked at it ... looked at it for several minutes. This must be the place, he reasoned as he had reasoned many thousands of times before, reading significance into weather variation, town names, people names, until he could no longer separate reality from the countless variations that may or may not lie ahead.

Wayside.

It sounded right.

Hell, it felt right. Wasn't there an expression about falling by the Wayside? There was, he was sure of that. Maybe that expression had been forged from the same Cenozoic goo that had birthed him, the perpetrator and the prophecy; Yin and Yang ... the two elements that would provide the whole. He would fall in Wayside. It made sense.

It was just after six a.m.

The coming summer's light sang to the weeds in the cracks in the sidewalks of Wayside, casting shadows of the sycamores and the oak that lined Bluffs Road (strange name, he thought ... another omen. Was he not the greatest bluffer in the world?) in the sharpest relief they would have all year.

Mister Mellor moved forward, changing as he did so, to start work.

Johnjo MacDaniels's wide-eyed pit bull, Driver, cocked a leg and peed against Maggie Henderson's old Dodge – the one her boy Drury had piled into the wall of Cy Simmons's General Store over on McLintock Avenue – and the steaming yellow liquid ran down the door beneath the now-crusted bloody handprints that littered the window like a frantic mosaic.

If he could have talked, Driver would have told a couple of stories to anyone who had the time or the inclination to listen. He would have told about how he'd like to stick his pecker way up inside Fred Krueller's Pekinese – so deep he'd split the little bitch into two ragged pieces – and about how some nights, when the wind was just right and whirling the dust and soft soil up into the air, and a gibbous moon held court, a dark-stained spectral teenager reappeared behind the wheel of that car and clawed at the door with broken hands while, all around him, silent white flames licked across his broken face and teased the blackened upholstery.

But not now.

Now, smelling of sweat, axle grease and rotting vegetables, Driver sniffed the air and let out a throaty rattle the way all dogs do when they see or sense something which humans can't. The hair along his back and above his sawed-off tail stump rose up, bristling, and he gave a low moan, occasionally snapping at the flies to show how tough he really was. Soon, Johnjo would step out of his trailer and tell Driver to shut the fuck up before he unscrewed the top off of his Old Granddad and mouthed the glassy teat for the first shot of the day.

It could even be that Johnjo would be feeling so plain mean and hungover, the way he did most every day when he woke up, that he wouldn't notice some things had gone from against the trailer. Things like a saw, a tyre-iron, a couple of wrenches and an old pitchfork with a splintered handle. But they were so rusted up from years of ignorance that he probably wouldn't even notice. And Driver would be mighty pleased about that, seeing as how he got blamed for everything that went wrong around the place . . . from a blown tyre on Johnjo's Cherokee to a busted faucet on the water supply.

But Driver figured there comes a time when discretion makes for the better part of valour. He further figured that the well-dressed young man who tipped his hat to him and gave him a wink as he pulled together all of these things was not about to take kindly to a whole mess of barking and snapping. So he stayed real quiet.

And so neither the new season nor the well-dressed young man paid Driver any attention as the two of them, man and season, drifted off – slithered and slid, Driver might have said if he'd been able to speak – along Fairfax, towards the Good Neighbour grocery store where Wilhemina Sherbourg, the biggest and fattest woman outside of a carny sideshow, lay spread-eagled on her queen-size bed, her flabby elbows reaching over each side towards the dusty floor.

The first ray of sunshine spun and pirouetted through the torn curtains and drifted across Wilhemina's slumbering naked bulk, lighting the pock-marked flesh and the feeding bed bugs, each one bloated with chocolate- and pizza-flavoured blood, and lingered on the wide spillage of breasts so big you could tear them off, hollow them out and then carry thirty or forty pounds of apples home in them.

But while the new season drifted past, heading on for the hills and the valleys, the plains and the fields, the tiny Main Streets and the mighty Interstates, something it had brought with it, like a seed on the breeze, slowed down and finally stopped at the paint-peeled door, sniffing, relishing the aromas that wafted through the gaps in the aperture, the grain in the woodwork, and even the walls themselves.

Why this door and not another was not certain. More than that: was not *known*. The truth of the matter was that there was no plan to such an event, no schedule to follow, no criteria to achieve, no standards to maintain, and no accounts to be settled. An entirely random visit.

Inside, a knock sounded at Wilhemina's door . . . gently insistent but somehow lazy, too. Kind of relaxed but inevitable, like the person knocking was in no hurry but, equally, was not going to go away. No way.

Wilhemina shouted, "Who is it?" half not caring and half not expecting any answer.

"It's your destiny!" a voice announced, a voice that sounded for all the world like one of those guys on the TV quiz shows, all toothpaste and toupée, set to offer her her wildest dreams and make everything she had ever fantasized about come suddenly wonderfully true.

Wilhemina could hear, from somewhere off in the distance, that damned dog creating a stink about something. Mutt sounded like it had its dick caught in a gate, making all that noise.

"I don't have no destiny," Wilhemina called, petulant and sad, half-lifting her head from her pillow, a once-white cotton affair marked with a hundred nights of dribbled saliva and lost hope.

"Oh, but you *do*," the voice said, gently correcting her. "*Everyone* has a destiny," it said.

Wilhemina said, "Shit!" and rolled over across the bed to allow her gargantuan legs to spill off the mattress in wobbling folds of Jell-O flesh, slightly grainy with yesterday's and the day before's dirt and smelling like old meat, sweet and dangerous.

She pulled on an old robe, tied the cord tight around her belly, and shuffled to the door. She leaned against the wood panelling to hear if the guy was still out there, but she didn't hear anything. "You still there?"

"Still here," the voice confirmed. "Destiny never goes away," it added.

"Whatcha want anyways? This some kinda sellin' stunt? 'Cos I can tell you—"

"No kind of selling stunt at all," the voice said. Then, after a pause, it said, "This is the real thing."

"Oh, hell," Wilhemina muttered as she shifted the deadbolt and turned the latch. She took hold of the door-handle and gave it a good tug, seeing as how last fall's rains and the lengthy winter had warped the wood right in the frame. And as it opened wide, she gave a small gasp.

There on the stoop was a fine-looking young man, a big smile beaming on his face and his hat held in one hand. "And it's a fine good morning to you," he said. "Might I come in for a while?"

Wilhemina tried to speak, but suddenly found that her voice had snuck off and hidden itself somewhere deep in the myriad folds of her ample bosom. She wanted to ask him who he was and what he wanted. She wanted to ask if she knew him – though she was pretty sure she didn't – or who had sent him. More than anything, though, she wanted to know why a fella dressed so mighty fine was carrying a whole load of old tools, all rusted and broken, so's they made a mess of his good suit. But somehow, she didn't really want to know the answer to that one until it became absolutely necessary.

Wilhemina Sherbourg took a faltering step back into the hovel of her life while the young man answered that move with a couple of steps forward.

He kicked the door shut behind him and breathed in deeply the collective aroma of sweat and dirt and old food. "My," he said, "now that smells good!"

He laid the tools down on the floor and turned, dropping the latch-lock and shifting the deadbolt back into place. "Tell me," he said as he turned back to face her, "do you have any young ones – you know, children – around the place?"

Wilhemina shook her head and suddenly felt like she needed to pee.

The man looked disappointed at first but then he shrugged and smiled, tossing his hat on to the chair alongside the door. "Ah, well, not to worry," he said. "We can proceed with just the two of us."

Wilhemina took another step back and tried to speak. It was still no use.

"I see you're interested in why I'm here," the man said as he bent down to rummage through the things he had brought. He picked the saw and the tyre-iron and stood up again.

"They say that inside every fat person there's a thin person trying to get out," he said. "Let's see if that's true."

And the two of them set to playing.

MICHAEL MARSHALL

Failure

IT IS ALWAYS difficult to discern the boundaries of existence. Children valiantly insist upon putting black lines around the shapes and people they draw, in an attempt to divide and master the continuum of being, but real life does not come with such clear separation. It's hard to tell where your existence stops and the external world begins, and equally tough to determine within that what counts as work, and what is merely "life": or, perhaps, what is merely work, and what has been the thing that, when you look back from the final precipice, will constitute the life you have lived.

Many people never even stop to consider these questions. Jonathan did, however. He monitored his progress, paying increasing attention as he entered his late-fifties and became ever more aware of his position on life's journey. Often the process of scrutiny was reassuring. He felt broadly content, for example, with his performance as Operations Director of a growing chain of copy shops, and had reason to believe they were content with him too. His thirty-year marriage to Elaine was similarly successful. They'd weathered storms large and small with patience and good humour, and there was no one in the world with whom he'd rather spend time. They always found something to talk about. They told each other they loved one another, with patent sincerity.

Even as solid a relationship would ultimately be terminated by death, however, and Jonathan would one day retire. The things you do by your own hand pass and fade away. The most important and lasting marks, therefore, are the ones you leave behind, the deeper scratches you make on the world – and it was here that Jonathan had begun to lose confidence in what he'd achieved.

Here, and specifically in the shape of his son.

He told Elaine he was going for a drive. This had long been his habit in the evenings, and she wished him well without bothering to look up from the copy of *Sunset Magazine* she was reading on the sofa. He picked up the keys to her 4Runner – the area's default domestic vehicle, and less noticeable than his own Boxter (itself a rare indulgence in a life that was otherwise remarkably unshowy) – and walked out into the evening. It had been unusually hot all day, without the welcome breeze that normally freshens Northern California afternoons, and the air retained warmth even in twilight.

As he opened the car door he raised a hand in greeting to his neighbour, who stood peaceably watering her front yard. Everyone in the neighbourhood employed teams of very competent Mexicans to perform such tasks – in most cases aided by automated sprinkler systems – and so this could only be a self-imposed diversion, an excuse for being out of doors on a pleasant night. And why not? She waved back as he drove away.

He passed a car parked fifty yards away down the street, in the shadow of trees. Beyond noticing it was another 4Runner, he did not give it any thought.

He found it hard to recall when he'd first started to feel concern that things were not going as they should. Ryan had been a mercurial toddler and a fractious boy, sure, prone to pout and to sweep things to the floor while possessed by inarticulate fury, but Jonathan suspected you could say the same of most children unless you were determined to maintain a pretence of perfection in front of other parents. There were other times when the child was as sweet and helpful as you could wish for. The two poles balanced, for the most part, more or less.

Nonetheless Jonathan gradually became aware of how many times he'd picked up some treat or trinket while away on business, telling himself he'd give it to his son to reward a notable piece of good behaviour, only to discover the object in a drawer six months later, no obvious occasion for celebration having presented itself in the meantime.

Ryan grew more even-tempered as he entered his teens. His schoolwork was uniformly better than adequate, keeping him in the second tier of students year after year. He was a good-looking boy, decent at sport, charming when it suited him. This combination meant that, after he entered high school, his father and mother became accustomed to meeting and welcoming the girls with whom their son became involved. And it was at this point, perhaps, that Jonathan had started to observe more closely, though he hadn't been consciously aware of it at the time.

There were four girlfriends worthy of the name during the teenage years. All had been attractive, polite and evidently enamoured of their son. Then, a few months later, the liaison would prove to have been discontinued. Ryan never volunteered anything beyond saying it hadn't worked out, and hadn't seemed to suffer any particular emotional turmoil or distress when this happened. There would simply be a period where he did not have a girlfriend, after which a new one would materialize.

The pattern did not have long enough to assert itself as notable, however, before Ryan finished school and left town to attend law school on the other side of the country.

Jonathan drove in an aimless fashion for an hour, tracing shapes around a town he had known for most of his life. When it finally got the other side of nine o'clock he looped back and headed for The Jury Room.

Santa Cruz's most barefaced example of a hardcore drinkers' bar, The Jury Room lurks at the northern end of town, close to the highway, a ramshackle sign above the door proclaiming it has been proudly manufacturing and servicing hangovers since 1976. It's open from six in the morning until two on the other side of midnight, after which the staff presumably crash out on the floor for four hours before starting again. Jonathan had never been inside.

He drove into the lot and to its darkest corner. He turned off the engine and settled to wait.

Ryan emerged from university with a good degree. He'd always been skilled at arguing, presenting the facts of a situation – or selected subsets of them – to his advantage. He'd evidently developed the ability to perform this task on behalf of clients. His mother was delighted when he elected to return to Santa Cruz, and Jonathan had been pleased too, while privately wondering whether it betrayed a lack of ambition. Ryan quickly got himself taken on by a small local firm, however, and used this as a stepping stone to a larger and more prestigious outfit over the hill in Los Gatos. His success was not conspicuous, but solid and sustained. The kind of success, in fact, that his father had always counselled him to seek.

After six years, he got married. Jonathan liked Maria the first time they met, an informal bar-snacks meal upstairs at The Crow's Nest restaurant, by the beach. She was very pretty, of course, but he could see at once that she possessed a good deal more character than the previous girls his son had been aligned with. She was smart, and excellent company, and Ryan's parents were delighted when the engagement was announced.

For several years all went well. Ryan achieved further promotions, taking him within a step of junior partner. He and Maria moved into a large house in Scott's Valley, halfway between his work and Santa Cruz. The two couples met for dinner once a month (Maria's family lived on the opposite coast, and were not involved in these events). Elaine increasingly allowed herself to speculate – with pleasure, and only to her husband – about how long it would be before they became grandparents.

Then one night Maria was absent from a dinner. Ryan brought her heartfelt apologies, explaining that an excess of Dungeness crab the night before (they were in season, and Maria an ardent fan) had turned bad on her. Jonathan and Elaine emailed their condolences. At the next gathering, Maria was amusing at her own expense.

Four months later it happened again.

Crab was no longer in season. This time it was a revised deadline for a report relating to the environmental agency for which she worked. A shame, but Ryan's parents agreed that her commitment to her job was admirable, and sufficiently within character that it raised no flag.

Two months after that, it was the flu.

By chance, Jonathan's schedule took him through Scott's Valley the following afternoon. He stopped by his son's house with a vial of the foul-tasting herbal concoction Elaine swore by when plagued by viral demons (and which genuinely seemed to lop a few days off the recovery period). At first there was no answer, but Maria's car was in the driveway and so he persisted.

When she eventually opened the door she stood well back, and the extra make-up had been well applied. The bruising was obvious nonetheless.

By the end of the year, the marriage was over. Aided in the closing stages by Elaine (who remained ignorant of what he'd seen that afternoon, and the previous instances which had prevented Maria's attendance at other meals), Jonathan did what he could. The relationship could not be saved, however, and privately he admired his daughter-in-law for her decisiveness in determining that there was a point after which it was no longer worth trying.

She finally left town one Thursday morning. She stopped by Jonathan's office, told him what she was doing, and explained that Ryan did not yet know she wouldn't be there when he got home from work.

Jonathan hugged her tightly and implored her to keep in touch. He watched her drive away toward the highway south, his hands bunched down by his sides. He then drove to his son's place of work, hauled him from his office and into a discreet corner of the parking lot. Within ten minutes he had secured a promise that Ryan would never behave in this way again. So far as Jonathan knew, he had not.

Not in that precise way, anyhow.

After forty minutes Jonathan saw his son coming up the street. He watched him head into The Jury Room. He knew Ryan couldn't have walked the ten miles from Scott's Valley, and so he must have parked on the street nearby. That was something, at least.

Jonathan put his head in his hands. He thought about going home, or calling his wife, but not seriously, and not for long. The love between a boy and his mother is a wonderful thing, of that there is no doubt.

The responsibility for a son and his life, however, lies with the father.

Of course it does.

A year-and-a-half after the break-up of his marriage, Ryan made partner. That night there was a celebratory dinner with Jonathan and Elaine, three at a table that would have felt better with four. The regular dinners they'd enjoyed during their son's marriage had never resumed. Instead there had been occasional brief encounters with Ryan and a succession of partners, most of whom appeared rather bemused by the experience. Few of these women lasted long. None was on hand to help celebrate his partnership.

Eventually the tickling in the back of his mind grew too acute to ignore, and Jonathan tracked down his son's most recent girl-friend (the only thing he remembered her saying was that she worked in administration for the Santa Clara mall, but that had been enough). Six weeks after the end of her affair with Ryan, a limp was still discernible. She declined to discuss their relationship.

By now wearily, and with a growing, leaden anger that felt horribly impotent, the next week Jonathan found and spoke to one of his son's high-school girlfriends, making it look like an accidental encounter. Jessica Friedkin had gained three children and sixty pounds in the intervening years. She remained as cheer-ful as he recalled, however, until the subject of her break-up with Ryan came up (or had been laboriously engineered). At this point she became evasive. Jonathan persevered gently.

"He was my first," she admitted, eventually. "He was ... I don't know. Well, I didn't know *then*. I had no comparison. But ... he was kinda ... *rough*. I'm sure he was just finding his way, though, right? None of us knew anything about that whole kit and kaboodle back then."

Jonathan nodded and smiled, and stayed long enough to steer the conversation back to more positive matters. Then he paid for coffee and left.

On the way back to the house he took a detour and parked close to the vast expanse of meadow and redwood forest that bordered the upper west side of town, stretching unbroken up

into the Santa Cruz Mountains. He walked out into it, not knowing what to feel or what to do. Along the path he came across the
sturdy sign showing a map of the area. He had walked past it
many times before. Occasionally, as now, there was a handmade
addition stuck on one side, warning of recent mountain lion
sightings.

Wild animals, in the neighbourhood. Creatures that could not
be trusted to treat humans kindly – who did not even compre-
hend the rules by which others felt honour-bound to live; and
who in the dead of night lifted their heads to listen to the silent
call of the wilderness.

Jonathan looked at the sign for a while and then walked back to
his car.

He didn't know how much to blame himself for not having
connected his son to the intermittent spate of local rapes. Area
women enticed from cafés and bars, then brutalized in cars or
alleys: all resistant to the idea of discussing their assailant, a man
whose methods of operation seemed different every time. Local
police – and the *Santa Cruz Sentinel* – took this to indicate that a
number of men were attacking women within the same period.

Jonathan was less sure. He came to fear – though he tried to
push the idea away – this merely meant that one man was being
crafty about his deeds, and that he'd been able to firmly impress
upon his victims the dangers of trying to identify him to the
authorities.

Why did Jonathan care? Because one long evening after his
wife had gone to bed, it finally occurred to him to wonder whether
he might know who that man might be.

There was no reason to think it was his son. Not really. Ryan
evidently nursed a tendency toward excessive physical domi-
nance with women, but there were plenty of marriages and part-
nerships that worked this way, and (though the idea was abhor-
rent to Jonathan) he could see how, within the strange shorthands
and hidden language of relationships, such a situation might
continue without a couple splitting up. Maria had clearly tolerated it for a number of years, and Jonathan would always ask
himself whether his visit to her the day after the alleged flu might
have provoked her departure; whether, had he been engaged in

business on some other side of town, things might have gone differently. Having your weakness and pain witnessed makes it real. Jonathan had done that for Maria, for better or worse. And she had left.

He'd only received one email from her afterward. He knew enough about technical matters to notice it had been sent via a means that stripped all geographical information from the chain of servers that had delivered it to his computer. Either Maria had not been sure whether or not to trust her erstwhile father-in-law, or had simply been very cautious indeed. He didn't blame her. In the conversation they'd had the afternoon of the opened door and facial bruising, she'd eventually – in a whisper, her head hung low with shame – revealed some of what it was like to share a sex life with Jonathan's son.

This was despite the fact that Ryan had loved Maria. Of that Jonathan had no doubt. The nagging question was what he might be prepared to do – what dire avenues he might feel drawn to explore – with girls casually picked up in clubs and bars.

Somebody was doing this to women in town. Once the idea had entered Jonathan's head that it might be his son, it proved tough to dislodge, however hard it might be to reconcile with his internal collection of images of Ryan as a little boy, looking up at him with amusement, or love.

It was also difficult to dislodge the notion that, should someone not step in, the results could get worse.

Thirty-five minutes later Jonathan sat upright when he saw a woman striding along the street toward The Jury Room. It was hard to tell much in a darkness slashed by harsh street lights, but she looked young and had a tight body in a short dress, and also – despite the confidence in her walk – betrayed signs of drunkenness. About twenty feet from the door she lost her balance for a moment, teetering on very high heels. Jonathan's window was open. He heard her swear under her breath. She regained control. He watched as she went inside, poise more-or-less re-established.

The die was cast, he knew.

Three weeks previously, Jonathan had spent the evening in a similar way. That time the bar had been The Grinder, in

Watsonville, a twenty-minute drive from Santa Cruz. It, like The Jury Room, had featured in news reports as a place where a victim had been picked up. This evidently hadn't been enough to stop women coming there.

Or Ryan, either.

Jonathan had recognized his son's car in the lot as soon as he arrived. He parked and went over to check. Then he returned to his own vehicle and sat in darkness for two hours.

At a quarter of eleven a couple emerged from The Grinder, spilling loud music and light for a moment before the door slammed behind them. The man had his arm around the woman's waist, and was leading her firmly.

The woman was very drunk.

The man was Ryan.

Brazen, calculated, or dumb? It was hard to be sure. This didn't prove that Jonathan's son was the attacker, of course. He could simply have been at The Grinder hoping to score cheap and easy sex, coincidentally visiting a venue the local attacker had also frequented. Nonetheless Jonathan was glad he'd taken the opportunity to shove an expensive four-inch vegetable paring knife – borrowed from Elaine's kitchen, purchased at some expense from Williams-Sonoma in Los Gatos – into three of the tyres of his son's car.

Ryan's fury at seeing the damage had been enough to convince his companion that he wasn't the right guy to be going home with. She tottered back to the bar and went inside. Ryan watched her go, hands on his hips, then got out his phone to call AAA.

Jonathan started his car and drove quietly away.

It wasn't proof.

But it was.

Brazen, calculated, dumb.

Or innocent?

That was the question that had plagued Jonathan over the last three weeks. Had Ryan gone to The Grinder because he was too arrogant to believe he might be caught, because he was crafty enough to think the cops would assume no one would be dumb enough to return to the scene of a previous crime, or because he was too dumb even to consider the question?

Ryan wasn't dumb. He never had been. So he was brazen or calculating.

Or . . . innocent, of course.

Still there remained that possibility, and that's why Jonathan had come out again tonight, to wait in the dark outside The Jury Room. He'd waited there the previous night too, and the night before, and the night before that – in vain. But tonight Ryan had finally come, and an hour-and-a-half later he emerged back into the night, lurching slightly, the hard-body girl in the short skirt by his side. Jonathan didn't think Ryan's stumbling was genuine, but tonight he'd left the tyres on his son's car alone.

To be sure.

He watched, his breathing shallow, as Ryan led the girl across the lot and let her into his car. He waited as his son drove out on to the street, and then followed.

He thought it would only be a little while before he saw his son indicate and turn on to a side road, somewhere close by. That's what had happened in the previous attacks, according to the victims' accounts. His heart sank – and his stomach turned cold – as he realized this wasn't going to happen. Before long he understood that Ryan was heading on to Highway 17 instead, taking the most direct route back to Scott's Valley. Where he had a house.

Innocence remained possible. But if not, then neither brazen, calculating nor dumb would describe Ryan's actions any more. If his son *was* the attacker, and had now decided to take a woman back to where he lived – with the far higher risks for identification that entailed – then it was likely he'd done so in order to give himself the time and freedom in which to do *very* bad things.

If that's what he had in mind, Ryan was now out of control. And, as his father's position on his tail demonstrated, incapable of adequately covering his tracks.

Jonathan stopped following when Ryan's car turned off the highway. He was horribly confident of the destination now. He parked a mile from his son's house, around the back of a *tacqueria* long-ago closed for the night. He walked at a steady pace up the long incline that led into the upscale neighbourhood where his son lived. His palms were damp. The front of his mind felt empty, the back heavy and dark.

He drew to a halt at the end of the driveway. This was long, snaking through a front yard that had once been striking in its design and planting. Maria's work. It was still presentable – this neighbourhood had its share of hard-working Mexican gardeners, too – but had lost focus, and looked dead in the moonlight. Ryan's house was hidden from the street by a stand of cypress trees, but Jonathan could hear the faint sounds of music. There was a party going on, evidently. A party for two.

He took a deep breath and started up the driveway, knowing this was an event he had to break up, before a little boy grown big started to snarl and shout, before he swept his arm across the table. Before something got broken.

On the other side of the trees he saw a light in the kitchen. The music was coming from there, too.

When he got to the window, however, he could see the room was empty. A bottle of wine stood on the counter, half-empty. Ryan's jacket had been thrown over a chair. Nearby on the floor lay a pair of black high-heeled shoes.

Jonathan moved silently to the French doors. He let himself in. The music was very loud. Grotesquely so. He hadn't done much preparation for this moment. All he saw ahead was telling the girl to get out of here, then trying to have a conversation with his son.

Assuming he wasn't too late.

He felt panicky, wondering whether he should have driven right up to the street instead of parking down the way. Surely half-an-hour wouldn't have been enough for things to have gotten out of hand, even if that's what Ryan had intended all along?

And assuming his son wasn't innocent after all?

In a break between songs Jonathan heard the sound of a voice, deeper in the house. A woman's voice.

That was a relief, but he had to stop wasting time.

He hurried into the corridor on the other side of the kitchen and toward the door which led to the large living space at the heart of the house. He heard the woman's voice again, raised now.

He started to run, bursting into the living room. The main lights were off, the area illuminated only by dim lamps. He stopped, staring at the figure tied to the chair in the centre of the space, head slumped forward. At the pool of blood on the floor in front of it.

"Who the fuck are you?"

Jonathan whirled to see the woman standing right behind him. Her eyes were hard too but she looked amused. It was the girl his son had picked up from The Jury Room, and she was holding a long, sharp knife.

Seen closer, he half-recognized her. It was not Maria, however. "What . . . are you doing?" he asked.

"Oh," she said, stepping closer. "It's daddy. Huh."

The figure tied to the chair raised his head. "Dad?" he said. His voice was hoarse. "Is that you?"

Jonathan saw that his son's face was badly cut. One eye appeared punctured. When he took a step closer it became more evident that the liquid on the hardwood floor around him was not just blood, but urine too.

He turned back to the girl. "Let him go."

"Sooooooo not going to happen," she said, flipping the knife so it spun in a languid 360 degrees. The handle smacked back into her palm, loudly establishing her level of acquaintanceship with the weapon. "This isn't good, Jonathan. This is . . . *not okay*."

"I can make him stop."

"Doubt it. That's not the point anyway, as you well know. The *point* is that he's crap at it. The cops in this town are dumb as a sack of rocks, but if *you* managed to put it together, sooner rather than later they will too. Then what?"

"He gets arrested. And it stops."

"No. Then the police and the media start nosing around your family. Are you sure all *your* bodies are buried deep enough, Jonathan? That none of the girls you've met on your evening drives are ever going to be found? And are you sure Ryan won't remember some evening when he was super-small and supposed to be asleep, a night you and Elaine held a party for our special friends, and little boy Ryan peeked out his window and saw bad funky stuff happening out there at the dark back-end of the garden? From what I hear Elaine was *quite* the party girl once, though she always left the wet work to you. Personally, that's my favourite part."

"He won't talk. He never saw anything. I made sure of it."

"No? So how come he's out there hurting people? And how come he's so fucking *bad* at it?"

The girl picked a bag off the nearest chair and put the knife inside. She didn't put the bag back down, however, or pull her hand back out. "You know the deal," she said. "Either the kids don't know anything about what we do, or else you train them up so they're *better* than you at it. Generation upon generation. This *has not happened* here, Jonathan. Your boy is the worst of both worlds – and whose fault is that?"

"Mine," he said, numbly.

"Dad?" Ryan said, his voice slurred. "What are you talking about?"

"Let him go," Jonathan asked, again. What was the girl's name – Miranda? Cassandra? Something like that. He now recalled seeing her, briefly, at a very private party at someone else's house, down in Los Angeles, seven or eight or ten years ago. She'd been very young then, not much more than a child, but laughed and clapped with ferocious glee when blood started to spill: the kid of someone who'd done a much better job of passing their secret world on. "I'll make it right."

"Too late," she said.

"You're nobody. You don't get to make that call."

"Screw you, and anyway I'm not making it. This is from the top. The Upright Man himself. You failed. End of story."

"Not just me," he said, grimly. "You think no one will remember you being with him in that bar tonight? If he dies, someone who looks like you will be suspect number one. The assholes in The Jury Room may be drunk out of their minds, but they'll remember you – and *they'll* talk to the cops."

"It won't get that far. Not with the neat father-ends-his-errant-son's-miserable-life-and-then-takes-his-own scenario we're going to be giving them."

She brought her hand out of her bag, and held out a gun to him.

"Seriously? You expect me to do that?"

"I know you will. And not just because you understand the consequences if you don't. You'll do it because you're one of us, and you know the rules."

Jonathan took the gun. He looked at Ryan, still peering blearily at him with his terribly damaged little boy's face. They hadn't wanted him to kill. He and Elaine had done everything they could to keep him from the life, in fact, going against everything the group was supposed to stand for. They had loved Ryan, very much, even when he was bad and ill-tempered. Even when he'd been hard to love. Jonathan had tried to be a good father. He'd tried to bring his son up to be happy and healthy, even at the risk of putting himself in danger by failing to mistreat the boy in the ways prescribed.

In vain, it turned out, because somehow Ryan had found his own path to the same destination.

"Elaine's already dead, isn't she?"

The woman gestured toward a side-table. On it, Jonathan now realized, lay a copy of the current issue of *Sunset Magazine*. He doubted this was a periodical that Ryan read, and he knew where he'd very recently seen it, and in whose hands, and he remembered the 4Runner he'd seen parked just down the road from the house when he came out.

"You bitch. Why?"

"We tie up the loose ends. Have to. You know that."

Jonathan took the gun and walked over to Ryan. He put his hand on his son's head, gently.

"I loved you," he said.

"Dad?"

Jonathan shot the boy through the temple. Then he raised the gun to his own head, and closed his eyes. "And I loved you most of all, my dear," he whispered quietly, to Elaine. "I'll fight through all the ghosts we made, until I am by your side."

He pulled the trigger a second time.

When she was convinced that neither of the men was going to move ever again, the girl – whose name, the one she used most often at least, was indeed Cassandra – left the house, and walked away down the driveway.

She took the copy of *Sunset Magazine* with her.

She hadn't read that issue yet.

KIM NEWMAN

The Only Ending We Have

T HE WINDSHIELD WIPERS squeaked ... like shrilling fiddles, scraped nerves, the ring of an unanswered phone. Another reason to trade in her '57 Ford Custom. For 1960, she'd like something with fins. Not that she could afford next year's showroom model.

Unless Hitch coughed up the ransom.

For the thing it was all about. The *MacGuffin*.

The thing the audience doesn't care about, but the characters do.

"Good eeeev-ning," Hitch said, every goddamn' morning ... like in his TV show with that nursery/graveyard tune burbling in the background. "Funeral March of the Marionettes". *Dump-da-dumpity-dump-da-dump* ...

"Good eeeev-ning, Jay-y-ne ..."

His gargling-with-marbles accent was British. Not like David Niven or Peter Lawford, but British crawled out from under a rock. Hitch was a wattled toad in a grey-flannel suit, with inflating cheeks and jowls. His lower teeth stuck out like the Wolf Man's. His loose, babyish lips got moist when she came on set. Even before she took off the bathrobe. When she unwrapped the goods, he was spellbound. After a half-hour, he'd have to gulp down drool with a little death-rattle.

"Jayne Swallow? Do you *swallow*, Jayne ... do you?"

Every morning the same routine. Even before the robe came off.

"Take a bird name, chickie," her agent, Walter, had said ... "bird names are good."

So, goodbye Jana Wróbel ... hello, Jayne Swallow.

She should have gone with Joan Sparrow or Junie Peacock. By

the time she signed on for Hitch, it was too late. She'd heard all the lines.

The set was festooned with dead birds. They stank under the hot lights. Chemicals. The glass eyes of the mountain eagle perched above a doorway reminded her of Hitch's watery ogling.

Hitchcock. That was a bird name, too. And a dirty meaning, which no one threw in the director's face every morning.

"Good morning, Mr Softcock ... Good afternoon, Mr Halfcock ... Good eeev-ning, Mr Cocksucker ... how do you like it?"

He'd screech like a bird at that ... *Scree! Scree! Scree!*

There was a bird name in his damn' movie. Janet Leigh's character. Jayne's character. Crane. Marion Crane.

... which made Jayne and Janet Hitch's Marion-ettes. The whole shoot was their funeral, scored with the slow, solemn, ridiculous tune. Jayne danced and strings cut into her wrists and neck.

In the end, the wires were snipped and she fell all in a heap, unstrung. Over and over. Like a sack of potatoes. Like a side of beef with arms and legs. Chocolate oozed from her wounds. Then she got up and died all over again.

Dump-da-dumpity-dump-da-dump ... Scree! Scree! Scree!

She drove north on the Pacific Coast Highway.

To disguise herself, in case anyone from the studio should be crossing the road in front of the car, she'd worn sunglasses and a headscarf. Marilyn's famous I-don't-want-to-be-recognized look. She'd taken off the disguise when she was safely out of Los Angeles and the rain got heavy.

Even without the shades, it was hard to see the road ahead. Short-lived clear triangles were wiped into the thick water on the windshield. A deluge. Mudslide weather. After months of California sun, you found out where the ceiling leaked. There wasn't much traffic, which was a mercy. The car weaved from side to side as the wheel fought her grip. Her tyres weren't the newest. She struggled, as if she'd been force-fed booze by a spy ring and set loose on a twisty cliff road to meet an unsuspicious accident.

The squeak of the wipers. The beat of her heart.

The voices in her head. Hitch's. Her agent's. Hers.

"Do you swallow, *Jayne* ... do you?"

Tony Perkins's. "I like stuffing . . . birds."

Scree! Scree! Scree!

The window-seals were blown. Water seeped into the car, pouring in rivulets over the dash and inside the doors. Droplets formed this side of the glass, too many to wipe away with her cuff. Her seat was damp. She shivered. She'd been fighting the flu since her first day in the shower. With all the water, no one noticed her nose was streaming . . . except Becca, the make-up woman, and she kept secrets like a priest in a confessional.

She could still feel water on her body. For days, she'd been pounded by studio hoses. The temperature varied from luke-warm to icy. The pressure kept up. Extra steam was pumped in, to show on film. She'd been scalded and she'd been frozen, but most of all she'd been soaked. She thought she'd never be dry again.

Before Jayne got into the fake bathtub each morning, Becca had to apply three moleskin patches which transformed her into a sexless thing, like that new blonde doll her niece had, Barbie . . . or a dressmaker's dummy with a head.

She might as well not have a head . . . her face would not be in the film. Janet Leigh's would be. The most Jayne would show was a tangle of wet blonde hair, seen from behind, as the knife scored down her unrecognizable back.

. . . in the book, the girl in the shower had her head cut off with an axe. One chop. Too swift for Hitch. He preferred the death of a thousand cuts. A thousand stabs. A thousand edits.

She was the only person on the crew who'd read the novel – not especially, but by coincidence, a few months ago. Something to read while a photographer got his lights set *just so.* The first rule of showbusiness was always take a book to read. There was so much waiting while men fiddled before they could start proper work. On the average Western, you could read *From Here to Eternity* while the bar-room mirror was being replaced between fights.

Hitch disapproved of Jayne's book-learning. He intended to make a play of keeping the twist secret . . . not letting audiences into theatres after the movie started, appearing in jokey public-service messages saying "Please don't tell the ending, it's the only one we have". But the picture's last reel wasn't an atomic plan guarded by the FBI. The paperback was in every book-rack in America. If it were down to Hitch, he'd confiscate the whole run and have the books pulped. It wasn't even *his* ending, really. It was Robert Bloch's. The writer was seldom mentioned. Hitch pretended he'd made it all up. Jayne sympathized . . . Bloch was the only participant getting a worse deal out of the movie than she was.

A clot of liquid earth splattered against the windshield, dislodged from the hillside above. The wipers smeared it into a blotch. She saw obscene shapes in the mud pattern, setting off bells at the Catholic Legion of Decency. Soon, the dirt was gone. Eventually, water got rid of all the disgusting messes in the world.

After a few hours in the movie shower, those patches would wash off Jayne's censorable areas. It didn't matter what spirit-gum Becca tried. Water would always win.

Then, spittle would rattle in Hitch's mouth. He would observe, lugubriously, "I spy . . . with my little eye . . . something beginning wi-i-i-ith . . . N! Nipple!"

Always, the director would insist on pretending to help Becca re-apply the recalcitrant triangles . . . risking the wrath of the unions. The film's credited make-up men were already complaining about being gypped out of the chance to work with naked broads and stuck with be-wigging skeletons or filling John Gavin's chin-dimple. There was an issue about whether the patches were make-up or costume.

Jayne had posed for smut pictures. Walter said no one would ever know, the pay was better than extra-work, and the skin game had been good enough for Marilyn. For *Swank* and *Gent* – she'd never made it into *Playboy* – they shot her as was and smoothed her to plasticity with an airbrush. For the movies, the transformation was managed on set.

"Have you shaved today, Jayne Swallow? Shaved *down there*?"

Unless she did, the crotch-patch was agony to get off. No matter how many times it washed free during the day, it was always stuck fast at the end of the shoot. She was raw from the ripping.

"I thought of becoming a barber," Hitch said. "If you need a hand, I have my cut-throat . . ."

At that, at the thought of a straight-razor on her pubes, he would flush with unconcealable excitement . . . and her guts would twist into knots.

"You'll love Hitch," Walter said. "And he'll love you. He loves blondes. And bird names. Birds are in all his films."

Sure, she was blonde. With a little help from a bottle. Another reason to shave *down there*.

We can't all be Marilyn. We can't all be Janet Leigh.

Being Janet Leigh was Jayne's job on this film.

Body double. Stand-in. Stunt double. Torso dummy.

Oh, Janet did her time in the shower. From the neck up.

The rest of it, though . . . weeks of close-ups of tummy, hands, feet, ass, thighs, throat . . . that was Jayne.

"It's a shower scene," Walter said.

She'd thought she knew what that meant. She'd done shower scenes. Indoors, for sophisticated comedies. Outdoors, for Westerns. Show a shape behind a curtain or a waterfall, and then let Debra Paget or Dorothy Provine step out wrapped in a towel and smile.

They always joked about shooting a version "for France". Without the curtain.

In France, Brigitte Bardot showed everything. Hitch would have loved to have BB in his sights. But Hollywood wasn't ready yet . . .

So, a shower scene . . .

A *Hitchcock* shower scene.

Not a tease, not titillation – except for very specialized tastes (i.e. his). Not a barber's scene, but a butcher's. Not for France, but for . . . well, for Transylvania or the Cannibal Islands or wherever women were meat to be carved . . .

There were caresses . . . the water, and the tip of the blade.

Not a single clean shocking chop but a frenzy of *pizzicato* stabs.

"This boy," Hitch said, embarrassing Tony Perkins, "he has an eye for the ladies . . . no, a *knife* for the ladies."

She'd been prodded, over and over. She'd been sliced, if only in illusion – the dull edge of the prop drawn over the soft skin of her stomach, again and again. After the fourth or fifth pass, it felt like a real knife . . . after the fourth or fifth day, she thought she was bleeding out, though it was only chocolate syrup, swirling around her dirty feet . . .

Some shower scene.

Her skin still burned with the rashes raised by the knife . . . with the little blisters made when the lights boiled the water on her shoulders. The sores scraped open and leaked as she was wrapped in a torn curtain, packaged like carved meat, suitable for dumping in a swamp.

She was uncomfortable in her clothes. She might never be comfortable in her clothes again.

If she kept driving North (*by North-West?*), she'd hit San Francisco . . . city of ups and downs . . . But before then, she'd need to sleep.

Not in a motel. Not after this week's work.

Her blouse was soaked through. No amount of towelling would ever get her dry.

"Do you swallow, *Jayne* . . . do you?"

The soles of her feet were ridged, painful to stand on.

"I spy . . . with my little eye . . . something beginning wi-i-i-ith . . . P."

Pigeon? Psychopath? Perkins?

"Pudenda!"

Every time the crotch-skin came off, Hitch sprung another letter on her . . . another word for vagina. F. C. T. Q. P. M.

M for Mousehole? Whoever said that?

Sometimes Hitch took the knife himself and got in close. He said Perkins wasn't holding it right, was stabbing like a fairy . . .

Perkins's eyes narrowed at that. They didn't slide over Jayne's body like Hitch's, or any of the other guys on the crew.

. . . but it was an excuse.

The director just plain liked sticking it to a naked woman.

Any woman? Or just Jayne?

He'd have preferred doing it to Janet, because she was a Star. Really, he'd have wanted to stab Grace Kelly or Ingrid Bergman, who were more than Stars. But he'd make do with Jayne Swallow . . . or Jana Wróbel . . . or some blonde off the street.

Oh, he never touched her with anything that wasn't sharp. Never even shook hands.

"How do you shake hands with a naked lady?" he'd asked, when they were introduced – she'd been cast from cheesecake 8 x 10s, without an audition – on set. How indeed? Or was that his way of avoiding physical contact with her? Did he not trust himself?

Others *had* auditioned, she learned . . . but turned him down. They'd found out what he wanted and preferred not to be a part of it. Blondes who did naked pin-ups, strippers, *girls who did stag films* . . . they didn't want to be cut up in a shower, even with Janet Leigh's head on top of their bodies.

So, Jayne Swallow.

Scree! Scree! Scree!

Now, she really had what Hitch wanted . . . and he'd have to pay more than scale to get it back. But it wasn't the money. That wasn't her MacGuffin. She wanted something else. What? Revenge? Retribution? To be treated like a person rather than a broken doll?

It wasn't just Hitch. She stood in for Janet Leigh. He stood in for everyone who'd cut her.

Since driving off the lot, she'd been seeing him everywhere. In the broken side-mirror, through the misted-over rear window. In every film, there he was, somewhere. If only in a photo on the wall. Unmistakable, of course. That fat, double bass-belly . . . that caricature silhouette . . . doleful, little-boy eyes like raisins in uncooked dough . . . the loose cheeks, like Droopy in the cartoons . . . that comb-over wisp.

He was waiting for a bus. He was smoking a cigar. He was getting a shoe-shine. He was wearing a too-big cowboy hat. He was smirking in a billboard ad for an all-you-can-scoff restaurant. He was fussing with dogs. He was the odd short fat boy out in a police line-up of tall, thin, unshaven crooks. He was up on a bell-tower, with a high-powered rifle. He was in a closet, with a bag full of sharp, sharp knives. He was in the back seat with a rope. He wore white editor's gloves to handle his murder weapons.

She looked at the mirror, and saw no one there.

Nothing beginning with H.

But there was a shape in the road, flapping. She swerved to avoid it.

A huge gull, one wing snapped. The storm had driven it ashore.

It was behind her now. Not road-kill, but a road casualty. Suitable for stuffing and mounting.

Hitch said that about Marion Crane too, in a line he'd wanted in the script but not snuck past the censors. They were Jesuits, used to playing word games with clever naughty schoolboys.

Birds . . . Crane, Swallow . . . suitable for stuffing and mounting.

Another dark shape came out of the rain and gained on the car. A man on a motorcycle. A wild one? Like Brando. No, a highway cop. He wore a helmet and a rain-slicker. Water poured in runnels off the back of his cape. It looked like a set of folded, see-through wings. His goggles were like big glass eyes.

Her heart-rate raced.

. . . *stop, thief!*

Had the studio called the cops yet? Had Hitch denounced her sabotage?

"*I'll take it out of her fine sweet flesh,*" Hitch would say. "Every pound of meat, every inch of skin!"

She was a thief. Not like Cary Grant, suave and calculating . . . but a purse-snatcher, vindictive and desperate . . . taking something not because it was valuable to her but because it was valuable to the person she'd stolen from.

The cop signalled her to pull over.

He had a gun. She didn't. She was terrified.

Cops weren't your friends.

She'd found that out the minute she got off the bus in Los Angeles. She'd been young and innocent then, with a hometown photo-studio portfolio and a notion to get into the movies. She learned fast. Cops locked you up when you hadn't done anything. Cops squeezed the merchandise and extracted fines which didn't involve money. They let the big crooks walk free and cracked down on the hustlers. They always busted the wrong man. Beat patrolmen, vice dicks, harness bulls, traffic cops. The enemy.

Her brakes weren't good. It took maybe thirty yards to pull over. With a sound like a scream in the rain.

The wipers still ticked as the motor idled. The screech slowed.

In the rear-view, she saw the cop unstraddle his ride. The rain poured off his helmet, goggles, cape, boots. He strode through the storm towards her. He wasn't like the city cops she'd met, bellies bulging over their belts, flab-rolls easing around their holstered guns. He was Jimmy Stewart lean, snake-hipped. A cowboy with an armoured skullcap.

If she put on a burst of speed, would she leave him here?

No, he'd catch her. Or she'd go off the cliff into the Pacific.

The knuckle rap came at her window. The cop didn't bend down. She saw the leather jacket through his transparent slicker. A wild one, after all.

She tried to roll the window down and the handle came off. It did sometimes, but there was a trick to fixing it back. She didn't bother with the trick. She opened the door, first a crack, then halfway, using it to shield against the rain, and ducked her head out to look up at the cop.

His goggles gave him the eyes of Death.

Two little television sets strapped to his face, playing the opening of that show. *Dump-da-dumpity-dump-da-dump* ... there Hitch was, in a fright-wig, being funny, holding a noose or a big bottle with POISON stamped on it. A non-speaking woman boiling in a pot or strapped to a saw-horse.

"Good eeev-ning," he said.

Not Hitch, the cop. And not with a British accent.

She waited for it. The come-on. Tonight's *stawww*-ry.

"Going mighty fast?" "Where's the fire, lady?" "The way you look, the things you do to a man ... that ought to be against the law ..." "See what you've done to my night-stick, ma'am ..." "Swallow, huh? Well ...?"

"Licence and registration?"

He was unreadable. Not a movie cop.

She didn't ask what she'd done wrong. She knew enough not to open up that debate. She found her documents, sodden and fragile as used tissue, in the glove compartment.

Whenever she showed her papers, she was irrationally afraid they'd turn out to be false – or the cop would say they were. That blanket of guilt was impossible to shuck, even when she hadn't had things to feel guilty about. She *knew* these papers were legit, but they weren't in the name she was using. In the photo on her driver's licence, Jana wasn't as blonde as Jayne.

Her papers got wetter as the cop looked them over.

"Wróbel," he said, pronouncing it properly.

Then he asked her something in Polish. Which she didn't speak.

She shrugged.

"Not from the Old Country, then?"

It might as well have been Transylvania.

"Santa Rosa, originally," she admitted.

"Hollywood, now," he said, clocking her address.

She was too cold to give him a pin-up smile. Usually, cops asked if she was in pictures . . . she must be too bedraggled for that now.

"You must be in pictures . . . dirty pictures," was the usual line. Said with a grin, and a hitch of the belt buckle into the gut.

"You must be in pictures . . . horror pictures," was the new take. "You must be in pictures . . . Alfred Hitchcock pictures."

"Watch your driving," the cop actually said. "This is accident weather. How far have you got to go?"

She had no definite idea, but said, "San Francisco."

"You won't make it by nightfall. I'd stop. Check into a motel."

"That makes sense, sir."

"No need for 'sir'. 'Officer' will do."

The cop's skin, under the rain, was greyish. This weather greyed everything out, like a black-and-white movie. The hillside mud should have been red, like blood . . . but it washed over the road like coffee grounds. Dark.

"Makes sense, officer."

"Good girl," he said, returning her licence and registration.

A motel. Not likely. When Hitch's film came out, people wouldn't check into motels without thinking twice. People wouldn't take showers. Or climb stairs. Or go into fruit cellars. Or trust young men with twitchy smiles who liked to stuff (and mount) birds.

If the film came out now. She might have scratched that.

The cop turned and walked back to his motorcycle. Rain on his back, pouring down his neck.

Why had he stopped her? Suspicion, of course. But of what?

The theft couldn't have been reported yet. Might not be until Monday morning. Word couldn't be out. This cop wasn't rousting a woman motorist for kicks, like they usually did. Maybe he was just concerned? There had to be some cops like that . . .

While she had the door open, water rained in. Her shoes were soaked.

She pulled the door shut and tried to start the car. The motor seized up and died. Then choked, then drew out a death scene like Charles Laughton, then caught again ... and she drove on.

Damn, December night fell quick.

Now, she was driving through dark and rain. The road ahead was as murky as a poverty-row back-projection plate. Her right headlight was on the fritz, winking like a lecher at a co-ed.

The cop was right. She had to pull over. If she slept in this leaky car, she'd drown. If she drove on, she'd end up in the sea. The Ford Custom did not come with an optional lifeboat. She wasn't sure hers even had a usable spare tyre.

Through blobby cascades on the windshield, she saw a flashing light.

VACANCY.

A motel. She remembered her vow. No motels, never again ... she knew, really, there was little chance of being butchered by a homicidal maniac. That was just the movies. Still, there was every chance of running into a travelling salesman or an off-duty cop or an overage wild one, and being cajoled or strong-armed or blackmailed into a room with cheap liquor and "*Que Sera Sera*" on the radio. The ending to that story would surprise no one.

She'd been photographed in motel rooms. She'd been interviewed in motel rooms. She'd auditioned for movie projects that didn't really exist. If some dentist wanted to call himself a producer and play casting-couch games, he hooked on to a script about giant leeches or dragstrip dolls just to set up his own private orgy. She'd checked into a motel with a young actor – not Tony Perkins, but someone a few steps behind him – and posed for bedroom candids leaked to the scandal sheets to squelch whispers that the rising stud preferred beach boys to bikini babes. In print, they put a black bar across her eyes.

She'd been abandoned in motels, too ... left with bills for booze and damages. Some guys couldn't have a party without breaking a lamp or knocking a picture off the wall. Or hurting someone, just to hear the squeal and see blood on their knuckles.

VACANCY.

The light flashed like a cliff-top lantern on a cliff in a three-cornered hat picture, luring storm-tossed ships on to the rocks to be looted.

She was more likely to die on the road than in this place.

So, she pulled off the highway and bumped downhill into a parking lot. There were other cars there. The lights were on in a single-storey building.

HACIENDA HAYSLIP.

Like every other place in California, this motel impersonated an Old Spanish Mission – protruding beams, fake adobe, concrete cactus, a neon sombrero over the name.

Once, the Pacific was the far edge of the world. The Jesuits got here first, even before the bandits. Jayne had been to Catholic school. She was more afraid of priests than outlaws. Priests were worse than cops. Beyond the shadow of a doubt. Cops just played the game by rules which favoured them. Priests took the same liberties, but told you it was God's will that you got robbed or rousted or raped.

She parked as near the office as possible and made a dash from her car to the lit-up shelter. By now, she couldn't get much wetter.

Pushing through the front door, she was enveloped by heat. The office was built around an iron stove which radiated oppressive warmth. Windows were steamed up. Viennese waltz music came from an old-fashioned record player.

In a rocking chair by the stove sat a small thin woman, knitting. On a stool behind the front desk perched a fat young man, reading a comic book. They both turned to look at her. She must be a fright. Something the cat would drag in.

"Arthur," said the woman, "see to the customer . . ."

Her voice was like a parrot's, chirruping words it couldn't understand. The thin woman had a grating, shrill tone and another British accent . . . a comedy fishwife or a slum harridan. *Cockney.* Jayne had heard other Englishmen say Hitch was a cockney. He went tight around the collar if it was said to his loose-jowled face. It was a put-down, she guessed – like "polack" or "hunkie". David Niven and Peter Lawford weren't cockneys. Cary Grant *for sure* wasn't a cockney. Hitch was, and so was this woman who had somehow fetched up on the far side of the world, in the country of Jesuits and outlaws and Indians and gold-diggers.

"In the fullness of time, Mahmah," said the fat young man.

He didn't sound cockney. He had a James Mason or George Sanders voice. A suave secret agent, a bit of a rogue . . . but coming out of a bloated, cherubic face, that accent was all wrong. Jayne wondered if Arthur was another fairy. Was that why mother and son – "Mahmah" must mean "Mother" – had said goodbye Piccadilly and farewell Leicester Square?

She stood there, dripping and steaming.

Arthur finished reading to the end of the page, lips moving as he mouthed the balloons. Then he neatly folded over the top corner and shut the comic. *Journey Into Mystery*. He tidied it away with a stack of similar publications, shuffling so the edges were straight as if he had just finished an exam and wanted his desk neat.

"What might the Hacienda Hayslip do for you, madam?"

"A room, for the night."

"Nocturnal refuge? Most fortuitous. We do indeed rent rooms, nightly. Have you a reservation?"

Before she could answer, his mother piped up . . . "A reservation! What does she look like, a squaw? Who ever has a reservation, Arthur?"

"Formalities must be observed, Mahmah. Did you, madam, have the foresight to contact us by telephone or telegram . . . or is this more in the manner of an impromptu stopover?"

"The second thing," she said.

"Spur of the moment? Fortunate for you, then, that one or two of our luxury cabins are unoccupied at present and can therefore be put at your disposal . . . are you of a superstitious or numerological bent?"

She shook her head.

"Don't give her Thirteen," said the old woman.

Arthur sucked his cupid's bow lips between his teeth, making his mouth into a puckered slit. He was thoughtful or annoyed.

"I don't mind," she said.

So far as she could recall, none of the rooms she'd been groped or duped or roughed up in had had the unlucky number. Ordinary numbers were bad enough.

"It's too close to the edge, Arthur," said the old woman. "Be the next to go."

"How would you like a cabin on the beach?" Arthur asked Jayne.

"Normally, that would sound nice. Just now, dry and warm is all I want."

"It's not nice," shrilled Arthur's mother. "Not nice at all. My son is trying to be funny. We sit on the cliff here and it's crumbling away. The dirt's no good. The rain gets in, loosens it up. The far cabins have gone over the edge. They tumble on to the beach. In pieces. You should hear the fearful racket that makes."

Arthur blew out his lips and smiled.

"Indeed, madam. We are in a somewhat precarious position. Some might opine that my mother made a poor investment. Others might rule this our just lot. For we have incurred the ire of the Almighty, by our many, many sins. My mother, though you'd not think it of her now, was once a very great harlot. A woman of easy virtue, baptized in champagne. Powdered and painted and primped and pimped and porked and poked and prodded and paid. Showered with gifts of opal and topaz and red, red rubies. She dragged fine men to ruin. Duels were fought. Balconies jumped from. Revolvers discharged into despairing brains. Foolish, feckless and fickle were her many, many admirers. All dead now, though their sins remain."

At this speech, the old woman cackled and grinned.

Jayne looked again at Arthur's mother. Her skin had shrivelled on to her bones. Her face was a pattern of wrinkles and her hands were vulture claws. She smiled and showed yellow teeth. She wore a black, feathery wig which matched her dress.

"Did you think, madam, to find the notorious Birdie Hayslip sat by the stove at this stop on your journey through life? Knitting her own shroud?"

"Shut up, Arthur, you're making her blush!"

Birdie! There was a bird name and no mistake. Walter would have loved it.

"Just sign her in, boy. Sign her in. Don't let her get away. We can't afford to lose customers. Not in these trying times. Income tax and the Bomb."

Arthur took the registration book from beneath the desk. It was bound in fleshy red leather.

She hesitated before signing. She was a thief in flight, she remembered. She wouldn't want to be tracked and traced. Her situation couldn't be unusual. Couples who stayed in joints like this mostly passed themselves off as "Mr and Mrs Smith". She wrote *Jana Wróbel*, but with a scribble – so it couldn't be read, let alone pronounced – and gave her address as Century City, Ca.

"Madame Wobble," said Arthur, without irony, "you shall have Cabin Number Seventeen . . . come this way . . ."

Reaching behind him, he took a key from a board. It was attached to a fist-sized plaster cactus.

He slipped off his high stool and came out from behind the desk.

Arthur Hayslip was not a dwarf but was well under five feet in height and balloon-bellied. His hair was thinning, though she thought him not much more than twenty. He wore a velvet Little Lord Fauntleroy jacket and child's slacks. He was a plump, ageing baby – but precise and delicate, as if performing all his gestures for television cameras.

"Galoshes, Arthur," Birdie reminded her son.

He slipped his pumps into waterproof overshoes, and took down a big yellow fisherman's slicker with attached hood. The protective clothing was made for a hardy six-footer and he disappeared into it. He looked like a fairytale character, but she wished she had a more rainproof topcoat too.

"Shall we venture out, Madame Wobble? Into the storm?"

"It's Miss Wobble," she corrected.

"You hear that, Arthur! *Miss*. I saw straight away. No wedding band. She's *available*!"

Birdie cackled again and the laughter turned into a coughing fit. She did not sound like a well person.

"I have to fetch some things from the trunk of my car."

"The boot, Arthur," said Birdie. "She means the boot."

"You always misremember, Mahmah . . . you took steps in 1939, dragged me from our native shores. When I was but a babe, the Jerries started dropping whizz-bangs. There was something in the newspapers about a war. There was a term for British subjects who fled to safer climes for the duration. Gone With the Wind Up. I am a naturalized American, a real-life nephew of my Uncle Sam . . ."

He didn't sound it.

"Or was it Uncle Irving, Uncle Montmorency, Uncle Yasujiro, Uncle Fedor, Uncle Harry or Auntie Margaret? Mahmah has never confided which, if any, of my many uncles might also have been my . . ."

"Arthur, don't be vulgar. She's not interested. Can't you tell?"

He took an umbrella from a rack by the desk and pushed open the door with it. The storm roared, and the waltz record stuttered after the music stopped. He opened the umbrella to shield them as they stepped outside. He had to stretch his arm like the Statue of Liberty's to get above her head. They still got soaked.

They trudged across muddy asphalt to her car and she popped the trunk.

In the dark, in the cold, in the wet, her face still burned.

There it was. In a sack, tied like a post-bag.

Arthur reached into the trunk with his free hand and took . . . not the sack, but her overnight bag. He ignored the MacGuffin.

"I'll just bring this along," she said, picking it up casually.

"That is your right and privilege, my dear."

The trunk wouldn't catch the first time she slammed it down, nor the second. Arthur had both hands full, so he couldn't help. Finally, she wrestled it and locked it. The sack started to get wet. What was inside might be dangerous when wet.

A covered walkway kept some of the rain off. They went past the main building.

Lights were strung up, but several of the bulbs were dead. Darkness encroached. The cabins were originally in a square around a swimming pool, but – as Birdie had said – the cabins at the far edge were gone, leaving only stumps. Beyond, unseen, was the cliff. A crack ran through the concrete bottom of the pool. It could no longer hold water, though temporary puddles collected, swirling and eddying into the fissure. This was an empty pool you could drown in.

The hacienda would eventually wind up on the beach.

Her cabin was well away from the crumbling edge of the property. No immediate danger.

Arthur put her overnight bag down and unlocked Cabin Seventeen. He reached in and turned on the lights, holding the door open for her. She took her bag and walked across a squelching WELCOME mat. Arthur let his umbrella down and followed.

There were twin beds. No, *two* beds. One a single for a giant, the other a cot for a circus midget. Between them was a low table with a two-headed bedside lamp, a crystal ashtray that fit the definition of blunt instrument and a Gideon Bible open to the Flood.

Above the table was a picture in a heavy gilt frame. A chubby naked woman was being bothered from behind by a giant swan with human eyes.

"A classical subject," Arthur commented. "Leda and Zeus. So *earthy*, the Gods of Greece."

Other pictures hung around the room, less ornately framed, less immediately eye-catching. Slim, big-eyed women dressed in the style of the Roaring Twenties. Fringes and feathers.

"Do you recognize Mahmah? She was always photographed, at the height of her infamy."

Jayne wasn't even sure the pictures were all of the same woman. She couldn't fit them over the Birdie who sat by the stove.

"The cabin has the full amenities, Miss Wobble. Through there . . ."

He indicated a closed door.

"Modern plumbing, a flush toilet, wash-basins, a bath-tub . . ."

"Shower?"

Arthur shrugged, non-committally.

"I could do with a long soak in a hot tub, after the rain and the drive . . ."

"I regret to inform you that . . . temporarily, there is no hot water. It seems one can have light but no hot water or hot water but no light, and after dark the need for illumination takes primacy . . . tomorrow morning, perhaps, after sun-up, something warm can be arranged."

Jayne tried to live with the disappointment.

She wanted at least to get out of her wet clothes and towel off.

Arthur showed no sign of leaving. Did he expect a tip? His waterproof dripped on the rug. He strolled about, looking at the pictures.

"Once, Mahmah was a nymph, a naiad . . . now, she is a gorgon, a harpy . . . time can be so cruel, don't you think, Miss Wobble? Though it is no more than she deserves, for was Mahmah not cruel when she had the chance . . . is she not still cruel, when she gets the opportunity?"

"I wouldn't know."

"Of course not. You are an innocent party in this situation . . . my m-m-mother deserves to die, don't you think? And not naturally. No, that would not be just. She is a most exquisitely *m-m-m-murderable* personage."

He had worked hard to overcome a stutter, but it slipped back.

"Shootable? Poisonable? Throttlable? Bludgeonable?"

Arthur's fat-wreathed eyes came alive. He reminded Jayne of . . .

"Stabbable? Slashable? Beheadable? Deadable?"

His recitative was almost a tune. *Hump-da-dumpity-dump-da-dump* . . .

He broke off.

"Happy thoughts, Miss Wobble."

"But morbid," she ventured.

"Practical. What do you do for a living, Miss Wobble? Presuming that you do live . . .?"

Normally, she would say she was an actress – which was partially true. But that always prompted the same response. "Have I seen you in anything?" And that led, if the enquirer was at all interesting, to "If you've watched most of my pictures, you've seen me in not much of anything at all . . ." Then, smiles, drinks and a happy ending.

Now, she was a thief, a saboteur. She had to be careful. Arthur was *not* interesting, not in that way.

"I'm in motion pictures. Make-up girl."

"An interesting expression. Make-up girl? What do you make up for?"

"Hard nights, mostly. Filling in the cracks so the camera doesn't see."

Arthur unbuttoned his slicker. He took it off and hung it on a coat-tree, as if it belonged there. She hadn't invited him to stay.

"The camera sees all, though," he said, pointing at one of the portrait pictures. A dramatic, Satanic pose – a big-eyed vamp resting her chin on her crossed wrists, under a stuffed goat-head on a pentacle. Jayne thought she *could* see Birdie in this Jazz Age sinner. The eyes were the same.

"The laughter is frozen and the rot shows through," said Arthur. "The pleasure garden in spring is a family plot in autumn. Photography makes corpses of us all. Snatches little dead moments and pins them down for all eternity. You apply make-up to the dead, too."

"Not me. I work with actresses."

"Actresses *should be* dead, don't you think? Mahmah once called herself an 'actress', though she never set her dainty foot on the boards. Stage fright, would you believe? Who would you wish dead, Miss Wobble?"

Men. Hitch.

"Me? Oh, no one. I say live and let live, you know. I like love stories. Not stories with murders."

"All great love stories end in murder, though. Or *could* end in murder . . ."

He sat down in a cane armchair, crossing his stubby legs and settling his stomach into his lap.

His torso was like a big egg, with another big egg – his head – set on top of it. Soft-boiled, unshelled. If she had a knife, like the movie prop knife, could she cut into those eggs? Find the yolks still molten and trickling.

Arthur's murder talk was getting to her.

"How would *you* like to murder my mother, Miss Scribble?"

That was like a stab to the chest.

"You couldn't be traced. Not with your signature, your *phoney* address . . ."

Phoney. That stood out. A wrong word. American, not consistent with Arthur's British manner of speaking.

"I can be counted on to give a most misleading description. You wouldn't even be a woman. You'd be a man . . . a swarthy, horny-handed man . . . the type my mother is attracted to, but who are no good for her, no good for anyone . . . a man's man, a man from the Isle of Man . . . a man with big hands, workman's hands, neck-snapping, larynx-crushing hands. Afterwards, we would both be free . . ."

"Free?"

"Yes. I would be free of Mahmah, of this place. You would be freer, free of . . . of the constraints of petty Protestant morality."

"I'm Catholic."

"Well, easy to do it then! You sin on Saturday night, and are washed clean Sunday morning . . . just take care not to die unshriven between the two sacraments. The sacraments of murder and confessional."

"I don't really like this, Mr Hayslip. I'm not comfortable."

"We're just talking, Miss Alias . . . shooting the breeze, yarning away the night hours while the storm rages without . . . without what, I always think, without what?"

"I'm not going to kill anyone," she said.

"A bold, sweeping statement. Would you kill to protect yourself from, say, a vile ravisher?"

Too late for that.

"Or to secure an inheritance, a fortune which you could use on good works if it were liberated from a miser who makes no use of it?"

"Is your mother rich?"

"No, she's *strange*. She hasn't a bean, Miss Alibi. Just this place. Half on the cliff. Half on the beach. She has only her memories. Her *disgusting* memories."

"I'm sure she's not as bad as that. She's just a woman."

Arthur leaned forwards, eyes shining. "*Just* a woman? *Just?* Maybe . . . maybe, at that . . . but it's no excuse, is it? It's no reason she should be spared from God's judgement. Quite the opposite. It was Eve, was it not, who led mankind into Sin? Eve, the *femme fatale* and the farmer's wife. Eve who brought about the Fall. Should not Eve be punished, *over and over and over . . .?*"

A thin line of spit, like spider-silk, descended from Arthur's wet mouth. He repeatedly slammed a pudgy, soft, tiny fist into the palm of his other hand.

It struck Jayne that Arthur Hayslip was hateful, but harmless.

If she killed this stranger's mother, what would he do for her? What wouldn't he do for her? Rain rattled the windows. The cabin shook, like a train compartment on an express.

"You don't know how to do it to a woman, do you?" she said. "You blame her, your mother, but it's your weakness."

He drew back. "I am a man of the world, my dear," he said. "Your sex holds no mystery for me. I know too much for that."

She tittered. He flushed red.

"You couldn't hurt a fly, if you wanted to. You don't want to murder your mother, you want *someone else* to murder your mother. But that would be the end for you, the ending you didn't guess was coming. The twist in the last reel. There would be nothing. Without her, you'd be a dummy without a ventriloquist . . ."

"Mummy," he murmured, "Mummy's dummy . . ."

All at once, she didn't want to press on. There was no point in it, in making an unhappy wretch more wretched. That wasn't heroic, that was bullying. She'd been bullied enough herself to hate that.

How many times had she been stripped and stabbed this week? In play, in fun, for *entertainment*? She had been murdered, over and over . . .

"Has he asked you to top me?" shrilled a voice from the door. "He asks all the lodgers to top me. All the ones he fancies, at least. Girlies and boysies, he's not too particular . . ."

Birdie flapped into the room, trailing a soaked shawl. Her wig shone with rainwater.

She pinched her son's pendulous earlobe and yanked.

"Naughty Arthur, bothering the girlies . . ."

Arthur's face screwed up with pain.

"Lord knows I've tried, ducks . . . but my boy's just a nasty little shit. No other words for it. I'll get him out of your hair and you can turn in. He tell you about the hot water?"

"There isn't any?"

"That's right. Pity, but there it is. Come on, Arthur . . . time to say nighty-night."

Birdie pulled Arthur out of the chair. She was taller than him.

"Be polite," she insisted, twisting the earlobe.

"Nighty-night, Miss," he said, through tears. "Nighty-night, Aphrodite in a nightie . . ."

Birdie took the umbrella and dragged her son back through the cabin door. They disappeared into the rain and darkness.

Jayne shut the door.

Her heart was pounding and her face burned. She was more embarrassed than afraid. She would leave early tomorrow.

For where? They'd be after her, by then. Hitch's agents. Paramount *and* Universal. Walter.

Think of that later. After sleep.

The door blew open again and Arthur was there, breathing heavily. He had broken free from his mother.

"What's in the sack?" he asked.

The question knifed into her heart.

Birdie came up behind Arthur, fingers hooked into talons, screeching . . .

Scree! Scree! Scree!

Jayne backed away and clutched the sack.

"What would you *do* for what's in the sack?"

"Nothing. There's nothing. Nothing. A negative."

Arthur smiled wickedly as Birdie dragged him away again, kicking the door shut.

Jayne sat down on the big bed and hugged the sack. It was heavy, lumpy, hard. Useless, yet beyond value. A measure of her suffering, but just deadweight. She threw it away and it lay like an extra pillow.

She would sleep on the other bed, the small one.

If she could sleep . . .

She went into the bathroom and turned on the light. It was tile-floored. The mirror had a scrollwork border etched into the glass. The claw-foot bathtub bled rust into the cracks between the tiles. There was no shower attachment.

She ran the tap, just to make sure. Icy cold bit her fingers.

At least there were towels.

She breathed mist on the mirror and wrote *JANA* in it, then watched her name vanish as the exhalation evaporated.

She undressed, not like she did for pictures. Not for show, but to get out of her heavy, sodden clothes. She unpeeled damp, sticky layers – cardigan, skirt, blouse, slip, brassière, shoes, stockings, panties. She would have to wear most of these again tomorrow, since she'd not thought to bring more than a change of underthings. They wouldn't dry completely by then.

What was she doing?

The towels weren't wet but they weren't warm. The rough nap rubbed her skin the wrong way. She saw herself naked in the mirror. Without moleskin patches. She didn't look the way she did on film. She looked already dead. Her next make-up artist would be a mortician.

There was a bathrobe. She pulled it on, wrapping it tight over her stabbable breasts, her slashable back, her sliceable limbs.

She turbaned her dried, scraggly hair with another towel.

Turning out the bathroom light, she stepped back into the bedroom.

Arthur was sitting on the big bed, the sack open. He had scratches down one side of his face. His velvet jacket was soaked. His slicker still hung in the cabin.

"What is this?" he asked.

The pie-shaped can lay on the bed, sealed with tape.

"Negative."

"Answer me," he insisted, angry. "No word games."

"Negative," she said. "*Film* negative."

Arthur smiled, the penny dropping.

"Motion pictures," he said. "*Dirty* pictures?"

"I'm naked in them," she admitted. "And dead, like you said. Snatched dead moments. Useless moments."

He ran his fat fingers over the can. She knew he wanted to *see* . . . but it was hopeless: he'd need to make a positive print, run it on a projector . . .

"It's the thing you're chasing after, Arthur. A woman, me, being cut up. It's the only evidence it happened. The only evidence it happened to *me* . . ."

She had stolen *weeks* from Hitch. Weeks it would take to stage again, with Janet or some other stand-in . . . if he could ever get it just so, just the way he wanted, which she doubted was possible, or hoped wasn't possible.

The studio would pay, if Hitch wouldn't.

Arthur scratched at the tape seal with his fingernails.

Jayne heard Hitch in her skull, ranting at her, raving at his loss . . . swearing vengeance and retribution and blood . . . impotent fury. "I shall make sure the chit will never work in this town again!" She'd heard that before . . . so had everyone. Sure, she could be blacklisted, but blacklists were broken all the time. Being dead to one producer just bumped you up on another's books. Plenty would hire her *because* she'd pissed off High and Mighty Cocky Mr Hitch. Directors without TV shows, who no one would recognize in the street . . . David Selznick, William Castle, William Wyler . . . the giant leech and dragstrip doll guys. She'd do all right.

The tape tore away in Arthur's fingers and the can popped open. A coil of 35mm negative came loose, like guts spilling from a wound. Arthur tried to grasp it, but the edges scored his palms.

He saw the reverse image of her naked in the shower – a thin black body bleeding white – repeated over and over.

He smiled and she saw Hitch's slobbering leer imposed briefly over the fat boy's face.

M-m-m-murder!

She grabbed the film and looped it around and around his fat neck.

Arthur yelped.

She wound it tighter. The edges bit into his soft throat. There was blood, which made the film slick, tough to hold.

Jayne didn't say anything. She just tried to kill a man. Any Hitch with a cock would have done.

The murder weapon was a murder. A negative murder.

Good eeeev-ning, Jay-y-ne ... do you *swallow*? Do you, do you?"

Shootable? Poisonable? Throttlable? Bludgeonable?

Dump-da-dumpity-dump-da-dump ...

Stabbable? Slashable? Beheadable? Deadable?

She made a noise in the back of her throat. More a croak than a screech.

Scree! Scree! Scree!

His fat hands flapped against the sleeves of her bathrobe. His sausage fingers couldn't get a grip on the flannel.

Dump-da-dumpity-dump-da-dump ...

It was like wrestling a marionette, strangling it with its own strings.

Doo-doo-doo ... Doo-doo-doo ...

The door opened again and Birdie came in – wig gone, showing a mummy-like scalp, scaled with the last wisps of white hair – an umbrella raised like a dagger.

"Get your hands off my boy," she screamed. "My precious, precious boy ..."

"Mummy," Arthur gargled, tears flowing freely, "*Mummy!* She's hurting me."

The umbrella blows were feeble, hurt less than a prop knife, but the words – the panic, the love, the desperation! – cut through Jayne's hot fury, dashed cold water over her homicidal impulse.

She let go of the film. She let go of her rage.

The old woman hugged her son and stroked his wounds. The fat young man shoved his face against his mother's shrunken breast. They held each other, locked together in an embrace tighter than death. They rocked together, crone and baby, crying away the pain, all the pain ...

"I didn't mean any harm," Jayne said . . .

. . . she wouldn't kill, after all . . . she wouldn't hurt a fly.

This was it, she realized, looking at mother and son, monsters both, bound by a ferocious love that seemed so much like murderous hate it was hard to recognize until the last moment.

This was it. The only ending they had.

RICHARD CHRISTIAN MATHESON

Kriss Kross Applesauce

<u>DR MARTIN ZIESLING</u>

<u>Private Notes: 23–29 April</u>

<u>EVALUATION / UPDATE OF JANET HARRIS</u>

Ms Harris (38), despite chronic, lifetime depression, eats and sleeps normally. She remains resilient and listens to Christmas Carols as often as possible. Attached herein is her most current letter:

20 December

Dearest Family and Friends,

Well, it's that time of year, again!! Just when you thought it was safe to go back in the mailbox!

Ready or not, here's the official <u>HARRIS FAMILY Annual Christmas (and almost New Years!!) Newsletter</u> for all our family members and friends, far and wide, we never see enough and always think about! We miss you guys!!

Mister Jack Frost himself is nipping at our noses, the Christmas Carols are on the stereo out here in scenic Ohio and the kids are all begging Mom (yours truly) to make my world-famous Walnut Fudge. I'm still on that diet I've been on my entire life so, I said what the heck! I'll somehow manage to get it done in-between sewing thirty (you read right!) costumes for the Christmas Show at the school for our spectacular twins Elena and Emma's class and ALSO making sure the rest of our little hoodlums do their homework. How about a round of sympathetic applause for Mom? At this rate, it'll be Easter soon and I'll be sewing all the Pageant's bunny and carrot costumes. No sleep for the weary!

Since we moved to this little slice of heaven, four months ago, we've been loving having such a BIG yard where the kids and critters can play. Of course, I still miss our old house and good friends in my beloved Simi Valley, California where as many of you will remember, I went to high school and attended my prom which was a dream come true, never to be matched by real life! I'M NOT KIDDING!!! Simi is still my home, in my heart, no matter where Bob's consulting work takes us. But we're making a go of it out here and we've fallen in love with this part of the country! The quiet and the nature everywhere is the kind of solitude poets talk about. It gives you time to think and feel and be who you really are deep down because it nurtures the soul. And it's so quiet at night. You feel like you're completely alone. But down the road we have super neighbours, and there are lots of new friends the kids are making at school and every weekend there's lots of fun events! Last week we went to the local Farmers' Market and I even got to judge a contest for the perfect goat, which might sound a little strange but you have obviously never gotten to know a beautiful goat (unless you count my ex!). AND NOT JUST THAT! My delicious fudge recipe took second prize. It should have gotten first prize but you can't have everything.

Our angel Molly is turning twelve tomorrow and ready for Junior High School next term and finally starting to get the knack of that violin! Can you hear our ears saying THANK YOU?! She's also starting to get asked for dates at a much younger age than I ever was but she's a lot prettier than I was!

Remember my acne and leg braces? OUCH! So, Bob and I have agreed if we meet the boy she wants to date first she can go out to a movie, but I told her to be a lady and if any of the boys want more, "KRISS KROSS APPLESAUCE" – or, in plain English, keep your legs together, young lady! Take my word for it!

And a huge Hooray to Bobby Junior who went out for Varsity Football and got a first-string position which is amazing given his size and shyness. He still hardly talks and his therapist back home says it will probably change. I hope so! Trying to get a word out of him is like pulling a rusty nail! Well, we're not big talkers in this family anyway about personal stuff unless you consider the Super Bowl personal! HIKE! We know he'll get over all that stuff at the old house between me and Bob. And it's almost spooky how much Bobby and I are so close, like we read each other's thoughts!

The Twins are growing up so fast it's making our heads spin twice and we can barely keep up with them growing out of their clothes! They can't stop playing with our new puppies who adore them and it's cuter than a pink tush to see them all rolling around next to the Christmas tree. Of course, when they knock ornaments down, during Christmas, Mom has to be the disciplinarian since Dad doesn't have the heart, the big softie! Speaking of my world's greatest husband, Bob may be getting a verrrry big promotion now that the other guy in the department passed-on in a car accident last month. We feel terrible for his wife and family. You just don't know what tomorrow will bring. That's probably why we all keep showing up the next day! With this promotion, we'll be able to re-do the kitchen and (if they're all nice and stop acting like rabid badgers!) take the family to DISNEYWORLD in Orlando which they are pretty much obsessed with. I've always loved Mickey Mouse!

ALIEN ALERT!!! We have a snail invasion in my new garden and even if those little guys are slowwww they're smarter than I am! They're eating my plants and vegetables like it's their own private salad bar and even though I hate to moosh them, sometimes you just have to moosh them! ICK! I've also discovered the other snails eat the dead ones. Talk about low dietary standards!

I've been teaching the kids in my Sunday School class about the miracle of life and brought in Miss Tigg who just had kittens and they are the cutest things you ever saw. Our kids wanted to keep them but we just couldn't do it. So, I gave them to other families. They were sad but it won't last! Get ready for some BIG automotive news! We took the plunge and bought a PRIUS because everyone is thinking green these days and we are, too! Either we love this planet or it will throw us off! Hey, that's life, as Frank Sinatra pointed out!

Well, that's about it from planet HARRIS! We all miss you like CRAZY and I have to get back to wrapping a million presents and getting the walnut fudge out of the fridge. We hope everything is great with you all and we send MERRY XMAS wishes to you and yours and everyone in between! Hope Santa doesn't get stuck in your chimney and hope no Elves make trouble!

Much love from the HARRIS FAMILY: Bob, Janet, Bobby Junior,
Molly, Elena & Emma, the puppies (and the snails!!)
HAPPY HOLIDAYS!!!!
xoxoxo
Janet

EVALUATION/ UPDATE OF JANET HARRIS (continued)

Photographs of Ms Harris's family remain displayed on her walls
and she still has no apparent memory of the tragedy twelve years
ago. She continues to wear a red and green vest as she did when
Police discovered her family's poisoned bodies on Christmas
Day.

As she has every day, for the past eleven years, she continues
to hand-write "Christmas Family Letters" to friends and relatives. These letters (per above), as previously documented, are
always precisely the same and Ms Harris composes one hundred
per day. As of today's date, she has written over forty thousand of
them.

JOHN LLEWELLYN PROBERT

Epilogue: A Little Piece of Sanity

"WOULD YOU LIKE to meet some of the patients now?" Dr Lionel Parrish replaced the yellowing clinical notes he had been reading from into a black box file shiny with age. The file went back on to one of the lower shelves, and then he turned to his companion.

"What I want," said Robert Stanhope, with the weariness of a man who had spent many hours sitting in Parrish's office and listening to the seemingly never-ending series of cases described to him, "is my interview."

"And I have told you," said the doctor, moving back to his desk, "you'll get it. Now, that last story – true or false?"

"It's certainly believable," said Stanhope, rubbing his eyes. "The world is full of people in denial, and the greater the atrocity they feel they have committed, the deeper I imagine they would push it into their subconscious. Janet Harris is just another example of that. I suspect what you've read me about her killing her own family probably is true, unless of course it's a trick?"

"Oh, that's not the intention of this, Mr Stanhope," said Parrish, uncapping his fountain pen for the last time and preparing to make a mark in his notebook, "that's not the intention at all." He gave the reporter a piercing look. "You're saying 'true', then?"

"Yes, all right, whatever," said Stanhope, not really caring one way or the other any more.

"Good!" Dr Parrish wrote in his notebook and then closed it. "Now to the other question I asked you – would you like to see some of the patients?"

"I want my interview, Dr Parrish," said Stanhope, tired and annoyed. "I've done what you asked. I've given you my opinion on whether or not every case you've described to me is real or imagined, by you or whoever else might have wanted to add to the casebook of horrors you've been recounting to me. Now all I want is what you promised."

"Don't you want to know how many times you were right?" said Parrish, putting away his pen and regarding the man opposite with a gleam in his eyes.

Stanhope shook his head. "Not really," he replied. "My guess is I probably managed about fifty-fifty but . . ." he looked at his watch and then at the darkening landscape outside ". . . it's getting late, I'm getting tired, and despite having been here for hours we still haven't started work on the real reason I came."

"Oh, but we have," said Parrish, almost under his breath, "you just haven't realized it yet."

"What do you mean?"

Parrish opened the left-hand drawer of his desk and removed a heavy bunch of keys. "Come and see some of the patients. It'll help you understand what we've been doing here, and I think you'll get a lot out of it, especially now that you've had a chance to hear many of their stories." He held up a hand as Stanhope began to protest. "I promise I will answer all your questions once we are upstairs. I just want you to get the full picture." He pointed at the machine Stanhope had long since put aside during the lengthy afternoon. "Don't forget your little tape-recorder."

"So you're saying that every story you've presented to me is true?" said Stanhope, getting to his feet and preparing to follow the doctor. At least it would get him out of this room, he thought, as the blood began to crawl back into his legs.

"You'll find out – all in good time," said Parrish as he opened the door to his office. He paused for a moment, his hand resting on the ornate brass doorknob. "One last question, Mr Stanhope, if you don't mind?"

Stanhope shrugged and gave Dr Parrish the resigned look of one who has been bested. "Go on then," he said.

"Would you consider yourself a sane man?"

A chill gripped Stanhope as he considered how best to answer, the nagging, worrying feeling that had begun at some point while he had been trying to pay attention to all those damned stories now starting to pick at him in earnest. Was this why he had been brought here? He looked at the empty cups on the desk. Had the tea been drugged? He looked through the window. Near-pitch darkness stared back. Was any of this actually happening? He looked at the doctor, calmly awaiting an answer.

Was he, Robert Stanhope, actually already a patient here? And his life outside this place – his job, his past, his marriage, his family – was that all make-believe? Was that what Parrish had been trying to get him to realize in this session, a session which had not been an interview at all but a consultation? Perhaps the most recent of many?

All this occurred to Robert Stanhope in the seconds it took him to answer. Parrish's expression gave him no clues, but then, thought Stanhope, it wouldn't, would it? He pulled himself together, licked his lips and said, with all the confidence he could muster, "Yes. Yes I would."

Parrish nodded thoughtfully before giving Stanhope a smile that made all of the journalist's concerns melt away. "Good!" replied the doctor. "I think so, too. Follow me."

They reached the upper floor via a narrow staircase with heavy security doors at both top and bottom.

"There is a main staircase," Parrish explained as he went through the ritual of ensuring each door had been re-locked after they had passed through it, "but it's actually quicker if we go this way."

The corridor Stanhope found himself in was poorly lit and, as it stretched away into the darkness, he could just make out doors set into its walls at regular intervals.

"Are your patients afraid of the light?" he asked.

"No," replied Parrish, "not the light. The lack of bulbs is just a consequence of government spending cuts, I'm afraid – something I would be very grateful if you could note in your article. You'll soon get used to it."

Stanhope stayed close behind Parrish as they made their way down the passage. There were cracks in the walls, and Stanhope found that if he stared at them for more than a few seconds he could almost imagine them moving, as if they were the tendrils of some black and terrible organism that had taken root in this building and was now trying to ensnare him, too. In the distance he could hear dripping and, when he looked up, the plaster above him seemed to shine with an unnatural dampness. Stanhope tried to suppress a shiver, but it did not go unnoticed.

"Sorry if it's a bit chilly in here," said Parrish, "but there's not long to go now. I thought it best if we all met in the theatre."

"I beg your pardon?" Stanhope's voice echoed briefly before the sound was swallowed up by the damp blackness that surrounded him.

"The theatre," said the now almost-invisible shape in front of him. "One of the ways in which we try to provide the residents with something to pass the long hours here."

Despite the gloom, Stanhope could now see that they were close to the end of the corridor. It ended in a heavy iron door, featureless except for the steel rivets around its border and the heavy locks that held it shut. He also realized that what little illumination there was in the corridor was coming from the strip of white light beneath it. He tried to shut out thoughts that the light might be the only thing that had ever managed to escape from the room he was about to enter.

"Nearly there," said Parrish as he reached for his keys.

"Thank God for that," said Stanhope as the door was opened and his eyes were hit by a blinding white light. As he shielded them, his throat felt the prick of a needle.

It was blinding light that was the last thing Stanhope remembered before unconsciousness, and it was blinding light that was the first thing he saw when he awoke. It took him a little longer to appreciate that he was lying on a hard surface and, as his eyes began to adjust, he realized he was staring at a white-painted vaulted ceiling high above him.

He was also unable to move.

From his right came a rustling noise like the autumn wind disturbing a heap of leaves piled in the hospital grounds, or perhaps a cascade of water down brittle stone.

Or an audience in the stages of preparing to watch a performance.

"Ah, you're awake!" said a familiar voice. "Excellent!"

The rustling noise settled down as the face of Dr Lionel Parrish came into view. "I'm sorry about all that, but it really was the easiest and most painless way to get you ready," he said with a smile.

Stanhope tried to speak. The words eventually came out as a croak. "Ready for what?" he said.

"Ready for my interview of course!" said Parrish. "Well, my interview-cum-demonstration. I said it was time for you to meet the patients, and here they are."

At that Parrish depressed the pedal beneath the table on which his charge was lying and tilted it so that Stanhope was now at a forty-five degree angle and could look around him.

It took him a little while to take in his surroundings.

On the wall to his far left was a blackboard on which a number of anatomical diagrams had been drawn, the blood vessels, nerves and lymphatics accurately depicted using a number of different shades of coloured chalk. Between the blackboard and where he was lying were two stainless-steel tables on which had been arranged a number of surgical instruments. Some were clean, bright and sparkling in the glare of the light. Others had obviously been used before and not been cleaned properly.

Stanhope gave an involuntary gasp, which in turn elicited a response from the other side of the room.

Stanhope turned his head the other way, and saw the patients.

There must have been close to a hundred of them, all sitting patiently, all obviously eager for whatever was about to happen. The banked seating that went back as far as he could see reminded him of a Roman coliseum.

He looked back at Parrish. "What is this?" he said.

"Exactly what I told you," said Parrish. "A theatre. Of course it's an operating theatre rather than the kind I probably led you to think it was, but in a way I wasn't really lying. In the days of the real Dr Parrish it really was a playhouse for us." He looked around him, eyes misty with nostalgic reminiscence. "We did quite a few of the greats here, you know. *Hamlet*, *Macbeth*, *The Tempest*." Then his eyes were on Stanhope again. "I played Prospero in that one."

Stanhope frowned. "What do you mean, 'the real Dr Parrish'?" he asked. "Who are you, then?"

The man standing over him frowned. "I'm afraid I have a little bit of trouble remembering that," he said. "But I know I'm not Dr Parrish because he's gone. That's why I had to take over. I mean, these poor people," he gestured at the audience, "they had no one to look after them after he killed himself."

"But what about the other doctors here?" Stanhope knew he should be feeling fear now, but his over-riding emotion was one of anger. Anger that he had trusted this man; anger that he had wasted all that time downstairs and hadn't even realized he was talking to an impostor; and most of all anger that he had let himself be tricked in such a ridiculous way.

"They didn't understand," said his captor. "When I found him ... it was my consultation period, and we had reached an understanding that within these walls we would very much respect each other as equals. One of my few privileges was to be able to come down from my room to his office unassisted, if you see what I mean. I remember that day so well, finding his body slumped over that lovely desk where you and I have been having such a nice chat, the blood from his slashed throat still soaking into the newspapers." Now his expression hardened. "The newspapers with your stories in them."

"A few news stories, most of which weren't even about this place, shouldn't have been enough to drive someone to suicide," Stanhope sneered.

"Not on their own, no," agreed his captor, "you're probably right. But Dr Parrish had been under a lot of strain recently and, well, I'm not really the right person to comment about that. You see, I've never really believed that diseases of the mind can be treated with talking and chatting and prolonged procrastinations over this drug or that drug and this dose or that dose. I've always believed in a rather more direct approach to such problems."

Something in the way the man's tone had changed during his little speech suddenly brought it home to Stanhope that he might not be making it out of wherever he was alive. "Where are the other doctors?" he asked, his voice little more than a whisper now.

"We put them away," was the reply. "Once we realized they didn't have our best interests at heart." The man who had claimed to be Dr Lionel Parrish pulled on a pair of surgical gloves as he continued. "I told you when you arrived that there were no psychiatrists upstairs, and now I hope you understand how honest I was being with you." He gave Stanhope a broad smile. "There are none downstairs either."

"So you're not even a doctor?"

Stanhope's captor looked indignant. "I most certainly am, Mr Stanhope. In fact for many years I was the very finest neurosurgeon in my field. You might even say that I was a star. That is, until my research, and the methods by which I obtained my results, turned out to be too unpalatable for the general public at large, and the General Medical Council in particular."

"Neurosurgery?" Stanhope croaked.

The man nodded. "I was very good at it, too. Very good indeed. And I still am." He leaned closer. "For example, I imagine you are in no pain at all at the moment, are you?"

Stanhope felt a gnawing horror squeeze his insides. What had this man already done to him?

"I can see what's going through your mind," said the surgeon, nodding, "so perhaps I had better show you." He picked up a large oblong of silvered glass that had been lying next to one of the instrument trolleys. "There's a mirror behind your head, so if I hold this one up in front of you, you should be able to see how we've progressed so far, thanks to the miracle of local anaesthesia. And of course my skill in applying it."

But Stanhope was no longer listening. Instead he was staring in horror at his shaved head, at the way in which his scalp had been incised and dissected off his skull, the flaps of tissue pinned back to expose the bone beneath.

Some of which had been removed.

Tears of shock, terror, and desperation filled Stanhope's eyes as he viewed his own exposed brain in the glass.

"As I said, Mr Stanhope," said the surgeon with a chuckle, "I can literally see what's going through your mind. What's wonderful is that soon my patients will be able to enjoy the benefits of your thoughts as well."

Stanhope blinked away the wetness and coughed at the tears that were already tickling the back of his throat. "What do you mean?" he asked.

"Just a theory of mine," said the surgeon, indicating the audience to Stanhope's right with a sweeping gesture. "The patients in this room can all walk, talk, and look after themselves. Many of them are capable of holding highly intelligent conversations on science, literature, religion, politics. The only thing that's really wrong with most of them is that a tiny part of their brain doesn't work properly, a tiny malfunctioning area resulting in psychotic impulses that have caused them to end up here."

He walked over to the nearer of the two stainless-steel tables and selected a pair of fine forceps with serrated teeth at the tips, and a scalpel with a small pointed blade. "That's where you come in, Mr Stanhope. You are going to give each of my patients here a little piece of your brain – a little piece of your sanity, if you like. Now please don't protest, not after doing so well in that little examination I set you. I may as well tell you now that you got all of the questions right." The surgeon paused. "At least, I think you did." Now he sounded a little unsure. "I must admit I do get confused sometimes, but you certainly acquitted yourself admirably, and your answers felt right, which at the end of the day is all that matters."

His confidence returning, the surgeon took a step forward, the instruments held high, as the man bound to the table began to struggle. "Come come, Mr Stanhope, there's no need to be upset," he said. "After all, you did get your interview, didn't you? You got to find out all about me and what's really going on in here, and how I propose to do the very best I can for the patients in my care."

The surgeon looked up at his audience, members of which were already getting to their feet in eager anticipation. He addressed them in the authoritative tones of someone used to being obeyed without question. "I would be grateful, ladies and gentlemen, if you would form an orderly queue down the left-hand aisle. There's no need to rush. Everyone will receive their treatment in due course."

Stanhope could hear the shuffling as the patients made their way towards him, forming a line the way schoolchildren might to receive a vaccination. Out of the corner of his eye he could see that the nearest was only feet away, close enough for him to be able to make out the hole that had been drilled in the man's skull. It was just above the bridge of the nose – an empty black socket that stared at him with a voracious, all-consuming hunger for his sanity.

"I've always prided myself on having my patients well prepared," said the surgeon as he came closer, knife at the ready, forceps poised to take the first tiny piece of Stanhope away from him.

The man bound to the table could think of nothing more to say and nothing more to do. So he did what any sane man in his situation would.

He screamed.

It lasted a very long time.

CASE NOTES

ROBERT BLOCH (1917–94) was born in Chicago and later moved to Los Angeles, California, where he worked as a script-writer in movies and television. His interest in the pulp magazine *Weird Tales* led to a correspondence with author H. P. Lovecraft, who advised him to try his own hand at writing fiction. The rest, as they say, is history.

Despite having published more than two dozen novels and over 400 short stories, he will always be identified with his 1959 book *Psycho* and Alfred Hitchcock's subsequent film version. His many novels and collections include *The Opener of the Way*, *Pleasant Dreams*, *Yours Truly, Jack the Ripper: Tales of Horror*, *Atoms and Evil*, *The Skull of the Marquis de Sade and Other Stories*, *Fear Today Gone Tomorrow*, *American Gothic*, *Strange Eons*, *Such Stuff As Screams Are Made Of*, *Psycho II*, *Lori*, *Psycho House*, *The Jekyll Legacy* (with Andre Norton) and *The Early Fears*.

In his 1993 "Unauthorized Autobiography", *Once Around the Bloch*, he explained about writing "Yours Truly, Jack the Ripper": "There was nothing particularly unusual about this story's composition ... it was just more product of the second-hand typewriter mounted on the second-hand card table in a corner of our one-room apartment, as well as a product of my interest in those whose lives were overshadowed by the looming of their own legends.

"The real-life Ripper had captured the imagination of millions, but he himself had never been caught, or even accurately identi-fied. Bringing the Ripper into modern time and using an American city as a new setting for his successfully unsuccessful operations required the addition of a supernatural rationale which

I had no difficulty supplying. And which others since then, I might add, have had no difficulty borrowing for their own.

"But in 1943 my idea was fresh, and after stealing the usual penny a word for it, I received a thirty-day sentence on various newsstands. As usual, aside from a few comments in the letter column of *Weird Tales*, the story went unnoticed."

In fact, the story was first dramatized in January 1944 on CBS Radio's *The Kate Smith Hour* starring screen Ripper Laird Cregar, before being adapted again for *The Molle Mystery Theatre*, *Murder by Experts* and Bloch's own *Stay Tuned for Terror*. Barré Lyndon (no stranger to Ripper movies himself) scripted a version for the 1961 TV show *Thriller*, hosted by Boris Karloff.

Bloch returned to the Ripper theme in his 1967 *Star Trek* episode "Wolf in the Fold" and the 1984 novel *The Night of the Ripper*.

"Over the years I've been asked my opinion of the Ripper's true identity," revealed the author. "After much study and consideration, I now firmly believe that Jack the Ripper was actually Queen Victoria."

LAWRENCE BLOCK has been writing crime fiction for over half a century. Best known for his long-running series about PI "Matthew Scudder" and gentleman burglar "Bernie Rhodenbarr", his awards include the Cartier Diamond Dagger from the Crime Writers' Association of the UK, numerous Anthony, Edgar and Shamus Awards, and in 1994 he was named a Grand Master by the Mystery Writers of America. As if all that is not enough, he has also been presented with the key to the city of Muncie, Indiana.

His most recent novel is *Hit Me*, the fifth book about a wistful hit man named Keller.

Of "Hot Eyes, Cold Eyes", Block says: "I wrote this story twice. The first version, dashed off in the late-1950s, was sold to a bottom-of-the-barrel pulp magazine, and I lost all track of it. Twenty years later I remembered it – but all I remembered was the last line.

"So I wrote it again. Actually I wrote a whole new story, leading up to the last line, which was all I remembered. (Who could forget it?) And I sent it to an editor who liked my work, and he wanted to buy it, but felt the ending was too vivid for his readers. So he'd take it, but he'd have to drop the last line.

"Drop the last line? Without the last line there was no story. So I displayed an uncharacteristic artistic integrity and took the story back, and in due course a *Playboy* imitator called *Gallery* printed it, last line and all."

RAMSEY CAMPBELL is described in the *Oxford Companion to English Literature* as "Britain's most respected living horror writer". He has been given more awards than any other writer in the field, including the Grand Master Award of the World Horror Convention, the Lifetime Achievement Award of the Horror Writers Association and the Living Legend Award of the International Horror Guild.

Among his novels are *The Face That Must Die*, *Incarnate*, *Midnight Sun*, *The Count of Eleven*, *Silent Children*, *The Darkest Part of the Woods*, *The Overnight*, *Secret Story*, *The Grin of the Dark*, *Thieving Fear*, *Creatures of the Pool*, *The Seven Days of Cain*, *Ghosts Know* and *The Kind Folk*. Forthcoming are *The Last Revelation of Gla'aki* (a novella) and *Bad Thoughts*.

His collections include *Waking Nightmares*, *Alone with the Horrors*, *Ghosts and Grisly Things*, *Told by the Dead* and *Just Behind You*, and his non-fiction is collected as *Ramsey Campbell, Probably*.

The author's novels *The Nameless* and *Pact of the Fathers* have been filmed in Spain, his regular columns appear in *Prism*, *Dead Reckonings* and *Video Watchdog*, and he is the President of the British Fantasy Society and of the Society of Fantastic Films.

"'See How They Run' was written for an anthology about psychopaths edited by my old, and now lamented, friend Robert Bloch," explains Campbell. "Bob was happy with the tale but not the title, which he'd used for a story of his own, and so I re-titled mine 'For You to Judge'. I still preferred my original title, however, and after Bob's death I used it for a reprinting by another much-missed friend, Karl Edward Wagner.

"Not many days before Bob died I was able to speak to him on the phone for half-an-hour and tell him he was loved. He told me that he was able to see a pattern in his life. I hope I shall in mine."

MIKE CAREY was born in Liverpool, but moved to London in the 1980s after completing an English degree at Oxford. He taught English and Media for several years before resigning to become a freelance writer in 2000.

Initially he worked mainly within the medium of comic books, coming to prominence with the *Lucifer* ongoing series at DC Vertigo. Since then, he has written *Hellblazer* for DC, *X-Men* and *Fantastic Four* for Marvel, *Vampirella* for Harris and *Red Sonja* for Dynamite Entertainment. He also scripted the Marvel Comics adaptation of Orson Scott Card's *Ender's Shadow*, and has launched a creator-owned book at Vertigo, *The Unwritten*, which (in collected format) has made the *New York Times* graphic novel best-seller list several times.

More recently, Carey has moved into prose fiction with the "Felix Castor" novels, a series of supernatural crime thrillers recounting the exploits of a freelance exorcist, and (under the pseudonym "Adam Blake") with mainstream thrillers such as *The Dead Sea Deception*. Along with his wife Linda and their daughter Louise, he has co-written the fantasy novel *The Steel Seraglio*, published in the UK by Gollancz as *City of Silk and Steel*. His movie screenplay, *Dominion*, is in development with US producer Intrepid Pictures and UK's Slingshot Studios.

"This story grew sideways out of another story," explains the author. "The earlier tale was about Sherlock Holmes and Moriarty as collaborators in a big creative enterprise – an enterprise that involved the endless, repetitive building up and breaking down of mysteries. Almost like they were two different versions of the same compulsive personality. Then someone showed me an essay by David McKie that said exactly the same thing in about one-tenth of the word count. So I threw that story away and came up with this one.

"I'd like to issue a small disclaimer, though. This incarnation of the story might give the impression that I have a poor opinion of reviewers, which isn't true at all. Some of my best friends are reviewers. And I've never killed any of them . . . even once."

R. CHETWYND-HAYES (1919–2001) was born in Isleworth, West London. Known as "Britain's Prince of Chill", in 1989 he was presented with Life Achievement Awards by both the Horror Writers Association and the British Fantasy Society.

The author's first book was *The Man from the Bomb,* a science-fiction novel published in 1959 by Badger Books. His subsequent novels include *The Dark Man* (aka *And Love Survived*), *The Brats, The Partaker: A Novel of Fantasy, The King's Ghost, The Curse of the Snake God, Kepple, The Psychic Detective* and *World of the Impossible,* while his short fiction was collected in *The Unbidden, Cold Terror, The Elemental, Terror by Night, The Night Ghouls, The Monster Club, A Quiver of Ghosts, Tales from the Dark Lands, The House of Dracula, Dracula's Children, Shudders and Shivers, The Vampire Stories of R. Chetwynd-Hayes* (aka *Looking for Something to Suck*), *Phantoms and Fiends* and *Frights and Fancies,* amongst other titles. A "best of" collection/bibliography is forthcoming from PS Publishing.

In 1976, Chetwynd-Hayes ghost-edited and wrote almost all the one-shot magazine *Ghoul.* He also edited the anthologies *Cornish Tales of Terror, Scottish Tales of Terror* (as "Angus Campbell"), *Welsh Tales of Terror, Tales of Terror from Outer Space, Gaslight Tales of Terror, Doomed to the Night,* and the posthumous *Great Ghost Stories* and *Tales to Freeze the Blood: More Great Ghost Stories* (both with Stephen Jones), along with twelve volumes of *The Fontana Book of Great Ghost Stories,* and six volumes of *The Armada Monster Book* series for children.

The author of two movie novelizations, *Dominique* and *The Awakening* (the latter based on Bram Stoker's *The Jewel of Seven Stars*), his own stories have been adapted for radio, TV and the movies, including *The Monster Club* (in which the author was portrayed by veteran horror actor John Carradine).

"The Gatecrasher" was adapted in the 1974 anthology film *Beyond the Grave,* for an episode starring David Warner. "When I was informed that Milton Subotsky was considering making a film based on four of my tales, I went over the moon!" recalled the author. "I thought, 'Gosh, a film! My fortune is made!' Alas, it wasn't, but I did have fun visiting the set and realizing that all of the dialogue that these famous people were speaking was mine.

"'The Gatecrasher' was supposed to be based on Jack the Ripper, though that point was completely overlooked by the scriptwriters."

BASIL COPPER (1924–2013)was born in London, and for thirty years he worked as a journalist and editor of a local newspaper before becoming a full-time writer in 1970.

His first story in the horror field, "The Spider", was published in 1964 in *The Fifth Pan Book of Horror Stories*, since when his short fiction has appeared in numerous anthologies, been extensively adapted for radio, and collected in *Not After Nightfall, Here Be Daemons, From Evil's Pillow, And Afterward the Dark, Voices of Doom, When Footsteps Echo, Whispers in the Night, Cold Hand on My Shoulder* and *Knife in the Back*.

One of the author's most reprinted stories, "Camera Obscura", was adapted for a 1971 episode of the anthology television series *Rod Serling's Night Gallery*.

Besides publishing two non-fiction studies of the vampire and werewolf legends, his other books include the novels *The Great White Space, The Curse of the Fleers, Necropolis, House of the Wolf* and *The Black Death*. He also wrote more than fifty hardboiled thrillers about Los Angeles private detective Mike Faraday, and continued the adventures of August Derleth's Holmes-like consulting detective Solar Pons in several volumes, including the novel *Solar Pons versus The Devil's Claw*.

More recently, PS Publishing has produced the non-fiction study *Basil Copper: A Life in Books*, a massive two-volume set of *Darkness, Mist & Shadow: The Collected Macabre Tales of Basil Copper* and a restored version of Copper's 1976 novel *The Curse of the Fleers*, while the Valancourt Books imprint is issuing new editions of the author's novels *The Great White Space* and *Necropolis*.

In 1991, "The Recompensing of Albano Pizar" was dramatized for BBC Radio 4's *Fear on Four* series as "Invitation to the Vaults", introduced by Edward de Souza's The Man in Black.

PETER CROWTHER is the recipient of numerous awards for his writing, his editing and, as publisher, for the hugely successful PS Publishing (now including the Stanza Press poetry subsidiary and PS Artbooks, a specialist imprint dedicated to the comics field).

As well as being widely translated, his stories have been adapted for TV on both sides of the Atlantic and collected in *The Longest*

Single Note, Lonesome Roads, Songs of Leaving, Cold Comforts, The Spaces Between the Lines, The Land at the End of the Working Day and the upcoming *Jewels in the Dust*. He is the co-author (with James Lovegrove) of *Escardy Gap* and *The Hand That Feeds*, and author of the *Forever Twilight* SF/horror cycle and *By Wizard Oak*.

Crowther lives and works (and still reads a lot of comic books *and* buys far too many CDs!) with his wife and PS business partner, Nicky, on the Yorkshire coast of England. He is currently writing a sequence of novelettes set against a background of alien invasion and the implosion of the multiverse.

"It's all John W. Campbell's fault," he complains. "I just *loved* his (or rather Don A. Stuart's) 'Who Goes There?', first reading it in a collection of that name, and again in its original appearance (*Astounding* from the late-1930s – always try to read your favourite stories where they first appeared), and then as a movie (first Howard Hawks's 1951 production – superb, but *not* a good rendition of Campbell's story; and then John Carpenter's 1982 riff, closer to the original material and great fun but, for me, a weaker movie).

"Anyway, not surprisingly, I wanted to write my own yarn about a shape-shifting monster.

"The germ of an idea had sat in the back of my head for some considerable time, waiting for that all-important USP that would make it special. All was quiet brain-wise until I was asked to write a story for Robert Bloch's *Psychos* anthology (this was in the early 1990s). That was when the idea for 'Eater' presented itself – first off, the shape-shifting became a take on the old American Indian myth of eating your enemy's heart to gain his strength; and secondly, the milieu in which the story takes place moved from the cold isolation of the Arctic to a busy police station in suburban USA. I was all set.

"But I was immersed in two other deadlines and so, by the time I started writing, the anthology had closed. Undaunted (and with nothing else time-sensitive), I carried on . . . and created Mister Mellor. When the tale was finished, I sent it in to Rich Chizmar at *Cemetery Dance Magazine*. He bought it – very enthusiastically, I might add – and the story generated a lot of kind words (always embarrassing, but also always heartily well received) ... resulting in an appearance in CD's *The Best of Cemetery Dance* (along with another Crowther yarn, 'Rustle'). It was also adapted for TV on both sides of the Atlantic, first as an episode of *Urban Gothic* in the UK and, in the US, as part of *Fear Itself* featuring Elisabeth Moss ('Peggy Olson' from *Mad Men*).

"'Mister Mellor Comes to Wayside' is a previously unpublished vignette originally written for my first collection, *The Longest Single Note*. I must confess that I rather like the character. I hope you do, too."

SCOTT EDELMAN has published more than eighty short stories in magazines such as *The Twilight Zone, Absolute Magnitude, Science Fiction Review* and *Fantasy Book*, and in anthologies such as *The Solaris Book of New Science Fiction, Crossroads, MetaHorror, Once Upon a Galaxy, Moon Shots, Mars Probes* and *Forbidden Planets*. His many zombie stories have been collected in *What Will Come After*, while his science fiction can be found in *What We Still Talk About*.

He has been a Bram Stoker Award finalist five times, in the categories of both Short Story and Long Fiction. Additionally, Edelman currently works for the Syfy Channel as the editor of *Blastr*. He was the founding editor of *Science Fiction Age*, which he edited during its entire eight-year run, and has been a four-times Hugo Award finalist for Best Editor.

"'The Trembling Living Wire' was inspired by one of my favourite Edgar Allan Poe poems," acknowledges Edelman, "knowledge of which is not at all necessary to appreciate the story. (Though those who already know of the one 'who despisest an unimpassioned song' may pick up on certain background elements earlier than those who've never read the poem.) Poe's 'Israfel' got me to thinking of the places we go in the service of our arts. Some of those places are darker than others, yielding darker results. I hope never to go as far as in the story."

HARLAN ELLISON® has been awarded the Hugo Award eight-and-a-half times, the Nebula Award four times, the Bram Stoker Award five times (including Lifetime Achievement in 1996) and the Mystery Writers of America Edgar Allan Poe Award twice.

He is also the recipient of the Silver Pen for Journalism by International P.E.N., the World Fantasy Award, the Georges

Méliès fantasy film award, an unprecedented four Writers Guild of America awards for Most Outstanding Teleplay, and the International Horror Guild's Living Legend Award. In 2006, he was made a Grand Master by the Science Fiction and Fantasy Writers of America (SFWA).

Born in Cleveland, Ohio, Ellison moved to New York in his early-twenties to pursue a writing career. Over the next two years he published more than 100 stories and articles. Moving to California in 1962, he began selling to Hollywood, co-scripting the 1966 movie *The Oscar* and contributing two dozen scripts to such shows as *Star Trek*, *The Outer Limits*, *The Man from U.N.C.L.E.*, *The Alfred Hitchcock Hour*, *Cimarron Strip*, *Route 66*, *Burke's Law* and *The Flying Nun*. His story "A Boy and His Dog" was filmed in 1975, starring Don Johnson, and he was a creative consultant on the 1980s revival of *The Twilight Zone* TV series.

His more than seventy-five books include *Rumble* (aka *Web of the City*), *Rockabilly* (aka *Spider Kiss*), *All the Lies That Are My Life* and *Mefisto in Onyx*, while some of his almost 2,000 short stories have been collected in *The Juvies* (aka *Children of the Street*), *Ellison Wonderland*, *Paingod and Other Delusions*, *I Have No Mouth and I Must Scream*, *Love Ain't Nothing But Sex Misspelled*, *The Beast That Shouted Love at the Heart of the World*, *Deathbird Stories*, *Strange Wine*, *Shatterday*, *Stalking the Nightmare*, *Angry Candy*, *Slippage* and *The Essential Ellison: A 50-Year Retrospective* edited by Terry Dowling.

Ellison also edited the influential science fiction anthology *Dangerous Visions* in 1967, and followed it with a sequel, *Again Dangerous Visions*, in 1972.

More recently, he was the subject of Erik Nelson's revelatory feature-length documentary *Dreams with Sharp Teeth* (2008), chronicling the author's life and work, which was made over a period of twenty-seven years.

He lives with his wife, Susan, inside The Lost Aztec Temple of Mars, in Los Angeles.

"'All the Birds Come Home to Roost' took many years to write," recalls Ellison. "I had the idea back in the early-1970s. It came to me because a number of women with whom I'd had relationships, which relationships had broken up and the women vanished from my world, suddenly began reappearing.

"Nothing mysterious about it: when I'd known them they were young and they'd gone off to begin careers, to get married, to discover themselves. Now, eight, nine, ten years later they were going through transition. Marriages dissolved, career changes, youthful escapades having palled on them, they were returning to the scenes of happier times. And they were getting back in touch with those they knew in those brighter days.

"But with the mind of the fantasist I made the leap into a fictional construct: what if some guy found his life being run in reverse but only in terms of the women he'd known?

"And that meant something ominous had to be at the end of the chain."

DENNIS ETCHISON is a three-times winner of both the British Fantasy and World Fantasy Awards. His short story collections are *The Dark Country*, *Red Dreams*, *The Blood Kiss*, *The Death Artist*, *Talking in the Dark*, *Fine Cuts* and *Got to Kill Them All & Other Stories*.

He is also the author of the novels *Darkside*, *Shadowman*, *California Gothic*, *Double Edge*, *The Fog*, *Halloween II*, *Halloween III* and *Videodrome*, and editor of the anthologies *Cutting Edge*, *Masters of Darkness I–III*, *MetaHorror*, *The Museum of Horrors* and (with Ramsey Campbell and Jack Dann) *Gathering the Bones*.

He has written extensively for film, television and radio, including hundreds of scripts for *The Twilight Zone Radio Dramas*, Fangoria Magazine's *Dreadtime Stories* and Christopher Lee's *Mystery Theater*.

His next book is a much-anticipated collection of new stories.

"When I wrote 'Got to Kill Them All'," Etchison explains, "the latest American success story was the triumphant return of big-money quiz shows to prime-time network television. Such shows had been enormously successful in the 1950s, until a Congressional investigation revealed that some of them were fixed. It turned out that certain contestants, including the scholar Charles Van Doren, were provided with answers in advance to manipulate the outcome and guarantee ratings; when the scandal broke careers were ruined and such programmes quickly disappeared from the broadcast schedule.

"Eventually smaller, less serious game shows reappeared on daytime and syndicated TV, emphasizing humour and celebrity guests, but allegedly serious, intellectually challenging quiz shows remained lost to history for more than forty years.

"The first of the new wave of retro quiz shows was *Who Wants to Be a Millionaire?* An American version of the British original, it debuted without fanfare as a low-budget, limited-run replacement series on ABC TV. It became an unexpected hit, scoring such phenomenal ratings that it soon began airing several nights a week, opposite copycat shows on other networks, including a revived version of the infamous *Twenty-One*, another UK transplant called *The Weakest Link*, and even one simply and shamelessly entitled *Greed*.

"At around the same time (February 2000), one could not help but notice that millions of American children had caught Pokémon fever. The word is the name of a game, derived from a wildly popular Japanese *animé* series, involving trading cards that picture hundreds of cartoon 'pocket monsters'. One of the characters is a boy whose job it is to protect the world by tracking down these monsters and containing them safely in his pocket. His motto, the signature phrase of the Pokémon universe, is 'Got to catch them all!'

"It did not require much imagination to speculate that some shrewd, enterprising producer might attempt to combine these two hot trends and reach an even larger audience. Replacing the word 'catch' with 'kill' seemed obvious for the story's title, even reflexive to a horror writer. And what would the show be called? Well, green is the colour of American money, which is after all what commercial television is really about . . ."

CHRISTOPHER FOWLER is the multi-award-winning author of more than thirty novels and twelve short story collections, including *Roofworld*, *Spanky*, *Disturbia*, *Paperboy* and *Hell Train*. He has also written eleven "Bryant & May" mystery novels so far, the latest being *Bryant & May and the Bleeding Heart*. These follow the adventures of two elderly detectives who investigate impossible crimes in London. The cases are filled with dark humour and often gory, bizarre deaths.

PS recently published *Red Gloves*, a collection of twenty-five new horror stories by the author to mark a quarter-century in print, and he scripted the *War of the Worlds* video game featuring Sir Patrick Stewart. He currently writes a column in the *Independent on Sunday* and reviews for the *Financial Times*, and his latest books are *Invisible Ink: How 100 Great Authors Vanished*, the graphic novel *The Casebook of Bryant & May*, the sinister comedy-thriller *Plastic*, and a memoir, *Film Freak*.

"The great thing about writing the Bryant & May stories," explains Fowler, "is that they adapt so easily to any format. I can take them into black comedy and to the edge of the supernatural, or I can take them somewhere much darker.

"'Bryant & May and the Seven Points' came from a dark place – London's Camden Town, actually, where an exhibition of rare original carnival sideshow acts filled the Roundhouse last year. They were terrifically creepy, and I've always loved films about them, so, having also seen *The Funhouse*, *Freaks*, *The Mutations* and the forgotten 1973 horror film *Ssssss!* (strapline: 'Don't say it, hiss it!'), I couldn't resist putting my elderly detectives into a situation where no one would be surprised to meet a psychopath . . ."

NEIL GAIMAN is the most critically acclaimed British graphic novel writer of his generation. He co-wrote the best-selling novel *Good Omens* (with Terry Pratchett), is the author of *Neverwhere* and *American Gods*, and became the first person ever to win the Newbery Medal and the Carnegie Medal for the same children's novel, *The Graveyard Book*, which spent more than fifty-two consecutive weeks on the *New York Times* best-seller list. The book has also won the Hugo Award, the Booktrust Award and many others.

For the movies, Gaiman co-scripted (with Roger Avary) Robert Zemeckis's motion-capture fantasy film *Beowulf*, while Matthew Vaughn's *Stardust* and Henry Selick's *Coraline* were both based on his novels. He wrote and directed *Statuesque*, a short film starring his wife, singer/songwriter Amanda Palmer, and his second episode of BBC TV's *Doctor Who*, "The Last Cyberman", was broadcast in 2013.

Recent projects include *Chu's Day* (illustrated by Adam Rex for small children), *Unnatural Creatures* (an anthology), *Make Good Art* (a speech, now designed by Chip Kidd), *The Ocean at the End of the Lane* (a novel for adults) and *Fortunately, The Milk* (a very silly book for kids and dads, illustrated by Chris Riddell in the UK and Skottie Young in the US).

"'Feminine Endings' was written for a book of love letters," explains Gaiman.

"In my head it is set in Krakow, in Poland, where the human statues stand, but it could be anywhere that tourists go and people stand still.

"Readers have assumed that the person writing the letter is male, and they have assumed the person writing the letter is female. I have been unable to shed any light on the matter.

"There is an odd magic to writing love letters, I suspect, even if they are scary-strange fictional love letters. Shortly after I wrote this story I met and, eventually, fell in love with a former human statue, and have been trying to tease out the cause and effect ever since – and, of course, whether or not I should be worried . . ."

BRIAN HODGE is the award-winning author of eleven novels spanning horror, crime, and historical. He's also written more than 100 short stories, novelettes and novellas, and five full-length collections. His first collection, *The Convulsion Factory*, was ranked by critic Stanley Wiater among the 113 best books of modern horror.

Recent or forthcoming works include *No Law Left Unbroken*, a collection of crime fiction; *The Weight of the Dead* and *Whom the Gods Would Destroy*, both standalone novellas; a newly revised hardcover edition of *Dark Advent*, his early post-apocalyptic epic, and his latest novel, *Leaves of Sherwood*.

Hodge lives in Colorado, where more of everything is in the works. He also dabbles in music, sound design, and photography; loves everything about organic gardening except the thieving squirrels, and trains in Krav Maga, grappling and kickboxing, which are of no use at all against the squirrels.

Of "Let My Smile Be Your Umbrella", he says: "There's something creepy about people who are so relentlessly upbeat and cheerful that they wear this persona like a shiny suit of armour. You just know something's going to blow eventually.

"I've always felt that to be an emotionally healthy, psychologically integrated person, you need to go through the dark times, the down days, without any filters in the way. Contemporary western society, particularly here in the USA, has developed a widespread aversion to this. Which no doubt explains the title alone of a 2011 entry from Harvard Medical School's Health Publications: 'Astounding Increase in Antidepressant Use by Americans'. This, while the multi-billion-dollar positivity industry preaches an end goal of 24/7 bliss, with strong implications that the failure to lock it down is a defect that needs to be fixed.

"So I felt like doing a piece that carries this ethos to its extreme.

"And just to show me that the story was intent on having the last laugh, its final word count clocked in at 5,150: California's law enforcement code for an involuntary psychiatric hold."

MICHAEL KELLY has been a finalist for the Shirley Jackson Award and the British Fantasy Society Award. His fiction has appeared in *The Mammoth Book of Best New Horror Volume 21*, *Supernatural Tales*, *PostScripts*, *Tesseracts 13* and *16*, and has been collected in *Scratching the Surface* and *Undertow & Other Laments*.

He also publishes and edits *Shadows & Tall Trees*, and is series editor for the *Chilling Tales* anthology series (EDGE Publications). More fiction is forthcoming in *Black Static* and *The Grimscribe's Puppets*, and his latest book as editor is *Chilling Tales: In Words, Alas, Drown I*.

"'The Beach' is another of my tales that examines how our childhood experiences, good and bad, help shape us into the people we become," reveals Kelly. "I was struck by a vision of a desolate beach that stayed with me for days. Once I had the setting, the story fell quickly into place. As well, I've long been fascinated with the giant monoliths on Easter Island, and I saw an opportunity to incorporate that into the tale.

"You truly can't bury your past."

JOEL LANE lives in Birmingham, England. His publications in the weird fiction genre include four short story collections, *The Earth Wire*, *The Lost District*, *The Terrible Changes* and *Where Furnaces Burn* – the latter a book of supernatural crime stories set in the West Midlands – as well as a novella, *The Witnesses Are Gone*.

His short stories have appeared in various magazines and anthologies including *Black Static*, *Weird Tales*, *Cemetery Dance*,

Gutshot, The End of the Line, Evermore, Gathering the Bones and two "Mammoth" series: *Best New Horror* and *Best British Crime*. A booklet of his short crime stories, *Do Not Pass Go*, was published in 2011.

As the author observes: "'The Long Shift' stems from my long experience of the 'scientific management' culture that swept the corporate world in the 1990s. Managers are supposed to identify with their firm – which means they take on its sickest aspects as personal values. We should not assume that psychopaths are always social outsiders: in business, a psychopath might be considered a prime corporate asset, and end up on the New Year's honours list."

JOE R. LANSDALE lives in Nacogdoches, Texas, with his wife, Karen. He is the author of more than thirty novels and twenty short story collections, with over 200 short stories, articles, essays and stage plays to his credit.

Best known for his popular "Hap Collins and Leonard Pine" series of mystery novels (including *Savage Season, Mucho Mojo, Two-Bear Mambo, Bad Chili, Captains Outrageous* and *Devil Red*) and the "Drive-In" horror series (*The Drive-In: A "B" Movie with Blood and Popcorn Made in Texas, The Drive-In 2: Not Just One of Them Sequels, The Drive-In: A Double-Feature* and *The Drive-In: The Bus Tour*), his other novels include *Act of Love, Dead in the West, Magic Wagon, The Nightrunners, Tarzan: The Lost Adventure, The Bottoms, Zeppelins West, All the Earth Thrown to the Sky* and *Edge of Dark Water*.

His short stories are collected in *By Bizarre Hands, Bestsellers Guaranteed, Writers of the Purple Rage, High Cotton, Mad Dog Summer and Other Stories, God of the Razor and Other Stories* and *Deadman's Road*, and he has edited numerous anthologies, including *Razored Saddles* (with Pat Lobrutto), *Dark at Heart* (with Karen Lansdale), *The Horror Hall of Fame: The Stoker Winners, Retro-Pulp Tales, Lords of the Razor, Cross Plains Universe: Texans Celebrate Robert E. Howard* and *Crucified Dreams*.

Lansdale has also written numerous comic books, graphic novels and animated TV series, his novella *Bubba Ho-Tep* was made into a cult favourite movie by director Don Coscarelli in 2002, and his story "Incident On and Off a Mountain Road" was filmed for Showtime Network's *Masters of Horror* series. He has received numerous awards for his work, including the British Fantasy Award, the Edgar for Best Crime novel, eight HWA Bram Stoker Awards, the "Shot in the Dark" International Crime Writers' Award, the Sugarpulp Prize for Grand Master of Crime Fiction, the Herodotus Award for Best Historical Crime fiction, the Critics' Choice Award, a *New York Times* Notable Book Award and the Grand Master award from the Horror Writers Association.

"The psychology of these kinds of humans has always intrigued and frightened me," Lansdale reveals. "What is it that makes them see the world in such a different and shaded light, and what is it about them that ties sexual passion and violence together? I don't have the answers, but the thing that disturbs me most is the certain truth that like all of us they have many of the same needs and concerns, and can seem so much like the rest of us, while in other ways being as alien as a being from a faraway galaxy that might look upon us as nothing more than things to be manipulated and used for perverse pleasure."

BRIAN LUMLEY started his writing career by emulating the work of H. P. Lovecraft and has ended up with his own highly enthusiastic fan following for his world-wide best-selling series of "Necroscope"® vampire books.

Born in the coal-mining town of Horden, County Durham, on England's north-east coast, Lumley joined the British Army when he was twenty-one and served in the Corps of Royal Military Police for twenty-two years, until his retirement in December 1980.

After discovering Lovecraft's stories while stationed in Berlin in the early-1960s, he decided to try his own hand at writing horror fiction, initially based around the influential "Cthulhu Mythos". He sent his early efforts to editor August Derleth, and Arkham House published two collections of the author's stories, *The Caller of the Black* and *The Horror at Oakdene and Others*, along with the short novel *Beneath the Moors*.

Upon leaving the Army, Lumley began writing full-time, and in 1984 he completed his breakthrough novel, *Necroscope*®, featuring Harry Keogh, a psychically endowed hero for the Great

Majority – the teeming dead – with whom he is able to communicate as easily as with the living.

Necroscope® has now grown to sixteen big volumes, published in fourteen countries and many millions of copies. In addition, *Necroscope*® comic books, graphic novels, a role-playing game, quality figurines and, in Germany, a series of audio books, have been created from the series. Moreover, the original story has been regularly optioned for movies.

Lumley is also the author of more than forty other titles. He is the winner of a British Fantasy Award, a *Fear* Magazine Award, a Lovecraft Film Festival Association "Howie", the World Horror Convention's Grand Master Award and the Horror Writers Association's Lifetime Achievement Award.

The author's most recent books include a new collection of non-Lovecraftian horror stories, *No Sharks in the Med and Other Stories*, from Subterranean Press, and he has also completed a new *Necroscope*® novella for the same publisher.

"Back in 1974," recalls Lumley, "when I wrote the story in this volume, I was still writing very much under the influence of H. P. Lovecraft. In addition to which, fancying myself as something of a limner in Indian inks, I was also much taken with the work of the weird and macabre artists (as this story will no doubt, er, 'illustrate'?) – the old, the new, and the upcoming, from Hieronymus Bosch down to Virgil Finlay and Lee Browne Coye, and further yet through Stephen Fabian and Dave Carson – not to mention the unmentionable Richard Upton Pickman.

"And so in 1965, having laid down the pencil and taken up the pen (at the urging of none other than Michael Moorcock, then editor of the British reprint *Tarzan* comic to whom I had sent some comic strips, who told me as gently as possible my scripts were way superior to my artwork), I suppose it was inevitable that I should write 'The Man Who Photographed Beardsley'.

"Any reader not already acquainted with Aubrey Beardsley's marvellous black-and-whites, do yourself a favour and get on down to the library; that way you'll also have a much better understanding of the story."

RICHARD CHRISTIAN MATHESON is a novelist, short story writer and screenwriter/producer. He is also the president of Matheson Entertainment, a production company he formed with his father, famed author Richard Matheson, which is involved with multiple film and television projects.

He began his career in the late-1970s as an advertising copywriter and writer for stand-up comedians. At twenty, he became the youngest writer ever signed to an overall deal with Universal Studios and was made story editor of the critically acclaimed *Quincy M.E.* He also wrote and co-wrote scores of episodes for *The Incredible Hulk, Battlestar Galactica, Simon and Simon, Amazing Stories, The A-Team* and many others. After leaving Universal, he worked as head writer and producer for comedy and dramatic series at every studio in Hollywood.

Matheson moved quickly into feature-film writing, working with Steven Spielberg on *Harry and the Hendersons* and *Three O'Clock High,* a spec feature script he co-wrote that Spielberg bought. To date, he has written, co-written and sold over twelve spec screenplays – considered a record. He has also scripted a number of TV mini-series, and adapted the double Emmy Award-winning "Battleground" episode for Stephen King's *Nightmares and Dreamscapes,* along with three episodes of *Masters of Horror.*

Matheson wrote and created *Splatter,* a web-based horror project for Roger Corman, directed by Joe Dante, and the web-series *Shockers,* which Matheson also directed. He recently adapted H. G. Wells's *The Time Machine* as a four-hour mini-series for TNT.

Matheson is considered a master of the short-short story and has published more than seventy stories of psychological horror in magazines and major anthologies. Thirty of his critically acclaimed stories are collected in *Scars and Other Distinguishing Marks,* with a Foreword by Stephen King and an Introduction by Dennis Etchison. His second collection, *Dystopia,* gathers sixty stories with an Introduction by Richard Matheson and an Afterword by Peter Straub. The volume also includes tributes to the author's writing from Clive Barker, Ellen Datlow, Stephen King, Dean Koontz, Ray Bradbury, Ramsey Campbell and many others. Matheson's debut novel, *Created By,* was a Bram Stoker Award nominee, and his magic-realism novella *The Ritual of Illusion* is available from PS Publishing.

He has worked as a paranormal investigator with the UCLA Department of Parapsychology on numerous cases, including the notorious house upon which the 1982 movie *The Entity* was based. He is also a professional drummer and studied with legendary Cream drummer Ginger Baker. Matheson has played with The Smithereens, Existers and Rock Bottom Remainders. His latest band, As Above So Below, was founded with guitarist and best-selling novelist p.g. sturges.

About "Kriss Kross Applesauce", the author recalls how, "As the Yule nears, annual 'family' letters, high-beaming chipper updates, arrive in my mailbox from people I have failed to dodge, barely know or can't believe I'm related to; a blur of miscellany and pep, blaring with exclamation marks and numbing detail. No narcotic can match their effect.

"Psychiatrists suggest madness is defined less by what the insane do and more by why. A short list would include chronic punning, bowties and cannibalism. A complete one would include holiday letters."

PAUL McAULEY is a former researcher turned full-time writer who lives in North London. He has published nineteen crime and science fiction novels, including *Fairyland*, which won the Arthur C. Clarke and John W. Campbell Awards, *Mind's Eye*, *The Quiet War* and *Gardens of the Sun*. His latest novel is *Evening's Empires*.

McAuley has also published more than eighty short stories, winning the British Fantasy Society award for "The Temptation of Doctor Stein", and the Theodore Sturgeon Memorial Award for "The Choice".

"This story about a science fiction fan who takes everything far too literally was written for a psychological horror anthology," he explains, "and is set in a town that has a passing resemblance to the Cotswold town where I spent most of my childhood.

"Things are always worse in reality than in fiction – even horror fiction. The last time I visited the place, a drive-through McDonald's had sprung up next to the bus station."

MICHAEL MARSHALL is the author of six international bestselling thrillers, including *The Straw Men* series, *The Intruders* and

Killer Move. His most recent novel, *We Are Here*, was published in the UK in 2013.

Writing as Michael Marshall Smith, he has also produced more than seventy short stories and three novels – *Only Forward*, *Spares* and *One of Us* – winning the Philip K. Dick, International Horror Guild, and August Derleth Awards, along with the Prix Bob Morane in France. He has been awarded the British Fantasy Award for Best Short Fiction a total of four times, more than any other writer.

Recent projects include a new story collection entitled *Everything You Need*, a 10th Anniversary Edition of *The Straw Men*, and his next novel. He lives in Santa Cruz, California, with his wife and son.

"'Failure' is a first for me," reveals the author. "Though I've written a lot of short stories in my time – and began my career with them, as have so many writers – I'd never written one as Michael Marshall before. All I can say is that I found the process different, but not so very different. The two Michaels have always been sides of the same coin.

"This story is set very close to where I now live, Santa Cruz in Northern California. It's an addition to the *Straw Men* mythos, but it's also about being a parent. Writing the story actually helped me realize that's what the *Straw Men* books have always been most fundamentally about, in fact – the struggles involved in trying to tame and civilize the childish mind, how hard it is to succeed, and the potentially huge cost of failure when you don't.

"Children invade your life. They take over. I've heard it wisely said that you're only ever as happy as your unhappiest kid, and that's very true. But it's perhaps also the case that you're only ever as safe as your least cunning child, and that's what someone discovers in this story."

MARK MORRIS is the author of over twenty novels, among which are *Toady*, *Stitch*, *The Immaculate*, *The Secret of Anatomy*, *Fiddleback*, *The Deluge*, and four books in the popular *Doctor Who* tie-in range. His short stories, novellas, articles and reviews have appeared in a wide variety of anthologies and magazines, and he is editor of both *Cinema Macabre*, a book of horror-movie essays by genre luminaries for which he won the 2007 British Fantasy Award, and its follow-up *Cinema Futura*.

His recently published work includes the official tie-in novel for zombie apocalypse computer game *Dead Island*, a novelization of the 1971 Hammer movie *Vampire Circus*, several *DoctorWho* audio dramas for Big Finish Productions, a short story collection entitled *Long Shadows, Nightmare Light*, and *The Wolves of London*, book one of the "Obsidian Heart" trilogy from Titan Books.

"Part of the reason why I write is to try to understand how people think and feel," explains Morris, "particularly those whose values and opinions differ wildly from my own.

"Like many people, I'm both repelled and fascinated by the psychopathic mind – by why certain people are driven to kill, and particularly by the reasons why they lack compassion for, and empathy with, their fellow human beings.

"Lone psychopaths are frightening enough, but what I have always found most horrifying are male/female couples, such as Ian Brady and Myra Hindley, and Fred and Rose West, who hunt, torture and murder their victims together.

"Repellent though the subject is, I have always wanted to write about such a couple, and so when the chance to contribute to this book came along, I jumped at it – and oddly the idea for 'Essence' leaped instantly and completely into my head, as if it had been waiting for just such an opportunity for years."

LISA MORTON lives in North Hollywood, California. She is a screenwriter, author of non-fiction books, award-winning prose writer, and Halloween expert whose work was described by the American Library Association's Readers' Advisory Guide to Horror as "consistently dark, unsettling, and frightening".

Her feature-film credits include the cult favourite *Meet the Hollowheads*, the vampire film *Blood Angels*, and the mutant-shark thriller *Blue Demon*.

She is a four-times recipient of the Bram Stoker Award for horror writing, and her 2012 release, *Trick or Treat?: A History of Halloween*, won the Grand Prize at the Halloween Book Festival.

Her most recent books include the novel *Malediction* and the novella *Summer's End*.

About "Hollywood Hannah", she will say only that certain parts of it might be autobiographical . . . but she won't say which parts.

KIM NEWMAN is a novelist, critic and broadcaster. His fiction includes *The Night Mayor, Bad Dreams, Jago,* the *Anno Dracula* novels and stories, *The Quorum, The Original Dr Shade and Other Stories, Life's Lottery, Back in the USSA* (with Eugene Byrne) and *The Man from the Diogenes Club,* all under his own name, and *The Vampire Genevieve* and *Orgy of the Blood Parasites* as "Jack Yeovil".

His non-fiction books include *Ghastly Beyond Belief* (with Neil Gaiman), *Horror: 100 Best Books* and *Horror: Another 100 Best Books* (both with Stephen Jones), *Wild West Movies, The BFI Companion to Horror, Millennium Movies* and BFI Classics studies of *Cat People* and *Doctor Who*.

He is a contributing editor to *Sight & Sound* and *Empire* magazines (supplying the latter's popular "Video Dungeon" column), has written and broadcast widely on a range of topics, and scripted radio and television documentaries.

Newman's stories "Week Woman" and "Ubermensch!" were both adapted into episodes of the TV series *The Hunger,* and the latter tale was also turned into an Australian short film in 2009. Following his Radio 4 play *Cry Babies,* he wrote an episode ("Phish Phood") for BBC Radio 7's series *The Man in Black,* and he was a main contributor to the 2012 stage play *The Hallowe'en Sessions*. He has also directed and written a tiny film, *Missing Girl*.

The author's most recent books include expanded reissues of his acclaimed *Anno Dracula* series and the "Professor Moriarty" novel *The Hound of the D'Urbervilles* (all from Titan Books), along with a much-enlarged edition of *Nightmare Movies* (from Bloomsbury).

As the author points out: "I should say that I don't subscribe entirely to the vision of Alfred Hitchcock as a sex pest/perv set out by the play *Hitchcock Blonde* and the films *Hitchcock* and *The Girl;* he seemed always – and especially in the years of *Vertigo, Psycho, The Birds* and *Marnie* – to be more obsessed with his work (and his reputation) than his leading ladies.

"Obviously, *Psycho,* the subject, resonated with Hitch first of all, and then with audiences world-wide, because of the major relationship in Robert Bloch's novel and Ed Gein's life, between the murderer and his mother.

"I first saw *Psycho* when the BBC broadcast it as part of a season of archetypal American films (along with *The Music Man*) over the Bicentennial 4 July weekend in 1977 – a witty piece of scheduling that Hitch would have loved."

REGGIE OLIVER has been a professional playwright, actor, and theatre director since 1975. Besides plays, his publications include the authorized biography of Stella Gibbons, *Out of the Woodshed*, published by Bloomsbury in 1998, and six collections of stories of supernatural terror, of which the fifth, *Mrs Midnight* (Tartarus Press), won the Children of the Night Award for Best Work of Supernatural Fiction in 2011 and was nominated for two other awards.

Tartarus has also reissued his first and second collections, *The Dreams of Cardinal Vittorini* and *The Complete Symphonies of Adolf Hitler*, in new editions with new illustrations by the author, as well as his most recent collection, *Flowers of the Sea*. His novel *The Dracula Papers I – The Scholar's Tale* (Chômu Press) – is the first of a projected four.

An omnibus edition of Oliver's stories entitled *Dramas from the Depths* is published by Centipede, as part of its "Masters of the Weird Tale" series, and his stories have appeared in more than fifty anthologies, including several in the "Mammoth" stable.

"It was the editor who suggested a late-nineteenth-century Paris setting for 'The Green Hour'," reveals the author, "and the idea immediately appealed to me. I love the literature of the period, and some of my most successful theatre writings have been adaptations from the French of plays by, among others, Maupassant, Feydeau and Hennequin.

"All three of them died insane as a consequence of syphilis, a tragic illness for which in the nineteenth century there was no known cure. From that morbid thought came many others, and who better to find his way through the dark labyrinth I had made of them than Edgar Allan Poe's immortal Auguste Dupin?"

EDGAR ALLAN POE (1809–49) has been described as "the father of modern horror" (as well as scientific and detective fiction). Born in Boston, Massachusetts, the death of his mother and the desertion of his father resulted in Poe, aged three, being made the ward of a Virginia merchant who later disowned him.

In 1836 he married his thirteen-year-old cousin Virginia

Clemm, who died prematurely of tuberculosis eleven years later. Suffering from bouts of depression and alcoholism, Poe attempted suicide in 1848 and, the following year, he vanished for three days before inexplicably turning up in a delirious condition in Baltimore, where he died a few days later.

Poe published a volume of poetry, *Tamerlane and Other Poems*, in 1827, and his first short story, "Metzengerstein", appeared in 1832. His tales of madness and premature burial never gained him wealth or recognition during his lifetime, but among his best stories and poems are "The Fall of the House of Usher", "The Murders in the Rue Morgue", "The Pit and the Pendulum", "The Black Cat", "The Premature Burial", "The Raven" and, of course, "The Tell-Tale Heart", which is included in this volume.

Originally published in *The Pioneer: A Literary and Critical Magazine* in 1843, the author's classic tale of creeping madness has been adapted for film, television and radio on numerous occasions, most notably on screen in 1941 (as an MGM short directed by Jules Dassin), 1953 (an animated version narrated by James Mason), 1960 (as a feature starring Laurence Payne and Adrienne Corri) and in 2012 (featuring Peter Bogdanovich as the Old Man). However, none of these dramatizations can match the intensity of Poe's original short story.

JOHN LLEWELLYN PROBERT had to re-sit his psychiatry exams at medical school. This both helped confirm his chosen career as a surgeon, and gave him more experience to draw on when he was asked to write the wraparound story and linking segments contained within this volume.

The author's stories have been collected in the award-winning *The Faculty of Terror*, *Coffin Nails*, *The Catacombs of Fear*, *Against the Darkness* and *Wicked Delights*, while his latest books are *The Nine Deaths of Dr Valentine* (Spectral Press), which is a tribute to the classic Vincent Price horror films he grew up watching, and *Differently There* (Gray Friar Press), a novella inspired by his own recent experiences at the other end of the scalpel-blade.

"The relationship between medicine and the media has always been quite shaky," explains Probert, "and so what better forum to explore that in than an Amicus movie-style framework story?

"I've always admired Robert Bloch's ability to present quite an acerbic world view in his stories, but at the same time make them very entertaining for the reader who wanted nothing more than that. It has therefore been a pleasure to be allowed to try and emulate the kind of framing device Bloch himself used in the 1972 Amicus film *Asylum*.

"So, presented here for your delectation, and for you to think about a little more if you so wish, is my imaginary encounter between a journalist and a psychiatrist – either or both of whom might not be who they claim."

JAY RUSSELL is the pseudonym of a writer born in New York, aged in Los Angeles, and currently living in London with his wife and two daughters.

"Hush . . . Hush, Sweet Shushie" is the latest adventure in the fantastical/comic life of reluctant supernatural detective Marty Burns, who also stars in a handful of cleverly titled short stories and the novels *Celestial Dogs*, *Burning Bright* and *Greed & Stuff*. Russell's other books include *Blood*, *Brown Harvest* (a World Fantasy Award nominee for Best Novel), *The Twilight Zone* novelization *Memphis/The Pool Guy*, and the short story collection *Waltzes and Whispers*.

The author claims that his lack of literary productivity is a consequence of having lost his lucky "Balso Snell" autograph model fountain pen down the back of a sofa in 2004. He borrowed Kim Newman's to write the present tale, about which he notes: "Marty Burns is back! Hullo? Anyone there? Testing, testing . . . is this thing on?"

He goes on to add: "The real psychos I've met in my life don't wield knives or axes or have secret torture chambers with industrial-sized rolls of cling-film. They're people who give you no clue about their mania(s) until it's too late. Which is also the definition of ex-wives/husbands, I suppose. Marty has several ex-wives, and Shushie is the sanest of them. So look out.

"This is also the latest in an absurdly occasional series of short Marty tales riffing on movie titles/themes. The editor has done everything humanly possible to pry more out of me. I can only pray he never gives up . . ."

DAVID J. SCHOW is a short story writer, novelist, screenwriter (teleplays and features), columnist, essayist, editor, photographer and winner of the World Fantasy and International Horror Guild awards (for short fiction and non-fiction, respectively).

His association with New Line Cinema includes such horror icons as Freddy Krueger (*A Nightmare on Elm Street: Freddy's Nightmares* and an episode of the TV series *Freddy's Nightmares*), Leatherface (*Leatherface: Texas Chainsaw Massacre III* and the story for *The Texas Chainsaw Massacre: The Beginning*), and the eponymous Critters (*Critters 3* and *Critters 4*). His most recent film credit is *The Hills Run Red* starring William Sadler.

In 1994 he co-wrote the screenplay for the modern classic *The Crow* and has since worked with such directors as Alex Proyas, James Cameron, E. Elias Merhige, Rupert Wainwright, Mick Garris and William Malone. He wrote more than forty instalments of his popular "Raving & Drooling" column for *Fangoria* magazine, later collected in the book *Wild Hairs*.

For the premiere season of Showtime Networks' *Masters of Horror*, Schow adapted his own short story "Pick Me Up" for director Larry Cohen, and for Season 2 he wrote "We All Scream for Ice Cream" (based on a story by John Farris) for director Tom Holland.

Among his more recent books are the novels *Gun Work* and *Internecine*, and the short story collections *Zombie Jam* and *Havoc Swims Jaded*. He has appeared on many documentaries and DVD supplements, contributing material to *Creature from the Black Lagoon, Incubus, Reservoir Dogs, From Hell, The Shawshank Redemption, The Dirty Dozen*, and the two-disc reissue of *Dark City*, amongst others.

ROBERT SHEARMAN is an award-winning writer for stage, television and radio. He was resident playwright at the Northcott Theatre in Exeter, and regular writer for Alan Ayckbourn at the Stephen Joseph Theatre in Scarborough. *Easy Laughter* won the Sunday Times Playwriting Award, *Fool to Yourself* the Sophie Winter Memorial Trust Award, and *Binary Dreamers* the Guinness Award for Ingenuity in association with the Royal National Theatre. Many of his plays are collected in *Caustic Comedies*, published by Big Finish Productions.

For BBC Radio he is a regular contributor to the afternoon play slot, produced by Martin Jarvis, and his series *The Chain Gang* has won two Sony awards. However, he's probably best known for his work on TV's *Doctor Who*, bringing the Daleks back to the screen in the BAFTA-winning first series of the revival in an episode nominated for a Hugo Award.

His first collection of short stories, *Tiny Deaths*, was published by Comma Press in 2007. It won the World Fantasy Award for Best Collection, and was also short-listed for the Edge Hill Short Story Prize and nominated for the Frank O'Connor International Short Story Prize. His second collection, *Love Songs for the Shy and Cynical*, published by Big Finish Productions, won the British Fantasy Award and the Edge Hill Readers Prize, and was joint winner of the Shirley Jackson Award. A third collection, *Everyone's Just So So Special*, won the British Fantasy Award. In 2012, the best of his horror fiction – half taken from these previous collections, half new work – was published by ChiZine as *Remember Why You Fear Me*.

"I had a doll when I was a kid," reveals Shearman. "It was a boy's doll – an American GI soldier, very macho – but let's face it, it was a doll nonetheless. Maybe it was something I'd picked up in a jumble sale; that would explain, perhaps, why it had no clothes. I certainly don't recall it ever having clothes – my Action Man was always completely naked, save for some silver medallion that was glued to his chest and that I could never prise off, not even with a knife.

"I used to play such games with my Action Man. Some days I'd send him into space by throwing him high out of the upstairs window. He'd become the first man to breathe underwater for half-an-hour – I pressed him down hard against the bottom of the bathtub and how he squirmed! I'd try to burn off his furry stubble with a light bulb; from the banister-rail I'd hang him high with a wire noose, and then I'd pull on his legs and imagine his neck snapping.

"A little while ago, on a visit to my parents, I was asked if I could get rid of all my old junk that had been boxed up in the attic. I'd completely forgotten about my Action Man – but there he was, lying face-up amongst loose blocks of Lego, and he was smiling, and he seemed happy to see me. I was happy too, and I reflected on what a shame it is that we can so easily forget our childhoods, how we discard what we once loved and what helped shape us into who we are. I threw Action Man on to the bonfire with all the other rubbish. I think I heard him scream.

"I hope you enjoy 'That Tiny Flutter of the Heart I Used to Call Love'."

ROBERT SILVERBERG is a multiple winner of both the Hugo and Nebula Awards and he was named a Grand Master by the Science Fiction and Fantasy Writers of America in 2004.

He began submitting stories to science fiction magazines in his early teens, and his first published novel, a children's book entitled *Revolt on Alpha C*, appeared in 1955. He won his first Hugo Award the following year.

Always a prolific writer – for the first four years of his career he reputedly wrote a million words a year – his numerous books include such novels as *To Open the Sky, To Live Again, Dying Inside, Nightwings* and *Lord Valentine's Castle*. The latter became the basis for his popular "Majipoor" series, set on the eponymous alien planet.

Although he is basically now "retired", the author's most recent publications include *When the Blue Shift Comes*, a two-novella book in which the first novella is by Silverberg and the companion piece was written by Alvaro Zinos-Amaro, and *Tales of Majipoor*, a new collection of the stories he has written about that world over the past ten or fifteen years.

As he explains: "'The Undertaker's Sideline' was written at a time (1958) when science fiction magazines seemed to be going out of fashion and monster movies were the rage in Hollywood. A good many magazines of horror fiction with 'Monsters' in their titles were started then, among them *Monster Parade* and *Monsters and Things*, both of them edited by Larry T. Shaw, for whose science fiction magazines I had been a prolific contributor.

"When those magazines folded, Larry asked me to write some horror stories for the new magazines, and I turned in about a dozen of them over the next year, working under a host of pseudonyms."

DAVID A. SUTTON is the recipient of the World Fantasy Award, the International Horror Guild Award and twelve British

Fantasy Awards for editing magazines and anthologies. He was co-editor of *Fantasy Tales, Dark Voices: The Pan Book of Horror Stories* and *Dark Terrors: The Gollancz Book of Horror*.

He has edited *Phantoms of Venice* (reprinted by Screaming Dreams in 2008) and *Houses on the Borderland* for the British Fantasy Society, while his short stories have recently appeared in *When Graveyards Yawn, The Black Book of Horror #1, #2* and *#4, The Mammoth Book of Best New Horror Volume 19, Subtle Edens: The Elastic Book of Slipstream, Estronomicon* and *The Ghosts & Scholars Book of Shadows*.

The author's debut short story collection is *Clinically Dead & Other Tales of the Supernatural* (Screaming Dreams), and he is the owner of the small press Shadow Publishing, which has produced a number of anthologies and collections.

"In writing 'Night Soil Man' I wanted to briefly evoke the atmosphere of the Black Country and life for the working man in Victorian times," Sutton reveals. "Wrapping that around a horror tale, it was a delight to write. A number of my ancestors were chimney sweeps and I wanted to incorporate that as well, and also a nod to the antics of Mr Gamfield in Charles Dickens's *Oliver Twist*."

STEVE RASNIC TEM's recent projects include *Onion Songs*, a collection of off-beat stories from Chômu Press; *Celestial Inventories*, a collection of contemporary, slipstream dark fantasy from ChiZine, and *Twember*, his first collection of all science fiction stories from NewCon Press. Also forthcoming is a new novella, *In the Lovecraft Museum*, from PS Publishing.

"Sometimes stories come from the oddest places," admits Tem. "Now and then we all do crazy things at home we probably would never do in public. Upon occasion I've been known to imagine voices coming from various household items. Usually it's the TV saying, 'You should turn me on', or the trash bin saying, 'You should take me out'.

"When our kids were at home, I'd share these domestic announcements with them and ask them to do something about them. Sometimes the dishwasher or the clothes washer would make some sort of music and I would dance to it (a cross between the watusi and the twist). Surely I'm not the only one who does this? My children would usually leave the room.

"So one afternoon, while conducting a dialogue with our new electric juicer, 'The Secret Laws of the Universe' came to mind. If you'd like to see other examples of my version of *noir* fiction, check out my collection *Ugly Behavior*."

CONRAD WILLIAMS is the author of seven novels, four novellas and over 100 short stories, some of which are collected in *Use Once Then Destroy* and *Born with Teeth*. In addition to his International Horror Guild Award for his novel *The Unblemished*, he is a three-times recipient of the British Fantasy Award, including Best Novel for *One*. His debut anthology, *Gutshot*, was shortlisted for both the British Fantasy and World Fantasy Awards.

He is currently working on a novel that will act as the prequel to a major video game from Sony, as well as a novel of supernatural horror.

"'Manners' is a story that had its origins in an old ideas folder of mine that is filled with scraps of paper, photographs and articles from newspapers and magazines. One such article was about a man who lived off road-kill. He hosts dinner parties for his friends and they never know what he's going to serve up. One of his big successes was a 'two-owl risotto'.

"There's also a line in a song – 'Something in the Way' by Nirvana – that pushed me in the direction of creating a character who zoomorphizes the few people with whom he has been acquainted.

"As many as one-in-ten of us exhibits psychopathic tendencies (if Jon Ronson's excellent book, *The Psychopath Test*, is to be believed). I wanted to get away from the slew of Hannibal Lecter Über-psychos and write about a quieter maniac, a character who poses no immediate danger to society, but is no less creepy for that."

RIO YOUERS' debut novel, *End Times*, was released by PS Publishing in 2010, followed by his first short story collection, *Dark Dreams, Pale Horses*.

He is also the author of *Mama Fish* (Shroud Publishing) and *Old Man Scratch* (PS Publishing) – the latter earning him a British Fantasy Award nomination. His novelette, "This is the Summer of Love", was the title story of PS's first new-look *PostScripts* anthology, a publication in which the author has appeared three times. His latest novel, *Westlake Soul,* is out from ChiZine Publications, while available soon from Cemetery Dance are a new novella, *The Angels,* and the collection *All That I See.*

"I recently reconnected with a friend from school," recalls Youers, "who I hadn't seen in years. We spent some time catching up, but mostly we talked about old times. I left his house feeling wistful, childlike . . . yet *old* at the same time.

"It also occurred to me that I had just spent the weekend with someone I didn't really know. Yes, we were friends at school, but a lot of years had passed, so much had happened . . . and people can change.

"I found this more than a little frightening – that I had given my trust without so much as a second thought. It had all turned out okay, of course. But what if it hadn't? What if my old friend had a secret – a *darkness* – that he'd been keeping inside for years? Needless to say, my mind whirred with the possibilities, and 'Wide-Shining Light' came to life."